I0818602

Praise for *Aegis Evolution* by Amazon bestselling author S.S. Segran

"Continuing with their expert pacing and growing lore, the *Aegis League* books provide constant thrills and excitement. This installment is arguably the finest example of those qualities yet."

— *The US Review of Books*

"I discovered the Aegis series back when there was only Book One. I was impressed then. After reading Book Three now, it reinforces my original opinion that this is a writer worth watching! She is in my top ten favorite indie authors, and I'll be waiting rather impatiently for book number four!"

— *L.J. Capehart, Author of the Trevalian Magic series*

"Exceptionally well written . . . this intriguing series promises much and delivers—gripping suspense and nail-biting action, as well as timely questions for today."

— *Amazon Reviews*

"Five Stars! An amazing adventure of epic proportions, *Aegis Evolution* whisks you away into a story that is X-Men meets Percy Jackson and spins a truly engaging and enjoyable tale."

— *Readers' Favorite Reviews*

"This has it all! Sci-fi, action, and adventure. Can't wait for the sequel. One of the best series I have ever read."

— *Bob Meredith, Amazon Reviews*

Publication Information

AEGIS EVOLUTION by S.S. Segran

First Published by INKmagination Feb. 2018. Second edition Sept. 2019
Printed in the United States of America

Cover Design and Illustrations © 2019 by S.K.S.
Book Teaser & Trailer by: INKmagination.

S.S. Segran asserts the moral right to be identified as the author of this book.

ISBN: 978-0-9910813-6-3 (hardcover)
ISBN: 978-0-9910813-7-0 (paperback)
eISBN: 978-0-9910813-8-7 (eBook)

Receive free short stories, exclusive giveaways, advance reader opportunities, and updates directly from the author.
Visit **www.sssegran.com** to subscribe as an Aegis Insider.

AEGIS EVOLUTION

AEGIS LEAGUE - BOOK THREE

S.S. SEGRAN

To my mom and dad once again,
because one can never thank their parents enough times.
I love you.

"The mind is not a vessel to be filled but a fire to be kindled."

— Plutarch 46-120 AD

"Just as we have faith in the rising of the sun at dawn,
we must believe that darkness cannot prevail, for
truly, darkness is but the absence of light."

— Elder Nageau

PROLOGUE

Box in Carmel's Possession

Roman Siege of the Jewish Fortress in Judea

Judea, 74 A.D.

Screams shredded the warm evening of the Judean Desert.

"*Run!*"

A massive force threw the girl to the ground as a colossal rock crashed mere feet from where she'd stood a second ago. Reverberations shook the earth. The nearby walls collapsed into a pile of rubble and dust swirled into the air, mingling with smoke. The girl wheezed in pain; the small wooden box she was carrying had jammed into her ribs.

Before she could catch her breath, she was hauled to her feet. Two hands grabbed her head and she found herself looking into a pair of turquoise eyes, identical to her own, under a carpet of honey-colored curls.

"Carmel!" Her brother, only a few years older than herself, frantically examined her face. "Carmel, are you alright?"

The girl gently removed his hands and picked up the box, then squared her shoulders. "I'm fine, Ezra."

As she adjusted the shawl over her head, she sized up the giant rock in its shallow crater. It was one of a few that had breached the fortress walls, which sat atop the plateau that rose a thousand feet above the desert floor. The Romans' main objective appeared to be to penetrate the Jewish rebels' western gate, but often their *ballistae* would also land a boulder inside the walls.

"We are not going to last much longer here, are we?" she asked.

"I do not think so." Ezra jumped out of the path of two women, both carrying small children as they pelted away from the mounting conflict. He watched them go, then turned back to his sister. "We must find a way to leave before—*Carmel! What are you doing?*"

With the brass-clad case tucked protectively under one arm, the girl had taken off toward the western end of the fortress that loomed above its surroundings. There she could feel the reverberations as the Romans feverishly battered at the wall with a ram. Torches and flaming arrows had set ablaze the rebels' hastily-made wooden barrier behind the outer stone fortification. Despite loathing them, Carmel grudgingly admired the legion's tenacity and engineering prowess.

Access to the mountaintop stronghold was limited to a narrow, zigzagging pathway; the Romans' solution had been to construct a circumvallating wall to seal the mesa in before beginning work on a massive ramp at the western side. Using Jewish slaves and Roman masons, they'd completed its construction in the span of just three months.

Nearly four hundred feet tall, the ramp held their siege tower and battering ram. The men and women cornered in the stronghold had been powerless to do anything but watch helplessly in growing horror as the legionaries laboriously pushed onward.

Carmel hopped up to the wall to join the onlookers as they threw stones at the besiegers, who in turn fired arrows. There wasn't much the rebels could do to defend themselves from the onslaught, but there was a lot of yelling from both parties; the Jews hurled insults at the legion, and she heard the Romans respond in kind.

The setting sun behind the colossal siege tower cast a bloody hue on the legionaries' burnished armor and bright red cloaks. She watched as soldiers under the tower used ropes and chains to swing the large battering ram back and forth, smashing the wall; fervor fueled their movements, their voices burned with rage, and their eyes gleamed with the lust for battle.

Carmel shuddered, then hastily dropped to avoid another volley of arrows. She waited for a count of five, then peered over the wall once more to glimpse the archers provide covering fire for the soldiers working the wooden ram.

Why can't they just leave us all be? she screamed silently, hugging the box to her chest. The bravado she carried when away from the action had dissipated. She felt small now, as she always did whenever she peeked past the barrier. The nine hundred and sixty souls trapped in the fortress were outnumbered ten to one.

As she dodged the projectiles zipping overhead, she spied a peculiar sight. Among the horde of uniformed monsters a young soldier stood still, staring blankly up at the line of rebels behind the wall. His bow was drawn but he never fired his weapon.

Their eyes locked, and for a brief moment the two were frozen in time. He looked as one dead to the world, but when their gazes met, emotion flitted across his handsome face—was it pain? Guilt?

Captivated, Carmel didn't register another hail of arrows had been released until they were already rocketing toward her. She watched, rooted to her spot, a gasp caught in her throat.

The next thing she knew, she was flung flat on her back behind the wall; the volley whistled harmlessly overhead. Ezra looked down at her, face flushed, a vein throbbing at his temple. "You almost got yourself killed!" he hissed. "You are far too senseless, you know that? Where would you be if I weren't around?"

She smiled weakly. "Probably not in the dirt as often."

Ezra grabbed the box from her and inspected it for damage. "Next time you want to run off toward danger, at least leave this with me. We cannot afford to let it fall into Roman possession. Or anyone's, really."

"They would have no clue how to properly use it even if they *did* possess it."

"And that's the danger. It should not be out of our hands. You and I are the only ones left entrusted to take care of it."

The wall beside them shuddered as the battering ram pounded against it. A few stones broke loose and dropped to the ground. With his free hand, Ezra gripped his sister's arm and pulled her away. Before they could get far, a deep bellow stopped them in their tracks. They turned around to see a striking, muscular man atop the stone wall, his dagger thrust into the air.

"They will soon break through!" he warned the multitude of people before him, black hair swept back from his face. "Now, listen, all of you! Listen to me!" He jumped down into the throng, who watched him raptly.

Ezra's jaw tightened. "What does he want now?"

"We should find out." Carmel made her way over to the group. Her brother was far from a loyal supporter of the man who stood before them—with reason, she supposed. But in a time of conflict, they needed to band together and he was the best they had, a resilient leader.

"They will break through the wall by the first light of morning!" The black-haired commander surveyed the hundreds of men, women, and children looking at him. "We will not make it through this. We have known that since the beginning. They cut off our routes of escape and, though we may have food and water, our end is nearing. Since we, long ago, my generous friends, resolved never to be servants to the Romans, nor to any other than to God Himself—Who alone is the true and just Lord of mankind—the time is now come that obliges us to make that resolution true in practice."

As he spoke, Carmel saw the faces of those around her darken. She swallowed.

"We were the very first that revolted from them," continued the commander, "and we are the last that fight against them; and I cannot but esteem it as a favor that God has granted us, that it is still in our power to die bravely and in a state of freedom, which had not been the case of others." His voice shook slightly. "It is very plain that we shall be taken within a day's time. But it is still an eligible thing to die after a glorious manner, together with our dearest friends. This is what our enemies themselves cannot by any means hinder, although they be desirous to take us alive."

Beside Carmel, Ezra stared at the man with deep, unmasked loathing. She nudged him, temporarily tuning out of the speech. He glanced at her, his demeanor softening minutely and tainted with sorrow. She squeezed his hand, then turned back to the leader.

"Let our wives die before they are abused, and our children before they have tasted slavery," the man roared. "And after we have slain them, let us bestow that glorious benefit upon one another, and preserve ourselves in freedom, as an excellent funeral monument for us."

Carmel bowed her head, shoulders trembling. They'd all known they were good as gone from the very start, and had held out on hope alone that they'd make it through.

No, she realized bitterly. *Not hope. Denial.*

"We are leaving," Ezra whispered fiercely into her ear as the man persisted in his speech, flaming arrows soaring overhead and landing around them to create pockets of fire.

Before Carmel could register his words, he was already dragging her away. "Ezra!" she cried. "What are you doing?"

"I will not kill myself, nor will I let that happen to you!" His tone was firm, befitting the twenty-year-old he was. "Whatever happens, this must be protected." He let go of her and held up the wooden box. Carved into the cover was an intricate pattern, laced with gold thread plaited into a clover-leaf design.

Carmel stared at it for the longest time before steeling herself and straightening her spine. She nodded. "Shall we find a place to hold out, then?"

"Nowhere within the fortress," he said immediately. "We will have to climb down and find a cave in the mountainside."

She let out a long breath. She'd rather race down the mountain, but they would never get past the circumvallating wall. Soldiers in the watchtowers would also surely pick them off with their arrows if they tried to climb over. And, if by some miracle they did safely scale the wall, the legion's eight camps around the base of the fortress left no paths to freedom save an arrow to the head or a sword through the chest.

Taking one last look at the hundreds of people they had lived with for the past few years, Carmel skulked away with a heavy heart, trailing her brother. He led her around the enormous, once-lavish palace by the western gate. She skimmed her hand over the stones of the building as she moved past, remembering stories some of the women had shared about the fortress. Decades ago, a king known for his paranoia had turned the mountaintop plateau into what it was now, with its extravagant palaces, swimming pools, bathhouses, a synagogue, and more.

He made history here in his own way, she thought. *What of us? Will we all perish as stories, or simply perish?*

The sun had already set. In its stead an army of stars glittered luminously, as if following the lead of the moon. They shone down upon dwellings that were both standing and torn, and those that had been stripped of their roofs. Carmel's heart grew even heavier. This was as close to home as she'd ever had since she and her brother were orphaned years ago. She was not ready to leave it behind, but she had an obligation and it rested within the box Ezra carried.

The siblings traversed toward the fort perched on the southern edge of the mesa, weaving their way between residences, cisterns, and a columbarium tower. Walking ahead, Ezra kicked loose rocks from his leather sandals irritably and cursed under his breath at the atrocity about to happen to those they'd left behind.

As they approached the fort, they were met by a surprising sight. A group of over twenty people were preparing to scale down the side of the mountain. They eyed the newcomers warily. Most were young men and women in long-sleeved garments, along with a few small children. A tense moment passed between the siblings and the group before understanding dawned in either party. One of the men dipped his head at the pair before disappearing over the edge of the cliff.

Ezra brought his mouth close to Carmel's ear. "They must be taking refuge in the caves below, too."

She tightened her shawl. "If this many of us have thought of the caves, surely the Romans will think to look there as well?"

"Perhaps not. But if they do, there are many openings in the mountainside, and some are better hidden than others. In either case, it's the best option we have."

She gritted her teeth, bracing herself. "Lead on, then."

They were the last ones to scale down; the others had already disappeared into openings in the declivity. *Thank the heavens above we grew up with this kind of terrain*, Carmel mused. *Bless that old, beautiful tribe.*

Ezra's voice reached her from below. "In here!"

Gripping the rock face, she glanced down. Her brother's head jutted out of a cave. He held a hand out to her and helped her in. She landed roughly on her hands and knees, grimacing. "Ouch!"

"I'm sorry." Ezra rubbed her back. "But look. Safety."

She squinted in the darkness. As her eyes adjusted, she made out seven huddled shapes: three men, two women, and two children. Acknowledging them with a nod that she wasn't sure they could even see, she moved to the farthest side of the small cave, right under a crescent-shaped mark in the ceiling. Ezra joined her, holding the box tightly. She rested her head on his shoulder and stared out of the opening to the neighboring mountain.

Nothing we can do now but wait. She shut her eyes tight. *God help us.*

Carmel was roused by the sound of bloodcurdling cries. Her eyes flew open and a hand quickly covered her mouth. Ezra, a finger to his lips, shook his head. She nodded and he removed his hand. The screams were coming from near their hideout.

Oh, no. Oh, please no. Her breaths came out short and ragged. *They must have found the others.*

Ezra put an arm around her, pulling her close. The group stared, transfixed, at the opening of the cave. The women hugged the young ones, tears trickling down their cheeks.

The last cry cut off abruptly. Carmel buried her face against her brother's chest, feeling his arm tighten further around her. Terrified silence soaked the cave.

A sudden scream sounded just above them. One of the children let out a yelp before being hurriedly shushed by the frightened woman holding him.

Ezra withdrew from Carmel to look at her properly. "This is not going the way I had hoped." He rested his forehead against hers. "We need to hide the box. Do you understand me? We need to bury it and let the Elders know of its location."

In his eyes, Carmel saw her own dread reflecting back at her. "We will die here, won't we?" she whispered.

She searched his face, waiting for him to contradict her, to give her some false hope. Instead, tears caught his eyelashes as he offered a faint, sad smile and kissed her forehead. "I love you," he said.

With wet cheeks and quivering fingers, she clawed at the ground. The screams continued. She tried to shut her ears to it, and her chest heaved as she dug. Out of the corner of her eye, she saw her brother go still for a few moments, as if in meditation, before snapping back to reality.

"Done," he breathed. "The Elders will know where to find it someday."

Eerie silence had replaced the chaos above. Then, a small rock bounced past the cave's opening; they could hear it hit bigger rocks on its way down the mountainside. The group held its breath, and even Carmel and Ezra forgot what they were supposed to do.

The clinking of metal against metal broke the siblings from their daze. Ezra shoved the box into the hole just as the women beside them inhaled sharply. Carmel looked over her shoulder.

Two legionaries, their swords drawn and dripping red, stood at the opening, observing the prey before them. The first one leapt forward and ran his weapon through the nearest victim, ending her cry. The second impaled one of the men. Carmel covered her mouth to stop herself from making any sound.

"Help me cover it!" Ezra shouted over the earsplitting shrieks.

Carmel, about to join him, froze when she noticed a third soldier standing at the mouth of the cave. It was the young man—the one who didn't seem to belong with the legion. Just as he had then drawn his bow but hadn't release an arrow, he now had his sword in hand but didn't move forward. He watched the slaughter, eyes glazed.

Then, as though he felt that he was being watched, he turned his head toward Carmel. His vacant look melted into alarm and his gaze darted between her and his fellow legionaries.

Ezra roared. “Carmel! Watch out!”

She twisted around to see a sword plunge into her brother’s chest as he dove in front of her. A scream was pulled from her heart and through her throat. *“Ezra!”*

He looked at her, blood dribbling from between his lips. With a voice softened from pain but still lovingly firm, he said, “Bury the box, Carmel.”

She watched as the sword was dragged out of him. He fell to the side. With the last bit of strength he had left, he crawled away from her, drawing the Roman’s attention. The soldier snarled in triumph as he drove the sword through Ezra once more. This time, her brother didn’t move.

In a fit of uncontrollable emotion she swept the dirt over the box, barely able to see through the torrent that rained down her face. With the hole covered, she pressed her back against the cave wall. The young soldier had watched her the whole time. She looked at him, pleading, hoping against hope that the Romans wouldn’t unearth what was buried. He didn’t make a move or utter a word to the others. Carmel pulled her knees to her chest, sitting in shock as she witnessed the gruesome end to the last member of the group.

The Romans turned to her, but all she noticed was her beloved brother. He lay in a pool of blood, his honey-colored hair tainted crimson, his lifeless eyes staring into the void.

The biggest of the legionaries advanced toward her and grabbed her locks, pulling her head back. He examined her features, suspicious. She knew that she and her brother, with their blond curls and turquoise eyes, looked nothing like the Jews they had lived and grown up with.

The brute snorted. He swung his sword back, preparing to bury it in her body, but a shout stopped him. He turned to square off with the Roman soldier who’d hung back from the murders.

Their low-pitched exchange was rapid; the young man sounded adamant, and the other was clearly arguing.

Finally, the bigger man sheathed his weapon and hoisted Carmel up. He shoved her toward the third legionnaire. She stumbled and would have fallen if the young man hadn't caught her. She looked up at him; he couldn't have been much older than Ezra. He wore a hesitant expression, but there was no mistaking the kindness in his eyes. Even his hands were gentle as he gripped her arms.

The brute marched ahead with the other soldier and they climbed up the rocky face back to the fortress. The legionnaire holding onto Carmel motioned for her to follow them. She took a step forward, then turned to find him staring into the cave, directly at the spot where the box was buried. Her mouth went dry. He looked back at her and motioned again for her to climb. Helpless, she obeyed. When she reached the top, the two gore-covered soldiers pulled her up. They spoke quickly to each other, then the brute pulled out his sword.

The hilt slammed into the side of Carmel's head. Light exploded behind her eyes and agony shot through her skull like a fist through a wall. Another violent blow sent her to the ground. As consciousness slipped away, she heard the young Roman bellowing behind her, a sound rivaled only by the scream she'd loosened at her brother's death. Then blackness devoured her whole.

South Kivu Region, Democratic Republic of Congo, Present Day

With a silent flap of its wings, the white-chested crow swooped down and perched on the branch of a tree. Its glossy black head shone in the afternoon sun as it glared at its surroundings. Before it lay a small village with dusty, red-dirt streets leading away from the main road that cut through the settlement in an east-west direction. Huts, wooden vendor stalls, and mud-brick buildings with old, whitewashed tin roofs mapped the south side of the road while scattered maize fields flanked the north.

At an isolated corner of the French-speaking settlement sat a large hut. An ebony-skinned woman with a single black braid hanging down between her shoulder blades strode toward it. She was in her early thirties and dressed in a tan shirt and blue jeans, something that had been frowned upon when she first arrived in the village some weeks before. Women in the region wore cotton skirts with their tops, while men were the only ones who wore pants. Though she had quickly earned the villagers' respect and friendship, they still regarded her wardrobe with raised eyebrows.

For the past few years she'd traveled around her country of birth, mainly from village to village, helping those in need as was her duty. Though she would use her real name, she kept her actual identity to herself. The villagers were welcoming, not often grilling her for information, which made it easier to blend in.

She stepped somberly into the hut through its doorless entrance. Her gray eyes adjusted to the dim lighting of the shelter as she walked into the scene of heartbreak that met her each time she entered.

Men, women, and children, all diseased, filled twelve beds, but this was like no sickness she'd ever seen. In the span of two weeks, the afflicted had seemed to age decades. A quarter of the village had been infected during the disease's initial sweep, including the chief and elders responsible for appointing the next leader.

The chief's son had taken up the position in his father's stead and reached out to health authorities for help. It took them a week to respond and, when they did, all they could afford to send was an inexperienced and ill-prepared nurse who could do no more than draw blood samples for testing at the nearest hospital.

Ongoing skirmishes in the region, exacerbated by the widespread crop destruction, had led to a complete breakdown in civil order. The weakened government, in no position to respond to any emergencies in places far from the capital, fought to stay in power.

"Dominique," someone to her right called feebly.

She made her way to the third bed and knelt beside a man, lighting a lamp and gazing into his sunken eyes. There was hardly a trace of fat or muscle on him. His skin sagged and his bones protruded sharply. Behind his ear was a tattoo of three triangles that had faded over the years. He was the village's forty-five-year-old medicine man but could have easily been mistaken for a sickly ninety-year-old.

How could this have happened? she wondered, grief tightening her throat.

The man reached out weakly. She took his hand, forcing a reassuring smile. "How are you doing today?"

"Terrible," he croaked. "I feel so faint. Every part of me aches . . . it's as if my body has completely turned on me."

She wiped away a tear that escaped from the corner of his eye. "You'll get better. We'll figure out something soon."

"Oh, please, my dear. I'm going to end up like the others. Dead in no time."

"Don't speak like that," she murmured.

"But it's true. Ah . . . forgive me, my ancestors. I should not have deserted you."

"You've said that every day this week. What do you mean?"

He didn't answer, but his grip on her hand suddenly tightened. "You have been valiant in the face of this curse, Dominique. We are deeply in your debt for everything you've done for us, but it seems that this disease is out of your control. If we could be cured by your will alone, we would all be working the fields, dancing at the fires, and embracing our families. But . . . this is not to be."

Dominique had to force down the mounting emotion in her throat. *You need to keep it together*, she told herself fiercely. *For him. For all of them.*

The man slumped back onto the cot. "You must not bear all these deaths on your shoulders, nor in here." He pointed to her heart with two quivering fingers, a gesture that sapped his strength. Yet he continued, wheezing. "To know that you do would cause a great hurt to our people. We carry you in our hearts when we leave and we would have you carry us in yours, free of guilt. Do you understand?"

She pressed her cheek to the back of his hand and nodded, her lower lip trembling. *These people are remarkable. Why is this happening to them?*

The man suddenly bolted upright. He grabbed her by the front of her shirt and pulled her close, whispering incoherently into her ear. *"Adiha kilazi! Adiha kilazi!"*

Then he collapsed back onto his bed, completely spent.

Startled, Dominique took a few moments to recover from the sick man's strange outburst. She shook her head, sighing, and held his hand until he fell asleep before getting up to check on the rest of the patients. Three other women, wearing colorful headscarves and skirts, rushed about, making the ill as comfortable as they could, fetching them water, and helping them eat.

A child, seven years old, rasped Dominique's name. He looked just as aged and haggard as the ailing adults. Though unsettled, she gave the boy a smile as she wiped his forehead with a cool cloth. She'd seen so many perish at the hands of the disease, but it never got easier to deal with.

The world has gotten darker. So much loss. So much pain.

Only two months ago she'd received word that her cousin in America had died, and now an abominable disease ravaged her new home. Her lower lip trembled again, this time at the thought of her cousin, her best friend. Gwen had been on an important mission, tracking a carful of men who'd kidnapped two extraordinary teenagers. Unfortunately, the abductors had discovered they were being followed.

"Madame Dominique!"

Snapping back to reality, she dropped the cloth into a bucket of water and rushed outside just as two children and a teenager were about to barrel in. They doubled over, winded.

"What is it?" Dominique demanded.

"Soldiers are coming," the teenager puffed, pointing behind him at the hilltop. "They're still some ways away, but they're heading here."

She narrowed her eyes, then asked them to call for the chief. A couple of minutes later they returned with a tall, long-limbed man and were dismissed.

With a knowing look, the newly appointed head of the village nodded at Dominique and the pair took off running up the hillside. When they crested the knoll, they squinted against the sun, discerning dark shapes rumbling along the paved main road.

"I see two jeeps, a truck, and a tank," the chief muttered. "It must be a raiding party. Coming for our food, no doubt."

Dominique's heart sank. The global outbreak of crop destructions that began several months prior had devastated the region's major farms, destroying the main crops of maize, rice, and cassava. Renegade military units had started going after smaller rural farms that hadn't yet been hit. It seemed their village was the next target.

"What do we do?" she asked.

"The smartest thing would be to flee, but . . ." By the look the chief wore, she knew the gears in his mind were spinning. They'd worked closely for a while now, each fond of the other, almost like siblings. Since he'd taken up his father's position, he would often approach her for advice.

She cocked her head. "Sébastien? What is it?"

"We need to warn the others first." The chief turned and sped downhill, his voice booming across the village as he called every able-bodied man into his presence. They quickly gathered and, once the situation was explained, most had their minds set on abandoning the village.

"We can't fight them," one argued. "They have guns, and all we have are machetes."

"We have two rifles," another corrected.

"That's not going to be much help! We don't have enough ammunition, either!"

"Friends," Sébastien said, hands raised. "If you want to go, go. There is no shame. But if there are some of you who are willing to stay and fight, then I will join you."

"We don't have anything to fight for," someone from the back of the crowd called out. "They'll take all our food. And those who are sick—we can't do anything for them. They're dying. We know that. They're dying just like the others, and all we can do is lie to them and tell them that they'll be fine!"

"I'm staying," Dominique announced. She gave the chief a quick, tight smile that he returned.

Mutters and whispers stirred through the gathering. Dominique and Sébastien waited, on edge, until a man at the very front raised his chin. "Alright. We'll stay. This is still foolish, but we won't let you face them alone."

Sébastien nodded. "Good. Thank you. I need two people to help evacuate the women and children. The rest of you, arm yourselves. I have a plan."

The convoy rolled steadily through the village in single file; one jeep led the tank and truck while the other brought up the rear. Dominique rested on her stomach behind a row of houses twenty yards south of the main road. On the opposite side was a large field of maize. She stole a quick look around the corner as the vehicles approached. Sébastien and his eighteen-year-old nephew, both equipped with rifles, had taken up position a couple of houses away, waiting for her signal.

The soldiers, clothed in green camouflage and berets, rode in their doorless, open-roofed jeeps, armed with AK-47s. The first jeep passed Dominique, then the tank and the truck. A gunner stood in the commander hatch of the tank, both hands on the machine gun atop the turret. Dominique knew that the military hardly, if ever, used the old T-54 tanks. They'd been left behind by the Russians decades ago and were useful mainly for intimidation.

Still, I wouldn't want to find out if they've got a shell or two left to use, she thought.

The truck was big, with canvas covering the box-like rear. It didn't appear to be weighed down, which likely meant it was empty and ready to have the village's food supply tossed in.

As soon as the jeep at the end of the four-vehicle convoy passed her, she nodded at Sébastien. He and his nephew slithered on their stomachs to get a good view of the first jeep, then fired two shots each.

Alarmed shouts broke out as the convoy came to a halt. Dominique took another quick peek. The soldiers had jumped from their vehicles. Some dropped to the ground and aimed their weapons, searching for the source of the gunshots, while most took cover on the other side of the convoy. The tank's turret swiveled, the muzzle of its main gun pointing toward the row of mud-brick houses. The soldier behind the machine gun surveyed the buildings, watchful.

Movement on the other side of the road caught Dominique's attention. The tassels of the maize stalks quivered, and the crops were pushed aside as a group of thirty-five villagers, machetes in hand, silently emerged behind the soldiers. She held her breath, willing them onward, hoping the soldiers would keep their focus on the houses.

Her eyes flicked to the gunner on top of the turret when he moved. Something must have alerted him; he glanced over his shoulder. As soon as he saw the approaching villagers, he barked a warning and turned the machine gun around, the turret following.

Dominique clenched her teeth. *They were halfway there!*

The villagers broke into a sprint, roaring. The soldiers leapt to their feet and let loose a spray of bullets. A few villagers collapsed in bloody heaps, but most got close enough to swing their machetes. One soldier distanced himself from the commotion and shouted frantically into a radio.

Sébastien's nephew stepped out from behind the house, took aim, and fired. The soldier dropped and his radio fell with a clatter. Two others spun around when they heard the gunshot and opened fire. Dominique looked on in horror as the boy collapsed with a cry.

Sébastien bellowed and ran out into the open in a haze of rage, firing a dozen rounds at the assailants. They hit the ground, dead. He bolted toward his fallen nephew. From where she stood, Dominique could see that the youngster was alive and had likely been shot in the leg. Relief flooded through her. They could deal with an injured limb.

The sound of the tank's turret rotating reached her ears. With growing dread, she saw the soldier behind the machine gun bring his weapon to bear on uncle and nephew. She would have screamed at Sébastien but they'd never get away in time. She had one option left.

Desperate times. She took a second to ready herself, then careened out into danger. She was a blur, moving with inhuman speed. In the blink of an eye she was by the two men, their shirt collars in each hand. Using her momentum, she hoisted and carried them behind a hut just as a storm of gunfire erupted where they were. She waited until it stopped before emerging again, fury shooting through her veins.

The soldier on top of the tank swung the gun toward her

and discharged a barrage of bullets. She faced them head-on. Her shift in speed slowed her perception of each projectile and she dodged them all, somersaulting forward, bending backward, and twisting her body with agile grace.

The gunner stared at her with sheer incredulity as she tore toward him. She launched herself at the tank, sailing over the twenty-foot distance that separated them. Landing astride the soldier, she swung a foot at his face. His head was thrown back and, before he could recover, she lifted him up like a toy. He screamed curses at her, legs flailing in midair.

She bared her teeth. *"Petit diable enfoiré."*

With that, she threw him over the side of the tank and into the chaos of the soldiers and villagers before dropping through the command hatch, startling the two men inside. She grabbed one behind the head and jabbed the other sharply in the face with her elbow, knocking him out. She put her free hand on the first soldier's shoulder, then threw her head toward his. His nose crunched and he went limp. Once she'd ensured the men were properly unconscious, she pulled herself back outside and stood on top of the tank to survey the battleground.

The villagers towered over the raiders, bodies heaving as they panted. Scarlet stained the road. Several combatants lay motionless, but most of the soldiers had surrendered and were kneeling on the ground, hands behind their heads, refusing to look at the machete-wielding men.

Dominique drew an arm over her forehead, wiping the sweat away. Despite the turn of events, their ambush had worked. She jumped down from the turret and made her way to Sébastien, who was attending to his injured nephew. The boy's shirt was tied tightly around his wound, and Sébastien patted his leg. "We'll get you taken care of, don't worry. You'll be okay."

He called for two villagers to carry his nephew away so the healers could tend to him. Once they were gone, Dominique asked, "What happens now?"

Sébastien circled the convoy, gun slung across his back.

Dominique's gaze was drawn to the lifeless bodies splayed at their feet.

"I don't know," he finally answered. "More of them will come when these pigs don't return. We could be in over our heads." He covered his face. "I really don't know what we're going to do."

Dominique put a hand on his shoulder. "We'll figure it out. We always do."

Despite her words she felt hollow inside, wishing she could do more, wishing she could ask for help. But the League was already stretched thin around the globe, handling the devastation brought by the crop destruction.

Sébastien dropped his arms to his sides. "I'll deal with the mess out here," he said softly. "Why don't you help tend to the sick ones?"

She dipped her head but, before she could move, Sébastien added, "And, Dominique? We're going to have to talk about how you did what you did back there."

She paused, then said, "We'll save that for another day," and left the scene.

Evening was nearly upon them. In the distance, Dominique noted the glow of the oil lamps from the entrance of the hut. Her stomach churned. If the past couple of weeks were any indication of what was to come, the people inside would soon perish and the next wave of diseased would take their place. As terrible as that was, it also meant there would be fewer people to defend the village should another raid occur.

She halted in her tracks and looked up at the darkening sky, searching for a solution. *I can't let this happen. I just can't.*

Lowering her head, she caught sight of a beady-eyed, white-chested crow staring at her from a tree to her right. It shrieked, as if cackling at her, then spread its wings and took off into the evening.

PART ONE

Sentry Lodge in the French Alps

Dubai Skyline & the Burj Khalifa Skyscraper

Fresh, soft snow covered the forest surrounding a valley that fit snugly between two majestic mountain ranges. The air was cold, invigorating, befitting an October morning in northern Canada.

From the sky, the valley appeared uninhabited, but in reality it housed an uncharted village. A narrow, mostly frozen river meandered through its length. While the northern bank mainly hosted clusters of five-sided abodes, called *neyra* by the residents, the southern bank accommodated a small school, a community hall, a youth center, storehouses, a large barn, a stable, a convalescence shelter, and even a greenhouse. The roof of every building was expertly fashioned and camouflaged to mimic the appearance of the surrounding foliage.

The scenic village of Dema-Ki was home to just over seven hundred inhabitants, all descendants of a hybrid race of people with an incredible range of abilities, from telekinesis and omnilingualism to extreme speed, agility, and strength, as well as a plethora of other gifts that varied from individual to individual. As extraordinary as this would be in the outside world, it was part of everyday life for the peaceful villagers.

Toward the western end of the valley, a wall of granite encircled an expansive training ground. Spruce, aspens, firs, and other species of trees dotted the mostly open and tranquil space. In a wide clearing, Mariah Ashton bounced on the balls of her feet as she blew into her hands to keep them warm. Her copper-blonde hair, tied into a bun, was hidden under a beanie. Ten yards across from her, in a royal purple headband and moose-hide tunic, stood Saiyu, her mentor and one of the five Elders of

Dema-Ki. Though the Elders were advanced in years, they hardly looked it and moved with the vigor and nimbleness of youth. Combining grace with a regal demeanor, they cast an ethereal presence wherever they went.

"It's so *cold*," Mariah complained to the redheaded teenager standing beside her; he had a hood on and seemed at ease despite the chill in the air. "My fingers are gonna be blue by the time we're done."

Aari Barnes grinned and held up his gloved hands, wiggling his digits. "I'd offer you my gloves, but I'm not that much of a gentleman."

"Pfft. Jerk."

"Pfft. Brat."

Aari was one of the most intelligent people she knew. His ice-blue eyes, often perceived as intense by those who were only acquainted with him superficially, now glittered with amusement at her predicament.

The rest of their group were elsewhere in the training grounds with their own mentors. Mariah cupped a hand over her reddened nose to warm it up. *Ten weeks*, she thought. *It's taken us ten weeks to reach the final stage of training.*

On a trip to Canada over a year ago, the plane carrying her and her friends had crashed near the Yukon–Northwest Territories border. The people of Dema-Ki had taken them in and nursed them back to health. As they healed, the Elders revealed that the teenagers were part of an ancient prophecy, and that they were to halt a cataclysmic threat to humanity. After an initial deep bout of disbelief and skepticism, the friends had eventually agreed to stay and develop their latent abilities. That life-changing decision had opened up a whole new world.

During their first months in Dema-Ki, they'd completed the first stage of their training: self-defense techniques and learning how to harness their individual powers; as well as the second stage, which was similar but far more rigorous.

Before the friends could begin the third and final stage, the

Elders had sent them back to their families with the memories of their time in the valley suppressed. On a trip to California just a few months ago, their recollections had been triggered by someone they'd learn was a Sentry, a descendant of the people of Dema-Ki living in the outside world. From then on, their entire trip to the Golden State became a cross-country race to stop a calamitous scheme set in motion by a clandestine organization bent on wiping out most of humankind and establishing a new world order.

Mariah felt her head spin as she recalled everything that had happened.

The final stage of the training they were now in was the longest and most demanding, focusing on the friends using their abilities in tandem. Even for the Elders this was uncharted territory, as it was outside the range of their own capabilities. Guided by the prophecy that stated the friends were chosen because they possessed this unique and powerful ability, the Elders embarked on training the teenagers with unquestioning faith. That they had to use their gifts jointly was essential in order for the group to fulfill their roles as the Bearers of Light against the gathering storm.

Mariah hoped they were on the right track. So far, they'd had minimal luck with the banded approach. Or, at least, she had.

Up ahead, Saiyu waved Aari aside. Aari removed his gloves and tossed them to Mariah, then went to the far end of the clearing, taking up position behind the Elder. The language barrier used to be a problem—Mariah's and Aari's respective mentors didn't possess the gift of omnilingualism as some villagers did—but in the past two and a half months in Dema-Ki, they had learned enough for basic conversation.

Mariah gratefully slipped on the gloves, then rolled her shoulders back, ready for her warm-up. Saiyu had laid out a variety of objects on the ground between them. Before Mariah could get a good look, the items were suddenly airborne and careening toward her.

She focused on the first object—a stubby branch—and altered its direction with her mind, the same method Saiyu was using to launch the projectiles. She deflected a leather pouch filled with sand in the next millisecond, then faced an incoming water pelt followed by three large pinecones in rapid succession. By the time she recovered from her efforts, she noticed too late a melon-sized ice ball rocketing toward her.

Thunk!

Mariah landed on her back, groaning. *There's another bruise to add to the count . . . Great. Pretty soon I'll have a full constellation on my body.*

She brushed away the ice fragments and got up. Aari, at the far end of the clearing, was hiccupping with laughter.

"Hey, 'Riah"—he could barely get the words out through his giggles—"you should probably get some ice for that!"

She scowled, then pointed her finger at him. His hand involuntarily jerked up and he smacked himself in the face. He staggered back, grabbing his nose. "Oy vey," he moaned. "Ever since you started practicing telekinesis on people, you've been a hazard."

"That's what you get for making a lame joke!" she yelled; it was a feat she would not be able to attempt again for a long, long time, but it was worth it.

Saiyu must have been doing her best to not smile or give the friends any kind of encouragement, but the mirth was plain on her face.

A gruff voice called out. Elder Ashack, Aari's mentor and Saiyu's mate, made his way over, carrying a large pinewood cube. Mariah eyed the man's bare, muscled arms. *Is that all he has in his wardrobe, sleeveless shirts? How is he not freezing?*

The black-haired Elder plunked the cube in the middle of the clearing next to six others and beckoned his apprentice over. Mariah and Saiyu watched as Aari conducted his warm-up. Each cube began to shimmer and, within moments, all had disappeared from sight.

Mariah smiled slightly. It was nice to see how far they'd come. The two of them were now quicker with their abilities, and capable of handling multiple objects at a time.

The second part of Aari's warm-up required him to cloak a grove of four trees. He struggled a bit but managed to conceal three. As he started on the fourth, Mariah used her ability to fling a pebble at the back of his head, distracting him just enough that the very top of the spruce remained visible, floating incongruously in the air. He pulled a grotesque face at her and she grinned.

The first exercise the pair did together required Aari to hide two objects from sight and Mariah to then move them. It was something they'd been struggling with for a week, and it was an infuriating task. The Elders did their best to help but this was new territory, and so they treaded it carefully.

In order to move an object, Mariah needed to see it or at least be able to visualize it if she had seen it previously. Since she didn't know what the objects were, her next best option was to connect with Aari in the novasphere, a dimension of higher consciousness, to sense the object's position. Much easier said than done. She closed her eyes and concentrated.

All there was at first was a shroud of nothingness, speckled by flashes of gray. She breathed slowly and observed the flashes as they pulsed softly then disappeared. When the darkness gave way to a gradual brightening in her mind, she began to sense Aari's presence and instinctively reached out.

She gasped. It was as though she was suddenly seeing through her friend's eyes but there was no actual image, merely an awareness, as if she could feel the physical outline of everything around him. She sensed the objects—the leather pouch and water pelt from her warm-up—and willed them to move. The objects wrestled gravity, then rose a few feet above the ground.

Beside her, Aari murmured, "There you go!"

She moved the objects slowly toward the Elders, who waited with their hands out. She dropped them into their palms and opened her eyes. Their mentors were staring at their empty hands in astonishment, which looked funny until Aari ceased using his ability and the objects became visible.

He pulled her into a victorious hug, whooping and rocking her from side to side. "You did it! You actually did it!"

She squealed and hugged him back. "I did! That was the weirdest thing ever!"

Saiyu ran over and wrapped her arms around her apprentice as well. The comforting scent of pine needles and mountain air wafted into Mariah's nose.

"Well done," the Elder said in her native tongue, beaming.

"Thank you," Mariah replied, words muffled by the sandwich hug. She lifted her index finger over her head at Aari. "I think it's his turn now."

Aari's exercise was to render one of the log cubes invisible while Mariah levitated it from side to side, but she didn't feel it was challenging enough and took it upon herself to make it harder for him. As he worked on concealing the cube, she flung it around willy-nilly, like it was on a roller coaster. Aari frowned, but to his credit he didn't complain. It took a while until he finally managed to make the cube disappear.

Mariah was impressed. "Good job."

He puffed his cheeks. "That was tough."

"That's the point!"

They took turns shuffling through other challenges until the Elders decided they'd had enough teamwork for the day. Ashack and Aari had the run of the place while Saiyu led Mariah to where the trees were denser. Mariah breathed deeply, taking in the freshness of the forest while relaxing her mind and body.

"I have one more task for you, then you are dismissed," Saiyu told her. They came to a small stream; in it sat a boulder the size of a car. The Elder nodded at it. "I want you to lift it."

Mariah rubbed her arms nervously. "That looks pretty heavy . . ."

"I know, youngling. But try."

Mariah sighed inwardly. She'd never attempted to lift anything this size before and knew it would be strenuous. Channeling her attention to the boulder, she willed it to move. It budged ever so slightly. She tried again, and this time it rolled sideways then stalled.

"Keep going," Saiyu urged. It looked as though she wanted to say more, but she didn't. Mariah knew what it was her mentor would have said: it wasn't about how high she could lift the boulder, but about overcoming her fears and believing that she could achieve what might seem impossible.

Saiyu's intense gaze implored her to try again. "Lift it."

Though Mariah had no desire to continue, her mentor was too much of a motherly figure for her to say no. *I'm gonna need two mega-sized aspirins after this*, she thought as she focused on the giant rock.

The boulder lifted a couple of inches off the ground, but that wasn't enough. She pushed herself further, face flushing from the effort, and became increasingly aware of a tension in her head, as if someone had tied a belt tightly around it.

Keep going . . .

It took nearly a minute, but the boulder finally rose a foot above the water. Black spots grew before Mariah's eyes and her head throbbed. When she felt something warm and wet trickling down her nose, she let out a grunt and the boulder dropped. "There," she rasped.

Saiyu looked pained but proud. She passed Mariah a handkerchief and gently massaged the teenager's temples, giving her words of praise as Mariah dabbed the blood from her nose. Once she felt better, they headed back to the clearing where Ashack and Aari were also wrapping up their session. They waved goodbye to the Elders and headed off to check on their friends.

As they strolled through the trees, Aari remarked somewhat sarcastically, "I like how some training sessions are short but intense, and on other days they're long *and* intense."

"I guess we don't have the luxury of relaxed training," Mariah said. "Not with the entire planet spiraling out of control. It's so easy to forget what's going on out there when we're here. Dema-Ki's such a world of its own . . . and I have to admit, I love it."

"Me too."

They neared another clearing and quieted their movements, observing the girl with dark locks who sat cross-legged with her back to them. Peacefully seated directly in front of her were three massive timber wolves. The wolves were still for a few moments, then stirred and looked around in an uncanny, human-like manner.

Mariah's jaw dropped. "She can control more than one animal *at the same time*?"

"I think she's jumping into each one quickly," Aari whispered. "It seems seamless, though, doesn't it? Look at the way they're moving. That's totally Tegan in control."

Tegan Ryder was present in two places simultaneously. Her physical self, Mariah knew, would be motionless until she ended her mindlink with the wolves she was now guiding. Or, at least, that used to be the case. Like those of the rest of the group, Tegan's abilities had grown by leaps and bounds, and sometimes she could engage in a full conversation with others while controlling an animal.

Mariah searched for her friend's mentor. "Where's Elder Tikina?"

"She's around somewhere," Aari said. "Probably figured Teegs could hold her own for a while—which, I mean, she is." The corner of his mouth lifted in wonderment. "Man, I'd give anything to know what it's like to mindlink with an animal. It's a shame we'll never get to find out for ourselves."

The pair watched for a while longer before heading toward the adjacent training ground to scout out the remaining two members of their group. They moved with great care, watching their footing as even a cracking branch might interfere with their friends' training.

A faint *whoosh* sounded above them. They craned their heads back to see a phantom leaping from tree to tree with stealthy dexterity.

"Follow the big monkey," Mariah murmured. She and Aari took off after it, suede boots making hardly any noise in the snow.

They soon found themselves at another training area within the forest. Kody Tyler, an African American teenager sporting an old ball cap turned backward, spotted the pair and grinned. Then, signaling for silence, he scanned the trees, searching for the phantom.

Mariah and Aari retreated behind a frost-covered shrub. Two Elders observed the proceedings calmly from the other side of the training area. One was a tall, stately man with tanned skin and sparkling blue eyes, his ever-present black-and-silver cloak standing in stark contrast to the snow. The other Elder, who was visibly younger, had flaming red hair with matching brows and a beard concealing a mischievous smile.

One more *whoosh* drew Mariah's and Aari's attention up into the trees. The figure they had followed peeled off, circling around Kody as it soared from one tree to another. Its movements were muted but, with his enhanced senses, Kody tracked its every move. The figure dove onto him, arms spread wide to take him down, but Kody easily rolled out of the way. The phantom bounded back into the trees, nothing but a blur, and melted into the shadows.

Kody kipped up and scoured the trees again, concentration etched on his face. He reminded Mariah of a hunter being hunted as he moved slowly, quietly, ears perked. He stiffened suddenly, preparing to lunge to safety, but was pounced on from behind and flattened into the snow. He flailed, then got his head up just long enough to spit out slush and yell, "I could've dodged that! I could've definitely dodged that! Somebody please get this *Sasquatch* off of me!"

Mariah and Aari snickered as they exited the area to save their friend from any further humiliation. The so-called Sasquatch who'd dropped Kody like a sack of potatoes was the last member of their group, Jag Sanchez. He'd gained substantial lean muscle mass from his training in extreme speed, agility, and strength. Kody, though a huge eater, was slim and no match for Jag even without the latter's enhanced abilities.

The sun had begun its descent by the time Mariah and Aari made it out of the training grounds. They crossed a bridge over the river that split the valley in two and passed clusters of *neyra*. As they approached a lone cabin away from the others, Mariah rubbed her temples. "Think I'm gonna skip having dinner with you guys tonight."

"Headache?"

"Yeah."

"I'll make sure Tegan brings you your dinner and *rytèrni* once it's ready," Aari said, referring to the sustenance drink that aided the growth of both their bodies and abilities, and sped the healing of any aches or injuries.

"Thanks, Brainiac. Tell Huyani I'm sorry I'll miss her company."

"Sure thing. Get to sleep early, okay? You'll feel better in the morning, especially after the *rytèrni*." He gave her shoulder a warm squeeze and disappeared into the abode.

Mariah continued down the valley, not noticing her surroundings with her reemerging headache. Muscle memory guided her feet toward the small *neyra* she shared with Tegan. Once inside, she turned on a couple of lamps and shimmied into more comfortable clothes before burrowing under the blanket on her soft bed, her journal in hand. No matter what state her body or mind was in, she made it a point to record the events of each day.

When she'd finished, she flipped through her earlier entries and came across a particularly tense day in mid-July. It described the evening Elder Nageau, Kody's mentor and the leading Elder of the village, arrived at the five's hometown of Great Falls, Montana to meet their parents who knew nothing of Dema-Ki and the prophecy, and divulge the friends' destined roles as the Chosen Ones. Needless to say, the following two weeks had been stressful.

But that was an entry she'd read another time, when exhaustion wasn't bearing down on her.

She tucked the journal under her pillow. The pounding in

her skull had grown in force and all she wanted to do was sleep it off. Pulling the blanket over her ears, she was dead to the world within seconds.

A few days later, the friends strolled along a snowy path on the southern bank of Esroh Lègna, the river that divided the valley. As they headed toward the temple to meet the Elders, they passed the community square where the villagers would assemble for gatherings and special occasions. It was empty this evening, but the friends could clearly remember their first time there. More than a year ago they'd stood nervously in the amphitheater, facing a large crowd as the Elders introduced them as the Chosen Ones to the people of Dema-Ki.

Kody reached for the pendant hanging around his neck. The brushed metal was beautifully engraved with intricate details. A pentagonal crystal of a striking green shade matching his emerald eyes rested in the center, and had a five-pointed star woven from twigs engraved in the middle. He clung onto it, drawing strength. The others carried similar ones, albeit with crystals of a different color and with different designs; they were sacred gifts from the Elders, capable of enhancing their abilities.

The blue-tinted, translucent greenhouse with a pyramid roof soon came into sight on their left. In such a remote setting, a massive building like it should look out of place, but the friends had learned long ago that Dema-Ki was not an ordinary village—and neither were its people. Given all that had happened to them in the past year, Kody would have liked to learn more about the valley, but time was short and they had more pressing matters at hand.

As the group passed the stable and barn beside the greenhouse, a fair, doe-eyed little girl with a long ponytail ran up to Kody and tugged on his sleeve. He smiled and, using his limited knowledge of the language, greeted her. "Hey, little one, what can I do for you?"

She held her arms over her head. He knew exactly what that meant. Picking her up, he placed her on his shoulders. When he saw the grins his friends bore, he grunted good-naturedly. "Not one word from any of you."

For some reason, upon the teenagers' return to Dema-Ki, the younger children had decided that Kody was a perfect steed for their travels up and down the valley. He didn't mind, really, but with Jag's strength and speed he had to wonder why the kids preferred him over his friend. Jag had offered to carry the children, twice, but both times they'd just giggled and pushed his hands away. Mariah's hunch was that Kody, who smiled the most, looked a lot friendlier and the kids probably liked that.

"Hey, check it out," Tegan said, indicating with her chin. "Up ahead. Isn't that Magèo?"

"Can't be," Kody scoffed. "That old coot hates sunlight. He only comes out—oh, would you look at that, it *is* him. What in the world is he doing outside his lab?"

Straight ahead through the trees, a balding, chubby old man with a flowing white beard bent down to observe something in the snow. Beside him was a girl, perhaps in her late teens. Her shoulder-length hair looked strange; it was black on one side and ginger on the other.

"There's a bad joke in there somewhere," Kody said, observing them, "but I can't find it yet. What's going on?"

"Huyani mentioned that Magèo's found an apprentice," Jag told him. "That's probably her."

Not wanting to bother the pair, they gave them a wide berth. Soon the trees thinned out and an incline rose before them. Kody gently placed the little girl on the ground. "Looks like this is where your ride ends."

She pouted, then broke into a toothy grin and scurried back the way they'd come. Kody shook his head in amusement, then followed his friends up the incline. A magnificent, five-sided temple sat atop the terrace. Polished wooden columns stretched thirty feet tall, topped with statues of slender human figures holding up the dome of the building. An impressive stream of colorful fire rose from a marble cauldron at the center of the open foyer, the iridescent flames dancing day and night. It was impossible to walk past without being dazzled by the display.

Inside the temple, four of the Elders were already seated at their regular spot in an alcove at a far corner of the grand hall. Elder Tayoka entered a minute later, his flaming red hair bright against his pasty complexion. He wore a sheepish grin and bowed apologetically to everyone gathered.

Kody laughed to himself. *The fastest Elder is also the tardiest. Now that's irony for you.*

Greeting their mentors, the friends took their places on curved benches facing the Elders. Kody listened to the quiet gurgling of two small water fountains behind the benches and inhaled deeply. The temple was a place of meditation and tranquility where the villagers would come to find peace and spiritual healing, but was now empty as the people of Dema-Ki prepared for their evening meals, allowing the Elders and the friends to have the entire hall to themselves.

Nageau welcomed the teenagers with a warm smile. Kody reciprocated, but noticed tension on his mentor's face. He'd grown more attached to the Elder since the group had returned to Dema-Ki. Nageau was a source of guidance, a foundation of reason and contemplation. Though it was well concealed, after being under the man's tutelage for so long, Kody could easily detect the stress weighing him down.

"How did you find training today?" Nageau asked in an accented baritone. In addition to heightened sensory capabilities, the Elder was gifted with omnilingualism, which made communication a breeze.

He chuckled at the mumbled chorus of "Good" that had become the standard response, then turned his studious gaze to Mariah. "Saiyu tells me that you have been having nosebleeds and headaches again, youngling."

Mariah sighed. "It started when I tried moving a big boulder a few days ago. But I'm okay now. The effects lessen as I get better. I guess it's expected when we take training up a notch. No pain, no gain, right?"

"That may be so, but your well-being comes first. If it does not improve by tomorrow, Saiyu has said she will give you a couple of days to recuperate."

Kody knew what Mariah's response would be before it left her mouth.

"No, thank you," she said firmly. Kody rubbed her shoulder. She returned his gesture with an appreciative pat on the hand.

Nageau dipped his head at her, then addressed the group. "The Elders and I are incredibly proud of each of you. We know the final stage of your training has been challenging, but you have shown unyielding determination to master your abilities. We are astonished by your expanding capabilities with each passing day. We are indeed honored to have the opportunity to be your mentors, though it seems that you are well on your way to surpassing us with your abilities. In fact, some of you already have."

Elder Tikina spoke up, adjusting her green blouse; like her mate, Nageau, she possessed the gift of omnilingualism. "I cannot agree more. This is unexplored territory for us and, just as Kody did during the summer, you may find yourself unlocking different levels to your current abilities, or even attaining new ones altogether. But, as we promised when you returned to Dema-Ki nearly three moon cycles ago, we will continue to help you learn and grow as much as we can."

"We appreciate that," Aari said earnestly.

"What happens when we're done with our training?" Jag asked.

"We will wait," Nageau responded. "The Sentries are on the lookout for disturbances."

Kody blinked. "But aren't the crop destructions disturbing enough? I mean, we've got riots and raids and a war going on."

"There are Sentries who are doing all they can to minimize the effects of the fallout from these events," Tikina said. "But there is an awareness of something far worse lurking just beyond the horizon."

"And what about Reyor?" Tegan asked. "Do we know what that monster's up to?"

"We continue to probe the novasphere, but the harbinger's presence is still masked."

Jag scratched his ear, frowning. "Okay . . . how about Tony and his men? Are we getting anything out of the interrogation?"

On either side of Kody, Tegan and Mariah scowled. The girls harbored an intense hatred for the young man who'd kidnapped them after duping the group with his feigned friendship during their trip to California.

"All that we have managed to extract for now is that he works for the harbinger directly," Nageau said. "His henchmen are not part of Reyor's Inner Circle. They simply follow Tony's instructions without question."

Jag's amber eyes flashed. "*That's it?* We haven't gotten anything else out of them?"

Kody flinched at the sharpness in his tone. *He still holds Tony responsible for his grandmother's death. It's Reyor you should be focused on, man. Keep your eye on the ball.*

Nageau looked rueful. "Tony is remarkably resilient. He is loyal to the harbinger, and it is not merely out of fear. He truly believes in their cause."

"Oh, that we know," Tegan muttered.

Tikina reached out and placed a hand on her apprentice's knee. "We remain confident that the Sentry conducting the interrogation will draw out the necessary information in due time."

The friends glanced at one another with uncertainty. They lapsed into silence for a while, letting the gurgling of the fountains soothe them. Kody rubbed his fingers idly, then said, "I have a question."

Nageau raised a brow. "Yes?"

"That sphere in Reyor's possession—I don't remember what it's called, but you talked about it a little when you met our parents over the summer. You said there were more just like it. Where are they?"

"The *lathe'ad*," Nageau said solemnly. "As I mentioned before, it is an ancient artifact of mysterious origin discovered by our ancestors. The other Elders and I possess four of the five. Elder Tayoka was meant to have the fifth, but the harbinger stole it before being banished from Dema-Ki. It is a device of supreme force and, in the wrong hands—"

A loud commotion outside the temple cut him off. A tanned, broad-shouldered young man with cropped black hair hurried inside, looking anxious and apologetic as he interrupted the meeting. The Elders rose to their feet at once.

"What is it, Akol?" Nageau demanded.

"You might want to see this, Grandfather," the young man replied. He gave the teenagers a quick nod and led the way out of the temple, then broke into a run. The Elders kept pace with him, and the friends followed closely. They wove through the trees, past the community hall, convalescence shelter, and school. A small crowd had gathered around one of the bridges that connected the two sides of the village, and more people were coming out of their homes.

The group slowed when Akol did. Kody heard shocked whispers among the villagers. A few of them looked livid. He frowned. *What's going on?*

Akol pushed his way through, parting the throng of people. He finally came to a stop, glaring at the sight ahead. The Elders and the friends fanned out on either side of him, and froze.

Two youths stood before them. Their clothes were tattered, their bodies gaunt and bruised, their eyes vacant as though they'd gone through hell and back. One of the young men swayed, his legs close to giving out. A large predator's incisor, attached to a black string, hung around his neck, swinging from side to side as he tried to remain upright.

The other youth looked just as battered. Kody remembered the last time he'd seen those eyes; they'd been cold, calculating, and manic. Now they were dull, clouded, almost remorseful.

A silence fell over the crowd until Nageau stepped forward. "Hutar," he said. "Aesròn."

The young men flinched weakly at the authority in his voice but looked up.

"We searched for you. We thought you were dead. Where have you been?"

Tremors of rage coursed through Kody as he silently seethed. *Yeah, where did you run off to after your attempted mass murder?*

Hutar wavered, then dipped his head until his chin touched his chest. "Elder Nageau." His words came out feebly. "The world outside . . . it is not for us."

Beside him, Aesròn attempted to dip his head as well. He faltered, and his eyes rolled to show their whites before his legs buckled.

Tayoka surged forward, lifting Aesròn and slinging him over his shoulders with ease, then instructed two villagers to help the other youth. Reluctantly, the villagers half-carried Hutar and followed the Elder toward the convalescence center.

Akol watched, jaw tight, before turning and striding away, the friends on his heels.

"Akol!" Jag barked as they caught up to him. "What is all this?"

"I do not know," he said through clenched teeth. "But I was glad when they were gone, Hutar especially. Now they are back, just like that, out of nowhere?"

Kody's tremors hadn't ceased. "They should be rotting in a hole somewhere. They're bad news."

"What are the Elders going to do about this?" Tegan asked, brow pinched.

"I have no idea," Akol answered, "but there is something very wrong with this picture."

"We have been at this for *two* days, Nageau! This is the best option we have!"

"It is too drastic! They can still be rehabilitated!"

Ashack leaned forward, a storm whirling in his dark blue eyes. In a quiet, clipped tone, he asked, "And just how well did rehabilitation work for them the last time we attempted it?"

The white-haired Elder sitting across from him averted his gaze to the fire. Ashack watched him, but when he received no answer he sat back, lips pressed together firmly.

The Elders were seated on low, hide-padded wooden benches around a small fire pit in their assembly *neyra*, a place they would gather to meet and discuss community affairs. Against every wall of the shelter were long, polished pinewood shelves. Each held a beautiful carving of a grizzly bear, Tiki-like statues with ancient Phoenician-style inscriptions, and a variety of small plants in terracotta pots.

At the far end of the *neyra*, an exquisitely detailed representation of an island rested atop a marble table. Golden beaches and a glistening turquoise sea surrounded the island, and a volcanic mountain rose grandly from the center, as if watching over everything. Numerous small houses and marketplace shops were positioned around the base of the mountain.

Ashack returned his attention to Nageau when the older man spoke; he sounded drained. "I do not wish to give up on them. They ran away during their rehabilitation, yes, but now they are home and we must look out for them. With our treatments, they are nearly back to full health. All they need now is more nourishment and they will be strong again, and we can then restart their rehabilitation."

"They will indeed be strong," Ashack growled, "but once again we must ask, is that a good thing? Especially in Hutar's case. His lineage is one to question—"

"We do not, and *will not*, judge anyone based on their bloodlines," Nageau said sharply.

Ashack noted the agony in the other Elder's eyes but refused to look away. "We cannot ignore it. What I suggest—"

"What you suggest is far too extreme. It will forever alter their personality."

"It will help them and keep everyone safe!"

"We ought to find out what happened to them after they fled," Saiyu interjected, gazing at Ashack; her expression forced him to settle down. How his mate could give such a pointed yet loving and understanding look was beyond his realm of comprehension.

Tayoka swept his hands through his hair. "Does it really matter? We know what they are capable of. What happened to them outside of Dema-Ki is, in my opinion, of little consequence."

Ashack nodded. Tayoka seemed to be the only one who was ready to side with him. Saiyu and Tikina were not indicating their preference, but he was certain that they would eventually agree with Nageau. Sighing, he tilted his head back to stare at the pointed ceiling of the *neyra*.

His recommendation to use *kah'dloc* was extreme, there was no denying that. The ancient method of resetting an individual's personality required excruciating techniques that would burn away a person's corrupted characteristics and tendencies.

Hutar had always been an unpredictable force, but after his attempt to murder the Elders and their apprentices one night, Ashack could not ease his distrust of the youth. Aesròn, strong, quiet, and manipulative, followed Hutar closely as if he were second-in-command. *Kah'dloc* would be required for him as well.

"Perhaps we could simply suppress their memories," Tikina said. "It is far less intrusive and they will not recall the horrible things they have done."

Ashack crossed his muscled arms over his chest. "That will merely conceal the problem. We need to get to the root of this curse if we hope to eliminate the threat. It needs to go deeper than suppressing memories."

"What you are demanding will affect the core of a person, the soul," Nageau said wearily.

"I hope you understand that this is not an easy thing for me to propose."

"I do. And I also understand what is behind your thinking."

"There is a reason we have *kah'dloc*, Nageau. It may have only been employed a handful of times in our history, but it is useful."

"That is a handful of times in nearly three millennia," Nageau pointed out. "And there is another reason for that. Need I remind you of the records that prove it was not always successful? Hutar and Aesròn are young, they can still change. We merely need patience."

"There was a time for patience," Ashack snapped. "We are past that. We have seen what they are willing to do. I saw no remorse during their nearly year-long period of rehabilitation with us." He stared at Nageau, the flickering fire between them reflected in his eyes. "I know you look for the goodness in everyone. I know you believe in second and third chances. I know you want to forgive and help, but we are past that with these two. You—we—need to realize that."

There was an irritatingly stubborn set to Nageau's jaw. Ashack tempered his exasperation and pressed on. "If they remain as a threat hanging over our people's heads, the village will not take well to that. As it is, their mere presence here has sparked disagreements among our kin. These two will not be treated the same as before. And, unfortunately, our brethren are right to do so, for their safety and for the safety of their families. We cannot endanger them, nor can we forget Hutar's hatred for the Chosen Ones!"

Nageau lowered his head, mouth working as he searched

for words. Ashack waited impatiently for a response, then felt Saiyu's hand on his arm.

"We have been here all morning," she said. "I think we should take some time to reflect, then return in a bit and continue to search for a solution. Come, Ashack. Some fresh air will do us good."

He followed his mate out into the cool midday sun, then turned to her. "We have a solution," he said through his teeth. "Nageau is too stubborn, too attached to the idea that everyone can be reformed. As much as I wish that were true, it is clear that this is not the case with Hutar and Aesròn."

Saiyu placed her hands on either side of his face. At her touch, the storm ebbed out of him. He exhaled his frustration and slowly closed his eyes, feeling her fingers slide through his hair.

"I see how upset you are," she said softly. "This is a difficult thing to consider, and it is also an option we cannot ignore. You are right, Nageau is a hopeful man who sees the best in everyone. But that is his gift. He feels he made a mistake with Reyor's banishment and wishes to avoid a rash decision with Hutar and Aesròn."

"His gift will be his downfall."

She wrapped her arms around him. "Let us hope not, my love."

He hugged her, taking in her strength. They remained together in silence until he murmured, "If Hutar and Aesròn remain here and all that we focus on is their rehabilitation, I fear for everyone's safety. They were not above murder before, why would they be any different now? Think of the people, the children, the youth. What will we say to their families should the worst happen?"

Saiyu stiffened. "I know. A parent should never have to bury their child." She placed her cheek on his shoulder. In a quiet voice, she said, "I miss him, Ashack."

He felt her tears slide down his bare arm and held her closer. "I miss him, too. It does not get easier with time."

A hunting accident had taken the life of their sole child nearly three decades prior; he was only fifteen. They were heartbroken parents, and still now it hurt. Saiyu had wept every night for a long time after that, the sound of which filled Ashack with so much pain. They'd eventually tried to have another child but could not conceive. Ever since, they had dedicated their lives to serving their people and were, in time, admitted as Elders after the passing of the previous ones.

Saiyu pulled back and dried her eyes with the hem of her sleeve. Ashack kissed her cheeks a few times, and together they entered the *neyra* and took their place around the fire. He returned to his usual gruff self as he acknowledged the others.

Nageau held up a hand. "I hear hurried footsteps heading this way."

A knock sounded on the door moments later. Saiyu went to open it and a tall girl with straight raven-colored hair tumbling over her slender shoulders stepped in. She smoothed her buckskin tunic, then dipped her head to the Elders.

"Is something the matter, Huyani?" Nageau asked.

"You wished to be informed when Hutar and Aesròn were fully awake. They are now, Grandfather."

The Elders glanced at one another, then rose to their feet in unison. They left the *neyra* with Huyani and strode toward the convalescence center near the riverbank. Outside the door of the large wooden building, they took a moment to compose themselves before entering. Akol straddled a chair at the far corner of the ward, arms folded on the backrest, looking cross. Huyani joined him.

The Elders passed two rows of empty beds lined against the windowed walls. Upon reaching the young men, now sitting upright in their cots, they spread out and stood by the beds; Tayoka, Saiyu, and Ashack facing Hutar, and Nageau and Tikina by Aesròn. The youths placed a fist over their heart and bowed their heads at the Elders. Ashack eyed the pair with mistrust.

"How are you feeling?" Nageau asked.

"Much better, Elder Nageau," Hutar answered, avoiding the older man's gaze. "Thank you."

"You ought to give your thanks to Huyani, as it was her skill that has healed you."

"Yes, Elder Nageau. We are very grateful to her."

"You realize that we have much to discuss."

"We know. We also wish to ask for forgiveness for running off."

Ashack noted that Aesròn was quiet and withdrawn, light green eyes distant. His hand twitched under his blanket as if Hutar's chastened words were giving him spasms.

"Why did you do it?" Saiyu asked. "You were being cared for. We did all we could to help you rather than punish you."

"Being here was humiliating," Hutar said, glaring at the foot of his bed. "Everyone looked at us like we would turn around and . . . and hurt them. We were not welcome. We felt that we would never be."

Ashack's nostrils flared. "And yet you returned. What you tried to do was beyond pardonable. There are consequences to your actions. Did you really think all would be easily forgiven?"

"We returned because the outside world was too foreign for us," Aesròn retorted. Ashack shot him an acidic look.

"That is another issue," Tayoka said flatly. "We scoured the novasphere for your presence and could not find you. Clearly, you were not dead and yet you were hidden. How did you do that? And why did you go to the outside world to begin with?"

"And," Tikina added, "why did you not reach out to us when you learned the outside world was not for you?"

"It is a technique that we practiced and perfected for ourselves," Aesròn answered. His hand twitched again under the blanket.

"We did not reach out to you because we"—Hutar's face flushed—"we were too proud. We were too proud, and—"

Aesròn suddenly threw off his blanket. Something sharp glinted in his left hand as he lunged toward Nageau.

"Aesròn!" Hutar roared. *"No!"*

None of the Elders moved fast enough, not even Tayoka. As the knife arced down, Hutar hurtled out of his bed and leapt in front of Nageau. The weapon sank into his chest. He screamed and buckled, falling to the floor, a scarlet stain growing on his shirt. A look of horror shadowed Aesròn's face and he stumbled away from his friend.

Tayoka dove at Aesròn, slamming him to the ground. The youth swore and fought against him, clawing, biting, and kicking. Ashack shot forward to help, though Tayoka could have easily managed on his own, and they kept Aesròn pinned in place.

It was as if time had slowed to a crawl and Ashack was seeing everything around him move agonizingly slow. He looked over his shoulder where the others were leaning over Hutar, working to staunch the bleeding. Then sharp pain clamped around his wrist. Aesròn had dug his teeth into Ashack's skin, madly rocking his head to and fro. The Elder tried to wrench his arm free but the younger man gnawed harder. Ashack felt his skin tear and warm blood trickled out. Agony flared white-hot in his arm.

Tayoka seized a fistful of Aesròn's hair and forcefully yanked his head back. The youth, his mouth stained red, bared his teeth at the Elders. Ashack glanced down at his open wound to assess the damage. In that moment, Aesròn, who had worked one of his arms free, tore off the incisor he wore around his neck and thrust it deep into Tayoka's side.

The Elder bellowed and his hand immediately flew to the injury. Aesròn jammed his knuckles into Tayoka's face before kicking loose. Ashack made a grab for him, but the youth knocked him down, stomped on his wounded wrist, and took off running. Akol let out a shout as he gave chase, and they disappeared out the door.

Ashack gasped, holding his limp wrist. Tayoka had pulled the incisor out of his rib and flung it aside. He got to his feet but couldn't get more than a few steps before doubling over, blood spilling past his hands as he held his wound.

Ashack's mind was whirling. He tried to process everything through the blazing pain, unaware that Saiyu and Tikina had hastened over and were tending to him and Tayoka.

What just happened?

The sky overhead in Swansea, Wales, was bright blue with scattered clouds. People milled about the Maritime Quarter, many making their way to the beaches to stroll with their children on the shoreline despite the bite in the air. The adults were taut-faced while their little ones padded along happily, oblivious to the blight afflicting the world. A man reading a newspaper on a park bench glowered at the headline: 'UN SECURITY COUNCIL CONVENES 5TH EMERGENCY MEETING.'

Two younger men passed him, one enjoying a cone of ice cream. He raised a disapproving eyebrow at their breezy attitudes, wondering how anyone could act carefree at such a time, before burying his nose back in his paper.

Gareth Vaughn chomped down on the last bit of his waffle cone. Though it was mid-autumn, the cold, creamy delight was his favorite dessert at any given time of the year. His only grievance was the inflated price he'd had to pay. Beside him, his identical twin brother held an enormous bouquet of colorful flowers, sneezing and complaining about the strong fragrance. Both men were tall with brown hair and had cheeky glints in their chestnut eyes. But behind the impish gazes were brilliant minds that few could match.

The brothers were similar in many ways, but their tastes in music and clothing differed greatly; Gareth was into rock 'n' roll and leather jackets, while Deverell's wardrobe consisted of blazers and his go-to playlist was filled with blues and jazz.

As the pair ambled toward the small hospital ahead, they engaged in an animated discussion about the state of their city's football club. It was a common topic the two could go on about for hours; a lifelong passion that now doubled as a diversion to get their minds off the troubling condition of the world.

"I'm telling you, Dev," Gareth said, shaking his hair away from his face, "the Swans need to bring back the Monk."

"That would just be like patching a hole, not finding a solution," his brother replied. "We need to get us a coach like Ranieri. Build us up from zero."

Gareth rolled his eyes. "Come *on*, mate. Finding a coach like him is just blind luck, and that's not something we can count on."

"I says they should build around Ayew and start from there." Deverell opened the door and walked into the hospital. "One day . . . one day we shall attain the realms of Swancelona."

"Swaaaancelona," Gareth chanted in reverence. The women behind the reception desk looked up at them, frowning.

Deverell whacked his brother on the shoulder. "Shh, there're sick people around!"

"Then they need cheering up, don't they? I mean, we all do." In a whisper, Gareth continued, *"Swaaaancelona."*

Stifling a laugh, Deverell approached the desk. *"Bore da,"* he greeted. "We're here to see Owen Vaughn."

After signing the visitor sheet, the pair took an elevator up and tromped down the long corridor to a room marked A14. Gareth knocked on the door before they stepped in.

An older man, with thick gray hair and prominent sideburns, opened his eyes from where he lay on the bed. He beamed when he saw his guests. "Deverell! Gareth!" He sat up and held his arms wide open. "Gimme a *cwtch*, the both of you!"

They hugged him warmly in response, then presented him with the bouquet.

"They're proper lush," he said, taking it. "Are these for your aunt?"

Gareth rolled his eyes again and smiled. "We thought these would add some color to this dull room. We picked the best for the only person who would dare babysit us when we were tykes." He reached into his jacket and pulled out a box of chocolates.

"We also got these for you, just in case."

"Now, that's more like it." Their uncle took the box approvingly and opened it. "How long has it been since I last took care of you two? You were, what—four, five years old?"

"Around that, yeah."

"Nearly thirty years . . ." The old man's lips twitched, wistful. "*Tempus fugit.*" He pointed at Gareth. "You need to get rid o' that mop on your head. Look at your brother. That's a right proper short cut, that."

"I'm quite happy with it, actually," Gareth replied, feigning annoyance. "In any case, how are you, Uncle?"

"Better. I should be out within a couple days, I think. It's nothing major, but the doctors want to keep an eye on me anyway."

"Has Dad come to visit you yet?" Deverell asked.

"Hah. That no-good brother o' mine said he might drop by tomorrow. Don't get me wrong, I love the old butt, I do. He just tends to put work ahead of everything and everyone else, including himself. How he ended up with a gem like your mother is beyond me." He shook his head in wonder. "Her love and patience is truly a testament to her character. And the way you two were raised . . . Well, that speaks volumes about her, too. There's something very special about that woman. Quite the enigma, she is."

The brothers gave each other secretive smiles. They were incredibly proud of their mother, and she was indeed a special woman of a distinct lineage with a significant obligation—an obligation that had been passed on to her two sons.

"So, what of you both?" their uncle asked. "Still freelancing?"

Deverell shared another quick smile with Gareth. "Aye."

"Good to hear it. And you're still traveling often?"

"Wherever the job is, that's where we go, Uncle."

"I never get to hear what these jobs are," the old man mused.

Gareth patted his hand. "We're not always at liberty to talk about it, but they're important, I promise you that."

Their uncle snorted. "'Not at liberty,' my arse. For all I know, you could be running around for MI6 or the CIA." He grew wide-eyed. "Oh, no."

Deverell and Gareth leaned in, worried. "What is it?"

"Don't you dare go James Bond on me. He's not even Welsh!"

The twins chuckled. They sat at their uncle's bedside, munching on the chocolates and sharing stories for nearly an hour, when a shrill voice from the hallway interrupted their conversation.

"What do you mean, you're not able to do anything? My husband's barely fifty-five! Look at him!"

Gareth and Deverell swapped inquisitive looks before tiptoeing to the door and poking their heads out into the hallway. A woman dressed in a bright red coat was screaming deliriously at a doctor a few doors down from them. The poor man winced, looking as if he wanted to be anywhere else in the world.

"She sure is tampin'-fumin'-ragin'," Gareth whispered. "Wonder what's got her all riled up."

He looked at his brother, who nodded in response.

"We'll be back soon," Deverell promised their uncle.

The old man waved his hand at them. "Go on, you two. Always were meddlesome . . ."

The twins waited until the woman and the doctor disappeared into the room, presumably that of the ailing husband, before slinking down the hall. They stopped at the open door and peeped in.

The woman was blocking their view of the patient. "Does this look right to you?" she demanded, crying now. "Does this look *normal?*"

The doctor pinched his nose. "I am so sorry. This is unlike anything we've ever dealt with before."

"He's been in your care for nearly a week!" she shrieked. "And all you can do is *apologize*?"

She spun around and walked to the corner of the room, hands covering her face, not bothering to hide the sound of her sobbing. The brothers were left agape at the sight that met them.

Lying on the bed was an emaciated man with pale, sagging

skin; there was hardly a trace of fat or muscle on him. He was mostly bald, with liver spots inked on his head and deep wrinkles engraved on his face. If anything, he resembled a gaunt and sickly octogenarian.

Deverell stepped into the room and cleared his throat. "Did you say he's fifty-five?"

The doctor's head snapped up. "Sir, I must ask you to leave—"

"Yes!" The woman ran up to the twins, eyes red. "He was in peak health only a few weeks ago. They've run test after test, but the bloody doctors can't tell me what's wrong!"

"Hey, now, look here," the doctor began to protest before stopping himself and facing the brothers. "I need you two to leave right now, alright? This doesn't concern you."

Deverell and Gareth complied and retreated to their uncle's room. He'd been dozing but sat up attentively when they closed the door behind them. "Satisfied your curiosity?"

Deverell flopped down on one of the chairs. "Not even close."

"What is it, Dev?"

His nephew shuddered. "There is a patient in one of the rooms down the hall. He looks like a corpse, Uncle. Just skin and bones. And terribly aged."

"He's just fifty-five," Gareth added, hushed. "According to the wife, he was perfectly fit only a few weeks ago. It's as if he aged years in mere days."

The old man frowned. "That sounds terrible. Could it be some kind of disease?"

"Entirely possible. Like progeria, where premature aging occurs. But—"

"—those who do have that disorder rarely live past their teens," Deverell said. "In fact, the oldest known progeria sufferers were—"

"—a fellow from South Africa who only lived to be twenty-six, and an American woman who lived until twenty-nine. The bloke in the other room is in his fifties and it's only now affecting him. It's completely unheard of."

"How awful. Just . . . so, so awful." The old man rested his head back on the pillow. “It’s times like these when I can’t help but think of how unfair this world is, how buzzing it is.”

“It’s not all that bad,” Gareth lied, adjusting his uncle’s pillow.

“Are you touched in the head? Don’t you see what’s happened to the world in the last few months?”

The twins went quiet.

“War has broken out! China and India have gone after *Russia!* People around the world are *dying* of starvation because of the bloody crop destruction! We go on with our lives because *we* weren’t affected too badly, but we’re only pretending that we aren’t really surrounded by hellfire!” The old man’s voice shook. “As I said, lads, the world is buzzing.”

The brothers looked down at their feet.

Their uncle sighed wearily. “I’ve ruined a perfectly good visit. I’m sorry.”

Deverell managed a smile. “It’s alright. We’re just worried you’ve tired yourself out more than you should’ve.”

“I did. That was foolish of me.” The old man coughed. “Go, the both o’ you.”

“Are you sure?” Gareth asked, biting his lip.

“Very. I feel a nap stalking me, and I doubt you’d want to be around when I start snoring.”

The pair hugged him, reluctant to go. “Take care, Uncle,” Deverell said as they headed out. “We’ll make sure Dad visits tomorrow.”

“Glad to hear that.”

As soon as they exited the elevator on the ground floor, they heard hysterical shouting coming from the reception area next to the Emergency Room. They sprinted down the hallway to where a young couple was confronting the receptionists, both of them weeping.

“Please,” the man begged, “please! Get us a doctor! We need help!”

The brothers came to a grinding halt, the blood draining from their faces when they saw the bundle in the woman’s arms.

Something peered out at them, but they couldn't call it a baby. With deep lines across its face, it looked so haggard, so sickly . . . so *old*.

Gareth was unable to take his eyes off the child as a doctor rushed to examine it. He felt Deverell grip his arm tightly. "That's not right," his brother said. "That's not right at all. He looks just like the man in the room, Gareth. This can't be a coincidence."

Gareth turned his back to the family. "There's something wrong about all this," he murmured. "And with all that we've learned these past few months . . ." He glanced over his shoulder at the baby, fear trickling into him. "We should look into this. If it's more than a rare disease, we'll have to contact the League."

My name is Tony Cross. That rotting corpse crawling toward me isn't real. Neither is that cobra. I'm—come on, keep it together. Keep it together. Where was I? Right . . . my name is Tony Cross. That rotting corpse crawling toward me isn't real . . .

The blaring death metal was certainly real enough, though. The speakers in the opposite corner of the tiny, cramped room were small, mobile, and packed a punch, but with one arm cuffed to the steel bed frame, Tony couldn't reach them. He would kill for five minutes of silence.

He stared up at the ceiling through bloodshot eyes and licked his dry, cracking lips. The grinning face of the Cheshire cat stared back down at him. He closed his eyes.

Not real. Obviously.

Using sleep deprivation as one of several interrogation tactics was a smart move on his captor's part, but Tony wouldn't fold. Though physically on the smaller side, he was resilient, and ferociously loyal to his leader.

The holding cell he'd been living in—for the past weeks, months, who knew—looked like a windowless storage room. He assumed he was being kept in a warehouse, most likely an abandoned one from the brief glimpses he got whenever his interrogator opened the door to enter or to leave.

The interrogator, strangely, was treating him decently enough in some aspects. A travel-sized porta potty was just within his reach. A musty mattress lay on the bed. He received food twice a day, sometimes, although it was hard to figure the passage of time while being holed up in a room continuously lit by a single incandescent bulb.

He'd tried asking what had happened to his team; they'd all been locked in a shipping container on the Sanchez farm in Kansas, but after being blindfolded and moved to this new place, Tony had found himself alone. The only answer he'd gotten was that the interrogator had seen to it that his men were now behind bars, which didn't entirely surprise him given their long rap sheets.

His ears pricked when he heard the door click open and swing outward. *Interrogation session number . . . I don't know anymore.* He'd long since given up trying to figure out the interrogator's routine and now just went along with it.

A man entered, slipping a car remote into the pocket of his parka, and hung the coat on a nail in the wall beside the door. A black balaclava covered all but his hazel eyes, and the hood of his sweatshirt was pulled over his head. He turned off the music and the sudden quiet rang in Tony's ears just as loudly as the pounding death metal.

Tony raised his head and sneered, tongue resting between his teeth. "You just can't keep away, can you?"

The man twirled the silver rings he wore on his middle fingers as he looked down at his captive. The unpredictability in those intense eyes was disconcerting. "You know the deal." The voice was toneless and husky. "You give me what I need to know, I let you go. It's that simple."

"And you know my deal," Tony replied evenly. "You answer my questions and perhaps I just *might* comply."

"You're more delusional than I thought. You're not in a position to negotiate." The man cocked an eyebrow at Tony's handcuffs. "I don't have time for this."

"Really? Because you've been doling out this interrogation for a while now. I'm sure you could spare a few minutes."

The man slowly crouched in front of him, not once breaking eye contact. Tony's sneer wavered slightly.

"You know something?" the interrogator murmured. "I think

I just may have a cure for your delusion." He turned to the open door and let out a low whistle. A canine form stalked into the room, the silver-gray fur on its shoulders and back bristling. Tony instinctively moved away from the wolfish beast as it licked its chops.

"Where is your boss?" the interrogator asked.

"Bite me," Tony spat.

"I'm sure my partner here would love to."

The animal lunged forward, jaws snapping inches from Tony's nose. He recoiled, tousled blond hair falling into his face. He yelled and tried to kick the creature away, but weeks of being inert had rendered his muscles nearly useless. "I'm not talking!"

"Back, Chief," the interrogator said calmly. The animal obeyed its master and retreated from the room, growling deep in its throat.

"You can try to threaten me," Tony said, breathing heavily, "but you haven't hurt me as much as you could have. Either you have some kind of a personal code, or you're under orders not to seriously harm me."

The man ignored him and turned the music back on. Tony shuddered involuntarily at the sudden discharge of throaty screaming over raucous guitar riffs. He watched as his interrogator grabbed his coat from the wall, slipped it on, and exited the room, shutting the door behind him. This had been one of the calmer and shorter sessions. Still, Tony tugged angrily on the handcuff, trying for the thousandth time to break free, but he was locked in. Bruises around his left wrist taunted him about his previous failed attempts.

With great effort he climbed onto the stale-smelling mattress and lay askew, one leg off the side. It wasn't so much the fact that he was captured that annoyed him, but rather that he was unable to be at his leader's beck and call.

Of course, having been caught is embarrassing. I'm probably the laughingstock of the Inner Circle.

A barely perceptible glint at the far end of the bed pulled him away from his self-pity. He stretched out, pushing two fingers into the hole in the mattress until he felt something thin and smooth against his fingertips. Pinching the object, he raised his hand to inspect it. To his surprise, it was an old paperclip.

How come I've never noticed that before? he wondered, confused. But his confusion grew into cautious delight. This could be his ticket out.

He straightened the clip, stuck it into the lock of his handcuff, bent it until it was the right shape then turned it, working the end back and forth. There was a small, distinctive click and the cuff opened. He slid his hand free, tenderly touching his bruises, thrilled that he could finally move. Despite the disgusting music that made his skull throb, he was much more at ease.

And he had a plan.

* * *

It felt like hours before the interrogator returned. Tony was already positioned to look as though he was still cuffed as the door opened. "Hey, big fella," he greeted as the man turned the music off. "Thought I'd never see you again."

Only the interrogator's eyes were visible, but his gaze conveyed his scathing smirk well enough. He shrugged off his coat and hung it on the nail.

Tony counted the man's steps as he approached. When he was a couple of feet away, he launched himself at the masked figure, throwing him off-balance and into a wall. With the interrogator momentarily stunned and winded, he grabbed the man's coat and ran out of the room, bare feet making no sound on the dirty concrete. His legs protested at the sudden exercise but he pushed on. Though the building was dark, he saw stars through a skylight in the high ceiling. Frigid gusts of wind billowed through broken windows, and fading light outlined a single, ill-fitting door.

It's a warehouse, alright. Looks like it's been out of commission for ages.

From the darkness, his interrogator's voice thundered

through the building. "Chief! On him!"

A howl echoed inside the warehouse. Unable to pinpoint where it was coming from, Tony sprinted and shoved against the door, which opened into the cold outside air. He rounded the edifice, frantically clicking buttons on the car remote. A blaring alarm went off and he followed the sound to the front of the warehouse where an old, dirt-caked red pickup hailed him. As he hobbled over, the smashing of glass made him look back.

The muscular, wolf-like creature had crashed through a window and was making a beeline for him. He jumped for the truck, slamming the door just as the animal leapt onto the hood. He fumbled the key into the ignition and the vehicle roared to life. Speeding away from the warehouse in reverse, he did a one-eighty. The animal held on for a few seconds before being shaken loose.

Shifting gears, he tore down a dirt road past other decrepit buildings. Graffiti defaced the brick and stone walls. He was driving too fast to make out most of them, but one stood out starkly: *NO GREEDY CORPS. NO CORRUPT GOVT. BURN THEM ALL DOWN.*

A layer of frost on the dirt and grass reflected under the truck's headlights. There were no streetlamps until he approached a main road, where the crumbling industrial zone gave way to residential buildings. He kept checking his rearview mirror. Though he could see no indication of pursuit, paranoia drove him to step on the gas.

More signs of life appeared. A handful of cars came and went. He peered around for street signs but couldn't make out the names in the dim light. *Where am I?*

Another check in his rearview mirror caused his heart rate to shoot up. A pair of headlights had materialized some distance away. *Is he following me? Or is that a local heading somewhere?*

Either way, he wasn't keen to find out. He floored it. The truck picked up speed and barreled straight through a four-way stop sign. Brightness suddenly flooded into the vehicle from Tony's right. He spun the wheel but couldn't stop, and the truck smashed into the side of a small car. He jolted forward, smacking his head on the steering wheel. Groaning, he pushed through the pain and made sure the pickup was still functioning, then backed up and sped away from the scene. A middle-aged woman who had staggered out of the car screamed at him.

Oh, shut up. At least you're alive.

The truck's headlights lit up a large green sign by a freeway ramp—*Edmonton 400 km*. Tony's eyes stretched wide.

"Edmonton . . . *Canada?*" he exclaimed. "You've got to be kidding."

He entered the freeway, which was almost devoid of other cars. Something dripped down the bridge of his nose. He wiped it with his hand and crimson colored his palm. Grumbling, he pressed his arm against his forehead so his sleeve could soak up the blood. The cut hadn't looked too bad in the mirror.

He eyed the gas gauge. *Full tank. Good, 'cause I don't have my wallet or phone. I need to figure something out, fast.*

The pickup's dash clock read just after ten p.m., which meant it was nine p.m. in California. He knew a man there who could help him with his situation, who was most likely working late in Phoenix Corporation's office.

He checked his mirrors and did a double take. Was that the same pair of headlights from earlier? Making a split-second decision, he took an exit into a gas station to see if the vehicle would follow, but the black Dodge truck cruised past without slowing. Tony let go of the wheel and leaned back, swallowing in relief.

Okay. It's okay. I'm good.

He parked and scoured the glove compartment for loose change. He found some, and was about to step out when he realized he was still barefoot. Fishing around behind the driver's seat, he dug out a pair of old work boots. Then, with his head down, he slunk toward a payphone to make a collect call.

As he waited to be connected, he examined the newspaper stand outside the door of the gas station. *'Food riots continue across province'? Really? In Canada?*

A man on the other end of the line answered, businesslike. "Hello?"

"Adrian. It's Tony."

There was the slightest pause. "Tony who?"

"Tony Cross."

A longer pause. Tony sighed and supplied a few nonsensical phrases to give the man time to electronically verify his voice.

"Tony! What in the—how? What happened? Where are you?"

"I'm two hundred and fifty miles from freakin' Edmonton, Adrian."

"Canada?"

"Yeah."

"But what . . . who—"

"Listen to me. I get it, you have a lot of questions, but I need to talk to the Boss right away. I'm not on a secure line so you gotta patch me through, scramble my call."

"I . . . yeah, sure. Will do. Stand by."

Tony drummed his fingers on the payphone box. Without warning, a voice spoke in his ear, almost metallic from the effect of a vocal modulator. "Anthony Evander Cross."

The world around him ceased to be, and a piercing chill coursed down his back. "Hello, Boss."

"You're alive."

"I am. I—"

"Get to Edmonton and call Adrian for instructions. I will make arrangements for your safe passage."

Taken aback by the curtness, Tony stammered, "I-I'm forever and always in your debt. Thank you, Boss."

"I will see you soon, Tony." The call went dead.

He hung the receiver in its cradle, hurried back to the pickup, and pulled onto the freeway; he had a death grip on the wheel. While doggedly faithful he, along with everyone else under the Boss's management, had a healthy amount of fear for Phoenix's founder. Failure of any kind was not tolerated.

But that's to be expected. The Boss's vision is glorious. A better world. A brighter future. A small, crooked leer played on Tony's lips. And we're almost there.

The black Dodge truck parked under an overpass waited for the old pickup to zoom back onto the freeway. Starting the engine, the driver inside wore a ghost of a smile, hazel eyes tracking the vehicle as he kept at a good distance. The wolfdog in the passenger seat beside him observed the pickup with the same cool, intense gaze as its owner.

Steering with one hand, the man scratched the animal behind the ear. "We got him right where we want him, Chief."

The friends stood under one of the gazebos bordering Dema-Ki's community square as they watched the villagers disperse after the evening's gathering. The swaying flames from a fire pit cast a soft glow on their faces. Still pondering the Elders' dialogue, Jag heard murmurs of uncertainty and concern from the people as they left the square. He empathized with them. How were they to make sense of Hutar saving Nageau's life when he'd attempted to kill all the Elders the previous summer? Add to that Aesròn's escape from the valley, and it was no wonder they were troubled.

Then there was the matter of something the Elders had said during the gathering that had left Jag unsettled.

"I hope it isn't true," he murmured.

"What?" Kody asked, turning around to warm his back.

"That because Reyor now knows about us and our connection to Dema-Ki, the village might be in the crosshairs."

"It's not *because* of us," Aari corrected. "It's because the Elders are aware of Reyor, and Reyor is aware that they're aware. It's no longer a secret that Dema-Ki is actively engaged in thwarting Phoenix's plans. Guess it's only prudent to be prepared for any eventualities."

Mariah exhaled loudly. "You guys say that name so freely."

"What name?"

"You *know* who!"

"What is this? A He-Who-Must-Not-Be-Named moment?"

Kody clutched his chest as if having a heart attack. "No, please, don't say the Dark Lord's name!"

Jag could tell Mariah was biting back a laugh. "You know the people around here don't really like hearing it," she said.

"We're the only ones here right now, 'Riah," Aari replied. "But alright."

Jag traced the path of a minute piece of burning ash as it floated upward, a glowing orange speck traveling to the gazebo's ceiling. A quote from Leo Tolstoy that Mariah had shared some weeks back returned to him, as it often did since he'd first heard it: "*There is something in the human spirit that will survive and prevail. There is a tiny and brilliant light burning in the heart of man that will not go out, no matter how dark the world becomes.*"

He glanced over at Mariah. She seemed lost in contemplation. Tegan, too, had retreated into her thoughts. He smiled slightly. It was amazing watching their growth over the years, to see how they were both developing into their own persons when, as children, they'd been particularly attached at the hip.

Tegan had grown to command respect from others for her tenacity. Her penetrating gray, almost silver, eyes would sweep a room, observing everything and everyone with a sharpshooter's astuteness. Mariah was all spunk yet cautious, and she enjoyed retreating into a fortress of books, stories that took her to other worlds and on great adventures. Together, the two could become a force to be reckoned with—and they had proven as much when they'd commandeered a four hundred-ton mining truck to escape their abductors. Jag was still awed, thinking about it months later.

Aari, standing across the pit from him, tightened the drawstrings of his hoodie. "I wonder how things are at home. It sucks that we haven't been able to talk to our families for . . . how long has it been? Two and a half months now?"

"I'm sure they're fine," Kody said, fidgeting with his ball cap. "Worried sick, but fine."

"That's quite the oxymoron, Kode-man."

"You're the oxymoron . . . moron . . ."

Tegan yawned. "As much as I'd love to stick around for more brilliance from Daffy Duck and Elmer Fudd, I'd like to turn in. It's been a long day."

Mariah nodded. "Me too."

"Aw," Kody pouted. "I thought we could all head over to Huyani's and hang out with her and Akol for a bit."

"Tomorrow. Promise."

Jag pulled Tegan and Mariah in for a hug. "Rest well, you two."

They smiled, bid the boys goodnight, and headed to their *neyra* across the river. Once they were out of earshot, Kody whispered, "Guys' night!"

Jag slung his arms around his friends' necks and, together, they made their way up the valley to meet Huyani and Akol.

* * *

Tegan fell into her bed without changing and was out in a heartbeat. Mariah removed her friend's boots and covered her with her blanket, then quickly donned her own pajamas. She turned off one lamp, keeping the other lit before rummaging through her heavy backpack. She'd filled it with everything she needed from home: her essentials, a large yellow envelope containing photos, and her phone and charger. In retrospect, bringing her phone along might have been useless, but it did give her comfort.

She'd also crammed in as many books as she could, alongside an extra journal and plenty of pens. In a small pocket was a bottle of cologne that had belonged to her father before her parents' separation, and his subsequent passing after a battle with cancer. The bottle was almost empty. Anytime she felt alone she'd pull the cap open, inhale the scent, and reunite with him in her memories.

She was tempted to reach for it, but instead grabbed a pen and withdrew to her bed. Picking up her journal, she jotted in small, neat writing the happenings of the day. When she finished, she flipped back to one particular entry.

It was agonizing to look over the events of the week after Nageau had visited the friends' parents at the Sanchez house. Equally difficult was the memory of the meeting itself. Mariah rested her head on her pillow and closed her eyes as her mind wandered involuntarily to that fateful afternoon, every detail as sharp as if it had occurred only moments ago.

The Elder's stately presence had filled the space as he addressed the parents. To Mariah, the familiar scent of forest pine elicited entrancing recollections of Dema-Ki.

The large group was seated on couches and chairs against each side of the living room. Jag had offered Nageau his family's heritage leather chair in one corner, usually reserved for special guests and family members, earning questioning looks from his parents.

Marshall Sawyer, who'd brought the Elder to the Sanchez home, stood behind Aari with folded arms. A former Marine with a short beard and dirty-blond hair, he was an American-based Sentry who had worked closely with the friends over the summer as they fought the blight that destroyed crops across North America.

Jag rubbed his hands nervously. "Uh, everyone, I'd like you to meet Marshall"—he motioned at the Sentry with his head—"and Elder Nageau."

Nageau had smiled disarmingly from where he sat on the leather chair, and in a rich, accented voice said, "I am sure you have many questions as to who I am and why I am here. Please allow me to put those questions to rest. As Jag said, my name is Nageau, and my home is a remote village quite far north of here. My people nursed your sons and daughters back to health after their aircraft crashed near our valley over a year ago."

Aari's father was stunned. "They . . . they were with you all those months?"

Nageau nodded, glacial-blue eyes sweeping over each parent. The hush that followed was thunderous to Mariah's ears.

"I'm lost for words." Roberto Sanchez, a spitting image of Jag, turned to his son and placed a hand behind the boy's head with a look of alarm only a parent could possess.

"I must tell you," Nageau continued carefully, "that the healing of your children was not all that took place during their time with us, nor was their accident a completely random event."

Mariah's foot tapped a rapid beat. *Nageau's actually gonna talk about it. Ohhh, my goodness.*

Tegan noticed the tapping and put a hand on her knee to stop her.

Mariah watched the adults as the Elder recounted, with some help from the teenagers, the full story, from the moment the friends were brought to Dema-Ki to their training and the Battle of Ayen'et, to the suppression of their memories and the trip to California that had turned into a mission to stop the crop destruction.

He then went on to explain some of the history of his people, as well as the prophecy that foretold a coming global conflict. The parents listened in muted shock. Kody's father, who had piloted the plane that crashed, sat with his hands clasped together against his forehead.

Turning to what Mariah figured was the final proof in his arsenal, Nageau called on the friends to demonstrate their abilities. Aari, hesitant, directed the assembly's attention to the large television and made it disappear from sight, part by part. Mariah chose to believe that the yelps from their families were those of amazement.

When it was her turn, she pointed at the coffee table and levitated it. At this point, she was surprised her own mother hadn't fainted, though she did seem on the brink. The other teenagers followed suit, each demonstration quicker than the one before.

"As you can see," Nageau said once some semblance of calm had returned, "your children have extraordinary gifts."

"Apparently," Mrs. Barnes whispered, staring at her son. Aari gave an awkward smile.

"There is one more thing—a very important finding—that I would like to share with you." The Elder swung his gaze to the friends. "This is something that is essential for you to know as well, younglings. As you are aware, the Elders are conscious that a certain individual is behind the attacks that we have seen around the world. All we had was a vague feeling of who this person might be since we had no concrete evidence. Until recently, that is. Now we know with certainty the identity of this individual."

The teenagers stirred. Jag had mentioned that Nageau had reached out to him after the nanomite ordeal and revealed that their enemy was someone who had been exiled from Dema-Ki.

"This person," Nageau said, "this harbinger of darkness, holds a twisted view filled with a deep hatred for humanity, and is plotting its demise. The horrific events that we have witnessed across the planet in the past several months were initiated by this—"

"Sorry to cut in," Aari's father interrupted, "but if you're so sure about who it is, then we should go to the authorities and let *them* deal with this murderous psychopath. Why do we and our children have to be involved with this mess?"

"The authorities must not be brought in," Nageau responded sharply. The parents were taken aback. "There is far more to this individual that you need to understand. There is an artifact, known to my people as the *lathe'ad.* A long time ago, five of these devices were found by our ancestors on our home island. No one knows for sure where they came from, but somehow, we were intuitively able to decipher their capabilities and came to understand that the *lathe'ad* is an exceedingly powerful device, capable of creation and destruction on a planetary scale. It has the potential to, how do you say . . . terraform worlds. In the hands of a person with the right knowledge and ability, the *lathe'ad* could become biologically linked to the bearer. Once that link is established, no one except the bearer is able to sever it. One of these devices is now in the possession of this individual."

"Why would anyone want to link with the la . . . the lath . . . that thing?" pressed Mariah's mother.

"Because it works as a deterrent. Should the bearer be harmed or killed, the *lathe'ad* will sense the disruption in the flow of energy in the host's body and its destructive power will be unleashed on the planet. And, if the bearer chooses, he or she could activate the device with a mere thought."

Kody's father looked horrified. "Are you saying that this . . . this person is a living, breathing weapon of mass destruction capable of an extinction-level event?"

"Yes. And that is why the authorities cannot be involved. They are not equipped to handle this situation. Any debilitating attack on this individual will be countered by the *lathe'ad* in accordance with its internal code, and it will wreak nothing but devastation in its purest form."

Everyone had gone still. Mariah swallowed and looked down at her toes. *That would have been really good to know earlier on, Elder Nageau.*

Jag's father shook his head, aghast. "Then how can this person be stopped? It's an impossible situation."

"There is only one way to end this peril," the Elder said. "From our prophecy we know who can put a stop to this, but we are still trying to ascertain how it will be done."

"What do you mean?" Tegan's mother asked.

"The five Bearers of Light." Nageau nodded at the teenagers. "They have been appointed by the prophecy for a reason. They are the only ones armed with the capability to disrupt the symbiotic connection between our foe and the *lathe'ad*, and eliminate this threat. As to how it will be done, we are confident that will come to light soon. Be assured the Elders are working to decipher the prophecy."

"Why our kids?" Mariah's mother demanded.

"Because," Nageau answered gently, "the prophecy deems it so. With their abilities combined, they will be the ones to stop the catalyst at the center of this storm."

Mariah could see the sheen of unshed tears in her mother's eyes. "But why them? Out of the nearly *eight billion* people on this planet?" Her voice cracked. "Why our kids?"

Nageau's demeanor softened further, his visage showing deep compassion. "Some things in life are carved by the hands of destiny. We are not always able to understand the reasons behind these occurrences, but time has a way of unlocking the wisdom within. We are called upon to have faith. Just as we have faith in the rising of the sun at dawn, we must believe that darkness cannot prevail, for truly, darkness is but the absence of light. Your children are preordained to cast away the storm gathering on our horizon." He took in the concerned, uncertain faces before him. "But in order to fulfill their destined roles, they need to continue their training with us. With that in mind, I would like to ask for them to return with me to Dema-Ki so that they may complete their preparations."

Nageau's request was met by stony looks. Mariah sat anxiously, not daring to speak. The Elder let the silence stretch for a few moments, then graciously dipped his head to conclude the meeting. He rose to his feet, unfurling his six-foot, five-inch frame. Marshall moved to his side. Before leaving, Nageau added, "This is a very important decision. Perhaps the most important one that you will make in your life. I understand you will need time to reflect upon such a weighty consideration. With your permission, I will return in one week to inquire about your choice. My gratitude to each and every one of you for granting me this audience."

The two men departed, leaving the room engulfed in what was the most nerve-wrecking stillness Mariah had ever experienced.

The topic wasn't addressed as a group until the parents had met to discuss the situation a couple of days later. Most were opposed to the notion in varying degrees, Mariah's mother being the one most staunchly against letting her only child go. They didn't want their sons and daughters to be taken away and put directly in the path of danger, though some of the parents were on uncertain ground.

They struggled with Nageau's proposition and scrambled for reasons to keep their children safe at home. The most convincing reason they could think of was education, but even if they had unanimously decided that their offspring were better off attending their senior year of high school, it would have been in vain. The start of the school year had been indefinitely delayed due to the growing social unrest across the state.

All factors considered, it was ultimately the problem of the *lathe'ad* and the small comfort in knowing that the teenagers would be in good hands that made them eventually, though unenthusiastically, shift their stance. The end of the week came around and they gave Nageau their answer. The days after that were miserable as the teenagers spent the remainder of their time in Great Falls packing and bidding vague farewells to their other friends.

When the day came to leave, the goodbyes were extremely difficult for the families. Mariah hadn't been able to stop sobbing. At that moment it hadn't mattered what lay ahead; the last thing she wanted was to leave her mother all alone.

Mariah now opened her eyes, slammed her journal shut, and shoved it under her pillow. She bit her lip. That was the one thing that constantly hurt the most to think about: her poor mother, the woman who cared for her and loved her unconditionally, languishing by herself in their apartment.

She turned off the lamp and, as she curled up in bed, thought, *I may not be there with you right now, but you're not alone. I'll see you again, not too long from now.* She breathed out slowly. *I love you, Momma.*

For the past forty-eight hours in their studio apartment in Swansea, the Vaughn twins had been monitoring the news and scouring the Internet. Since they moved around so much, the place was furnished simply, with a bed, a pull-out sofa, a dining table with two chairs, and a small television.

At the table, Deverell had several tabs open on his laptop, each with different search results for terms such as *progeria*, *accelerated aging*, and *progeroid symptoms*. Nothing quite matched what they'd seen at the hospital, but a trending social media topic in Wales was also gaining some momentum across the United Kingdom, France, and Belgium. The Welsh called it *marwolaeth*, or "the death." The other countries used variations of the word, and the messages were often accompanied by images and videos of people stricken by the disease.

Sitting on the end of the table with his back to his brother, Gareth flipped through news channels on the TV while keeping an eye on the Twitter feed on his phone. "It hasn't made headlines yet," he said, "but we could be on the verge of seeing something go viral."

"It's just a matter of time," Deverell agreed. "Reckon we ought to call Marshall?"

Gareth muted the television. "Yeah."

Marshall, who'd worked closely with the Chosen Ones over the summer, now watched over their families with two other Sentries to ensure their safety while the teenagers trained in Dema-Ki.

The American picked up the call after a few rings. "Well, look at you two," he teased. "No telepathic ability so you're stuck chatting over a phone. What a shame."

"Nice talking with you, too," Deverell said, sharing slightly amused looks with Gareth.

"What's up, fellas? How've you been?"

"We're alright, which is more than we can say for some others."

"Come again?"

Gareth spoke up. "Marshall, there's something going on here. Some kind of disease, we think. It's like nothing we've ever seen before. We're still not sure what it is or how it spreads but, mate, it's damned disturbing."

"What is it?" All merriment had left Marshall's voice.

"Adults and children alike are going through some sort of accelerated aging," Deverell said. "*Babies*, even. And then they die because their bodies can't handle the sudden decay. No one's spared. These little six-month-olds look like they're ninety. Here, I'll send you a photo."

There was a short silence on the other end, then: "Son of a—that's a *child?*"

"Yeah."

"This isn't good."

"We know. That's why we called you."

"No, no. I mean . . . Do you guys remember Dominique Mboya?"

"Dominique . . ." Deverell sifted through his mental dossier of all the Sentries he knew. "Aye, we met briefly for a mission in Cape Town a few years back. Strong woman with a smile that could melt an iceberg. What about her?"

"She reached out to me a couple of weeks ago and again earlier this week. She's been in a remote village in Africa for the past two months. The first time we connected, she mentioned that several villagers had come down with a strange sickness that seemed to cause rapid aging. I advised her to contact the health authorities immediately, but when we connected the second time she said the authorities were doing jack all thanks to the incapacitated government. No test results came back, no help came. And, on top of that, they were attacked by renegade soldiers looting villages for food supplies. The villagers fought them off, but Domi and I decided to call other Sentries from the region to protect the survivors. Many of the villagers have died, and none of the cures she knows are working."

Deverell's head snapped up. "That's horrible!"

"It is. And Domi, bless her, she's still pushing on. All she's managed to learn is that it's highly infectious and not containable by any of Dema-Ki's treatments."

"That's just bloody perfect." Gareth rubbed his forehead. "So it's only this one village?"

"That's what she told me, yeah."

"Hold on," Deverell said. "As far as we can tell, this disease appeared in Europe less than a week ago, but from what you're saying it's been confined to that village for at least *three* weeks."

"I know," Marshall said. "Quite the geographical leap. I reached out to the Elders earlier to let them know what was going on, but I'll have to update them on your find. And I think it's time we gather up some of the field Sentries for a meeting at the Lodge, just to touch base at least."

"When?" Deverell asked. "And which Lodge?"

"I'll let you know, and the one in Europe."

"Wait," Gareth cut in. "Marshall, you said Dominique's been in that village amidst this breakout. How is she doing?"

"That was the first thing I asked her. She said she's not affected, which is a huge relief, but she doesn't know why."

Gareth scratched his head. "That's interesting."

"Yeah, and that's an understatement. Look, fellas, I gotta run. The sooner I let the Elders know what's happening, the better. Talk to you soon, alright?"

"Cheers." Deverell ended the call and sat back, stretching.

Gareth stared at the phone for a long time. "It feels ominous, doesn't it? It really can't be mere coincidence. This . . . *disease* . . . breaking out with everything else that's going on."

"I think so too. I'll tell you what, though. This is exactly what

I'd do if I had Reyor's twisted mind."

"What d'you mean?"

"Think about it." Deverell went to the sink to splash his face with cold water and dried off with a small towel. "It takes more than just one blow to knock humanity to its knees. You need to keep hitting it until it's too bruised and battered to get back up. Until its spirit is too broken to rise again. Then you deliver the *coup de grâce*."

Gareth's brow furrowed. "So, step one's obviously the crop destruction. Step two—"

"The war and unrest that's broken out, a direct consequence of the global food crisis."

"Right. Turn people and nations against each other. And step three—"

"A deadly and virulent disease that we're not equipped to handle. This just can't simply be happenstance."

Gareth raked his fingers through his shaggy hair. "If that's really what this is, what are we to do? Reyor probably has everything in place. Who knows what else is in the works."

"Let's see what the Elders have to say to Marshall. In any case, he's right. We ought to convene a Sentry meeting as soon as possible."

Gareth got off the table. "Well," he said tightly, "it's been a long couple of days. I don't know about you, but I could do with a nap right now."

"Me too. Take the bed this time, I'll take the couch."

"Thanks."

"What are big brothers for?"

"You're older by *eleven minutes*, for heaven's sake." Gareth flopped onto the bed and shut his eyes, arms around the pillow.

"Still older."

The couch looked inviting but Deverell knew he wouldn't be able to sleep, not with the way the gears in his mind were spinning. If it was capable of wiping out nearly an entire village, what did that mean for the countries where the disease had begun to rear its head? If it continued its pattern eastward, all of Europe would be engulfed, as would Asia and, eventually, the rest of the world.

"*Ach-y-fi*, it's going to get bad," he said to himself, tapping his fingers on the tabletop.

We may need to prepare for the worst-case scenario. No rest for the weary.

The strange aircraft with its twin proprotors in full forward position flew through Blue Mountains National Park, with Sydney's distant skyline to the east. The stars had mostly faded as dawn commenced its gradual creep into a new day in Australia. All was quiet apart from the beating of the aircraft's blades.

Keeping low between sandstone plateaus to avoid radar detection, the V-22 Osprey traveled northward over the man-made lake behind Warragamba Dam. The pilot, ignoring the three-mile wide exclusion zone around the reservoir that supplied drinking water to Sydney, flew close to the calm, blue-green waves and admired the view. The park hosted a range of habitats, home to countless animals and trees. Mist hugged the gorges snugly, giving the entire forest an ethereal feel.

The pilot guided the Osprey toward a preselected landing zone atop a small plateau. The aircraft's nacelles rotated upright, allowing it to hover, and the grass below swept to and fro under the downwash of the enormous rotors. The Osprey gently touched down, its ramp facing the coastal city.

The access door on the copilot's side opened and a woman in a yellow biohazard suit jumped down. She went around to the back of the aircraft and waited for the ramp to open fully. When it did, she stepped on, her skin prickling at the eerie silence within. A large cage had been installed, taking up the entire length and width of the cargo hold. Inside the cage were over a thousand ravens. They stood absolutely still on their perches.

The woman did a quick inspection, observing the odd slickness on their dark feathers and the discharge from their eyes. She pressed a button on the wall and, when a click sounded, gripped a lever beside it and pulled down with all her strength. As the doors of the cage hissed open, she bolted out of the aircraft and retreated a safe distance.

A fiendish screeching inside the Osprey grew in timbre until the woman thought she would bleed out of her ears. A dark storm cloud exited the aircraft, spreading out like a demonic sigil against the lightening sky. A few birds peeled away, but most were on a fixed trajectory toward the beautiful city ahead, now aglow with luminous trails of the rising sun.

Once the ravens were far enough away, the woman climbed back into the plane and took her place beside the pilot. They looked at each other without a word. The pilot closed the ramp and the Osprey lifted off the ground in a vertical ascent. Once in the air, the aircraft's nacelles rotated forward and the plane headed away from Sydney and its approaching threat.

The young black bear lumbered through the forest as if drunk, stumbling into a bush and conking its cranium against a tree. Shaking its head vigorously, it staggered backward and fell onto its rear, crushing the bush under it.

Oh my goodness, would you please *cooperate with me?* Tegan could barely keep the creature under control with the way its will overwhelmed her. When it moved in one direction, she'd try to guide it elsewhere and the bear would end up cross-pawed before toppling onto its face.

It was so much easier controlling that shark in Carpinteria, she grumbled. *Ugh.*

Something suddenly piqued the bear's nose and Tegan recognized it immediately: a hare.

Oh, no. Wait just a—AGH!

The bear careened in the direction of the scent. It felt just like the time both of Tegan's big dogs, a Belgian sheepdog and a Beauceron, caught the mouthwatering aroma of a barbeque while on a walk. They'd nearly yanked her arms out of their sockets when they took off.

Stop! Stop! Please stop! For the love of everything, please stoooop!

In her panic, she lost all control of the bear but remained linked to it. She was helplessly dragged along for the ride as it came upon a hare's nest against an outcrop of rocks on the forest floor. The hare inside looked frightened out of its wits with nowhere to go. The bear opened its jaws wide as it approached the defenseless creature.

Don't eat it! Tegan bellowed. *Do you hear me? Do. Not. Eat. It!*

Just as the bear was about to snap its maw shut, Tegan kicked into overdrive and wrenched its head away. *No! Bad bear!* She forced it into a breakneck sprint until there was a healthy distance between it and the hare, then severed the mindlink.

When she opened her eyes, she was sitting on the snow in her training area. Groaning, she flopped onto her back. "That was awful."

Tikina, seated across from her, opened her eyes and smiled. "Quite."

"Ha. Thank you."

"The bear was a difficult one, it seems."

"It had a lot more willpower than I imagined. I controlled *three* wolves a while ago, and they were super cooperative."

"There will be some individuals within a species who will be harder to mindlink with."

"Like the Marauders. Though it's more like we just flat-out can't link with them properly."

"The Marauders are man-made creatures designed specifically to guard and kill," Tikina reminded her. "Those beasts were not created by nature. Accessing their minds will always be a futile task when one's ability is rooted in the natural order of the world."

"Yeah, I guess." Tegan sat back up. "Well, I failed that exercise. So where were you? I couldn't find you when I did have full control of the bear."

The Elder winked. "Flying quietly through the trees with Akira."

"I thought you were going to pick a land animal, not her," Tegan complained. Akira was a golden eagle that had formed a close bond with Tikina. "How was I supposed to spot you?"

"Not to worry, youngling. We will keep practicing." Tikina went still for a brief moment. Before Tegan could ask what was wrong, the Elder snapped back. "I am afraid the rest of your training has been called off for today. Nageau would like to speak with all of us."

"What?" Tegan asked, disappointed. "Why? What's happened?"

"I do not know, but it sounded urgent." Tikina got up, pulled her student to her feet, then marched briskly off to the middle of the training grounds, Tegan rushing to keep up.

The rest of the Elders and their apprentices were already waiting when they arrived. Tegan immediately joined her friends while the mentors exchanged quiet words, their faces shadowed by distress.

The teenagers took in their surroundings—an oval clearing with a creek that cut through each of the training grounds, and a cluster of boulders beside two log benches—until Nageau finally addressed them. "I will get straight to the point, younglings. Marshall just connected with me. There might be a situation developing."

The friends brightened a little at the mention of the faithful, amiable Sentry. Then the rest of Nageau's sentence sunk in and they became grim.

"Is it more crop destruction?" Jag asked.

"No," Nageau answered. "It is far worse—some sort of disease. We first heard of it about half a moon cycle ago, and at that time it appeared to be localized in a remote village in the continent you call Africa. Reports from Sentries indicate that this disease is now spreading across Europe. Our Sentry in Africa reported that the majority of the people in the village have died."

Tegan, dumbfounded, stuttered, "What's this disease?"

"It ages people rapidly, no matter if they are a newborn or an adult. The rate at which it spreads is alarmingly quick."

"And you think that Reyor is behind it," Aari ventured.

"We are unsure," Tikina said, "but the signs seem to point in that direction."

"What do you mean?"

"We suspect that it is part of a larger plan," Nageau said. "It looks as though the crop destruction, and this disease, may have something in common besides being global in nature: They aim to strike down humanity but not harm the planet. This disease does not seem to kill animals, at least not the livestock in this particular affected village. The harbinger of darkness is fiercely protective of Earth but has a distinct hatred for humanity."

"Yeah, Aari and I heard the speech to the Stewards of New Earth." Tegan remembered with disdain the fervor of the crowd that had gathered in an underground sanctuary to hear Reyor speak a few months back. "Question is, why so much hate?"

"And are we any closer to finding Reyor?" Jag added.

"The Sentry interrogating Tony is trying every avenue to get the answers we need," Nageau said. "He is currently treading on the risky side, but we leave it to him to play his hand. He is more than capable." He then bowed his head at Tegan. "To answer your question, youngling, the . . . harbinger . . . as you know, is from Dema-Ki, and is therefore well-versed in our ancient prophecy. The prophecy is a tool to guide us but, like any tool, its possible outcomes are dependent on the motive of the user. For instance, a knife is a tool. It can be used to prepare a meal or take a life.

"Allow me to use the first lines of the prophecy as an example: '*From the flames of Cerraco, five will arise.*' The people of Dema-Ki now understand it as the arrival of the five of you after your aircraft caught on fire and crashed, thus resembling our fiery bird of legend. Reyor always took that passage to mean a metaphorical fire that would destroy humankind in order for it to rise anew from the ashes and reorganize into five distinct classes. Echelons, if you will. This interpretation—or rather, misinterpretation—of the prophecy reinforced the harbinger's twisted view of humanity wherein we are a persistent, cunning sort with uncanny adaptive capabilities that led to us being the dominant species on the planet. This is why it can be expected that, in order to execute a plan to annihilate humanity, there will need to be a series of coordinated attacks. I should know this." Nageau smiled sourly. "I have been inside that warped mind, trying to untangle the web of misguided self-righteousness and loathing for mankind that lies within."

Kody removed his baseball cap to rub his temples. "So we're

nothing more than parasites that need to be exterminated."

"Precisely."

"What gives Reyor that kind of superiority and arrogance?" Mariah demanded.

Nageau looked up at the teenagers. "Evolution."

"Evolution?" Aari echoed. "How does that play into this?"

"Perhaps we should take a seat first, then I will explain."

The friends settled on the small cluster of boulders, leaving the log benches for the Elders. Nageau continued. "The people of Dema-Ki have unique abilities. You are no strangers to that. Even with the coming together of two very different peoples—the Islanders, advanced for their time, and the natives of this land who had an uncanny bond with nature—these traits were not diluted or lost. These higher mental and physical capabilities are the result of what you would call a leap in evolution. Using our gifts to live ethical lives in harmony with our planet and each other is the hallmark of our people.

"The Elders, not just us but those who took up this mantle before us, always believed that the rest of humanity would, in due course, join us on this path; in other words, evolve out of their self-centered and afflictive conditions. We see the phase that humanity is presently in as its collective and turbulent adolescence. We are confident that mankind will eventually emerge wiser and more mature in how it treats each other and the Earth, and this will continue to be our belief. But Reyor insisted that humanity would only destroy itself and the world, and that intervention was needed. Unfortunately, that meant speeding up the species' demise. And, to the harbinger, that is mercy."

"So, in a nutshell, Reyor is someone from Dema-Ki with a different take on the prophecy," Tegan said.

"Very different, yes. The banishment happened over three decades ago. The harbinger is a compelling orator and many of our brethren fell under the spell of these perverse beliefs. After countless attempts at reasoning, it became clear that change would be less and less likely to occur. It started to tear the community apart, and grew into an even more pressing problem with the harbinger's desire to be appointed as an Elder."

Nageau paused, pressing two fingers to the side of his forehead as though recalling the past caused him physical pain. "Then . . . there was a murder. All evidence linked back to Reyor. I was, at the time, a newly inducted leading Elder, and the hefty responsibility fell onto my shoulders to banish the monster from our community. The streak of evil I saw there darkened with each passing day. There was even fear among our people that Reyor would usurp the Council.

"You must keep in mind that the harbinger is unusually gifted, even for our people. So, yes, expulsion became necessary. We stripped Reyor of every possession, including the crystal—the one given to each individual to help enhance our abilities—and with a single sack of sustenance, the harbinger was banished from our home."

Tegan felt a pang at the profound grief in the Elder's eyes. Nageau glanced away, and when he looked back, the sadness had been replaced with resentment. "Later on, it became apparent that a handful of crystals had gone missing from the temple, and so did one of the five *lathe'ad*. But it was not until recently that we were able to determine for sure it was Reyor who stole them."

Tegan, perched on the tallest rock on the outcrop, looked down at the others. They were absorbed, trying to make sense of what had been divulged.

"So . . ." Aari stuck his hands into the pockets of his jacket. "All that's happened, or will happen, is basically just to reboot humanity?"

"Humanity 2.0," Jag said.

"Why didn't we know about this sooner?" Kody asked.

"Because," Nageau said, "we wanted to be sure that we had sufficient evidence that proved our assumptions were correct. If you recall the Battle of Ayen'et, the only possible link we had to the harbinger at that time was this." He held out his hand and Tikina pressed something into his palm. When he displayed the silver object between his thumb and forefinger, the friends sat straighter.

"That's the coin I found at the mining site after the fight, isn't it?" Mariah asked.

Nageau passed it to her. "It is."

Tegan shifted closer to better see the dark symbol carved in the coin's center as it lay in Mariah's hand. The rune bore a loose resemblance to the letter zee, with a short horizontal line crossing midway; meaning destruction, it was part of a pair of symbols that spoke of the duality in all of existence, the other of which was creation.

"That coin was not substantial proof of anything, though it was startling to see," Nageau said. "Even so, when we sent the five of you home soon after that battle, we suppressed your memories for your own protection. We believed that if this harbinger was indeed the one behind the operation on the mountain, there would eventually be interest in you during your time with your families. It was best if you remembered nothing of your experience in Dema-Ki."

Jag fiddled with the pendant hanging around his neck. "Guess it does explain everything that's been going on."

"There's one thing that sticks out," Tegan said. "You mentioned that the people of Dema-Ki made a leap in evolution that gave you all these abilities. How did that happen?"

Tikina responded in Nageau's stead. "We do not know the exact details, but what we can say is that from time to time in history, certain groups within a given population have been known to take such leaps. They become recipients of a genetic code that takes their species to the next evolutionary level. All we know is, for our people, this leap occurred within a generation or two after our ancestors, the Islanders, found the crystals in different parts of their home. Another artifact they found during that time were the five *lathe'ad*."

Tegan saw Aari's interest suddenly spike and she quietly laughed to herself. *He's gonna be scratching his head over this, the dork.*

"Then what about us?" Jag asked. "We have some of these abilities, too."

Tikina leaned closer. "And that is the most important question of all. It goes to the heart of the matter. The fact that the five of you exhibit these abilities is not only a fulfillment of the prophecy, but it is also evidence that a leap in this vein of evolution is not confined to just our people. In other words, you are the proof of the fallacy of Reyor's theory and beliefs." She regarded the friends, green eyes shining with an emotion Tegan couldn't decipher.

"You," the Elder said, "are the chink in Reyor's armor."

In the passenger seat of a parked white Camaro, the wolfdog lounged in the afternoon sun, dozing. A click, followed by the driver's door opening, made him raise his head to greet his owner. The hazel-eyed man pulled off his sunglasses. His dark, textured hair was neither styled nor combed, and he sported some stubble. Though he was approaching forty, he had nary a gray hair and he could match the athleticism of a man half his age.

He stroked the dog between the ears. "Hey, Chief."

Chief wagged his tail before resting his head back down. The man hooked his sunglasses onto the open neck of his faded red Henley. "I can't stand San Francisco," he told the dog. "City's so broke, the bylaw officers are forced to fine people for the smallest violations." He crumpled up a small piece of paper and tossed it over his shoulder into the back seat. "I've fed that friggin' meter four bucks every hour for the past day and a half. Missed the last pay by a *minute* and I get a stupid ticket."

Victor Colback, the Canadian Sentry in charge of interrogating Tony Cross, had tailed the younger man since his escape from Fort McMurray, Alberta, and followed him to Edmonton.

Well, it's not really an escape if it was planned, he thought. *Kid's wily. He actually knew how to get out of his cuffs with a paperclip. Good for him. And me.*

In Edmonton, Victor had eavesdropped on another call Tony made. Along with the ability to harness and manipulate acoustic waves to use it as a concussive force, among other things, the Sentry was endowed with the partial gift of enhanced senses that gave him acute hearing. Tony had again spoken to someone named Adrian, and with a swift glance at Phoenix Corporation's web page on his smartphone, Victor surmised that it was Adrian Black, the company's chief executive.

The Sentries had come to know Phoenix as a bona fide business that dealt in a broad range of industries, but underneath the legitimacy was a clandestine operation working to bring the world to its knees. The people of Dema-Ki and the Chosen Ones had had multiple run-ins with the corporation, and they'd never been friendly.

Tony had received instructions to make his way to a small airstrip just outside of Edmonton, where a private plane would take him to San Francisco. He was to show up at the head office as soon as possible. Victor flew out with Chief after getting a flight later that morning, putting them a few hours behind their quarry.

Now the Sentry and his faithful companion sat in their rented car, parked in a public lot right across from the corporation's office in downtown San Francisco. The gray-colored tower was perfectly nondescript, blending in with the other tall buildings in the financial district. Busy locals and tourists flocked from one place to another, lost in their hectic bustling.

Drizzle pattered on the windshield, taking Victor by surprise. It had been a sunny afternoon mere moments ago. He turned on the wipers. *Great. If the rain picks up, Tony might not even come out at all.*

He'd staked out the HQ for over thirty hours with no sleep. Tony had only left the building during the evenings for a casual stroll, then would return to the office and not come out until the following evening. Victor suspected that there was some kind of accommodation in the building where the younger man was staying.

But what is he doing here? What's he waiting for?

Victor needed to get in, but there was no way to slip past the security detail in the lobby without an ID. He'd loitered just outside the building, listening in on the guards' conversations, and learned that a new guard would be joining the night shift at eight p.m.

He reached for the coffee cup in the drink holder. Realizing it was empty, he crushed it in his fist. "Need to get some liquid energy or I'll crash in an hour. Coming, Chief?"

The wolfdog grunted.

"No, of course you're not. Why did I even ask?" Victor got out of the car and headed to a coffee stand a block away just as the drizzle ceased and the few clouds dissipated. He put his sunglasses back on and stood in line behind a girl. When she left, he stepped forward and ordered an espresso.

"How are you doing today?" the woman behind the counter asked, flashing a smile.

"I'm good, thanks." He reached for some change in his pocket. "And yourself?"

"I'm just fine, honey." She cocked her head at him curiously. "I can almost place that accent . . ."

Accent? He was somewhat tickled by the statement. "I'm from Canada."

The woman looked excited. "Really? I have an aunt in Canada! She moves around so much, though. I don't remember where exactly she lives now. But, hey, enjoy your time in San Francisco!"

Victor paid her, returning her smile with a small one of his own. Despite the hustle and bustle of city life, he had to hand it to the locals; they were very much an open and welcoming bunch. He turned to leave and his heart suddenly leapt into his throat.

Tony Cross stared back at him.

Decked in a few bruises from his interrogation sessions, he seemed not to have recognized the Sentry. Victor's thoughts raced at the speed of light. *No, of course he wouldn't recognize me. He's only ever seen my eyes and I've got shades on.*

He gave Tony a short nod as if he were just another stranger, then headed back to his car. Inside the vehicle, he slouched in his seat, blew a raspberry, and patted the wolfdog's rump. "You'll never guess what just happened, Chief. Tony actually came out of the building in broad daylight. Good thing I didn't bring you along, or else he would've recognized us immediately."

As he downed his drink, he kept a close eye on Tony as the young man retreated inside Phoenix's office with his coffee and muffin. He looked at his watch. "Four more hours until the security detail rotates. Nothing to do but sit tight."

* * *

Victor rested against a railing on the steps that led to the HQ's entrance. With his phone against his ear as if he was on a call, no one would guess that he was tuning his hearing to the conversation of the two guards in the reception area inside.

"Hey, Martinez," the older, tank-bodied guard said, "welcome to Tower 51. Let's get you up to date, hey?"

"Yes, sir," the new member responded. "Uh, Tower 51, sir? Like Area 51?"

"Hah, yeah. Just a nickname for this place."

"Why? You got spaceships hidden around here somewhere?"

"Wouldn't be surprised if there were, honestly. Alright, let's get down to it. So, anyone walks through those front doors, they need to hand you their Phoenix ID card. You scan it on that doodad by the computer and it logs their identification and check-in time. Same thing happens when they leave. If you're dealing with visitors, they'll have a letter with a stamp. You cross-reference it with the daily visitors' schedule and if it's all good, you issue them these guest ID cards and they're clear to go. If not, you kick 'em right out, and they ain't welcome back till they've got their papers together."

"Just like that?"

"Just like that. Next thing you need to know is that most of the folks here are out by nine, though the senior execs sometimes stay back till after midnight. That ain't our business. They occupy the top floor, and no one's allowed up there apart from myself and the supervising janitor. It ain't rocket science, right?"

"No, sir. Do the jannies have cards that I scan, too?"

"Yeah. They're here three times a week. Tonight's night

number two. They're prompt, always here by nine sharp. They come into the parking garage with their van and enter the lobby from that door by the desk. The supervising janitor's gonna need a special access card for the elevator to get to the top floor and all the rooms up there. That keycard is in the middle, locked drawer to your right. Got any questions?"

"No."

"Good. You're better than the last guy, ha-ha. I'll be with you for a bit, making sure you're doing everything right, then I'm heading off to do some patrols. Once everyone's gone, lock up the front door. I'll send Sullivan over to show you around the place."

Victor waited for a few minutes, then pretended to hang up his call. He strolled away, zigzagging around cars and buses in case anyone was watching, before slipping into the Camaro. Chief, fully rested, sat attentively, looking at the Sentry with his head tilted.

Victor smiled slightly. "I've got an idea, Chief, but it's risky. Bark if you see a janitorial van, eh?"

It was ten minutes to nine when a gray box van turned in at the building's parking entrance. Chief snuffled, eyes on the vehicle.

"Yeah, I see it too." Victor took out a small bottle of painkillers and swallowed two capsules—he loathed them, but they helped keep his chronic headaches at bay—then quickly removed his silver rings and his top. As he grabbed a dark green button-down shirt from his duffle bag and donned a black cap, Chief watched him quizzically.

"For the cameras," the Sentry explained, stuffing into his back pocket a flat leather pouch. This housed all the tools he needed, among them a lock picking kit and other paraphernalia. "Don't want to look the same as I did earlier today. Now, stay put. Good boy."

He hopped out of the vehicle and stole into the garage as Tony stepped out of the front doors of the tower. *Out for the usual walk. Slick timing.*

Inside, the garage was large, well-lit, and nearly empty save for a few sleek cars. The gray van was parked in a stall near a door on which 'LOBBY' was stenciled. A group of six men in beige coveralls and ball caps were busy gathering their supplies from the back of the vehicle. Victor lurked behind a concrete pillar out of the nearest security camera's line of sight, trying to figure out which of the janitors was the supervisor.

One of the men whipped out a clipboard and spoke loudly, the echo of the garage aiding him as he listed off duties on the checklist.

Maybe him? Victor thought. *I've only got one chance at this.*

As the team filed through the door to the lobby, the man with the clipboard took up a position between the van and the wall and lit a cigarette. Victor lowered the brim of his cap and approached while staying in the camera's blind spot. "Hey, pal, you the supervising janitor?"

The man looked up, surprised. "What? Yeah, wh—"

Victor swept his arm forward. A powerful wave of concussive energy shot headlong into the janitor, hurling him against the wall. He crumpled to the ground, knocked out. Victor checked him for injuries and only found a small bump on the back of his head. He quickly stripped the janitor of his coveralls, then pulled out the pouch from his back pocket and went to work on the man's identification badge, deftly replacing the photo with his own. Once done, he tugged the coveralls over his own clothes, tucked his black cap into one of the big pockets, and put on the beige one. He dumped the man inside the van, then hauled the last of the janitorial supplies onto a cart and wheeled it into Phoenix's warmly lit lobby.

The new guard was on his own at the front desk, watching him expectantly. Victor headed over and rested an elbow on the counter. *Confidence counts for something. Act like you belong.*

"Hey," he said.

The guard held out his hand. "Evening, sir. Your badge, please."

"Sure thing." Victor unclipped the ID and passed it over.

The guard ran the badge over a scanner. It beeped twice. He frowned, then wiped the card on his sleeve and tried again, eyeballing Victor suspiciously. Victor stared back with an air of impatience. This time there was only one beep. The Sentry exhaled quietly. When the guard didn't hand over the badge quickly enough, he gave the other man an unimpressed look. "I'm gonna need the keycard to get to the top floor, too, by the way. Didn't your boss tell you about that?"

The guard turned red. "Y-yes, he did. Sorry, one sec." He unlocked the middle drawer of the desk and handed a white card to Victor. "Here you go."

"Thanks. See you when we're done." Victor touched the brim of his cap and wheeled the supply cart through the massive lobby toward the elevator. The cart glided smoothly on the polished marble floor, past luxurious couches and beautiful decorative plants.

Entering the elevator, he tapped the keycard against a scanner below the buttons on a panel, pressed Level 40, and traveled to the top floor. He stepped out into the long, carpeted corridor with mahogany walls and posh lights that gave the place a lavish glow. Against the wall, on Victor's right, was a glass table with a gorgeous crystal sculpture of a majestic phoenix rising from its ashes.

He took a swift look around. One CCTV camera was perched on the wall behind him, and another glared from the far end of the hallway. Angling his head down, he guided the cart past a few offices to his left and a large boardroom on his right. The corridor ended at a door with a plaque that read 'Executive Suite'.

Called it. Victor swiped the card on the scanner under the door handle and stepped in, shouldering the backpack vacuum cleaner for authenticity's sake under the cameras' watchful gaze.

The door swung shut behind him and he found himself staring at a well-appointed apartment. A generous pantry and kitchen greeted him on his left. At the other side of the room, a comfortable king-sized bed with a nightstand beside it was pushed into the far corner. A sleek television set atop a teakwood console faced the bed, and a bathroom was located between it and the pantry.

This is really nice, Victor marveled, *staying poker-faced. I wouldn't mind crashing here for a few days myself . . . No wonder Tony barely leaves.*

He stole a glance at his watch. Tony's walks took anywhere from half an hour to forty minutes. Nearly fifteen minutes had passed since he'd seen the man leave the building, so he had to work fast. Problem was, the room looked spotless. Nothing seemed misplaced. The bed was neatly made, the wastebasket empty.

Kid's got to be a neat freak. It's like Mr. Clean was let off the leash.

He split the chamber into sections, combing through everything thoroughly but careful to leave nothing out of place. All he found was a small overnight bag with fresh clothes. He stood in the middle of the room, forlorn. Ten minutes of scouring and nothing to show for it.

His gaze lingered on the bedside table where a pencil and notepad lay. His tongue slowly traced his bottom lip and his brow creased. Grabbing the pencil, he started to shade the topmost page of the notepad. White lines forming letters appeared through the lead. First an E, then M, a P, an O, R—

The door clicked.

Victor grabbed the paper and tore it off, spinning around to face the new arrival as he slipped the note into his back pocket. Tony stood in the doorway, like an animal defending its territory. "What are you doing?" he snapped.

The Sentry tightened the muscles in his throat and pitched his voice higher. "Cleaning this floor, sir, this room included. I'm almost done."

"Ah." Tony regarded him cagily. "Why are you squinting at me? And are you sick? You sound sick."

"Sorry, really don't mean to squint. Just nearsighted. And it's just the tail-end of a cold, I promise. Didn't contaminate anything of yours. Can't afford to miss work. Have to put food on the table, you know?"

". . . Right. Well, thanks, I guess." Tony scrutinized Victor for a second longer before going into the bathroom and shutting the door.

The Sentry maintained his squinted eyes as he exited the room in case Tony came back out. As he put one foot out the door, he heard the elevator at the end of the hallway open and a voice singing gruffly to himself. "Mama, just killed a man, put a gun against his head, pulled my trigger, now he's dead . . ."

Victor quickly pulled back. *Crap. Head guard. He'll know my charade. There's a stairwell—agh, the cart. I'll have to drag it down somehow. And . . . is he singing Bohemian Rhapsody?*

He knelt and channeled his energy, then placed his hand on the ground. He looked around the corner just as the guard stepped out of the elevator. Before the big man could turn and see the impostor, Victor sent a blast of focused acoustic waves through the floor. It traveled down the hall, shot up through the table where the crystal phoenix sat, and sent the sculpture flying behind the guard. It smashed against the wall, shattering into thousands of pieces. The guard spun around at the noise, away from the Sentry.

Victor hastily pushed his cart into the stairwell and, with some difficulty, went down a flight to the floor below, then took the elevator all the way to the lobby. It was empty. He headed out to the parking garage, opened the back of the janitors' van, re-dressed the still-unconscious man back in his overalls—with the keycard in a pocket—and switched the picture on the ID badge back again. He replaced all the supplies and left the van doors open to expose a janitor, who appeared to be sleeping on the job, then left the scene with his own ball cap back over his head, once more taking a long route to his car.

Chief greeted him enthusiastically. Victor put an arm around the dog and rubbed his belly. "Hey. Been cooped up for a while, huh? And having the windows down doesn't really do anything, I know. I'll take you for a walk in a bit. But first . . ."

He pulled the paper from his pocket and searched around his duffel bag for a pencil, then finished shading until the entire note was gray. Sitting back, he gave a half grin. "I think we've got something here, Chief."

Against the car's interior light, the words were spelled out clearly:

EMPORIO RULLI, SFO
DR. NATE, THURSDAY 11 a.m.

Victor flipped the small piece of paper between his fingers. "Looks like the jaunt was worth it. It's Wednesday today. What comes after Wednesday, Chief?"

Chief's ears pricked as he looked at his owner. The Sentry scratched the dog under his chin. "Thursday, indeed. And . . ." He gazed up at Phoenix's tower as it loomed in the darkness. ". . . We finally get to meet the infamous Dr. Nate."

Victor lurked inside a newly opened bookstore in San Francisco Airport's international terminal, flipping through a *National Geographic* magazine. He wore a fitted gray jacket with a beanie covering his hair and a scarf around his neck, aiming to look different than the night before.

Thirty yards away, Tony was seated in front of the Emporio Rulli café, sipping a hot drink and scrolling through his new smartphone. *Phoenix probably provided that*, the Sentry thought.

A young, attractive barista worked around Tony, cleaning tables and putting used dishes on trays, often looking over at him. She was obviously trying to catch his attention, but he was glued to his phone. Victor raised his eyes heavenward.

From his left came a bespectacled man no taller than five feet, with a round face and no eyebrows. His oily black hair was combed against his skull. He had a strange fashion style: black pants with creases that could cut a person, and a white poet shirt loosely tucked in. He carried a briefcase half his size—*that's comical*, Victor smirked—that he plunked down as he took a seat opposite Tony. Despite his diminutive stature, there was something chilling about the man that the Sentry couldn't quite place. He honed in his hearing on the pair, canceling out other sounds and amplifying their voices.

"You look like 'ammered crap," the newcomer said, pushing his glasses further up the bridge of his nose. He spoke as if he had sandpaper in his vocal cords. "Did you give out any information?"

Tony slowly set his phone down and stared emotionlessly at the man. "Pleasure seeing you as well, Doc. Didn't Adrian fill you in? I gave them nothing."

"That kind of interrogation, surely you spilled some information?"

"Don't you dare question me like that. I've already told Adrian what happened. I will not repeat myself, do you understand?"

Dr. Nate shushed him and peered around; Victor quickly turned his back to them. "Keep it down, Tony. Now, tell me 'ow you escaped. One minute you were in Kansas where you were bested in your own game by children, next thing you're in Canada, cuffed in a cell. And you escaped. 'Ow?"

"Look, I've spelled out all the details for the Boss in my report. Get to business already. Why did you want to meet me here?"

"You never 'ave patience with me. Alright, fine, we'll get to it. The Boss wanted me to pass along a message to you."

"Wha—are you joking?" Tony sounded stunned; hurt, even. "What's this, a demotion? I can't talk to the Boss myself now?"

"Let's just say there's a different plan for you."

"Which would be . . ."

"The Boss is putting you in charge of the New Mexico Sanctuary."

There was a sharp intake of breath. "Excuse me? Vladimir and his walking, one-eyed tree trunk are running that show, aren't they?"

"They're being pulled out for another assignment, so we need you to get to the Sanctuary within forty-eight hours to relieve them."

Victor could hear Tony's teeth chattering in anger. "And . . . for how long . . . do I have to be stuck in that hole in the ground?"

"Watch your words," Dr. Nate chided icily. "That so-called 'ole in the ground, all six of them, are our Noah's Ark. Once the world flatlines, you'll appreciate it."

"*Don't preach to me.* I know what it's all for." Tony drew in a long inhale as if to calm himself. "How's the second project of the Arcane Ventures going? I've been told it's already begun."

"We did initial testing in an isolated village in Africa some weeks back, and it turned out quite well."

"Very nice. And now?"

"It's picking up. It will make the Spanish flu and some of the other recent outbreaks look like the common cold. I suggest you keep an eye on the news—while you're doing your job in New Mexico, of course."

"Of course," Tony said. "Now, I ask again, how long exactly will I be stuck doing this?"

"If you do your duty right this time, you might be able to ask the Boss yourself soon."

"I—what?"

"You may get a surprise visit at the Sanctuary. Maybe."

Victor nearly dropped the magazine he was holding. *What?* He risked a glance at the pair, noting that Tony's demeanor had lightened considerably. The young man was silent for a time. When he spoke, he sounded genuinely more cooperative. "So, where are you headed?"

The Sentry saw Dr. Nate give an ugly smile. Tony frowned at the diminutive man's expression, then leaned back, eyes wide. "My God. You're not really going *there*, are you? You are. You're actually going to the Hea—"

At that moment, the barista working around them dropped an entire tray of dishes. The cascading crashes jarred Victor and he stumbled back against a pillar, covering his ears, eyes squeezed shut. Through the painful ringing, he heard the barista apologizing profusely, humiliated. Tony got up to help her and the floor was cleaned within a minute. Sitting back down, Tony looked at Dr. Nate expectantly, as if their conversation hadn't been interrupted. Victor grimaced, the ringing in his ears starting to fade.

"I'm afraid I'm not allowed to reveal that to you," Dr. Nate said.

"Wow. So that's it, then. That's how far down the ladder I've slid."

"Don't take it personally. I'm sure you'll get back up quickly as the go-getter you are. No more blunders and you'll be fine."

"Don't patronize me, you ass," Tony muttered.

Victor watched them out of the corner of his eye. Dr. Nate swung off his chair and fluffed his shirt. "Well, thank you for meeting me 'ere on such short notice. I'm off. You know what you need to do, and don't forget to call Adrian once Vladimir 'as 'anded the operations of the Sanctuary over to you."

Tony didn't look at him. "Say hi to the Boss for me."

Dr. Nate smiled without replying, picked up his briefcase, and trotted off. Victor looked from him to Tony, then back again. *One is heading somewhere important, maybe even to meet Reyor. The other is heading to New Mexico, where Reyor might show up.*

He was fine with letting Tony go. His main objective had always been to locate the head of the snake, but would following the doctor increase his chances of finding Reyor?

From the moment I'd let the kid go, it's been one gamble after another.

He decided to stick with Tony. It helped that he knew where the younger man was headed; the Chosen Ones had been there and the information they'd gathered about the Sanctuary had been passed on to a number of Sentries, himself included.

Victor waited for Tony to leave the airport before finding his way to the Camaro in the packed parking lot. Chief was sitting inside, happily gnawing on a juicy bone.

"We've got another flight to catch," he told the wolfdog as he started the car. "There's more work ahead. We need to keep pushing—the Elders are counting on us."

Aari left the training grounds with Tegan, Jag, Kody, and Mariah. His friends were furious. The group had been informed that Hutar wished to see them at the temple, and none of them wanted to entertain the thought of meeting the would-be murderer.

"I don't care what he wants!" Mariah exclaimed. "I'm not going!"

"Neither am I," Kody said. "And you *know* how easily I forgive people."

Aari shut the heavy wooden gate of the training grounds with Jag's help, then dusted off his hands. "Maybe he wants to apologize."

Tegan scoffed. "And maybe I'm the Queen of England."

"I don't like him any more than you do, but would it actually hurt to at least hear what he has to say?"

"We're not going to meet with him, and that's final," Jag said as they descended the slope with the back of the temple in sight. "Some people you just don't go near. The Elders have been dealing with him, and I think it's best we leave it that way."

"The Elders also told us that this choice is ours to make," Aari pointed out. "Jag, I'm not saying we sit down for a latte with the guy and discuss world issues. I'm not even saying we forgive him if he does apologize—which I think is highly unlikely. Let's just see what he wants."

"No."

"Fine. You guys go ahead and enjoy what's left of the afternoon, and I'll go meet him."

Jag looked as if he wanted to restrain Aari. Then he sighed.

"If you really want to, alright. Just . . . be safe."

Aari smiled. "Always."

As the others continued down the valley, he strode up the stairs to the magnificent temple. He paused in front of the incandescent stream of flames at the center of the foyer to compose himself, then entered.

The temple was completely devoid of people, which was strange considering there were usually at least a few villagers meditating or reading at this time of the day. At the far end, light glinted off a set of ancient swords set decoratively behind some benches. Passing by the corner where he and his friends would usually sit and discuss matters with the Elders, Aari turned left and found Akol by a pillar just outside the temple's library.

Nageau's and Tikina's grandson had a staff slung across his back and a hunting knife sheathed on his belt. He looked displeased. "I had hoped that you would not come."

"Well, hello to you too, compadre," Aari said lightheartedly.

"Oh hush, my friend. I just do not understand what the point is in meeting Hutar."

"I'm the only one who agreed to see the monster. The others tried to talk me out of it, but I thought it would be fair to at least find out what he wants." He indicated Akol's staff and knife. "I have to admit, it's weird seeing anyone armed in such a spiritual place."

"It is merely precaution. Your safety is important."

"I appreciate that, Akol. Really."

Akol dipped his head.

"You know, I couldn't help but notice that it's empty in here."

"And it will remain so until . . . he . . . leaves."

"Let's get to it, then. The sooner this is over with, the sooner people can get back into the temple."

Akol led the way past the doorless entrance of the vast library. Sunlight streamed through wide windows, catching on the leaves of numerous colorful flowers and plants. Frankincense burned on hot coals in stone trays by the bookshelves, releasing a soft, pleasant scent both sweet like myrrh and crisp as forest air.

Aari scanned the large collections of leather-bound books and scrolls on long wooden shelves, then turned his gaze to the center of the library where five wingback chairs faced one on which Hutar sat. The young man was reading peacefully. Two youths were positioned on either side, armed and alert. Akol went to stand behind Hutar, a hand on the hilt of his knife, and signaled for Aari to approach.

Aari wet his lips, then cautiously took the center chair opposite Hutar. Hutar didn't acknowledge him for a full minute until he finished the page he was on and slowly closed the book. His dark sapphire eyes locked with Aari's ice-blues, unblinking. Aari tried to hold his stare but ended up glancing sideways before looking back. *I can't read this guy. It's like he just doesn't show emotion.*

Hutar put the book aside and leaned forward, arms resting on his knees. "I see you are the only one who has agreed to meet with me. That is one more than I thought would come."

"I can't believe I'm sitting here, talking to you," Aari blurted before catching himself and mentally kicking his rear end.

"I am surprised you came at all. Why did you?"

"To hear you out." Aari crossed his arms. "And to say that what you did, saving Elder Nageau . . . that was selfless."

Hutar's face remained inscrutable. "Where are the others?"

"They don't really want to be anywhere near you."

"I cannot say that I blame them."

A pause came between the pair. Aari jerked his chin at Hutar. "How's the injury? It's only been a week and you're out and about."

Hutar studied his fingernails. "Better. Huyani is a great healer, and it helps that she is skillful with our remedial solutions." He halted his preening and looked directly at Aari. "You have a question."

"I'd just like to know why you wanted to speak with us."

"I wanted to speak with you because I wished to apologize for what I did in the past, and I would like for bygones to be bygones.

However, I am certainly not a fool. I know that will not happen overnight, but I was hoping the healing would begin."

"That's it?" Aari asked flatly.

"That is all." Hutar absently touched the center of his chest as he let his eyes wander around the library, ignoring the guards on either side of him. "I am curious, Aari. How is your training? I have heard mutters from my people that you and your friends have begun to exhibit some great abilities as a group."

Aari tucked his chin against his neck, face hardening. "Training's fine."

For the first time, he saw a flicker of emotion in Hutar's eyes. "I would like to make amends, Aari. I really would. Maybe one day . . ."

Aari stood up. To himself, he thought, *Not likely.*

"If that's all, I've got somewhere to be," he said.

Hutar picked up his book and resumed reading. Aari raised his hand to Akol and the other guards, all of whom placed their fists over their hearts in farewell. When he was far enough from the library, he rushed out of the temple, nearly running into a towering figure.

"Whoa! Elder Nageau, hi." He gave the man a pinched smile.

Nageau clasped his hands behind his back. "I take it the talk did not go too well?"

"You could hear?"

The Elder chuckled. "I may have the gift of enhanced senses, but I would never use them with imprudence."

"Fair enough. The meeting wasn't bad, I guess. He mainly wanted to apologize, but I just can't help feeling unnerved being so close to him again. He's saying all the right things, and yet it's like there's a shadow lurking somewhere deep inside."

"I understand. It is going to take time for him to win back the trust of the people. This will not be an easy journey for any of us, Hutar included. It takes vigilance and continued effort to cast away darkness once it has sunk its claws into the soul." Nageau ambled along the partially frozen river, Aari beside him.

The snow crunched beneath their boots. "Let us pay Mariah a visit. She is giving some of the youths a hand with the horses."

Aari followed the Elder down the slope to the stable. Inside, he peeked through all the stalls until he found Mariah happily brushing the glossy coat of a regal black stallion. "Hey," he said. "How's it going?"

"Great! This guy is such a sweetheart!" She hugged the horse and it nuzzled her lovingly.

Nageau appeared at the door of the stall, beaming. "Ah, I see you are caring for my favorite scoundrel."

"Yeah," Mariah grinned. "Korv is amazing. I heard his story, too; about how he's named after a heroic horse from your island ancestors' home." She stroked the animal's flank. "I'd love to take him for a ride some time, if that's possible."

"What's your goal, to ride every horse in Dema-Ki?" Aari asked. "You've ridden six of them already."

"Yes, perhaps you can, Mariah," Nageau interjected. "Though I suppose I should first warn you that you may be called upon to return to the outside world at any moment."

Aari spun around to face the Elder. "What?"

"The Sentries may soon need your help, younglings."

"I'm confused," Mariah said. "Why do they need us? I mean, honestly, what is it we can do that the Sentries can't? How are we of any use besides being extra hands?"

"Never in all my years have I seen the things that you five have begun to manifest as a group," Nageau answered. "And you have proven, by fate or by chance, that you can perceive things the Sentries cannot."

"But what about our training?" Aari asked. "We're not through, are we?"

The Elder slid his fingers from the horse's forehead down to its muzzle. "Truthfully, we do not know. There is no further guidance as to what needs to be done to tap into your latent capabilities. Perhaps your training has, in reality, already ended and we are merely pushing against a wall that can no longer be moved.

But if your training is yet to be concluded, we will know in time and continue accordingly. Your abilities will grow when they are truly tested, but from what the Elders and I have witnessed thus far, your individual powers have flourished dramatically. Your combined capabilities have proven to be exponential as well. Not only in intensity, but also in variability. This is something that the people of Dema-Ki have never seen."

Mariah swept her thumb over the bristles of the brush. "How will we know when and where we're needed? Will the Sentries ask for us?"

"The signs will show us when we must send you out," Nageau answered. "It could be soon or a little further down the road."

"Something tells me it's going to be the former." Aari leaned against the stall door and tapped his lips slowly. "Elder Nageau, something's been nagging at me. If Reyor does learn about our abilities and our role in the prophecy, won't our families be in danger? I'm aware you have Marshall and two other Sentries watching over them, but are there better alternatives if . . . you know . . . ?"

"The Elders have been discussing this. For the moment, your families are safe, but we do have a plan in place should the harbinger's shadow fall over them."

Aari nodded. Nageau smiled warmly at the friends, then bade them a good evening and left. Aari picked up some hay and fed it to the horse as Mariah worked on picking the animal's hooves clean.

"We put a lot of faith in the Elders," he thought aloud.

"They haven't given us reason not to," Mariah said. "And they put a lot of faith in us as well."

"Talk about pressure."

"I know, but at least it feels like we're working with family and not a soulless organization, you know? A family with a reliable support system."

"True." Aari waved at a girl as she brought in a sweaty mare after what looked like an intense ride; she smiled and waved back.

As Mariah moved around the horse, she said, "Something feels really different."

"Hm?"

"We initially agreed to train last year because we were excited to unlock our abilities. Yes, there was the prophecy and all that, but it was sort of in the background. Then there was the battle on the mountain, and that whole road trip to California that gave us our first taste of Reyor's plans. But *this*. You can almost touch the darkness that's growing out there. It's not just crops dying anymore. It's people. All over the world. And something tells me we're really, truly going to get our feet wet and our hands dirty."

"I know what you mean. It *is* different now, and I'm pretty sure we're all starting to feel it."

"I'm scared, Aari."

"Me too."

They looked at each other, a silent conversation passing between them, before she returned her attention to the horse. Aari slunk out of the stable, lost in the storm of his thoughts and the thunder of his growing fears.

"Ladies and gentlemen, this is your captain speaking. We are currently one hour away from Dubai International and will be arriving earlier than expected. Our descent will begin shortly. It's a bright, sunny day in the City of Gold. Temperature's close to forty degrees Celsius with high humidity—for our American passengers on board, that's one hundred-and-four degrees Fahrenheit. And for those of you getting onto connecting flights, enjoy the cool comfort of the airport. Everyone else, hope you brought your bathing suits! You'll find some relief from this heat with a nice dip at some of Dubai's beautiful beaches and pools."

The Aboriginal Australian captain of the A380, the world's largest passenger airliner, released the switch to end his transmission into the cabin's PA system. He stretched his arms over his balding head, rotating his shoulders. *Gotta quit these long-haul flights. Can't wait to get back to Sydney. Hope Janice and the kids are enjoying the family reunion . . . should give 'em a call once we land.*

The flight was at full capacity, with nearly five hundred passengers and crew members. Behind the pilot and his first officer was the relief crewmember, a beaming blonde in her thirties. The pilot had been fond of her since the day they'd met; she always came to work with a bright face and kind words.

"Thank goodness for that tailwind, huh?" she said. "Saved enough fuel to make the bean counters in the office smile."

The tanned, square-faced first officer looked absolutely disgruntled. "Who cares? I can't wait to get this thing on the ground. It's so bloody hot in here, I'm this close to taking my clothes off."

"What are you on about?" the pilot asked. "The ECS is doing great. We've got optimal cabin climate."

"Doesn't feel like it."

The pilot sighed. "How's the headache, mate?"

"I think it's gotten worse since yesterday. It's been coming like the devil's hitting my skull with a jackhammer, then it goes and returns worse. I can feel it starting up again."

"Hang in there. We'll be landing soon."

"Not soon enough," the first officer grumbled.

"Maybe Paige ought to take over for you?"

"Nah, it's alright. I'll tell you what, though. Once we land, I'm taking everything Dubai's got to cure this headache, if you know what I'm sayin'."

The captain grinned, shaking his head. Ten minutes later, the autopilot began to lower the massive aircraft from its cruising altitude of forty thousand feet. The small talk died down shortly after as the flight crew prepared for their descent over the Gulf of Oman. The pilot hit the comms switch on the sidestick and spoke into his headset. "Dubai approach, good afternoon, Zeus 183, level twenty thousand."

A smooth, Arabic-accented voice from Dubai International Airport's air traffic control responded. *"Zeus 183, Dubai approach, turn left heading three-two-zero, descend and maintain ten thousand feet."*

"Left to three-two-zero, down to ten thousand feet, Zeus 183."

As the pilot reduced the altitude, the first officer let out a cry, savagely beating his fists against his head. The pilot jumped. "Whoa! Mate, what are you—"

"Make it go away," the first officer groaned. "Make—it—go—*away!*"

"Hey, *hey!* Listen to me, okay? Listen to my voice! You gotta—"

The first officer unleashed an agonized roar. He stopped pummeling himself and held his head in his hands, every inch of him trembling.

The pilot, fighting to remain calm, turned to the relief

crewmember behind the first officer. "Take over from him," he ordered.

Nodding, the woman unfastened herself and got up. As she approached the first officer, he thrashed and bared his teeth at her. Stark red veins stretched around the whites of his eyes. The woman stepped back instinctively, but quickly gathered her wits. She reached out to hold the man and spoke calmly until his thrashing subsided and he'd more or less regained his composure. Once she'd unbuckled him, she guided him to the seat behind the pilot's and secured him with the seatbelt.

"Everything alright?" the pilot asked.

"I think so." The woman exhaled, shaking a little, then took the seat beside him and slipped on the headset.

"Good." The pilot pressed the comms switch. "Dubai approach, Zeus 183, we have a medical emergency."

"Zeus 183, Dubai approach, state nature of emergency."

"Dubai approach, first officer experiencing seizure of some sort, request EMT upon arrival."

"Zeus 183, Dubai approach copy, arranging medical response upon landing."

The pilot let go of the switch and glanced at the jittery crewmember next to him. "Paige."

She started. "Yes?"

"Deep breaths."

She did as instructed, then asked, "Do you think we should get one of the cabin crew to remove him from the cockpit?"

"And let the passengers see him in this state? No. He's strapped in, anyway. Let's not make a scene without reason."

She didn't seem happy, but she didn't argue. Tense silence filled the space until the pilot pressed his comms switch again. "Dubai approach, Zeus 183, approaching ten thousand, information Foxtrot."

"Zeus 183, Dubai approach, maintain three-two-zero, descend to five thousand, visual approach runway three-zero left."

The pilot turned back to look at the first officer. The man

seemed to have calmed down, though his breathing was labored. The pilot allowed himself to release the tension from his shoulders. "See?" he told the relief crewmember. "It's fine."

The plane descended to five thousand feet and angled to line up with the runway. As the desert landscape drew closer, Dubai's skyline began to shimmer at a distance.

"There it is," the female officer murmured. "Burj Khalifa."

Up ahead and slightly to the left, an immense reflective structure rose half a mile into the sky, befitting its title of the world's tallest building. Thousands of hand-cut glass panels glinted in the desert's sunlight, and high-intensity strobes mounted on the building's spire flashed in warning to passing aircrafts.

Moments after the plane descended below a thousand feet, the pilot took manual control in preparation for landing, but furious stomping from behind wrenched his attention away.

The first officer glared at him, body shuddering as if he was being subjected to electric shocks. Blood dripped from his tear ducts and nose, staining his white uniform. But something in the way he acted baffled the pilot; it was as though the man was petrified of his companions. He swung his head wildly, sweat coating his skin, teeth gnashing as his hands slapped at the seatbelt until it unfastened.

"Secure him!" the pilot shouted. *"Now!"*

The woman threw herself at their delirious colleague. The first officer, already on his feet, spun around just as she made contact. He bellowed, grabbing her head, and slammed her mercilessly into the side panel of the cockpit. There was a distinct snap and she slid to the floor like a ragdoll, her face frozen in an expression of shock.

The pilot screamed at the first officer to sit down. The authority in his voice must have worked; the bloodied copilot went still, staring blankly at his captain.

The plane flew over the outskirts of downtown Dubai, and the airport was just within reach. Perspiration dripped down the captain's forehead. *Need to request an emergency go-around!*

As he reached for his comms switch, something grabbed him by the throat and squeezed. He let go of the controls to pry himself free, but the first officer had an iron grip locked around his neck. The pilot unbuckled his seatbelt to fight back, digging his nails into the first officer's hands. He heaved short gasps, lungs burning, heartbeat pulsing in his head.

Desperate, he tried to reactivate the autopilot but only managed to reach the comms switch with his fingertips. *"Help,"* he rasped. *"First officer—st-strangling . . . hel—"*

The hands suddenly forced him down, smashing his head into the controls. The plane's nose dipped and the aircraft banked violently to the left. Holding onto the last bit of his will, the pilot tried to fight for control of the aircraft but was hauled out of his seat. He came face-to-face with the first officer and could only scream before being thrown to the floor and stomped on.

Alarms in the cockpit blared earsplitting warnings, but the pilot couldn't do anything. He saw the sole of the first officer's boot coming down onto his face, and the last thing he felt was its bone-crushing impact moments before the plane struck the ground.

* * *

"Gareth!" Deverell yelled. "Get out here and look at this!"

Startled, Gareth nearly slipped as he scrambled out of the shower. He tore out of the bathroom with a towel wrapped around his waist, leaving wet footprints behind him, and found his brother staring agape at something on the television in their flat. "What is it?"

Deverell turned up the volume in response. The news channel showed a live shot of a massive mall in downtown Dubai. The entire west wing of the building was engulfed in flames and the base of Burj Khalifa was on fire, tendrils working upward and burning the interior. People could be heard screaming, and a few ran out of the tower, hysterical, their clothes smoldering.

Gareth leaned against the table beside his brother. "What happened, Dev?"

"A huge passenger plane just crashed a few minutes ago. Look, right there." Deverell pointed with the remote. On one corner of the split screen, a video taken by a tourist showed the A380 falling out of the sky and plowing into the mall, a meteor of death. The twins watched, aghast.

"I can't see how anyone on that flight would have survived," Gareth murmured.

"And all the people in the mall," Deverell added quietly. "How could that have happened?"

In the midst of the cacophony of sirens and flashing lights on the screen, an icy wave of turbulence rolled in Gareth's chest, nearly knocking the breath out of him. He rested a hand over his heart, feeling its frenzied beating below his skin. "Do you . . . do you feel it?"

Deverell sat heavily on one of the dining chairs. "The fabric. It's been disturbed. Again."

"Yeah." Gareth turned away, pensively apprehensive. "Something else is afoot, and it slipped right under our noses."

"We can't be the only ones who felt the disturbance." Deverell picked up his phone. "The flight originated in Sydney. Let's see if the Sentries in Australia know something."

Jag shut the door of the van and stared up at the stately three-story chalet. The building, known to the Sentries as the Lodge, was used as their base in Europe. Located on one of the smaller, snow-covered mountains in the French Alps, it overlooked a lake that hadn't yet frozen over. Coniferous and deciduous trees wreathed the luminous, serene surroundings that could put a tempestuous heart at ease.

This is so unexpected, he thought. *The Elders said we might be called out on a mission soon, but I didn't think that meant two days after we were told about it . . .*

"Quite a place," Kody said as he and Aari joined Jag.

Marshall, who'd met them in Mayo, the town nearest to Dema-Ki, rounded the vehicle and grinned; Jag was still getting used to the man's now clean-shaven face. "Glad you like it. Come on, let's get our stuff inside."

The girls suddenly appeared beside them, looking ecstatic. "We just saw an ibex!" Mariah whooped. "The horns on that thing were *huge!*"

"There are a number of animals up here." Marshall opened the back of the van and passed the bags to the friends. "Bears, a few types of deer, wildcats, wolves, bouquetin—"

"What's that?" Tegan asked.

"Bouquetin? That's French for ibex."

Kody rolled his eyes. "Why not just say ibex?"

"Hey, don't ask me. I'm not French."

"I'm asking why *you* didn't just say ibex, dum-dum."

The Sentry snickered in response.

"Marshall, whose bike is that?" Jag asked, pointing at a black dual-sport motorcycle parked at the base of the Lodge.

"Everyone's. We keep it here as one of the emergency vehicles. I see you eyeballing it, kiddo. Do you ride?"

"My brother bought one earlier this year. He never let me near it, so I'd take it out for a spin whenever he was out of the house."

"Cheeky."

Jag shouldered his bag and followed the group up the stone steps to the Lodge. The large timber door opened before they reached the last stair, revealing a tall black woman with steel-gray eyes, looking cozy in her jeans and white pullover. She smiled dazzlingly and welcomed them in, introducing herself as Dominique Mboya from the Democratic Republic of Congo.

"I am so honored to meet you," she told the friends in a thick French accent. There was such profound emotion in her eyes that Jag thought he would drown in them if he didn't avert his gaze.

The friends blushed in unison at her words and mumbled awkwardly, making Marshall laugh. Once the group introduced themselves and shared some pleasantries, Dominique gave them a tour of the place. The main level housed bedrooms where the friends and others would bunk. A third of it was occupied by an electronics room; some field Sentries used it to experiment with Dema-Ki defensive and offensive technology as inspiration to create new equipment. Below them, the massive basement hosted as a training and recreation area, complete with a gym, an open space with mats for self-defense practice, a pool table, and a dart board. A medical bay was tucked at the far end.

The top floor, with its large, open floor plan contained a common room with a fireplace, a kitchen that Jag knew made Kody's heart leap for joy, a few more guest rooms, and a meeting area with a ten-foot-long maple veneer table and a huge corkboard on the wall beside it. Two separate staircases led to lofts on either end of the building.

"I'm in love," Jag heard Tegan say dreamily behind him. "The furnishing is minimalist. The carpet is so soft. And the windows are *so big!* Look at all that natural light coming in!"

"Forget that, just look at this kitchen!" Kody bent over the marble countertop of the island, arms spread out to embrace it. "If this is what heaven's like, I'm no longer afraid of death."

Dominique seemed pleased. "I'm glad you like it here. The Lodge was willed to me by my father when he passed away, but it really belongs to all of us. This used to be a boutique hotel for many years before my father decided to turn it into a safe house for Sentries. Many of us have used this place over the years to meet or rest between travels. Some even took the liberty to renovate and upgrade the furnishings, as well as other things. Though we are quite off the grid, we have generators and enough technology to power the Lodge without a problem."

The friends were impressed. Kody raised his hand. "What's the Wi-Fi password?"

Dominique's lips twitched from refrained laughter. "You will get it shortly. Now, come, let me show you the rooms. Pick whichever one suits your fancy."

When she led them to the first room, Jag knew it was the one he needed and he claimed it instantly, grinning from ear to ear.

"Are you sure you don't want to look at the others?" Dominique asked, surprised.

Jag dropped his bag and took stock of the space. "I'm good, thank you."

"You can have it," Kody sniffed. "An entire wall that's just a window? No thanks. Too much light for me."

The Sentry led the others around the main floor, leaving Jag to marvel at his new bedroom. The massive floor-to-ceiling window opposite him granted a view of snow-covered trees and distant mountains. There was a double bed, and the fresh linen hugged his face when he belly-flopped onto it. He groaned happily. The room was barren of anything else except a few built-in shelves, but it was still elegant.

He allowed himself to rest for a few minutes before unpacking, then went to check on the others, first going into the smaller room beside his. Aari's clothes were already neatly hung on a rack next to his bed, and his toiletries were arranged on the short dresser below. The redheaded teenager rested on the mattress, checking his phone as it charged. His laptop rested on the carpet, also plugged in.

"I see you wasted no time getting all your electronics out," Jag said, poking Aari's cheek.

"It's the twenty-first century. Unfortunately, we kinda need it all."

"Makes you wonder how up the creek we'd be if everything suddenly stopped working."

Aari blanched. "*Please* don't talk like that. I'm not built to take on a world devoid of tech."

"Yeah, I hear you." Jag turned to leave.

"Where you going?"

"To check on the others."

Aari bounced up. "I'll come."

They found Kody passed out on the bed in his room. Two rows of shelves built into the wall above him already displayed his comic books and bobbleheads of Boba Fett and Master Chief. A small bay window offered a view similar to the one from Jag's room.

Aari tutted. "He couldn't even wait until he unpacked his clothes."

He went over to Kody and shook him. Kody turned over, grumbling. "Five more minutes. Jet lag."

"As if," Aari retorted. "We've traveled with you and you have never had jet lag."

That earned him a pillow to the face. Jag chuckled, leaving the room so his friends could squabble in peace.

He found himself in front of Mariah's room next. She was carefully placing books on a single shelf. He knocked on the open door. "Hey, can I come in?"

Mariah beckoned him to enter. "I already love it here," she gushed. "I mean, it's kinda bare, but something about this place makes me happy, you know?"

"Yeah." Jag dug his toes into the soft round rug beneath his feet. "How are you doing, 'Riah? I know leaving home was . . . was really hard for you. Probably harder than it was for most of us."

The glow in Mariah's face faded. She sat on the edge of her bed, hair covering her eyes. "I'm okay."

He took a seat beside her, saying nothing. Neither of them moved until she rested her head on his shoulder. Feeling her quiver slightly as she held back tears, he leaned his head against hers and stroked her hair.

"Your mom's a strong woman," he said. "She'll be alright, knowing she raised a daughter as strong as her."

Mariah let out a bark of laughter between sniffles. "I'm nowhere near as strong as she is. I freeze up when I'm all alone in a crowd of strangers, for Pete's sake."

"You've gotten a lot better the last two years," Jag pointed out. "No one has to hold your hand when you go to the mall now."

She punched his arm. "Har, har."

"Seriously though, you *are* doing better. Be patient with yourself and you'll get there."

"Thanks, Yoda. Really."

"Welcome, you are."

Mariah dried her eyes, giggling. Jag smiled, then indicated the books on the shelf. "I can't believe you managed to fit all that *and* your clothes into one bag. You know you can live without books for a while, right?"

"What, that? That's nothing. I had a dozen more I wanted to bring, but they wouldn't fit and Tegan didn't have room in her bag for them."

". . . Readers are crazy people."

"We *are* crazy. And books are our medicine."

"I'll leave you to take your daily dose, then." Jag gave her a side hug and exited, only to crash into Tegan who was power-walking down the hall with a toothbrush in her mouth and her hair in a bun.

He reached out to wiggle the back of one of her many earrings.

"You do know the bathrooms are the other way, right?"

She mimicked his sarcastic tone and smacked him upside the head before continuing to her room. Jag covered himself and followed her, keeping at a safe distance. She grabbed her toiletry bag and rushed back out just as toothpaste started to dribble down her chin. "You can wait there!" she yelled.

"That's so attractive!" he called back.

"I will shove this toothbrush up your nose, Sanchez!"

Jag recoiled. "Sorry!"

Tegan returned a minute later, all cleaned up. "So, how are you liking our new digs?"

"I'm liking it a lot."

"Me too. I don't think we'll be here for too long, though."

"What makes you say that?"

"If we were staying here for a while, then that's time we could have been training in Dema-Ki. We're out here because things are going to start moving pretty quick. But don't hold me to that."

"Leave it to the most observant person on our team to notice that."

"Team?" Tegan arched her eyebrows at him as she unpacked the last of her clothes. "Since when have we called ourselves that?"

"Sorry, it just . . . came out."

"No, don't apologize. You're not wrong. We're a team now, not just a group of friends. And the fact that you called us that means it's starting to sink in for you, too, whether you realize it or not. That's leadership, Jag."

Jag slouched against the wall, mouth closed tight. Tegan noticed his posture and her expression hardened. She threw her clothes onto the bed and stormed up to him, jabbing a finger at his chest. "No. No second thoughts. We talked about this last year. You know you're the one to lead us. We've been following you since we were little, and you're the one we'll follow as we walk toward whatever lies ahead."

Jag knew that if he tried to argue with her she'd put him in his place, and his pride wasn't ready for that. He bowed his head and only raised it when she went back to unpacking. Her room, like the others, was simple and elegant with only a bed, some shelves, and a window. Jag noticed she'd already started to hang up her sketches, as well as a few completed pieces of artwork.

"I've never seen these before," he remarked.

"I did them while we were in Dema-Ki."

"You managed to carve out time for art? That's amazing." He outlined a particular illustration of a group of superheroes, admiring it. "They're really good, Teegs. You've come a long way."

"They're works in progress, but thanks."

A chorus of voices further down the main floor made the pair look up.

"The other Sentries must be here," Jag said.

As they hurried along the wide hallway, the others emerged from their rooms and fell in step behind them. When they reached the front door, they found Marshall and Dominique hugging the new arrivals who, upon seeing the friends approaching, let out exclamations and greeted them with warmth—love, even. The teenagers, astonished, couldn't help but reciprocate the genuine enthusiasm as they introduced themselves.

The two men with cheeky grins were the Vaughn twins, whom Marshall was particularly fond of. Beside them stood a Sentry from India, Benny Kumar. He was younger than the other Sentries at twenty-six, with a full head of wavy black hair and a dark mocha complexion. Lei Shao, a tall and slender Chinese woman, had a razor-sharp look that could strike down a serpent.

Wouldn't want to get on her bad side, Jag thought.

Coolly observing the gathering from behind the other newcomers stood Zoe King, the Australian Sentry with a well-toned surfer's body, beach-blonde hair, and the darkest pupils Jag had ever seen. She came across as amiable but had an air about her that warned off casual conversation.

Behind him, he heard Mariah whisper to Tegan. "What it is with Dema-Ki people being all tall and graceful? If they had pointy ears and long hair, I swear they'd be elves."

Tegan giggled, and even Jag failed to suppress a grin.

Benny rubbed his hands together cheerfully. "Should we get on with the meeting?"

Marshall led the way to the top floor where they convened around the conference table, none of them opting to sit. Deverell and Gareth used the corkboard to display papers they took from a folder.

Marshall made a call and put it on speaker. When a man picked up, the Sentry said, "Hey, Colback, is this a good time? We're starting the meeting."

"Yeah. I'm en route to the New Mexico Sanctuary as we speak. Should be there in an hour."

"Awesome. By the way, guys, this is Victor Colback on the line. Some of us know him, some don't. He's in charge of locating Reyor."

"Hey, everyone."

The other Sentries seemed surprised about who was on the other end of the call; Jag caught a couple of them sharing awed glances and heard Benny mutter, "The Knight of the North? That's *him?*"

Marshall placed his hands on the table, his tone changing from casual to businesslike. "Okay, this is what we know. Six months ago, crop failures started to spread in America and, a month or two later, around the world. We traced the blight to Phoenix's REAPR project—nanomite pods strategically located to decimate major crops across the planet. In June, we managed to completely shut down the pods in North America but the struggle still continues globally. Other Sentries are working on destroying the pods and, last I checked, it's estimated that sixty percent have been dealt with. Of course, the fallout from this has been famine, riots, and pillaging, not to mention what appears to be a war of attrition launched by China and India against Russia. News is, because the Russians were for some reason largely spared by the REAPRs, the Chinese and Indian governments are convinced they're the culprits behind the systematic crop failures.

"Then, in August and September, Dominique was serving in a remote village in the Democratic Republic of Congo when the villagers began succumbing to a highly virulent disease that caused rapid aging. She was, and remains, unaffected but the fatality rate was one hundred percent. The entire village has since perished." Marshall reached out to Dominique, placing a hand on hers. She looked down, faintly motioning for him to continue.

"Cut to Wales, early October. Gareth and Dev happened to be in a hospital where a man and a baby had both shown symptoms of the same disease. The guys spent the next two days monitoring every media outlet and saw that the disease was starting to work its way eastward through Europe.

"Now it looks like there's another disease originating from Australia—with Sydney being the epicenter—and it's a whole different beast. Those affected turn into noxious wind-up toys. When the key's turning, they seem fine, but when it comes to a stop, they explode in a burst of violence for a brief period before succumbing to death. It isn't pretty."

As Marshall spoke, the Vaughns worked behind him, Deverell putting up printed articles and photos while Gareth stuck pins in the map on the places Marshall mentioned.

"I assume we're all aware of the Dubai plane crash that's been all over the news?" Marshall asked.

"Worst in aviation history," the Australian Sentry, Zoe, said solemnly. "Over a thousand dead. Five hundred passengers and crew members, as well as those in the mall and Burj Khalifa."

"Yes. And what we're now learning is that there may be evidence in the recordings between the pilot and air traffic control to indicate that the copilot was affected by the Australian disease. He attacked the flight crew at a critical moment as the plane was landing."

Jag's brows knitted. "Obviously we're looking at it from the angle that this is Reyor's doing, but apart from dots that seem to connect, how do we know for sure that this is actually the case and not just two random diseases running wild?"

"We do have more evidence," Marshall said. "Colback, you there?"

"Yeah," the Sentry on the phone replied. "I was hot on a trail a couple days ago and listened in on a conversation between Tony Cross and Dr. Nate. They made a reference to something called the Arcane Ventures and spoke about a second project that had been launched globally after successfully conducting initial tests in Africa. What are the chances, right? I'm also willing to go out on a limb and say that their first project was the REAPRs."

Lei tapped her foot against the floor in a rapid, anxious beat. "So Reyor is really taking things up a few notches?"

"Great," Aari muttered. "Go unleash two vicious diseases in the midst of a global chaos, why don't you."

"Speaking of the chaos," Tegan said, "we were kind of under a rock in Dema-Ki. What's actually happening on the Russian front?"

The Sentries looked uncomfortable. Benny rested his elbows on the table and chewed his lip. "The invasion has been bloody. The Chinese and Indian forces combined have a huge numerical advantage over the Russians, but it hasn't been anywhere as easy as they thought. People just don't learn from history. Russia isn't known for rolling out the welcome mat to invaders. But I'll give credit to the Indo–Sino forces—their troops managed to secure large areas of agricultural land and some grain silos. Still . . . many of them have been cut off by Russia's scorched-earth policy, like what they did in World War Two with the Nazis. Plus, the Russians are isolating enemy troops and strangling supplies. Oh, *and* they're threatening the use of tactical nukes. So far it has been a conventional war, thankfully, but the situation is still explosive and I wouldn't put it past the Russians to throw a nuke into the mix."

Jag was appalled. "What's the U.N. doing?"

Zoe snorted. "The ever-so-effective Security Council called for cessation of hostilities that, as expected, fell on deaf ears. Now they'd be content if they could broker a 'de-escalation and containment.'"

"And it's not just Russia, China and India that are fighting," Lei added. "Wandering military units are going after grain supplies in Africa and Southeast Asia, especially Indonesia and the Philippines. It's a free-for-all."

"What's America doing?" Mariah asked.

"There's a lot on their plate, dealing with the consequences of the crop loss," Marshall said. "With riots, social unrest, and high food prices, they've got enough to contend with. No one's in the mood for military intervention."

Jag rolled a chair to the table so he could collapse onto it, then rested his head heavily in one hand. *Ugh.*

"Do we have any more information about the disease?" Tegan asked, leaning against the chair's high backrest. "Like how it spreads, what the early symptoms are, and how infectious it is?"

"We don't know much, except that it's extremely contagious," Marshall answered. "No one has a clue as to how it spreads or how it's carried."

"Actually," Dominique interjected, "I think I do know the symptoms. At least, for the disease that causes aging."

The gathering gave her their full attention.

"It starts with a cough," she said, "and then blurred vision that comes and goes. After that, there is weakness and pain in the joints that grow until people who have it can't move because of the extreme agony and exhaustion. Visual signs of accelerated aging like hair loss, tooth decay, cataracts, and failing memory begin appearing between the last two symptoms."

Jag suddenly saw an image of himself, nearly eighteen, with his skin sagging and his whole body aching, a tooth dropping out each time he tried to speak and hair graying before falling in clumps. He swallowed hard, goosebumps popping all over his arms.

"I'm assuming the CDC's handling this?" Aari asked.

"They've been asked by other countries to aid local efforts, yes," Marshall said. "Authorities in parts of Europe, Australia, and Southeast Asia are scrambling to get to the bottom of this mess before it gets out of hand and the public starts to panic."

Jag slumped back. "So where do we go from here?"

Marshall raised his index and middle fingers. "Our job is two-fold. One, contain the outbreak, whatever it takes. Two, stop the scourge at its source."

"The disease, you mean?" Mariah guessed.

"No. Everything."

Jag looked at Marshall, thoughtful. "Reyor."

"Precisely. We'll need a location first, though, and that's Colback's mission."

The twins went to stand on either side of Marshall. "Where should we begin?" Deverell asked.

Zoe placed a metal canister on the table. "Here."

Gareth eyed it. "What's that?"

"Tissue and blood samples from victims in 'straya."

"How . . . ?"

Zoe smiled, her dark eyes twinkling. Gareth pulled a face. "Fine, don't tell. So, what do we do with this?"

"I have an idea," Marshall said, "but let me speak with the Elders first."

The gathering remained respectfully quiet for a few minutes, allowing him to establish a telepathic link. Jag absently reached into his T-shirt and pulled out the pendant hanging around his neck—an amber crystal shaped into the paw print of a wildcat embedded in carved metal. He gripped it tightly as his mind warped into a wormhole where countless thoughts raced through. He glanced at his friends. All of them had the corners of their mouths pulled down.

Marshall suddenly clapped his hands. "Alright, here's the plan. We're going to send the samples Zoe brought to a go-between in Mayo. She'll meet Magèo's apprentice halfway between there and Dema-Ki, who'll then pass the samples to Magèo so he can run some tests and see if he can't reverse engineer a cure."

"A go-between?" Tegan repeated.

"Yeah. She's a Sentry, but her duty is to stay in Yukon and

keep in contact with the Elders once in a while. It's a new thing they implemented just before they sent you home last year."

"So we've got the Australian sample," Deverell said, stroking his chin. "We should get the European one as well, and ship both to Magèo."

"How would we get it?" Kody asked.

"You'll see. Want to come?"

Kody blinked. "What?"

"To get the European blood and tissue samples. Care to join Gareth and me, mate?"

Kody looked to Marshall for direction. The Sentry smiled, understanding. "We're not your parents, Kody. We're here to fan the flames of good in this world, and back you five up if you need us. Out here, you call the shots for yourselves."

Jag felt icy fingers tracing down his spine. *They're stepping back and letting us grow into our roles in different ways. We're going to be getting more responsibilities. That means more will be expected of me.* The fingers turned to claws that dug into his lower back. He shifted uneasily in his chair. *No. I can't do this. Tegan's better suited. She's cool under pressure. She's focused. The group would benefit if she led.*

The sound of people shuffling around returned him to reality. He watched them, confused. Tegan leaned down and whispered, "Space cadet, where you at?"

"In orbit," he answered tersely.

"I'll fill you in. Kody's leaving with Deverell and Gareth to get the samples we need, Mariah and I are going with Marshall to get some grub and supplies in the nearest town, and you and Aari are staying back to monitor and map disease patterns."

"What? I didn't agree to that."

"Yes, you did. You nodded when you were asked."

"I did?"

"Man, you are out of it. What's going on?" She placed the back of her hand against his forehead. "Are you sick or something?"

He brushed her away and got out of the chair. "I'm fine."

Mariah sidled up to them. "Teegs, the Sentry who's going to the New Mexico Sanctuary . . . should we brief him properly on what to expect?"

"Yes!" Tegan turned to Marshall as he was about to end the call. "Wait!"

While the girls spoke with Victor, Aari popped up beside Jag, his laptop tucked under his left arm and another, taken from the electronics room, in his right. "Let's get to work."

The girls departed with Marshall once they were done with the call. Jag and Aari took over the table while everyone else dispersed to unpack.

Jag opened his laptop, then looked at the map hanging across from him. He wished he was out getting supplies with the others; something deep inside told him that the map, with only a handful of pins stuck in it, would soon fill up. And he wasn't ready to see that. He wasn't ready to face the reality that the world he knew was slowly, but surely, slipping away.

15

Mariah watched the scenery roll by as the van cruised down a winding road toward the nearest ski town. The beauty of the snowcapped mountains glimmering under the cobalt sky took her breath away. She preferred warm weather but could see why people like Tegan and Kody loved winter.

In the front passenger seat, Tegan quietly drew in a small sketchbook. Mariah leaned forward to catch a glimpse of the work in progress. In the middle of the page was a shaded lion-head door knocker. It was surprisingly detailed for a sketch. She marveled at it for a bit, then sat back. "How long till we're there, Marshall?" she asked.

"Seven, eight . . . hundred miles," the Sentry said.

"Wait, *what?*"

"Jokes, jokes. Just a couple of miles after this bend."

Mariah caught Marshall grinning in the rearview mirror. She flicked his ear. "Meanie."

In the distance, the ululating wail of a siren reached them, growing louder with each passing second. The Sentry quickly pulled to the side of the road as an ambulance emerged from the bend up ahead and raced past them, then continued on until the small ski resort village came into view.

It's so quaint and peaceful, Mariah thought, examining the colorful ornamental lights that decorated the streets and the rustic structures that gave the town its character. *Or maybe not . . . What's going on here?*

As they drove along the main street, two ambulances pulled away from a lonely house, their sirens blaring. Mariah stuck her fingers in her ears as the vehicles rocketed past the van and retreated from view. "What in the world?"

Tegan gripped her respirator mask; Marshall had grabbed a boxful from the Lodge and, as a precaution, handed them out to everyone before they left. "Should we put these on?" she asked.

As the Sentry parked, he said, "I don't think there's a need for it right now, but keep it with you at all times."

They arrived at a grocery store just as a middle-aged woman inside turned the hanging sign from Open to Closed, but when she saw them she hastily unlocked the door and let them in. In English that was surprisingly good, she apologized for attempting to close early. "I wanted to visit my husband in the hospital. I haven't been able to leave the store all day."

"We're so sorry to hold you back," Marshall said.

"It's okay. It's just a few minutes. Anyway, my husband is probably enjoying the solitude."

As they worked through the aisles, Tegan asked, "He's okay, then? Nothing serious?"

"I hope not," the woman answered. "It started as a cough. A couple of days later he began to get terrible aches in his joints and limbs. I thought it would be a good idea to get him checked. I was told he'd be fine, but the doctors decided to keep him for observation." She laughed sheepishly. "I worry so much, my husband sometimes says it's like he married his mother!"

Mariah gave her a quick grin, then to her delight found a row of soda cans at the back. "Oh, Dr Pepper! I've missed this so much!" She snagged a few. "So, what's with the ambulances?"

The woman fiddled with the end of her graying ponytail as she looked out the window. "You know, I'm really not sure. It's almost winter and some of the older people do get sick, but we don't usually have this many paramedics come at the same time. My husband told me that someone he works with started coughing and getting aches, too, like him." She suddenly gasped, hands clenching her ponytail. "You don't . . . you don't think it's that disease from the news, maybe?"

Mariah looked over the aisles at Marshall, who returned her alarmed stare with a barely perceptible shake of his head. "I doubt it," he answered pleasantly. "We're too far away from any densely populated areas. That's where the disease is right now."

"But we do get tourists here sometimes," the woman said, "even though this is just a small town. And they come from all over the world. You just can't ever know these days. I mean, we've seen things I never thought I'd see in my lifetime! Crop failures across the world, the awful unrests, everything else . . ."

"We're living in disturbing times, but I'm sure things will settle down eventually." Marshall gave her a warm smile, then addressed the girls. "Got everything?"

"Yep." Mariah picked up a few bags of chips and headed to the counter. "Now let's get a move on so this sweet lady can be on her way."

* * *

The moment the trio set foot in the Lodge, Aari and Jag yelled for them to hasten upstairs. They bolted up the steps, groceries and supplies in each hand. When they got to the top floor, Mariah's chest was heaving.

"What's going on?" Tegan demanded.

"Look at this," Jag said darkly.

The girls and the Sentry approached the meeting table and looked over the boys' shoulders at their laptops. Aari fluttered his hand impatiently. "Not the screens. The map. Look at the map."

Mariah lifted her eyes to the large chart hanging on the wall across from them. She raised an unsteady finger at it. "I don't remember there being that many pins on it before we left."

"That's because more cases have been popping up, most of them in Europe," Aari said. "We've been monitoring social media, along with regular news. The outbreak is centered in the U.K., and it looks like Wales is ground zero. See, the green pins are reports of the first disease, the aging one. The red pins are the violent outbreaks."

"More greens than reds," Marshall noticed.

"Not for much longer, I don't think."

"How many cases have you got on the record?"

"Thirty-five for greens, twelve for the reds."

Mariah noticed something on the map and paled. She slowly put her bags down. "Wait a minute . . . guys, you've got pins in North America."

Jag took in a long breath before acknowledging her statement. "We do, yeah. There are several cases we caught online in and around Atlanta, Chicago, New York, and L.A., as well as a few in Toronto and Vancouver in Canada."

"Why there?"

"Probably due to airports." Aari drummed his fingers on the tabletop. "Flight hubs. Same thing's happening in Indonesia, China, and Russia. These countries have some of the busiest airports, too."

"I'd hoped home would've remained clear," Tegan murmured. "At least for a little while longer."

"In a highly interconnected world?" Marshall sighed. "Not a chance."

"Hey, Jag," Aari muttered, frowning at his laptop. "How much time elapsed between the first reported outbreak in Wales and Asia?"

Jag scanned the spreadsheet he had open. "Huh, that's weird. They came at around the same time."

"And, meanwhile, there was a twelve- to fourteen-hour lapse between Europe and North America."

Mariah peered at Jag's screen, resting her chin on his shoulder. "What does that mean?"

"Normally, you can trace an outbreak to one epicenter," Aari said, "but if there are simultaneous outbreaks around the world, then it's not following typical viral outbreak patterns."

"Meaning?"

"Nature doesn't scheme. This definitely doesn't seem natural."

Tegan crossed her arms. "One thing we know for sure is that

Reyor isn't stupid. Or careless. If it's this easy to figure out that the outbreak is engineered, then Phoenix must be confident that it can't be traced back to them. At least, not in time to stop them. Which means they're ramping things up."

"This is crazy!" Mariah exclaimed. "It's spreading so quickly! Where are the authorities? What are the governments doing? Where's the CDC?"

Marshall put a hand on her arm. "We'll hear from them, hopefully soon. But we know that at the heart of this madness is a darkness that only the five of you are tasked to defeat. We need to make sure you're prepared to deal with things out here. You're going to have your work cut out for you."

Mariah's eyes flicked toward him, her mouth tight.

Jag chewed on his pen. "We'll stay on top of this and keep monitoring everything."

"Great," the Sentry said as he headed to the kitchen. "But we can't work on empty stomachs. Domi, Benny, and I will prepare dinner."

Mariah, still fixed on the green and red pins on the map, felt lightheaded from apprehension. "I think I'm going to call Mom and chat for a while, see how she's doing. I'll catch you guys in a bit."

* * *

"Yes, Momma, we're fine." Mariah closed her bedroom door and put her phone on speaker, placing it on the bedside table. She changed out of her clothes and into her pajamas even though it was still early in the evening.

Her mother sounded relieved. "Oh. Okay. Good."

Mariah smiled to herself. "I miss you."

"Even my nagging and my one hundred and one questions?"

"Well . . ."

"Shush, I don't want to hear an answer to that." The older woman chuckled. "I miss you too, baby. It's been really quiet around here. I don't get to hear you go on and on and on about your books or TV shows anymore."

Mariah sat on the floor by her bed, her smile ebbing. "I hope you're not spending too much time alone, Momma. You know you've got a giant support system in Great Falls."

"I do know. Don't you worry about me. So, you're in Europe now, huh? Are you eating well? How was Dema-Ki? How did your training go?"

Mariah fiddled with the hem of her pajama pants. "Yes; yes; it was beautiful as always; and it went well."

There was a brief pause. "You're not as chatty as you usually are with me, Mariah. Is something wrong?"

"No . . . no, nothing's wrong. Just really wanted to hear your voice."

"Then, maybe for this call, I'll do the talking and you can listen. Next call, we switch it."

"Deal."

Mariah rested her head against the bed and listened as her mother recounted stories from work or within her circle of friends; the comforting voice put her entirely at ease. Occasionally, her mother would interrupt herself to murmur much-needed tender words before continuing to regale Mariah with entertaining anecdotes.

Mariah lost track of time until someone knocked on her door. "One second, Momma. Come in!"

The door opened and Aari poked his head inside. "Dinner's ready."

"Okay. Be out in a bit."

He chucked little pieces of crumpled paper at her. "No. Now."

"Ugh, you're annoying."

"I know."

"Hi, Aari!" her mother called loudly.

Aari beamed at the sound of her voice. "Hi, Mrs. A! Sorry to interrupt your call. I thought Mariah was done."

"No worries, sweetie. You guys go and enjoy your dinner. Mariah, thank you for calling. Talk soon, baby?"

Mariah half smiled. "Yes, hopefully."

"Tell everyone I said hello, okay? Be good! I love you!"

"I love you too, Momma."

"Love you too, Mrs. A!" Aari hollered.

Mariah picked up the pieces of paper littered around her and threw them back at him. He ducked out the door. Sweeping her phone off the nightstand, she hit the end call button and tromped after him, feeling the heaviness that had settled within her pushed away for the moment.

Tony Cross sat alone in the spacious conference room located inside the administrative building for the New Mexico Sanctuary, a subterranean enclave located adjacent to a mining operation run by one of Phoenix's subsidiaries. He watched the holographic image before him, nervously tapping a pen on the long mahogany table. The figure, well over six feet tall, stared back from under the gold hood of a knee-length black coat. Or, at least, Tony guessed that the figure was staring back; the hood cast a shadow over most of the face.

In a voice turned deep and metallic by a modulator, the Boss said, "There are consequences to all actions, both good and bad. You're merely paying for your failure."

"I know."

"You first disappointed me when you failed to capture the five children. Then, in an even more stunning bungle, *you* were instead captured by *them*. Considering these momentous lapses, you should be grateful that you even remain relevant in our plans. You now have the opportunity to redeem yourself by taking responsibility for the operations of the New Mexico Sanctuary. Construction is almost complete, as scheduled, so it shouldn't be too hard to keep everything in check."

Tony nodded, stifling the tempest of objections whirling in his head. The Boss must have seen it on his face, though, because the cold voice added, "You could be worse off, Tony. I could have sent you to the Sanctuary in Kazakhstan. That site's having a lot of issues and needs some serious attention. Perhaps I should send you there anyway . . ."

"So," Tony interrupted hurriedly, "why did you pull Vladimir and Elias out of here? Dr. Nate was pretty cryptic about it."

"Right now, that's none of your concern. Complete your work in the Sanctuary, then we'll talk."

Tony's face flushed. *I've been pushed so far down the totem pole. The flush reached the tips of his ears. I'm done playing nice with those kids. If I see them again, they'll get no sympathy.*

The holographic figure stirred slightly. "Tony."

The metallic voice had adopted a somewhat milder tone, something Tony was not used to. He looked up at his superior.

"You must understand that this is simply penance, and that my disappointment stems from the fact that I expected more from you. You have been a committed champion for our cause—I would hate to lose you. Just do the job right and know that your spot up here awaits you once you're ready."

Tony bowed his head, profound adulation rising within him. "I will do my best to return to your side." His lip curled impishly as he added, "My liege."

The Boss let out a short chuckle. Considering how seldom that happened, Tony took great pride in making his superior laugh when he could. *Third time in nearly as many years*, he thought. *I'm getting good at this.*

He leaned back in his seat. "Dr. Nate told me that you might visit," he said, hopeful. "Is that true?"

"I'd considered it, but I thought it best to check on other sites that are dealing with inefficiencies."

"Of course." Tony swallowed his disappointment. "By the way, did Phoenix find out who was masquerading as the supervising janitor at the HQ?"

"No. The man seemed to know what he was doing and kept his face hidden from the cameras. You said he was in your suite?"

"Mmhm. He told me he was cleaning. As far as I could tell, nothing was out of place."

"Security insists the same about the rest of the office, except that the real supervising janitor had been knocked out. They've been instructed to keep digging." The hologram looked upward, then back at Tony. "The Inner Circle meeting will be starting soon. I wanted to speak with you briefly before we began, seeing all that's transpired lately and the fact that this will be your first rodeo as the Head of a Sanctuary. They are waiting for us now. Are you ready?"

"I am."

"Good. We'll be connected in five seconds."

Tony quickly fumbled to sit upright and adjusted his tie as the large screen beside the Boss's hologram turned on, revealing a six-way video conference with the other Heads of Sanctuaries around the world and Phoenix Corporation's CEO, Adrian Black. Black was flanked by the bow tie-loving Jerry Li, the company's Chief Financial Officer, and Dr. Albert Bertram, the Chief Scientific Officer who resembled an intimidating, grouchy Santa Claus.

Tony frowned. *Where's Dr. Nate and Vladimir?*

"Greetings." The Boss's voice resonated through the speakers. "Thank you all for your attendance. I don't wish to tarry, so let's begin with the Sanctuary updates. The American Sanctuary in New Mexico, which for the time being is under the command of Tony Cross, is approaching full operational capacity."

Tony, flustered about his new position, toyed with his pen.

"The Sanctuaries in Mali, Brazil, New Zealand, and the Heart are also progressing as scheduled," the Boss continued. "As much as I am pleased with the development at these sites . . ." The metallic voice turned acidic. "There is a thorn in our side that needs to be dealt with immediately. I am, of course, referring to the Sanctuary in Kazakhstan."

Tony noticed that one of the two women on screen, a brunette in her forties, was picking invisible lint from her jacket, keeping her gaze averted. He leered, knowing what was coming.

"A series of delays due to sheer incompetence has put the project way behind the other five Sanctuaries," the Boss said. "In view of this, I have decided to visit the Kazakhstan site to see what I can do to help accelerate progress there."

The brunette froze mid-pick, fear painted across her face.

The rest of the Inner Circle fell silent, no one daring to utter a word.

"Zarya." The Boss addressed the terrified woman. "Expect me seventy-two hours from now."

She jerked her chin in an attempted nod.

"Continuing on. As stated in our last meeting, the test results from the DRC were positive and we have since started dispersal of the pathogen in Europe and Australia, followed by several other countries."

"What about North America?" Tony asked.

"Inevitably, some cases will appear due to global travel, but the plan is to let them watch the world burn first. They are the catalyst of humanity's decline and I would like to see them squirm as the fire of our retribution licks ever closer. Only then will we unleash the virus upon their shores."

"If anything, the Americans are quick on the draw," one of the women on screen said. "They will shut down their borders and all forms of international travel immediately if they have to."

The Boss chuckled once more, low and distorted. "The virus is already within their borders. All that is left to do is release our carriers. In any case, thanks to the brilliant work of Dr. Bertram, there are now reported cases on every continent on the globe. His countless days and nights spent perfecting the bio-agents EVO-1 and EVO-2 have ensured that it is spreading at the rate we projected."

There was a polite round of applause for the tubby, white-haired CSO. The man cracked a smile and said modestly, "It is an honor to be a part of this global undertaking to restore our world. I would be remiss if I failed to mention the crucial role played by Dr. Deol at Quest Biotech in the success of this project. Her dedication has been exemplary. From creating the Marauders to producing the EVO pathogens, she has proven to be quite a visionary."

"And your services are indispensable," the Boss acknowledged. "The Arcane Ventures will indeed reorganize and revolutionize the world as we know it, but at the heart of this endeavor lies the task of eliminating the most destructive life form this planet has ever known. Humans are adaptive, intelligent—hence their dominance. Commendable qualities, really. But humankind has failed to live up to its higher purpose and, instead, devolved into a pestilent, self-obsessed, corrupt species that has done nothing but wreak havoc on the planet. Tell me, before we launched the Ventures, how many times would you watch the news only to despair at the state of the world? The people are unified only in their division."

The Inner Circle members nodded slowly. Tony noticed several of them had glazed expressions tinged with sadness. *Harden your hearts,* he advised them silently. *This is a battle for the soul of the planet. We will create a new world. Harden your hearts. It's the only way we can make it through this.*

"Humans are on a path toward a cataclysmic end," the Boss said. "All we are doing is mercifully accelerating their demise. Elimination, although difficult, is not impossible. It requires a multifaceted strategy that is precisely timed. With the Ventures, we successfully launched the REAPR incursion that has strangled global grain supplies and exposed the baser elements of this species, easily sending them into riots and war. With the EVO project we have begun to strike the species directly at its root, its very existence. Morale, which is already in short supply, will be devastated. In due course, we will follow up with another lethal blow aimed at crippling them completely."

"If you didn't care so much for the planet," one of the other Heads of Sanctuary cut in, "we could nuke them. I'm sure we have the capacity. Better still, let them do it to themselves. Russia's probably on track to launch one anyway."

"I have discussed this many times, with you especially. I should hope you understand this sooner rather than later, or we *will* have a problem. Earth is our home. It has done us no wrong. Nature has given us much, but it is humans who corrupt all they touch. We cannot, under any circumstances, harm it. Why do you think we went to such extensive lengths to ensure that the animal carriers of the disease are not permanently harmed? When we want to be rid of pests in our homes, do we burn down the house?"

The man stifled a sigh. "No, we don't."

"Good. Now, I have said that we—"

A jarring crash, followed by yells outside the administrative building, made Tony jump. He gripped the edge of the table, cringing. *Oh, come on! During my first meeting as Head of Sanctuary? Seriously?*

He righted himself and, through clenched teeth, said, "Excuse me. Unfortunately, I think I may have some matters to attend to."

The Boss gave one wave of a hand. "Take your leave. Adrian will fill you in later."

Tony swiped across the tablet built into the table and both the screen and holographic projector shut off. He yanked off his tie and stormed out.

The moment Victor heard the crash, he flattened himself against the wall of the administrative building where he'd been painting, keeping out of view as the door around the corner opened. Tony's furious shouts filled the cavern as he charged out to investigate the source of the din.

The Sentry waited until he was sure the younger man had passed beyond the large workshop directly in front of him before confirming the coast was clear, not wanting to risk accidentally bumping into Tony while sneaking away. *I can probably go around the other side of the workshop,* he thought.

A firm hand gripped his shoulder. He whirled around and reflexively jammed the heel of his palm into his assailant's face. As he drew his arm back for a surer strike, he stopped.

The silver-haired boy in front of him stood a head shorter, was most likely in his late teens, and had blood trickling down his face that lightly flecked his bright orange coveralls. The boy pinched his nose, groaning. "I'm not gonna hurt you or rat you out, man!"

With his free hand, he grabbed Victor and pulled him along to the other side of the workshop, directly under a lone camera planted on the cave wall so they were safely out of its field of view. "Follow me. I'll get you someplace safe. Trust me, okay? I'm not one of these people, I swear."

"How'd you find me, kid?" the Sentry asked, eyes sweeping the vicinity. "Thought I had a good cover."

"I've been watching you since you got in. Been here long enough and I never forget a face. I've never seen you before, so I got curious." The teenager peered around the workshop. "The forklift that dropped its load is on the far side of the Sanctuary, so we're good. Walk with me like you belong here."

Victor followed the boy's lead, head low. Several paces further along, they passed a wooden structure the size of a tennis court; the sound of chickens clucking from inside surprised him. The silver-haired youth saw the look on his face and grinned.

Just past the poultry barn was a lush, open space filled with shrubs and small colorful plants set on a gently undulating terrain of grass and pebbles.

"What's this?" Victor asked.

"We call it Eden. A lot of us come here after work."

The Sentry could almost feel the thick, verdant grass through his boots as they traversed the garden. The sweet fragrance of jasmine filled his nose, putting him at ease despite himself. To their right, a long brick wall came into view, covered with vibrant murals of George Washington, Socrates, and Lenin.

"That's an impressive piece of work," he said.

The teenager looked irritated. "Not all that glitters is gold. You see that door right there, in the middle of Lenin's face? That leads down to the CUBE."

"Care to give me more than that?"

"It stands for the Center of Understanding, Betterment, and Enlightenment. Pretty words for indoctrination chambers where cerebral reprograming is carried out. Like Project Monarch, except this one's on steroids and uses high-tech tools. Every person you see here is a victim of the God-awful procedure."

"But not you?"

"Right. You, uh . . . you don't seem too surprised about any of this."

"That's because I'm not." Victor used a tone that said not to push the topic further, and the boy smartly obeyed.

They left the garden and weaved between two rectangular buildings that were, according to Victor's young guide, a seed bank and a recreational center. *It's not exactly a prison camp*, he thought, *but it's definitely not a resort either.*

"What's your name?" he asked.

"Kenzo," the boy replied. He came to a stop in front of a group of honeycomb-shaped structures, looked around, then led the Sentry into the second one. They hurried down a hallway lined with doors before he suddenly turned toward a room, punched in a code on a keypad, and ushered Victor inside.

The living quarters were decent in size, just slightly smaller than a studio apartment, and consisted of a bed, a nightstand, a kitchenette, a small bathroom, a desk, and a large-screen TV.

Kenzo rushed into the bathroom to wash off the blood from his now-swollen nose. "So, tell me," he called, "how did you get in here?"

Victor shrugged as he took stock of the room. "Got into the mining site above as one of the truck drivers, knocked out a guard at the entrance to the Sanctuary, and entered."

"No, come on." Kenzo walked out, clean-faced, holding a red-splotched tissue to his nose. "First we had two girls break out of here, now you trespass *after* they tightened security. How'd you do it?"

Victor regarded him for a while, considering his question. "As I said, I hijacked one of the trucks, knocked out a guard at the entrance, and got in." He didn't think it was the best time to tell Kenzo that he'd rendered the guard unconscious with his concussive blast and used a special tape to lift the man's fingerprints for the scanner at the Sanctuary entrance.

Kenzo tilted his head. "You didn't even blink when I mentioned that two girls had broken out of here."

"I know they broke out. I'm here looking for the person who had them abducted in the first place. I actually spoke with the girls, and they told me to keep an eye out for a guy with"—Victor motioned at the boy's silver hair—"who helped them escape."

Kenzo, eyes like saucers, stuttered for a bit before catching himself. "What's going on? Who are you?"

"Let's just say that the world is spiraling into a void and the individuals setting up these Sanctuaries are behind it. Some people are trying to stop all of this. You've figured out that a form of indoctrination is happening in here. And I'm sure you know why."

"Yeah. We're meant to be stewards to the planet once the Paterfamilias has, and I quote, 'hastened humanity's demise.'"

"Paterfamilias . . . is that what you guys call your leader?"

Kenzo got a bag of crushed ice from his freezer. "Yup. Head of the house and family or, in this case, Sanctuary and SONEs. No idea what this person's real name is, and I've only ever heard the higher-ups refer to them as the 'Boss.'"

"It's probably best if you don't know. Who are the sons you mentioned?"

"SONEs. Stewards of New Earth." Kenzo lay on his bed, keeping his head elevated, and placed the ice pack on his swollen nose. "All of us in the Sanctuary, the kids, the guards, the electricians, whoever."

"I see." Victor paced at the foot of the bed. "So, what? These poor shmucks are zombies with no memories of their past?"

"Oh, they have their memories, but their minds have been repurposed. For them, those memories have become a kaleidoscope of meaningless events."

"Jeez. Alright, tell me more about the Boss."

"We really don't know much," Kenzo said. "We've only been addressed once via a huge screen. The Paterfami—the Boss used a voice modulator, I think, and had a hood on, and was rolling this purple sphere in one hand. The speech was about our roles and—"

"I know. I was given the details."

Kenzo eyed him. "Was it the girls?"

"One of them. Soon after escaping she was caught again and forced to watch the address as it was broadcasted to all the sites." Seeing the look of concern on the teenager's face, Victor added, "But she's safe now. They all are."

"All? There's more than just the two of them?"

"It's a long story. All you need to know is that we're the good guys and, yes, there are more people like me out there. The girls and their friends play an important part in this."

Kenzo chucked his ice pack aside and sat up. "Look, I've been stuck in this place for nearly two years. I've had to walk around pretending I'm one of *them*, scared that if I do or say something even remotely off, they'll throw me back into the indoc chamber and repurpose me. *Properly*, this time. Or maybe kill me, who knows. They've got these beasts—the Marauders—for it. Those who tried to escape early on were hunted down. We watched the kids get torn to shreds." His breathing started to labor. "I have never been so alone in my life. My only family here, my cousin, she's one of them. I can't talk to anyone. And I don't want to try to escape without her. So all I'm asking is that you tell me how screwed up our situation really is and if there are any plans to get us out of this mess and what I can do."

Victor glanced away briefly, then sat on the edge of the bed. "Why do you think you have a role in this?"

"Because . . . because . . ." Kenzo threw his hands up with a frustrated cry. "I don't know! Look, I need to do something before I go insane. You're here to help, aren't you?"

"Yes, but we have to tread carefully. There are forces at play that are unexplainable to society at large. This is why we haven't gotten the authorities involved. They have no idea of the existential threat that's hanging over their head, and they aren't equipped to stop it."

"I'm not gonna pretend that I understood everything you

just said, but at this point I don't care. I want an end to all this. I want to help end it. Just, please. I feel like I'm going to go out of my mind soon if I don't do something."

Victor reached into his pocket. "I was hoping you'd say that." He pulled out a small smartphone. "Here."

Kenzo took it from him. "What's this for?"

"To stay in touch. It's been reprogrammed to securely contact only two people. I'm one, and Tegan is the other. She's one of the girls who was here. Also, the phone's prepaid and set up for automatic reload."

The boy ogled the device. "You . . . you came prepared."

"Truth is, I was hoping to bump into you. The girls told me to keep an eye out for you, said your sympathies may not really be with the people running this place. I think their intuition was right. And they asked that I thank you on their behalf for taking the risk in letting them escape."

Kenzo, stunned, appeared to be at a complete loss for words.

Victor continued. "If you're ever on the verge of committing murder, just message me, eh?"

The teenager met the Sentry's eyes, his own conveying gratitude. "Thank you."

"Don't mention it." Victor tilted his chin toward Kenzo. "I do have an assignment for you, though."

"An assignment?"

"I need you to get close to the higher-ups in this place. I need you to be my eyes and ears so I know what's going on." He noticed the boy swallowing hard at his words. He hesitated, then reached out and clasped Kenzo's arm. "You'll need to be careful about how and who you approach. But from what I've seen, I'm sure you'll be able to carry this out safely. You've got good instincts, kid. Trust your gut."

Kenzo closed his fingers around the phone. "I'll do it."

"Good. I've checked out the cell signal down here. Best place is at the spot you found me, near the admin building. Just make sure no one catches you with that phone. Seems like you've got a pretty serious Big Brother thing going on down here."

"Actually, not really. They figure that once our brains are rewired, there won't be any more attempts to escape. We never had many cameras in the Sanctuary to begin with, and a few new ones were installed after the girls got away, but they're only in the general area and a few high-value buildings."

"So you're free to roam anywhere you want, whenever you want?"

"Yeah, except we can't go outside. And these kids in here; I used to think they were drones, but they're not. Not really. Their beliefs were altered, that's it. Once indoctrinated into their new cause, they're gung-ho to do their part as SONEs. Life really isn't all that bad here. If you've been repurposed, that is."

"We're gonna have to find a way to reverse the damage that's been done to these kids, but it won't be for a while. Our resources are limited, and the priority right now is to stop the mess that's happening." Victor looked at his watch. "I really need to get out of here. I've got a lead on a location and the sooner I can get there, the better."

"Where are you going?"

"Kazakhstan. I've got seventy-two hours to get there and figure out where the Boss will be."

Kenzo fell back, laughing hard. "Good luck with that!"

Victor allowed himself to join in on the amusement, but only for a second. "Yeah, thanks. You wouldn't happen to know about the Sanctuary there, would you?"

"No. Sorry." Kenzo's mirth subsided and he studied the Sentry for a moment. "You know, you actually look less intimidating when you smile."

"I've been told that." Victor got off the bed. "I need to get going. Could you point me to the tunnel that the girls used to escape?"

"Heh, you can't use it. They've sealed it up properly."

Victor stopped short. "I was counting on that to be open. Are there any other options?"

"Dunno. They're not exactly big on posting exit signs down here."

"Well, I can't go back the way I came in. It's been a couple hours since the guard's little accident and he's probably nursing a headache while someone else took over his post. There's got to be some other way."

Both the Sentry and the teenager took in a long breath and exhaled as they pondered. There was a peculiar pause, and then their eyes met in realization. Victor spun around, scanning the room. "There has to be an air circulation system in place down here. Where is it?"

"Circulation system," Kenzo repeated. "Circulation sys—the huge fans! There's four of them in the Sanctuary."

"How big are they?"

"Uh . . ." Kenzo stretched his arm over his head. "Like, that tall?"

"About eight feet?"

"Yeah. There are two on the east side, and two across on the west end."

"Worth a shot. Do you know if there's any air filtration system in the shafts, anything that I'd have to cut my way through? And are the intake and exhaust wells at the surface patrolled?"

Kenzo shrugged. "All I can say is that first you have to get through the fans, and stopping them will attract attention." He tapped his fingers on his thigh. "But the maintenance people do stop them when they check on stuff."

"We're not maintenance."

"No, we're not. But . . ." A spark appeared in Kenzo's eyes. He jumped off his bed and ran to the door. "Wait here. I'll be right back."

* * *

No one gave the two men clad in navy blue coveralls and white hardhats a second look as they walked past the poultry farm and around the workshop, out of everyone's line of sight. When they reached a locked gate erected between the cave wall and a partition, one of the men used a set of bolt cutters to chomp through the padlock.

Victor stuffed the lock into his coveralls, threw the cutters and hardhat into the canvas bag Kenzo had found, and stepped through the gate. The teenager followed, looking over his shoulder every other second.

"Relax," the Sentry muttered. "You're making me nervous." He opened a control box mounted beside the massive swirling fan. "Huh, there's a setting to slow this thing down."

"Great!" Kenzo breathed. "We don't have to stop it and raise any alarms."

Victor turned the dial to its lowest setting. The fan slowed, but the gap between the moving blades was still too small for his liking. He hefted the canvas bag and gauged the rotation of the fan, then threw it. It just barely sailed through an opening and landed with a muted *thunk* inside the shaft.

"No one thought of using this to escape?" he asked. "Really?"

"It used to be that the priority of the security system was to make sure no one in here gets out," Kenzo replied. "But now that the indoctrination proved to be so successful, the focus is on preventing outsiders from getting in. Nobody here would dream of wanting to escape. The word's not even in their vocabulary."

Victor turned to Kenzo and shook his hand. "Thanks for your help." Though he knew the answer, he asked, "I know I gave you an assignment, but you sure you don't want to come along?"

"As much as I would like to, no. My cousin's here and I'm not going to leave her behind. Besides, an absent SONE? That's going to raise a few red flags. I'd be more useful to you in here anyway."

"True." To himself, Victor thought, *You're admirable, kid.*

"Oh, and remember that when you get out, there could be cameras watching the shaft."

"Appreciate the heads-up. Take care of yourself. And remember, eyes forward." Victor paused, then added in a lower tone, "One more thing. If you hear from the Boss again, get ahold of me immediately. Please."

"Count on it."

The Sentry saw hope beginning to brighten Kenzo's dark eyes, and a dull pang struck him in the chest. He wished he could guarantee that everything would work out for the boy, but how could he when there was no same assurance for everyone else involved in taking Reyor down?

Facing the spinning fan, Victor timed the rotations, then dove headfirst through the gap. He landed perfectly on the other side, just missing the moving blades. As he gathered his bag, he heard Kenzo call quietly: "I never got to ask! What's your name?"

The Sentry faltered, then said "Victor" and swiftly began making his way up the gentle incline of the circular air shaft.

The shaft ascended to the surface that lay forty feet above the Sanctuary roof. At what Victor estimated was the halfway point, he came face-to-face with his first obstacle, a metal grid that spanned the breadth of the shaft and held activated charcoal filter panels. With a wrench, he removed bolts at the top and bottom of the lowermost panel, allowing the filter to pivot and give him space to wiggle through.

Three feet beyond was a bank of different filters, which gave him barely enough room to secure the charcoal filter behind him. He repeated the process with the second filters, breathing a little hard from the effort, and continued upward. The shaft wasn't completely dark, which meant the surface was near.

Here we go. With a grunt, Victor pulled himself up the final few feet and squinted at the daylight seeping from the surface. *What in the . . .*

A large concrete slab, held twelve inches above the shaft's entrance by iron bars no more than six inches apart, blocked his escape. Wire mesh zigzagged between the bars, most likely to keep small animals from wandering into the air duct. Shrubs had been planted around and on top of the slab, allowing it to blend with the landscape.

Victor peered through the foliage, trying to get a feel for his surroundings. Through the greenery, he caught a sharp glint as sunlight hit and reflected off something on a tree. *That's probably a camera, isn't it? Yeah, looks like it.*

Reaching into his bag, he fished out one of his favorite devices. The handheld cutting torch weighed a mere two pounds in his hand and used thermite cartridges to produce a five thousand-degree-Fahrenheit jet of flame shaped like a blade. He pointed it at one of the iron bars on the side of the slab opposite the camera. The bright stream of superheated vapor sliced through it like a hot knife through butter. He had to cut through the top and bottom of three more bars to create an opening wide enough to squeeze through.

At last, he wormed out into the shrubs to spy on the camera. *There's no way I can make a break for it without getting caught on tape. But maybe . . .*

He swept up a pile of earth with both hands and focused for a few seconds. Then his hand shot out and energy from his body forcefully whirled the dirt into the air to create a small dust storm that roiled toward the camera. Victor scrambled to his feet. Gripping the canvas bag close, he sprinted past the camera and down the hillside. He stumbled and nearly fell more times than he cared to count, but didn't stop until he reached the bottom.

He doubled over to catch his breath, then gazed up the slope. Feeling a small twinge of guilt as he left the site, he gave a curt salute to the boy who was forced to remain alone in the Sanctuary.

17

Adrian Black could not believe he'd been dragged to Sausalito for the second time in just a few months. He loathed the artsy atmosphere that dripped from the city's figurative walls. On the bright side, the Spinnaker was a decent restaurant to dine in and he was with good company—although even that wasn't enough to wholly allay him.

"We have a perfectly good saloon at the office and an excellent chef on call," he grumbled, scowling around the table. "Why come out here?"

Beside him, a short man with black hair, thick-rimmed glasses, and a colorful bow tie that clashed with his gray business suit grinned. "Because, despite how lovely the view of San Francisco is from HQ, it's good to get away from the boardroom every once in a while."

"Okay, no, you're supposed to back me up, Jer."

Jerry Li's grin widened. "Alright, how about . . . This celebration is for Luigi, and it's a big deal, so he gets to choose where we go."

"Mmph, fine. Makes sense." Black smirked. "After all, this place is as pretentious as he is."

Across the table, Luigi Dattalo sputtered a sound that was something between indignation and a laugh. "Sorry you can't appreciate the finer things in life, knuckle-dragger!" he hooted.

"Gentlemen," rumbled the last member of the group, a trace of a German accent in the word. Dr. Albert Bertram hoisted his glass. "The drinks have arrived and I'd like to ask our resolute CEO to make a toast."

The others picked up their drinks. Black met Dattalo's eyes.

The Italian looked worn but content, and he flashed Black an amiable smile. Black nodded once, then lifted his voice. "All four of us are here for a reason. We *earned* the Boss's trust, which is no small feat. We're playing our parts to usher in a new world through Phoenix and the Arcane Ventures beneath it. Jerry, our wizard CFO; Al, the best chief science officer Phoenix could have asked for. But today is about Luigi, the head of Quest Defense and, now, the fledgling Quest Aerospace. Congratulations, you lucky dog."

"Cheers!" Li hailed, and the others echoed him.

"Cheers, friends," Dattalo murmured.

There was a space of silence as they sipped their beverages, then Bertram clapped Dattalo's shoulder. "You are a busy fellow with two subsidiaries in your portfolio!"

Dattalo shrugged, glancing down at the table, but he couldn't hide the upward slant of his mouth. "Quest Aerospace is merely a growing department in my subsidiary."

"An extremely well-financed one," Li pointed out, "with funds that account for more than half of Quest Defense. I'd say that's a *lot* more than just a department. Has all the markings of a full-fledged entity."

"Well, it does take quite a bit to get stuff into space. After all, breaking the bounds of gravity is an exceptionally costly proposition."

"Would be far more practical if we worked out of a moon base, I'll tell you that," Black joked, then thanked the waiter as hot meals were placed in front of them.

"Yeah," Dattalo said. "Comparatively speaking, though, the other Arcane project at Quest Defense costs significantly less. It helps that the material we're using isn't as troublesome to procure as the damn fenixium we needed for the REAPRs. And it doesn't hurt that it was already on the black market. The only challenge is the delivery. My people are scrambling to keep everything on schedule for next year. I'm glad that we've at least launched the rest of our satellites, finally."

Li carefully cut into his steak. "Speaking of the REAPRs . . ."

Black noticed Dattalo bristling slightly before smoothing his hackles. "What can I say?" the Italian told them cheerfully. "Our North American pods were compromised before the project could run its full course. I still think the nanomites did their job well enough regardless. Just look at the news. Many of the global pods remain functional and are causing mayhem, as promised."

Black pushed his dark hair away from his forehead. "You did well, Luigi, and you deserve the promotion you got."

Dattalo gave him a look of gratitude. The men ate in quiet ease for a while before Bertram asked, "How are things topside, Adrian?"

Black allowed himself to feel a little self-satisfied. "All our lawful operations have never run smoother. See the smile on my face? And we're actually reporting increased revenue across all subsidiaries. The coffers are overflowing, we're doing great financially . . . heh, the irony of it all. Just before the world goes boom, our profits go boom-boom."

Li groaned laughingly into his plate. "Good God, Adrian!"

Bertram tapped his fork against his lips, thoughtful. "That's just the way it works, I suppose. Before you can raise a new edifice, you must raze down the defective structure. But I'll tell you this: Your stewardship of Phoenix has been nothing short of astounding. Without that, funding the Ventures to realize the vision of our global undertaking would have been impossible."

"I appreciate that, Al," Black said. "But you can thank the Boss for the astute investments to begin with."

Li waved his knife at Dattalo and Bertram. "It just blows my mind, what you guys are doing. I know what all these things cost but, for me, the science is still so out there. Al, tell me about the virus. The EVO-1 strain."

Bertram's normally grouchy exterior crumbled at Li's compliment. "It's a really simple concept. Stupidly simple, actually. Each one of us has a biological clock built into our cells. All my people and I did was put together a bunch of proteins and give them the smarts to speed up that clock. Ta-da!"

The other men stared at him, unamused. Bertram looked from one to another, then chuckled. "Ah, you want the actual science? Alright. Well, DNA is the genetic code at the heart of our cells, we all know that. Each strand of this double helix is capped with telomeres—it's like the aglet at the end of a shoelace. They protect our chromosomes. Every organ in our body is made of cells that renew by copying themselves. Each time a cell replicates, the telomeres get shorter but the DNA remains protected. At some point, though, the telomeres get too short to do their job, causing our cells to age as they wear out and are not replaced. As I said, there's a kind of aging clock in every cell. So, what does EVO-1 do? It eviscerates the telomeres. Without them, accelerated aging occurs. When cells can no longer reproduce, our tissues degenerate and eventually die."

Li whistled. "Well, paint me purple and call be Barney. I can't believe you actually created an organism that does that! *And* it doesn't affect the birds and other animals we use as carriers! That must have been the trickiest part."

"Technically, a virus isn't a living organism," Bertram said. "It's a string of protein molecules that carry enough genetic information to do its bidding and replicate. And in our case, do it stealthily."

"And EVO-2?"

"Same concoction of proteins, different set of smarts. This one goes after the fight-or-flight response in the nervous system; specifically, the amygdala in our brain. The virus manipulates it, which then triggers a neural response in the hypothalamus. This creates a reaction in the pituitary gland and bada-bing, bada-boom, you have a tsunami of epinephrine kicking in. It has a cascading effect on emotional regulation and perception of control. The bleeding that often results is a side effect."

Li frowned. "Sounds like EVO-2 should work almost immediately, so why does it take several days for it to kick in?"

"The body fights to find an equilibrium. The initial ebb and flow of hormones build up over time into a roller coaster of confusion and agitation. It causes an increase in the core body temperature, as well as increased blood flow to the muscles by diverting it from other parts of the body. The increased blood pressure, heart rate, and glucose levels supply the extra boost of energy and augments muscle tension to provide greater speed and strength. This initial surge eventually takes its toll, leading to stroke, seizure, and cardiac arrest."

Li looked gobsmacked. "Astounding."

"I'm just glad our families will be protected through everything," Dattalo said. "But it's a shame we're not allowed to include extended members."

"Ho-ho!" Li slammed his palm on the tabletop, making the others jump. He beamed wickedly. "Did I tell you that my ex came crawling back, asking for another go?"

"Oh no," Black said. "This is news to me."

"Yeah, it happened last week. Before you ask, hell no, I didn't take her back. Turns out her actor boyfriend walked out on her. Ha! Serves her right. And now she'll wave goodbye to me with the rest of the world. Good riddance."

Bertram eyed the smaller man. "You have a mean streak I have only ever seen in my niece's Chihuahua. That thing will bite off fingers and toes."

"Says the man who engineered two strains of a deadly virus."

"Dr. Deol did much of the actual groundwork."

"That woman is a brilliant star in this organization," Dattalo said. "Hopefully the Boss will be willing to induct her into the Inner Circle soon."

Black reclined in his seat and looked out of the Spinnaker's numerous large windows, admiring the view of the bay, then returned his attention indoors to the sparsely occupied tables. He cocked his head, watching the few people present eat, smile, and breathe despite the events of the summer and, now, the spread of an incurable disease.

Bertram's voice reached his ears. "Penny for your thoughts?"

He blinked. "Sorry. It's just . . . can you believe all of this will be coming to an end soon? There are times when I find it hard to grasp the sheer immensity of what we're doing."

Bertram raised an eyebrow. "Is that doubt I'm hearing?"

"No, of course not. It's just a bit jarring. But, when you're on the right side of history, it doesn't matter."

"Never doubt that a small group of thoughtful, committed citizens can change the world. Indeed, it is the only thing that ever has."

"Hm. Margaret Mead?"

Bertram nodded approvingly. "Very good, Adrian."

"Yes, well, it's an apt quote." Black gazed down at his empty plate for a few moments. "We live in exciting times, and we get to help steer the course of destiny." He looked back up, meeting the eyes of each of his cohorts. "This is an honor, gentlemen. We are the change we've been waiting for."

Kody flipped though channels on the Lodge's satellite television; some of the broadcasts were in English and others in French. Annoyed, he called out, "There's nothing much! The newscasters are just quoting parts of the CDC media statement. I guess we missed the actual thing."

"Hey, I found the full transcript," Aari said from the conference table around which he, Tegan, Jag, Mariah, and the Sentries sat. "It was just posted on the CDC website."

Kody trotted over to his friends, who were all seated across from the Sentries, in front of the giant map on the wall. He bumped fists with Deverell as he passed the Welshman. He and the twins had returned from Zurich earlier in the morning after obtaining lab samples of the aging disease, and Dominique had shipped everything off to the Dema-Ki contact in Yukon—including blood and tissue samples from the teenagers and the Sentries present.

Deverell and Gareth had also added a gift for Magèo: a microsphere nanoscope, a high-quality optical microscope that used extremely tiny beads to allow the viewing of objects between two and three hundred nanometers, giving the user the ability to study microorganisms and viruses.

Kody took a seat between Mariah and Tegan. Aari tilted his laptop's screen back and as he cleared his throat to read the statement aloud, they heard the front door open then slam shut. Kody looked over at the stairs, eager to meet the newcomer.

A broad-shouldered, rugged man in a faded black utility jacket and jeans climbed the steps, a duffel bag on his shoulder and another in his hand. Kody had to do a triple take at the creature following him.

Is that a wolf?!

"About time, Vic!" Gareth grinned. "How was the drive from Geneva?"

"Long." Victor gave a short nod to the other Sentries, a few of whom were staring at him with something akin to poorly disguised hero-worship.

When his gaze landed on the friends, Kody suddenly felt incredibly small and unwelcome. The man had a quiet fierceness about him, and the intensity in his eyes reflected blatant disapproval.

The stretch of silence was painful. Victor turned to walk away, then paused and looked back at the teenagers. "Nice to meet you."

The friends glanced at each other. Kody noticed a cold expression cross Marshall's face as the Sentry watched Victor retreat to one of the loft rooms.

"Um." Gareth rubbed the back of his head. "Aari, let's get to the CDC's statement."

"Right." Aari cleared his throat again. "*The Centers for Disease Control and Prevention confirms an outbreak of a previously unknown disease and is working with public health officials in Australia, the United Kingdom, and the European Union. Two possible variations of the disease have been observed and, due to their highly infectious nature, the CDC has issued a travel warning for these regions. Although the vector, or vectors, remain unknown at this point, the CDC is not ruling out any possibilities, including zoonotic transmission.*"

"One more time in English, please," Kody said, taking a granola bar out of his pocket to munch on.

"They're not sure what kind of agent is spreading the disease," Aari explained, "and they're not ruling out the possibility of the carriers being animals."

"Animals make sense," Lei said. "The more widespread they are, the more devastating."

Marshall shook a finger in agreement. "Lei's right. You know what I'm thinking the best mode of delivery is? Birds. Wide range, huge population. Perfect carriers."

"I'm bringing an umbrella with me the next time I walk outside," Kody muttered.

"While studies into the pathogen and possible vectors are ongoing, the CDC is able to confirm the symptoms for one variation of the disease . . ." Aari quickly scanned the report. "We know this already. They're talking about the accelerated aging strain. It's exactly as Dominique described."

"Anything else?" Mariah asked.

"Yeah, the unconfirmed initial symptoms for the second variation, the violent one: mild headaches, increase in heart rate, blood pressure, and body temperature."

"It's like a fever," Zoe murmured. "And that's just the early symptoms."

"Investigation into the advanced symptoms of this variation is underway, and details will be made available once determined," Aari continued. "Honestly, it looks like the simultaneous outbreaks around the world has them baffled, and it's gonna be a huge challenge for them to find Patient Zero." He slumped back, fingers laced behind his head. "That's about all they've got for now. I'll keep an eye out for more updates."

"Alright." Benny, the Indian Sentry, got up. "I need to start packing."

"Where are you going?" Kody asked.

"Home. Zoe's heading back to Australia, Lei's returning to China, and I'll be leaving for India tomorrow. We've got our work cut out for us."

"We were just getting to know you guys," Kody grumbled.

Benny smiled warmly. "I'm sure we'll see each other soon. It was very much a pleasure—and an honor—meeting you five."

The Sentries slowly dispersed, either to pack or to catch a well-deserved nap, leaving the teenagers around the table. Marshall was the last Sentry to go, but when he did, he headed to Victor's loft. The cold look had returned to his face. Curious, Kody honed in his hearing and directed it toward the topmost floor.

Marshall's voice filled his ears. He sounded livid. "Really? That's it? That's all you've got for them? 'Nice to meet you'?"

"I'm sorry. Should I have showered them with rose petals?"

"You're unbelievable. What's up with you? They're the Chosen Ones!"

Something fell, making a stark clatter.

"They are not *messiahs,*" Victor snarled. "They're kids. Is this what we do to kids? Throw them into the jaws of a world driven by cruelty? It will chew them up and spit them out, and we're going to have to pick up the pieces." A heavy thud sounded, like a fist against a wall. "I just had to leave a kid in a lion's den. He was going out of his wits. I saw the look in his eyes—it was almost suicidal. And not only did I have to leave him behind, I gave him an assignment that could put his head on the chopping block."

There was dead silence from Marshall.

"And now, I walk in here and see those five staring back at me. I don't know how you and the others can sit around and smile and laugh with them because all I see"—Victor's voice was low, rough, angry—"are kids thrown into an adult war, who believe they'll make it out unscathed when you and I both know that's a lie."

"No one ever said this was going to be easy, or safe." Marshall softened his tone. "But the Elders have been preparing them for this. And we've been doing what we can here, developing their self-defense techniques, giving them crash courses in first aid, CPR, survival skills—"

"Do you hear yourself? Do you really believe they'll be okay, or are you just trying to convince your conscience?"

"Listen, I had my doubts, too. I really did. Everything you mentioned was everything that went through my head, so believe me when I say that I am not blind to the risks they will face. But I had the opportunity to work with them. I saw what they were capable of, and this was *before* they completed their training with the Elders. I know it doesn't seem fair that they have to bear the burden of the prophecy, but that's just the nature of it. It's the universe at work."

"Screw that. Blood will be spilled no matter how this turns out. And it'll be on our hands. Can you stomach that, Sawyer?"

Kody snapped away from the Sentries' quarrel. He sat in silence, mouth dry, while his friends conversed among themselves. Marshall came back downstairs a minute later, expression taut, but gave a smile when the rest of the group noticed him.

"Sorry about Colback," he said. "He's, ah, a bit rough around the edges. Doesn't do a whole lot of socializing, either."

"That's alright," Jag said. "What's he up to now?"

"Using his layover to restock on supplies and reach out to Sentries in Russia and Kazakhstan. There's a Sanctuary somewhere there that Reyor will be visiting soon and he needs to find out where exactly, preferably before his connecting flight tonight. This is the closest anyone of Dema-Ki blood will have ever gotten to Reyor in . . . decades."

"Godspeed to him," Mariah said softly. "What's he gonna do if he does find the Sanctuary?"

"My guess is he'll report to the Elders. A plan will probably be put in place, and we'll be let in on it when the time's right. Colback doesn't talk much about his work. He's a bloodhound with a trail to follow and that's what he does best. Hopefully this will bring us closer to ending Reyor's schemes once and for all."

"It's interesting," Tegan observed, "that the Sentries openly refer to Reyor by name, whereas the Elders and villagers do everything they can not to. Or they try not to, anyway."

"Most of the Sentries never knew who Reyor was. That name doesn't carry as much weight to us as it does to our brethren in Dema-Ki."

Marshall stuck around to chat with the friends for a few minutes more before retiring to his room. Kody waited until he heard the door on the floor below them shut, then said, "Victor's not fond of us."

Aari snorted. "Yeah, no kidding. He sounded nicer on the phone."

"I don't mean it that way." Kody wavered. *Should I tell them what I heard . . . ? Probably.*

He quickly filled his friends in. Jag looked at him disapprovingly. "You eavesdropped?"

Kody nodded, earning himself a smack on the head from Mariah. He rubbed where she'd hit him, glaring.

"I think it's good that he did," Tegan said. When the others stared at her, she shrugged. "I'm not saying eavesdropping itself is good, but I'd sure like to know if the people we're working with have problems, especially if it relates to us. Victor seems standoffish."

"That concerns me," Mariah muttered.

"I'm just curious, really. I can't decide if he's a pessimist or a realist."

"You can relate, I'm sure," Aari teased.

Jag pushed away from the table and got up. "I don't think we should pry into this anymore. We're not working with Victor directly, so it's not really an issue for us. Let's squeeze in some training before dinner. It'd be a better use of our time."

The friends followed him to the basement's steps. Kody looked up at the now-quiet loft, head tilted, then headed downstairs with the others.

* * *

Midnight found Kody in the kitchen devouring cookies, the lights to the entire third floor switched off. He was sure almost everyone else was still awake, but they were all in their rooms winding down. With an earbud in one ear, he nodded along to his phone's playlist to dispel the silence.

The stairs to one of the lofts creaked. He stopped chewing and peered into the darkness without engaging his enhanced vision. He could just make out a silhouette carrying two duffel bags crossing the living room to head down to the main floor.

"Leaving without saying goodbye?" he asked as he resumed his snacking.

The silhouette paused, then flicked on a light. "There are more important things than goodbyes."

Kody pulled out his earbud. "Any luck with what you needed to find?"

"Yes." Victor looked down at his four-legged companion. "Sit."

The dog obeyed. Kody examined it closely. "Is he, like, a real wolf?"

"Half."

"That's cool. Tegan would love him. She's nuts about animals."

"I could tell. She perked up at the sight of Chief when we walked in. Mariah seemed more apprehensive. Not big about wild animals, is she?"

"Yeah," Kody said. "How does he handle all the traveling that you do? Must be hard, constantly being cooped up in a crate in the cargo hold of some plane."

"He's a service dog. He stays with me at all times."

Kody, surprised, looked the man up and down. "I don't mean this disrespectfully, but you seem . . . fit."

"Service dogs aren't just for physical issues."

Seeing Victor's sour look, Kody, suddenly feeling rather stupid, decided it was best not to pursue the topic. As he followed the man down the stairs, his stomach suddenly rumbled. He patted his belly with a sigh, and thought he saw the swiftest twitch of amusement flicker across the Sentry's face. But it was gone so quickly he figured he'd imagined it.

Victor reached into one of his bags and pulled out a handful of energy bars. "Here. These fill you up within a couple of bites."

Kody took them. "Thanks." He slipped them into the pocket of his track pants, storing them for later. "Sooo . . . do you only know us by name, or can you put faces to 'em?"

"You're Kody. Tall guy with a constant guarded look is Jag. Redhead with the inquisitive energy is Aari. And I talked to the girls on the phone."

"Guess that answers that."

Victor reached for the knob of the front door, then stopped.

"What do you turn to in times of trouble?"

"What?"

"You heard me."

Kody blinked. "Um . . . my friends. And my family."

"Anything else?"

"I guess I turn to humor, too, but that's kind of preprogrammed in me."

"It's mankind's greatest blessing, a writer once said." Victor opened the door and strode out into the night, Chief following closely. As he melted into the blackness, he warned darkly, "No matter what happens, what *will* happen . . . don't lose your humor. If you do, your house of cards will crumble and hope will be lost in the wreckage. Trust me, that's the last thing you want. Don't lose your humor."

Kody stood in the doorway long after the taillights of the Sentry's car had disappeared from view. He barely noticed the snow beginning to fall, nor the biting cold that pinched every inch of his body until he realized he could no longer feel his face. His appetite lost, he shut the door and returned to his room. He lay awake half the night, staring up at the shadows cast on his ceiling by a tree outside his window as it rocked to and fro in the wind.

When he finally did close his eyes, he dreamt of a colossal pyramid formed from a deck of playing cards towering above him against a starry night. A gust billowed through the great structure. Kody watched in terror as the topmost card tipped over and the cackling face of the Joker rushed to meet him, its mouth open wide in a gruesome laugh, devouring him whole.

The elderly man knelt beside the body, lips trembling as tears trailed down his weathered face. He softly stroked the girl's black-and-ginger hair, silently weeping apology after apology. Then, with shaking hands, he pulled the sheet over his lifeless apprentice, concealing the face of the person who was the closest thing he'd had to a daughter.

Corpses covered with sheets littered Dema-Ki's community square. Rain beat down around the old man, the heavens lamenting, as Magèo did, for the lives that had been ripped away by the plague. Lightning struck on the opposite bank, momentarily illuminating the afflicted villagers as they moved through the trees. They were on edge; the disease had reduced them to beasts that assailed each other when their paths crossed. Magèo crouched low among the bodies, staying out of sight. Thunder roared, echoing through the valley. The old man had never felt so defeated.

Slowly, he backed away from the community square. He needed to get to his laboratory, barricade himself within the safety of its walls, and find the cure. The rain soaked him to the bone and tightened his tunic around his rotund body, restricting his movement. When he thought he was a safe distance away, he spun on his heel to make a break for his lab. Another flash of lightning erupted in front of him. Sparks of electricity lit up the darkness and he let loose a scream that beat out the thunder.

Nageau stood before him, foam dripping from his clenched teeth, blood trickling from his nose and ears. In his hands, a sword glinted in the lightning's wake. Delirium shrouded the Elder's gaze as he locked eyes with Magèo.

The older man stepped back, begging softly as Nageau lifted

the sword over his head. "Nageau, please, put the weapon down. Please, dear friend, please . . . Nageau? No! No! Please, Nageau! *No!*"

Magèo awoke with a cry. Above him, his apprentice looked down worriedly. His hands shot up, cupping her cheeks, his eyes searching hers. "Nal! Are you alright?"

The girl was startled. "I am fine, mentor. I heard you scream and ran to see what the matter was. You must have had a terrible dream."

"A dream," Magèo muttered, sitting up from his divan and rubbing his different-colored eyes. The shutters of all twenty windows high up in the building's walls were open, letting in rays from the sun. He glared at the daylight in distaste. "Yes, it was a dream. Of course it was. Help me up."

"You really should rest, mentor. You have gone almost four days without sleep trying to find the cure."

"And still we have not discovered it. Help me up."

Nal pulled the old man to his feet. "I did what I could while you were here, but my own work has not amounted to much."

"So we must keep plowing onward."

"I agree, but you have not eaten in hours. Let us return to this after our midday meal."

"I cannot stop, Nal! I have wasted too much time as it is!"

"Mentor, you must eat! I will make you something myself if I have to. We have to keep up our strength!"

Grumbling, Magèo shuffled into a glass enclosure at the far corner of the building. A construction team comprised of ten villagers had quickly erected the quarantine zone while the samples had been flown halfway across the world for him. His lab was now the only place in the village with access to minimal electricity, which was generated from Dema-Ki's thermal springs. It was fitted out to operate equipment necessary for his work, including the Vaughn twins' special gift that absolutely fascinated him.

He pulled on a pair of gloves and goggles, then stepped into the enclosure and peered through the nanoscope at the tissue samples. Both strains of the infectious agent were hardy, aggressive, and had clearly been created with deadly intent. What he found most intriguing were the results of his examinations on the tissue and blood samples from the Sentries.

He'd ran the tests several times to be certain, but the samples did not appear to be affected by the pathogen. Elated, he'd gathered samples from a few of the villagers, including himself and Nal, and discovered that they, too, were immune from both strains of the disease. He concluded that, for some inexplicable reason, those of Dema-Ki blood were safe from harm.

The second thing he learned, however, was concerning. Having tested the tissue samples from the Chosen Ones, he found that although they did not react to the aging strain, the violent strain of the disease affected the samples at random. Despite puzzling over it for two days and running a series of experiments, he couldn't identify the cause for the pathogen's arbitrary behavior. When he reported his findings to Nageau, the Elder was just as confounded but did express some relief.

"It is good to know that they are safe from one strain," he had said, "but it worries me that we cannot prevent them from possible suffering at the hands of the other. I know you are already working tirelessly but please, old friend—I cannot stress this enough—do all that you can to find a cure. The world needs it."

Magèo stepped away from his nanoscope and paced around the table, mumbling furiously to himself, hands clasped behind his back; he barely heard his apprentice call out before she left to prepare a meal for them both.

* * *

Akol trudged several steps behind Hutar in the shin-high snow, keeping a watchful eye on the young man as they strolled along the bank of Dema-Ki's river. The Elders permitted Hutar two short walks a day as long as he was accompanied by guards.

The other youth beside Akol, a twenty-something woman,

regarded Nageau's grandson bemusedly. She leaned in, voice soft. "You look as if you have just eaten a sour tart, my friend."

Akol dragged his fingers through his short-cropped hair that was growing out for the colder days ahead. For whatever reason, being close to Hutar made his scalp prickle. "Believe me, I would much rather have eaten a sour tart than follow *him* around."

The woman tutted as she regarded Hutar's back. "He seems much different now, Akol. Look at him. There is an aura of tranquility there, and I venture to say shame, too."

"Yes, I suppose so."

"He does not request to go out unless he is certain that most everyone is tucked away in their homes. He does not wish to be seen by the people."

"I realize that."

"The lad is embarrassed."

"You are sympathizing with him quite a bit, I see."

"Do not think much of it. I only say what I observe."

"You really believe he has changed?"

The woman took time to carefully craft her answer. "I believe that when we are faced with incredible tests and difficulties, we are forced into transformation whether we realize it or not, and whether we want to or not. He said that he encountered terrible things in the outside world—"

"Which he has not disclosed."

"True. But some things really are too personal, too horrifying, and it may be for the best that no one speaks of it. Hutar especially does not like to talk much, more so when a bruised ego is in question. And he keeps to himself by nature. Perhaps in time he will open up." She lowered her voice further. "And, do not forget, he has lost every member of his family. Aesròn ran away. He is well and truly alone, and he knows that he is not entirely welcome here. Even the youths who were by his side last summer are keeping their distance."

That was more than accurate. Akol had tracked the movements of Hutar's old accomplices since his arrival, but none of them dared to come anywhere near the young man. There was a growing curiosity in him as well, and he wished he could squash it. *What in the world did Hutar face when he was away from Dema-Ki?* he wondered. *What compelled him to go from wanting to murder the Elders in cold blood to nearly sacrificing himself for Grandfather?*

Akol battled with himself. His family meant everything to him, and the thought that Nageau could very well be dead but for Hutar's actions left an awful taste in his mouth.

He looked back at Hutar as the other youth paused to silently admire an eagle gliding above the valley and felt, for the first time, a pang of sadness. *How time changes us. We used to be friends in our childhood. Carefree, innocent. Unsullied. Now look at us. Once you walk into a storm, you come out a different person.* He was caught off guard by the lump that suddenly formed in his throat and quickly swallowed it.

Just ahead, they saw Nal hurrying toward Magèo's laboratory from her family's *neyra*, basket in hand. When she spotted them, she waved. Akol saw Hutar balk, then wave back. Nal waited by the bridge and greeted them as they came. "Akol, Venya, how are you?"

"Very well," Akol replied, smiling slightly; Nal, a year younger than himself, was introverted but friendly, and her keen mind was one of the reasons why Magèo had chosen to mentor her in his field. "How is everything?"

"Truthfully? It could be a lot better."

The other guard, Venya, hugged her. "I smell something mouthwatering, Nal!"

Nal opened her basket, revealing a plate of baked salmon and some greens. "It is for Magèo. The crazy old man refuses to eat or rest while we work."

Hutar stepped away from his guards and looked into the basket. "You take good care of him, Nal. He is lucky."

The girl turned rather pink and mumbled awkwardly. Hutar gave her a small grin. Akol regarded the exchange, nonplussed.

"They have met before, on his previous walks," Venya whispered to him. "If you ask me, Nal is a tad smitten."

Akol pinched the bridge of his nose. *How?! Ech, I should be part of these walks more often. I cannot allow this.*

Using his body, he nudged Hutar away from Nal. "It was nice seeing you," he said. "Good luck with Magèo."

Nal scrunched her nose adorably. "Thank you!"

Hutar watched her leave, a certain softness in his eyes. Akol noticed, and decided it was time to take him back to the convalescence shelter. Hutar didn't complain.

Two other youths were waiting to relieve Akol and Venya of their duties. The number of guards assigned to watching Hutar had dwindled over time; the Elders had reduced it from four to three, then from three to two. They felt more assured now that Hutar would not try to cause problems. Akol was opposed to it, but there was nothing much he could do except keep voicing his concerns.

As the new guards guided Hutar into the convalescence shelter, Akol and Venya bid each other goodbye and parted ways. Akol absently reached over his shoulder, seeking the comfort of the staff slung across his back.

He passed the five Elders as they made their way to the temple and placed a fist over his heart, bowing his head. They beamed and Tikina embraced him warmly before they continued on.

Akol took a step forward, then stopped and turned to look back at them. He hadn't meant to, but a few nights prior he'd ambled past their *neyra* and heard his name through an open window. The subject of conversation seemed to be that the time might soon be approaching to prepare him. Akol had hurried past, not wanting to be caught eavesdropping, but his inquisitiveness was piqued. What did they need to prepare him for? He would be turning twenty the winter after this. Did they want him to find a mate? The villagers did not believe in arranged marriages, but that didn't mean Tikina and Nageau weren't eager for him to start a family so they could be great-grandparents.

Akol pulled a face. *No, marriage is not it. They want to prepare me for something else. But they have yet to mention anything . . . I should leave this be. If they require something from me, they will make it known.* He continued toward his family's home. *I really would like to know what they meant, though.*

"It has been six days since Magèo received the samples," Ashack said as the Elders sat around the fire pit in their assembly *neyra*, "and nothing useful has come out of it."

Saiyu frowned at her mate, the light from the setting sun spilling onto her bronze features through a window. "I disagree. We have learned that we are immune to the disease and that the younglings—"

"I meant by way of a cure. By no means do I intend to diminish the work Magèo and Nal have done. Truly, their efforts are remarkable."

"Indeed," Nageau said. "And I understand your frustration, Ashack. We all do. We want a cure so badly, but we must be prepared for this to take time. If anything—"

The door of the *neyra* banged open; the Elders jumped. Magèo marched purposefully in, his long beard flowing. He didn't seem to realize that he'd walked in on a meeting.

"Old friend, what are you doing?" Nageau asked, bewildered; he'd been too deep into the conversation to pick up the scientist's approaching footsteps outside the *neyra*.

Magèo, not appearing to hear him, strode to the opposite end of the timber lodging. He pulled open a trapdoor in the floor and climbed down the wooden steps which led to a subterranean vault. The Elders, after a delayed reaction, clambered after him.

The large room had wall-to-wall shelves packed with leather-bound books amassed over centuries, all from the villagers' ancestors. Two long log tables stood at the far end, atop which were several crates filled with scrolls and various other forms of ancient records. Magèo had already lit all the lamps and was working his way through one of the shelves by the time the Elders joined him.

Saiyu gingerly began to place the books back where they belonged, making sure the well-worn bindings didn't fall apart. "What are you looking for, Magèo?"

"There is something . . . something . . ." the old man muttered, pushing aside more books until he arrived at one of the tables that held crates of scrolls.

The Elders watched him, mystified but patient. The scientist was dearly loved by all of Dema-Ki but he was eccentric, and the villagers had long since become accustomed to his peculiar ways.

"Can we help?" Tikina asked.

Magèo stared at the shelves for what felt like an age, then snapped around and shooed the Elders up the stairs. "Leave me to my work!"

"Do you want us to call Nal?"

"No, no. Let the poor girl rest. Now, out!"

The trapdoor slammed shut once the Elders were back on the main floor of the *neyra*. Tayoka jerked his thumb at it. "Did he just throw us out of our own cellar?"

"Yes, he did." Nageau returned to the fire pit. "We may as well continue our meeting. I do not foresee him leaving anytime soon."

As they resettled around the fire, they could hear muffled thuds as the old man worked. The Elders shared looks, then picked up their discussion from where they'd left off . . . until a crash in the cellar brought the meeting to an abrupt halt a while later. They scrambled to their feet and barreled down the stairs, and to their horror found countless parchments and volumes strewn everywhere.

"Look at this mess," Ashack muttered. "I feel as though I am wading through a war zone."

Books upon books were piled around Magèo, who sat in the center of the clutter, breathing hard, his face contorted. As the Elders made their way to him, they took great care to avoid treading on anything that wasn't solid ground.

Tikina knelt beside Magèo and held his shoulders. "Dear one," she said, "talk to us. What is it? What are you searching for?"

The old man's eyes were sunken from lack of sleep, and glassy with tears of frustration. He pulled away from her and went to sit on a small bench at the far end of the vault.

"The world," he rasped, "is descending into chaos. I have done everything I can to find a remedy but it seems to elude me. There is nothing out there I know of that can cure this despicable plague."

"You mentioned that we are impervious to the disease," Nageau said. "Can we not use our immunity to create a cure for the rest of the world?"

"That will not work," Magèo answered sullenly. "I have learned that what protects us from this disease is what makes us who we are."

"Meaning?"

"This pathogen strikes at the kernel at the heart of our cells, where instructions for our biological existence reside. These instruction-bearing kernels make us who we are, at least physically. For whatever reason, ours appear to be exempt. It is not something that can be transferred to those in the outside world to give them immunity. The other option is to destroy it, and I have tried every compound, herb, mineral, and everything in between, applying all the knowledge I have gained over the years. Every single possibility has been exhausted and nothing has worked. This *thing* is just too hardy. I have been picking at my brain so much, I am surprised it has not yet bled. But . . . but then, a shadow of a memory echoed in my mind." He fluttered his fingers beside his head. "Something I heard when I was a child. It was about the Tree of Life."

Saiyu slanted her head. "The what?"

"The Tree of Life," Magèo repeated, looking from one Elder to another as though stunned that they weren't understanding. "Surely some of you have memory of this?"

"What are you talking ab—oh." Ashack covered his face,

heaving a long sigh. "Oh, for goodness' sake, Magèo. I am sorry that I sound disappointed, especially after the days of work you have put in, but is this really your answer? A mythical cure-all?"

Magèo shot up, shaking a fist at him; Ashack returned the gesture with a disgruntled stare. "Why do you call it a myth?" the old man demanded.

"Because we have so much lore that dates back to the time of our Island ancestors. For there to be a cure that sounds too good to be true, it must be a myth."

"Wrong!" Magèo poked the Elder's forehead. "You call it a myth because we do not have it with us. We do not have it; therefore it must not be real. Yes?"

"I—"

Magèo leaned in closer, his finger stuck to Ashack's brow. "Yes?"

Ashack gritted his teeth. "Yes." He looked even more disgruntled now and it didn't help that Tayoka, beside him, was trying to hold back a laugh at the ridiculous scene.

Magèo removed his finger, pleased with the Elder's affirmation. "The flaw of our species is that unless we have tangible proof of something, that thing does not exist. It is fabricated. A myth, a lore, a tale. A dream is not tangible. Emotions are not tangible. A thought is not tangible. And yet we know with certainty that they are real." He placed his hands on his hips and spoke more slowly. "But you may still be right, Ashack. It could be a myth after all. We do have a lot of those. And I *have* asked myself if I am just so desperate that I will grasp at anything, no matter how absurd." His gaze drifted around the room, finally resting upon the crates filled with journals. He pointed. "How far back do these date?"

"Just over two or so millennia, though some go back to our Island ancestors," Nageau answered. "Why?"

"I found something while you were all upstairs." Magèo pulled out a torn parchment from within his tunic. The Elders instinctively moved closer to get a better look. Magèo let out an exclamation and waved his arms wildly, forcing the Elders to stoop low to avoid getting hit. "Give me room, all of you! You know I need my space!"

The Elders took a big step back, forming a semicircle around the scientist. Magèo lifted the timeworn parchment to the light, tapping it repeatedly. "These are written records with sporadic mentions of seeds scattered throughout the narrative, and not just any seeds. Seeds to the Tree of Life!"

"It is a *myth*," Ashack growled. "We have many parchments dedicated to all kinds of legends and tales. This is merely another one."

"Help me search for more mentions of these seeds," Magèo begged the others, ignoring Ashack. "I need to try all avenues and I refuse to stop now." He went up to Nageau, grasping the Elder's arms. "Please. I beseech you."

Nageau placed a hand on the older man's face. "We will help you, old friend."

Ashack didn't look happy but Nageau, though not optimistic about the endeavor himself, knew that Magèo would not leave the vault until he had combed through every page of every book and read through each line of each scroll.

We might as well help him figure out that the solution may not be in this vault, he thought morosely, turning to the many shelves. *This will be a long night.*

* * *

It was well past midnight when Nageau closed the sixteenth book he'd picked up. It was an almanac of sorts, detailing curious happenings during the initial period when his ancestors first established Dema-Ki. A particular story had grabbed his attention; a few of the original Islanders had vanished one night from the newly formed tribe, never to be seen again. The chronicler of the book had named them the Lost Ones, and as much as Nageau wanted to continue reading there were more pressing matters at hand.

Lodged on the floor between two bookshelves, he placed the almanac aside and observed the others. Tikina and Saiyu sat together, cross-legged, squinting and blinking often as they categorized the ancient records by relevance. Ashack was by himself in a corner, eyes slowly closing and snapping open, only to slowly close again. They were all exhausted, and the desire to give up hung heavily in the air. Only Tayoka and Magèo showed some hint of vigor. They stood by the tables, shuffling through the contents of the crates.

Is it possible, Nageau mused silently, *that we are not meant to find a cure at all?*

He dismissed the thought quickly, blaming his tired state for such contemplations. Then he noticed Tayoka's shoulders stiffen. The man did not move for a minute, and when he did turn around, his hands shook. Resting upon his open palms was an ancient journal that, by all rights, should have been falling apart.

"Have you found something?" Nageau asked.

Tayoka delicately passed the book to Magèo. The old man's finger zipped over the words on the pages, his mouth moving silently as he read.

"This," he whispered. "This is it!"

"What is it?" Ashack sighed.

"The cure!"

"For the disease?"

"No, for my arthritis," Magèo snapped. "Yes, for the disease!" His face glowed as he skimmed the pages. "This is the journal of Arka'th. He was one of the fifteenth-generation Elders of Dema-Ki."

All lethargy vanished, like mist dissipating above their heads.

"What have you found?" Saiyu asked.

A tantalizingly slow smile crept across the scientist's lips. "An entry about the seeds of the Tree of Life."

"No!" Tikina gasped. "They *are* real?"

Magèo bobbed his head, looking down at the journal. "There is an account—well, more of a preface to the actual entry—about a smaller group of survivors who escaped the destruction of the home island, but they were not with the Islanders who made it here. One of the families was the Keeper of the Seeds, the ones responsible for the Tree of Life. They, along with the Keepers of Remedies, were one of the various groups of people under the auspices of the Custodians of the Temple, who in turn were supervised by the Council of Elders on the island."

"But where did they go?" Tikina pressed.

"Remember the trading vessel our ancestors escaped in?"

"It carried fifty-one survivors to this continent," Saiyu said. "One lineage of Dema-Ki."

"Yes," Magèo said. "But there was another ship. A smaller fishing vessel that carried two families from the opposite side of the Island in a different direction. One family did not survive the voyage, but the other did and ended up on a coast near a desert. They resided there in a small settlement and eventually melded with the local people, just as our ancestors did here."

Nageau started to nod. "I remember hearing this story as a boy, decades ago. But nothing was mentioned about the Tree of Life. All we were told was that the family lasted a few generations, and that they kept in touch with the Elders here."

"Indeed. The last of that bloodline, a brother and a sister, made contact with the Elders one last time before their presumed deaths."

"What happened?" Tayoka asked.

"According to this journal, what they called 'Roman conquerors' seized the fort that they and others from their village were using as a safe haven. The siblings managed to escape the siege and hide in a cave. The brother, being the only one with telepathy, reached out to Arka'th before the warriors found them. He transmitted a message that a box containing the seeds was safely buried there. Sadly, the siblings were never heard from again and it does not seem like any attempt was made to retrieve the box, most likely because the Elders did not have an accurate enough location, nor did they have the means to travel to such distant lands."

"Fascinating." Nageau stroked his chin, mind reeling.

"Absolutely fascinating. So, these seeds, they really do grow into trees that cure any and all diseases?"

Magèo picked up the parchment he'd found earlier which detailed the seeds. "It seems so. It says here that it was routinely used by the Custodians of the Temple on the Island to create medicines that cured ailments. Of course, since the discovery of our crystals, our ancestors hardly ever fell ill, but in the rare instances they did, they were cured by tonics made from the sap of this tree. That could explain why even though the tree had potent capabilities, there is hardly any mention of it elsewhere in our history."

"Perhaps our ancestors viewed it as another fixture among the numerous curious finds they had discovered on the Island," Saiyu suggested.

"Quite likely. They were able-bodied and, as I said, rarely unwell, so a tree such as this would not have been a part of their daily conversations."

"Even if by some miracle we do find these seeds, trees take a long time to grow," Ashack pointed out.

Magèo looked down at the scroll again. "True, but . . . perhaps not this tree. If what is stated here is veritable, then the Tree of Life will reach maturity"—he smiled, the corners of his eyes crinkling—"very quickly after a seed is planted. Very quickly indeed."

"That seems too convenient."

"The scroll appears to be missing a portion," Tikina noted.

"That it is, but it does not matter because we have the important part right here." Magèo caressed the parchment. "The ink has faded but much of it is still readable. What matters now is that we know with certainty that this is not a myth. We *must* find those seeds."

"It does seem to be the only lead we have," Tayoka agreed.

"It could very well be a lost cause, a wild chase," Ashack cautioned. "We do not know where to even begin the search."

"We may not, but perhaps the Sentries will."

“We must do everything we can to obtain these seeds,” Nageau said, standing taller. “I will reach out to the Sentries and the Chosen Ones. Their mission is about to begin.”

21

Aari flopped against the wall, sweat dripping from his brow. "I'm done," he wheezed. "I'm done. Kode-man, you get in there."

Kody put away a bo staff he'd been studiously practicing with and bounced on his toes a few times before squaring off against Mariah in a boxer's stance. He struck out and she easily blocked with her gloves. He brought his left arm up for an uppercut, but she ducked and threw him off-balance with a well-placed kick to his knees. Kody fell with a heavy grunt, then made a face at her.

"Okay, I see how it is." He sprang to his feet, back in his ready stance. "Come at me, woman!"

Mariah hurled a jab toward his head but he dodged inward and clamped his arms around her torso. Before she could counter, he lifted her up and flipped her over his shoulder. She landed on the mat with a thud. Groaning, she gave him a thumbs-up. "Nice."

Using his teeth, Aari undid the Velcro fastener of one of his gloves and removed it. He stretched his fingers, watching his friends spar. The group took every opportunity they could to be in the training room—though sometimes they had to be dragged out of their comfortable beds—since not much else could be done while they waited for Magèo's full results on the tissue samples.

Kody was knocked onto his back again. He leapt up, roared comically at Mariah, and they continued sparring for the next few minutes until a voice called out. Aari turned to see Tegan and Jag coming down the stairs, both grinning with flushed faces.

"How's it going in here?" Tegan asked.

Kody wiped the sweat off his face. "Good. Mariah's determined to kick my butt, as usual."

"Attagirl."

Mariah smiled. "How was the outdoor training?"

"Great," Jag beamed, rummaging through a box of martial arts equipment and pulling out a pair of focus mitts, "but we're still figuring out how to use our abilities in tandem. And we had some fun with parkour. It's pretty cold, though. My ears and nose have gone numb."

Tegan deftly snagged the mitts from Jag and slipped them on. "Alright, who's up?"

Aari looked away, like a student avoiding eye contact with a teacher when the class is asked a question. Tegan smirked. "On your feet, Brainiac."

"I was just up against Mariah," he complained.

"And it looks like you've caught your breath. Come on. On your feet."

Aari put his glove back on and faced off against Tegan. She had a calm, cool look in her eyes. He blew a raspberry. *Wonder if she'll beat her record today. Last time it took her eight seconds to throw me to the ground.*

Six seconds later, he found himself on his rear end on the training mat, groaning. "I'm done! D-o-n-e, *done*. I've been getting served all day!"

Jag chuckled. "Then you need more training, genius."

Tegan pulled Aari up. "One more round. I'll go easier on you this time."

He scowled. "Don't you dare."

They squared off again. Just as Aari leaned forward for a jab, Marshall called out to the group from the third floor. They immediately threw off their equipment and raced up the stairs, bare feet stomping on the hardwood. They found the Sentry in the meeting area, a sheet of notes in his hand. He had them all sit around the table, not wanting to waste time.

"Elder Nageau just reached out to me," he informed them, "and it looks like we may have a breakthrough."

"The test results came back?" Aari guessed.

"Yes, and there are some strange findings. It seems that anyone of Dema-Ki blood is immune to both strains of the disease."

"Weird," Tegan said. "That makes it look like it was specifically designed to spare you guys. Either that, or your kind of evolution protects you from stuff like this."

Jag folded his arms. "What about us?"

Marshall licked his lips and glanced down at the paper. "The good news is that you're immune to the aging strain."

Aari felt like a weight had been dropped onto his chest, forcing the breath out of him. "But not the violent one."

"Not a hundred percent of the time, no. I'm sorry—I really wish I had better news."

"Great," Mariah said sarcastically. "Well, I don't want to tempt fate. Guess we'll just keep carrying our masks with us."

"Why aren't the Sentries and villagers affected?" Kody asked.

"Tegan may have hit the nail on the head with that," Marshall said. "Magèo's theory is that it may have been designed that way, specifically to target anyone who doesn't share our DNA."

"But why would Reyor want that?"

"Beats me, kiddo. And for some reason that Magèo can't pin down, it seems that if one of you does get infected, the pathogen just stays with the host."

"Meaning we won't be contagious," Aari said.

"Yes."

Tegan rested her feet on the edge of the tabletop, frowning. "That's odd. And was Magèo able to find a cure?"

"Sadly, no. But he did find some evidence for a possible solution." Marshall placed his notes on the table; Aari tried to get a peek. "Which brings me to my next point. We've finally got a mission."

The group sat up straight.

"The Elders believe that there's a cure out there in the form of seeds," Marshall said, "that, when planted, grow into the Tree of Life . . . a tree that can cure diseases."

The friends looked skeptical, and Aari voiced what they were all thinking. "That sounds like something right out of a fantasy novel."

"You're forgetting the people you're dealing with. The Tree of Life was thought to be a myth even by those in Dema-Ki, just one legend among many. Turns out, there are actual historical records of it. A few of our ancestors managed to escape the devastation of their island with a box containing the seeds, but they weren't on the trading vessel that carried most of the survivors to North America. Instead, they got on a fishing boat that ended up on the shores of an arid land."

Kody leaned forward eagerly. "Like a desert? Africa, maybe?"

"That's the thing. We don't have a specific place, or an exact location, because the last that was heard about the fate of the seeds and those who guarded them was back in the first century."

The teenagers' jaws dropped. Mariah held up a hand. "Wait, let me get this straight. We're hunting for the seeds of a cure-all tree that was lost, like, two thousand years ago? And we don't know where exactly on planet Earth to start searching? Oh, yeah, that's gonna work out just fine."

"We do have *some* information," Marshall countered. "Here's what we know: This happened sometime during the first century A.D.; it took place in an arid region not far from where my ancestors' home island used to be; and the last Keepers of the Seeds, two young siblings, were barricaded in a fort on a mountain being attacked by Romans and so they snuck off to hide in one of the caves in the mountainside. Unfortunately, it's believed that they were killed. The last connection they had with Dema-Ki was when one of the kids reached out to the Elders and informed them of their situation, and that they'd buried the box in the cave."

"That's not giving us much," Jag said. "We don't have a location."

"But we can search for it online," Kody suggested. "There's got to be some kind of record somewhere for an event like that, right?"

Aari lifted a finger. "I . . . I think I know where this all happened."

For a moment, the room went deathly quiet. Marshall leaned toward him. "You do?"

"It wouldn't hurt to double-check online, but what you described . . ." Aari steepled his fingers together, index fingers pressed against his lips. "It sounds familiar. My grandfather's a Polish Jew, and he's got a keen interest in the history of his people. He managed to survive the Holocaust thanks to my grandma and her family. Together, they emigrated to Israel after the war ended, then eventually moved to the States and settled down. I remember sitting with him in front of the fireplace when I was younger, completely absorbed in the stories he'd tell me whenever he visited. One in particular came to mind as you talked about what happened to the siblings. Like, it fits the description of a god-awful event that happened in Israel to a tee, except for one important part."

"And what's that?" Marshall asked.

"There were no survivors among those trapped in the fort—all nine hundred and sixty of them committed suicide," Aari replied softly. "When the Romans were expanding their empire in the first century, they took over Jerusalem. That was in response to the Sicarii, who were pretty much the earliest form of an organized assassin unit, after they tried to drive the Romans from their homeland.

"The Romans executed a three-pronged attack, and Jerusalem fell. It felt like the literal End of Days for the Jews . . . So many were killed. Those who survived fled to a safe haven, a fort built by Herod the Great on a mesa in the Judean Desert. The Romans followed them and laid siege to the fort for over a year. Then they made a massive ramp using engineers and Jewish slaves to build it, which took two or three months of backbreaking labor. The Jews in the fort—and the Sicarii zealots—really couldn't do much except watch and probably scream curses. As the Romans used a battering ram to break into the fort, the people inside knew that their end was near. And, yeah, they couldn't escape or fight, so they decided on mass suicide."

"I can't imagine that kind of desperation," Mariah murmured.

"Me neither."

Marshall scanned his notes again. "Your story does seem to match what little I was told by the Elders. Except, as you said, for the mass suicide pact."

"But it looks like there could have been survivors, and we may have a location now," Jag said. "Israel."

Aari looked up. "And I think I know where in Israel. It's by the Dead Sea."

"Does it have a name?" Marshall asked.

"Masada."

Kody threw open the laptop sitting at the center of the table and quickly typed a search. "Would you look at that. It's actually one of Israel's most popular tourist spots. It's even a UNESCO World Heritage Site."

Aari pulled the laptop toward him. "There have been archaeological digs all over the place. They've even found a few remains in the caves you mentioned earlier, Marshall."

"Looks like only the plateau is accessible, though, not the caves," Mariah said, peering over his shoulder. "If it's a popular tourist site, we're gonna have an issue getting down there."

Tegan shook her head. "Given the state of the world right now, tourism's probably slow. More than that, if the place has already been excavated, wouldn't the box have been found? Who knows where it could be now."

"It might be in a museum somewhere," Jag said.

"Good point. Give me a sec." Aari typed a new search entry and scrolled through pictures and articles. The others hovered around him; he could almost smell their impatience.

At last, he pushed the laptop away. "If they did find the box, there isn't a single mention of it anywhere. Which is pretty strange, seeing as ancient seeds would be the one thing that would get both scientists' and historians' knickers in a bunch."

Mariah glumly drew her nail in circles on the tabletop. "No mention of seeds at all?"

"They did find some, but unless Judean date palm seeds in clay jars are what we're looking for, that's not it."

"So the box is still buried in one of the caves?" Kody asked.

Aari shrugged. "Maybe."

"We need to check it out," Marshall said.

"There are a lot of caves. How do we find which—"

The Sentry held up his paper between two fingers. "That's where the last piece of information comes in. The cave we're looking for has a mark on the ceiling that's shaped like a crescent moon. It's supposedly located near a double cave."

"A double . . ." A light switched on in Aari's head. "I just read about that! That's where some remains were found, in a double cave at the southern slope of Masada."

The energy in the room grew so palpable, he thought electric sparks might go off if they moved even an inch. Smiles began to form all around.

Then his face fell. "This is all fine and dandy, but so what if we get the seeds? Trees take a *long* time to mature. By then, who knows how many people will have died."

"That's what I thought, too," Marshall said. "But when I asked Elder Nageau, he said that these seeds, once planted correctly, grow fast. Insanely fast. We're talking four weeks, tops."

Jag rubbed his temples. "Dema-Ki people, man. You guys have some crazy stuff. Borderline sorcery." The side of his mouth curved up. "And I'm glad."

"Even if that's all true," Tegan interjected, "a lot can happen in those weeks."

"Which is why we need to find those seeds ASAP." Marshall slid his folded notes into the back pocket of his jeans. "I'm gonna start searching for flights. You guys should get packing. Fit as much as you can into a bag, and maybe a carry-on just in case. We're heading out as soon as we can."

The friends trickled down to the main floor and stood in a circle, saying nothing, allowing the exhilaration on their faces to speak for them. Then they dispersed to their rooms.

Aari stared out of the huge windows by the foot of his bed, observing the snow-covered trees. He would miss the view, and the Lodge. They'd been living in the French Alps for just over a week but the friends already considered it home. Even so, he was eager to head out at last.

After all the waiting, all the training, all the preparation, he thought, this is it! The mission is finally about to begin. A slight thrill danced up his spine. *I can't wait.*

PART TWO

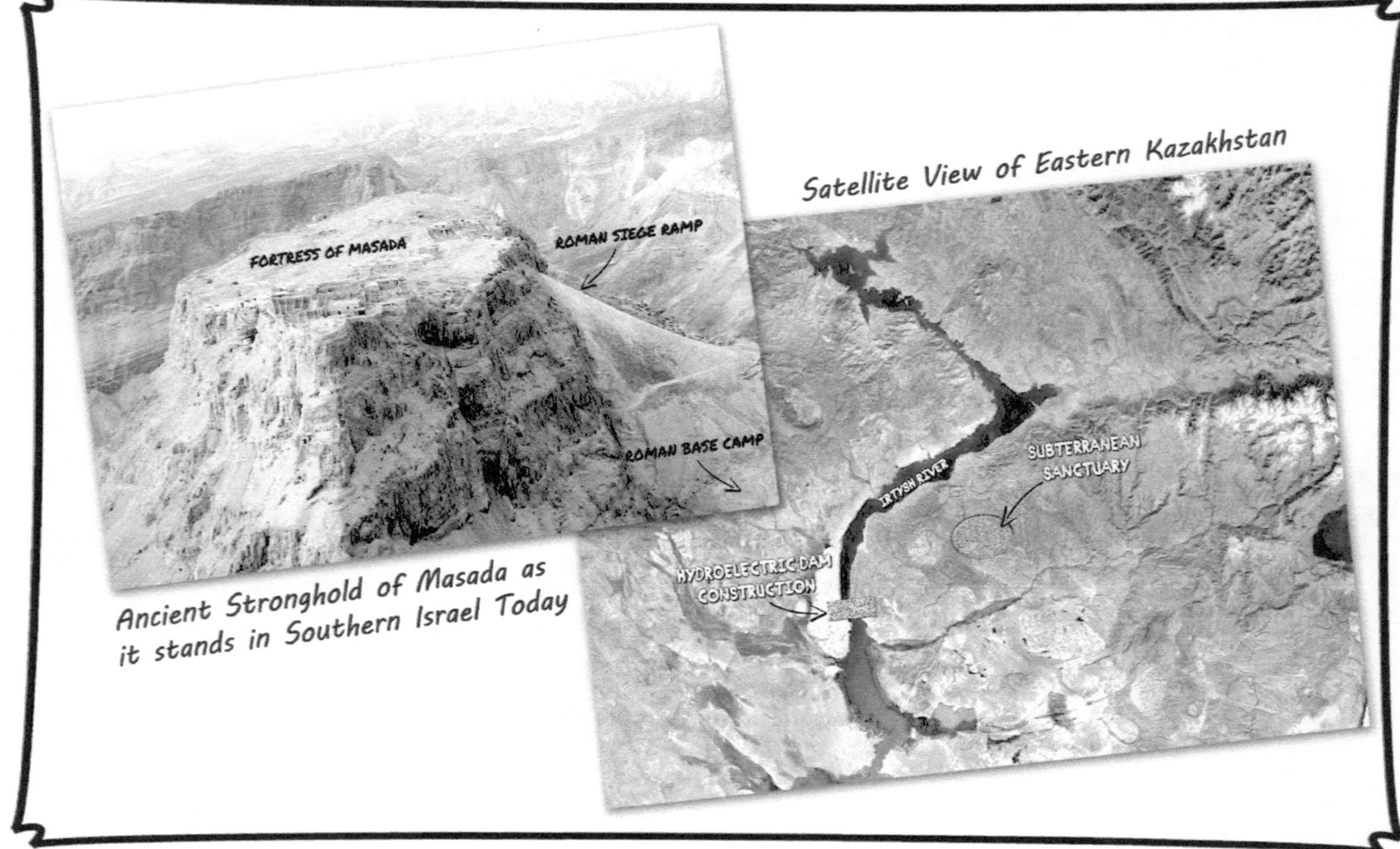

Ancient Stronghold of Masada as it stands in Southern Israel Today

Satellite View of Eastern Kazakhstan

Jag watched Ben Gurion Airport recede in the passenger-side mirror of the rented Ford Expedition. Almost immediately upon leaving the facility, he already had a feel for the pace of life by how aggressively the locals drove.

Airport security was ludicrously tight. There had been a three-hour delay as Israeli health authorities tested a new screening method, pioneered by their own scientists, on every passenger entering the country, taking blood samples and cheek swabs. The friends were relieved to receive a clean bill of health after the long wait.

The SUV accelerated under several overpasses before matching with the flow of traffic as they headed away from Tel Aviv. Clusters of red-roofed buildings were scattered among stretches of farmland. A curious assortment of rundown houses standing next to modern mansions caught Jag's eye. *Interesting*, he mused. *Do people live like this across the country?*

As he sat beside Marshall, quietly taking in the passing scenery, he was struck by a brief flashback of their road trip to his grandparents' farm in Kansas just a few months before. It was after Tegan and Mariah had broken out of the New Mexico Sanctuary, where they'd been held by Tony.

Jag slumped in his seat, his mood darkening. It was bad enough that Reyor's personal lapdog had abducted the girls and tried to capture him and the others, but then Jag had lost his grandmother as a result of the crop destructions. It left a searing void that continued to haunt him. All the love from his family and the thoughtful advice from the Elders had done little to quench his thirst for retribution. If they couldn't get to Reyor first, Tony would have to suffice.

“The weather’s much cooler than I expected,” Kody noted out of the blue from the back of the seven-seater, yanking Jag out of his reverie.

“We’re a couple of weeks out from November,” Aari said. “Guess it gets cold here, too.”

Jag glanced in the rearview mirror. Mariah, in the middle row beside Aari, studied a travel brochure she’d picked up at the airport. “Israel’s so tiny!” she gasped. “According to this, it’s barely the size of New Jersey, but the amount of conflict that goes on around here is crazy. Wars, skirmishes . . . why?”

“Many reasons,” Aari said. “History, politics, religion. I mean, this is ground zero of the monotheistic world. More than half of the planet calls this region their Holy Land.”

“Okay, well, why does it all happen here? Why not somewhere else?”

“Funny you should ask that. I asked Mr. Gregson that exact question once after History class. He answered my question by holding up his snack.”

Kody’s voice popped from the very back again. “Snack?”

“Sit down, Scooby. Gregson held up an apple. He said asking why this part of the world turned out special is like asking why the stem of the apple is at the center and not somewhere else on the fruit. Then he walked over to the world map on the wall, asked me to point out Israel, and weirdly, it’s pretty much in the center. For some reason, when we defined East and West, this region ended up nearly smack in the middle. I’m not saying it’s providence or anything but, just like the stem on the apple, it is what it is, I guess.”

“This is also a land of mystery and prophecies,” Marshall added as he pulled down his sun visor. “It’s actually really interesting stuff.”

“For example?” Tegan asked.

“Like when it was said that the Jews would be exiled from the Kingdom of Ancient Israel and it would happen over and over, and that they'd go through a lot of tribulation. History aligns with that."

"So it's come to pass a few times, then."

"Yeah. They were scattered far and wide. It was also said that they'd come back to Israel once the Messiah returned at the End of Days."

Jag raised an eyebrow. "But they're already here. So, what? Is it the End of Days?"

"Kinda does feel like that, doesn't it?" Marshall shrugged. "The Jews started returning when the Edict of Toleration was signed between the British and the Ottoman Empire in—"

"1844," Aari finished. "Well before the formation of the State of Israel after the second World War."

"Are you *kidding* me?" Mariah exclaimed.

"Uh, what?"

"Seriously? The Edict of Proclamation in eighteen . . . whatever? I can't even remember what I had for lunch yesterday!"

Jag could see Aari trying not to smile as he said, "You mean the Edict of *Toleration*."

Mariah grabbed his head and shook it. "Give me your brain!"

Giggles filled the car as Aari pulled away. Once the merriment subsided, Marshall spoke again. "What you said was right, Aari. So, yes, it would seem that there are quite a few parallels to prophecies. If you believe in that sort of thing."

Jag started to laugh, hard, and couldn't speak for a full minute. He tried to collect himself and, still snickering, said to his bemused friends, "I guess that's ironic, isn't it?"

"What is?" Tegan asked.

"Ending all that with 'if you believe in that sort of thing.' Look at us. We're literally at the center of a major prophecy. We can't really claim to be skeptics anymore, can we?"

There was a collective, amused snort from his friends. Even Marshall smiled. "No, I suppose not . . . Hey, what's this?"

The car rolled to a stop behind long lines of vehicles. Jag moaned. "Look at this traffic!"

"The cars further ahead are moving," Marshall said. "Maybe there was an accident."

Jag eyed the time on the dashboard. *11:23 a.m. As long as we get to Masada well before closing hours, we're good.*

He held his hand out the window, feeling the parched air on his skin, then twisted around to take a proper look at the others. They were anxious about what was to come, he knew, and did what they could to keep themselves occupied. Mariah had pulled out a novel and was already engrossed. Aari looked out at their rolling surroundings, seemingly lost in thought. Kody, in the back, flipped through one of his favorite superhero comic books and shared an earbud with Tegan, who had her eyes closed.

It's a good thing we got to rest at the Lodge, Jag thought. *Dunno how much of that we'll be getting from now on.*

A discord of honking erupted ahead, startling him. There was yelling and shouting, though whether in Hebrew or Arabic he couldn't tell.

"Heads up," Marshall murmured. He tapped the controls on his door and all the windows automatically closed. Jag leaned over to the Sentry's side to get a better view of the situation.

A driver several cars ahead had jumped out of his vehicle and was running in their direction, screaming and pointing. Jag, befuddled, turned to look out his window. A face straight from the depths of hell smashed against the glass. He tried to pull away but was jerked back by his seatbelt as it locked with the sudden motion. His heart beat madly in his chest. The man's red-rimmed, bloodshot eyes were partially glazed. Crimson dripped from every orifice on his face, and saliva and specks of blood flew from his mouth. Through the gruesomeness, there was something in his expression that Jag couldn't quite place, but it brought about a grief so deep he felt almost ill.

Marshall reached over, protectively placing his arm between Jag and the window. He seemed unfazed as he watched the demented man beat at the glass. "He's sick."

Two soldiers in olive green uniforms approached, shouting,

their assault rifles trained. The man faced them, staying perfectly still as they neared. Jag's eyes darted between them. He had his hand on the door handle, ready to help, but Marshall gently removed it, shaking his head.

The man let loose a feral cry. He flew toward the soldiers, ignoring their yells of warning. Two shots sounded. The man dropped to the ground, convulsing. Jag went limp in his seat, unable to shift his gaze from the sight.

It took half an hour before emergency responders dealt with the scene and traffic began moving again. Neither the friends nor the Sentry spoke, and it wasn't until the SUV was cruising down the highway that Jag whispered, "He was scared. He was reduced to an animal, and he was sick, and it was either fight or flight and he fought. Or he tried to. But he was scared and trying to find help."

"There was nothing we could do," Tegan said quietly. "If we'd stepped out, we could have gotten the disease. We're vulnerable. It sucks, but it wasn't our place to step in."

Jag cupped his hands over his face. *It was like looking at a terrified child. And then a violent beast. Oh, my God.*

"I'm gonna find a spot to disinfect your side of the car, Jag," Marshall said carefully. "For the time being, don't roll down the window. You too, Aari."

They passed a number of small towns until they came upon an empty gas station and pulled off the highway. The Sentry gave the SUV's doors and windows a quick wash, then thoroughly scrubbed the exterior using a spray bottle of disinfectant. Jag got out to lend a hand but Marshall shooed him back into the vehicle.

Inside, he found Mariah sitting absolutely still, her hands pressed tightly between her knees. He rubbed her leg. "'Riah?"

She stared into the distance, unblinking. "Do you remember when we got caught in that riot during the summer?"

"I do. Unfortunately."

"I'd never felt so sick and helpless in my life . . . until that man came up to your window and got shot."

Jag, not knowing what to say, reached out and pressed a kiss the top of her head. Marshall retuned a minute later and as they veered back onto the highway, said, "I know I keep mentioning this, but make sure you've got your masks with you at all times." He glanced briefly at Jag, then into the rearview mirror at the others. "I couldn't bear it if anything happened to you guys. You are too important. Don't ever forget that."

As strange as it still felt to be the Chosen Ones, Jag knew Marshall was right. For the sake of bringing an end to a growing apocalyptic nightmare, they couldn't take unnecessary risks.

He subconsciously slid his hand to his backpack on the floor. To avoid attention, they'd opted not to bring their masks from the Lodge onto the flight, so Marshall had asked one of his friends from the Israel Defense Forces to meet them outside the airport arrivals area with new ones. The former commando readily supplied six full-face masks that were designed to protect against biological agents.

Traffic slowed as more residential and commercial buildings appeared. Jag checked the car's GPS. "We've just entered Jerusalem, ladies and gents."

Aari and Kody were the most thrilled. They took out their phones, eagerly snapping photos. "Did you know," Aari started to ramble, almost breathless from excitement, "that over four thousand years ago Jerusalem was called Urusalima, which means the City of Peace? Which is ironic because the amount of war and destruction that Jerusalem has seen in its lifetime is beyond ridiculous. And did you know that there are over *two thousand* archeological sites here? And, also, did you know that—"

"I'm just super stoked to be visiting a historical place that's in one of my favorite video games," Kody said, bouncing in his seat. "Marshall, any chance we'll be passing by Acre or Damascus? Or Masyaf?"

"Acre is behind us and to the north," Marshall replied. "And Damascus and Masyaf are *way* north. In Syria."

"I was kidding about the last two. But will we be passing the

Dome of the Rock, at least?"

"If only. Believe me, I really want to see all these places too, but with what happened earlier, the disease has probably already found its way here. We should stick to our plan and avoid population centers, which means we shouldn't drive into Jerusalem."

"Bummer."

"Hey, when this whole thing with Reyor is done and over with, I'll gladly bring you guys back here for sightseeing and all the other good touristy stuff. As long as the world hasn't burned down completely by then, of course."

"We're holding you to that, Marshall," Tegan said; there was a smile in her voice as she spoke. "Don't disappoint."

The Sentry chuckled. "Love you too, kiddo."

They came upon several checkpoints as they drove but were always waved through without incident. *Having American passports sure helps*, Jag thought.

They left the district of Jerusalem and coasted along the highway. Most of the traffic was destined for the city, leaving the lanes practically car-free. All around them was desert, a stretch of golden nothingness save for some shrubbery. The sun shone brightly, forcing Jag to pull down his own visor. From the back of the SUV, Kody cleared his throat. Jag rolled his eyes good-humoredly, knowing what was coming.

"So, it's one in the afternoon," Kody started slowly.

Marshall hummed. "Well, we're pretty far from crowds, and I *do* see a restaurant coming up on the GPS . . ."

"*Yes. Yesss.*"

Jag swapped amused looks with the Sentry, then suddenly sat up straight. "What's that?"

"I think," Marshall said, "that's some kind of a rest stop."

They turned onto a smaller road, surrounded by a stunning vista of the Judean Mountains. Next to a parking area, a large stone retaining wall with a giant teal plaque read 'SEA LEVEL' with accompanying Hebrew and Arabic script.

"Check out the Bedouin." Marshall nodded at a man garbed

in a long white tunic and a red-and-white headdress. He stood beside a placid, colorfully accessorized camel. "He probably lets tourists take photos for a small fee."

"But I don't see any tourists," Tegan said. "And it's likely there aren't going to be any for a while . . ." She trailed off. "Marshall, could you stop the car?"

The Sentry complied. Tegan got out and ran over to the Bedouin. Jag watched as she flashed the man a wide smile. He let her stroke the camel, then took a photo of her with it. She handed him a few coins, then asked him something. He beamed and swept out a hand. She stood beside him, held her phone at arm's length, and snapped a picture. She passed him a few more shekels and gave a shallow bow. The Bedouin returned the gesture, surprise and joy radiated from him.

Jag smiled. *It's always the ones you least expect, isn't it?*

Tegan ran back. She didn't say anything to the others but waved to the Bedouin and his camel as Marshall put the car in drive.

"Okay, I've got this figured out," Aari said a few moments later, indicating a hill with a long green sign stretched across it. "Those are altitude markers. Where the rest stop is, that's sea level. Altitude was zero. As we keep going down toward the Dead Sea, more markers are probably gonna pop up as the altitude drops."

"Makes sense," Mariah said. "The Dead Sea *is* below sea level."

As they returned to the highway, Marshall said, "Food's coming up, Kody. I swear I can hear your stomach growl from here."

Kody sighed dramatically. "It's an embarrassing problem, really."

Small stores, empty parking grounds, and numerous lots with rows upon rows of clay sculptures, fountains, and flowerpots started to crop up. A few camels rested by the roadside, watching, unruffled, as the SUV sped past.

"What's all this?" Jag asked. "It's kind of in the middle of nowhere."

"Tourists often pass through here on their way to the Dead

Sea," Marshall explained. "Guess these folks cater to them, hoping to make a living and—ah, here we go. Last Chance Restaurant."

They turned off the asphalt road and onto loose gravel. Despite sitting at the very back, Kody was the first one out of the SUV and into the quaint yellow building, leaving Jag and the others to catch up.

Inside, Jag's olfactory just about overloaded with the delightful aromas of Middle Eastern cuisine. He reached out to grasp Kody's shoulder as a sudden wave of hunger crashed over him. Kody gave a knowing grin as if to say, 'Welcome to my world.'

The man behind the counter, a cheery, tanned fellow with a whitening beard greeted them enthusiastically in near-perfect English. "*Shalom!* Welcome, friends!"

"Thank you," Marshall said. "Got a table for six?"

The man spread his arms out, showing off the cozy, though empty, restaurant. "I think we can squeeze you in."

As they pulled a couple of tables together, the man glanced at the respirator mask Tegan had strapped to her leg. "What's that for, young lady?" he asked kindly.

"Can't be too safe," she replied.

The man's cheery appearance faltered. "That's true. Business has been down the past few days around here, but people still come and go. They have a need for some normalcy, some fun." He passed them their menus, took down their orders, and offered them drinks. Then he turned to Marshall. "And for you, sir, a nice cold beer?"

The Sentry gathered up the menus and returned them. "I'll just stick with water, thanks."

Once the man left, Kody, sitting beside Marshall, poked his arm. "You can have a drink, you know. One of us can drive."

"I think your parents would kill me if they found out I let you drive because I decided to order booze. Besides, I don't drink."

"You don't?"

"To perform our duties as Sentries, we need to be clear-minded and present at all times, and completely in control of all our faculties. And"—he slung an arm around Kody's neck in a headlock—"I would wholeheartedly advise all of you against anything that would inhibit you as well. Being the Chosen Ones and all that, you gotta be in top form at all times. Agreed?"

Kody flailed. "*Gak!* Agreed!"

The Sentry regarded the boy warmly and released his hold. "Good."

Jag, seated between Tegan and Mariah, rubbed their backs. "You two doing okay?"

Mariah nodded, but Tegan was distracted by her phone. Jag looked over her shoulder and saw her changing her lock screen photo to the picture of her and the Bedouin. When she caught him looking, she connected with him telepathically. *Peekaboo, Sasquatch. Can you hear me?*

Oof, it's been a while since we've chatted like this.

Yeah. Sorry. Don't really feel like talking out loud right now.

All good. I'm actually glad you reached out. He paused. *I've been thinking.*

What about?

The fact that you're usually more driven by logic than emotion. I'm the other way around most of the time. Or, even if I'm acting out of logic, emotions can overpower me.

She squinted at him. *Continue.*

It's like . . . you're the Spock to my Kirk.

I don't know where you're going with this, but I hope this isn't turning into a session of Dr. Phil.

No, nothing like that. He paused again, hesitating. To himself, he thought, Spock would make a better leader. But I should probably shut this down or she'll punch me in the face. To Tegan, he said, *You know what? Never mind. Ignore me. I'm just hungry.*

She shot him a look. *You okay?*

I'm fine. Hey, lunch is here.

Not wanting to waste a second more than was necessary to get to Masada, the group inhaled their falafels and shawarmas and downed their drinks.

"Enjoy your day!" their host boomed from the bar as they got up to leave.

"Thanks!" Marshall said, holding the door open as the friends filed out. "You too!"

It wasn't long before they found themselves on yet another stretch of desert highway. The GPS guided them south, with a sign pointing toward Masada. As they rounded a curve, greenery gradually appeared, as did signs of life, only to be replaced by mountains.

To the left, Jag could just make out the Dead Sea in the distance. The car whizzed past another sign. "Qumran," he read aloud. "Whoa, look at how crowded it is over there."

"This is where they found the original Dead Sea Scrolls," Aari explained, face up against his window to watch the people climbing out of tour buses. "Nearly a thousand different ancient texts were discovered in the caves. It's considered one of the greatest archaeological finds."

"Ancient texts of what?" Tegan asked.

"A lot of them are biblical. They found things like the oldest copies of the Hebrew Bible and one of the earliest known copies of the Ten Commandments. There are even scrolls that talk about the final battle at the End of Days."

"End of Days, huh?" Jag repeated. "That term has come up quite a bit today alone. Is that why there are so many people visiting Qumran?"

"Possibly," Marshall said. "I don't think those folks back there are your typical tourists. They're probably more like religious groups. Guess it's beginning to feel a bit like Armageddon." He clicked his tongue. "Temples, synagogues, and churches around the world will start experiencing a groundswell of believers in the coming months, I guarantee it."

"Prayer can be comforting," Tegan said. "But we need to follow that with action."

"And that's where the five of you come in."

"No pressure."

"No pressure at all."

The Dead Sea finally came into full view, glittering under the stark sunlight. "It's gorgeous!" Mariah exclaimed.

Jag had to agree. Though he hated swimming in salt water, he was tempted to take a dip in the shimmering blue depths of the hypersaline sea.

They rocketed by a nature reserve as the GPS showed that the group was fast approaching their destination. Jag sat forward, ready. The mountains continued to stretch to the right and yet another sign blurred past. He knocked on his window rapidly. "That said Masada!"

"Keep your shirt on," Marshall chided. "You're making *me* restless."

The mountains began to edge back, as if distancing themselves from the car. Then there was a sudden eruption from the teenagers and Jag hollered. "There it is!"

There was a distinct sound of several seatbelts unbuckling as the Sentry steered off the highway toward the large tourist center and parked in the near-vacant lot. The building's exterior matched the sandy color of the historic mesa behind it.

Marshall removed the key from the ignition. "Let's go."

23

Tegan picked up a tour map of Masada inside the bright, polished visitors' center and hurried after the others as they loped through the building to get to the cable car, forgoing the charming little museum and an audiovisual display about Masada's history. A smiling woman behind the counter had advised them to board the next car, as the last ride back for the day was in two hours. The center was fairly empty, giving the place an eerie, deserted feel.

I knew tourism would be down, but this is crazy, Tegan thought. *There's just one family here. Wait, what's that?*

She veered away from the group to study a gray model of the mountaintop fortress. It looked exactly as their research had shown. They'd scoured photos upon photos of Masada and studied every available online map to try and identify the cave in which the box of seeds might be hidden. All of them knew the place in detail, albeit theoretically, but Tegan was still eager to see the real thing.

She circled the model, hoping to spot the caves they'd singled out as possibilities, all of which were on the southeastern slope of the mesa. The cable car would take them to the northeast sector and drop them by the remains of King Herod's grand, three-tiered palace. They'd only have to follow the fortress walls to reach the other end of the plateau.

Unable to properly distinguish the caves, Tegan ran to catch up to the others as they went out back. Their cable car awaited them at the base station on an open platform. Relieved that they had the roomy cabin to themselves, Tegan stepped inside first.

With the disease going around, I'd hate to be crammed in with tourists like sardines.

The ground below her withdrew as the glass gondola ascended at an angle. They traversed over the Snake Path, an ancient dirt track that zigzagged from the fort to the base of the mesa, in silent observation. A lone couple trekked down, evidently having finished their tour of the two-acre fort.

The cable car docked a few minutes later. The group marched onto a wooden pathway and climbed the steps to the main entrance to the fortress.

"Look at this place," Aari breathed.

Before them sprawled a flat expanse of land. The ruins of Herod's other residence lay some two hundred yards ahead. Known as the western palace, it was where Herod was said to have conducted his business. Tegan knew from their research that the king's throne room sat in one corner of the edifice. Next to it stood the remnants of an ancient Byzantine church.

To their right was the northern complex which had housed an administrative building, a quarry, a commandant's headquarters, and storerooms among other things. The northern palace, with its three terraces, was perched on the steep slopes behind it, out of view.

Kody pulled the brim of his cap lower over his eyes. "You know, it's a lot barer than I thought it would be."

"This fortress is over two thousand years old," Aari said hastily, "and it's seen its fair share of conflicts. If we could get closer, we'd see so much more of the—"

"Nope." Jag shepherded them all in the opposite direction. "Not today, brother."

They trooped along the eastern wall, rubbernecking past the rubble to glimpse the glossy blue waters of the Dead Sea below. Tegan smiled to herself. *For something with such a grisly name, it looks really pretty from here.*

A handful of tourists meandered about, snapping photos and taking videos, seeming to be at ease.

Nothing like being in the middle of nowhere, away from the noise and problems of the world. Tegan looked on ruefully as a young couple strolled by. *Either one of them could be sick right now, or they could get sick, or someone they know . . . We really need to find the cure. No one should have to deal with any more deaths and heartaches.*

Her gaze wandered to Jag as he walked ahead between Marshall and Kody. *Poor guy. Not a single word from him about his grandmother's passing since we left home. He's still angry, and now it's seeped into his bones.*

The meager fragments of two small palaces stood near the center of the plateau. A few tourists sat on the large stones, taking in the stunning view of the desert and the sea. Tegan nodded a polite hello and they grinned back.

"Teegs," Jag called suddenly.

She looked up at him. He pointed at a bird balanced on the rubble, barely longer than the distance from her wrist to the tips of her fingers. Its lustrous black plumage was dashed with an orange strip on either wing. Tegan stared at Jag in blank confusion, then understood. *Oh, right!*

The friends and the Sentry settled beside the tourists. Tegan closed her eyes. When she opened them a moment later, she found herself observing through the eyes of the bird. *Alley-oop! Come on! Up you go, you little thing.*

Having full motor control of the creature she took off, soaring above the heads of everyone below. A slight breeze ruffled the bird's feathers as she guided it toward the southeastern slope of Masada. She banked left, taking a thorough, long look at the cavities in the mountainside; the friends hadn't been able to gather how many caves there were exactly, so their next best option was to have Tegan reconnoiter from the air.

She approached one of the caves and hopped inside. *Agh, the sun's setting on the other side. It's too dark to see anything in here.*

She hopped back out and took flight, then severed the mind-link with the bird. The others were waiting expectantly for her report when she returned to herself.

"I counted eight openings," she said. "They're about twenty to thirty feet apart, although a couple looked too small to be caves."

"Did you go in and check them out?" Jag asked.

"It was too dark to see much inside."

He uttered a sound of disappointment. "Then we'll have to check each one. Are there footholds and handholds we can use?"

"I think so."

"Gotta wait until everyone's gone," Marshall muttered, "or we won't be able to get into the caves without drawing attention."

"You mean we're staying past closing?" Tegan asked, alarmed. "Then we need to move our car. Leaving it in the parking lot will raise suspicion."

"I'll do it," Jag said, holding out his hand to Marshall.

The Sentry slapped the keys into his palm. "Be quick."

"Hey, that's my specialty."

Once Jag took off, the group scouted for a place to lay low. The ruins of the small fort at the southern tip of the plateau provided some feasible cover to slouch behind. Tegan transmitted their location to Jag, then she and Mariah settled against the half wall of rubble next to Marshall. Kody and Aari sat on his other side, making sure to stay out of view of the railed pathway that circled behind them.

"Do you think there are guards who come up here after hours?" Mariah asked.

"Dunno," Marshall said. "Considering the state of the world and the fact that Israel is already in a pretty volatile position, it's possible."

"Not to mention, this *is* a historical landmark," Aari added. "Logically, they should have some form of security up here."

The sound of wrapper crinkling made everyone look to Kody, who munched happily on a protein bar. When he noticed them, he waved the bar in their direction. "Want some?"

They shook their heads.

"Always prepared when it comes to food," Mariah sighed.

"And still, he barely gains weight."

"Victor gave me some of these before he left the Lodge," Kody said. "Apparently they should last me better than the other stuff. Boy, was he right."

Mention of the Canadian Sentry triggered a thought. Tegan turned to Marshall. "We haven't heard any news from Victor's end. It's been more than a few days since we saw him, hasn't it?"

Marshall shrugged. "I hardly hear from the guy to begin with. He usually gets a mission and goes on total radio silence for a while."

"How do you know if each other's okay, then? Actually, how do you keep in contact with every other Sentry?"

"Our network's a bit funky. The original Sentries put a system in place that allows us the chance of knowing a Sentry who knows another that we don't. And, with technology, it's even easier now for those without telepathy. For example, Deverell, Gareth, and I are in a text group. They spam it with funny photos—what are they called, memes?—and interesting articles, so I know they're fine. Victor, on the other hand, will be in touch maybe once or twice a month. More so now because of everything that's going on."

"I'm guessing you all keep in contact with the Elders, then," Aari said. "At least, if you have telepathy."

Marshall combed his fingers through his styled hair. "We never really did up until the past year or so."

"How come?"

"We're Sentries. Our main duty, before the five of you came along, was to live among regular folks in our communities and help keep light alive—and to protect it, and the people, when required. There was never a need to contact the Elders until you entered the playing field and Reyor began moving the chess pieces."

Something still nagged at Tegan. "You said that Reyor would be visiting a Sanctuary somewhere in Kazakhstan real soon. That was a week ago. Shouldn't we have heard from Victor by now?"

"Not necessarily," he said. "Relax, kiddo. I know him well enough. And if anything's wrong, all he has to do is reach out to me. He's got telepathy, too."

"You've worked with him, then?" Kody asked as he took a peek over the rubble wall. Tegan followed suit and saw Jag approaching from afar, but Marshall's clipped tone brought her attention back to him.

"I can count on one hand how many times we've worked together."

Tegan lightly bonked her head against his shoulder. "There's a bit of friction between you two, huh?"

Marshall smiled sheepishly. "I do a bang-up job of hiding that, don't I?"

"You sure do."

"Colback was good back in the day, brighter. Not that he was necessarily easy to talk to. The guy's solitary by nature, but he'd always listen when people came to him. Then several years ago . . ." He hesitated. "Mmh—you know, it's not really my place to tell."

What would make someone go from okay to hard around the edges, maybe even hard on the inside? Tegan wondered to herself, tapping her jaw. *An issue of the heart, right? So . . .*

"He lost someone?" she ventured.

Marshall hesitated again, then nodded. "More than one. I can't even begin to fathom the pain. And that was on top of . . . Let's say he's been through rougher patches than most folks I know. And I feel bad for him, I really do, but he fell into a dark place and pushed a lot of people out. Working with him got harder, at least for me. He gets along well enough with Dev and Gareth and a handful of others. It's the strangest thing, but for some reason I feel as though he loathes me."

Kody gently nudged Marshall with his knee as if to comfort him. "Well, we definitely don't loathe you, and I for one am glad we've got you here, Mr. Poster-boy Sentry."

Marshall threw his head back, laughing, and smacked it

against the stone wall. He winced, rubbing the sore spot. "Ouch."

The group let out a short laugh just as Jag rejoined them. "What'd I miss?"

"Marshall hurting himself," Kody said cheerily.

"Brilliant."

"Everything good?" Marshall asked.

Jag passed him the keys. "Yeah. Our ride's in the parking lot of a hostel just down the road from the visitor center."

"That was quick. Who needs the cable car when we've got a speed demon?"

"I made sure no one was on the Snake Path. Don't wanna spook the tourists or the locals."

The six of them waited, conversing softly as the fortress grew quieter. Tegan checked her phone. *Four p.m. Last cable car would have just left, and it should get dark in about fifty minutes.*

Sure enough, the sun began to sing its goodbye for the day in a glow of golden ichor that trailed through the Judean Desert, its echoes heard for another hour until twilight appeared. The heavens started to wink with emerging stars, and the waxing moon painted the fortress in its pale sheen.

Tegan felt warm on the inside as she watched the cosmos run its course. There was something just so utterly magical about the world when day gave way to night, about the way it made her entire being come alive.

Marshall stood up, grumbling. "I'm getting stiff in my old age."

"You're thirty-three!" Mariah admonished. "My mom would whack you with her ironing board if she ever heard you complain. I can hear her now: 'Thirty-three! *Thirty-three?* And he has the gall to say that's *old?* If that's the case, then I'm ancient!'"

Marshall pulled Tegan and Kody to their feet. "Your mom's such a sweet lady. She'd never assault me with an ironing board."

"Don't test her."

"You can see where 'Riah gets her spunk from," Aari said.

"Don't you test me either, Aari."

"That was a compliment!"

Tegan scanned the area, ensuring there were no stragglers or security detail, before taking the lead. They headed past an open water cistern and stopped between two small buildings adjacent to the eastern wall. "Here's a good place to drop the gear."

Marshall removed a pouch from his backpack and pulled out an ultralight tactical ladder. As he drew out a couple of climbing ropes from his bag, he said, "Before we do this, I need to ask: Are you guys okay going down? Free-climbing isn't exactly safe and I'll gladly do it on my own if you aren't—"

"You're not getting rid of us that easy," Jag told him firmly.

Marshall's mouth quirked up. "Alright. So if there are eight caves like Tegan said, then four of us can go down, take two each, and be done with this in no time. Who's keen on joining?"

"I am," Jag said.

Tegan stood beside him. "I'm coming, too."

Kody raised his hand. "I'll go, but I gotta say that ladder looks pretty sketchy to me."

"It's designed for combat situations," Marshall assured him. He threaded the climbing ropes through the two eyelets of the ladder and fastened them around a sturdy boulder at the edge of the mesa. "Look. Reinforced steps and Kevlar sides. It's military grade, Kody."

"Mmkay . . ."

"Mariah and I will stay topside," Aari said, "keep an eye out for guards or whatever else shows up."

Tegan grabbed three small walkie-talkies from her backpack and tested them, then put the volume on the second-lowest setting. Since she, Jag, and Marshall were the only ones with telepathy, the others would need radios to keep in touch.

She passed one to Mariah and another to Kody, then gave the last to Marshall before she went to scrutinize his handiwork with the ladder. "Are we gonna lower the ladder over each opening to drop one person at a time?"

"Nah." Marshall clipped the radio to his belt. "It'll be faster if we just climb down from the middle, then scale sideways."

He tugged on the ropes, tossed the keys for the SUV to Aari for safekeeping, and started to descend, quickly leveling with the row of caves. Using hand and footholds on the mountainside, he made his way to the westernmost openings. Kody went down after him and moved to the two caves on the east cautiously.

Tegan followed, taking the openings between Kody and the ladder, leaving Jag to check the remaining ones on the other side. She'd never had a problem with heights, but it was a bit unnerving to see the desert floor a thousand feet below her shoes.

"Good luck, guys!" Mariah whispered. "Be safe!"

Aari and Mariah watched as Jag disappeared below their line of sight. "And then there were none," Aari murmured. He grabbed their bags and stuffed them into a small, unidentified stone building near the tip of the plateau.

As he returned, Mariah stepped away from the edge and craned her neck to look up at the sky. "This is such a treat," she said. "I've never seen so many stars in my life. Even away from city lights back home it was never anything close to this."

"There's hardly any light pollution for miles, and the air is real dry here. Picture-perfect for viewing."

Mariah was motionless for a while as she stargazed. "You know, if these were normal times, we'd be in our senior year. In a few months we would've graduated and gone our separate ways. Kody to the Air Force like his dad, Jag and Tegan probably sticking around until they figured out what they wanted, and you to some Ivy League university if they accepted you. Hah, who am I kidding? They definitely would have accepted you."

Aari grinned. "No, no Ivy League school for me. I wanted to go to MIT."

"And what did you want to study there?"

"Computer science and artificial intelligence."

"AI? Really? Haven't you learned anything? Do the words *Terminator* and *Cylon* ring any bells?"

Aari unconsciously dug into the dirt with the heel of his shoe. "Pfft. And what exactly did you want to do? Last I remember, you were pulling your hair out over what academic route to take."

Mariah twirled around to examine the vast fortress behind them. "I really wanted to go into scriptwriting for TV, and maybe eventually movies."

"Seriously? That would've been awesome." Aari's heel struck something hard. He bent down and picked up an inch-and-a-half-long rock resembling an arrowhead. "And your mom's cool with that?"

"She had lots of questions, as always, but she did eventually get on board. Even if she hadn't, it wouldn't have mattered because, hey, look where we are now."

Aari faced the fortress with her, bouncing the rock in his palm. "Where we are," he repeated, almost inaudibly.

It came out of nowhere. A quick flash behind his eyes, somehow both bright and dark. Bodies upon bodies lying in red rivers that tainted the ground and pooled at his feet. Women, children, men. Glassy-eyed, unbreathing.

He dropped the rock, blinking fast, and the image disappeared. Mariah was holding his arms to steady him. "Hey, hey! You okay?"

"Y-yeah." He turned his back to the fortress, struggling for breath. "Can you . . . can you feel them?"

She let go of him. "Feel who?"

"Them. The ones who died here. The ones who took their own lives."

"What, are you into the supernatural now?" she joked. When he didn't react to her attempt at humor, she seemed mystified. "Yeah, I can feel this . . . this deep kind of sadness and the historic weight of the place, but I don't think I feel *them*. Are you sure you're alright?"

The radio clipped to Mariah's back pocket crackled softly, and Marshall's voice came through. *"Hey, eyes in the sky, everything kosher up there?"*

Mariah pulled out the walkie-talkie. "Everything's swell. How's it going with you?"

"We've almost cleared our first caves. Nothing to report yet. Will keep you informed."

"Copy that." She clipped the device back to her pocket and

returned to the conversation as if they hadn't been interrupted. "What happened, Aari? You're pale."

"I was here," he murmured. "Not here-here, more like farther back in the fortress. Bodies—the suicide that happened. I saw it. Am I crazy? Because I swear I saw them, but my mind is telling me that's impossible."

"What in the world are you talking about?"

"It's like I was there. Mariah, it *felt* real. I don't know what it was, but I . . . I just . . ."

Her eyes scoured his face, as if assessing his mental state. Aari moved closer to her, voice soft. "You really didn't feel them?"

"Not the way you just described. But maybe . . ." She pursed her lips. "We were told by the Elders that we would uncover more of our powers."

He snorted. "Sure, but seeing into the past? Come on. That's a stretch, even for us."

"We'll talk to Marshall about it, okay? We'll talk to him and find out what happened to you. It was just that one thing you saw, right? Nothing else?"

"Yeah. But this is ridiculous."

She fiddled with the pendant around her neck. "I think just about anything is possible now, don't you?"

Aari looked at her, miserable. She rubbed the side of his head. "Right, I forgot. You need hard facts for everything."

"Preferably."

"That's funny, considering your favorite movie of all time is *Contact*."

It was a thinly veiled attempt to lighten the mood, but she was trying to shake him out of his funk and Aari felt he ought to indulge her. "Hey, it's not like *Contact* was a B-grade horror flick. Okay, yeah, there's a reference to an alien civilization, but it's really about the conflict between science and faith. Plus—"

"And here I thought it was about you going googly-eyed over the idea of Marvin the Martian hiding somewhere in outer space."

"If you'd just watch the movie like I keep telling you guys to, then you'd know better," Aari complained.

"Bah, fine, I will. One day. Sorry for interrupting. You were saying?"

"I like *Contact* because of the story's underlying conflict. And now with all that we've gone through, I'm learning more and more every day that the physical and the metaphysical are basically different branches of the same tree. Whether it's science or spirituality, we're just viewing reality from different angles. But I'm not saying that it isn't hard to wrap my mind around everything we're going through." He stopped, then grinned. "And besides, Matthew McConaughey and Jodie Foster in one movie? Total OTP."

"*Now* you're speaking my language!"

"If you ever tell anyone I said those words—"

"Oh, bite me. There's nothing wrong with that."

"Yes, there is."

"No, there isn't."

"Yes, there is."

"*No*, there—"

"*Atsor!*" a voice thundered.

Aari's blood ran cold. Slowly, he and Mariah turned around to face a powerful beam of light. They raised their hands to shield their eyes, both moving instinctively to block the boulder behind them.

If he sees the ropes, we're in trouble, Aari thought.

The guard lowered the flashlight; Aari could only see a silhouette as his eyes tried to adjust to the sudden shift in brightness.

"*Atah medaber ivrit?*" the man asked.

Ivrit . . . that means Hebrew. He's asking if we speak Hebrew. Aari shuffled through the few words he knew in the language. "*Loh, loh ivrit. Anglit.* We speak English."

The guard became disgruntled upon hearing that. In stilted English, he asked, "What you doing here?"

Aari swallowed. "Uh . . ."

Mariah suddenly rounded on him. "I told you!" she screeched.

"I told you we shouldn't have come up here!"

Aari nearly tripped over himself in his surprise. "What—"

"No! Don't even try! I *told* you, there's no need for something overly romantic! A simple day trip to the Dead Sea's a good enough date! But do you ever listen to me?"

It took a moment for Aari to catch on and when he did, it took everything he had to keep a straight face. "I was trying to do something nice for you!" he yelled back. He noticed that she'd slipped her hand to her back pocket where the radio was, just out of the guard's view. "But you always have to go and make a big fuss about it, don't you?"

"*A fuss?* Look at where your harebrained idea landed us. Thanks *so* much! What a fan-freakin'-tastic night! I'd rank this as the worst date of all time!"

"Hey, hey!" the guard boomed. "Calm down!"

Mariah stormed past the guard, taking his attention with her. Aari quickly faced the boulder and deflected the light, rendering it and the ropes invisible. He backed up so he and Mariah stood together, forcing the guard to turn toward them, away from the big rock. From the corner of his eye, he saw that the white-haired man sported a gray shirt and black pants, a holster on his hip.

Definitely a park guard, he concluded. *Old guy, but he sure doesn't move like one.*

"My mother warned me about you," Mariah hissed.

Aari stifled an eye roll. *Of course, pick the most clichéd of clichés.*

"What you doing here?" the guard demanded again. "Hours closed!"

"This complete *idiot* thought that staying here after hours would be romantic," Mariah snapped. "I told him no, we really shouldn't, but he kept insisting. I am so, so sorry!"

"Show ID." The guard, though gruff, was obviously thrown off by the quarreling.

Aari, needing to keep the boulder in his line of sight to hide it, reached into his pocket and pulled out his passport, as did

Mariah. The guard took the documents, then stopped. Aari knew the man's eyes were on him.

Probably wondering why I keep looking past him, he thought.

The guard whirled around. "What you looking?"

Yep.

"What you—" The man halted. He peered straight in the direction of the boulder. In his peripherals, Aari could see the guard's mounting perplexity, as if something was missing.

"Nothing, sir," he said. "I just don't want to look at her, because she's so bloody ungrateful when all I did was try to be more romantic like she *wants* me to!"

"Don't you dare!" Mariah screamed. "I am so done with you!"

"Yeah? Well I'm done with *you*!"

"Quiet!" the guard bellowed. "My God!"

Aari's heart raced as he watched the man go through their passports, alternating his flashlight beam between the documents and their faces. Then he slipped the passports into his shirt pocket and motioned for the teenagers to walk ahead of him, back to the north side of the mesa.

"Are we in trouble?" Mariah asked. "Please, it was an honest mistake! I'll never date another moron!"

"I send you down. Other guard will get you. Walk, please."

Aari fell in step with Mariah, very conscious of the guard behind them. *Oh no. Oh no, no, no. What are we gonna do? Where are they gonna take us?*

"What's that?" the guard asked harshly. "Madam, back pocket. Radio?"

Every ounce of color drained from Aari's face.

"Is that radio?" the guard repeated.

Mariah cleared her throat. "Yes. But it's not on." She pulled it out, and as she did, Aari caught sight of her thumb on the dial, discreetly turning the radio off. "See?"

"Where other one?"

Aari whipped around furiously. "She chucked it over the side of the mountain! She threw it away in one of her stupid fits!"

Mariah kicked dirt at him. "Don't make *me* look insane!"

"I don't have to! You're doing a damn fine job on your own!"

"Enough!" the guard shouted. "Okay, that's it! You go down. Now. And you will not come here again."

Jag didn't need a walkie-talkie or Kody's acute hearing to overhear the raised voices on top of the mountain. He opened his mind to Tegan. *Jeez. If I didn't know better, I'd think there's actually a lovers' quarrel going on up there.*

Did you hear Mariah, though? Tegan asked. *'My mother warned me about you'?*

She's adorable.

She is. But I guess we're compromised now.

No, we're not. They are. Question is, what's the guard gonna do with them?

They were caught trespassing at night on a romantic date, and they're teenagers with American passports. That can't get them into too much trouble . . . can it?

Jag bit his lip. *I don't know. We're entering a whole new world with all that's going on. They may want to be more cautious and hold them in a cell or something.*

You wanna check with Marshall, see what we should do?

Yeah. Jag ended the link with her and established another. *Hey, Marshall.*

The Sentry heaved a sigh. *Well, that was something. I think Mariah purposely held down the transmission on her radio so we could hear what was happening.*

Smart girl for sure. What do we do now?

We need to find those seeds, but we can't lose Mariah and Aari. It's your call, Jag.

Jag, sitting in the hollow of the first cave he'd searched, bowed his head and grunted as he thought to himself. *Seeds, friends. Seeds, friends . . . Actually, no. Save the world, friends. Save the world . . .*

He reestablished the link with Marshall. *We need to keep*

searching. But let's make it quick.

Wilco. I'll let Kody know.

Jag linked back with Tegan. *Find the box.*

Roger that, Captain.

Stop it.

Sorry. She withdrew from his mind, though Jag suspected she wasn't sorry at all.

He backed out of the big cave, expertly finding footholds as his hands worked across the hard surface. It had been a while since he'd done any rock climbing; as much as he loved it, the activity haunted him. All he could think of was Roderick's face as the defective cam gave way; his friend screaming as he plunged toward the ground far below and landing with a sickening, gut-wrenching crunch.

Jag dug his fingers into the rock face. *Stop. Stop it. Stop thinking about it. At least Roddy's alive.*

Another voice, pervasive and dark, wormed into his ear. *He's alive, yes, but paralyzed from the waist down. Stuck in a wheelchair. Because of you.*

The cam was defective. I never thought—

You led that team up the mountain! You promised you'd look out for them! You told them it would all be fine, that they were safe in your expert hands. You cocky son of a—

It wasn't my fault!

It was! You didn't check the equipment as thoroughly as you should have! Now Roderick's paralyzed for life! And you, you have the audacity to think that you can lead your friends into this battle against an enemy undoubtedly more powerful than you? Watch them all fall! Step by step, THEY—WILL—ALL—FALL.

Jag pressed his forehead against the rock wall, teeth gnashing as he did everything he could to expel the voice from his mind; it had been gone for so long, he'd dared to hope that it would never return. But it always did.

He timed his breathing until his jaws unclenched, then continued along, crossing the twenty-foot gap to the second cave and pulling himself in. Fishing out the small flashlight from his pocket, he crouched in the space and ran the beam over the ceiling. *Zilch.*

He reported back to Tegan and Marshall; neither of them had had any luck either. Kody radioed the Sentry to say his search had also turned up nothing.

Jag lay on his back in the hollow, the crook of his elbow covering his face. *Is there another cave we missed?* he asked Marshall.

No, the Sentry said. He sounded peeved. *I guess it's the curse of finding a cure. It won't be where it's supposed to be.*

Jag then remembered how Marshall, Aari, and Tegan had flown to Nevada during the summer to search for the dopant, a countermeasure to stop the nanomites from laying waste to the Great Plains. They were told it should have been in a lake, but it ended up being somewhere else entirely.

He hurled his flashlight deeper into the cave. It hit the wall and rolled back to him, flickering. *Great. So what now? We don't have the seeds, Mariah and Aari are caught, and we can't contact them. Just . . . great.*

He got no response.

Marshall?

The man's voice returned, and he was animated. *Sorry about that! Kody just radioed in, said he thinks he might have gotten a visual of another cave sixty or seventy feet below him.*

Jag scooped up his flashlight. *Really? He's sure?*

Ninety percent sure.

That's good enough for me. I'll head down and have a look.

Jag, no. I'll check out this one. The ladder only goes another twenty feet down. That's maybe fifty feet of free-climbing. Let me handle this.

But I should be the one to go. This is our mission. You said we call the shots, right? Then I'm calling this one. It's okay, Marshall. I'm in my element.

So am I.

Jag started to work his way out of the cave. *I'm going.*

NO!

He faltered. The Sentry had never used that tone before.

No, Marshall reiterated, calmer this time. *Not for this. This bears too much risk and I will not put you in that position.*

We're supposed to learn how to call these shots for ourselves. Your words.

Fine, you're right. I did say that. You decide if you want to go, but keep in mind that we can't afford to lose you. Or the others.

Jag hunched forward. *I'm trying to be a leader,* he thought to himself. *Doesn't that mean their safety comes first? How can I ask people to take risks while I remain protected? This is messed up.*

Clenching his jaw, he finally relented. *Alright. You go.*

Thanks, kiddo.

Jag leaned out of the cave, watching Marshall work his way toward him. He moved with a certain ease and comfort. When he arrived at Jag's cave, he looked up and patted the teenager on the cheek with such affection that Jag managed to crack a small smile. Once he passed, Jag climbed out and followed him. The moon lit the ground far below with a ghostly luster.

That's a fatal fall, he thought. *Be careful, Marshall.*

Jag waited until the man had descended to the edge of the ladder before getting on it himself and hanging tight. He spotted Tegan and Kody watching from their respective caves; they looked as apprehensive as he felt.

Below them, Marshall navigated the terrain like he'd been raised on it. His effortlessness should have put Jag's stomach-churning to rest, but it didn't.

Marshall made it to the cave and slipped in. Jag allowed himself to let go of the breath he'd been holding and exchanged weary smiles with his friends. They shook their heads, simultaneously stressed and relieved.

The beam from Marshall's flashlight suddenly appeared in their faces as his voice filled Jag's head. *It's here! The crescent! It's right here just like the Elders said!*

Jag almost let out a whoop but quickly slapped a hand over

his mouth. By the jubilant grins Kody and Tegan shared, he guessed that the Sentry had passed the message on to them.

That's great! Jag said. *Is the box there?*

Haven't checked! I wanted to tell you guys first—be right back.

The light and the Sentry disappeared into the cave again. Jag impatiently readjusted his grip on the ladder. *Come on, come on . . .*

The minutes marched on; five, then ten. There was no sign of Marshall. Jag waited a few moments before deciding to reach out telepathically. Just before he did, Marshall reemerged and started to scale up the rock wall.

Do you have it? Jag asked.

The Sentry paused to meet his gaze, face dark. *No.*

The elation in Jag's chest fell like a cement block. *What?*

It doesn't look like that soil's been turned over in ages. Marshall continued his ascent, testing each foothold and handhold with care. *I dug and I dug. It's not there.*

Jag shut his eyes. *We're back to square one.*

He opened his eyes, and everything he saw moved as though time had slowed.

As Marshall reached up to grab the next handhold, the rock under his left foot gave way. He slipped, hands and feet scrambling, fingers digging into the disobliging wall of the mesa. He looked up at the friends, terror slashed across his face, before gravity pulled him backward.

Paralyzed, Jag watched the Sentry plummet toward the ground, a falling angel gone to meet his end.

25

NO!

Jag pushed his feet into the rock wall and released his hold on the ladder. The force of the Earth yanked on him as he activated his speed and propelled himself groundward. In an instant he was rocketing down the slope. The world around him slowed as he outraced the acceleration of gravity. Adrenaline blazed through his veins. Wind slapped at his hair as dirt and rocks jet-washed behind him in a turbulent wake.

As he drew even with Marshall, the Sentry turned his head to him, face frozen in horror. Their eyes met for a microsecond. Jag pulled ahead as the dry riverbed in the canyon below rushed to meet them. Now with enough distance between them, he slowed just enough to match the Sentry's velocity.

Marshall crashed onto Jag, back-first. A burning like he'd never felt before flared through Jag's legs as he plowed his heels into the slope, trying to slow their fall. Marshall's full weight bore down on him more with each passing moment. A realization hit him, then—at this speed, a soft landing would be impossible.

He shot past the dusty riverbed at the base of the mountain, Marshall fused to his back by inertia, and traveled nearly a quarter of the way up the opposite slope, using its gradient to soak up his momentum. As the world around him edged toward its normal speed, his pace dragged and he lost his footing. He raked his toes into the incline but had no traction and tumbled backward. He twisted around, frantically making a grab for Marshall, but his grip loosened and the Sentry toppled after him.

Everything was a dizzying whirl of earth and rocks and pain. Jag felt something snap but had no breath to cry out. He finally rolled to the bottom, landing spread-eagle on his back. His vision blurred, eyes damp with shock.

A second later, Marshall landed on top of him. The cords in Jag's neck pulled as he fought not to scream. Trembling, he forced himself to sit up and weakly put his arms around the Sentry. "I got you," he wheezed. "I got you. I . . ."

He collapsed, blacking out.

Kody had witnessed the entire scene, horrified. He zeroed in his vision on the crumpled bodies nearly a thousand feet below, his mouth dry. When he saw their chests just barely rise and fall, he groaned in relief. "They're alive!"

Tegan swung out of her cave and worked her way toward the ladder. "We need to get to them!"

They climbed back to the top of the mesa, scraping arms and knees in their haste. Kody started to sprint toward the entrance of the fortress, but Tegan hissed. "Wait! The ladder!"

He did a one-eighty and ran to the boulder to untie the climbing ropes. "Where are our bags?"

She cursed. "Aari and Mariah probably hid them. I'll look around."

"Hurry! And watch out for the guard!"

He unknotted the ropes and pulled up the ladder, checking over his shoulder every few seconds until Tegan returned with their bags. They packed everything and, staying close to the eastern wall, moved quickly toward the entrance. A beam of light worked down in the opposite direction, but it was on the other side of the plateau.

"The cable cars wouldn't happen to be working, would they?" Kody whispered, though he knew the answer.

Tegan led him out of the entrance and down the steps to the Snake Path. "Brace yourself," she warned. "I don't think it'll be an easy hike."

That was an understatement.

The rocky path wound for two and a half miles and though

Kody, like the rest of the group, was in peak physical condition, he soon felt fire searing in his legs. At one point, Tegan had to use the railing to steady herself. They passed a water bottle between them as they ran down, sweat coating their skin in spite of the cool night.

The vastness of the mountains was lost on Kody. Any other time he would have felt small among them, and in complete awe, but in his head he kept playing Marshall's fall and Jag's rescue over and over.

When they reached the riverbed, his legs instantly turned to jelly. He stumbled but Tegan hoisted him to his feet. "Up!"

He sucked in air and, trying to block out his body's screeching protests, fell in step with her as they veered into the canyon. *It took longer to get down here than I thought . . . I hope they're okay.*

They found Marshall slumped, unconscious, on top of Jag. Both were battered and bloodied. Kody wrapped his arms around the Sentry's chest and pulled him away, then pressed two fingers to the man's neck and felt for his pulse.

"Check them for injuries," Tegan said, kneeling beside Jag.

Kody carefully did a head-to-toe assessment on Marshall. "Apart from some bleeding and bruises, I think he's okay," he reported. "Jag took the brunt of the fall."

"Seems like it." Tegan sat back on her heels, completing her own check on Jag. "I could be wrong, but I'm pretty sure his left leg is broken."

"What do we do?"

She got up and paced, hands on her hips, lips tightly pressed together. Kody watched her anxiously. "Teegs?"

"I . . . I don't—"

The radio clipped to his belt suddenly crackled to life. *"Marshall? Kody?"*

Kody whipped the device to his mouth. "'Riah! Are you guys okay?"

"Yeah! The other guard let us go with a warning after checking our passports again. He said we could wait till the first tour bus

comes in the morning to leave, but we told him our car's parked at the hostel and we're staying there for the night."

Tegan took the radio from Kody. "Glad to hear you're okay, but we've got a situation. Get to the canyon north of the visitor's center and be prepared to punch the gas out of here."

"Okay. We're half a mile out. We'll be there in about two minutes. The guards might see us, though."

"I know, but there's no other way."

"Did you find the box?"

"No. Just get here and we'll fill you in on the way out."

Tegan passed the radio back to Kody and he clipped it onto his belt. She took out an extra T-shirt from her bag, ripped it in half, and doused the strips with the last bit of water from the bottle. Kody grabbed one of the cloths as well, and together they worked on cleaning the blood off their unconscious friends.

"I can't believe that just happened," he murmured. "I still haven't processed—"

"Don't think," Tegan advised him curtly. "Save it for later. Here they come now."

The rented SUV was making its way along the riverbed; its headlights were off but the roar of the engine echoed in the quiet night. It skidded to a halt beside them and Aari and Mariah leapt out, mouths hanging open.

"What happened?" Mariah squeaked.

"Later!" Tegan barked. "Get them in first!"

They carried Jag and Marshall into the SUV and clambered in after them. Tegan dove into the driver's seat and Kody jumped in beside her, beating the dashboard wildly. "Go, go, go!"

With hearts hammering they tore out of the canyon, not bothering to see if the guards had spotted them, and left Masada shrinking in their rearview mirrors.

A dirty white sedan trailed the SUV from a distance as it raced back toward Jerusalem. Behind the wheel sat a monster of a man, with irises as black as the pits of hell and a hulking body scarred in ink. A cigarette stuck out from the side of his mouth, the glow from the cherry barely lighting up a visage marred by an untidy scar that stretched from the forehead, past the partially blind left eye, to the chin.

A much shorter, auburn-haired man in the passenger seat watched the SUV with the sharpness of a hawk; his square face twitched in distaste.

The giant glanced at him. “What is that look for, Mr. Ajajdif?”

“It’s thanks to Tony’s stupidity—*nyet*, ineptitude—that we’re stuck out here keeping an eye on these brats. I could be running the mine site and Sanctuary in peace. Dr. Deol just rolled out the new line of Marauders, too, and they’re even better than the last.”

“All I heard was that they’re not hindered by daylight anymore. A minor upgrade not worth wetting yourself over, if you ask me.”

“I didn’t ask you. Besides, that’s only the tip of the iceberg. Point is, they were supposed to bond with each Head of Sanctuary and I wasn’t there.”

“You still have the first field models, sir. Those love you . . . or something. I don’t think killing machines created in labs are able to feel love, are they?”

“Elias, would you please shut up and drive?”

“Ah, come, come, this isn’t bad. I like the change in pace. Better than being holed up at the Sanctuary. We get to stretch our legs out here.”

Vladimir Ajajdif grimaced. "Once a mercenary, always a mercenary, hm?"

"Of course, sir." Elias Hajjar blew smoke out the window. "Agh, those little punks. Do you know how hard it was to keep a cool head around Tony when the girls escaped the Sanctuary? It was humiliating that they got past *me*, but I couldn't let Tony see that or he'd—"

"Get over yourself. I honestly can't tell what gets under your skin more, the brats or Tony."

"I'd gladly strangle them all if I could." Hajjar patted the pistol sitting in the open console between them. "It would be so easy to grab the kids right now. It'd be hassle-free, too, with the new tranquilizers we got from Dr. Deol. I swear, Quest Biotech creates the best toys."

"We're not here for that," Ajajdif said. "Not yet, anyway."

They passed through a few darkened towns in silence, always keeping the SUV's taillights within sight. Ajajdif wound down his window and lit a cigarette for himself. He hated the taste of it, but it was something to occupy him.

Hajjar blew out another cloud, wearing a look of contemplation. "Did you see what happened back there? Did you see how *fast* that kid moved? Right down the mountain!"

"You're no stranger to this. You've seen things. In Canada, in New Mexico."

"And here I thought those forest hillbillies were the only ones with these powers."

"It's another reason we can't just swoop in on them right now, and why we have a team waiting for my call. Be patient, my friend."

"Oh, sir, you've never called me that before."

Ajajdif shook his head, unable to help grinning. "How in the world did I get stuck with you all these years, huh?"

"Crap luck."

"Tch, I believe it."

Hajjar hummed deep in his throat, then said, "I'm thinking,

you know, to have been assigned this job . . . that means we're in the Boss's good books."

"I've been in the Boss's good books for a long time, Elias. It's nothing new."

"You can't let me enjoy this one moment, can you, sir? Yes, we all know about the great Vladimir Ajajdif, from a poor town in Russia who found himself homeless in America at eighteen. Then the Boss saw him one day and picked him off the street like the garbage he was sweeping!"

"I could clock you for that."

"You could, but how many of our sparring matches have I won?"

Ajajdif flicked his cigarette ashes at the big man. No one could ever converse with him the way Hajjar did. Despite the difference in their positions in Phoenix's hierarchy, they maintained a professional but amiable camaraderie.

Which is to be expected after nearly a decade of working together, Ajajdif thought. *But long years of service don't always guarantee good company. I wouldn't mind breaking a few teeth of some of the Inner Circle idiots.*

Now at the edge of Jerusalem, they followed the SUV as it came to a halt a quarter mile from the colossal St. Louis French Hospital. Blue and red flashes strobed against the baroque Renaissance architecture as nearly half a dozen ambulances blocked the area around the building. EMTs pulled people on stretchers from the backs of their vehicles.

"They're all sick," Hajjar rumbled. "Poor schmucks. At least we don't have to worry about that."

The SUV reversed and did a U-turn, speeding past them. Hajjar allowed it a short head start, then took off after it. Ajajdif nodded in reluctant approval. "Not going into a hospital full of possibly infected people. Wise move."

Keeping to the edge of the city, the SUV wove through minimal traffic before turning into a residential area and continuing on until arriving at a row of small houses across from a long apartment building. Hajjar turned off the headlights, maintaining a healthy distance.

The teenagers parked in front one of the residences and jumped out. The front door flew open and a man, silhouetted by the light inside, ran out to help them lift a body from the SUV while the rest guided another man out of the vehicle.

"Looks like Mr. Sawyer's conscious," Ajajdif muttered. "Turn into the apartment complex, Elias."

Hajjar did as ordered. He parked a few levels up in an empty stall facing the street, a half wall providing sufficient cover.

"They're probably resting here for the night," he said. "I'll take first shift. You need some sleep. You're looking gaunter than I've seen you in a while."

"It's because I hate being out here." Ajajdif tossed his cigarette out the window and reclined his seat. "If they so much as step out that door, wake me up. I want to make sure we don't screw this up like Tony did."

* * *

Tegan slumped against Mariah on the couch. She was drained now that the adrenaline of the dash to Jerusalem had worn off. In the small open-plan kitchen beside the living and dining room, Kody and Aari spoke quietly, each with a glass of water in hand. Despair polluted the environment, as thick and heavy as smog.

Marshall limped out of a room across from the couch. His cuts and bruises had been cleaned, but he looked a little green from his near-death experience. He'd regained consciousness in a fit of panic just as the friends were about to arrive at the hospital in Jerusalem, and instead directed them toward the home of his IDF associate who'd spared them protective masks upon their arrival in Israel.

The girls scooted over so Marshall could sit between them. "How are you feeling?" Mariah asked.

He smiled tiredly as Kody and Aari made their way over. "I think I'll be seeing that fall in my dreams for a while, but there's no permanent damage. I got off almost scot-free, and that's all thanks to Jag."

Tegan looked toward the room with its door ajar. "Is he okay?"

"Danny took a look and said that he's got a broken tibia and some other injuries. That'll take some time to heal."

Aari paled. "He's out of commission? For how long?"

"A few weeks."

Tegan buried her face against Marshall's arm. "Oh, my God."

"Hey, hey. At least he's okay." Marshall placed a hand on the side of her head, lifting it. "You should go see him. He came around as we were putting the cast on, said he wanted to talk to you."

"He's awake?"

Marshall's friend emerged from the room, wiping his hands on a small towel; Daniel was as tall as the Sentry, though darker in complexion with short black hair. "He is." He had a slight accent but his English was impeccable. "I've done all I can, but I hope you know that he's in no condition to travel."

"Yeah," Marshall said. "Thanks again for letting us crash here, Danny."

"C'mon, Mars. Don't mention it."

Marshall gently nudged Tegan so she'd get off the couch. She gave Daniel a tight-lipped smile as she passed him and entered Jag's room. The man was incredibly friendly and not nosey in the slightest, which was exactly what the group needed. He trusted Marshall, and Marshall trusted him. That was good enough for Tegan.

Jag lay in bed, his leg wrapped in a thick white cast, his head propped up by pillows. His feet, red and blistered, were lathered in ointment. A glass of water and some pain medication rested on the nightstand, and the lamp on the tabletop was the only lighting in the room.

Tegan took a seat in the vacant chair beside the bed. "Hey."

Jag looked at her, eyes barely open. "Hey."

"I see you're already on the good stuff."

"Daniel only gave me two pills."

"Ha. You never were good with meds."

His gaze wandered to the ceiling. "So. No seeds. No cure."

"No."

"Square one."

"Yes. Although, honestly, as disappointed as I am, I'm not really surprised. Nothing's ever handed over on a silver platter, is it?"

"Tegan Ryder, ever the pessimist."

"Realist, thank you very much." She examined his injured leg. "How's this doing?"

"The cast is solid. Marshall put in some of his homemade Dema-Ki healing powder. He said it should accelerate the mending."

Tegan leaned back, resting her feet on the corner of the bed. "You're insane, you know that? And brave. What you did—"

"I agreed to let him climb down, and what happened was the result of that decision."

"He's alive. That's all that matters."

Jag tilted his head toward her, half his face buried in the big pillow, and held out his hand. She took it.

"Maybe this needed to happen," he said. "Me breaking my leg and being stuck here for a while, I mean."

Tegan noticed his eyes shifting away before returning to her. She knew where he was going. She knew it when he'd called her the Spock to his Kirk in the restaurant. She pulled her hand back. "I will not take your place, Jag."

Dumbfounded, he couldn't form words for a full minute. She held his gaze with icy calmness and repeated, "I will not take your place."

"How did you know I was gonna—"

"We've known each other all our lives. I *know* you as much as you know me. The five of us, we're all open books."

"Then you know I can't do this. Right now is the perfect time for you to step in. With all the uncertainty of this mission and the world spiraling out of control, we need someone reliable to lead it. And I know you'll do well."

Tegan looked away. *Why is he still doubting himself? Does he ignore all the years we followed him just because it happened when we were younger? He's cutting loose and trying to slip away again . . . Mmph. Maybe pushing him like this will only keep him at bay forever. Maybe I could keep the gears moving, then by the time he recovers the team'll be all set for him to take the reins again. Yeah. Maybe that's all he needs.*

"Tegan, please—"

She held up her hand. "I'm not going to debate this, so I'll make you a deal. I'll do it. But the moment you're well enough to be in the field with us, you're back on the job."

His expression leapt from pleased to confused, then to surrender. "Alright."

She patted the blanket and got up. "I should let you rest. You look like you're about to pass out."

As she headed to the door, Jag asked, "How are the others?"

"Tired," she said. "Extremely dejected that the seeds weren't in the cave. But you and Marshall surviving the fall is quite literally a lifesaver for all of us."

"We'll find the seeds. It's just a matter of time."

"Time isn't a luxury we have. But I hope you're right." Tegan walked out and found the couch and floor covered with blankets. "What's going on here?"

"Welcome to the communal bed," Kody announced, windmilling his arms. Tegan stared at him blankly. When he realized what he'd said, he looked mortified. "That came out really weird. We're bunking here for the night is what I meant."

Mariah, curled up on the couch, had wrapped herself in a blanket like a burrito. "How is he?"

Tegan grabbed another blanket from the floor and wound it around herself. "He's fine, considering. He was about to knock out so I let him be."

As Marshall helped Daniel pump up an air mattress, he said,

"You four wanna rock-paper-scissors to see who gets this bed?"

"You take it," they piped in unison.

Daniel grinned. "Good bunch of kids you got."

"They're awesome," the Sentry agreed. "But, really, it's been a long day and—"

"And the guy who had a brush with death needs that bed," Tegan finished. "Yes, Marshall, we completely agree."

Daniel capped the mattress's air valve. "All done. So, guys, I have to run an errand early in the morning. I'm going to bed, but *mi casa es su casa*. Eat what you like, watch what you like. Just don't use my toothbrush, okay?"

Marshall bumped the side of his fist against Daniel's. "Thanks, Danny. Again, we really appreciate it."

Aari turned on the TV once Daniel had retired and they were all snug with their blankets on the couch and floor. He flipped through a few stations until coming across an American international news channel. A blonde anchor was listening to a reporter who stood outside the CDC headquarters in Atlanta, Georgia, where a press conference had just concluded.

"Those were definitely some terse remarks from Ruben Flint, the director of the Centers for Disease Control and Prevention," said the reporter, glancing down at a sheet of paper in his hand. "It looks like the United States' decision to close its borders early, though opposed by some, appears to have been its saving grace. We may have staved off large outbreaks. However, we have seen sporadic infections in bigger metropolitan areas. All available resources have been channeled into the investigation of this virus. The pandemic has taken the world by shock and is spreading at an alarming rate, with a hundred and fifty thousand reported cases, and over fifty thousand fatalities globally from both strains."

The anchor looked aghast. "You're saying the mortality rate is thirty-three percent?"

"In all likelihood it's probably higher, because those inflicted by the aging variant will eventually increase that rate."

"Is there any news of a cure? Is a vaccine in the works?"

"I'm afraid not. As we heard from Dr. Flint, this is an entirely new type of virus and there's nothing in the CDC's database that provides a clue about the pathogen. As I said earlier, it's taken health authorities by shock. No doubt experts around the world are scrambling to make sense of this virus and engineer a cure. Vectors are now suspected to be zoonotic, meaning the carriers are most likely birds and/or other animals. It's also believed to be airborne and capable of surviving in the air for about seventy-two hours."

"Is there any additional information, maybe about the incubation period and more about the symptoms?" the anchor asked.

Kody poked Aari's ribs. "Incubation period . . . isn't that the time it takes for the symptoms of an illness to show after a person's been infected?"

"Yeah," Aari said.

"Shh," Tegan whispered, eyes glued to the television.

The reporter held up his notes. "Yes, actually. We do know more now than we did earlier this week, and the picture isn't good. The incubation period is said to be between two to seven days for both variants of the disease. The period of communicability is from the time a person is infected until the moment the victim succumbs. Now, add to that the survivability of the virus in or outside of the deceased host for several days . . ." He let the sentence hang and looked up briefly, ashen, then continued. "Initial symptoms for the first form of the virus, which authorities are calling the Alpha Strain, includes coughing, blurred vision, bleeding in the digestive tract, and signs of accelerated aging such as loss of hair, teeth, and mobility."

"And the second one?"

"At the CDC's last public address, we were told that the initial symptoms of the second variant, known as the Omega Strain, are fever-like. Now we know that the mild headaches the victims experience grow in intensity within days, until they become completely unbearable, resulting in bleeding from the eyes and ears and possible seizures. At that point, those infected erupt in sudden violence before they . . . expire. The reason for this is still unclear."

The anchor stared into the camera, at a loss for words. The reporter on the split screen jumped in to fill the void. "Many countries around the world are considering shutting down all non-essential travel in the coming days and weeks if things get worse."

Mariah took the remote from Aari and turned off the TV. "Okay, I'm done. I don't want to go to sleep feeling even worse."

"Fifty thousand gone, just like that," Aari murmured. "In almost two and a half weeks. That's brutal."

Tegan wrapped herself tighter in her blanket and burrowed deeper into the couch. "And we're at a dead end now."

Marshall, lying on his back on the mattress, said quietly, "If there's one thing I've learned, it's that there are no real dead ends."

Kody turned off the light, and one by one the group fell asleep. Tegan, exhausted, sent a plea to the universe before she, too, nodded off.

Help us.

Along an arm of the partially frozen Irtysh River at the eastern tip of Kazakhstan, construction of a hydroelectric dam was in progress. A ramshackle barge made its last rounds for the year, plying between both banks before winter set in. The rolling, snow-draped slopes on the southern shore gave way to a miniscule town by the water, beside which lay a vast staging area for the hydroelectric project.

Since its independence from the Soviet Union in 1991, Kazakhstan had become the strongest economy in Central Asia. In spite of global turmoil, the nation's economy was relatively sound due to oil exports. Though the country maintained a stable government with an authoritarian form of democracy, greed and corruption in public and private undertakings benefited Phoenix Corporation's construction division, as well as its more clandestine operation. Free from government oversight, the hydroelectric project provided cover to build a Sanctuary.

Like Russia, Kazakhstan had been mostly spared by the nanomite scourge—though certainly not due to magnanimity—and the government-controlled media kept this fact as closely guarded as possible to avoid raids on its grain reserves. Sitting between Russia and China as they warred earned the country a great profit from skyrocketing oil prices, but that didn't protect it from the virus. Even so, while the illness affecting those in larger cities had started to spread outward, the workers at the remote project site seemed to be faring well.

The hills to the east of the small town both supplied construction materials for the dam and concealed the entrance to the underground Sanctuary, which resembled the five others in layout. Inside the main administrative building of the subterranean complex, two pairs of footsteps echoed down the extended hallway, the pitter-patter of one as it tried to keep pace with the stark snapping of the other.

Dr. Nate stole a quick glance at the looming figure beside him. The Boss, garbed as usual in a long black coat with the golden hood pulled up, walked in silence. The doctor had instructed employees to vacate specific areas within the administrative section upon their arrival three days prior, leaving them exclusively to him and his superior.

He looked down at the tablet in his hands, scrolling through a file he'd put together just minutes before meeting the Boss. "Increased productivity in the Sanctuary 'as been nothing short of remarkable since our arrival," he said jauntily. "I suppose sometimes all that's needed is the motivation of a strong presence."

When the Boss answered, the deep, digitally distorted voice that emerged made the doctor jump. "It would seem so. All the same, I would—you look startled, Doctor. Did the vocal modulator catch you off guard?"

Dr. Nate smiled, embarrassed. "Ah, yes, yes it did. Seeing as you're wearing it, I assume that means you're waiting for a call?"

"I am. As I was saying, I intend to remain here for at least two more days. Don't want to lift my foot off the neck prematurely."

"Sensible. I'll notify Zarya."

"Good. Anything else?"

"Mm, yes. Dr. Bertram emailed me a few minutes ago, said that we need to speak soon on an important matter."

"Is something wrong?"

"There's very little information in the email, for security reasons, I assume, but it's about Dr. Deol."

The tall figure halted at the mention of the woman heading Quest Biotech, one of Phoenix's most crucial subsidiaries. Dr. Nate craned his neck to look at the black void where the Boss's face was. *That damned hood sucks all the light like nothing else. I may as well be looking at the grim reaper.*

"Dr. Deol," the Boss said flatly, "is vital to our plans. I want to know what the problem is, if any, as soon as you do."

"Of course."

They continued down the hallway. Dr. Nate swiped upward on his tablet and six passport photos appeared. "Jag Sanchez. Tegan Ryder. Aari Barnes. Mariah Ashton. Kody Tyler. Marshall Sawyer."

His superior bristled. "Annoyances. At least they haven't yet found what they're looking for. And how many Sentries have we identified?"

"Aside from Mr. Sawyer, there's the pair in Montana acting as guards for the urchins' families, the three that were caught on camera at our nanomite production center in South America, one in Afghanistan, and another in Germany. And of course, there's the . . . other one."

"We need to uncover their network and take them down. They've been destroying our REAPR pods, and let's not forget what happened to the Quest Defense manufacturing facility in Nevada over the summer."

"The damage *was* substantial," Dr. Nate said feebly. "And yes, regrettably many pods in North America were destroyed, but we've just about won that battle globally."

"That's not the point. The Sentries are undoubtedly coordinating with Dema-Ki. I grow tired of reminding you, Doctor. Under no circumstance should you underestimate them. They have proven to be determined adversaries."

"I'm sorry." Dr. Nate rubbed his forehead, feeling the hairless space where his eyebrows had once been. "Is the plan still to detain the five?"

"Yes. But we must wait until they find the seeds or abandon the effort, else other Sentries will continue the hunt. And if the seeds do still exist, I want them in my possession."

"I most definitely don't mean to point out shortcomings, Boss, but when we tried to grab the urchins a few months ago, it didn't exactly go as planned."

"I am quite aware, thank you, but Vladimir has a bigger team this time around."

"And what is the plan once we 'ave them?"

The Boss grunted. "If I had it my way—"

Dr. Nate looked up at his superior, frowning. "But you do 'ave it your way."

"Yes. Yes, I do." The Boss sighed. "I'm a little tired today, Doctor. The plan is that they will be brought to the Heart, alive, where I will deal with them. That's all you need to know for now."

"I understand." Dr. Nate adjusted his thick glasses and scrolled down his tablet, searching for his next talking point in the file. "As you know, we've already begun work on the division of echelons for the Sanctuaries. While most are yet to be rolled out, we've been occupied with getting the martial arm in place, vetting candidates who are fit both physically and mentally. Some of your, er, 'ired 'ands are assisting with the training."

"Hired hands? That's a very politically correct thing to call my mercenaries, Doctor. So I take it all is going well?"

"I dare say it's better than well. Our candidates so far are performing excellently. I think they'll be ready just in time for the final stage of the Ventures next year."

The Boss hummed contentedly, though with the vocal distorter it sounded more like the growl of a wild beast. Dr. Nate patted back his greasy hair, suddenly nervous. *Oh, stop it. It's just the modulator.*

He cleared his throat. "Is the asset faring well? I 'aven't seen 'im since we landed."

"He's resting. It was a long journey and he's proven to be valuable. Don't worry about him."

"As you wish." Dr. Nate continued scanning through his tablet, bringing onto the screen an image captured by a CCTV camera. He wrinkled his nose.

The Boss leaned over to glimpse the photo. "I see you're still sour about our visitor."

"I want answers and I'm not getting them!" Dr. Nate snarled.

"We know the guard found 'im lurking in the town and we know the bugger was at the other Sanctuary, but that's it!"

The Boss surprised him by placing a hand on his shoulder. "It won't do to go in all excited. Calm down."

He forced himself to take slow breaths. They came to a stop by a long frame of glass set in a wall. The Boss turned to it, arms crossed, and Dr. Nate imagined he felt an icy gust emanate from the hooded figure. He climbed onto a box, placed there specifically for him, and looked in. His blood started to boil.

On the other side of the two-way mirror, a man sat in a chair facing them, wrists bound to the armrests and legs tied securely. Dried blood crusted parts of his face from cuts and a split lip. He smirked, like he knew they were watching him. A few feet away, a wolfdog lay chained to a wall, heavily sedated.

Without looking at Dr. Nate, the Boss said, "Get to it, Doctor. He's waiting."

Even standing, Dr. Nate didn't reach Victor's eye level. Beside him, a small metal rolling table lined with syringes glinted in the harsh light of the room. One had been emptied into the Sentry's veins when the doctor entered nearly an hour ago. It was like clockwork; every couple of hours they injected him with a dose.

From the moment a guard had found Victor reconnoitering with Chief in the adjacent town and shot him with a tranquilizer, they'd kept him drugged. The doses suppressed his abilities somehow, not allowing him access to his enhanced hearing, his telepathy, or his concussive blasts. He'd been held for two days in the same room and given a single meal. Armed guards were posted right outside the door; he'd been warned that only one of them had a tranquilizer gun.

He side-eyed Dr. Nate, then looked past him to the two-way glass. *I know you're there.*

Those of Dema-Ki blood were, to varying degrees, attuned to the flow of psycho-emotional energies in the biosphere that they called the fabric of existence, and only powerful events or presences affected it. The instant Victor's plane had crossed into Kazakhstan, he'd felt a disturbance like no other; for the briefest moment, it even frightened him. In this room, the sensation came in suffocating waves. It was surreal to be mere feet from the epicenter of the disturbance, separated by a mirror. The room felt colder and even the air felt thinner.

A sudden slap to his face shook him. Dr. Nate grabbed Victor's chin roughly and pulled him close. Victor tried not to show it, but the doctor's rancid breath nearly made him gag.

"I know you're a Sentry, so there's no point in 'iding it," the short man whispered. "Cooperate. It will be so much easier."

Victor's lips twisted in a derisive smile.

"'Ow did you find this place? What are you doing 'ere?"

The Sentry's expression didn't change.

"What were you doing in the New Mexico Sanctuary? You dodged the cameras like you knew your way around. Which urchin in there 'elped you?"

An image of Kenzo flashed in Victor's head. "Apparently I didn't dodge *all* the cameras."

"No. You were in the corner frame of a camera outside. We saw you touch the ground and a moment later, the guard at the entrance blacked out. We doubt it's coincidence."

"You keep saying 'we,' little man. Who might your plural counterpart be? Your almighty boss?"

Dr. Nate shoved Victor's face away. "You worthless piece of filth. You will never get the bounty of being in the presence of the Boss."

Victor lazily jerked his chin at the glass. "I think I'm pretty friggin' close to that murderous psychopath, don't you?"

He watched with satisfaction as Dr. Nate clenched and unclenched his fists. *Come on, little man. Lose your cool. Do it.*

Dr. Nate turned away, then wheeled around and struck the Sentry across his jaw. Pain exploded in the side of Victor's face but he gave another scathing smile. *Good. Keep it up.*

The doctor wound his arm back to strike a second time, then stopped and glanced at the glass behind him. His face contorted for a moment before he slowly lowered his hand and straightened his shirt. "Make this easy for everyone. The bag you 'ad when you were caught—we found the blue overalls issued by our facilities. We did a full inventory, and there's one like it missing from our site in New Mexico. You were 'elped by someone inside the Sanctuary."

"I didn't need help."

Dr. Nate removed his glasses and wiped them savagely, a

throbbing vein appearing in his forehead, then put them back on.

Must be so frustrating, Victor thought, *finding a guy with just a bag and his dog. No wallet, no keys, no ID, no phone.* Those were safely tucked away in a car in a town across the river. He couldn't help but be amused at the turn of events. *I was interrogating an uncooperative man just last month. How the tables have turned.*

Dr. Nate slid his ice-cold fingertips over Victor's hands, coming to a rest on the silver rings on each of his middle fingers. "Do these mean something to you?"

Victor tensed. The doctor pulled the rings off, watching the Sentry carefully as he slid them into his pants' pocket. Victor's mouth twitched as he fought back a snarl. *Don't react. You can't allow that. You'll get them back later. Don't react.*

Dr. Nate moved closer, holding the armrests, and brought his face right up to the Sentry's. Victor hated having his personal space invaded and tried to press back into the chair, away from the doctor and his fetid breath. "Whoa, hey. You ought to buy me dinner first if you want to get any closer. I'm kind of old-fashioned like that."

The doctor didn't blink. "Listen to me very closely. Are you listening? Good. We know where your five precious teenagers are." He paused to study the Sentry's reaction. "Ahh, *yes*, there it is. I see the fear in your eyes now. We know where they are, and we 'ave a team waiting to grab them with just a call from us."

"If that's really the case," Victor said, "why haven't you picked them up already?"

"That will 'appen when it 'appens. Just know, we're following them diligently. They're all the way in Israel, are they not? Taking refuge in a 'ouse that belongs to a friend of one Marshall Sawyer. If you cooperate with me, I give you my word that they will not be 'armed."

Victor looked into the man's black eyes and realized at that moment that he could never despise another person as much as he did the vermin in front of him.

"You," he murmured through gritted teeth, "will die one day.

And I will be the first to kick your ashes into the wind."

The doctor leered. "And I was under the impression that Dema-Ki people were supposed to be much kinder, even to your foes."

"You indoctrinate kids and turn them into drones. You stole them from their families in the name of, what, a benevolent cause?"

"Actually, most of these urchins are foster kids. Orphans. They won't be missed."

Victor felt a stab in his chest. "You took advantage of kids without homes? Without families?"

"Why?" Dr. Nate asked, mouth quivering in an intrigued smile. "Does that 'it close to 'ome?"

When Victor remained silent, the shorter man waved his hand dismissively. "We only 'ave one life and what we do with it is all that matters. My work 'as given these kids purpose. My work will save them from what's to come."

"Yeah, you keep telling yourself that."

Dr. Nate pulled out his phone and looked at it. "I've spent nearly two 'ours 'ere already but, believe me, I 'ave all the time in the world. I'll 'ave no trouble using 'arsher methods to get what I need. Now tell me about your group, the lot that you call Sentries."

Victor just stared at him.

Dr. Nate walked around the rolling table to pick up his giant briefcase and opened it. He pulled out a blue, gel-like helmet populated with electrodes and micro-LED lights. Victor knew immediately what it was; Tegan and Aari had been threatened with it before.

"I'm sure you've noticed the drugs we use 'ave suppressed your abilities," Dr. Nate said, displaying the helmet like a proud father. "This 'ere is a wireless optogenetics controller. It—"

"I know what that is. You reprogram the minds of kids with that hat from hell."

"Call it whatever you want. It will give me the information I need." Dr. Nate stroked the helmet tenderly. "Unfortunately, in order to use it, your system 'as to be more drug-free, which we can't afford at this moment. But, please, I dare you to push our buttons further. It will grant me the opportunity to make my case and use it anyway. As a bonus, I'll get to alter your mind and wipe your identity clean."

Victor snorted and looked back at the two-way mirror. *Why don't you come in here yourself, instead of letting your cronies get their hands dirty?*

Dr. Nate's phone rang. He checked the caller ID and clicked his tongue but didn't answer it. He returned his attention to the Sentry. "Eh? What's the matter with you?"

Victor's eyes were closed, his head lolled to the side. Dr. Nate grabbed his face and shook it. "Stop fooling around. I am not falling for this trick, you 'ear me? Open your eyes." The shaking got more frantic. "'Ey! Open your eyes! Open! *Damn it!*"

A modulated voice came over the intercom. "Is there a problem, Doctor?"

"I . . . I'm not sure. It could be that the dosage of the last injection was a bit much."

"You filled it up yourself, didn't you?"

"I did the other ones, but a guard 'elped me with this batch. Boss, I 'ad a 'undred different things to deal with today and I wasn't trying to—"

"Is he faking it?"

Dr. Nate delivered a powerful backhand, leaving a stark red mark on Victor's face, but the man didn't budge. "I don't think so."

"I want him alive, Doctor. Will your mistake kill him?"

"N-no! It shouldn't. I mean, it won't. This ape should come out of it shortly."

"Keep an eye on him until he does. I have some matters to attend to."

"Yes, Boss. But . . . permission to step outside? Dr. Bertram called my cell."

"You have two minutes. Have the guards with him while you're out."

All three guards stepped in moments later, shutting the door after Dr. Nate left.

Victor was perfectly fine, aside from the slap he'd received; that had smarted quite a lot. He'd felt the effects of the drugs slowly waning over the past few minutes and didn't want to have another injection numb his abilities again. One by one he tested them. *Concussion blasts aren't working. Telepathy's kind of okay, I can sense some people in the novasphere. Hearing . . . let's try it out on the little man.*

Working through the drugs to access his abilities was like wading through a pool of molasses, and the exertion forced a budding migraine to rear its head. As painstakingly slow as the process was, he managed to tune his hearing just enough and picked up Dr. Nate's voice, along with a second one on the other end of his call.

"I've had my doubts for a while, Ian. Dr. Deol hasn't been herself lately. It's like someone killed the chatterbox in her. She's been reporting to me for almost six years now and I have never seen her like this. She's been quiet and aloof the last couple of weeks. I think . . . I think she might be losing faith in the cause."

"This is a woman who's been unshakably loyal to the Boss's vision," Dr. Nate said. "Are you certain about this? For goodness' sake, *she* created the Marauders and engineered the virus, so you'll excuse me if I find it 'ard to believe she'd jump ship now."

"I know! But you have to remember, she's a doctor and a scientist first. Creating the Marauders was more of a pet project. She never really got to see the devastation the beasts caused. With the virus, it's different. We're seeing its effects everywhere, and she knows her hands are stained with blood."

"She's made of stern stuff, Al."

"All the same, I think this has to be contained."

"First, 'ave you tried talking to her?"

"No, but I will."

"You do that. See if it's worse than it seems or if it's just a case of 'er needing a pep talk."

"I'll do what I can, but my gut tells me that we're losing her."

"Keep me posted. I want to know if she's salvageable."

"If not?"

Dr. Nate sighed. "She's too valuable and she knows too much. It's a shame that an adult brain is unable to actually be repurposed. You're not overly attached to 'er, are you?"

"She's a delightful woman and a good friend, but this cause is bigger than any one of us. And she has the anti-viral formula in her head. It's a potentially volatile situation."

"Precisely. Is she still at the Moscow lab?"

"The last I checked, yes. She's called in sick twice this week already."

"I'll inform the Boss. Get back to me immediately once you've spoken to 'er."

"I will."

Victor forced his hearing back to normal. The crushing migraine had clamped itself like a vise around his temples, the pain now unbearable. He remained as still as he could but the electric throbbing was too much; he flinched, hands clenched, just as Dr. Nate returned.

When the diminutive man saw his captive's movement, he sprinted toward the table and grabbed a syringe. Just before he plunged the needle into the Sentry's neck, Victor sent out a broken telepathic blast to Marshall with the last bit of energy he could muster.

As the drug burned its way into his system, he roared, thrashing his head from side to side. It was as though his entire head was on fire from the inside out and someone kept pouring on gasoline. When the agony finally eased, he was drenched in sweat, chest heaving. He bared his teeth at Dr. Nate, barely able to think straight.

If this . . . goes on . . . it might . . . actually . . . kill me. He let his head fall back. *Hope you . . . got my message . . . Sawyer. The kids . . . aren't . . . safe.*

A hard smack on the forehead startled Deverell out of his slumber. "What the bloody—"

His twin towered over him sleepily, the smartphone he held illuminating his face. "Get up. Marshall's on the line."

Deverell sat up in his bed, rubbing his eyes as Gareth plopped down next to him and tapped his phone's screen. "Okay, Dev's here. What's the matter?"

Marshall's voice filled the dark room. "Sorry to wake you up in the middle of the night. I got a message from Colback about twenty minutes ago. It was a weak connection and I've been trying to reach him since then, but I can't find him in the novasphere. I'm worried something bad—"

"No," Gareth jumped in. "No, Marshall. There are many reasons why you can't sense him. Vic's a tough fellow. He's pulled through rough situations before."

"I don't know too many reasons why someone would go black, Gareth."

"Reyor's learned the trick of hiding from the novasphere," Deverell said, trying not to come across anxious. "Maybe Vic has just now mastered it too?"

"Maybe." Marshall didn't sound convinced. "There's something else. He called me Mars."

Deverell glanced at his brother sharply. "He stopped calling you that since you guys fell out a while ago, didn't he?"

"Yeah. I think he's really in trouble."

"What was the message?"

"Mars—cure. Dr. Deol. Moscow. Kids not . . . Someone watching."

"That doesn't sound intelligible."

"I know, and that's almost word for word. Like I said, the connection was weak. What could cause that?"

Deverell traced the top of his ear, thinking hard. "The brain functions through synaptic transmissions, right? If those impulses were interrupted somehow—"

"—by extreme pain or alcohol or drugs—" Gareth added.

"—that might explain the broken message. His abilities may be suppressed, but he could still be alive."

Marshall grunted. "That beats the other prospect. He was hot on Reyor's trail, so that's bound to be a lot dicier than anything we've ever done. He might've gotten caught. Whatever it is, he's in trouble."

"So are you and the others, I think." Deverell motioned for Gareth to follow him; the brothers headed up to the kitchen to brew some coffee. "That last part, something about the kids and someone watching. Or is someone watching Vic?"

"Believe me, I've been on a whole new level of alertness since I got the message," Marshall said. "I'm looking out for the kids. But I'm worried about Colback. If only that stubborn son of a gun had at least told me where he was headed . . ."

The brothers exchanged grimaces.

"You tell him," Deverell mouthed to Gareth, who mouthed back indignantly with a firm shake of his finger. Deverell darted to the other side of the kitchen and promptly stuck his head in the fridge. He could hear his brother exhaling curses at him before clearing his throat and saying, "Actually, mate, we . . . uh, we do have an idea where he went. He called us on his drive to the airport when he left the Lodge."

Marshall paused. "Oh."

Deverell winced at the other man's tone as he pulled out a carton of milk.

"He told us that he had evidence pointing to a hydroelectric project in Kazakhstan," Gareth continued. "We don't know where, exactly, but we could dig it up. What I'm curious about is that bit about Dr. Deol. Does this man, or woman, know anything about a cure? It would make sense, wouldn't it? They'd need some big brains to concoct this pathogen, which means those same brains could have the formula for the cure, or at least a way to reverse engineer one. And they'd've inoculated their people, including the SONEs in the Sanctuaries."

"If what Colback said meant that this doctor really has the cure," Marshall said, "it would be a good move to grab it. If you two could look into this, that'd be great. Hope you weren't about to go on a mission or anything?"

"We were planning to catch a flight to Brazil in the evening, actually."

"Brazil?"

"Aye. We've been monitoring the escalating riots, the virus, and the nanomite incursions since you left yesterday, trying to figure out where we're most needed. Turns out the Sentries in Brazil are having a huge issue getting the nanomites under control. The buggers have begun attacking coffee bean farms on top of maize and rice crops."

Marshall blew out a breath. "Come again?"

"It's brilliant, really. A third of the world's coffee supply comes from Brazil. It's another effective way to crush any remaining semblance of normalcy. Look at America. Over eighty percent of adults need coffee just to get started in the morning."

"So the Sentries in South America decide to call for help when the coffee supply slows to a drip?"

Gareth snickered. "Ha! No, they'd lit the Bat-Signal prior to that, but with our limited resources it's been a challenge to assign more support there."

Deverell removed the coffee pot and poured the dark, steaming liquid into two mugs. "But we'll have to put that on hold," he said. "We have a situation with Vic. If he did stumble onto a lead for a cure, this will have to take precedence. Speaking of cures, are you any closer to finding the box of seeds?"

The twins listened as Marshall recounted the events in Israel, intrigued at first and then horrified.

"You are so lucky Jag made that split-second decision," Gareth whispered. "We could have lost you, Marshall."

"I owe the kid my life, literally," Marshall said, sounding almost weary. "But, as it is, we've got no more leads and I've been wracking my brains trying to think of something."

"You scoured all the caves, yeah? Not just the one with the crescent mark?"

"Yes, but the box wasn't in any of them."

Deverell leaned on the counter across from his twin and took a careful sip of his drink. "I'm sorry, Marshall. There's nothing much we can offer. When you left, we did more research and called different contacts, but no one's even heard of our box."

"What if the box was removed soon after it was buried?" Marshall asked.

"The Elders would have been told if it was dug up."

"Maybe it wasn't one of our people who did it."

"You reckon the Romans had a hand in this?" Gareth asked.

"It's all in theory, but yes. Maybe."

"So, assuming the Romans did have a role and the artifact did survive, where in the world would it be today? Italy?"

Deverell grabbed the phone from Gareth and scrolled through the contacts list. "Marshall, there's a good man we know in Israel. A friend. He's a collector of sorts and is incredibly knowledgeable of the history of the region. He's the only associate left who we haven't been able to get in touch with. Doesn't like phones very much. He works in Haifa as a landscaper at the Bahá'í Gardens. I'm sending you his contact info and address. Hopefully you'll get to meet him personally. Just mention that the Welsh brothers sent you."

"You think he has answers?" Marshall asked.

"I think you need a lead. This is all we've got right now. Let Gareth and me worry about this Dr. Deol character and Victor, okay?"

"Right, yeah. Okay. And listen, I just . . . I'm really glad you're both around."

The brothers gave each other small smiles. "Likewise," Deverell said. "Take care of yourself, mate. And good luck with our historian friend."

"Thanks, Dev. You two be good."

"When are we not?" Gareth quipped.

"Ha!"

Deverell ended the call and looked at his twin through the steam swirling from his mug. "Shall we?"

They left the kitchen and went downstairs to the tech room, turning on two computers. Within seconds, all that was to be heard were clacking keyboards with the occasional pause as the pair jotted notes on legal pads.

Deverell yawned loudly and poured the rest of his coffee down his throat. *Bugger. There are at least a dozen major dams in Kazakhstan. Where to begin . . .* He rolled his chair over to Gareth, who was staring at Russia's White Pages. "Any luck?"

Gareth pushed back his shaggy brown hair. "Seems that Deol is an East Indian name. You'd think there'd only be a couple of them in Moscow, but no, there are seven. Four men, three women. None of them are listed as doctors, and a couple don't have any jobs tagged under them. Looking at two of the men's profiles, though, I don't think either is our target."

"Why not?"

"It says they own a grocery store. Unless they're hatching nefarious plans from behind the counter, they're not who we're looking for."

"At least you're narrowing it down."

"Mmph. What about you? Found anything?"

Deverell sunk low in his chair. "There are a number of dams. It could be any one of them."

"Are they all operational?"

"Most are. One is being refitted as part of a modernization plan and two are under construction."

"Hmm. Have you tried looking up the stakeholders in the project? Information about contractors, subcontractor, suppliers . . . might lend a clue."

Deverell snapped up, suddenly more awake. "That was the next thing I was about to do, I swear!"

Gareth rolled his eyes. "Suuure. As usual, I come up with a solution, you swoop in and take the credit."

"Pisho bant."

"Oi! Don't you tell me to piss off!"

Deverell rolled back to his computer. "You're too chopsy for your own good sometimes. And don't pretend to be miffed. I've definitely heard worse come out of your mouth. Mum would have had a heart attack if she heard you the last time the Swans lost a match."

"I'm a thirty-year-old man. If you think I'm terrified of Mum—"

"I'll call her, then. You can tell her exactly what you said that day."

"Shh. Go do your research."

Deverell clicked his mouse furiously, scanning different pages of Kazakhstan's hydroelectric dams. *All of them were commissioned in the last century . . . except for the two that are under construction. Hmm. One's being built by a Chinese contractor and the other by what appears to be a local builder. The Chinese firm is based out of—ah, here it is. Guangzhou. Been around for nearly forty years, too. I think we can rule that out. And this local contractor, Izdenw . . . what, did a cat walk across the keyboard when they were naming the company? Alright, let's see what we can find.*

His fingers darted over the keys. *Huh. A relatively young outfit that sprang up three years ago. How does a fledgling business win a bidding war for a massive project like this? It doesn't smell right. This could be the one. But why call it Izdenw?*

He entered the name into an online translator but couldn't find a direct definition. He sat back, contemplative. *If that really is a Phoenix subsidiary, wouldn't they name it Quest, like Quest Mining and Quest Biotech? That seems to be their modus operandi elsewhere.* He paused briefly, a smile forming on his face. But what if . . .

He typed in 'quest' and translated it to Kazakh. *Agh, that's not it either. Oh, wait, what's this teeny second translation down here?*

He clicked the Cyrillic script in a little panel below the translation box, and the Romanization appeared: *Izdenw.*

He nearly wrenched his neck from laughing so hard. "Oh, come *on*. Couldn't they be more creative?"

"What?" Gareth asked.

"Nothing. I found the dam."

"Fantastic. Meanwhile, it looks like I've got some scouting to do in Moscow. I've ruled out all the men, which leaves the women. I haven't been able to find anything on them yet. Their social media profiles aren't giving much, either."

"Whoa, who said you were going to Moscow?"

"I did, just now. What? You want to go?"

"Maybe."

Gareth rummaged through the drawers of the desk and found a coin. "We'll do a toss, then. Heads or tails?"

"Tails."

Gareth flicked the coin upward and slapped it onto the back of his hand. It landed heads up. He grinned. "Maybe next time, Dev. In all honesty, I think your abilities may be better suited at the Kazakh Sanctuary. Also, we need to cancel our flight to Brazil. Can you do that while I get new tickets for us?"

"I'll do it now, in a minute." Deverell grabbed his mug. "I think there's still some coffee left in the pot. Want more?"

"Nah."

Deverell headed back up to the kitchen and got his refill. He sipped his drink, watching hefty snowflakes fall slowly outside the floor-to-ceiling windows of the living room. Despite the serenity of the empty Lodge, he felt a sudden burst of agitation. His short nails scratched feverishly against the ceramic mug.

Vic may very well be at the mercy of someone bent on throwing the world into a forge and reshaping it into an entirely new entity, and I'm going to one-man it?

He gulped down the rest of his coffee in one swig.

Steady, Dev, steady. You've got this. It's not the first time you've had to get someone out of trouble by yourself. You'll be fine. Hang tight, Vic. I'm coming.

The sun was already setting by the time Gareth slipped into his rental car in Moscow. *Stroke of luck, getting the last seat on that plane*, he thought, *especially with the travel restrictions.* He looked down at a list of names and corresponding addresses in his phone, then keyed the first into the vehicle's navigation screen. With three women to investigate in different districts of Russia's sprawling capital city, he had no time to waste.

Despite Moscow's less than friendly facade, he loved the cityscape. Gorgeous skyscrapers intermingled with a host of Imperial and Soviet-era architecture with parks splayed out in between. The only thing he detested were the traffic jams; they were among the worst in the world. Even with the disease ravaging portions of the population and an ongoing war in the eastern provinces, a sizable number of vehicles still occupied the roads.

Gareth glanced at his watch. *Maybe I should've just taken the metro. If it's still functioning, that is.*

Convoys of military trucks and tanks rumbled down the streets, forcing civilian traffic to pull aside every so often. The ground shook as one of the tanks passed him. He turned to watch it, unable to shrug off the image as a beast patrolling the city.

Once free of the gridlock, he stepped on the gas and headed west. Within a half hour he found himself on a quiet suburban street, with a heavily wooded green belt on one side and two large mansions on the other. The houses sat on spacious acreages and were separated by a long masonry wall. He parked across from one of the buildings, an elegant property. An extensive stone walkway coiled between two rows of frosted firs and toward the terrace of the mansard-roofed manor.

He quickly pulled on a white face mask. Almost everyone he'd seen in the airports and in Moscow wore one, so he decided it best to play the part of a normal citizen worried about the virus. Then he grabbed a bouquet of flowers from the backseat and stepped out of the car. *Been a while since I've had to use the flower-delivery routine. Hope I'm not too rusty.*

Commotion erupted from the house. A streak of orange zipped over the front lawn and across the street, barely giving the Sentry enough time to jump out of the way as it shot past. *Agh! Watch it, cat!*

A sudden cry came from the house. Gareth spun around. A woman ran after a small girl who'd given chase to the animal. Shrieking excitedly, the child darted into the street as a car barreled down the icy asphalt, headlights illuminating her.

Gareth threw down the flowers and raced toward the girl. He dove, grabbing her, and rolled out of the way just as the car sped past, blaring its horn. The Sentry glared at the vehicle, then looked down at the child pressed to his chest. She blinked up at him, grinning, perfectly unfazed. He got up and took her by the hand, leading her back to her mother. The woman was almost in hysterics.

"Thank you," she gasped in Russian, holding her daughter close. "She . . . she's deaf. It's hard to tell her—to explain to her . . ."

Gareth smiled softly. "No worries." Something trickled down his temple and he wiped it with his fingers, surprised to see a thin trail of blood. *Must've gotten scraped on the road.* When he saw the woman looking at him with concern, he winked. "It's just a cut. I've had worse on the playground growing up."

As she looked him up and down, he took stock of her in turn. He reckoned she was probably a few years older than himself, and quite fit. Her black hair flowed in loose waves around her shoulders. His eyes drifted to her full lips but he quickly caught himself, though not before he saw her smirk. *Oops.*

"You're not from around here, are you?" she asked.

"No," he admitted, "but I'm not unfamiliar with the place.

And, if I may be so bold to assume, you're not from around here either."

"No. I moved to Moscow from New Delhi years ago. It's kind of become home ever since."

"Haven't really heard of many people moving *to* Moscow."

"I moved here to get married."

"My apologies. I didn't mean to pry."

"It's alright. If you don't mind my asking, what are you doing all the way out here?"

"I'm on an errand. I've got something for a Ms. Ina Deol."

The woman's eyebrows rose. "That's me."

"In that case . . ." Gareth loped over to the flowers he'd dropped, straightened them, and passed them to her. "A few of them are a little bent. Sorry about that."

She took the flowers in one hand, bewildered. "These are beautiful, but what are they for? Who are they from?"

"As I said, I'm just making a delivery."

"Well, thank you. And I apologize if I sound brusque. It's just . . . with all the worry about this virus and the war, people here have been even less open to one another than usual. It's nice—and surprising—to see kindness survive."

Gareth reached out to pull a piece of leaf stuck in the young girl's hair. She wiggled around in her mother's arms and beamed at him. He smiled back, then glanced at the manor and let out a low whistle. "This is an amazing property you have. You've done really well for yourself here."

The woman bashfully waved the bouquet at the house behind her. "Oh, this is all inheritance. My daughter and I have been fortunate that way."

Inheritance . . . from her parents? Or perhaps a late husband. She's using 'Ms.' instead of 'Mrs.', after all. Deciding to risk it, he offered another smile. "Undeniably. I'm sure you and your husband must enjoy raising your little girl here."

The woman turned away from him. "My husband passed."

"Oh. I'm so sorry."

She said nothing, but when she turned back to him, she frowned. "You're still bleeding."

"I'm fine."

She shook her head. "Come inside, we'll get you cleaned up."

"Aren't you worried I'll spread the virus?" he asked, half joking.

"You've been standing here with your mask all askew since saving my daughter. I've already taken my chances, but I'm going to send Anya upstairs, just to be safe."

In the sleek, marble-topped kitchen, Gareth removed his brown leather jacket and dabbed the scrapes on his temple with a paper towel. They were small, inconsequential, but the woman was insistent as she circled him like a mother hen.

"So," he said, taking a cloth from her and wiping his face, "what did you do for a living before the world started sliding into hell in a handbasket?"

"I'm an artist," she said, pouring water into a glass.

"Really? You've got a gallery somewhere?"

"God, no." She scrunched her nose in disgust, then passed him the glass. "My work isn't public. It's mostly for charity or private auctions within my network. I believe they serve better this way than if they'd gone to the masses. Besides, it's just a hobby, really. Something to do with my time."

No wonder her occupation didn't show up anywhere online, Gareth thought as he downed the drink. *Wealthy artist living on inheritance. Not too shabby a life.*

"And you?" she asked. "What do you do?"

"Me? I travel the world. Doing odd jobs here and there, meeting people, gaining new experiences."

"That sounds amazing," she said dreamily. "I've always wanted to travel but never had the courage. And now it doesn't look like I'll ever get the chance. You're certainly fortunate. You must have met many . . . interesting people during your travels."

Their eyes met, and she had a dangerously playful twinkle in hers. Gareth couldn't stop himself from grinning.

Then, from somewhere in the house, came the ringing of a handbell. The woman gave Gareth a remorseful look, the flirt in her suddenly vanishing. "That's my little one. She's tired and wants me to tuck her in."

Gareth shrugged his jacket back on. "I should be going, anyway."

She walked him to the door. "It was a pleasure chatting with you. It's really nice to see a face that smiles around here. And thank you for the flowers."

"I'm just the errand boy," he said. "It was lovely meeting you, Ms. Deol. And, please, try not to leave your home if you can help it. You've got a darling family here and I'd be remiss if I didn't beg you to stay safe."

She gazed at him with wonder. "You are a spark of light in this dreary place. Don't worry. I was planning a complete lockdown from tomorrow onward. Drive safe."

Once inside the car, Gareth crossed the first name off his list, then keyed the second address into the GPS. It took him eastward, past the famed Red Square plaza. Just after it was Lenin's Mausoleum, where the body of Russia's former leader lay preserved and on display for the world to see. Gareth thought it was a bit macabre.

In the far reaches of a quieter district, he headed up the stairs of a decades-old apartment building. The lights overhead flickered and buzzed as if they would burst any minute, and a constant cold draft seemed to follow him. Everything about the place gave him the creeps. The one thing he could not stand was horror movies, and the building radiated with all the wrong vibes.

He reached the eighth floor and double-checked the apartment number, then knocked on the second door to his right. A rat scuttled past his foot, making him jump. "Bwah!"

The door cracked open and one eye glared out. "*Da?*"

Gareth quickly righted himself. "Good evening. May I speak with Mrs. Deol?"

"Why?"

"I'm here on behalf of a neighbor who—"

The door swung fully open, revealing a short old woman with a kerchief tied around her head. She had a rolling pin in hand and she looked absolutely livid. "It's Petrov again, isn't it? I told him, I will not be sharing any more of my food! And now he pulls his lousy lackey in to help him? That wretched, no-good piece of—"

"Are . . . are you Mrs. Deol?"

"Are you stupid? Does it look like anyone else lives here? Yes, it's me! Now you go and tell Petrov that if he so much as tries to set foot in my house again, or even knocks on my door, he will regret it!"

"Madam, if you don't mind, I'd really like to—"

She screeched and swung her rolling pin like a bat, hitting him square in the abdomen. He doubled over, the wind knocked out of him, and backed off, holding a hand up in submission. "Okay! Okay! I'll let Petrov know!"

"You better!" She slammed the door on his face.

Gareth hobbled down the stairs to his car as fast as he could. *Well, I'm quite certain that's not who I'm looking for. A Caucasian with an East Indian name—must've taken her husband's after marriage.* He rubbed his sore abdomen. *Oof, that babushka has one heck of an arm.*

He typed the final address into the car's navigational system. It took him southward; he drove past the Kremlin and over the Moskva River toward the next district. As he passed the famed Gorky Park, he felt disheartened. The normally vibrant public square was completely empty, even the outdoor ice rink. He had fond memories of it from his mid-twenties when he and a group of friends had backpacked across Europe. The ice rink had given them bruises and sore feet, but also ear-to-ear smiles all around.

The GPS led him to a country-style house at the outskirts of the district. Two luxury cars were parked inside the gated property. The lights on the grounds were lit, but the house itself was not. Gareth pulled a face. *Guess I'll have to wait the night out here.*

He stationed his vehicle across the street behind other parked cars, turned off the engine, and hunkered down, pulling his jacket tighter and covering his ears with a beanie. Being from Wales he was used to the cold, but it didn't mean he enjoyed turning into an icicle. He was in and out of slumber the entire night, his subconscious too paranoid about missing whoever might walk out the front door.

Just before dawn, he startled himself awake. Momentarily forgetting where he was, he peered out his window as a tanned woman in a business suit strode out of the house. Her face flushed, she unlocked her car and got in, warily checking her surroundings.

Gareth slid lower to conceal himself as she sped past, then followed. *That looked secretive. She could be the one, driving to her office of horrors. Or that could also be guilty behavior. Maybe she left a lover in the house.*

She was the only one of the three women on his list who had some presence on social media. As far as he could tell, her main interests were cats, skiing, and fun nights out with her friends. It wasn't much to go on, but it was something.

He tailed her across the bridge back toward the heart of Moscow as daylight broke. They navigated the streets until she pulled up by an imposing structure with rows of glass windows. Gareth gawked at the large emblem high up on the building.

No. Way.

He was staring directly at the offices of the Ministry of Health.

So you leave out the most important part in your online profile? he thought, irritated. *I could've saved so much time if you'd stated this up front.*

As the woman headed inside, he fished a spare wallet from his bag, stuffed some rubles and kopeks into it, then removed his beanie to part and comb his hair, hoping to look sufficiently professional. Straightening his jacket, he jogged into the simple reception area of the building just as the woman stepped into an elevator to his far right. Not knowing if he could follow her, he hurried to the smartly dressed man behind a long counter and held up the wallet. "Excuse me, that woman who just got into the elevator dropped this."

The man took it without smiling. "Your Russian is good, even though you're obviously not from here."

"Um, thanks. Will you pass that to her?"

"Yes."

"Great." Gareth glanced back to the elevator, then awkwardly added, "She, uh, she's quite a gorgeous doctor, isn't she?"

"Doctor?" The man finally cracked a grin. "You are a funny one, foreigner. I suppose she could be a doctor, except for the fact that she's an accountant."

"My mistake. Thanks again."

Gareth returned to his car and put the heater on full blast. He was utterly lost, and he hated dead ends. Frustrated, he drove to a hotel and got the cheapest room available. As he took the elevator up, he muttered incessantly to himself.

Okay, calm down. There's no point in getting worked up. Go back. Retrace your steps. Do more research.

Hours later in his room, he slammed his laptop shut and tossed it onto the bed. There was nothing more to be found. None of his local contacts could help him, and most of the Russian field Sentries were on the frontlines doing what they could to stave off the devastation from the war.

He threw open the curtains and looked out over Moscow. The city glinted under the orange sun as if on fire. He rested his forehead against the cold window.

What did I miss?

31

In the small town adjacent to Phoenix's hydroelectric project, Deverell ate his breakfast by the window of a family-run diner. He fumed at the delays getting to his destination. He'd landed in Astana, Kazakhstan, two evenings before but had been trapped in the city due to a massive snowstorm. At the first sign of clear skies, he'd taken off in a rented pickup truck for an eighteen-hour drive, tormented by the thought that the longer Victor remained in Reyor's hands, the shorter his lifespan would be.

He'd arrived at the town less than twenty minutes ago, just before the night shift workers were relieved. Instantly, he'd felt it—the disturbance in the fabric. Reyor was somewhere around. But he couldn't focus on that now.

The once-sleepy settlement of four hundred inhabitants had swollen into a bustling municipality serving over three thousand people working on the massive project. Across the street from the diner, men and women in dirty coveralls swung in and out of the doors of a laundromat and a grocery store, seemingly happy to be off duty.

Deverell sized up two workers in green garments carrying full bags of clothes as they entered the laundromat. He quickly paid for his meal and hurried out, careful not to look out of place; most of the workers were Kazakhs, with some Mongols and others from Russia. With his pasty complexion and height, he hoped he could pass for the latter as a worker on his day off. He was also painfully aware that eyes watched the town; most likely Americans who, while dressed as civilians, carried themselves with the sharp bearing of military specialists. Deverell figured that if Victor really had been caught, Reyor would have beefed up security at both the Sanctuary and the project site.

He crossed the street just as the two workers left the laundromat. Bumping into one, he gripped the man by the shoulder to keep them both steady and apologized profusely in Kazakh.

The worker smiled. "It's okay."

Deverell returned the smile, then glanced up at the gray sky. "I heard we're going to get hit with another storm. Do you think they'll change the shifts around, maybe shorten them?"

The man followed his gaze. "No clue, but I'm not worried. I'm finally on my weekend."

"Ech," the second Kazakh grumped. "I've still got two more days to go."

The pair bickered as they strolled off. Deverell looked down at his hand and waggled his eyebrows at the nametag he'd removed from the first man's chest. *It's a lucky thing I'm one of the good guys.*

Inside the empty laundromat, he rummaged through the dryers, picked out coveralls like the ones the workers wore, and locked himself in a bathroom at the far end of the establishment. Once he'd shimmied into the stolen clothes, he rested his hands on the edges of the sink and stared into the mirror. He winced at what was to come, then focused on the structure of his face, just below the skin. Little breaths of pain escaped him as the cartilage in his nose and ears, and the bones in his face, slowly start to move. He could hear the dull crackling throughout his head for almost a minute until everything came to a rest.

The man in the mirror no longer looked like Deverell. Instead, he resembled the worker whose nametag he'd lifted. It wasn't a perfect mimicry, but it would do in a pinch.

He dug through his backpack and pulled a leather bracelet onto each wrist, both two inches wide. The one on the right had a thin wire connecting it to a small hoop that fit over his ring finger. *Time to take these prototypes on a test run.*

Leaving the town behind, he traversed on foot to the sprawling staging area located half a mile away, between the bank of the Irtysh River and a stretch of snow-covered hills to the left. As he approached a junction, he noted a dirt road that led inland through the hills, away from the staging area.

That's probably where the raw materials are excavated for construction, he mused. *The Sanctuary's most likely somewhere in the back, too. Mining activity would offer a perfect cover. I need to get there, but I'll look out of place just walking around.*

As he neared the bustling staging area, he noticed baton-bearing guards in gray uniforms posted at various locations around the site. *This must be the regular security detail for the construction project . . . But those two eagle-eyed blokes in black over there are packing some real firepower. Probably Reyor's bunch, protecting the Arcane Ventures.*

The two guards he'd spied only gave a quick glance at what must have been a familiar face as Gareth entered the worksite. He fished out a hardhat from a crate beside a row of dirty flatbed trucks, then checked the vehicles. The doors all opened, but keys were nowhere to be found.

I could hotwire one of these, but that might get some attention. Let's try something else.

He located the site office—a converted shipping container—and made sure the hardhat was pulled low over his eyes. His abilities allowed him to mimic the basic facial structure of whoever he'd had physical contact with, but it didn't change his voice, the pigment of his skin, or his eye color.

Inside, workers sat behind messy desks. Most were focused on their computers or paperwork, but one older Kazakh woman waved him over. "Serik? Why are you back? I thought you were done."

"I—"

"As long as you're here, would you mind going to Site Two? The excavator there is broken again. I tried to get ahold of the other mechanics but they're all busy."

"I'll take a look at it."

"Great." The woman jerked her thumb over her shoulder at

a large panel on the wall with keys hanging from hooks. "Use truck number six. I'll sign it out for you."

Deverell grabbed the keys and found the truck and appropriate equipment within, then left the staging area. *No excavators here, so it's probably in the mining area in the hills.*

He turned onto the dirt road he'd seen earlier. As he rounded the bend, he found a guard in black stationed there. Continuing down the wide, muddy track, he soon spotted the stalled excavator a quarter mile away. Then, something else caught his eye.

Another dirt road forked to the left of the main one and curved out of sight between two hills. He saw no vehicles taking the path.

Curious, he thought as he arrived at the broken excavator.

The operator, a Russian man, looked annoyed. "Finally! Do you know how long I've had to wait for you?"

"I apologize, we've been really busy. So, what's the problem?"

"The oil is overheating again."

"Alright, let me have a look."

Deverell got to work checking the gauges in the cab. It helped that he and his brother were knowledgeable in a wide range of occupations, a consequence of having an unquenchable thirst for knowledge and self-reliance. He finished his inspections and turned on the excavator. Within minutes the oil temperature shot up. He turned it off and plugged in a diagnostic analyzer, waiting until it beeped to check the readout.

The operator hovered near him impatiently. "Well?"

Deverell jumped out of the cab. "Looks like the oil cooler is malfunctioning. There could also be a problem with the relief valve pressure. Let me clean the valves and try again, otherwise I'll have to get replacement parts."

"Hurry up, then."

"Believe me, I'm trying," Deverell muttered. It would take about thirty minutes to confirm the problem one way or another. It was time he didn't have, but he needed to assimilate into the workforce to avoid raising suspicion.

Sure enough, half an hour later, he presented the bad news. "It doesn't look good, and I don't have any spares in the truck. I'll have to go to the main site and see if I can locate some. Hopefully we have them."

The operator responded with a string of profanities. Deverell left the man to himself and drove back along the muddy road. While the town had cleared its streets after the snowstorm, the powder at the worksite had turned into slush, making the ride more than a little dubious.

Ahead, a truck similar to his but orange in color, headed his way. It made a sharp turn onto the empty road that disappeared into the hills. Deverell ensured he was alone on the main track before hastily wedging his vehicle out of sight between two knolls. He clambered up the slope of one, using mounds of snow as cover. Peering over the other side, he saw more hills behind the secret road and, in the distance, dark shapes moving in pairs. Examining the shapes through a monocular, he realized that they were armed guards patrolling different sectors of the terrain.

Probably watching the Sanctuary's exit points and air vents, he thought. *Tighter security after Vic's breakout from New Mexico, no doubt.* He climbed a little higher just as the orange truck peeled into view and turned into a twenty-foot-wide hole in a hillside diagonally across from him.

No. Not a hole. A tunnel!

Just inside the tunnel entry, four giant guards, armed to the teeth and garbed in black, checked the driver's identification and the interior of the vehicle before waving him through a massive, sliding steel door. It would be impossible to sneak in on foot.

Deverell put the monocular away. *There's the entrance, but how do I get past the Orcs and into Mordor?*

His answer emerged from the Sanctuary a few minutes later: another orange truck. He rushed down the slope and grabbed his backpack from his vehicle. With no one in sight, he sprinted through the sludge and turned onto the hidden road before slowing to a walk. He held up his hand as the truck approached. The driver powered down his window and yelled at him in English, accent perfectly American. "Hey, you're not supposed to be here! Site Three is for authorized personnel only!"

Deverell went up to the window, putting on a thick Russian accent. "My truck broke down and my leg is already bad shape. Can I get lift to site office?"

The man looked as though he was debating with himself. Then he relented. "Yeah, sure. Hop in the back."

Deverell slid behind the driver, noting the toolbox on the passenger seat. Before the man could shift gears, the Sentry grabbed him around the neck. The driver flailed, fighting as hard as he could, but slowly weakened until he was unconscious. Deverell checked the man's pulse, then with a quick motion jerked his right wrist back so the hoop on his finger pulled on the thin wire. A small, hypodermic needle unsheathed from a concealed slot in his bracelet and pricked the man's neck before ejecting itself as another needle took its place. Under normal circumstances, the sleeper hold would have left the man unconscious for a few minutes, but with the tranquilizer he would be safely out of commission for two hours.

If I could just figure out how to make this compound take effect instantly, this prototype would be even handier, Deverell thought.

He quickly changed into the driver's white coveralls and helmet, hid the unconscious man in the back seat under a tarp, then got behind the wheel and watched in the rearview mirror as he altered his facial features. *Hopefully, since this fellow was just there, they'll let me in without checking the truck.*

A sharp beep sounded and a small light on a tablet resting atop the toolbox flashed. Deverell turned the screen on and grinned. *Looks like this is connected to the Sanctuary's systems. So what was that alert for?* He swiped down on the notification bar, tapping the latest icon. *Aha! A work order for some electrical malfunction. This lad must be an electrician. Perfect cover.*

He steered the truck around, slowing as he entered the tunnel. One of the guards, a muscular black man, came up to the window.

"Richie. Back so soon?"

Deverell did his best to mimic the driver. "Yeah. Just when you think you're done, another job pops up."

"That's the way the coin lands, my brother." The guard nodded at the others and they waved the Sentry forward as the steel door slid open.

Inside, Deverell continued down a long tunnel before emerging in the cavernous Sanctuary. Mounted high on the ceiling at well-spaced intervals, large, warm-toned banks of LED lights illuminated the subterranean stronghold, bathing the entire place in a soft golden glow and leaving only a few scattered shadows around some of the buildings and structures.

Deverell gaped. *This is like an underground city—a perfect preppers' haven!*

He stopped in a parking lot near the tunnel; it was already filled with several trucks, a couple of smaller vehicles, and a few Hummers. He surveyed his surroundings, then looked back at the tablet. In addition to work orders, the device contained a diagram of the layout of the Sanctuary as well as a highlighted note: *Eastern section of administrative building is off-limits this week, as directed by Head of Sanctuary Zarya Yussupov.* He paused, then zoomed in on a small box of statistics in the corner. *Each Sanctuary can house up to six thousand people? There definitely doesn't seem to be that many here. At least, not yet.*

He checked the details of the work order, grabbed the toolbox, and entered a building adjacent to the parking lot marked on the map as 'Aquaponics 3.'

Inside, a fish-rearing tank spanned the entire building, twice the length of a tennis court, with narrow walkways around it. Countless tilapia swam and splashed toward a dark-skinned girl as she tossed fish feed into the water. She wore a crisp gray shirt and black cargo pants, a utility belt around her waist. Deverell passed her and was stunned when he glimpsed her face. *She can't be much older than thirteen or fourteen!*

Two other similarly dressed SONEs tended to a range of crops in hydroponic trays suspended above the fish tank, harvesting tomatoes, lettuce, strawberries, and kale. Deverell gave a small nod and squeezed past them to the other end of the building where the control panels were located. According to the work order, the automated light timers—which he suspected simulated natural day–night cycles—were acting up.

It took him only a few minutes to get the lights working properly. On his way out, the girl feeding the fish grabbed his arm. “Hey!”

Deverell froze.

“Thanks for fixing the timers!” she chirped. “They’ve been driving me crazy all morning.”

The Sentry relaxed and gave a half smile. “No problem. I’m glad to be of service.”

The girl beamed, letting him go. “Of course. Everyone should be. This is all for a future that *we* will lead. A brave new world awaits us! Gosh, I’m so excited!”

“Let’s keep at it, then. We’re closer now to a fundamental transformation of the planet.”

“Yes! Absolutely!” The girl shook his hand and returned to feeding the fish, a big smile plastered on her face.

As he left, Deverell thought, *Fundamental? Humph. Emphasis on “mental.” What a mess. It’s so tempting to get rid of Reyor once and for all. That monster is here, right here. I can actually feel it in my bones. Ach, what an awful sensation. Even my hands are trembling.*

Stepping out of the aquaponics facility, he chanced a walkabout to get a feel of the Sanctuary. Teenagers swarmed the place, some tending to a variety of life-sustaining facilities, others trooping around with clipboards or tablets, and still others checking on structural and support systems. They wore differently colored shirts and black cargo pants with boots, but a few wandered around in civilian clothing.

Guess they get days off, Deverell noted silently. *This is fascinating. They’ve all been repurposed, but they don’t seem to be mindless drones. Free will does exist to some degree. Bravo, Reyor. This was very well thought-out. Still, it would be so easy to end it all here. Except, oh yes, the world would literally be obliterated. How twisted is this? Not only can we not eliminate Reyor, but we may actually have to protect that fiend against threats, including the authorities!*

He threw his arms up and bellowed in frustration, causing a pair of youths to stop and stare at him. He paused and awkwardly waved at them until they walked away.

The lathe'ad is Reyor's shield, he continued to himself. *The only shield. It completely rests on the Chosen Ones to deal with this, but are they even capable of that monumental duty yet? What if they're not? Argh . . . Okay, okay, focus on the task at hand. Think. Where would they hold Vic if they had him here?*

He glanced at the tablet, rereading the note from the Head of Sanctuary. *The admin building. It's worth a look. Maybe I can find a way to sneak into the restricted area.*

Rumbling engines emanated from the tunnel as a couple of Hummers rowdily rolled in and parked beside Gareth's truck. Three guards with backpacks got out, joking with each other. One checked his watch. "We're fifteen minutes early."

"Let's relieve the guys anyway," a second said. "They've had a long shift."

Deverell followed them as they headed past the lot. A hundred yards across from the parked vehicles, a platoon of SONEs in military fatigues participated in drills on an open gravel field. The teenagers, taller and beefier than the others he'd seen so far, looked hardened from physical training. Men and women with stony expressions inspected them while one stood in front and barked commands.

The three guards turned a corner and entered what must have been a locker room, because they quickly reemerged without their backpacks and ambled toward a sizable concrete building. Without anything to hide behind, Deverell tailed them as casually as he could. He checked the site map on his tablet, then smiled.

They're heading to the admin building, and yet it's off-limits . . .

One of the guards stopped short and spun around. Deverell hastily glanced down at the tablet as if to read something, then craned his head back to inspect the ventilation shafts overhead that led to an imposing steel enclosure. The enclosure stood out starkly against the warmer hues of the other buildings and had no windows, only a fortified door. Strange sounds came from within, almost like thunder.

Deverell didn't dare check if the guard was still watching. He wandered around, pretending to examine something or another as he tried to work out a plan to infiltrate the administrative building.

Moments later he heard approaching voices. Three different guards, all with shadows under their eyes, passed him. They gathered their belongings from the locker room, then trudged to the parking lot. Deverell followed them and made a show of searching for something in his truck's flatbed; all the guards had parked in the row ahead.

The guard closest to him, with a deep southern accent, searched his pockets and backpack, then groaned. "I can't find my keys."

"Check your locker," one of the others suggested. "We'll meet you back in town for a nightcap."

"Naw, you're waiting right here. Y'ain't getting a head start on the drinks."

"Sure, sure. No problem. We'll just . . . be here, of course."

As the first guard started back toward the lockers, the other two cackled and jumped into a Hummer, tearing toward the tunnel and out of sight. The remaining guard cursed out loud. He took a step forward and a metal jingle emanated from his pants. "What the—"

Before he could check his pockets again, Deverell slid behind him and applied the same chokehold and tranquilizer combination he'd used on the electrician. He crouched out of view when he caught sight of a SONE heading toward the aquaponics facility, then dragged the guard behind the truck he'd stolen. Once he'd again changed clothes and facial appearance, he dug the missing keys out of the guard's pocket before stowing both the limp guard and the electrician in the back of the remaining Hummer. Then he grabbed his bag and jogged to the administrative building.

Three doors twenty feet apart provided access. Deverell opened the first and found himself staring down a hallway with more doors evenly spaced along either side. *Looks like some kind of dormitory*, he thought. He looked up and saw a camera above his head, facing the long passage. *This probably isn't it.*

He opened the second door and walked in. When his boot touched the ground, a sharp snap sounded. *Whoa, that's some solid flooring. Can't sneak up on anyone like this.*

A few paces ahead, a darkened corridor extended to the left. It was empty except for a couple of brightly lit vending machines. To the right was a door with the word 'Boardroom' inscribed in Kazakh on a plaque. Deverell thought he heard voices on the other side. He stopped and pressed his ear against the wood, feeling a slight chill as he did.

There was a low drone of male voices, as well as a female one. They went silent within a few seconds. Deverell quickly turned and started down the corridor, only glancing back when he heard the door open. An incredibly short man with greasy black hair and thick glasses glared out at him. Deverell had never seen Dr. Nate before but knew it was him right away.

"Mornin'," he said crisply.

The doctor mumbled something and shut the door, though not before Deverell glimpsed a figure garbed in a long black coat with a golden hood at the back of the room. Terror shot through him. He steadied himself against the glass window of one of the office rooms. It was as if he'd completely forgotten how to breathe. He rode out the fear in silence, then gathered himself and continued down the hallway.

That was Reyor. My God, that was Reyor! He halted. *What if Vic is in there? There's not a chance I'll be able get in with just my adaptive appearance . . . Bah, why wasn't I born with additional abilities?*

The offices were all dark and empty but at the far end of the corridor, light spilled from a window of a corner room. A camera on a wall directly ahead made Deverell regret pressing his ear to the door earlier.

An Asian man with a rifle slung across his shoulder looked around the corner of the hallway as Deverell passed in front of the lit room. "Hey!" he greeted, his accent perfectly American. "I knew I heard footsteps. You're done with your shift, man. Why are you still here?"

"I lost my keys," the Sentry drawled. "Was wonderin' if I dropped 'em 'round here?"

"Not sure. We've stayed put, keeping our eyes on this chump." The guard nodded into the lit room.

Deverell turned to the large glass window. Fury made his breath hitch in his throat.

Victor sat slumped in a chair facing the mirror, his T-shirt torn, red and purple welts peeking through the slits. Blood caked the sides of his face and mouth. His head hung so low Deverell feared he was unconscious, but when the older Sentry raised his chin to glare, he let out a loud exhale.

"I know, right?" the guard beside him said. "It's creepy how he keeps staring directly at the mirror like he can see us. He always looks like he's ready to kill everyone."

Of course he does, you witless arse, Deverell thought, outraged. *Look at what you've done to him!*

He let the guard lead him around the corner where a pair of other armed men were stationed in between two doors—the left one leading to Victor's holding cell, the other directly ahead leading out of the administrative building into the open cavern—and a third to a room on the right. The Asian guard opened the last one. "Maybe you left your keys in the pantry. Have a look."

"Thanks." Deverell went into the converted office that served temporarily as the guards' break room and made an act of searching the place. *There are three of them and they're armed,* he thought. *They think I'm one of them. The camera is pointed down the corridor, not around the corner, which is perfect. But I can't take all three at once.*

He stepped back out, shaking his head. "They ain't there."

"You could always walk back to town." The Asian guard grinned. He wiped some sweat off his brow, which Deverell found strange in the chilly building.

"You alright?" he asked.

"Yeah. Had too much coffee, so I'm a little jittery."

"That's what you get for emptying the pot," one of the other men said crossly. "I really needed some caffeine. That's karma for you, Arnold."

"Well, I'm on my way to flush karma down the urinal. Hold the fort, hey?"

"Grab me a soda on your way back, would ya?" The third guard flicked a silver coin at his departing companion, who caught it easily.

Seeing an opportunity, Deverell followed the Asian guard down the hallway and turned into the bathroom. When the man shot him a questioning look, he said, "I might've dropped my keys in here."

The moment the door shut, Deverell pounced, knocking the guard out and pricking him with a tranquilizer. He picked up the rifle and coin, then locked the man in one of the stalls. There was no point in using his abilities when he could not pass as a non-Caucasian; the other guards would know something was wrong immediately. But he still had the element of surprise.

He bounced the coin on his palm, noting the symbols on either side; a rising phoenix on one and, on the other, the Dema-Ki symbol—similar to the letter Z, with a horizontal line through the center. *Strange. If the symbol was a lighter shade, that would mean creation. Darker, destruction. This is mid-tone. What statement are you trying to make, Reyor?*

The guards stationed outside Victor's cell looked up when

Deverell returned with a can of root beer. Confusion had just started to appear on their faces when he tossed the can high into the air. "Catch."

One of them instinctively grabbed the drink as it soared over his head. Deverell swung his fist into the man's face, then pivoted on his heel to grab the second guard around the neck. By the time the first man recovered from the punch and got over the shock of a broken nose, the Sentry had dealt with the other guard and had his gun pointed at him.

The guard grimaced, a red stream trickling down his lips. "Who are you?"

"On your knees," Deverell said. "And remove your gun."

The guard gave him a nasty look but obliged. Deverell reversed his hold on the rifle and jabbed the butt at the man's head, but the guard rolled aside and kicked out, catching the Sentry's knees. Deverell buckled, nearly dropping the gun. The guard shot up and slammed his forearm against Deverell's. The Sentry muffled a yelp and let go of the weapon, then found himself staring down its barrel. He put his arms up slowly, concentrating with all his might.

The guard's expression transformed into horror as Deverell's face morphed into his. *"Holy—"*

Deverell shoved the gun away from his head and slammed the confused guard into the wall before forcefully wrenching him to the ground in a reverse chokehold. The guard swung wildly, nearly landing a few punches before going limp and getting pricked with a needle. Deverell, breathing hard, pushed himself up and opened the door to the holding cell.

Victor turned his head to him as he entered. He bristled, fighting against his restraints and spitting imprecations. Deverell stepped back. "Whoa, hey! Vic, it's me! It's me!"

That only riled Victor more. Deverell, realizing his mistake, morphed back to himself and watched the hostility drain from his friend's eyes. As he crouched to unbuckle Victor's restraints, the older Sentry stared at him like he couldn't believe what he was seeing. "My message got through?" he murmured.

"Some of it, yes. Where's Chief?"

"They took him away."

"You think they'd—"

"No, they wouldn't kill him. Not when they know they can use him as a bargaining chip." Speaking those few words left Victor breathless. "It's good to see your dopey face, kid."

Deverell grinned as he released the last of the manacles. "Good to see you, too." He paused at the sound of several sets of footsteps hurrying down the long corridor. Victor tried to get up but his legs gave out almost instantly. Deverell caught him and sat him back down. "What did they do to you, mate?"

The man looked as though he was about to slip into unconsciousness. Deverell grabbed his head and shook it urgently. "Don't close your eyes, Vic. I'm getting you out of here, okay?"

He lifted his left hand and pulled back a cover on his second leather bracelet, revealing a compartment with a few capsules no bigger than beads. He held one up to Victor's nose and snapped it between his fingers. A spray of green mist puffed out and entered the other Sentry's nostrils as he inhaled. A couple of heartbeats later Victor threw his head back, eyes wide open. "What was *that?*"

Deverell pulled him up and passed him his black utility jacket that was strewn on the floor. "A combination of naturally occurring chemical compounds that Gareth and I created. What you're feeling right now is a rush of adrenaline."

"We're lucky you jokers enjoy experimenting and creating stuff. Got any more toys?"

"In my bag."

"Good." Victor shrugged on his jacket. "Let's get outta Dodge."

They headed for the exit but jerked to a halt when a hooded figure, taller than either of them, appeared in the doorway. Deverell could have sworn the temperature dropped ten degrees.

The Sentries hesitated. In that moment, Reyor swept out a hand and they were lifted off the floor and flung across the room. Their backs smashed against the wall; they groaned, hanging midway. The terror Deverell felt earlier came rushing back as he fought in vain to free himself from Reyor's telekinetic grip.

The towering figure took a step into the room, followed by Dr. Nate. A third figure stayed in the shadows at the threshold. Deverell threw a look at Victor. The battered Sentry gave Reyor a black stare of seething contempt, then flicked his wrist once. Nothing happened. Deverell realized too late what Victor was trying to do. As a warning cry pushed past his lips, Victor flicked his wrist again and Reyor lurched back a few steps, dropping the Sentries.

Deverell reached out to stop Victor but the other man leaned forward, raised his arms behind him, and with white-hot fury in his eyes, swept them forward. Deverell leapt back as a powerful concussive wave tore through the holding cell, shattering the two-way glass into fragments. Reyor staggered out of the room, colliding against a wall. Dr. Nate was sent tumbling backward like a helpless penguin in a storm, and the third man with them was knocked clear to the ground, facedown.

Deverell rounded on Victor. "What the hell were you thinking?" he snapped. "Hurting Reyor could have set off the *lathe'ad*!"

Victor gradually came to his senses. He stared down at his trembling hands, haunted. Deverell grabbed his arm and pulled him toward the exit. As they stepped over the man laying facedown, Victor stumbled against the doorframe. "I—just . . . suddenly weak . . ."

Deverell held him upright and guided him through the door. "It's the compound I used on you. Every time you use your abilities, it weakens you. You were already in bad shape and you just unleashed a massive blast in there."

"Temper . . . got the better of me. But I wasn't at . . . full strength. Could have been . . . worse."

"Let's hold off on the spectacles until you're better, alright?"

The hooded figure was nowhere to be seen as they shambled into the hallway. "Think Reyor bolted?" Deverell muttered.

"No," Victor said between wheezes. "Tactical retreat. Reyor

has no idea what . . . what other abilities we might have, and because I pulled a . . . a stupid stunt back there . . . it must have startled the monster. Reyor's not ready . . . to be a martyr . . . just yet."

As Deverell pushed open the door leading to the cavern, Victor steadied himself and pulled away to stoop over a dazed Dr. Nate, drawing out two silver rings from the diminutive man's pocket. "*These belong to me,*" he snarled.

An alarm sounded. Deverell slung Victor's arm around his neck and they hurried out. "Vic, there are some explosives in my bag. Grab one and—"

"Got it." Victor fished out a blue gel cube, armed it, and tossed it behind them. It landed a few feet from the exterior wall of the administrative building, exploding seconds later in a fiery display. The force pitched the Sentries forward, but they kept their footing.

Guards patrolling inside the cavern poured toward the commotion. Deverell, dragging Victor as though he'd been injured in the blast, shouted at them. "There was an explosion! There are people inside! Help them!"

The men and women in uniform sprinted to the administrative building. Deverell and Victor had only just made it past the locker room when they heard Dr. Nate scream, "What are you doing? They're getting away! *Appre'end them!*"

"We've been made." Victor extricated himself from Deverell and the pair took off toward the parking lot. "Dev, give me another dose of whatever you used."

"I can't."

"Come on!"

"I can't! One dosage, max, or you'll be so pumped with adrenaline your heart will give out!"

Victor glanced over his shoulder at the half-dozen guards in breakneck pursuit. "We're not gonna lose them."

"Don't even *think*—"

Victor turned around and let loose a roar as he unleashed another powerful concussive blast that flung the guards back.

Deverell caught him as he doubled over and threw up. *"Are you mad?"* he hissed.

Victor wiped his mouth, looking wan, then snapped his fingers and sent out a microblast Deverell knew was specifically for his wolfdog to respond to. The older Sentry listened closely for a few moments, then said, "I know where Chief is. I—"

Deverell's look of horror made him stop and do an about-face. SONEs dressed in military fatigues in the field across from the parking lot stared at them, expressionless. Then, in eerie uniformity, they flooded toward the Sentries like a single organism.

"Run!" Deverell yelled.

The men careened to the parking lot. Deverell removed his backpack as they neared the first row of vehicles and grabbed a red spherical gel, armed it, and tossed it over his shoulder. The device erupted, releasing a thick fog. The SONEs fell back, gasping for air and choking.

Deverell coughed and quickly covered his mouth. "Vic, you need to get Chief *now!*" He tossed Victor his left bracelet. "Use only one dose if he's sedated! And don't take any for yourself, you hear me?"

Victor took off, disappearing behind the parking lot. Deverell fell back against the hood of a Hummer, unable to stop coughing.

A battle cry erupted as four SONEs pierced the fog and converged on him, hauling him down by his legs. The back of his head smacked against the ground, temporarily blurring his vision and jumbling his hearing. He kicked out, feet catching one youth in the stomach and pushing him away. Another struck him with a baton, opening a stinging gash from his temple to his cheek. He howled and thrashed, boxing the SONE under her chin with a hard uppercut that threw her head back.

A youth on his other side grabbed his arm. Deverell put all his weight onto the teenager as he pushed himself up and, with their arms locked, rolled over the SONE's back. He lashed out with a kick that sent the youth staggering away, then stole a moment to hack out the smoke from his system only to have two more SONEs drive him back to the ground. His bellow was cut short as one of the teenagers gripped him around his throat, her hold as tight as a constricting python. He slapped meekly at her hands, air no longer finding its way into his body.

A roar reverberated through the Sanctuary, like the roll of thunder. As if on command, the SONEs stepped away from Deverell, distancing themselves until they disappeared into the haze. He sat up, gingerly touching his bruising neck, wondering what had just happened. The sound of thunder echoed again, this time closer. Deverell's gut twisted.

From the smoke, three pairs of green, crocodilian eyes emerged, followed by muscular, streamlined black bodies with cropped tails and ears. The creatures' elongated jaws peeled back, revealing three-inch fangs in double rows. They advanced on massive, silent paws, serrated claws unsheathed. Standing five feet at the shoulder and six feet in length, the beasts approached with hair-raising calmness, under which Deverell could sense an insatiable hunger for slaughter and mayhem.

He slowly got to his feet and backed up between two vehicles. His truck was some rows down. *If I can just get—*

Two of the beasts leapt, easily covering fifteen feet. They slammed down onto the trucks on either side of him, their weight crumpling the roofs like cardboard. Deverell stared at them, mouth hanging open, and they grinned murderously back. He fled among the vehicles, slamming into side mirrors but not stopping. The beasts followed, sending a boom throughout the cavern with each roof-crushing impact and snapping at him as he ran for his life. He had a sick feeling that they were toying with him, that they enjoyed seeing him panic.

His truck came into view. He pulled the door open, dove in, and slammed it shut. Gasping, he locked everything.

BOOM.

The roof of the truck collapsed inward, nearly crushing his skull. He yelped and looked up in time to see long claws pierce the vehicle's metal skin, almost impaling his eyes. He sank low in his seat and, just as he turned on the engine, a different thud sounded. Peering through the gap between the headrest and the seat, he spotted the second beast on the flatbed. It rushed at the rear window, ramming its head against the thick glass. Cracks appeared, growing like a spider's web.

As the beast prepared to slam the glass again, the driver's window shattered inward and the third monster shoved its head through, nearly filling the whole frame. Before Deverell could move, it clamped its jaws around his left arm. A guttural scream tore from the Sentry as bone snapped and flesh ripped. He lifted his other arm and repeatedly stabbed the creature in its eye with the remaining tranquilizers in his bracelet. The beast let go and stumbled back. It flung its head furiously from side to side, letting out a roar that wobbled the entire truck before finally falling to the ground. Whether it was unconscious or dead, Deverell couldn't tell, and he didn't care to find out. His arm hung uselessly by his side and the adrenaline kept him from feeling most of the pain as he bled over everything—the steering wheel, the seat, himself.

Keep it together, he thought, shivering. All his senses were heightened. He tasted the metallic tang of blood in his mouth and smelled it from his injuries, and nearly suffocated on the pungent reek of ammonia coming off the beasts.

As he reached for the gearstick, he heard the rear window shatter. He didn't get the chance to put the truck in reverse. The creature on the roof leapt down and shoved its head through the broken driver's window. It was bigger than the others but managed to squeeze its head in. Deverell scooted across to the passenger seat. The beast bared its teeth, tongue poking out between its fangs as if to say, *You can't run, and you can't hide.*

It tried to crawl in but found itself unable to fit, and retreated instead. Deverell took his place behind the wheel again but the beast shoved its head back in, bit down on the window frame, and tore the door clear off the truck, flinging it away. Before Deverell could register what was happening, the monster clamped down on his mangled arm and hauled him to the ground like a rag doll. Spittle dripped from its mouth onto his face as he fought to keep the creature away from his neck. He screeched as it opened its jaws wide, fangs rushing to meet him.

A blur of silver-gray barreled into the beast, knocking it off him. Deverell scooched toward the truck, stunned to find Chief grappling with the much bigger creature. As he neared the vehicle, he saw Victor running in the direction of the fray.

The beast in the flatbed jumped onto the truck's roof. Deverell pulled himself inside just as the creature leapt over his head and bowled Chief over, leaving the other beast to pick the wolfdog up by his scruff.

Deverell threw the truck in reverse and powered down the backseat window. "Chief!"

Chief, ears pinned and hackles raised, violently clawed his way to freedom. Smaller and lither than the beasts, he weaved past them and gracefully soared through the open window and into the backseat. Deverell backed up and spun the truck around so it faced the entrance tunnel just as Victor released a concussive blast that knocked the beasts over and shook the truck like a leaf in the wind.

Deverell steadied the vehicle with his good hand as Victor, visibly weakened, stumbled toward it and collapsed into the back seat beside his wolfdog. "I shorted the door control," he panted, "so the gate's wide open. Go!"

They took off. Glancing at his rearview mirror, Deverell's throat tightened. The beasts had regained their feet—even the one he'd stabbed with tranquilizers. A full-grown human would have died from two doses.

He stepped on the gas and refused to look into the mirror again.

The guards at the Sanctuary's exit were waiting, rifles leveled. As the truck neared, they let loose a torrent of bullets, striking the fenders and hood and shattering the windshield. From the back seat, Victor reached forward and pushed Deverell's head down, shielding him from flying glass and bullets. He made a grab for the wheel but was thrown back as the younger Sentry stomped on the gas pedal.

"Let me drive!" Victor barked.

"Like hell! You're not fit!"

"Says the guy with *one functioning arm!*"

When the guards realized that the truck would not stop, they threw themselves out of its path. Victor grabbed onto Deverell's headrest to keep himself steady. "Move over!"

"Have you lost your—"

"That's an order, Vaughn!"

Deverell knew better than to argue when he heard that tone. Keeping one hand on the wheel and one foot on the gas, he slid into the passenger seat.

Victor climbed over the center console and moved in behind the wheel, but the hasty hand-off made the truck veer and slip in the mud. He wrestled with the vehicle as it fishtailed down the road between the hills, half-blinded by the slush flying through the gaping hole where the driver's door had been.

He squinted into the rearview mirror, unused to natural light after days underground, and went wide-eyed. The pursuing beasts closed the gap between them with every ten-foot leap. *So those are the Marauders we've heard about,* he thought. *Freakish abominations.*

"How are they catching up so fast?" Deverell exclaimed as he ripped off part of his stolen uniform to bind his injured arm. He took another look into the mirror on his side, and suddenly guffawed.

"That's an outrageous sound to hear in our current predicament," Victor muttered.

"'Objects in the mirror are closer than they appear.' I swear I've seen this movie before."

"*That's* what you're thinking about right now?!"

The leading Marauder, with tranquilizer needles still sticking out of its damaged eye, drew even with the truck's rear. It nudged the vehicle with its muzzle, executing a PIT maneuver that sent the truck into a spin, flinging sludge and mud everywhere. The vehicle spun thrice before coming to a standstill—facing the oncoming beasts. Deverell cried out. "Vic!"

Victor threw the transmission into reverse and floored it. As they backed down the road with the engine screaming, the other Marauders caught up with the first. Two black Hummers roared out of the Sanctuary tunnel, covering the terrain as easily as the beasts.

Deverell hiccupped nervously. "Oh, cheers. Shall we just *Thelma and Louise* this whole thing?"

"I'm seriously considering pushing you out of this truck and getting away alone." Victor looked over his shoulder as the road curved left. "I hope that's an exit."

"It'll take you to an active mining road. Make a right and we're golden. Just don't back into it!"

"Too late." Victor spun the wheel and they swung into the main road in reverse. "There! We're—"

"WATCH IT!"

Victor slammed the brakes and they skidded past an oncoming double tractor trailer. The driver bludgeoned his horn, deafening the Sentries. Victor kept reversing as the colossal vehicle swerved to avoid the smaller truck. The tractor slid sideways in the mud and collided into the base of a hill, coming to an abrupt stop, but the double trailers—loaded with rocks and earth—barreled right past the cab and dragged the tractor along. The Marauders emerged from the concealed Sanctuary road just as the entire rig tipped on its side. Two of the beasts leapt to safety. The third was crushed by one of the massive trailers.

The Hummers veered around the wreck, scaling the banks on either side of the road. Victor, still speeding backward, yelled, "Hang on!"

He hurled the truck into a reverse one-eighty, then changed gears and ripped forward. In the back, Chief could be heard tumbling against one of the doors. Deverell, who'd been patching his arm, turned green at the sudden J-turn. "This feels like Istanbul all over again."

Victor grunted. "This is *nothing* like Istanbul."

They raced between the hills until the small town near the hydroelectric operation came into sight. Not wanting to put civilians in harm's way, Victor turned onto the road that connected the town to the staging area and sped toward the bank of the two-mile-wide river. Deverell pointed through the destroyed windshield. "Look!"

Moored to a dock, a barge and towboat were tied together with heavy ropes. The last of six cars that the barge had ferried across the river slowly rolled off a ramp. *It's the boat Chief and I took when we crossed over to recon*, Victor realized. *That's our way out.*

He struck the horn, sending out a warning. Upon seeing the chaos headed directly at him, the driver of the car up ahead swerved, tires slipping, and narrowly missed getting totaled as the truck charged up the loading ramp. The Sentries found themselves airborne for a moment before hitting the deck. Victor slammed on the brakes. The truck skidded toward the end of the ninety-foot barge, stopping just as the bumper kissed the railing.

"That was close," Deverell said through his teeth. He jerked his head at the fifty-gallon fuel drums secured to the railing beside him. "Good thing you missed those. Would've been really gutted if we were blown up after getting this far."

"Was that a morbid pun?" Victor asked in disbelief.

"Don't look at me like that, you curmudgeon! You're the one who always tells people not to lose their humor!"

They leapt onto the deck. Deverell jumped down into the towboat on the starboard side of the barge and yelled for the captain and his assistant to leave. As the terrified crew fled to dry land, Victor made a break for the mooring lines securing the barge to the dock. His chest hurt from breathing the cold air too fast, and his freezing fingers struggled with the ropes. As he cast off the approaching Marauders, less than forty yards from the ramp, seemed to pick up speed as they neared.

"Dev!" he shouted, dumping the ropes onto the deck. "Get us out of here! *Now!*"

A dull rumble of the towboat's engine responded. Victor released a long exhale as they started to put distance between them and the shore, his tense shoulder dropping. Chief slunk up to him, growling at the Marauders as they drew closer to the riverbank. He patted his companion's head wearily. "We're good, Chief. We're good."

The beasts let loose a roar that drained all the blood from the Sentry's face. They made it to the edge of the shore and, muscles bunched, leapt. Victor stared in horror as they soared nearly twenty yards in the air and crashed onto the unsecured ramp trailing in the water, half of their bodies in the river, claws gaining purchase on the metal gradient.

He grabbed Chief before the wolfdog could descend the ramp to go head-to-head with the Marauders and flung him toward the towboat. "Go!" he ordered. Chief hesitated, but when Victor shouted again, he dove over the side to join Deverell in the wheelhouse.

The Marauders, using their claws as hooks, had worked their way up to the deck. Victor faced off against them, reaching into whatever energy he had left, and cast out a concussive blast. It barely ruffled the beasts' fur. He tried again but the attempt was even weaker than his last. The Marauders' jaws parted in a mockery of a smile, their manic eyes following his every motion. Water dripped off their obsidian coats as they closed in like pincers. Victor backed toward the center of the deck. He glanced at the towboat, contemplating his chances of reaching it.

The beasts sprang, throwing him onto his back and covering him in a pungent flurry of fur and ivory fangs. Victor fought to keep their faces away from his exposed throat. He cursed at them, summoning his last reserves of energy, and released an acoustic wave that flung the Marauders off the deck. They splashed into the water and disappeared beneath the waves, then broke the surface, eyes locked on the Sentry. With frenzied rage, they propelled themselves after the barge.

Victor got up, swaying, before his legs gave out. He fell heavily onto his arms and knees, forehead against the deck. Despite the biting cold, sweat glazed every inch of his body and dripped off his face onto the rusty surface. His head hurt and his heart hammered against the confines of his chest. His vision tunneled for a few seconds but still he pushed himself up, steadying himself against the rocking of the barge.

The Hummers that had followed them from the Sanctuary veered toward the project's staging area. Victor pressed his hand against his throbbing head. *What are they doing?* His gaze slid ahead of the Hummers' path and he groaned. He stumbled over to the railing where the towboat was churning the water. "They're heading for workboats at the dam site!" he shouted to Deverell. "They'll be coming from the south! We need to go faster!"

Deverell poked his head out of the wheelhouse. "We can only do six knots with the barge attached! At this rate it'll take twenty minutes to make it across!"

"Six knots? The Marauders are doing better than that!" Victor turned back to the staging area. Three high-powered aluminum workboats pushed away from the shore and tore through the water toward them. "They're on the move!"

"Get over here! Let's lose the barge!"

A report sounded, shattering the air. Victor threw himself to the deck. Bullets whizzed around him from the direction of the staging area, striking the truck, the side of the barge, the railings, and the mast above the towboat's wheelhouse. *Can't let them close in,* he thought. *And the Marauders are catching up.*

He glanced toward the bow of the barge and spotted the fuel barrels beside the truck. At the first sign of a break in the shooting, he vaulted over the railing into the towboat and rolled into the wheelhouse. Grabbing Deverell's backpack, he rummaged through it.

"What are you looking for?" the other Sentry yelled as the gunshots resumed.

Victor shoved a few explosive cubes into his utility jacket. "These. And—" He pulled out a black-and-red tactical knife. "Are you kidding? I've been looking everywhere for this!"

"I meant to return it after the shindig in Novosibirsk!"

"That was two years ago!"

"Sorry!"

Grumbling, Victor put the hilt of the knife between his teeth and climbed back onto the barge. He'd only taken a few steps when something struck him, sending him spinning, before he slowly crumpled to the ground. A stream of red spilled from his head, tainting the deck.

It took a few moments for him to realize he was still alive. With shallow breaths, he shakily felt the right side of his head, aware of a sharp burning there. Blood curled over his fingers and into his eye. He wiped it away and continued to feel around.

No holes. Just a graze. That's a lot of blood. So much blood. It's okay. Just a graze.

He slid his thumb over his ear. It was jagged—part of the helix had been torn off.

You're fine. Get up.

He stepped over the scarlet puddle, doubled over, and ran to the truck. Using it as cover, he opened the cap to one of the fuel barrels and pulled a cube from his jacket. There were three indents on its surface, timers set to detonate the cube in two hours, half an hour, or forty seconds. If all were pressed at once, it would detonate within seconds. He pushed the forty second timer, forced it into the circular opening, then capped the barrel and cut the rope holding it in place.

He waited for another break in the gunfire and rolled the barrel toward the ramp. Bullets flew again. Victor kept close to the deck but a projectile scraped past his calf. The hot metal tore his jeans and skin. He fell onto the barrel, gritting his teeth, but didn't stop.

He made it to the edge of the ramp and looked down at the Marauders, less than thirty feet from the barge. He grinned at them, eyes cold, and with one final heave he pushed the fuel drum into the water.

The barrel exploded between the beasts, sending steel shards into the air. The parts of the Marauders exposed to the explosion were completely skinned. And yet they lived, braying in pain and rage. Then puddles of fuel ignited, engulfing the beasts in a furious firestorm.

Victor darted back to the truck amid another hail of bullets and tried to get the other two drums loose, but found that they were secured not just with ropes but chains as well. Frustrated, he looked around the vehicle. A couple of hundred yards from the other side of the barge, the workboats bounced over the waves toward the Sentries. Thinking fast, Victor armed the rest of the gel cubes, shoved two into each barrel, and dove over the railing into the towboat, landing on his side. His injured leg screamed in protest and his vision tunneled again. He dragged himself to the ropes that bound the boats together, struggling with them until they were released from their bollards.

"Go!" he yelled.

The smaller vessel surged past the barge with a sudden burst of speed, as if thankful to be rid of the excess load. They were now a quarter mile from the east bank, from freedom. Victor made his way into the wheelhouse. Deverell did a double take.

"Your head!"

"Just grazed," Victor said. The blood had already started to harden against his skin and jacket. He gripped the back of the wheelhouse seat. "I'd suggest holding onto something."

"What did you do?"

Victor watched as the guards, ignoring the loose barge drifting toward them, sped after the Sentries. "Detonation in three, two . . ."

Four explosives in a hundred gallons of fuel erupted in a massive fireball stretching hundreds of feet into the air. The discharge tore all the way through the barge. The shockwave and ensuing wall of water hoisted the workboats violently off the river before capsizing them, and the guards were flung haphazardly into the freezing river, screaming and sputtering obscenities. Smoke spiraled upward as debris rained down. Fire danced on splotches of fuel floating in the water, spreading quickly.

The wash from the explosion sent out swells that pushed the Sentries closer to the frozen shore. As they neared the bank, Victor passed Chief one end of a long rope and secured the other to a capstan on the towboat. The wolfdog leapt ashore, pulling the boat until it grounded, and the Sentries helped each other onto land. They collapsed on their backs to catch their breath, then propped themselves on their elbows, facing the river.

The flames on the barge, surrounded by a blanket of black smoke, reached out like glowing fingers in the cold air as the vessel began to sink. One of the workboats' fuel tanks ignited into a ball of cardinal fury, engulfing it.

Deverell started to cough, only it wasn't a cough but a weak snicker. Victor felt his lips pull into a smile and he joined in, holding one hand up. Deverell grasped it tightly, then they threw their heads back, laughing hysterically into the sky, hollering and whooping and crowing. Chief joined the merriment, loosing a howl that made them laugh even harder.

After a few moments, Victor rested his head back down. The last of the adrenaline had left him and now he could feel the pain of everything—his leg, his head and ear, his body, his face, even his teeth ached. By Deverell's fading laughter, he suspected the other Sentry was starting to feel the agony of his mangled arm as well.

"Reyor will probably have people watching the hospitals around here," he said, sitting up. "I've got a first aid kit in my car, but it's still a bit of a walk."

"Where did you park it?" Deverell asked.

"A small town about three miles south to keep away from prying eyes."

"Guess what they say about great minds is true. That's where I stashed mine as well. You can grab your things and we'll take my truck."

They moved as quickly as they were able to, but it still took almost an hour to reach the town. They ignored the puzzled expressions directed at them and got into Deverell's vehicle, patching themselves up as best they could. And, though they both loathed it, they were forced to take painkillers.

"I'll drive," Victor said.

Deverell smacked his hand away from the wheel. "No."

"You—"

"I *know* I've got a gimp arm, but whatever they did to you pushed you to the brink of death and I don't think you even realize it. And that's before your multiple injuries, not to mention the epinephrine boost I gave you has completely worn off. Mate, you look like you should be in a hearse right now."

"You sure know how to flatter people."

"I'm driving, and that's that. You should rest. We've got a long way to go."

Victor glanced into the back seat where Chief, exhausted, had fallen asleep. He reached out to stroke the wolfdog between the ears, then sighed. "Alright. But don't push yourself. The moment you need a break, you wake me up. We clear?"

"Crystal."

Victor crawled over into the back as Deverell started the engine. Hugging Chief close, Victor allowed himself to feel safe for the first time in days and willingly walked into the blackness that called out to him.

"Momma, are you okay?"

"It's nothing, sweetheart."

Sitting at the dining table with Tegan as they Skyped their mothers on Aari's laptop, Mariah leaned toward the screen. "You sure?"

One of the two women on the other end of the video chat, a near carbon copy of Mariah down to the copper-blonde hair and earnest cognac gaze, smiled meekly. "I'm concerned, that's all." She blew a kiss at the camera. "I love you so much, baby. Don't worry about me."

"We're taking good care of her," Genevieve Ryder added.

Tegan slid her arms around Mariah. "And we're taking good care of this one."

Krystal Ashton beamed. "I don't doubt it. The five of you have always looked out for each other. Speaking of which, how's Jag? His parents told us what happened."

"He's doing alright, all things considered," Tegan replied. "The boys are keeping him company while he's stuck in bed. He's actually healing pretty fast. The Dema-Ki compound is doing its thing."

The front door opened and Marshall stepped in, cell phone to his ear and grocery bags in hand. He saw the friends and gave them a shake of his head, then entered the kitchen. The girls exchanged glances. *Guess he hasn't found the people tailing us yet*, Mariah thought. The possibility they were being followed was one detail the friends decided to skip while updating their mothers.

"Marshall, come say hi," Tegan called.

The Sentry, still on his call, popped in to wave at the camera, then ruffled the girls' hair and headed back to the kitchen. Their mothers smiled tightly, lines appearing on their foreheads. Mariah gave them a look. "What is it?"

Her mother shifted in her chair. "I . . . we . . ."

"It's nothing," Genevieve said hastily.

Tegan cocked a brow. "It clearly isn't nothing."

Mariah's mother looked down, silent for a few moments. "This has been so difficult for us, letting all of you go because of some *prophecy*. There are times when we take a step back and wonder about what we've done. It's hard to make sense of it all. And then we remember Nageau's words . . . but still. Look at Jag. We could have lost him. Marshall, too. Sometimes we can't help asking if we made the right decision letting you go."

The girls didn't know what to say. Mariah's mother rubbed her face. "I'm sorry."

"You don't have to apologize," Mariah said softly.

Her mother glanced away and quickly wiped her eyes. "So, are you any closer to finding the cure?"

"We hit a bump on the road," Tegan said. "But we did get a break, and one of the Sentries is chasing a lead in Moscow. We were gonna visit someone in Haifa yesterday who may have some answers, but it was Shabbat. Today is an off day as well, so we'll go tomorrow."

"You sound annoyed."

"Well, yeah. We don't have the luxury of wasting time. We've tried calling the man but he never picks up." Tegan huffed. "Anyway, how're things at home?"

"There was talk about reopening the schools in March, but the virus has hit larger cities on both coasts. There's worry that it could spread inland, so there's a chance that it may not happen."

"We saw the news," Mariah said. "People are going crazy in New York and San Diego. And I read online that the government's about to impose martial law in harder-hit places."

Her mother shifted aside, letting Mrs. Ryder move closer to the screen. "Both strains were incubating for a while and now we're beginning to see the effects here, yes. About martial law . . . it's just a rumor as far as we know, but I wouldn't be surprised if the government decides to call in the National Guard to help maintain order."

Mariah noticed Tegan going still as she stared at her mother. She nudged her friend. "Teegs?"

Tegan ignored her. "Mom. Did something happen?"

The elder Ryder gave her daughter a helpless look. "Nothing escapes you, does it?"

"What is it?" Tegan asked, moving closer to the laptop.

"Honey, one of your dad's cousins . . . you remember Bill? We used to visit him in Florida when you were younger? He loved taking you and your brother to Epcot for the rides."

"Yes . . ."

"He's sick, Tegan. Dad and I spoke with his wife. He's not doing well. She said he's aged so much and he's so frail, so . . . so . . ." Genevieve's bottom lip trembled and she bit down to stop it. "The doctor said that, at this rate, he won't make it past next week."

Mariah turned to Tegan, stunned. Her friend had a glazed, faraway look in her eyes. Then, in quiet submission, she said, "Please give Bill and the family my love, Mom."

And there it is, Mariah thought, placing a comforting hand on the other girl's back. *The brave front.*

"How's Dad dealing?" Tegan asked, not looking directly at the screen. "I know how close they are."

"He's shaken. It barely hit home when we first heard that the virus had arrived here, but now . . ."

"I'm glad he has you and Damian to lean on. And Great Fall's entire police department."

Tegan's mother smiled slightly. "The PD's been so good to him, hon. They're looking out for him. For all of us."

"I wouldn't expect anything less. Is Dad on patrol now?"

"Mmhm. Police all over the state—all over the country, really—have been pulling extra shifts. The disease may not have made it to Great Falls yet, but there's still scattered unrest from the food crisis. And some people continue to take advantage of the situation to loot stores and destroy property."

Krystal glared. "I don't understand how some folks can be so selfish and awful."

"Surely it's not all bad?" Mariah asked; she hated to think that her peaceful city could be so obscenely turned upside down.

"No, it isn't," her mother acknowledged. "Times like these often bring out the best in us. Neighbors show love and concern, families come together. But it can also dredge up out the worst as well."

An exuberant yell rang through the house. The girls leapt out of their seats like startled cats. Their mothers gave them enquiring frowns.

"Guess we should let you find out what that's about," Genevieve said. "It was lovely catching up with you two."

"Stay safe," Mariah's mother added.

Mariah waggled her fingers at the screen. "We will, Momma. Love you!"

They ended the call and ran into the kitchen to find Marshall still on the phone, grinning broadly. Mariah tilted her head and he mouthed, "Sorry!"

Aari and Kody trotted out of Jag's room, curious about the commotion. "What's up?" Kody asked.

Marshall put his phone down. "I was talking to Gareth, trying to help him figure out what he might have missed with the three Deols he met in Moscow, when a call came in." He laughed, some of the stress dissipating from his face. "It was Colback. Turns out he *was* in some serious trouble. Dev found him and broke him out of the Kazakh Sanctuary."

The friends slumped against the counter. "Thank goodness," Mariah breathed.

"Yeah, especially since Reyor was there."

The group goggled. "*What?*"

"I can't imagine what that was like for them, being so close to that monster." Marshall rubbed his arm, as though uneasy. "And we're lucky. Apparently Colback nearly launched an apocalypse of biblical proportions."

Kody's eyebrows rose. "What do you mean?"

"He lost it and fired a major concussive blast. Thankfully, the *lathe'ad* didn't go off. I don't know why it didn't, but I'm not gonna argue with the universe over this one."

"Me neither," Tegan agreed. "But if an attack on Reyor could cause the *lathe'ad* to detonate, how are we supposed to fulfill our roles in the prophecy?"

Mariah's shoulders drooped. *So we have to find a cure for a disease before it kills off everyone on the planet, and stop Reyor without laying a finger on the beast. This is impossible.*

Marshall's baby blue eyes softened as he took in the downcast teenagers before him. He hesitated, then slowly pulled them all into an embrace. "I know I probably sound like a broken record," he murmured, "but you're chosen for a reason. Doors will open for you. We have to believe that, have faith in that. And you're my ki—you're family. I will be with you every step of the way, no matter what. This may be your destiny but know that I, and the other Sentries, will walk through fire for you."

Mariah burrowed her face into Marshall's side. *Gah, why am I emotional all of a sudden?*

Because we were just reminded that we are not alone in this journey. We're never alone.

Mariah stood still, not blinking for nigh over twenty seconds. It was not her voice that had just spoken in her head.

Hey! Oh, dang it, she's gone.

Mariah was sure of it now. There was a presence in her mind; tough, composed, thunder in the bones. She cautiously reached out. *H-hello?*

Mariah! You can hear me?

What... wait a minute. Teegs? She looked across Marshall's chest. Tegan, on his other side, smiled at her. Reeling, Mariah stammered, *But how?*

Remember what Elder Nageau said, that it's possible we'd achieve this at some point?

Mariah touched the pendant hanging from her neck. *No way.*

Yeah! Listen, this is new for you, so . . . Tegan trailed off, as though there was a bad connection, then her voice returned: . . . *hovering around in the novasphere, watching to see if you or Aari or Kody would wake up. Looks like you just did.*

I lost you for a second.

That'll happen. In the beginning the exchange is sometimes spotty, but it'll get better the more you use it. Hold on, I'm gonna let Jag know.

A few seconds later, Jag's presence appeared; he was like fire, simultaneously warm and powerful, charged with emotion. *Welcome to the club, Miss Ashton!*

Oh, why thank you, Mr. Sanchez. It's an exclusive club.

Incredibly exclusive, yes, because you can only talk to one person at a time.

Aw, are you serious? No conference calls?

That's not possible, as far as I know. I've asked Elder Nageau.

There was a prodding in Mariah's mind. *Uh, I think someone else is trying to reach me. Gosh, this feels so weird.*

You'll get used to it. Pick up the phone, see who's on the other end. Jag severed their connection.

Mariah reached out again. The new presence felt irrevocably altruistic, as well as soft-hearted and protective. *Hi?* she said.

Marshall's arm tightened around her. *Good of you to join the rest of us, kiddo.*

Mariah pulled away with a laugh. Aari and Kody stared at her, puzzled. "So," she said, "I just got telepathy."

Kody groaned. "Oh, great." He turned to Aari and dragged him into a separate hug. "It's okay, buddy. You and I will travel the lonely road of non-telepaths alone."

The redheaded teenager wiggled away, snickering. "You're an idiot." Mariah noticed that despite his bonhomie, Aari seemed a little down about her announcement.

Marshall clapped his hands. "You know what, I'm a big believer of rejoicing in even the smallest victories, so let's celebrate. Dev and Colback are safe, and Mariah can now enjoy a new ability. I'll make dinner."

Kody stuck his nose into the fridge. "I'll help! I'm a stupendous cook, just ask anyone. Ooh, we may have enough stuff here for Kung Pao chicken! Awesome."

Marshall grimaced. "No, please. No Kung Pao. That's a bad memory for me."

"Bad memory? Of what?"

"Long story short? Stumbling into the nanomite plot and nearly getting killed."

Mariah squinted. "Do Sentries routinely get themselves into life-threatening situations?"

"It's kind of a bad habit. I'll try to kick it."

Mariah, Tegan, and Aari left the kitchen and sat on the steps outside the house, eyes sweeping their surroundings. "You guys feel it, don't you?" Tegan muttered.

Aari pulled his hood over his head and scoped the apartment complex across the street. "That we're being watched? Yeah. If Reyor was there when Victor got out, then whoever's tailing us was probably warned that we'd be on the lookout. And maybe that's why even with his hypersensory abilities, Kody can never find them when he scouts around."

"But why haven't they swooped in yet?" Mariah demanded. "What are they waiting for?"

"I'm sure we'll find out soon enough."

Tegan lifted her chin; there was defiance in her steely gaze. "And when we do, we need to be prepared."

Gareth stepped out of a shopping mall, fixing a surgical mask over his face with one hand and holding a phone to his ear with the other. "So where'll you be heading now?" he asked.

On the other end of the line, his brother responded. "We're on our way south to Almaty. Vic's got a contact there who can help us get the paperwork we need to get to Tashkent."

"You're going to Uzbekistan?"

"Aye. Reyor'll most likely have eyes everywhere in Kazakhstan, so we'll have to take the long way 'round. From Tashkent, we'll fly to the Lodge and recoup there."

Gareth said nothing. Deverell laughed. "When you don't talk is when I know you're worried. Relax, Gareth. We'll be fine."

"You blokes are ridiculous. You must be in loads of pain, but you both sound like nothing's happened. And Vic lost his ear!"

"Not all of it," the Canadian Sentry corrected in the background.

Deverell sniggered. "What happened to you is rather ear-reversible, wouldn't you say, Vic?"

"Jeez Louise."

"Friends, Romans, Victor—lend me your ears!"

"You're making me irritable."

"Don't you mean ear-ritable?"

"Oh, my God."

"You walked right into that one, Vic," Gareth hooted.

"Shut up."

Gareth's mouth curved upward. No matter how choleric Victor sometimes was, he knew the older Sentry was fond of the twins . . . not that he would ever say so outright.

"Anyway," Victor continued pointedly, "I heard you're on the hunt for Dr. Deol. How's that coming along?"

"Horribly," Gareth confessed. "And it's really starting to eat at me. I've checked everything probably ten times over and there's nothing more to be found. D'you suppose you've any more information that could help?"

"I wish I did. All I can say is, I think she's our best bet. From what I heard during Dr. Nate's call, it sounds like she's losing faith in the cause. He and the other guy he spoke to seemed spooked. They were debating whether or not she's 'salvageable.'"

"That doesn't sound promising. What if they decide she isn't?"

"I doubt Reyor likes loose ends, especially if that loose end engineered the virus." Victor paused, then said quietly, "I don't want to put more pressure on you than you're already putting on yourself, but we need to get to her sooner than Phoenix's paranoia."

Gareth fidgeted with his mask, hand clammy, mouth shut.

Deverell spoke up. "We know you're doing the best you can. But, Gareth, remember that yours isn't the only play. The five and Marshall are following another solution as well. We're still in the game. Alright?"

"Mmh." Soft drizzle fell from the clouds overhead, catching Gareth by surprise. "Listen, lads, it's starting to rain and I need to drive. Check in with me when you reach Tashkent, alright?"

"We will," Victor said before Deverell hung up. "Remember, kid. Eyes forward. Always."

Gareth tucked his phone away and pulled up the collar of his leather jacket, hurrying past an empty concert hall toward the main road where his car was parked. As he unlocked it, a small, frazzled-looking group of people rushed by and darted across the street, unperturbed by the speeding vehicles and subsequent honking. Gareth frowned, watching the group duck into a black-roofed edifice directly across from him—the Yaroslavsky railway station. Upon closer inspection, he noted that the doors and windows of the building were broken, and the station was dark, vacant.

Now, why is it that one of the major railway stations in Moscow looks out of commission? he wondered. *And what would a group like that be running in there for at this time of night?*

He looked from his car keys to the building, then pocketed the keys and loped across the street. Atop the roof, a decorative ironwork emblem of the famed communist symbol glinted: a hammer and a sickle. Gareth pursed his lips at the motif, then tailed the group through the length of the ornamental but decrepit station. Glass shards from broken windows and light fixtures crunched beneath his shoes. His breath fogged in the chilly air.

The group vaulted over a row of half-height turnstiles and ran through the shattered glass doors that led outside, from where agitated voices could be heard. Gareth followed and found himself under the painful brilliance of floodlights. He shielded his eyes until they adjusted.

Before him was a crowd of thirty or so people wrapped in warm clothing. Razor wire fencing cordoned off all eleven platforms and sixteen tracks, but he couldn't see anything else through the throng of people. As he worked his way between the masses, the sound of crying filled his ears.

What's going on?

His heart missed a beat when he reached the front. On the other side of the fence, personnel in hazmat suits with military grade weapons shoved dozens of men and women onto the centermost railway track. The civilians crouched on the iron rails, rocking back and forth in the cold. The drizzle grew heavier, but the soldiers patrolled the platforms between the tracks without offering anything to the shivering people for warmth.

Beside Gareth, a distraught teenage girl with dark hair and pale skin held a little boy close to her. The Sentry grabbed her arm. "What's happening?" he demanded in Russian.

The girl turned to him, shooting a glare. He let go of her and held his hands up, softening his tone. “Please, tell me. What’s going on?”

She eyed him, guarded. “The infected. They’re being shipped out.”

Gareth looked back at the men and women on the railway tracks several feet below the platforms. A few of them clamped their heads between their knees or jammed the heels of their hands against their temples, moaning to themselves.

“Where are they being shipped to?” he asked.

“We were told that the trains will take them to a hospital away from the cities. But I’ve heard rumors that . . .” The girl’s voice shook, and the little boy in her arms burrowed into her hair. She glanced down at him, then back at Gareth. Catching her hint, the Sentry leaned in. She whispered, “I heard that they’re taking them away to be incinerated.”

Her words took a moment to sink in. Gareth slowly met her eyes. “That can’t be true.”

“That’s what we heard.” She raised her gaze upward, fighting against the forming tears. “This is not the only place where it’s happening, either, but it *is* happening. Quietly.”

“No, that can’t be. Who authorized it?”

“Nothing happens without the approval of the government.”

Gareth couldn’t to believe his ears. “And why are you here?”

She hugged the little boy tighter as the drizzle turned into a downpour. “Our parents are sitting on those tracks.”

Gareth turned away, running his hands through his wet hair. He wanted to do something, anything, to help, but he knew that he was powerless.

He pulled a small package of surgical masks from his jacket, passed one to the teenager and fit another on her brother. “You shouldn’t be out here without this.”

The girl adjusted her mask, a little surprised by his gesture. “Thank you. We just returned from visiting our grandparents outside the city and found out the military had taken our parents.”

“Are your grandparents here as well?”

"We lost them in the crowd." The girl looked up at him through the fast-falling rain, aggrieved. "Everyone here has someone they care about on the other side of the fence. But nobody can stop this."

An alarmed shout wrenched away their attention. An infected woman clambered onto a raised platform and screamed as the guards approached her. Using the muzzles of their weapons, they nudged her back into the gap. She spat at them, her words growing incoherent. Another woman shrieked, scrambling up the side of the platform. A man followed her, only to get a military boot in his face that sent him falling back onto the tracks.

The girl beside Gareth grasped his wrist. "Their eyes—they're bleeding out of their eyes!"

The guards started to back away as the infected crawled up to the platforms, beating their heads and moaning. Some clawed at their own faces. The guards moved with nervous energy as they tried to herd the sick group back onto the tracks, to no avail.

Then, silence fell. Those that had been banging their heads stopped and peered around, eyes like saucers, heads low. The rest of the infected kept clear of each other, wary.

They're acting like frightened animals, Gareth realized.

A feral cry ripped the silence. A man in a tattered suit threw himself at one of the guards, hurling him onto the ground and repeatedly bashing his head into the concrete until he moved no more. Two other guards filled him with bullets, and chaos broke loose as one after another the sick civilians surged onto the armed personnel.

"Shoot them!" an officer cried.

The crowd behind the fence screamed as submachine guns and assault rifles sprayed the infected masses. Bodies dropped. Sanguine splatters painted the ground. Within seconds it was over. All that could be heard was the fading echoes of the gunshots in the downpour.

A wail rose from somewhere within the throng of people. "You slaughtered them! *Animals!*"

Beside Gareth, the girl stood drenched in rain and shock. She'd held her brother's head against her so he would not witness the massacre that had taken place, so he could not see their parents lying among the rest of the shredded corpses. Gareth put his arms around the two of them. The teenager buried her face into his chest, body heaving. He stared over her head at the carnage as rain washed the blood along the platform and down the tracks. Some of the soldiers removed their gas masks. One fell to his knees, retching. Another sank to the ground and was enfolded in the arms of the others.

An older Russian couple cut through the traumatized crowd. The girl pulled away from the Sentry. Sobbing, she ran to them with her brother in her arms. Gareth watched for a moment, then turned and slunk back into the building. He pulled himself over the turnstiles but slipped and fell over to the other side. Pushing his back against the metal barrier, he sat in the dark, face covered, shoulders shaking. He could taste salt on his lips, and the pungent reek of blood wafted into his nose, making him feel ill.

Something vibrated in his pocket. He pulled out his phone; the caller ID was blocked. He wiped his eyes and cleared his throat, buying time to compose himself, then answered. "Hello?"

A coy voice responded. "Gareth Vaughn."

He was not in the mood for games. "Who is this?" he snapped.

"The woman you've been looking for. I'm Dr. Deol."

Aari removed his sunglasses to take in the grandeur of the expansive manicured gardens that cascaded over nineteen terraces, the entire length of Mount Carmel. *Whew*, he thought. *What a view.*

The Bahá'í Gardens in Haifa were divided into three sections; lower, middle, and upper. Aari, Tegan, Mariah, Kody, and Marshall milled on the topmost balcony of the latter, soaking in the serene aura of one of Israel's most popular tourist attractions. Palm trees, fountains, and countless vivid flowers flowed down the slope. A white marble structure crowned by a glinting, hundred-and-twenty-foot golden dome enthroned the center of the hillside. Two sets of stairs stretched from the summit to the bottom courtyard, flanked by rivulets. Just past the foot of the courtyard, a long road lined with restaurants and shops on both sides extended toward the port, opening into the dazzling Mediterranean Sea.

Aari shook his head in wonder. *The design of this garden . . . just stunning. Not to mention the Parthenon-esque buildings we saw while driving up! Man, what a place.*

Mariah, beside him, linked her arm through his. "I wish Jag could be here to see all this," she murmured.

"Some contrast, huh?" Marshall said, leaning on the marble railing, a breeze sweeping through his hair. "Being in an oasis like this while the world is on fire."

Tegan nodded. "And the irony is that, amid everything, we find solitude in the Middle East of all places."

The Sentry chuckled. "I guess Israel's security paranoia paid off. They're not completely free of the virus, but at least they're somewhat safer."

"Okay, I hate selfies, I really do," Kody said, "but can we take one picture?"

"Yes!" Mariah pulled the others close.

One of the guards at the entrance, no older than twenty, poked his head past the gate. "Hey, I can take that photo for you if you'd like."

Kody passed him his phone and the guard snapped away, then returned the device. "Thanks, my dude," Kody grinned. "You don't sound like a local. Where you from?"

"Chile." The guard jerked his chin at the entrance where an Asian girl was laughing with one of the local security personnel. "And she's from Australia. We volunteer here." He nodded down the slope. "How do you like it?"

"It's gorgeous," Mariah gushed. "Your gardeners do an amazing job."

To their left, a man came up the stairs to the balcony. "Some call it the Eighth Wonder of the World. I've worked here for years, but I never get tired of the view."

The man wore dirty gray pants and a black sweater. He looked to be in his early sixties and was deeply tanned with short, white hair. The corners of his russet-brown eyes crinkled as he smiled. "You must be the group the guards said is looking for me."

Marshall extended his hand. "Yes! I'm Marshall. That's Tegan, Aari, Kody, and Mariah."

"Asa." The man pumped the Sentry's hand. "Welcome to Haifa. What brings you here?"

"More like who—the Welsh twins."

Asa's face lit up. "Deverell and Gareth! Those rascals . . . good boys, them. Why did they send you?"

"We were hoping you could help us. They said you have extensive knowledge about the history of the region, and that you've also got a great collection of artifacts."

"They said that, hm?" Asa folded his arms. "And what are you looking for?"

"We're on a mission to hunt down a relic from about two

thousand years ago, give or take," Aari explained.

The man's eyes bore into the group. "A mission, you say."

They swapped glances. *He's not going to give things up easily,* Aari thought. *The only reason he's even entertaining us right now is probably because we mentioned Gareth and Dev.*

Asa studied each of them, his demeanor gradually softening. "I have another hour until I'm done for the day. Meet me at the entrance at the bottom of the mountain. We can talk then."

He strode away without waiting for a response, leaving the friends and the Sentry alone on the terrace.

* * *

The group milled around a fountain in the middle of the courtyard, waiting for Asa, until a voice called out. "*Yalla!*"

The gardener stood outside the entrance, waving at them. They quickly joined him, exchanging brief greetings.

"So, Asa," Marshall began. "We—"

"No, no, no." Asa smiled, courteous but firm. "I insist we talk business after tea at my place. Come."

Aari, seeing Marshall suppress a frustrated breath and rub his knuckles against the beard he'd grown out again, offered the man a consoling look.

Mariah gazed up the terraces at the lustrous, golden-domed building in the heart of the gardens. "Is that a temple?" she asked.

"It's a shrine," Asa replied. "The Shrine of the Báb."

"Shrine of . . . what?"

"The Báb. It means 'the Gate' in Persian. The Báb was the martyr–herald of the Bahá'í Faith. Kind of like John the Baptist."

"A herald?" Aari asked. "For who?"

Asa gave him a friendly slap on the back. "That, *habibi*, is a long story that we can maybe chat about later."

"What about you?" Tegan asked. "Are you a follower of this Faith?"

"Mm-mm, no. I'm a crusty old agnostic, my dear, and I'll probably go to my grave that way." He nodded to a passerby, then added, “But there are some tenets I can relate to.”

“Like what?”

“Well . . . it calls for impartial investigation of truth, of reality, so blind imitation is discouraged. That’s a big one for me.”

“Me too,” Aari said.

“What else, what else . . . ah. It has a very optimistic view of the world. That’s something I think I need. And it says that humanity is evolving to a point where it will need to recognize its essential oneness. Looking at everything, it’s hard to deny that we could use a little—or a lot—of that. It offers a good amount of spiritual pragmatism, too. As someone once said, it’s like treading the mystical path with practical feet.”

Aari leaned toward Marshall. “I think I dig that,” he whispered. “Kinda sounds like something the Elders would say.”

“I’ve noticed,” Tegan piped in, “that very few people in Haifa wear masks.”

“That’s because it’s quite safe here,” Asa told her. “The moment there was news about the disease in Europe, the Israeli government tightened security and began working on a method to identify those with the sickness. Just yesterday they handed out individual test kits to the public, trying to get them into the hands of every citizen here. And they’ve also delivered a bunch of them to the UN.”

“Yeah, my pal that we’re bunking with brought home several kits last night,” Marshall said. “We’re all clean.”

“That’s good. In all of Israel, there have only been six cases of the violent strain and less than a dozen of the other one. Those infected, and their families, have been quarantined.”

Kody let out a whistle. “You guys are really prepared.”

“We have to be. We’re a small country that’s constantly under threat.”

They turned onto another street and followed Asa up a walkway that led to a white, two-story stone house with an expertly manicured, pint-sized lawn. Asa explained that the first floor accommodated all the basic necessities of a home, and the top floor was entirely dedicated to his private collection of artifacts.

He sat the group down on two couches in the living room and served them hot tea and fruit, still insistent that they not speak of business until after. He settled in a chair across from them and as he took a small sip from his cup, the friends and Marshall knocked back their drinks. Asa, though surprised, consumed his tea at a more leisurely pace. Aari noticed Kody's impatient leg-shaking.

I know, Kode-man, he thought sympathetically. *It'd be nice if we could get a move on and see if this guy has any leads. Or even better, the box itself.*

"Alright," Asa finally said, putting his cup down. "Tell me everything."

"We've been searching all over for an artifact," Aari said, the words tumbling out of his mouth in a rush. "We went to Masada, where it was supposed to be buried. We scoured museum collections online. No one has it. No one's heard of it. We're hoping you can help because it could hold the answer to this outbreak. It could be the cure."

Asa seemed caught off guard by the outpour of information but recovered quickly. "A cure, huh?" He leaned back, interest budding in his tone. "But what is it?"

"Right, sorry. It's this wooden box—"

"Clad in brass," Mariah added.

"Brass, yes," Aari said. "And it contains these extremely rare seeds from an extinct tree."

"There are markings on the lid." Marshall nodded at the friends. "The pattern is similar to this."

The teenagers removed their pendants and placed them on the table, facing Asa. The gardener examined first the carved crystals, then the intricately worked metal around them. His finger traced the detailed engravings. "Patterns like this?" His forehead crinkled for a long minute. The group fidgeted in the quiet. Then, he shook his head. "I don't believe I have anything that matches the description of your artifact, my friends. I'm sorry."

"Are you sure?" Tegan pressed. "If it helps, the box was last seen during the Siege of Masada."

Asa's jaw worked from side to side, his brow furrowed. "Well, there is one thing . . . I think there might actually be a box somewhere in my collection. *Rega*."

As he disappeared upstairs, Kody leaned toward Aari. "What does *rega* mean?"

"Wait," Aari said.

"For what?"

"No, no. *Rega* means 'wait'." He looked over at Tegan; the girl had been peering out of the window every few minutes. "Teegs."

She shushed him. "I know what you're thinking, and of course Reyor's people won't be stupid enough to be standing right outside the house, but it doesn't hurt to check."

Asa called out for them to join him. The friends reached for their necklaces on the table but, as they did, the pendants quivered ever so slightly, drawing toward each other. They paused. Kody, his hand hovering midair, mumbled, "Umm . . . maybe that was an earthquake?"

"Nothing else in the house shook," Tegan said slowly. "Only the pendants."

They looked to Marshall, who offered them a bewildered shrug. They grabbed their pendants and ran up the stairs. A wall with a single entrance blocked off the entire second floor. They stepped through, into a decontamination chamber where powerful air jets blew dust from them and their clothing, then entered a second door into a cold, dim room. As Aari's eyes adjusted, his inner historian leaped for joy.

Small incandescent lights lit a long workbench at the center of the room. Against each wall, rows of shelves housed carefully preserved artifacts ranging from documents to various kinds of weapons. The windows were blacked out and the low-powered fluorescent fixtures had been darkened. *UV filters*, Aari thought. *Smart*. The quiet hum of an air conditioning unit and dehumidifiers filled the space.

Mariah shivered, pulling her jacket tighter around herself. "It's *freezing* in here."

"It helps preserve my collection." Asa placed a plastic tub with an airtight lid in the center of the workbench, then pulled on a pair of latex gloves and reached into the tub, removing a cubic object enclosed in linen. "This is very, very old, from the time the Romans were in Israel. It must be handled with care, so unfortunately I cannot let you touch it. I don't know where it was found, exactly. It was passed between a few collectors before me."

He unwrapped the linen, and the lights from the workbench bounced off the coppery shell of a wooden box. The group crowded around him.

"Is that it?" Kody whispered. "Is that our box?"

They moved closer to get a better view. Aari's face fell. "This is bronze, not brass."

"And the markings are different," Tegan said, holding her pendant above it. "The ones on the box look like a bunch of tiny Roman numerals."

"Asa, could we maybe take a look inside?" Marshall asked.

The gardener obliged. Aari peered in, feeling a surge of optimism only to have it slashed again. The box was empty. Asa, covering the artifact and placing it back in the tub, saw the despair on his guests' faces and apologized. "This is the only box I have from that era."

Marshall did his best to feign a smile. "It's alright. Thank you for your help. You've been incredibly gracious to a bunch of strangers."

"Any friend of the twins is a friend of mine," Asa said kindly. As the group headed toward the exit, he stopped them. "Tell me more about this artifact you're looking for. What is its story?"

Aari, his fingertips on the door handle, pulled back. The friends glanced to Marshall for direction, unsure how much they could divulge. He took in their expressions, then made his way back to Asa with the four of them in tow.

"The seeds we're looking for come from something called the

Tree of Life," he said. "These seeds were in the possession of a pair of siblings, a boy and a girl in Masada. But they weren't Jewish. Actually, they weren't even local, not really. They were part of an ancient race of seafarers who lived around the region. Last we heard, the seeds were kept in a special box and supposedly buried in a cave in Masada when the Romans attacked. But we checked and the box isn't there. It's believed that one of the siblings, the brother, was killed in the attack after the box was hidden."

"And the girl?" Asa asked, unable to hide his intrigue.

"All contact with her was lost."

"Contact? How were they in contact? With who?"

Marshall gave a sheepish grin. "That, we can't quite say."

Asa removed his gloves, mouth quirked sullenly to one side. "I'm sorry. I really wish I could be of more help. If these seeds of yours are really the cure for the virus, the world could use them right now."

Aari fell in behind Kody as Asa led the way back out through the decontamination chamber. The boys shared weary looks. As the gardener reached for the second door, he spun around, causing a pileup behind him. "Wait!" he cried, bulldozing back into the room. The friends and the Sentry hurried after him.

"What is it?" Marshall demanded.

Asa swung his head from side to side, scrutinizing the artifacts on the shelves. "It just struck me . . . that story of yours sounds a little familiar." He started to rummage through several large plastic tubs.

"Familiar?"

"Yes, I read it somewhere."

Marshall looked confused. "You read about the seeds?"

"I meant about what happened at Masada."

"It's in Flavius Josephus's writings about the siege," Aari supplied. "It's the only account there is."

"No, *habibi*. I'm talking about the girl and the box." Asa worked his way around the room. "Where did I read it . . ." He opened the cover of one tub. "Aha! It's in the letters!"

Tegan looked over his shoulder. "What letters?"

"The letters that never made it to Rome." Asa hoisted the tub onto the workbench and pulled on another pair of gloves. "I purchased these almost thirty years ago, from a collector who got them from another collector who got them from a thief. But we won't talk about that."

He removed eight long sheets of tattered papyrus, each mounted on separate four-ply boards in polyester coverings, and laid them out on the tabletop. Aari took in the faded black writing. "This looks like Latin, but I don't really know how to read it."

"I do," Asa smiled.

"You're a linguist too?"

"I have to be so I can understand what I collect."

"What do these say?" Kody asked.

"These were written by a Roman legionnaire named Lucius. He wanted to send the letters to his family but never found the courage."

Mariah frowned. "Why?"

"Because he ran away from the legion with a young woman. He wrote these letters to his family, apologizing for shaming them with his desertion." Asa tapped the first parchment. "In this one, he explains how he found a girl in a cave in Masada and stopped two other legionaries from killing her. He saw her bury something and, while she went back to the fortress, he dug it up. It was a box."

Aari perked up.

"When he returned to the fortress," Asa continued, "he saw the legionaries viciously strike the girl on the head with the hilt of a sword. She woke up having lost her memory due to the injury. Lucius, he didn't want to fight. He never did. So, with the girl and the box he escaped from Masada and paid a ferryman to take them up the Sea of Death—we call it the Dead Sea now—to the Jordan River. They trekked for *weeks*, past the Sea of Galilee and Tiberius."

Tegan tilted her head. "And they had the box the whole time?"

"They did. It says here that the girl was 'instinctively protective' of it. She wouldn't let Lucius touch it or open it. She couldn't remember why she buried it in the first place, but she always kept it with her. It says she learned his language extraordinarily fast and became fluent far quicker than he thought possible. And, according to the letters, they eventually fell deeply in love. Lucius speaks of her very adoringly."

Aari tapped his fingertips on the table. "What happened after they escaped?"

Asa scoured the rest of the letters. "They went west to the coast and settled in a small fishing village. Ahh, of course . . . I remember now. I researched this before acquiring the letters. They settled right here in Haifa before we came to know it as Haifa. At the time the Roman Empire was present in most of Judea, but this particular place was safe for a while. The young couple hoped they could disappear and live quiet lives. But—and this is why your story triggered my memory—the girl stood out. She had hair like the sun and eyes as blue as the sea. She was so fair-skinned, and she never tanned. People started asking questions about her heritage as she obviously wasn't a local. It became difficult for them to assimilate."

"What did they do?" Marshall prodded.

"Around then, they heard that the Romans were beginning to march toward Haifa. They thought it was best to leave. If the legion found them, they would kill Lucius. He was a deserter and she . . . well, she probably would have been taken as a slave, or worse. In his last letter"—Asa picked up the eighth parchment—"Lucius said they'd decided to leave for Africa."

"Africa!" Mariah gasped.

"Is there anything else?" Marshall asked. "About the seeds? About where in Africa they'd planned to go?"

The gardener took another look at the letters. "Aside from the girl protecting the box with her life? Nothing."

"So . . ." Kody fell heavily onto a stool and dropped his forehead against the tabletop. "Africa. A needle in the haystack that is an entire continent. *Ha.* This might as well be a dead end." He sounded bitter. "We're not gonna win this one. There's just no way."

Aari plunked down beside him, clawing his fingers through his hair, wanting to rip it out. *Maybe we really aren't meant to cross the finish line this time,* he thought. *Maybe this one is on Gareth. He needs to find Dr. Deol, and soon.*

36

Nageau's black-and-silver cloak swept the ground as he dragged Magèo by the arm. "Come, now, old friend! A walk will do you good! It is no use being cooped up here if there is no cure to be found."

Magèo whacked the Elder's hand away. "Alright, alright!"

Nageau let go and stepped out of the laboratory. The older man followed, grumbling as he slipped on a pair of sunglasses, a gift from Kody during the friends' most recent stay in Dema-Ki.

Nageau spread his arms wide. "See? Smell that fresh air. It does wonders for the body and mind."

"The air is not the problem."

"I know, I know. You have turned the sun into your personal nemesis."

They crossed the bridge to the other side of the river and headed westward, past clusters of *neyra* and up an incline upon which sat a spherical, glazed-clay structure—the village's hot water reservoir, fed by a thermal spring. Nageau smiled to himself, recalling with fondness the story the friends recounted of their attempt to escape from Dema-Ki the previous year, and how Kody had burned his fingers on the tank.

Past the incline loomed a rock wall that separated the village from Jov-Ki, the Pinecone Valley. A trodden path burrowed into the granite, disappearing into the darkness. The villagers, who knew the lay of the land just as well as the back of their own hands, hardly ever used a lantern to pass through the dim tunnel.

Magèo grunted as the hole swallowed them. "I think it is time we made this passageway taller, Nageau. I am tired of hunching whenever we travel through here."

"That can be the youths' next project," the Elder said, stooping to avoid hitting his head.

They emerged a few minutes later in the adjacent, barren valley. Magèo grumbled and brushed past Nageau, who caught up to him with an easy jog. "You seem more bad-tempered than usual," he said. "What is bothering you?"

"Generally speaking, everything."

"Right now, I mean."

"Aside from still being unable to figure out a cure that does not require the seeds?" Magèo sighed. "I am concerned about Nal. She seems to have befriended Hutar."

"Mm, yes. Akol did mention that she would appear whenever Hutar goes on his walks."

"I do not like that they have gotten close."

"Is this solely her mentor speaking?"

"I will admit that she has become like a daughter to me, but I will not apologize for my caution. I do not believe it is wise for her to nurture this growing amity with Hutar."

"The boy has been nothing but cooperative during his time here. I know you are looking out for Nal, but I have to wonder if all this mistrust might push Hutar away again. We have an opportunity now to truly guide him onto the right path . . . perhaps even with Nal's assistance."

Magèo bristled. "You are *not* putting my apprentice in the middle of this!"

"If they really have gotten closer, she can aid him to become a better man."

"*I will not* put her in the path of that . . . that . . ." Magèo inhaled deeply. "You know Hutar was a troubled child. Add to that his lineage—"

"We do not look at others' bloodlines."

"Sometimes we have to, Nageau! Sometimes we just cannot turn a blind eye!"

They skirted around the frozen carcass of a deer, remains of a meal likely left behind by a mountain lion. The Elder kept silent. Beside him, Magèo sighed again. "Has a decision been made about *kah'dloc*?"

"No. Ashack wants it, whereas I am opposed. Saiyu and Tikina are still undecided. Tayoka seemed inclined to side with Ashack, but after the boy saved my life . . ."

Magèo stroked his flowing white beard. "Humph. *Kah'dloc* is certainly a severe alternative. It is not an easy decision to make, and I cannot say that I envy the Elders."

"Believe me, I understand the other side of this argument. Yet . . ."

"Yet what?"

"Say we do go through with it and completely change Hutar for the better. While it may appear to be a victory, would it not be equivalent to what Rey—to what the harbinger is doing with the young ones in the Sanctuaries?"

Magèo winced. "I see. How can we, on one hand, condemn something but then justify it enough to use it ourselves? Similar means, same purpose, different hands."

"Exactly. We would be no better than the harbinger."

"I wish I could help, Nageau. I really do."

A red fox bounced out of the trees ahead. Nageau bent down and stroked the animal, feeling its soft, thick winter coat. The fox purred contently before continuing on its way. He watched it leave, a twinge of envy flickering in his chest at its simple life. Several creatures were known to be friendly with the villagers and would often pass through Dema-Ki as they pleased. Though the predators had to be closely watched around children and livestock, they understood that they would not be harmed if they behaved.

Magèo cleared his throat. "I do not think you dragged me out of my laboratory simply for my health. Shall we get down to business?"

Nageau smiled wryly. "You know, I do care about you."

"Oh, yes. I also know that something perturbs you. Get to it."

"The other Elders and I have agreed that the time is fast

approaching to move the families of the Chosen Ones to Dema-Ki."

Magèo nearly tripped over his own feet. "Oh! Alright. But?"

"I take it you have some reservations?"

"Not reservations, as such." The old man stroked his beard again, only more nervously. "This will be the first time that we will have a large group of outsiders in our village. It should be interesting to see how it plays out."

"I trust our brethren will do all they can to make the move as easy and comfortable as possible for the families."

"Of course, of course. Has something happened to spur this decision?"

"Aside from the disease now spreading faster in their homeland? I think if we continue to frustrate the harbinger's plans, it will only be a matter of time before the families are taken and used as bargaining chips, or worse. Especially as the Chosen Ones grow in power and continue to be a serious threat to our foe's scheme . . ." Nageau trailed off as something nagged in the back of his mind.

"Nageau?" Magèo probed. "What is it?"

"The families would be better off here than in the outside world," the Elder murmured, "but I wonder for how long Dema-Ki will remain safe."

"What do you mean?"

Nageau stopped in his tracks and steepled his fingers over his mouth, eyes shut. He felt the cold pinch his ears, heard the forest suddenly grow still as if listening in on their conversation.

"There will be an attack on Dema-Ki," he intoned softly. "The question is not if, but when."

Magèo's face tightened. "Why are you so sure?"

"Because we have the black crystal." Nageau opened his eyes, glacial-blue gaze clouding.

"But only the Elders, my predecessors, and I know about it," Magèo whispered.

"Reyor approached me some time before the banishment and caught me off guard, begging me to divulge its location—which

I did not, of course. I do not know how the harbinger became aware of its existence. That should have been a warning sign, but I dismissed the plea as eager curiosity."

"If I recall correctly, a chunk of the crystal is missing. Its location has been a mystery since the beginning of our ancestors' time in Dema-Ki. Who knows how much stronger we could have been with the whole crystal in one piece."

"And what we have is more than enough to extend one's lifespan for eons," Nageau said. "The harbinger will want to be there, alive and well, to ensure that everything goes according to plan once humanity has been eradicated and the Stewards of New Earth return to the surface."

"And you really think that monster will lay siege to our home for the black crystal?"

"Of that I have no doubt. Combining the *lathe'ad*'s symbiosis with the longevity afforded by the crystal, Reyor could potentially dominate the world, undeterred, for centuries to come."

"But—" Magèo snapped his mouth shut as they passed a group of youth on horses bringing back the haul of their morning hunt. The group placed fists over their hearts, heads bowed. The men returned the gesture.

Once the youths were out of earshot, Magèo continued in a hushed voice, pulling off his sunglasses. "But we have an effective method in place to safeguard against the misuse of the crystal. Only the leading Elder ever knows of the crystal's precise location."

Nageau dipped his chin in acknowledgment. "And only those who take up your mantle can administer it correctly, yes. Which means, when Reyor comes, it will be for us both. And if any of our kin steps in to protect us . . ."

Magèo spun into Nageau's path and gripped him forcefully by the shoulders, his different-colored eyes ablaze. "You must destroy it."

"You know I cannot do that."

"Maybe we are not as dependent on it as we believe. Maybe

we have evolved past it and our abilities are stable enough. And maybe this is a sacrifice we need to make in order to keep the crystal from falling into the wrong hands!"

"Do we really want to risk that?"

Magèo threw his hands up and stalked away through the grove of snow-covered firs, muttering under his breath. Nageau trailed after him, forlorn. *What if he is right? What if this calls for a sacrifice, even if it might weaken us as a people? But how then will we fend off an attack bereft of our full strength?*

As they circled a rocky outcrop, Magèo halted abruptly, causing the Elder to collide into him. "What—" Nageau started.

"Shh," the older man whispered. "A Guardian."

Nageau stepped around him and went still. In a clearing leading to the pool with a lofty frozen waterfall glimmering in the sunlight, a colossal creature stood on its hind legs. The silver-furred bear towered fifteen feet above the ground, dark eyes shining with curious light as it watched the men cautiously approach. They lowered their heads as the powerful being slowly lowered itself onto all fours.

The bear, a Guardian, was one of five that inhabited the forests around Dema-Ki, working to safeguard the people of the valley from trespassers and threats. A mutual bond of respect had formed between the first Guardians and the villagers' ancestors over two millennia ago, and the descendants of both groups maintained the union.

Nageau went down on one knee, the bear's shadow eclipsing him. The Guardian snuffled, head tilted slightly. Intelligence twinkled in its gaze as it touched its cold nose to the Elder's forehead. He smiled softly and looked up at the massive creature, recalling the first time the Chosen Ones arrived in the valley, unconscious after the plane crash, each one on the back of a Guardian.

His smile faded as he took in the bear's heavily scarred face. *You were a great help during the battle on Ayen'et,* he thought, *but we will need your assistance again. I do not know when the harbinger will move to attack, but I trust the Guardians will fight alongside us.*

The Guardian snuffled again and held Nageau's gaze for a moment. Then, with one last look at the men, the bear lumbered past them and disappeared into the trees. Magèo placed a hand on the Elder's shoulder. "Are you alright?"

Nageau patted his hand and got up, dusting the snow from his cloak and moccasin boots. "No," he said. "Magèo, regardless if the remnant of the black crystal is destroyed or not, the harbinger will wage war upon our home. We must be prepared."

A glint of sorrow fluttered over Magèo's face. "I understand. How may I be of help?"

"I need you to prepare defensive measures that we can put in place."

"And offensive ones as well, I would imagine."

"We must be ready for anything." Nageau looked up at the solid waterfall, shielding his eyes from the light as the rays bounced off the ice, then turned around to face the crescent-shaped tree line some yards away from the frozen pool. Five immense, majestic pine trees stood at the edge of the arc.

His eyes rested on the centermost tree a few shades darker than the rest. "One thing is for certain," he said. "Whether the attack is tomorrow, several moon cycles, or even a year or two from this moment—we will not go down quietly. We will not let Reyor win."

Gareth gave a tight nod of thanks as the waiter poured him some carbonated water and left. He picked up the drink, shaking it in his glass, but couldn't bring himself to take a sip and instead thought back to his surprise phone call the night before.

Her voice sounded familiar, but I still can't place it. Which Deol is she? How does she know who I am? How did she get my number? And why did I let her decide on the meeting location? For all I know, this café could be a bloody trap and I walked in completely underprepared.

He put the glass down and forced himself to take a bite of his muffin. The upside of Russia being mostly spared by the crop destruction was that food was never stale in the country. Coffee, on the other hand, had become a more difficult commodity to come by.

He could only manage a few nibbles before shoving the plate away. After the massacre at the train station twenty-four hours prior, he'd neither eaten nor slept. The gruesome scene played over and over in his mind, and the screams and gunfire still echoed in his ears. Now, with the meeting close at hand, he felt as though he was about to be sick. *What monster can look at the world and decide that she's perfectly fine with genocide?*

The bell above the entrance jingled as a woman stepped through the door. Gareth's face fell. *Not you. Oh God, not you.*

Ina Deol walked briskly to his table, surreptitiously throwing looks over her shoulder. Her black hair, done in a messy side braid, was tucked into her green jacket, and the bags under her eyes were stark against the warmth of her brown skin. She sat across from him, inspecting the small, mostly empty café, before at last resting her gaze on him. They were both guarded, both sizing the other up as if it was the first time they were meeting.

I don't understand, Gareth thought, heart sinking. *It can't be her. She seemed so . . . normal. And she's a mother, for heaven's sake. She can't be capable of something like this.*

His nostrils flared as a storm of conflicted emotions threatened to knock him over. "So. An artist. I assume that was a lie."

"I *am* an artist," she retaliated, "but it's only a hobby. I don't make a living off of it."

"And the house? Is that really inheritance?"

"No. My employer generously provides."

"Right. Phoenix."

The faint lines on her face tautened. "Yes."

He closed his eyes briefly. "Where's your daughter?"

"At home with a babysitter." She looked over her shoulder again.

"So how . . . how did you—"

"Find out who you are?" she finished. "It wasn't difficult. Firstly, my gut went into hyperdrive when you showed up. I have never, *ever* received flowers after my husband passed. Secondly, I have cameras that monitor my property and one of them is placed across the street from my house. You happened to park right in front of it."

"I didn't notice any cameras."

"Of course not. They're not meant to be detected."

"That's fair. What else?"

"I have access to some resources. Once I had your face and your license plate"—she swiped his glass and took a sip—"facial recognition scans pulled up some fascinating things."

Gareth's jaw tightened. "Such as?"

"You have a habit of showing up where interesting events happen. The Good Samaritan from Wales who never takes credit . . . both you and your brother."

Gareth sat back, arms crossed, and adopted a mask of

inscrutability. "And I'm assuming you somehow traced my license plate to the car hire agency and got my number."

"Exactly."

"That's crafty, I'll give you that. But why did you reach out to me?"

"Why were *you* looking for me?"

Gareth searched her face. *She's fearful about something. She's barely made proper eye contact the entire conversation. Should I tell her the truth, then? What have I got to lose?*

He licked his lips. "I've been looking for you because I think you have the cure."

She clasped the glass with both hands, red nails scratching the surface. "Cure? For what?"

"Don't do that. You know what. The outbreak."

"Why do you think that?"

"Because otherwise you wouldn't be here. Because I know you created the virus. I know you engineered the Marauders. I know that you work under a bloke named Bertram and he's been suspicious of your loyalty as of late."

She blanched, visibly stunned by his knowledge.

"If you really are Dr. Deol," he continued, "then I think you want out of this abyss."

"How did you—"

"You have your means, I have mine." Gareth softened his tone. "People can make wrong decisions. Horrible decisions. Decisions that they don't think they can ever come back from. You can't undo what has happened, I understand that. But you can make a difference, right now. The question is, will you?"

She drew away and hugged her shoulders as she gazed out the window. They sat in silence for some minutes. Then she clenched her teeth, suddenly looking as though she might shatter at the slightest touch.

"I . . . I lost my way when I lost my husband." Her shoulders hunched further inward. "When Dr. Bertram offered me a place in the company, it became more than a job. It filled a gaping hole in my life." Her voice trembled. "Maksim was killed on our third anniversary. The pigs that murdered him; they were never caught. They danced over his body as he bled out in the alley from his slit throat. They took whatever little money we had and told me that this was what he got for refusing to work with the Bratva, the mob. I was six months pregnant and . . . and kneeling next to my husband on the filthy lane, soaked in his blood. The pigs laughed as people passed through the alley, looking the other way out of fear. No one stopped to help."

Gareth listened, mouth closed firmly.

"I hated people that night," she seethed. "I hated people as the corrupt police refused to investigate the murder of my husband. I hated people as I learned more about self-serving public officials and politicians who were in bed with the mob. I hated people who'd rather save their own skin than be decent human beings. And yes, I . . . *hated* people . . . when I created the virus." A couple of tears trailed down her cheeks and she brushed them away. "The world had become a cesspool of the wicked, the corrupt. It needed to be cleansed. I refused to allow my daughter to grow up in the same world that took her father from us." She dropped her gaze to the floor. "I realized later, much later, that when you allow this kind of pain to consume you, it rages through your soul and leaves behind a husk. An abomination."

Gareth tilted his head back to look at the warm ceiling lights. *Pain is the devil that turns grief into madness. But nothing can justify the monstrosity that she's unleashed.*

Ina wiped her nose, then covered her face for a few moments to gather herself. "I was suspicious of you when you showed up with the flowers. But then you threw yourself in front of that car to save Anya, shrugging it off like it was nothing, and I . . . I had not witnessed such a selfless act in ages."

"If you were so suspicious of me," Gareth said, "why did you invite me into your home?"

"Besides the fact that you'd just saved my daughter's life? Well, you piqued my interest. There was something about you;

I couldn't place it. A certain goodness." When Gareth arched a brow, she hastily added, "And you were too careless with your mask. You didn't seem bothered that it wasn't covering your mouth and nose. Besides . . . you had some cuts and bruises that needed to be tended to."

Gareth expelled a breath as he realized what had happened. "I left you with a sample of my blood."

"Yes." She rested her elbows on the table and leaned toward him. "And when I tested it, I was completely floored."

Gareth closed the distance between them. "Why?"

"Before I created the pathogen, I was given a tissue sample. The instructions I'd gotten were that I needed to design a bug that would not affect those with certain genetic markers in their DNA. When I tested your blood, I found that it had a similar marker."

It was specifically designed to target anyone but those of Dema-Ki origin. It dawned on him, then. *Wipe out the whole world and leave the rest of us standing. But why?*

"So that's why we're not affected," he murmured to himself.

"We?"

"Ina, how well do you know your boss? And I don't mean Bertram, or Adrian Black."

"Well enough, but not on a personal level. Why?"

"My brother and I are descendants of a . . . certain group of secluded people. So is the head of your organization. That sample you initially received? I guarantee it's from your boss. That's why you see a pattern in our DNA."

Ina's gaze slid past him. "Dema-Ki," she said, slowly. "You're from Dema-Ki."

Gareth blinked. "How—"

"I overheard Bertram speaking with another man once. It was sometime last year. I didn't get to hear much and pieces of information were missing but, talking to you now, I understand better." Color trickled out of her face and tears began to spill anew from her eyes. She hurriedly dabbed them but more kept coming. "Sorry. I can't control this."

"It's alright."

"I know I'm beyond salvation. I deserve what's coming to me."

Gareth hesitated, then wiped her tears with his thumb. She's not wrong. *This is her cross to bear. But if she's willing to atone for her crimes, then we have to help her. And that means Reyor will come after her with everything under the sun. Hell hath no fury . . .*

"Listen," he said; Ina looked up, eyes puffy. "My people and I will do everything we can to protect you from your employer. We'll keep you safe, you have my word, but we *will* need your help to get the cure."

She pulled back a little and gave him a lackluster smile. "Phoenix is looming over me, Gareth. Don't make a promise you can't keep."

"I know a place where they won't be able to find you," he said. "It's off the grid. You'll be untouchable. You and your daughter both."

He could see her teetering on the precipice, wanting to believe him but wary of putting her faith in someone else. He took her hand in his. "You can trust me."

Her expression softened as she finally gave in. She picked up his glass again and downed its contents. "Ugh, I wish this was something stronger than water. Okay, first order of business: I'll need to get to my office. Not today, but tomorrow. Everything we need is stored on a secure server there."

Gareth squeezed her hand, letting himself smile in respite. "I was led to believe that you have the formula for the cure in your head."

"I do. Most of it. But we'll need details, blueprints. Plus, I think you'll want to know about the company's future plans. I've also got a file detailing how to properly deactivate the Marauders. Also, there are new, nastier creatures being produced and you will need all the help you can get dealing with them."

"That would be incredibly helpful." Gareth knocked his knuckles on the table. "Nastier creatures. It never gets easier, does it?"

"Not at all."

"Mmh. By the way, why did you decide to meet me three hours away from Moscow?"

"I wanted to make sure that I wasn't easily followed," Ina explained. "Like you said, Bertram—and by extension, the company—has become suspicious of my loyalties. I need to watch my back."

"You're not alone anymore," he assured her. "Do you have anything at home?"

"Relating to my work? Definitely not. You won't believe how paranoid Phoenix is about all this."

"I think I would. So what's the plan?"

"Before we do anything, we'll have to find a safe place for my daughter."

"Done. I have a couple of friends who can help. They're trustworthy."

Ina relaxed slightly in her chair. "Perfect. Once Anya's with them, I'll head to my office."

"I can drop you off."

"No! The workplace security parameters are wide. Even the parking lots are guarded. It wouldn't be wise if I stepped out of someone else's car. Just be ready. I'll leave for the office first, and you'll follow a few minutes later. It won't take long to retrieve what we need."

Gareth stopped her as she pushed her chair back. "Wait a minute, now," he said. "If it's all on a secure server, how do you plan to get the documents?"

She managed a grin. "By removing the hard drive. The alarm will go off, but I'll trigger the fire bell first to create a diversion. It should confuse the guards long enough for me to run out and hop into your car. Then we'll fetch Anya and you'll take us to safety. I hope you know what to do after that, because the company will be on us like bloodhounds."

"I'll have a getaway plan in place by the time we've secured Anya," Gareth replied.

They made their way to the door. As they trod out into the cold, Ina turned around and grasped the front of his leather jacket, pulling him close. His breath caught as he gazed down at her.

"Thank you," she whispered. "Thank you for giving a monster like me a chance at redemption."

Gareth glanced into the rearview mirror at Anya as she slept in her booster seat, bundled cozily in her little orange parka and boots. The six-year-old seemed so at peace, he couldn't help but smile just a bit. Beside him, Ina stared out of her window as bare aspen and birch trees blurred past against the wintry backdrop; she'd been silent for most of the ride.

After their meeting the evening before, she'd returned home to pack some belongings while Gareth pieced together their exit strategy in his hotel room. He'd stayed up all night finalizing the plan and slept through the day until Ina clocked out of work as usual late in the afternoon, just to make things look normal at the office. Once he'd picked up the Deols, they headed northwest where they would drop Anya off before returning to Moscow for the hard drive.

Gareth, noticing Ina's constant fidgeting, cleared his throat twice to catch her attention. "Tell me about Anya. Is she—was she—homeschooled?"

Ina lurched out of her reverie. "What? Oh. No, she wasn't, though I wish she had been. I don't like being away from her for hours at a time, especially considering that she can't hear. But, as it goes, my work requires my full attention. She has hearing aids, though she doesn't like to wear them much."

"She's not comfortable with sound?"

"More like she's not comfortable having things in her ears." Ina wore a sardonic grin. "I actually planned on setting up a surgery for her when she was a little older so she wouldn't need hearing aids at all. Phoenix has so much at their disposal, you wouldn't believe some of the projects they have on the legal side of things."

Gareth picked up the bitter melancholy in her words and tried to comfort her, but was held back by a painful truth. *Many others are suffering far more from her hands than she is.* His grip on the steering wheel hardened. *Then why am I struggling to not feel sorry for her?*

Ina turned to the back seat and brushed a few strands of hair from her daughter's face, her own knotting in grief. "My greatest fear," she confessed under her breath, "is that one day she'll find out just what kind of a fiend her mother is. And she won't look at me with love anymore, but with fear. Shame. Disgust. Hate."

"The only thing she'll know," Gareth said, finding his voice, "is that in the time of crisis, her mother did the right thing and helped put an end to the madness."

Ina gave one last, long look at her daughter before facing the front. "So, our getaway plan is in place?"

"Everything's ready. All we have to do is make a few hops after you get the hard drive to shake off anyone on our trail. Which reminds me; I have a few questions."

"Questions?"

"Aye. Before I get into anything, I like to have a feel for the lay of the land."

"Ask away, then."

"Have you noticed anything different or out of the norm lately? With your boss? With Bertram?"

Ina twirled the end of her side braid. "Bertram's been nice to me. I mean, he always is, but since I started being questioned, he's been extra nice."

"Hmm. Anything else?"

"Um . . . last week, we got a new set of guards at the office. They were appointed specifically from Arcane Ventures, so they have a good idea of what's going on with the clandestine part of the organization."

"Tightening security. Not surprising. Sounds like they're certainly on to you. That's it?"

"Nothing else has changed as far as I can tell. This site is where biotech prototypes are designed. Besides the tight security, this place is quite inconspicuous. The full production facility is farther east, in the wilderness, though I think we've opened up some new ones recently. That's where my creations come to life." She scowled to herself, then vigorously shook away the dark cloud over her head. "These friends of yours Anya will be with—"

"They're great people. I met them when some mates and I backpacked across Europe years ago, and I always drop by when I'm around. It's just a few hours, Ina. She'll be fine."

"A mother's worry never ceases."

"I know."

They turned right, heading off the beaten road and rolling along a lengthy driveway toward a farmhouse with a rusty old truck parked just outside the front door. They got out and, as Gareth rang the doorbell, Anya stirred in Ina's arms, blinking owlishly.

A slim woman and a plump man, both bespectacled with silver hair and sunny demeanors, welcomed the trio. Gareth planted a quick kiss on their cheeks and introduced them to the doctor and her daughter in Russian. Ina greeted them, though she was clearly still hesitant.

The elderly man gave her an understanding smile. "She'll be safe with us, dear."

Ina glanced at Gareth. He nodded reassuringly and watched her swallow her reluctance. As she passed her daughter to the couple, Anya shrunk away.

"Anya, darling, it's okay," she soothed, making sure the girl's hearing aids were properly placed. "They're Gareth's friends."

"You're staying, right?" Anya whined.

"We have to go for a little while, but we'll be back before you know it."

"No! Please stay! Don't go!"

"I have to, darling. Mommy has important work to do. We'll be back soon."

Anya squeaked and latched tightly to her mother's neck.

Gareth gently rubbed her back. "Hey," he said. "Hey, it's alright. Anya, come here."

The girl immediately reached out to him and he lifted her into his arms. "Uncle Sergei and Auntie Nika took very good care of me when I first came here. They'll take good care of you, too. Oh, and you know what?" He grinned. "Auntie Nika makes really yummy cookies. Mostly chocolate chip. I know you love those, don't you? Their pantry is full of them." When she still didn't look convinced, he added, "They also have a cat somewhere in the house."

Anya's eyes became full moons. *"A cat?"*

"Yes! His name is Isidor and he's always playing hide and seek, so you can help them find him."

Anya squirmed eagerly, forcing Gareth to put her down. Ina stooped to kiss her. "Be good, darling. And make sure you keep your hearing aids in, hm?"

"Okay!" Anya sang.

The elderly couple beamed as the girl shot past them, calling for the cat. "She'll be well taken care of," Nika promised, and Ina finally offered an appreciative, believing smile.

Gareth wrapped the old woman in a hug. "Of course she will. You're both here."

Sergei rested his hands on the Sentry's shoulders. "It's wonderful seeing you again, my mischief-maker. I know you're in a hurry, so go. Be safe, both of you."

As Gareth and Ina retreated down the driveway and sped back toward Moscow, Ina said, "Let's run by the plan one final time."

"We've done it four times already."

"Humor me."

Gareth acquiesced. "You go to the office in your own car. I'll wait a few blocks away, just outside of the security perimeter. It should take you ten minutes to get in and out of the server room."

"Remember, there won't be a cell signal when I'm inside."

"I'll try not to panic if you don't answer me, then," Gareth said. "Don't want to seem too clingy."

That got a twitch of a smirk out of her. "When everything is in place, I'll call you right before I pull the fire alarm and remove the hard drive. That'll give you—"

"Less than a minute to get to the front of the office and Speedy Gonzales us away," he finished. "Ina, I've got it. Really. Now try to relax. You can't go walking in on edge. You know what'll help? Music. For instance, classic rock calms me."

Ina laughed, delighted. "Me too!"

"What? No way."

"Mmhm. Lynyrd Skynyrd, ZZ Top, Blue Öyster Cult, Zep, Foreigner, REO, you name it."

Gareth turned to her, slack-jawed. She tucked her hair behind her ear, blushing. "Stop looking at me like that!"

"Sorry! It's just been so long since I've met someone who's more than a casual listener." He fished his phone out and connected it to the car's speakers. "Go on, then. Relax yourself. We've still got two hours of driving left."

* * *

Gareth leaned against the hood of the car, taking in the subzero night and the darkened office buildings on either side of the wide street. Though the entire area was empty, it nonetheless surprised him that Moscow had yet to impose a mandatory curfew on its civilians. *Can't really complain*, he thought. *If they had a curfew, tonight wouldn't be possible.* He checked his phone. *9:05. Ten more minutes. She's already been gone for five.*

He loathed the fact that her office was several blocks out of view, but the shots were hers to call. *And call them she does. Guilt is an incredible motivator when one wants to right their wrongs.* He turned on his screen again; the time hadn't changed. *A watched pot never boils, mate.*

Maxing out the volume on his phone, he placed it on the car's hood and stretched out the stiffness in his body. A short man waddled past, a beak-like mask covering his face. Gareth's skin crawled. *Why on God's green Earth would anyone casually own a plague doctor get-up? That's downright disturbing. Oh ho, and he's staring at me as if I'm the oddball! That's right, old fellow, keep walking. Perhaps you'll find your way to, oh, I don't know, literally any drug store that carries surgical masks to catch you up with the times.*

He finished his stretches and picked up his phone. *Ten minutes and no call.* He chewed his thumbnail. *Give her a bit more time. She might've run into someone and got stuck chatting with them.*

Five more minutes passed and still nothing. He paced around the car, picking up speed with every revolution. *I should go. Something must've happened. I should go. But what if she just got caught up? What if she misjudged how long it would take? Agh! If I go in now, it could blow everything!*

He dialed Ina's number but the call immediately went to voicemail. "It's alright," he muttered. "It's alright. She said there would be no signal in the server room. Just wait."

The seconds and minutes dragged on until the clock hit 9:20.

Gareth shoved his phone into his pocket. "Screw it." He threw himself into the driver's seat. The engine came to life and he took off, foot cemented to the accelerator. As he neared the office building, he noticed color bouncing and reflecting off nearby glass towers, hues of orange, yellow, deep red; flickering, dancing . . .

Ice-cold claws sunk into him when he realized what it was.

A blazing inferno engulfed the single-floor building. Three guards outside worked with a hose attached to a fire hydrant, but when Gareth looked closer, his face twisted gruesomely. *They're not really trying to put it out!* He saw the handguns tucked in their holsters. *And I can't go through the front or they'll kill me. Damn it!*

He reversed the car until he reached the intersecting road behind him and went around to the back of the fenced office. The fire had eaten away part of the roof, and smoke billowed through the gaping holes.

He pulled out a bandana from his bag, drenched it in water from his bottle and tied it around his mouth and nose, then raced toward the wrought iron fence. He scaled the ten-foot tall barricade and vaulted over, landing in a crouch.

Three windows, no guards. He sprinted over to the centermost pane, untouched by the fire, and slammed his elbow through the glass. Tightening his jacket to protect himself, he climbed in, ignoring the shards scraping his head and hands. Fumes rushed out of the broken window, temporarily blinding him. He dropped to all fours where the smoke was less dense and, blinking rapidly as scorching heat stung his eyes, kept still. His hearing temporarily left him as he focused on activating his powers.

A sensation akin to being compressed spread throughout his body, and a glacial cool unfurled under his skin until he no longer sensed the fire's fury. The chill radiated from him like an aura; the flames could not touch him. He grunted as what felt like frozen spikes pierced his chest and abdomen. Still he pressed on, lowering the kinetic energy of the molecules in his body as much as possible while maintaining the functions of his internal organs. Within moments, most of the pain had ebbed.

Through gaps in the wall of smoke, he saw flames licking the stairwell to his right. *Fire must've started in the lab . . . Think, Gareth. She said the server room was at the back of the building, on the right. Which means my left.*

The ground beneath his feet suddenly gave. He plummeted with a cry. At the last second his hands shot up, grabbing onto the edge of the hole, and he dangled above the burning laboratory. *Bloody wooden floor! The fire's eating right through it!*

Just as the flames below jumped to meet him, Gareth heaved himself back up. *Hurry, hurry . . .*

He could barely make out a fortified door, slightly ajar, to his left. The Cyrillic writing on the plaque read 'Server Room'. He dragged the heavy door open and entered.

What the—no. No. No! He spun around. *There's nothing here!*

Every single server rack, in all four rows, had been cleared out. The fire had worked through half the room, melting the empty shelves in its path.

Gareth's knees weakened. *They knew. They were on to her.*

He darted ahead of the flames, nearly slipping on the steel-coated tiles as he checked each row for Ina. *If the fire started in the lab, how did it get into a fortified room like this? And why hasn't the fire suppression system kicked in?*

The likely answer terrified him.

"Ina!" he shouted. "*Ina!*"

He rounded the last row of racks and froze. Ina lay on her side, hair covering her face. He ran over and dropped to the ground. *No, no, no . . .*

Delicately, he turned her over. Her eyes were closed, her face blank. He shook her, called her name, but she didn't respond. He brought his cheek to her mouth and nose but felt no breath. With trembling fingers he touched her neck, praying for a pulse.

Nothing.

No. No. Please, no.

The fire slithered closer. Gareth lifted Ina into his arms and escaped the room. He carried her through the smoke and dodged the flames, shielding her from the blaze as support beams and walls crashed and burned around him. He found an office room near the front of the building, still unscathed. Inside, he laid her down, unzipped her jacket, and started chest compressions. "Come on," he muttered. "Come back, Ina. Come back. Please."

He pulled his bandana down and tilted her chin up, placing his mouth over hers, and gave repeated breaths. As he readied himself for more compressions, he caught sight of a small puncture at the base of her neck. He pushed her hair away and moved closer. His throat constricted.

Hypodermic needle. He pressed his knuckles against his lips. His eyes stung again, but not from the smoke. *She was dead before the fires were lit.*

He stared at Ina's lifeless form. Most of the color had left her face, yet it seemed as though she was just resting. He shook his head, chest tight, before breaking down completely. He gathered her into his arms. *I'm sorry. I'm sorry. I shouldn't have waited so long. I should have left the moment I thought something was off. I . . . oh, God. Ina, I'm sorry.* He pulled her closer. *I'm so sorry.*

Through the open doorway, he saw the fire surging toward him. He picked Ina up, her body a heavy mistake he knew he'd have to carry for years to come, and left the room, finding his way to the front of the building.

The three guards outside dropped their charade with the fire hose the moment he stepped through the doors. They whipped their pistols out, demanding he let go of Ina's corpse. Gareth fixed them with a venomous look, honing in as he prepared to unleash the full extent of his ability. He distinctly sensed the frenzied rise of kinetic motion in every element in his body and released a searing stream of invisible current at the first guard.

The stocky man dropped his gun with a cry, contorting as though possessed. He fell onto the frozen pavement, ripping at his jacket and shirt as a wave of thermal energy pierced through him. The second guard flung himself into the spray from the fire hose and drenched his body as wisps of smoke rose from his skin and clothes, but the nozzle turned a glowing red and the water evaporated at Gareth's command. The last man had collapsed, shaking uncontrollably. Gareth reveled in it. Letting the fury take over felt good, liberating.

"One of you murdered her!" he roared. "And this—*this is what you get!*"

He pushed further. The guards had stopped fighting and lay spread-eagle on the ground, twitching.

Then something inside him suddenly thundered upon the realization of what he was doing.

Wait! Stop! You're killing them!

Gareth let go of his ability as he returned to himself. With one last disgusted look at the guards, he carried Ina around the block to his car just as the wailing of ambulances and fire trucks came within earshot. By the time the emergency vehicles arrived, he was already gone.

Tegan stirred, opening her eyes. In the darkness, she heard someone whispering but couldn't make out the words. The voice went on for some time, then fell silent. No movement followed, piquing her curiosity.

She carefully tiptoed around her friends as they slept and crept past the small dining room into the kitchen. She found Marshall hunched over the sink in the dimness, his back to her. His phone lay facedown on the countertop.

"Marshall," she said softly.

He turned; his cheeks were gaunt and his usually perfectly styled hair disheveled. "Tegan. You startled me."

"Sorry."

"It's three in the morning, night owl. Why are you awake?"

"What, are you my warden now?" she jested.

"Never been, never will be."

"I know." She leaned against the fridge beside her. "I just kind of woke up. Thought I heard someone talking back here."

Marshall spun his phone around with one finger. Hollowly, he said, "A lot has happened in the last twenty-four hours. I just got off the phone with Gareth. He found Dr. Deol. She was in a really bad place, teetering between darkness and light. Gareth showed up at the right time. And when she spoke to him, it was all the nudge she needed to join us."

"That's awesome . . . but you don't look happy."

"We were so close, Tegan. So close."

Tegan's limbs went heavy. *Oh, no.*

The Sentry dragged his bottom lip between his teeth. "They murdered her. They murdered her and took away everything we needed. And I mean everything. Formula for the cure, future plans, Marauder kill switch. *Everything.*"

Tegan slowly slid to the ground. She couldn't decide which was worse, the slain woman or the lost goldmine of information, and felt guilty. *Whichever way you look at this, it really sucks.*

"How's Gareth?" she asked.

"Not good. He's blaming himself. Big time."

"How can he? It's not his fault."

"They had a plan in place to get everything on a computer hard drive. Well, she did. Her office was ablaze by the time he got there. He found her in the server room but she was already dead via some kind of lethal injection. Gareth thinks that if he'd listened to his gut and moved in sooner, she'd still be alive. And a six-year-old girl would not be an orphan."

"That's awful," Tegan whispered. "Something like that can really mess with your mind."

"It does. I've seen it in the military, I've seen it with other Sentries." Marshall lowered his head. "He buried her on the outskirts of Moscow."

Tegan screwed her eyes shut.

Marshall pulled her up and they left the kitchen, taking a seat across from each other at the dining table.

"What now?" she asked. "What do we tell the others?"

He looked past her at the teenagers asleep on the couch and newly bought air mattresses. He didn't offer an answer. Tegan grabbed Aari's laptop from the other side of the table and opened it to scroll through Moscow's local news, using the search engine's automatic translator.

There it is, she thought. *Fire at an office. Bio lab completely burnt to ashes. Man, this bites.*

The two of them remained at the table, each lost in their own thoughts, even as the sun rose a couple of hours later. Mariah, the first one up, acknowledged them groggily, her hair in a messy bun. Jag limped out of his room, looking peeved about his cast-wrapped leg. Aari joined them half an hour later. Kody remained burrowed in his blanket from head to toe, snoring softly.

"It feels more doom and gloom than usual this morning," Jag noted warily. "I sense bad news."

Marshall didn't lift his gaze from the tabletop. "I'd rather talk about it once everyone's awake."

Mariah went over to Kody and prodded him with her foot. "Get up, you turtle. It's nine. Rise and shine."

"I hate mornings," Kody moaned, untangling himself from his blanket.

"You don't hate mornings," Tegan said. "You just don't like waking up."

"Like you're any different." He joined them, taking the last vacant seat beside Marshall, and saw the Sentry's dark look. "Oh boy. What worse thing has happened today?"

As Marshall recounted the events of the night, pensive dreariness met his words.

"Are the Elders aware of all this?" Jag asked.

"Yes."

"And?"

"As wise and knowledgeable as they are, they're not all-knowing. We've hit a brick wall."

Daniel walked out of his room, yawning, and saw the faces of his guests. "Whoa," he said. "Who died?"

"Someone who could have stopped the spread of the disease," Kody said, point-blank.

Daniel halted, then gawkily retreated back to his room. Kody left the table, muttering something about checking outside for their unseen pursuers. Jag and Tegan flopped despondently onto a couch and turned on the television. They increased the volume just as the anchor warned viewers of the graphic imagery that was about to be broadcast.

Mariah, Aari, and Marshall joined them as a shaky video from a Moscow train station unfolded. Screams and gunfire blasted through the speakers as armed personnel in military hazmat suits gunned down infected men and women. Some of the footage had been blurred but a few of the friends still turned away. Aari stumbled toward the front door, slamming it shut behind him.

"Gareth was there," Marshall said hoarsely. "He witnessed that."

Tegan looked down, running both hands through her hair over and over. As much as she tried to forget, the dead Dema-Ki villagers from the Battle of Ayen'et still lurked in the back of her mind; their lifeless bodies strewn in the dirt, the rest of the villagers having to carry their fallen brethren home and bury them. The massacre at the train station brought the raw images back to the surface.

Her eyes welled with tears but she quickly blinked them away as the images on screen switched to drone shots of civilians being taken into quarantine zones around the world, some even at gunpoint. One zone in Indonesia had gotten out of control and, as in Moscow, the infected were all gunned down.

A voiceover recited portions of press release statements and statistics throughout the photo and video reel. *"Dozens of countries have officially declared a state of emergency, with many grounding all flights to and from their nations. Urban centers and transportation hubs are most affected and many quarantine zones, as you can see on your screens, have been set up around the globe in an effort to contain the virus. Remaining governments have also begun closing their borders as the death toll continues to rise. According to the World Health Organization, at least four hundred thousand mortalities have been reported. There is no indication that this virus has even reached its peak as the world frantically searches for a cure. We have to hope that a breakthrough will come soon. Back to you, Lara."*

The camera cut to the anchor, but each time she opened her mouth to speak, only shaky breaths came out. "I, um . . ." She pressed her fingers to her closed eyelids.

Mariah sank onto the couch beside Jag. He put his arm around her. "It's happening," she whispered. "It's really happening. The world is spiraling out of control, just like Reyor wanted. And we're supposedly the 'Bearers of Light,' the Chosen Ones. Look at us."

The anchor managed to compose herself. "I apologize. Thank you, Thomas. Continuing on now, a recent report about the ongoing conflict between the Indo–Sino forces and Russia bears no suggestion that the war will end anytime soon."

"You'd think," Tegan said, "that an outbreak like this would slow down this stupid war."

Marshall shook his head. "They're just soldiers following orders, doing what they think is necessary for the survival of their country. Besides, most of these skirmishes are taking place in farmlands away from populated areas. They probably haven't seen the effects of the outbreak up close."

"Which means small villages and rural areas could still be safe?"

"Potentially, yes. And they might put up fences and security along their borders to keep away people fleeing the big cities."

On the screen, the anchor attempted to perk up. "In other news, a new phone app has started to make waves in Korea, Japan, Singapore, and Hong Kong, and is steadily being downloaded by countless users around the world. The app, Soteria, allows people to remain safely at home while government-sanctioned delivery mechanisms for food and other essentials are coordinated to minimize public exposure to the virus. This is a very helpful addition to the Israeli-provided test kits that help detect the virus in your system."

"That's good," Jag said. "If we can minimize people's movement, it'll help slow the spread of the disease and buy us more time to find the cure."

"Maybe," Tegan said. "But there are always more than a few morons who'll jack this up."

"And Soteria is a brand-new app," Marshall added. "Getting those government delivery systems in place worldwide will take time."

Tegan glanced at the front door, then passed the remote to Jag and headed outside. She found Aari and Kody sitting together on the steps in the cool morning and plunked herself beside them. "Got anything, Kody?"

Kody's head moved as if on a swivel. "Maybe, but I'm not gonna jump to a conclusion just yet. Also, if you're wondering why Aari looks like he might puke, I'd recommend listening to what he has to say."

Aari did indeed look nauseous. Tegan squeezed his shoulder. "Hey, Brainiac. Talk to me."

He pinched his eyebrows between his fingers. "Ugh. I wanted to ask Marshall that night on Masada, but then he nearly got killed and ever since then we've been busy, so I just put it on the backburner."

"Put what on the backburner?"

"On Masada, I picked up this old broken stone that I think might have been an arrowhead. When I did, I looked around and saw . . ." He clenched his teeth, pressing his palms to his face. "I saw hundreds of people, all dead. I could smell the blood soaking the air, feel the wind in my face. It's like I was *there*, Teegs. It's like I was there right after the mass suicide happened. It's just been festering in the recesses of my mind ever since, but when they showed the Moscow massacre on TV it all came rushing back."

Tegan turned his head toward her and searched his face. "You're shaking."

"I told you. It's like I was there. No, I *was* there. I don't know how."

"You saw into the past, then?"

"You believe me?"

"I would be stupid not to after all we've seen and experienced." She hoisted him up. "Come on. Let's talk to Marshall. You joining us, Kody?"

"One sec." Kody blinked a few times, getting his vision back to normal, then followed them inside.

"Marshall!" Tegan called.

The Sentry looked up from the couch, startled. "Yeah?"

"Aari thinks he saw into the past when we were in Masada. Possible, yea or nay?"

"You *what?*" Marshall jumped to his feet, grabbing Aari's arm as everyone crowded around them. "Are you serious?"

Aari seemed to wilt. "Is it bad? What's going on?"

"No! No, it's not bad. I've just never heard of anyone being able to do that."

"So, either this is really cool," Kody said, stroking his chin thoughtfully, "or the dude's a freak."

Tegan pushed him away. "Oh, go brush your teeth already. Marshall, Aari said it happened when he picked up a rock that might have actually been a really old arrowhead. My guess is that this ability activates by touch."

"Could be." Marshall found a decorative vase from the living room and handed it to Aari. "Anything?"

Aari stood still for a minute as everyone held their breaths. Then he passed the vase back. "Nothing."

Jag handed him the Dema-Ki pendant he wore around his neck. "Here, try this."

Again, Aari indicated no.

"This is so strange," Mariah said. "Maybe it was a fluke or something."

"Maybe not," Tegan disagreed. "You guys remember during the summer when Kody discovered another layer to his sensory abilities?"

"It was terrifying," Kody called from the kitchen as he started making breakfast for the group. "I had absolutely no control over it at the beginning. Do you know how disturbing it was seeing that dog in thermal vision? I almost had a heart attack."

Jag clicked his fingers. "I get it. Maybe what happened to Aari is the same thing that happened to Kody. His new ability is still developing, going through a metamorphosis, so it comes and goes when it wants."

Tegan smiled. “That’s what I’m thinking.”

“Let me check with the Elders,” Marshall said.

As he retreated into his mind, the others threw different items at Aari, hoping to find one that would open up his new ability again. Their efforts were in vain. As they gave up, Marshall returned to them.

“Elder Nageau wants to speak with you, Aari,” he said. “I’ll be the . . . let’s call it intermediary. Go ahead.”

Aari locked his fingers together. “Um, hi, Elder Nageau.”

“Greetings, youngling,” Marshall said. “Marshall has given me some stunning news.”

“So is it a real ability?”

“It is, but this power has not been seen since my Island ancestors were displaced from their home. It is even considered a myth by many in Dema-Ki. Youngling, what you have is a kind of extrasensory perception.”

“Extrasensory—like a sixth sense?”

“Not just any sixth sense. In your language, I believe it is called retrocog—”

“Retrocognition!”

“Yes.” Nageau chuckled. “Leave it to you to know these things. We do not have much insight into this ability, but I think I have enough for you to begin with. When you pick up an object whilst connected to the novasphere, glimpses of historical memories belonging to the object’s owner will be made available to you. There are, however, two conditions for this to work. The first is that the owner or creator of the object must be deeply bound to the item, or they must have created it at an intense emotional and spiritual level. In other words, for your ability to work, the person behind the object must be uniquely and powerfully connected to it.”

“Alright. And the second condition?”

“The second is that the owner or creator of the object cannot be presently linked to it in this, the biosphere.”

"What do you mean?"

"The person must have passed on. If he or she is still alive, the physical connection between them and their artifact will prohibit you from retrieving their memories. Once they have departed from this plane of existence, you may tap into the novasphere to access their memories. Even then these memories may only appear in bits and pieces, usually close to locations where significant events in their lives had transpired. A curious thing I have heard is that sometimes there tends to be brief flash-forwards to the next emotional geographical markers in the person's life."

Tegan was only half listening by the time Aari had given his gratitude and goodbyes to the Elder. She felt a knock on her mind and opened up. *Hey, Jag.*

I see it on your face, he said.

And I see it on yours.

We're thinking the same thing.

Yes, we are.

Should I bring it up, or do you want to?

You gave me the reins while you're out of commission, bucko. But it's your call.

Jag gave her an acquiescent grin. *Go on, then.*

Tegan put an arm around Aari's waist and wiggled him back and forth. "This is awesome, Brainiac. You know why? Shut up, I'll tell you why. Because we have hope again."

Aari looked like he was still trying to absorb the potentials of his newfound capability. "Huh?"

"Really? Smart guy like you hasn't caught up?"

"Asa!" Kody yelled from the kitchen where he was furiously cooking over the stove. "We go back to Asa and get him to hand over the Roman letters so you can do your freaky-deaky thing on them. Jeez, he's slow today."

"I think we can forgive him this one time," Jag said, grinning.

Mariah snorted. "And you really think Asa will just hand over something from his prized collections? We'll probably have to resort to theft."

"You're right," Tegan said. "He won't give it up. But it's still worth a shot."

"And if it doesn't work?" Aari asked, finally coming around.

"I think I know what to do if he resists us." Tegan looked at the Sentry across from her. "And I'm gonna need your help, Marshall."

40

"No! Absolutely not!"

Asa stormed through the swinging door into his kitchen as Tegan, Mariah, Kody, and Marshall hounded the poor man. Aari sat in the living room; he'd stopped watching their parade around the house twenty minutes ago.

Eh, who were we kidding? he thought, slouching all the way down. *Like he'd ever agree if we don't tell him why we need the letters. And, if we do tell him, he'd probably think we're completely nuts and kick us out anyway.*

Asa threw open the door and raged back into the living room, uttering a string of Hebrew phrases, most of which Aari understood to be curses. He ducked behind Aari's chair to use it as a buffer, then looked down at the teenager. "I like you. You're the only one not pestering me with this stupid request."

"Actually—" Aari started.

"No!" Before Asa could scurry away, Marshall and Tegan emerged from the kitchen.

"Asa," Marshall said, "if we could just see the letters out of their protective coverings—"

"Why?" Asa demanded as the pair cut off his escape route and closed in. "How does that help anyone? What aren't you telling me?"

"Please," the Sentry implored. "Asa, we just—"

"No! These are precious, fragile artifacts from two millennia ago. There's nothing on earth that will make me put them at mortal risk!"

"Okay, that's it!" Tegan whirled around and pointed at Marshall, growling. "Do it."

Marshall's expression hardened. He reached into his back pocket. Asa's gaze darted from the Sentry to Tegan. As Marshall approached him, the Israeli brought his fists up in a fighter's stance. Marshall raised one hand, then pulled the other from of his pocket and held his phone out to Asa. The man stared at the device, his hands still balled. "What is this?"

"Gareth and Deverell are on a conference call," Tegan explained. "They'd like to speak with you."

Asa shot them a look of suspicion, then snatched the phone before retreating to his bedroom on the other side of the house and slamming the door shut. Mariah and Kody trotted out of the kitchen to join the group as they listened to Asa shouting through the walls in Hebrew, Arabic, and English.

Aari bit his thumb. "Wow, he sounds really peeved."

"I hope the guys will get him to agree," Mariah said. "Hey, Kody, where are you going?"

Kody readjusted his baseball cap and straightened his oversized green sweatshirt. "I'm gonna look around for our tail."

Marshall stopped him. "Maybe it's not a good idea to step out. Can you get a look through the windows instead?"

Kody lifted the blinds from a pane that overlooked the front lawn. "I can give it a try."

As the others chattered among themselves, Aari sat with his hands clasped together in his lap. Asa was still shouting, but the intervals between yells had lengthened.

That's a good sign, he thought. *Right?*

A quarter of an hour later, Asa reappeared. He tossed Marshall his phone and rumbled, "Close all the windows and blinds and start boiling big pots of water. Don't cover them. Shut the kitchen door and turn off the lights."

He disappeared upstairs. The group, though unsure about what was going to happen, obeyed Asa's orders. As Kody and Mariah blacked out the kitchen windows, Tegan and Aari took turns filling large pots from the tap and setting the burners on the stove to their highest flame.

"I wonder what he wants," Tegan said, wiping spilled water from the counter and floor. "You gotta admit, those are some weird instructions."

"I hope this isn't some sort of Norman Bates thing," Kody said, shuddering. "Where's Jag when you need him?"

Asa returned with a large plastic tub and placed it on the table. With gloved hands, he pulled out long parchments in polyester coverings.

"Are those the letters?" Marshall asked delicately, as though Asa might suddenly lash out.

"Yes." Asa, aggrieved, removed the parchments from their protective casings. "I will leave the letters on the table. The boiling water will create just enough moisture in the air so that I can roll them up without damaging them." He placed the final letter down, then put a hand over his heart as if he'd just laid the artifacts to rest. "You may have these for only one week. When they are returned, I don't want to find a single tear in them. Understand?"

Marshall gave Asa's shoulder a quick squeeze. "Thank you. I know this is difficult for you but believe me, it's a great help to everyone."

We hope so, anyway, Aari thought. Since discussing his new ability with Elder Nageau earlier in the day, he'd been wracked with unease. His first impression of retrocognition had been ghastly and didn't leave a particularly delightful taste in his mouth. *I'd really rather not see any more dead people.*

Asa rolled up the letters, separating them with opaque polyester sheets, and slipped them into an airtight cylindrical canister. As Aari slung the canister's strap over his shoulder, he gave their host a firm handshake. "We'll take good care of them," he promised. "You won't be sorry, Asa."

Asa managed a wavering smile. "Go, all of you. Find what you need to find."

* * *

The group was on their way out of Haifa when Tegan said, "Question. Why wait to get to Daniel's house when we can just let Aari have a go at the letters here?"

"I saw an empty outdoor café some ways back," Mariah said, motioning toward a sandy stretch to their right. The royal blue waters of the Mediterranean Sea waved at the group as they raced past.

Marshall swerved off the highway and sped along a road leading up to the beach. "Let's do it."

Soon they were seated around a table under a spacious wooden overhang. Aari breathed in deeply; the briny scent of the beach under a bright sky always flushed him with a sense of openness and freedom. Beside him, Kody scanned around, concentration darkening his eyes. He was in his own world for a while before he snapped back and nudged Aari. "Well? Pick a letter."

"Yeah, yeah, don't get your boxers in a twist." Aari eyeballed the long parchments laid out on the table, then readied himself and touched one of the letters with his index finger, already flinching.

"You see anything?" Marshall asked.

Aari tucked his digits into a fist. "No."

"Try again, kiddo."

He reached out with two fingers this time, and thought he felt something scratch the back of his head and dig through his skull, but nothing happened. He withdrew. "No dice."

"Hold your hands out," Tegan directed.

He tentatively complied. Kody and Marshall, on either side of him, thumped his back encouragingly. Mariah, at the end of the table, observed intently as Tegan picked up a letter and placed it atop Aari's open palms.

There was a sudden flash behind his eyes, simultaneously bright and dark, just like before. A blonde girl not much older than him appeared in his vision, so real that if he reached out, he might have been able to touch her. When she locked eyes with him, a sudden jolt shot through Aari. He recoiled, flinging the letter away.

Kody yelped and dove off his chair, catching the parchment before it hit the ground. "Dude! What the heck? Asa's gonna *murder* us if we mess up his artifacts!"

"You saw something," Mariah guessed excitedly. "You've got that same look you had at Masada."

"It worked," Aari said, wiping his brow. "I saw a girl. Long blonde hair, kinda pale, had a bit of dirt on her face. She . . . was an absolute babe."

Mariah snorted. "Bah, typical male."

"Oh, please. I've seen the way you and Tegan look at some of the guys in school."

"Why did you freak out?" Kody asked, gingerly placing the paper back on the table.

"Because it caught me by surprise!" Aari snapped. "And it felt so real!"

"You need to go back there," Tegan said. "Can you do it?"

It took two tries before he slid into the vision again. The heat of the desert was almost unbearable. Sweat rolled down his skin. He saw the girl again; this time she wore a colorful shawl over her shoulders. Her turquoise eyes bore the weight of sorrow and loss as she looked away. Sunlight glinted off something gold around her throat—a necklace. He squinted, making out an inscription on the rectangular pendant.

That's block script, he realized. *Hebrew. C'mon, Grandpa taught you well. Don't fail him now.*

He struggled with the right-to-left alphabet just a bit before he got a name: Carmel.

Behind the girl, a small but busy village teemed with life. A vast, glittering body of water speckled with fishing boats rolled toward the shore. It struck him, then, why this place looked familiar. *That's the Bay of Haifa! That's where we are right now! It's Haifa before it was Haifa, just like Asa said!*

He found himself stepping back but had no control of his actions. *What the—*

An arm appeared, as if he'd raised his own, but it was too tanned to be his. The hand opened and the girl took it, her grip tender in his. There was still sadness as she gazed at him, but also deep adoration.

Holy smokes. The letters were written by Lucius . . . so everything I'm seeing is probably through his eyes. I repeat: Holy. Smokes.

Lucius's gaze drifted slightly down. Aari's heart skipped a beat.

Held against the girl's hip, in her free hand, was a small box clad in scuffed, coppery metal. The engravings on the lid matched the friends' pendants. He strained for the box but couldn't move. No matter how hard he labored, his host would not budge.

Come on, come on!

He blinked and was wrenched back to the café. He stood up so fast his chair fell back with a racket. "I saw the girl!" he crowed. "I saw the girl with the box! They were in Haifa!"

His friends threw their arms in the air, hollering. Marshall pulled Aari down, wrapped him in a headlock, and gave him a noogie. "Attaboy!"

Aari wriggled out of the Sentry's grip. "Let me go back in. Maybe I can find a clue about where they went."

He righted his chair and took the parchment. Another flash—he saw his, or rather, Lucius's hands frantically stuffing garments from a chest into a plain cloth bag; he was in a small room with a stone floor and clay walls. Carmel did the same with her wooden box and their sleeping mats. Moonlight streamed through the latticework that covered the single window, creating miniscule diamond patterns on the ground.

Lucius picked up a stack of parchments at the bottom of the chest. Aari, unsure why, felt displeasure envelop him. *Am I feeling what he feels, too? That's crazy. This is all crazy. I can't believe—hey, these look like the letters he wrote. Wait . . . what's he doing?*

The Roman knelt and removed a loose section of the dense stone floor. He arranged the letters in a depression in the dirt, touched his fingertips to his lips, and pressed them onto the topmost parchment in a symbolic goodbye, then replaced the stone into its slot.

Shrugging on his bag, he joined Carmel by the doorway and cupped the side of her face, kissing her long and soft before taking her hand. Together, they slipped out into the open-roofed central courtyard. Other rooms surrounded the quad and snoring could be heard from within. By a wall, a cooking pit smoldered from a recently extinguished fire.

They crept past a covered area near the front of the courtyard where a few cows, sheep, and a donkey slept. Pausing by the entryway of the home, they smiled at each other and strode out into the warm night.

Aari blinked, but instead of returning to the café, there was yet another flash. This time, he found himself in a bustling marketplace. Sweet fragrances filled his nose, perfumes of cinnamon, lily, cardamom, myrrh, and other scents he couldn't place. Bronzed, clean-shaven men attired only in loincloths or linen kilts tied at the waist worked the stalls or played board games in the shade, while women clothed in comfortable white sheath dresses perused the booths. Both sexes sported dark eye makeup and wore either amulets or vibrant pottery beads around their necks. Most had rings on their fingers, and bracelets or armbands. Children scampered by, all of them bald save for one long section of hair on the side of their head.

When Lucius glanced to the right, Aari found a beaming Carmel among some of the women. They ran their fingers through her blonde hair, markedly different from their own, and pressed the backs of their hands against her pale skin. Some of the children frolicked around them in a game of tag, shrieking and giggling.

Lucius slowly turned on his heel, allowing Aari to take in the lively marketplace. He marveled at the sight, soaking it all in for so long that it took him a while to focus on the backdrop. If he had control over Lucius's mouth, it would have hung open long enough for a horde of flies to buzz down his gullet.

Just a few miles in the distance, three prominent pyramids rose from the ground, sentinels overlooking the immense desert, blurred by waves of heat under the scorching sun. He blinked, and this time they were much closer. Aari tried to move Lucius toward the towering structures in vain. Then, with another blink, he returned to his friends.

"Are you back?" Mariah asked, face puffed in concern.

Aari flopped against his chair, groaning in response. Marshall stared at him in awe. "You were gone for almost fifteen minutes. Your eyes were open but we had to check for a pulse just to be sure you were alive. Good thing this place is empty, or people might've gotten spooked."

Aari started. *Fifteen minutes? Didn't feel like it at all.*

"You saw everything?" Tegan asked; there was a gleam in her eyes.

"Yeah. I—"

Kody clamped a hand over his mouth. "If you could, ladies and gents," he interjected, "please wait until we're in the car."

"Why?" Aari asked, voice muffled.

"Just pack everything up."

Once in the SUV, Kody took the passenger seat, put his finger to his lips as a warning to the others, then turned the radio volume on full blast.

"I didn't want to say anything until I was sure," he whispered as they all gathered close, "but seeing as we might have really valuable information right now, methinks I'm as sure as can be." He inclined his head toward the back of the SUV. "I'm pretty sure Reyor's guys are tag teaming. There are at least two cars, if not three, that seem to always be around. One is usually by Danny's house, normally in the multi-level parking lot of the apartment across the street. When we drive out to Haifa, another one is with us. And, I could be wrong, but I'm pretty sure a third car sometimes shuffles with the first and follows the third when we're on the move. They're always super quiet when I search around. Like, they don't talk. That's why I could never really pinpoint them. And I'm worried that they have listening devices, so let's keep the radio on, okay?"

Aari, sitting behind Marshall, nodded approvingly. "Clever."

"Aw, shucks. Thanks, Captain Smartypants. C'mere and gimme a kiss."

"Get away from me!"

"Okay, okay, behave," Tegan said. "Aari, where did Lucius and Carmel go?"

"Egypt," he answered, keeping Kody's head and puckered lips at a distance. "They were at a marketplace not far from the Pyramids of Giza and then got closer, but I can't imagine why. Asa said they were running away from the Romans, but Egypt was controlled by the Empire at the time. Why would they go there?"

"Whatever the case, at least we have a place to start searching again. Could you see anything beyond the pyramids?"

"The memory only stretches that far. Maybe getting close to the geo-markers of significant events will reveal more clues, like Elder Nageau said. Right now, that next marker is near the pyramids."

"Then that's enough for us," Marshall said.

Mariah lifted a finger. "Reyor's people will still follow us. It'll be hard to throw them off without giving away the fact that we can locate them now."

"We'll work out a plan," Tegan said.

"I'll get us tickets and we'll pack up," Marshall decided. "While you were traipsing in Lucius's memories, Aari, I checked the news. Turns out Egypt is one of several countries that'll close their international airports *tonight*."

"Talk about luck," Kody breathed, then added meekly, "Guess Jag's not coming, huh?"

The Sentry grimaced. "Afraid not. Can't have him trekking through Egypt with a broken leg when we still don't know the endgame."

"He's gonna be so bummed when we tell him."

Aari ran his hand over the canister in his lap, barely listening. Reverence had overtaken him. "It's incredible. By some providence we decided to check out these artifacts by the Bay of Haifa where Lucius and Carmel lived for a while, almost at the exact spot where the emotional geo-marker was created when they prepared to leave for Africa. Seriously. What are the odds?"

"As I said, if you're on the right path, the universe will open its doors for you guys." Marshall turned the volume up just a little more. "Now, let's start planning our way out of here. This should be interesting."

Kody trotted toward the parking lot of the apartment building across from Daniel's house, whistling. A tubby orange cat ambling beside him hissed. He glanced down at it, hissed back, then whispered, "Fine, I'll stop whistling. Party pooper."

All anyone observing would notice was a cat padding by its lonesome across the road—exactly as planned. Tegan, mind-linked with the animal, had joined forces with Aari in the novasphere so that he could use the cat's sight to deflect light from Kody, rendering him invisible to any other onlooker.

Armed with two wooden boards with protruding metal spikes, Kody entered the parking lot and went up to the third level. *I'm on my way, little piggies*, he thought giddily, *and boy do I have a surprise for you suckers.*

Most of the slots on the third level were filled. Kody narrowed his eyes until the world became dark gray save for some brightness, indicating cars that had just been in use. *Thermal vision is the coolest. Hopefully X-ray is next. I'd be such a terror with it.* He snickered to himself.

Since they'd received Victor's broken warning a week ago about possible watchers, he'd been hyper-suspicious of everyone and everything. His sensitivity to the surroundings caused him to notice one car in particular that seemed to always remain around the area, though sometimes he would not be able to find it. It was, as far as he could tell after days and nights of observation, the only vehicle that was constantly incredibly bright in his vision. There would be no reason for a parked car to project a heat bloom unless there were occupants who needed a little extra warmth in the cooler autumn nights.

He spotted the car now, a dirty white sedan parked between other vehicles, and picked up heat signatures from two bodies inside, something he was never able to catch through the half walls of the parking lot that overlooked the houses across the street.

Beside him, the cat meowed softly and he smiled at it. As he placed the spiked boards behind both of the car's rear tires, he tuned in his hearing.

"I hate this," muttered the tattooed giant in the driver's seat. "The loud music they've had going for the past few hours in that house . . . the parabolic mic is useless with all that noise. If we had any doubts that they knew they were being followed, this definitely wipes it all away."

"Hardly matters." The second man had a touch of a Russian accent. "They can't make a move without anyone knowing."

"Sir, what do we do? They're scheming, I'll bet on it. They must have learned something on the beach. And don't forget about the car that pulled into the garage two hours ago. It hasn't left."

"Shh, Elias. We sit and we wait. If anything happens, the others are just a few blocks away. Now stop talking."

"Yes, Mr. Ajajdif."

Kody crept out of the parking lot, scampered to the house, and crawled through a window in the back. Once inside, both Aari and Tegan ceased their exertions. Tegan nudged him. "Well?"

"Definitely Reyor's people," he said. "I think these guys were at the mining site on Ayen'et, too—the big security man, Hajjar or something. And his boss, Ajoojfid. Wait, no. Ajajdif."

In the dining area, Marshall raised his arm. The friends sidled up to him, joined by Daniel and one other IDF soldier, a small but fit brown-haired woman in her early twenties who Kody tried to play eye-tag with. She looked more amused with his attempts than anything else, like one might be toward an excitable puppy.

"Alright," Marshall said. "Well done, team. Everything's in place. We'll be leaving soon, so I suggest taking this time to say our goodbyes."

The friends glanced at each other, lips pursed, and busied themselves with rechecking their packed bags for the umpteenth time. Kody patted the pocket of his black cargo pants, hearing the crinkling of the last two power bars Victor had given him. He pulled one out and turned to Jag but the taller boy had stolen into the bathroom with a toothbrush, leaving the door open.

Kody joined him at the sink to splatter his face with cold water. Wordlessly, he passed his friend the power bar. Jag took it gratefully as he brushed his teeth. "You okay, Kode-man?"

"Yeah. You?"

"Never better."

"Liar."

Jag spat carefully into the sink. "Yup. I'm surprised my pants haven't caught fire yet. I just don't like leaving you guys, you know?"

"Hey, Superman, we can take care of ourselves. We may not have your speed, strength, or agility but we can still manage. Honestly, we're more worried about you."

"Why? Danny's taking me to a safe house. I think the worst part about all this is that I'm just additional weight with my bum leg. I can't be with you guys in Egypt. I'm useless."

"You're really not." Kody wiped his face with the sleeve of his T-shirt. "We're gonna miss you, man. It's been years since we've been split up."

"Except for most of junior year, when a handful of people talked smack about our amnesia and we stopped hanging out to avoid the attention."

"Not gonna lie, I'm pretty disappointed with all of us about that. Why didn't we stick together? It's what we've always done."

"I guess when you hear others say that there's something wrong with you over and over, jokingly or not, you start to believe it." Jag's tone picked up a faraway tenor. "But you're right. We should've stuck together."

Kody shook his head vigorously. "No. Nope. Nopity nope. Stop it, you."

"Stop what?"

"I can hear it in your voice. You're gonna start reminiscing about all our fun little misadventures before Dema-Ki and the prophecy. You'll get emotional, then I'll get emotional."

Jag turned on the tap and flicked water at Kody, who squawked and splashed him back. Mariah poked her head in. "Hey, you toddlers, some of us still need to use the bathroom! Move it or lose it!"

When the clock struck eight p.m., they reconvened by the dining table. As the friends held each other in a group embrace, Kody closed his eyes. *This feels right. This is family.*

All too quickly, they let go of each other. As they grabbed their bags, Jag gave Marshall a quick hug. "I know you'll take care of them," he murmured. "Just make sure to take care of yourself, too."

The Sentry regarded him warmly. "You too, kiddo." He held up his thumb to everyone else. "Let's go."

The IDF woman left first, backing her decoy car out of the small garage, and idled on the street. Marshall brought their SUV in from the side of the road, shutting the garage door to hide from Reyor's men; then Kody, Mariah, Tegan, and Aari piled in. Jag and Daniel slid into Daniel's truck and, together, both vehicles exited. Kody tuned his hearing to the two men watching them from the apartment parking lot. They spoke softly, but now that he knew where to direct his abilities, he could catch them easier.

"Sir, I'll say it again," growled Hajjar. "I don't like this. Three cars, all with tinted windows. We don't know who's in which vehicle. We don't know if they've split up."

"Start the car," Ajajdif instructed. "We're following them. I'll call the others."

Daniel and Jag took off down the street, tailing the decoy car for some distance before splitting off. In the SUV, Marshall stomped down on the gas and flew in the opposite direction. Kody, sitting on his own in the third row, tilted his head toward Reyor's men.

"Go, Elias!" Ajajdif shouted.

There was a second of silence before two resounding blasts were heard, followed by alarmed curses. "What was that?"

"Sir, our back tires are trashed!"

"*What?* How?"

A door slammed.

"What in the—how did this happen? Who put these here? *Elias!*"

"I swear, there was no one, sir! I don't know how but those punks got one over us!"

"Damn it!"

"That's one down," Kody told the others. "I'm naming them Huey. If I'm right and they've only got two other cars at their disposal, then Dewey and Louie will make an appearance soon."

"Nice work!" Marshall said.

"Ehh, all I did was place the boards with the nails. This was all Tegan's idea."

They raced down the street, merging with the few vehicles on the main road bearing north. Kody kept watch out of the rear windshield. A dusty, dark gray truck screeched out of a side road and fell in a few cars behind the SUV. "There's Dewey, folks."

Mariah, sitting in the middle row with Aari, hummed pensively. "The only advantage we have is that they don't know we're taking a flight to Egypt. But if we head toward Tel Aviv, they'll know we're aiming for the airport."

"We'll have to shake them off before that," Tegan said. "Any ideas?"

Mariah peered out of her window. "Traffic's slow enough. I could spin a couple of cars around and cause a pileup, but I'd rather not risk injuring anyone, even at low speed."

They followed a bend and a tunnel appeared ahead. "The turnoff to Tel Aviv is in four miles," Marshall informed them.

They zipped through the underpass and everything narrowed into darkness with flashes of yellow from the overhead lighting. Kody tuned his hearing again. An Israeli man in the truck was speaking. "What do we do? They're four cars ahead."

Over what Kody suspected was a phone, Ajajdif's voice barked, *"Stay on them. Don't mess this up."*

"I think they've got local baddies on their payroll," he called.

"Wouldn't be a stretch," Marshall said. "They need allies wherever they go."

The tunnel's exit came fast and they were back under the night sky. Oblong concrete planters with shrubbery and multihued flowers decorated the sides of the two-way road and arching streetlights.

"We need to shake them," Aari warned. *"Now."*

"I've got an idea." Mariah shimmied into the back seat to join Kody and looked out the rear windshield.

The cars behind them sped out of the tunnel. As the gray truck emerged, Mariah dragged two fingers through the air. One of the concrete planters swung onto the road, grinding against the asphalt. Kody, his senses still heightened, clapped his hands over his ears, recoiling. It was like nails on a chalkboard amped up a million times.

A second later he heard panicked yells from the truck's occupants just before they collided into the planter. Parts of the fender and the hood blew off. The windshield shattered and smoke erupted from the engine in a thick curtain.

"We're clear!" Mariah hollered.

They tore down the road and turned onto a freeway ramp under a sign for Tel Aviv. Kody kept an eye for any more tails, but he was cautiously optimistic that they'd made it. He pushed against Mariah's arm, triumphant. "I think we're clear!"

Aari grinned. "See? We're not helpless without Jag."

"Speaking of whom," Tegan said, "he just checked in. He and Daniel are out of danger. Louie went after the decoy."

Marshall puffed out a breath. "Nice."

Kody settled comfortably into the back seat, looking out at the city lights on the horizon. *It's funny,* he thought. *We've gotten so used to our abilities that it's become second nature. But if anyone else saw us, they'd freak. The corners of his mouth lifted. Man, have we changed.*

* * *

"I really don't envy you, sir. This is not a call I would want to make."

Ajajdif was hunched over in the passenger seat, his head in his hands. "Shut up, Elias."

His phone rested on top of the dash, beeping as he waited to be patched through to his superior. There was a click, then a modulated voice came on. "Vladimir."

Ajajdif swiped the phone and turned the speakerphone off. "Hi, Boss."

"I hope you have good news."

He would have rather had a drill bore through his head than deliver details of the mishap. The Boss listened as he gave the full rundown. All the while, he fought the urge to give excuses. There was an uncomfortable, prickly silence once he finished but he dared not utter a sound.

"So," the voice finally said, "you and Elias don't even get in the game because your back tires blew. One of your teams gets bested—by a *flowerpot*—and the other had to choose between two cars and went for the one that led them to a McDonald's drive-thru in Jerusalem. We're a multibillion-dollar outfit outwitted by a few kids. Is this what you're telling me?"

Ajajdif couldn't bite his tongue any longer. "You know these are not normal kids. They're smart and sharp, and"—he glanced at Hajjar, then stepped out of the car—"they have abilities. I got a concussion from that battle at the mining site two summers ago, remember that? I *know* I didn't throw myself headfirst through the ceiling of my office. I'm not sure if it was the girl or the woman with her who did it, but these kids have abilities just like you do, and—"

"Enough!"

Ajajdif swallowed. The Boss had never used that tone with him before, and he recognized a mortal threat in that single word. He wished he hadn't opened his mouth. Ajajdif, along with Dr. Nate, were the only people in the Inner Circle who truly understood the extent of their superior's capabilities. Even Tony Cross, the ever-faithful personal lapdog, had no clue.

Vydiot, Ajajdif thought. *You're an idiot for comparing the Boss to those kids. You'll probably get your tongue cut off now.*

"I'm sorry," he stammered.

The Boss disregarded his apology. "It's a good thing I didn't put all my eggs in one basket. Again."

"You've always been prepared like that. So what do I do?"

"Nothing. I'm sending Tony back into the field. You are to stand by until you get further instructions. If you fail me again, you will not see the outside of a Sanctuary, ever, until your last days—if I'm feeling gracious."

And yet, after Tony's ridiculous failure, all you did was demote him, Ajajdif accused silently. *I suppose you pick your favorites, too, just like everyone else.* He immediately felt guilty about his thoughts and vehemently expelled them.

"I understand," he said, clipped. "What's Tony's assignment?"

"To give us a compelling leverage against the children when the time comes."

"I'm sure Tony will be glad to be out here again. But what about the New Mexico Sanctuary? Will you be sending me back there?"

"No. I'll get Arianna Abdul to move. You remember her, don't you?"

"Mm, my chief geologist at the Canadian site. I thought she was working in the Heart now?"

"She is, though I'm sure she'll be happy to serve wherever she is most needed. Besides, work in the Heart is almost complete. I'll have Adrian call her."

"He's a busy man, running the topside of the company,"

Ajajdif said. "I know he's a key player in the Inner Circle but he's not the only person. I can arrange to transfer Arianna while I wait for further instructions."

"Already trying to work back into my good books, I see. I don't need you to do anything. Understand? Adrian can handle it."

"As you wish." Ajajdif swiped a finger on the vehicle's exterior, leaving a clean trail through the dirt. "I know I don't run the New Mexico Sanctuary anymore, but I can't help but worry about it. Has Tony managed to find the mole that helped the intruder escape?"

"That *intruder* said he had no help. A lie, surely. Nothing has come up yet but I'm certain Arianna can follow up just fine. It's no longer your problem, Vladimir. Get that through your head."

"Yes, Boss."

"Stay put. You'll get your instructions soon. And, Vladimir?"

"Yes, Boss?"

"I don't enjoy giving second or third chances. You're like a son to me, but make no mistake. If I have to, I will make an example out of you."

". . . Yes, Boss."

PART THREE

Cessna 206 over the African Savannah

The Pyramids of Giza Rising from the Desert Floor

Kenzo Igarashi stood near the back of the crowd as the Stewards, gathered in their tranquil garden aptly named Eden, eagerly awaited the Boss's address. The eighteen-year-old raked his fingers through his silver hair a few times, then reproached himself. *Look excited, not nervous.*

His cousin, Ren, chattered with a gaggle of her friends, her black locks barely distinguishable in the crowd. Kenzo felt a familiar stab of misery. *If I can't save anyone else, I'm going to save you,* he promised silently.

Ren and the rest of the SONEs had grown into their roles over the past year and possessed an air of determination and experience. He, on the other hand, felt more out of place with every passing day.

At the center of Eden, an immense, twenty-foot-tall projection screen displayed a golden phoenix emblem against a black background. Speakers around the cavern hummed along with the rest of the mechanical systems that kept the subterranean settlement habitable. Construction work in the Sanctuary had been completed the day before, and the entire night had been spent in celebration. Kenzo hated that he'd actually enjoyed the festivities; the atmosphere had been so unifying, so lively, that he almost forgot that they'd been taken from the outside world, brainwashed, and dumped underground.

Since encountering Victor half a month prior, he'd worked hard to expand his network, befriending numerous SONEs and administrators. Tony, often sullen and refusing company, was a problem he hadn't quite figured how to circumvent. He'd also kept watch on the SONEs, hoping against hope that at least one other youth was like him, impervious to Dr. Nate's cerebral reprogramming but acting as part of the masses out of fear. Unfortunately, that did not seem to be the case.

The speakers suddenly crackled, and a hush fell over the gathering. The emblem on screen morphed into an image of a figure in a black coat with a gold hood, concealing a face in its shadows. All around Kenzo, a thrill swelled through the ranks.

"Welcome," the figure said, a modulator altering the voice. "Thank you for joining me from different time zones across the planet. I would like to begin by expressing how proud I am of each and every one of you. All six of our Sanctuaries are now nearly complete and operational.

"You've demonstrated that you are hardworking and dedicated. More importantly, you are, day by day, proving yourselves to be worthy of the title of Stewards of New Earth. Or, as I've heard you call yourselves, SONEs. I must say, it has a pleasing ring to it. You are indeed sons and daughters of a new world."

The voice rose. "A world that will be free from the stranglehold of a society driven by greed and corruption. No longer will the cancerous culture that celebrates deviant obsessions in the name of progress be allowed to poison the soul of humanity. These people, these *parasites*, will be wiped off the face of our planet and we will return the glory to Mother Earth. And you, my Stewards, are the chosen ones who will bring about that change."

Kenzo joined the thundering applause but felt sick to his stomach.

"As you have undoubtedly noticed during the course of the past few weeks, we have begun distributing new uniforms according to the five-echelon classifications for the Sanctuaries. You've each been carefully selected for the echelon you're in. No one group is above the other in our collective, and each plays an important role that complements the rest."

The hooded figure disappeared from the screen, replaced by an image of a SONE in a black shirt, camouflage pants, and polished boots.

"The Vanguard," the voice from the speakers said. "You will

ensure tranquility, order, and safety, both now and in the future."

The next image depicted two SONEs in beige cargo pants, though the first wore a forest-green shirt and the other a gray one. "The Producers and the Builders. Many of you will serve your brethren through these two echelons. You play a significant role in safeguarding the survivability of each individual with the food you produce and the facilities you maintain."

Following that was a SONE dressed in dark pants and a shirt of royal purple. "The Administrators. You are a smaller group, but no less important. Your main duty is to establish the fair and just governance of our community. You will have weekly meetings with the Head of your respective Sanctuaries to discuss this further. Your future in the new world will be an exciting one, and it will be explored in the months to come.

"Finally, we have the Counselors. You are here to ensure our well-being and happiness, and to guarantee that we remain committed to our cause. As with the rest, you will attend meetings in the coming days to familiarize yourselves with your responsibilities."

Kenzo looked down at his navy shirt and white pants. *Guess I'm a Counselor. 'Here to ensure well-being and happiness.' Ha. More like keep a sharp eye on everyone. But this could be good. Think I heard someone say that this is the echelon that has access to the CUBE. If I can get my hands on one of Dr. Nate's devil helmets, I can toy around with it, see if I can put what I know to good use.*

The hooded figure reappeared on screen. "And there you have it. These five echelons are the foundation of a new civilization that we will build when we return to the surface. Speaking of which . . . you are aware that societal disintegration is accelerating around the globe at this very moment. It will lead to the complete collapse of civilization as we know it, but it isn't the first time humanity will experience near-extinction. Seventy-five thousand years ago a supervolcano erupted, almost wiping out the entire population and plunging Earth into six years of volcanic winter, leaving behind fewer than ten thousand survivors worldwide.

The ensuing genetic bottleneck led us along an evolutionary path to where we are today—and it is not a path that has brought out the best in this species."

A few among the crowd murmured.

"We will correct that. The apocalypse that is unfolding and the eventual rebirth of humankind is guided by our hand, not by a random act of nature. And, as such, the recovery will be swifter. Our approach is not one that harms the planet, but rather one that cleanses it of the vermin that decimate it. But should our venture be thwarted, I will not rule out extreme measures to reach our goal, knowing that we possess the ability to rehabilitate the planet."

The murmurs grew in intensity.

"Moving on to a matter that I'm sure will rouse your excitement and curiosity: In due course, you will be joined by a group of rare individuals whose unique blood will usher in a new stage in your evolution, giving the next generation an array of remarkable abilities. They will be equally distributed to all six Sanctuaries. And that, unfortunately, is all I can say for now."

Groans erupted from the gathering, followed by some good-natured laughter.

"These are exhilarating times as our plans fall into place," the Boss said. "Keep faith and work hand in hand, and I promise history will remember us as the ones who righted all of humanity's wrongs. To you, my SONEs, and to New Earth."

The crowd thundered, the echoes of their roars resonating throughout the cavern as they threw their fists in the air. "New Earth! New Earth! New Earth!"

As the screen went dark and retracted into a concrete slit in the garden, the Stewards dispersed into smaller groups, prattling animatedly with springs in their steps. Kenzo cut through the crowd toward the administrative building behind the massive workshop. Ducking out of sight of the lone CCTV camera, he checked the signal on his phone. *Victor said the best place would be around here somewhere . . . bam, here we go. Aw, man, one bar?*

He dialed one of the two contacts, named V, but got a long beep followed by dead air. He tried again, but no luck. After a few attempts, including shooting out a text that wouldn't transmit, he gave up.

Guess I'll have to keep checking this signal. He heard his name called from the other side of the building and shoved the phone into his pocket. *Should probably head back before someone misses me.*

* * *

As soon as the camera feed to the Sanctuaries was cut, the hooded figure turned a knob on the wall behind. The wall faded into transparency, revealing a window overlooking a sandy cove that hugged the shimmering waters of a lake speckled with sampans. A floatplane bobbed by the dock of the enormous villa.

Behind the camera, an older man, who would have towered even more in his youth, rose to his feet from a large rattan chair where he'd sat watching the speech as it was given. His full beard was dark around the mouth and chin, but the edges were widely gray. Life had carved deep lines into his stern, fair-skinned face, and his amber eyes flickered with vigilance. A tribal tattoo, its style unknown to the modern world, coiled around his left arm, disappearing into the short sleeve of his embroidered royal purple tunic.

"Not bad for your second address to the Stewards, Reyor," he rasped.

The hooded figure bowed slightly. "Thank you."

The man waited for the hood and voice modulator to come off, but neither did. "I assume you have another meeting shortly?"

"Yes."

He nodded, then scowled a little as he clenched and stretched his fingers.

"Are you alright?"

"Mm, yes. The effects of the black crystal can only take me so far. After all these years, age does catch up." He gave Reyor a pointed look. "And once you get your hands on the rest of the crystal, this will be your eventual fate, too—to live for centuries, see civilizations rise and fall, tyrants come and go, and then pass on and hope you made a difference for every generation you lived."

Reyor reached for the hood, as though to pull it back, but stopped short after seeming to reconsider. "There is no need for hope. I know I'm making a difference. The only civilization to come, Mentor, is the one we're building. I will cultivate it and sustain it for as long as the black crystal will extend my time on this planet. Our new world will evolve as the Stewards do. But . . . why do you tell me this now?"

The old man went to the window and gazed out, his strong hands clasped behind his back. "As I said, age does catch up. And, truthfully, I grow wearier of this world with each passing year."

Reyor moved to his side. "You speak as if you expect to leave me soon, Mentor."

A small smile tugged at the man's lips. "I have assisted you as much as I can, so that whenever my time here comes to an end, I can go to the grave knowing I've given you all I could. You are my blood, and I am proud of all you've accomplished in the last three decades. You have put in so much effort building this empire. But take heed, Reyor. Never allow anger to find home in your life. This will be my most valuable counsel to you. Rage burns away reason and clouds judgement. For those of us gifted with tremendous power, it can bring untold grief that will simmer in our soul for ages. Take it from someone who has lived through it."

Reyor looked away, and instead of responding to his words, said, "You've never quite told me why it is you wanted the five children brought to you so badly. Why the obsession?"

"Life does not allow a person to live so long without gaining some wisdom. If these five *youths* have truly made an evolutionary leap, and the Elders believe that they are the fulfillment of the prophecy, then . . ."

"Then nothing. They are freaks of nature, Mentor. Nothing more."

"Perhaps. Still, I want to see them. When can you bring them to me?"

"Soon."

"You've said that before."

"I'm putting a contingency plan in place. You will get them, you have my word. And I will bring you the seeds. That way nothing can impede our efforts."

"Very well." The old man tugged on his beard, then shot a grin at the hooded figure. "I'm glad to see you're still taking good care of my leather coat. It's a timeless piece of our history. I wore it on the ship that brought our people to a new home—where we eventually established Dema-Ki."

Reyor reached into a pocket and withdrew a small violet sphere. "Oh, I know." The *lathe'ad* rolled over smooth fingers. "You never cease to speak of it. And I see you're yet to outgrow the colors of our forefathers. That gaudy hue hurts my eyes."

"I will let that quip slide. This Tyrian purple is a nod to our heritage, Reyor, and a noble heritage it is. It was one of our ancestors, after all, who brought the abjad to the world. If not for that, the ancient Greeks would have been letterless! See how revered they are now, even to this day."

"The world has much to thank us for and soon, when it has been cleansed, it will thank us again." Reyor turned to the digital clock on the desk at the far end of the room. "I have a meeting with Tony in a few minutes."

"I'll leave you to it, then." As the old man walked out the door, he added over his shoulder, "Go easy on him, Reyor. He is entirely devoted to you, and you know it kills him that he's let you down. A good leader knows when to swing hard and when to give their people breathing room."

Once he'd left, Reyor turned back to the window and raised the *lathe'ad*, watching the sun refract in the sphere. "And, sometimes, a good leader knows that fear and an iron fist is needed to get the job done."

Mariah tugged on the ear loops of her disposable surgical mask. "I hate these things," she muttered. "They feel so flimsy compared to the full-face ones Danny gave us."

"Those ones are military grade," Marshall said. "Just hang tight. We've already cleared immigration and got our bags, so all we need to do is get through the health screening and you can use your personal masks."

"Is Dominique here yet?" Tegan asked, sounding eager to see the African Sentry again.

"She's making her way to the arrival hall as we speak."

Aari looked at his watch. "Midnight on the dot. I'm surprised she managed to get to Cairo on such short notice."

"Helps when you've got friends who can fly planes." Marshall slapped Kody's back. "Just like someone we know."

Kody staggered forward a few steps before Tegan caught him. "Whoa, hey, good sir," he said, brushing himself off. "I've only logged a couple hundred hours on a single-engine Cessna. Now if we're talking gliders, I've got that locked down."

The group stood in a lineup of nearly two hundred people from two separate flights, waiting to be transferred to the screening area. They all wore masks the airport staff had distributed before they'd boarded their planes to Egypt. As far as Mariah could tell, most of the passengers were Egyptians returning to their country before flights were grounded. At the very front of the queue, security personnel in white uniforms and full-face masks with assault rifles slung over their shoulders ushered the travelers into the arrival hall. Other armed guards were positioned at various entranceways.

Marshall cocked his head. “Hm.”

“What?” Mariah asked.

“I was remembering the last time I was here, a few years ago. Security was shamefully lax. Sure feels different now.” When his gaze drifted to a traveler a few rows ahead of them in the lineup, his face tightened a bit. Mariah turned to see what had caught his attention.

A disgruntled young woman in a mint-colored hijab sat on her suitcase. An older lady looked down at her miserably, then extended a hand only to have it angrily swatted away.

The crowd was soon led into a cordoned corner at the farthest side of the arrival hall. Rows of chairs had been divided into three sections by stanchions to segregate travelers from different flights. At the end of each section was a long table, two of which were occupied by nurses in hazmat suits ready to take blood samples and cheek swabs. The passengers from Tel Aviv were assigned to the center section marked B while those who’d arrived on the flight from Jordan sat in Section C. As the first passengers were called up to the tables, the flight crews from both planes arrived, taking their places with the others.

One by one, every person flashed their passports, gave the necessary samples, and returned to their seats to await the results. The friends did some people-watching to kill time, all of them impatient to get going.

“This shouldn’t take long, right?” Aari asked. “We were screened before we got on the plane.”

“It still might be a while before we get the all-clear,” Marshall said. “There’s a ton of people to go through, and only a couple of nurses this time of night.” He looked over to the exit behind them where fully armed military personnel were now posted.

“Guess we can’t make a break for it,” Tegan said. Mariah suspected she was only half joking.

Kody prodded Aari’s knee. “Hey,” he said, “wasn’t high fever one of the symptoms of the Omega strain? The violent one?”

“Yeah,” Aari replied. “Why?”

Kody surreptitiously indicated with his chin. "You see that girl there, with her head in her hands?"

Mariah scanned the crowd from the Jordan flight until she found the passenger—the young woman in a mint-colored hijab holding her head tightly, as if in pain.

"I see her," Aari said. "She was ahead of us in the queue."

"I just did a thermal scan of the crowd," Kody murmured. "Everyone's body temperature is normal except for hers and the woman beside her, probably her mom. The mother's is elevated a tiny bit, but the girl? She's off the charts."

"*What?*" Mariah hissed. "How did they get past the health screening in Jordan?"

Dread flashed in Marshall's eyes. "Maybe they didn't screen their passengers at all."

"The girl's all the way over there," Tegan said, pressing her mask flatter against her face. "And everyone's covered up, so we should be fine. Right?"

"Guys." Kody's voice shook. "There's blood dripping from the corner of her eyes."

The young woman suddenly screamed. She fell off her chair and onto her knees, banging her fists against her head. Her mother crouched next to her but was roughly shoved onto her back. Scarlet leaked from the girl's nose, staining her clothes even as blood trailed down her face from her tear ducts. She bashed her head against the ground over and over, wailing.

All hell broke loose as terrified passengers made a break for the exit. The soldiers standing guard pointed their rifles at the approaching crowd and shouted at them to stay inside. The passengers screamed, begging to leave, some even falling to their knees with their hands raised in supplication. The armed men forced them back into the screening area. A few retaliated but were struck with batons and shoved away. The passengers gathered behind the seats, putting distance between themselves and the sick girl. A couple of them wept openly. Marshall stepped protectively in front of the friends.

The sick girl turned to see two nurses escorted by airport security approaching her; one of the nurses had a needle in hand. She scurried backward on all fours, quivering, her eyes darting from one person to the next.

She looks like a terrified child, Mariah realized, heart twisting. As she watched helplessly, Tegan and Kody slid their arms around her, holding her from either side. Aari, standing next to Tegan with his hands tucked firmly under his arms, could barely watch.

"*Ummi!*" the girl cried, reaching for her mother. Blood dribbled between her lips. "*Ummi!*"

The older woman ran to her despite the guards' efforts to hold her back and knelt beside her daughter. The girl suddenly bared her teeth, ripped off her hijab and threw herself at her mother, fingers curved like claws, sweat dripping from her forehead. She screeched and swung at the older woman but missed, her sharp nails striking the ground.

The guards and nurses moved in. Sensing their approach, the girl leapt off her mother but was rapidly circled by the workers. They spoke in soothing tones as they orbited her, the guards with their hands on their holsters, the nurses holding up sedatives. She twisted around to keep an eye on all of them as they got closer, her body heaving with ragged breaths, her dark hair covering half her face. She'd started to bleed from her ears, and the whites of her eyes were almost completely covered in red veins.

What can I do? Mariah gripped Tegan's and Kody's arms tightly. *There has to be something. I can't just . . . just stand around!*

The girl stomped her feet, warning the workers to keep away as terror returned to her face. They moved closer. One of the nurses approached her from the side, but she saw the oncoming threat. With a bellow she hurled herself onto the woman, throwing her to the ground and savagely beating her with her fists.

The guards yelled for her to stop as they swung their guns up. Mariah frantically looked from the men to the girl beating and clawing at the shrieking nurse. As the guards' fingers slid to the triggers, she focused on the weapons.

But she was half a second too slow.

Two reports sounded. The girl froze for a moment before slowly slumping onto the nurse. A sickening silence followed as though all the air had fled the hall.

Mariah dug her fingers into her friends' arms. *No.*

"She's still breathing," Kody whispered. "But barely."

Newly arrived guards in hazmat suits helped the nurses carry the young woman through a door at the back of the screening area behind the test tables. The girl's mother sat on the ground, rocking back and forth, her lamentations echoing through the space and her face soaked with tears. The guards returned and one guided her through the same door. The other addressed the passengers and crew in Arabic, then in English. "We will be moving everyone to a secure facility, where you will all be tested again."

The passengers went into an uproar. They flooded toward the guard, shouting over one another in protest. Marshall headed over, signaling for the friends to stay put.

Tegan pulled Mariah close. "Hey, come here."

Mariah nestled into the hug, drained. "How are you so calm?"

"Because losing my head isn't a reasonable option . . . but it doesn't mean that that wasn't one of the hardest things I've had to watch."

"That girl could be dead."

"She was already dying, 'Riah. We need to remember that. She could have seriously hurt, maybe even killed, the nurse. And it really sucks, I know, because we have these gifts, these abilities, and we're powerless. But the only way we can help is by finding the seeds."

Kody fell into a chair. "It's hard to keep that in mind when something like this happens right in front of you. At the Battle of Ayen'et—yeah, we saw good people die, but at least we were able to help right then and there."

Marshall returned a while later, grim. "There's no way they're letting anyone leave after what just happened. We're all quarantined. They've got buses coming to pick us up."

"But even if we got sick, we can't pass it on to anyone," Aari countered.

"Try explaining that to the health authorities," Kody said, glowering.

Tegan crossed her arms. "Then we have to break out of here."

"Okay, Shawshank," Marshall said. "Got a plan?"

Mariah looked up at the Sentry. "You mean you're okay with this?"

"You guys call the shots, remember?"

"Alright, then," Aari said. "Anyone got any ideas?"

Tegan did a head count of the military personnel at the exit. "You said buses were coming to pick us up, right, Marshall?"

"Yeah."

She started to nod slowly. "Then I might have a plan. And it all rests on you, 'Riah."

Mariah groaned inwardly. *Somehow, I don't think I'm gonna enjoy this.*

* * *

"Ready?" Tegan asked.

Mariah scowled. "Are you sure there's no other way?"

"Unless anyone else has a better idea that doesn't involve getting in the crossfire of over fifteen military guys, then yes."

"This is gonna hurt. A lot."

"I know, but you'll pull through. And I've got some aspirin with your name on it."

Four red buses idled on the road next to the terminal, away from the main entrances of the arrival hall. The friends and Marshall made sure they were last in line as the crowd boarded with their luggage. Three buses were completely filled, but the fourth at the back still had plenty of room. As the soldiers shepherded the teenagers and the Sentry toward it, a dark vehicle with its headlights off crept around the bend fifty yards behind the last bus.

Good, Mariah thought. *Domi's ready.*

As the group neared the open door of the last bus, Tegan muttered, "Now!"

The bus at the front of the line lifted off its two right wheels, tilting toward the road. The passengers trapped inside screamed as they fell against the windows; Mariah had to shut her ears to them.

The armed men yelled at each other in Arabic and two of them ran to the first bus. Just as they arrived, the bus slammed heavily back onto the road, causing them to stumble.

Mariah jammed her knuckles against her temples, her legs almost buckling. *This hurts!* she shouted telepathically to Tegan. *It's like someone's jackhammering into my skull!*

You need to do this! Tegan barked. *One more! One more and that's it, I promise!*

Mariah's teeth chattered. She was barely able to see through the haze of agony, and she could have sworn it was as if something was gouging through her eyes into the back of her head.

Then warm hands rested on each of her shoulders, followed by a peculiar sensation against her chest as her pendant pulsated, like a heart. A surge of energy like nothing she'd ever felt before nearly threw her forward. *Whoa! What in the wor—*

Before she realized what she was doing, the first two buses rattled and bounced uncontrollably from side to side. More screams and wails threatened to suffocate her but she stubbornly pushed on. *I'm sorry, I'm sorry, I'm sorry.*

The hands lifted from her shoulders and it was as though her very bones had crumbled from rapid exhaustion. She heard Tegan say that she'd created the diversion they needed, but it sounded as if her voice was reverberating off the walls of a long tunnel. Excruciating pain shot through Mariah's head, and the last thing she saw before the asphalt rushed to meet her was the unlit vehicle approaching from behind the buses.

From the back of the minivan, a groan sounded. "What the . . ."

Aari, buckled in the center row with Kody, looked over just as Mariah groggily lifted her head from Tegan's lap. He closed his eyes briefly. *She's okay.*

"Welcome back to the land of the living," Tegan said softly.

Mariah dropped her head down, groaning again. "What happened? Why does my head feel like it's been run over by a truck?"

Tegan stroked Mariah's hair away from her face. "You blacked out. Those buses really took a toll on you."

"Blacked out? That's new. Explains why I feel so weak right now . . . How long was I out?"

"Nearly half an hour," Kody told her. "You also had one mother of a nosebleed."

"Ew. I must have looked like a mess."

"Without you we wouldn't have gotten away," Aari said, smiling over his seat at her. "We're proud of you for pushing through."

"Everything okay back there?" Marshall asked from the front passenger seat.

"Yeah!" Mariah called weakly. "Hi, Domi."

The radiant African Sentry behind the wheel beamed into the rearview mirror. "*Salut, ma chère!* It's good to see those beautiful brown eyes open."

"Mmh, thanks. If you guys don't mind, I think I'll lay off my abilities for a while. And I could sure do with that aspirin now."

Tegan shook a small bottle. "Got them right here."

Once Mariah gulped down two tablets, she said, "Hey, Marshall, have you ever heard of people being able to transfer their energy to someone else?"

"Never," he answered. "As far as I know, that's impossible."

"Are you sure? Because I don't know which two of you touched my shoulders earlier, but when you did, this new energy just flowed through me and I was able to keep going. But when you let go, I was completely drained."

Aari looked down at his hand, and then at Kody. Both of them were perplexed.

"That was us," Kody said uncertainly.

Marshall turned to frown at the teenagers. "This is strange. First your pendants vibrated all on their own at Asa's place, now this. I've never heard of anything like it before."

They drove through the city, nearing the desert. Aari knocked on his window. "'Riah. Sit up and look outside."

He heard her shuffling in the back seat as she rubbernecked around him. "Oh! Oh, my gosh. Is that—"

"The Pyramids of Giza, the last of the Seven Wonders of the Ancient World that remains."

"Don't feast your eyes yet," Dominique advised. "I'll drop you off first and park elsewhere. Just remember to stay away from the guards until I return. And wear something warm—it can get chilly out here at night."

The van rolled to a stop by the closed ticket office to the north of the pyramids. Aari, with the canister holding Lucius's letters, followed the group as they slunk into the shadows of the office's extended roof. As the vehicle retreated, Kody grabbed onto one of the support columns. "Marshall, could you give me a hand?"

"Gonna look for the security detail?" Marshall asked, boosting him onto the ledge.

"Yep."

As Kody scouted, Mariah sat heavily on the ground, still looking a little out of it. Aari joined her, distracting her by pointing out different constellations in the starry sky to marvel at.

"Wow," Kody gasped from above. "These pyramids are *amazing*. I can't believe they were built with only manual labor."

"Crazy, right?" Aari said. "Over two million limestone blocks were used for the Pyramid of Khufu alone."

"That's insane . . . Okay, back to business. I see one guard by a low wall near the first pyramid. He's on his phone. The other guy's circling the farthest pyramid. And, um, do they just let camels hang out in the open?"

"That's not what I remember the last time I was here," Marshall said, frowning. "I know they use tour camels during the day, but the owners always take them back once the place closes at night. Are you sure those are camels, Kody?"

"No, you're right, I must be looking at deformed giraffes."

"Alright, alright."

A rush of wind whooshed past them. Dominique appeared, clad in a black running jacket and sweatpants.

"Whoa." Kody leapt down from the ledge. "I forgot you're a speedster."

"And more." Dominique's teeth flashed in a grin. "Mariah, you don't look too well."

Mariah smiled faintly. "I'll be fine."

The six of them took off at a jog, cutting away from the road and onto the sand toward one of the ancient cemeteries near the first pyramid, which towered more than four hundred feet over the desert floor. Keeping low, the group ducked past short, crumbling walls and got as close to the distracted guard as possible. Aari counted sixteen camels sleeping in a semicircle behind the man, all tied to flimsy posts in the ground.

"They shouldn't be here," Dominique muttered. "Their owners must have paid the guards to look after them. I wouldn't be surprised if it becomes too hard to care for them with the disease spreading as it is."

"Then let's set them free," Tegan said roguishly.

A few seconds later, one of the camels awoke with a start, braying like a dying man. The others snapped up, joining the fracas and petrifying the guard, who about now probably wished his uniform didn't consist of white pants.

Aari's eye twitched. *This is the most disturbing thing I've ever heard. I could've gone my whole life not knowing what noises camels make. Good grief.*

The first camel yanked its head back, pulling the lead rope off its post. The guard could only take one step toward it before the animal bucked at the second camel's post, snapping it in half. The guard ran after the pair, trying to grab their leads, but the camel Tegan controlled galloped around the semicircle, rousing the rest of the herd. They danced and brayed around the guard until the lead camel took off westward, away from the pyramids and into the desert. He ran after them, yelling and waving his arms uselessly. The guard on the other side of the pyramid complex heard the commotion and took off after the camels to try and block their escape.

Tegan darted out of hiding. "Come on!"

The group followed her, trying to stifle their giggles. Marshall pulled a face. "Get it together, all of you."

"You first," Kody retorted.

As they approached the first pyramid, Aari removed one of the letters from the canister. "Alright. The last thing I remember was me—I mean, Lucius—heading toward the pyramids with Carmel. They were already pretty close, but I may be *too* close . . ."

With the others in tow, he loped away to put more distance between himself and the pyramids. When he got to a spot that felt right, he grasped the letter firmly, expecting a flash. All that appeared were some undistinguishable images with static, like an old television with a bad antenna.

"Do you see anything?" Tegan asked.

"No," he said. "I don't understand. I'm pretty sure we're at the same distance from the pyramids as Lucius was the last I saw him. How—" He slapped his forehead. "Agh, I'm an idiot!"

"What is it?"

"The pyramids. The largest one is to my left and the smallest one is to my right. But in my vision, it was the other way around. We're on the opposite side of where Lucius and Carmel were."

With the desert sky twinkling above, they raced between the pyramids. Aari was still admiring the structures when they reached the other side of the ancient masonry. *Human hands created all of this in a desolate land. Human hands created a disease to wipe out humanity. Human hands help and hurt. Human hands can do so much . . . so why do we waste them on hate and destruction?*

"Does this spot feel right to you?" Dominique prodded.

He looked around. The city lights a few hundred yards behind them casted away the darkness surrounding the pyramids. "This isn't it. I can only see two of them from here. I should be able to see all three."

Dominique nodded toward a seven-story-tall limestone sculpture to their far left. "The Sphinx. That should give you the right view."

When they reached the ropes that blocked access to the imposing monolith, Aari stared up in wonder. The enormous face, weathered over centuries, almost seemed to smile shrewdly at the sprawling cityscape before it.

No wonder Arabs call sphinxes The Terrifying Ones, he thought. *Sure wouldn't want this coming to life.*

He gripped the papyrus letter again. This time, there was a flash. When it waned, he could see through the eyes of Lucius the unforgiving desert sun glaring down on the pyramids. He and Carmel were concealed in the shadows of the Sphinx's massive paws. Carmel wore a dark wig and had lined her eyes with makeup in the manner of the Egyptians; she'd even donned a long white dress. Lucius motioned for her to stay put. Tightening the belt holding up the loincloth around his waist, he emerged into the open. Aari felt his apprehension like a heavy cape draped over his shoulders.

Egyptian workers milled about, and the Roman legionaries were scattered throughout the site, speaking among themselves and keeping an eye on the citizens. Lucius focused on a single centurion conversing with a young legionnaire. When he rubbed his head nervously, Aari realized that he'd shaved off all his hair, and his arms and torso looked even darker than when they'd been in the old Haifa fishing village.

He's trying to blend in with the locals, Aari thought.

As Lucius approached the centurion, the man halted mid-sentence and stared at the newcomer. Under his silver helmet, brief shock splayed over his scarred face. He held up a hand, gruffly ordering Lucius to stop, and dismissed the other soldier.

As soon as the younger man was gone, sternness melted away and disbelief returned to the centurion. "Lucius," he breathed, removing his helmet, "is that you?"

The apprehension fell off Lucius's shoulders. "Cassian. It is so good to see you, my friend."

"What are you doing here? I heard you deserted us a year ago! What happened?"

"I will tell you everything, I promise. But I need your help."

The centurion paused, then bowed almost imperceptibly. "Anything for you."

"Cassian, I travel with a woman. We need to get somewhere safe, somewhere far from the reach of the Empire."

"Your brain must have rotted if you came here to get away from the Empire." Cassian indicated the dozens of armed men around the pyramids. "They have not forgotten about you, Lucius. It is because of you that others found the courage to desert."

"Their actions are not to be blamed on me," Lucius snapped. "I was not the first to leave, and those who have fled won't be the last."

"It is not honorable," Cassian muttered, moving to shield Lucius from the looks of curious passersby.

"Do you fault me for leaving?"

Cassian said nothing.

Hurt and a touch of humiliation spiked in Lucius's chest. "I understand," he said bitingly. "We sit on different sides."

"Perhaps we do, but you were always my most loyal friend growing up. A brother. I will help you, Lucius." Cassian gave him a teasing grin. "And I must applaud your efforts to blend in with the Egyptians. I almost didn't recognize you."

"The things one does for love."

"I cannot argue that. Now, listen. I know a man who can get you someplace safe. I will tell him to wait for you by the river five miles east of here."

"Will he demand payment?"

"I will take care of everything. But, Lucius, I will not be there to send you off."

"I understand. Your help here is all I could have asked for."

Cassian's battle-hardened face softened. "Go. I will make preparations. If all is well, you should be able to leave two mornings from now."

"Thank you. It was good seeing you again, Cassian."

"Likewise. Take care of yourself, Lucius."

They shared final, sentimental smiles, then Lucius hurried back to the Sphinx, head low. As he turned to enter the gap between the paws, he stopped in his tracks.

Carmel was gone.

His heart pounded in his throat as he spun around, hoping to find her among the throng of Egyptians. Faces passed but none were hers. Then, from the other side of the Sphinx, away from the crowd, came sounds of struggle. He tore around the statue, the sand hot on his sandaled feet.

A legionnaire had his back to Lucius, his hands reaching for Carmel's dress. She backed away, hugging her bag close to her chest. Before Lucius could jump in, something stiffened Carmel's stance. She brought her arm up and the legionnaire found himself floating above the ground. He flailed his legs and as he opened his mouth to scream, Carmel swiped her arm across. He was flung into the shoulder of the Sphinx and slid down, out cold.

When Carmel spotted Lucius, the anger in her eyes dissipated into bewilderment at what she'd done. He approached her guardedly as she dropped to her knees and hurriedly unfastened her bag. Pulling out her precious brass-clad box, she opened it and peered in.

Five seeds rested in individual glass vials. All were unharmed.

Aari blinked twice and was pulled back to his time. He grabbed Kody to steady himself.

"What did you see?" Dominique asked. Her eagerness threw him off until he remembered that his newfound ability had not been observed in at least two millennia.

"They came here because Lucius had a trusted friend in the legion who could help him and Carmel get away from the expanding Empire," he said, crouching down. He'd been standing still for so long, his legs had locked. "He was told to go east to a nearby river, which I'm pretty sure is the Nile. It's a couple of hours away if they went on foot."

"You could understand them?" Kody asked. "Wouldn't they have been speaking Latin?"

"I didn't even realize that! You're right, it *was* Latin, but it's like I was fluent."

"You must get omnilingaluism when using retrocognition," Marshall said in wonder. "That's remarkable. Two for the price of one."

"Did Carmel have the box?" Tegan asked.

"She did," Aari said. "And, when she opened it, I saw five seeds in there."

"Five!"

"Yeah. Also, I now know why this spot is an emotional geomarker. I'm pretty sure it's the first time that Lucius witnessed Carmel's abilities, and maybe the first time she used them since losing her memory. They were both in shock." Aari rose to his feet and looked at Mariah thoughtfully. "She was just like you, actually. A telekinetic."

Mariah appeared pleased for some reason. "So was that all you saw? Did they really go elsewhere, or are the seeds here?"

Aari held up the letter. "Let me try again."

Another flash came and went. Lucius and Carmel were in a riverboat, pulling at the oars as the sun began to set. Behind them, Cassian's associate grunted with every breath as they steered the craft until they arrived where the river split around a small island.

"This is it," announced the captain. "My duty to you ends here, where the two rivers become one, just as I promised your friend."

Aari felt Lucius getting ready to protest, but the memory froze and faded. He returned to his friends, grumbling. "I couldn't get far, but I'm almost sure Carmel had her bag with her. They arrived at the place where two rivers meet in the Nile."

"Where the two rivers meet . . ." Dominique stared off toward the pyramids, her lips pressed together in a contemplative pout. "Of course. Khartoum."

"Where is that?" Mariah asked.

"Sudan."

Marshall harrumphed from behind the Land Rover's wheel. "Seriously, you guys?"

Kody didn't look up from his phone. "What?"

"Since we left Cairo, you've all either been asleep, on your phones, or reading. That's almost twenty hours of silence."

"I drove for a while!" Tegan protested.

"Yes, you did. Thank you again for that. But no one's spoken a word, so I'm putting my foot down. I want every gadget tucked away in a bag."

"But—" Aari started.

"Gadgets. Bag. Now."

"Yes, Dad," Kody grumbled.

They'd left Egypt with an older but more suitable ride than Dominique's minivan. With spare fuel cans and new waterproof supply bags in the back of the Land Rover, they felt ready for whatever Africa had to throw their way.

The friends passed their electronics to Kody. As he placed them in a bag he noticed a square device already inside. "Hey, Domi?"

"Yes?" she called, half dozing in the front passenger seat.

"What's this thingamajig you've got here?"

"Ah. It's something I recently decided to invest in: a portable satellite modem. We should be able to get Internet and phone coverage almost anywhere on the continent."

"Ooh, cool." Kody rummaged around until he found a pack of chips to share with Tegan beside him. "By the way, Teegs, how are Jag and Danny doing?"

"The last Jag checked in," she replied, taking a chip, "they were already at the safe house. Doesn't look like Reyor's people picked up their trail. Or ours, for that matter."

Mariah harrumphed. "My question is, how'd they find out we were in Israel to begin with?"

"Phoenix is a huge organization," Marshall said. "We've seen how far their reach can stretch, and they have our faces and names. I wouldn't be surprised if they've got contacts with their ears to the ground in almost every region."

"Aari," Tegan called.

"Yeah?" came the reply.

"I've been wondering. Is it just coincidence that Carmel and Mount Carmel in Haifa share the same name, or is there more to it?"

"I wondered about that too, but I'm, like, ninety-five percent sure there's no correlation. Mount Carmel was referred to by the Egyptians in sixteenth century B.C., if I remember correctly. And, anyway, the actual name in Hebrew is Har Ha-Karmel."

Kody tuned out the conversation, instead taking in the barren landscape outside. *Desert, desert, desert . . . and, oh look, more desert.*

Most of the settlements in the area rested along the banks of the Nile, interspersed with sandstone hills. Anger spiked in Kody's chest every now and then when the main road wound close to some of the villages, granting a view of vast acres of devastated crops. Strangely, he'd spotted a few tiny fields thriving among the colorless ones, all covered with thick meshes of chicken wire.

"How come some of these crops weren't destroyed?" he asked.

"I've seen this in the DRC," Dominique said. "These crops were planted after the nanomites' initial sweep. They're used to feed units of the army that have disbanded and disintegrated into highway bandits. Food is so scarce, the bandits strike a deal with the villagers—grow food for us, and we won't harm you or your family."

"That's sad."

"It is. That's how it works in this part of the world now. And you saw what happened at the border. The customs and immigration agents allowed *us*, non-locals, to cross from Egypt on land instead of using the ferry, even though it's forbidden. Yes, we had to cough up some money, but the point is that Sudan's government, like many other countries in Africa, is in disarray from the crop destruction and the disease."

"Egypt seems to be doing okay, though," Aari noted.

"Because the military's fully behind the president," Dominique said. "And that's only in Cairo. As I drove to pick you up, I heard on the radio that in some of the rural governorates, unrest has been brewing and is threatening to blow up. It's not pretty."

Mariah sighed noisily. "You know, even if we do somehow manage to stop everything Reyor's doing, the recovery will probably take decades."

"The important thing is that we *do* stop it," Tegan said.

Kody looked back out his window, toying with his sensory abilities. As he zoomed his vision toward the murky waters of the river on his right, he gasped. "Whoa!"

"Saw something?" Marshall asked.

"Crocodile!"

There was a *thonk* as Aari slammed his face up against his window. "Where?!"

"It just slid into the water. That thing was *huge*, man. Like, fifteen feet long."

Aari, still pressed against the glass, said, "Fun fact: Did you know that about two hundred people are killed each year by Nile crocodiles?"

"I think you need to review what the definition of 'fun' is, Mr. Encyclopedia."

"They're apex predators," Aari continued, as though he hadn't heard Kody. "Some have even been known to take down giraffes, rhinos, and hippos."

"That's comforting. Remind me to never swim in the Nile."

"Heads up," Marshall said. "Looks like a blockade."

The Land Rover trundled to a stop a few yards away from an old Jeep obstructing the road. Two armed Sudanese in worn-out green uniforms strode up, one with a radio clipped to his belt. He rapped on Marshall's window until the Sentry rolled it down, then prattled on in Arabic. Dominique translated. "They're saying that there's been an accident somewhere down the road and they want us to take the path through the hills by the river."

"Um . . ." Kody adjusted his vision. "Those hills are two or three miles away. If there's an accident, couldn't we, I dunno, drive around it? It's just one long road and a wide desert. It's not like there's nowhere to go."

Dominique conversed with the men, whose voices rose as they signaled angrily with their hands. She nodded, but even from the back seat Kody saw the distrust in her eyes.

"I'd rather not cause trouble," she whispered to Marshall. "Let's take the other route."

As they turned onto a dry riverbed to the right, Aari opened up a map of Sudan he'd referred to throughout the excursion, the paper unfolding across both his and Mariah's laps. "Unless I'm mistaken," he said, "these hills are part of a game reserve."

Tegan combed her fingers through her dark hair, uneasy. "I'm not the only one getting weird vibes from this, right?"

"Definitely not," Marshall muttered.

The rocky ride didn't ease as the riverbed narrowed through the hills. The tall sandstone mounds seemed to press in on them, and claustrophobia squeezed its grip around Kody. He checked to see if the Sudanese men were following them, but all was clear except for the clouds of dust the Land Rover's tires kicked up as it crossed the uneven terrain. A few hundred feet ahead were the muddy banks of the Nile.

Marshall turned left onto a dirt road that ran parallel to the river, then slowed. "Oh, boy."

Four uniformed men emerged from the bushes on either side of the path, rifles pointed straight at the vehicle as they blocked the way. Two of them held up their hands, motioning for the car to stop. When it didn't, the men fired warning shots over the roof. Kody and the others ducked instinctively.

Without taking his eyes off the human barricade, Marshall said, "Domi?"

When the other Sentry spoke, a snarl escaped her. "Highway bandits. The detour was nothing but a sham. They will rob us of *everything*, including Asa's artifacts."

"What's our best option?"

"Drive straight through."

"You want me to run them over?"

"Trust me and do it."

"Well, here goes nothing." Marshall white-knuckled the wheel. "Everybody *down!*"

Stooping so only his eyes were above the dashboard, he stomped on the gas and the Land Rover charged forward. The bandits unleashed a torrent of bullets, puncturing the hood and shattering the windshield. Glass shards flew inward, invoking cries, but Marshall kept his foot on the pedal. When the bandits realized their target wasn't slowing down, they leapt, rolling out of the way. The vehicle sped past, narrowly missing one of the men's legs.

Kody peeked through the rear windshield. Two of the bandits were already up, weapons in hand. He heard the pop of gunfire and dropped down just as the rear screen was obliterated. A bullet tore straight through his headrest and lodged itself in the back of Aari's seat. Another blew the rearview mirror away entirely, the shards cutting the Sentries. Marshall held firmly onto the wheel as bits of blood trailed down his scalp.

Two more pops sounded. Kody thought they were bullets hitting the body of the car until the vehicle lurched abruptly.

"They shot our back tires!" Dominique shouted.

Kody gripped his seat tightly as the Land Rover fishtailed out of control. The rear end swung onto the muddy shoulder of the dirt road. As sludge caught onto the destroyed tires, the car slid sideways toward the incline by the river.

"Hold on!" Marshall yelled.

The drag on the tires threw the Land Rover into an unexpected halt, tipping the vehicle over. Screams erupted as the car tumbled over the shoulder and down the low-set slope. Kody lost his bearings as the world around him vortexed.

The car flipped over and over, parts flying off mid-fall, until it landed upright in the shallows of the Nile. Water sloshed in through the broken windows. Marshall unbuckled himself with one hand and pressed the other against his head. "Everybody alright?"

Kody felt as if his brain was rattling around in his skull. "Define 'alright.'"

A quick head count determined that they were all fine, save for some minor injuries. Marshall opened his door and more water spilled in. "We're sitting ducks in here," he said.

They hastily waded out into the river, using the Land Rover as cover and making sure their heads weren't visible through any of the broken windows. Kody pulled a face at the murky, chest-high water. "Ugh, I didn't think the Nile would be like this."

"We have a bigger problem right now." Tegan peered around the car. "They've just split into two groups and are coming down the slope on either side."

"So, they want whatever we have, but they'll kill us if we don't cooperate?" he asked.

Dominique gave him a tight-lipped look, then faced Marshall. "I'll take care of this."

Marshall was appalled. "There's four of them and they're armed. Even if you take down the first two, the others will get the drop on you before you reach them."

As the Sentries exchanged rapid, tense words, Kody's ears picked up a low rumble. He slowly turned around. On the mud flats a couple of hundred yards behind them, four burly crocodiles slithered into the water, their bone-plated backs and tails the only thing visible as they swam toward the group.

"Uh, guys?" A chill crept up the back of Kody's neck. "Incoming."

Expletives escaped them all. Mariah pressed up against the Land Rover. "Four men with guns in front, four crocodiles behind. We're in trouble."

Tegan grabbed Dominique by the arm. "What if Aari covers you while you take the men out?"

"I'll need line of sight," Aari hissed. "If I show my head, it might get blown off!"

Dominique easily snapped off the car's side mirror and passed it to him. "Use this."

Aari fumbled with it. "Uh, alright, but—"

The second Dominique stepped around the front of the car, gunfire shattered the quiet of the hills. She slammed back into cover, forcing down a cry as she held her shoulder. Blood dripped between her fingers into the water.

"Domi!" Marshall made a move toward her but she waved him away.

"I'm fine," she said, jaw clenched. "It just grazed my shoulder."

"I'll do this, okay? Just—"

"You're not fast enough, Marshall." Dominique ripped off the hem of her T-shirt and Tegan quickly helped secure the strip around her wound. "Ready, Aari?"

Aari focused on her, and the Sentry shimmered until she disappeared. He stretched his arm past the car's fender, using the mirror to keep Dominique concealed. Kody looked into the glass, watching the unsuspecting bandits continue down the slope.

Without warning, one of the two men on the right flank had his gun ripped out of his hands. They watched in astonishment as the rifle pointed down at their boots. There was the crack of a gunshot and the first man dropped to the ground with a scream, holding his foot. The other moved to help but there was another blast. He hopped around before falling, cradling his own foot while yelling what were most likely obscenities to the invisible spirit that had attacked them.

Aari started unexpectedly. "Kody! The canister!"

"On it!" Kody stole a look at the scaly, primordial beasts traversing the halfway point of the river. Their reptilian green eyes ogled the group. He swallowed. "Guys, the crocs are closing in . . ."

Tegan faced the oncoming creatures. "I'll handle it."

The crocodile on the far left suddenly whipped around, clamping its jaws over the neck of another. The second beast rolled, catching the attacker's front leg and ripping it clear off. Tegan cried out at the same time the first crocodile unleashed a roar that reverberated across the dull gray water.

Stunned by the scene, Kody had to be thumped on the back by Aari. "Dude! The letters!"

"Right!" Kody glided through the side window of the Land Rover, trying to stay out of sight of the two remaining bandits on the left flank. He searched frantically, barely able to see through the mucky water. The straps of their bags were caught around the seats, keeping them from floating out the decimated rear windshield, but the canister was nowhere to be found. He popped his head through the open window. "It's not there!"

Aari kept his eyes on the mirror. "Check again!"

Kody returned inside, working from the front to the back. Water splashed against his face as he searched the center seats. When he stood up to get some air, he noticed something glinting in the sunlight fifty yards downstream. *No!*

He pushed himself out of the rear windshield to give chase but someone grabbed him by the collar, hauling him behind the vehicle just as a spray of bullets erupted in the water.

"Are you trying to get yourself killed?" Marshall demanded.

Kody pointed a finger. The Sentry spun around and his eyes widened as he spotted the canister rolling with the waves. He put a firm hand on Kody's chest. "Stay here. I'll get it."

With that he was gone, disappearing underwater.

A yell broke out. Kody risked a look over the hood of the vehicle and gaped. One of the bandits had been thrown two stories into the air. He hung for a second, mid-flight, flailing frenziedly before plummeting to the ground. He landed with a thud and was knocked out.

"Wait, Domi!" Aari cried. "You're moving out of my sight!"

Too late, Kody saw the Sentry shimmer into being some ways from the final bandit. The man witnessed her sudden appearance, nearly stumbling over himself, but quickly recovered and reached for the trigger. Realizing that she was no longer hidden, Dominique froze.

"No!" Mariah screamed.

The bandit's rifle was yanked upward by an unseen force just as he pulled the trigger. Bullets and shells hailed down around him. He yelled, trying to let go of his weapon. Before he could free himself, a blur rocketed toward him and Dominique delivered a massive body slam. He flew backward through some shrubs and smacked into the hillside before sliding down, unconscious.

"*Ohhh!* That looked like it *hurt!*" Kody rubbed the back of Mariah's head. "Quick thinking with the rifle."

She had paled. "That was too close. I wish I could have done more, but I—"

"Hey, it's okay. You're still recovering."

Tegan returned to herself and leaned against the car for support, breathing hard. The two crocodiles she'd locked into battle had rolled away from them, back toward the mud flats on the shore. The other pair had completely disappeared.

Kody fidgeted anxiously. *Where did they go?*

Tegan pushed herself away from the car. "Where's Marshall?"

All eyes turned downstream. The Sentry had reappeared near the canister, now a hundred yards away from the group. As he swam toward it, the two missing crocodiles emerged, their dark backs and powerful tails slicing through the water with fearsome speed.

"Tegan!" Aari yelled.

Tegan roared as she threw herself into the novasphere. Kody watched, hands on his head, as both crocodiles vanished underwater again. He could barely breathe.

As Marshall's hand gripped the canister, one of the beasts broke through the surface like a torpedo. It snapped its jaws shut, narrowly missing the Sentry as he dove under. It was about to follow when an explosion of water brought the last crocodile out. It was smaller but it launched itself at the aggressor, chomping down on the other's snout.

Tegan let out a choke when she returned to her body; Mariah caught her before she slipped underwater. "They're so strong," she panted.

"You did good, Teegs!" Aari called.

Kody pushed through the water, scanning around. "Guys, I don't see Marshall."

"His abilities let him stay under for a while," Tegan assured him, getting to her feet. "I know, it looks like it's all wrong but I've seen it. He'll be back."

Minutes passed and the Sentry still hadn't appeared. Kody treaded further into the Nile. *Come on, man . . .*

Marshall shot to the surface in front of him, water cascading down. He shoved the canister into Kody's arms, turned away from the teenagers, and retched. Kody blew out the breath he'd been holding.

The group allowed themselves to relax as they grabbed their bags out of the Land Rover. When Kody realized one was gone, he punched a headrest and it snapped off the seat.

"Whoa, Rambo," Marshall said. "What's wrong?"

"We lost one of the bags. It had our personal test kit."

At his words, Kody felt the group's heartbeats collectively skip. They all looked up the river as it gurgled past them.

"Nothing we can do now," Tegan said tightly.

They trudged up the slope toward Dominique, who'd made quick work of tying up the men and leaving them with a piece of dull flint to cut the ropes. "We'll be long gone by the time they free themselves," she said.

"You know, none of this would have happened if the guy that flew you to Egypt would've flown us out here," Aari grumped.

Dominique gave him a brilliant smile. "That man's a stickler for rules. If Egypt grounded all flights, then he can't be persuaded otherwise. I know a bush pilot outside of Khartoum who can get us where we want to go, though. He's an old family friend."

"Have you considered MMA, Domi?" Kody asked. "Because that body slam was deadly."

"I think I would be disqualified immediately for having an edge over everyone else, but I will take the compliment."

Marshall took out a water bottle and dumped it over his face and hair. "I'm so glad we decided to get waterproof bags." He nodded at the canister. "The letters are fine, right?"

Kody opened it, fearing the worst, but was delighted to find the letters perfectly dry. "Everything's good here. Except for the fact that we don't have a ride."

"There are settlements along the river. Maybe we can find some other means of transportation."

Dominique started up the bank. "Come. It's a long walk and we're losing daylight."

The hike through the hills to the nearest village had been a long one. By the time the group found a family willing to part with the older of their two boats—for a fee, of course—it was already mid-afternoon. It took them three hours to travel up the Nile to their destination in the eighteen-foot aluminum vessel. The teenagers had parked themselves at the front, making use of the breeze to keep cool. Aari didn't mind the hot weather and he knew Mariah didn't either, but Tegan and Kody looked about ready to melt. The Sentries sat at the back by the antiquated, noisy outboard motor.

Aari looked up from his map, then back down, and up again. "I'm confused," he said. "Are we in Khartoum or what? Because that city to our right is apparently called Omdurman."

"Omdurman is the largest city in the state of Khartoum," Dominique explained. "And Khartoum is the second-largest city in the state of Khartoum."

"Why do they have to confuse people like that?"

On either side of the boat, the banks of the river were matted with what must have once been verdant grain fields. The disheartening scene had been their view the entire ride up the Nile. Behind the fields were expansive, dusty cities.

It's so quiet here, Aari thought. *Too quiet.*

Dominique must have noticed, too. "The Alpha strain is prevalent in Africa," she said bitterly. "Something tells me that's why it's so lifeless here."

"The Alpha strain is the aging one, right?" Mariah asked.

"Yes."

"I see a few cars on that bridge up ahead," Kody said. "That's a good sign."

Dominique absently tugged at her single braid. "Maybe. From what I know, most of the interior is somewhat safe from the outbreak, but population centers like this are hit mainly by the aging strain."

"That's a bit of a relief for us," Aari said. "We're immune to it, right?"

"Well, yes, but there are some cases of the Omega strain, too. Which is why, for your sake, we need to stay as far away from the cities as possible."

"Hey, Brainiac," Tegan called. "Didn't you say your last vision was of Lucius and Carmel in a boat, and they'd stopped where the river split?"

Aari sighed. "Technically, it's where the two rivers *converge—*"

"Aari!"

"Sorry, sorry! Yeah, that's what I saw."

"Then come check this out."

Aari sidled up to the bow. A few miles in the distance, the two arms of the Nile met in a hug around an island. Aari retrieved one of the letters from the canister; as he did, static flashed behind his eyes. He waited for a vision, but nothing came. "We're still too far away," he told the others.

Marshall patted the outboard motor. "Let's get you closer, then."

They crossed under the bridge and followed the right arm of the river. The static persisted but faded in and out. "We're going in the wrong direction!" Aari exclaimed. "I must have missed something where the merge happened!"

Marshall guided them around the island, passing by a handful of rundown boats with silent fishermen watching them, and completed the loop. As they neared their starting point, Aari was hit with a blinding flash. He flinched. "It's got to be here somewhere!"

"We've made a full circle," Dominique said, bewildered.

Tegan stared hard at the island, tying her hair into a ponytail. "Maybe they docked?"

"Worth a shot." Marshall pulled the boat into a shallow cove and the group hopped out, careful not to tip over the bobbing vessel.

Dead stalks crunched and crumbled beneath Aari's shoes like brittle bones. The desolate, pallid acres of farmland stretched far and wide, shaded by groves of acacias. *This is so awful.* He gripped the parchment tighter. *This is someone's life, just taken away from them by a psychopathic—*

A brief burst of light threw him into Lucius's memories.

The grizzled Egyptian captain had grounded his boat onto the tip of the island flanked by the two arms of the river, but neither Lucius nor Carmel had stepped off.

"I am truly sorry," the captain said. "But no amount of pleading will change my mind. This was the deal I made with your friend in the legion. This is where your ride ends."

Lucius slipped a hand into his leather bag and produced a small satchel. He opened it and showed the captain a few blue gems. "Will this do?"

The captain's eyes widened and he smiled knowingly. "Sapphire?"

Lucius nodded.

"Yes, it will do." The captain made a grab for the gems but Lucius held them out of reach.

"I will give you half now and the rest when we reach our destination," the Roman growled. "I want your word that you will take us to the safest place possible, far from the Empire's reach."

"On my honor, I will get you to safety."

"And where is that?"

The captain sat down heavily, making the boat rock. Lucius quickly crouched to regain his balance. "I ask again," he said. "Where will you take us?"

"The safest place I know," the captain sniffed, "is at the foot of a white mountain that touches the sky. It rests about ten days' journey on foot, east of an immense lake where this river begins. All we have to do is follow it all the way to its source."

Lucius searched his eyes, suspicious. "That cannot be. No one has ever found the source of the Nile."

The captain smiled wryly. "That is what *you* think, son of Rome. My father once took me there, many years ago. I still know the way, but I must warn you that the journey will not be easy. We will have to hike around the treacherous parts of the river, which means leaving the boat and carrying your belongings over difficult terrain. Once we find safe river passage, we will have to build a raft to reach the lake. Are you prepared for the task ahead?"

Lucius turned to Carmel, who gave him a firm nod. He faced the captain, steel in his voice. "Yes."

The shorter man held out an open palm and Lucius passed him half the gemstones.

As evening fell they set up camp at the tip of the island, rolling out their mats and starting a fire while the captain regaled them with anecdotes. Lucius looked around, munching on a dinner of bread, lentils, and dates. The rich and fertile dark soil of the Nile banks teemed with healthy crops of wheat and barley that whispered as a light wind rustled them. The quiet peace of the arid, subtropical land welcomed the weary travelers with open arms.

Wow, Aari thought, observing the vivid memory. *This breeze, these sounds . . . they've already happened. I'm actually reliving the past.*

He blinked, and found his vision had gone completely black. *Uh . . .* A swell of panic started to rise when the void refused to leave. *Why can't I see anything? What happened? Oh God, what's going on?*

There was a yell and suddenly the darkness disappeared, like eyes opening. Lucius bolted upright, heart hammering in his chest. They were being invaded. Men in bright tunics rummaged through their bags around the dying campfire, but the moment Carmel had sounded the alarm they'd drawn sword-like sickles from their scabbards. Lucius rolled out of the way as one of the thieves swung at him, then leapt. They fell onto the dirt, fighting for control of the weapon until Lucius ripped it from him. A cry from the other side of the campfire made him look up. The thief kicked him off and scrambled away into the fields.

The captain was pinned to the ground, struggling against another thief who had the tip of a blade to his throat. Lucius hurdled over the fire toward them but wasn't fast enough; the bandit ended the captain's life with a flick of the wrist. Lucius screamed. As the thief whirled around, the Roman drove his blade into him. The man slumped to his knees, then toppled face-first into the dirt.

Lucius staggered back, nearly falling into the fire. He stared at his trembling hands. A rush of guilt and horror flooded him. He feverishly tried to wipe off the specks of blood that stained his fingertips, then looked down at the dead thief and, beyond him, the lifeless captain. Hopelessness threw itself into the tumult of his emotions.

Carmel cried out behind him. He spun around. The five remaining thieves circled the young woman like ravenous vultures, each trying to make a grab for the knapsacks she'd collected. One of them lunged at her and managed to get ahold of a bag—the one that contained her box of seeds. As he tried to yank it away, Lucius saw an awful fury in Carmel's eyes. She threw her hands out and the thief catapulted backward, soaring through the air and landing in the river with an unceremonious splash.

There was a few seconds of dead silence. Carmel fixed a cold stare on the rest of the thieves and they immediately took off toward the other end of the island, shouting hysterically. Lucius stumbled over to her, but the memory was shoved out of the way by reality.

Aari wheezed out a gasp. He was on the ground, and his friends knelt over him in concern. Marshall gently hoisted him up. "Hey, champ," he said, brushing the teenager off. "Take it easy. You were gone for a while."

"Lucius killed a man," Aari sputtered, a hand on his throat. "Oh, God, I feel like I'm gonna be sick."

"What happened?" Mariah murmured.

"They were camped out on the tip of the island and some thieves tried to steal their stuff. They fought back, the captain got killed, and Lucius—he . . . he . . ." Aari mimed the scene. "From what he was feeling, I think it's the first time he's ever killed someone."

"Hence this spot being an emotional geo-marker," Tegan said, nodding to herself. "That's dark. And Carmel still had the seeds?"

"Yeah." Aari waited until the urge to throw up had ebbed a bit. "But I still need to find out where they went. I think I have an idea, but just in case they didn't follow the captain's directions . . ."

Kody thumped him on the back. "Down the rabbit hole you go."

At the next flash, Aari faced a volcanic mountain with a distinctive collapsed side. Then Lucius turned around to gaze at another majestic peak in the distance, surrounded by savanna.

I knew it, Aari thought. *'A white mountain that touches the sky.' That's what the captain said.* Despite still feeling nauseous, he smiled to himself. *Hello, Kilimanjaro.*

"Kilimanjaro. Like, Mount Kilimanjaro?"

Aari exhaled noisily as he rolled up the letter. "Yeah, Teegs. That one."

Tegan stared up as the darkening sky bled from fire to twilight blue. *These seeds are really making us work,* she thought. *It's almost insane. But if it hadn't been for the highway bandits, we wouldn't have traveled by boat and it probably would've taken us way longer to find the exact location of Lucius's geo-marker. Or we could have missed it entirely. Marshall's right. Somehow, things do work out.*

"If we drive around the clock," Dominique said, poring over the map, "we'll probably make it there in about two days. But if my pilot friend outside of the city is willing to help, we could get there in seven or eight hours."

"We'll see him tomorrow," Marshall decided, "but right now we need to call it a day. It's past sunset, and I don't think it's a good idea to walk around these parts at night."

"Are we gonna camp out here?" Kody asked, snapping off a short wheat stalk and wiggling it under Tegan's nose until she sneezed.

"It'd be safer than wandering into the city," Marshall said, "since we don't know what it's really like in there."

"I'm not sure it's much safer out here," Mariah whispered, her back to them as she gazed out at the acres of dead crops. The silhouettes assimilated so well into the backdrop that Tegan didn't realize what they were until they moved—human forms clinging to the peripheries of the fields and lurking between trees like restless spirits.

"Uh, yeah, I'm not comfortable with this, either," Kody said. "There are people just chilling out there, watching us. It's very *Shaun of the Dead*."

Aari shrugged. "What are they gonna do, watch us to death? And anyway, I think we can defend ourselves if we have to. Or maybe it's nothing at all and they're just curious as to why a bunch of people are hanging out in these fields."

Tegan looked toward the city, contemplative. "If there are still cars going back and forth, then it can't be too bad in there, can it?"

"But why put yourselves at risk?" Dominique asked.

"We're totally exposed out here," Mariah said. "If we can find a motel or something, then at least we'd be in a closed space away from sick people."

As the group debated, Tegan mulled to herself. Then she placed two fingers to her lips and whistled to catch their attention. "I think it would be best if we found a place to stay the night. Mariah's right; four walls is better security than an open field."

Marshall seemed uncomfortable. "Are you sure about this?"

Tegan looked back at the forms creeping in the far shadows. "Positive."

They got into the boat, some reluctantly. Marshall steered them across the river until they reached the mainland and tied their vessel alongside large freighters docked by the shore. There were no signs of life as the group walked the streets of the straggly but seemingly empty city of Khartoum, all of them on high alert. Tegan kept a hand on the full-face mask strapped to her leg.

"Motel at two o'clock," Marshall said.

Aari looked skeptical. "You really think anyone will be running it?"

"Only one way to find out."

They cautiously entered the stout building's lifeless lobby. "This doesn't look too bad," Kody said, craning his head around. "It's like one of those boutique backpacker hostels you see in budget travel brochures."

"It needs to be decent," Marshall said. "Khartoum's a hub for tourists. At least, it was until all this happened."

A man in a perfectly pressed suit with a short gray afro greeted them with a wave from behind the marble reception desk. *"Ahlan wa sahlan!"* When his gaze drifted past Dominique to the Americans, he added, "Oh, welcome!"

Dominique gave him a smile, motioning behind her back for the teenagers to move to the far end of the lobby, away from the man. "Good evening. Do you have two rooms available for a night?"

"Every room I have is available."

"Ah, I'm sorry to hear that. How are your rates?"

As Marshall discreetly pulled out cash from his bag, the receptionist passed Dominique the keys and took a proper look at the group. "What are you doing out here? And, my God, it looks like all of you fell into a mud bank!"

"It's a long story," Dominique said politely, then made a show of looking around the austere lobby. "Business really isn't good, hm?"

The man laughed a little. "It's very bad. No one has booked a room in two weeks."

"Then why do you keep the place open?"

"Because it's all I have left in this half-dead city."

A teenager, dressed as impeccably as the man, emerged from a doorway behind him. "What, I don't count?"

The man gave the boy a light tap on the back. "Tsk, Atif. You know what I mean."

The teenager greeted the guests and went to peek out through the glass doors of the main entrance, biting his thumbnail. "Did you see anything on your way in?" he asked.

"If you're asking about people," Tegan said, "we saw no one."

The boy bumped his head against the glass. "It's the damn disease. I bet if you walk into any of the houses around here, you'll find old people on the floor, dead."

"Atif!" the receptionist snapped. "We do not worry our guests like that!"

"I'm sorry, Uncle, but it's true!" The boy turned to the group. "Sometimes, you can hear screaming outside. I went to see what it was a few days ago and . . . and a man was bleeding out of his face. He was so sick with the other disease. And he—"

The receptionist exchanged rapid, angry words in Arabic with his nephew. The teenager's expression darkened and he stormed back through the doorway he'd entered from.

The man sighed. "I apologize about that. My nephew has been agitated lately with all that's going on." He handed them their keycards. "Your rooms are on the second floor. And, don't worry, you'll be safe in here. We lock the doors at night."

The group rode up an old elevator in silence, then muttered their goodnights as they parted ways toward their neighboring rooms, the girls and Dominique taking the first door and the boys with Marshall taking the second. Tegan dove into the shower the moment they dropped their bags, only too eager to wipe the grime off her body. When she reemerged, clean and fresh, Mariah ran past her into the bathroom, yelling, "You always take too long in the shower!"

"I have a legitimate excuse this time!" Tegan yelled back.

Dominique heated a cup of instant noodles in the microwave. "This is dinner," she said remorsefully.

"I'm good with anything right now," Tegan said. "I'm famished."

The clock hadn't even struck nine by the time Dominique and Mariah had fallen asleep. As Tegan lay in the dark, playing a game of Snake on her phone while it charged, she heard a muffled curse outside her room. Curious, she peered out the door. Kody leaned against the wall between their rooms, rubbing his elbow.

Tegan smirked. "Spatial awareness woes?"

Kody nodded, wincing. "It's like my body keeps forgetting that I've grown and have longer limbs now, so I need more space to move. It's a chronic problem." He continued down the hallway and she followed. "Look at us, black sweats and T-shirt. We're twinning!"

Tegan wasn't amused. "Don't ever use that word again."

"Grump."

"How are the others?"

"Squeaky clean. Marshall's out like a light. I think being nearly eaten by a crocodile does that to a person. It's a good thing we had you, Teegs, or he'd probably be gone."

"I don't like his near brushes with death," Tegan muttered.

"Me neither."

She noticed a tightness in his face. "Kody? What's wrong?"

He shoved his hands into his pockets. "Aari's doing some timeline thingamajig on his laptop, where he keeps track of the spread of the disease. Teegs . . . three days ago, fifty thousand people had died. We're at four hundred thousand now."

Tegan turned away, fighting the bile rising in her throat. Kody ran his hand up and down her back. "I know," he said. "I know."

"Does . . ." She used the wall to steady herself. "Does Aari have a projection for how long it would take to . . ."

"Wipe us out? No. He slammed his laptop shut before he could get that far, but he did say that if the virus spreads at its current rate, it'll wipe out twenty percent of the global population in about six weeks."

"Kody . . ."

"I know."

Despondently, they headed to the elevator. Kody pressed the button a few times but nothing happened. "Guess it's the stairs for us."

"Where are you going, anyway?" Tegan asked.

"The drain in the shower is plugged. I'm hoping the receptionist can fix it."

They reached the main floor, turning past the lobby filled with empty chairs and divans, and headed to the reception on the right. Tegan, busy admiring some of the antique furniture, stopped short when Kody balled the back of her shirt in his fist. She turned to protest but he clamped his free hand over her mouth, eyes glued directly ahead at the reception counter. When

Tegan finally saw it, she let out a quiet whimper.

Crouched like an animal on the countertop with his back to them was Atif, the motel owner's nephew. His suit was bedraggled, half of it hanging off his shoulder. The sides of his white collar were inked red. His rough, ragged breathing grew louder with each lungful of air. He shrieked at the wall in front of him, hitting his head with his hands. Tegan's gaze slowly drifted to the ground. A body lay on the floor, only the legs clad in dress pants visible, the rest hidden behind the counter. A stream of slick blood steadily grew, coating the tiles.

Kody eased his hand from Tegan's mouth but didn't loosen the grip on her shirt. He tugged, pulling her with him. They backed away quietly through the maze of chairs and sofas. Tegan couldn't take her eyes off Atif. When he turned his head to look down at the body behind the counter, she saw crimson trails dripping from his ears and nose.

The friends neared the stairs, and as they whirled around to make a break for it, they collided into one of the divans. The drawn-out scrape of furniture against the floor demolished the silence like the klaxon of a foghorn. Tegan flinched. Slowly, they looked toward the reception.

Atif's head swiveled until his bloodshot gaze found them., He turned his body around. The front of his suit jacket was shredded and stained, as if he'd been in a fight. An unearthly scream ripped from his throat and he flew off the counter toward them.

Tegan vaulted over the divan and sprinted for the stairs. As she ran up, she realized that hers were the only footsteps she could hear. Without a second thought she hurtled back into the lobby and found Kody on the floor, thrashing as he tried to push Atif off him. The sick boy grabbed him around the neck and slammed him into the ground over and over.

Tegan spotted a fire extinguisher and ripped it off the wall. Screeching, she swung at Atif with all her might, driving the cylinder against his head. The boy was thrown clear off and slid across the floor. As he struggled up, Tegan hurled the extinguisher at him, nailing him in the face. Atif fell back and didn't get up. His fingertips twitched, but as quickly as the attack began, it was over.

Tegan returned to Kody as he got to his feet. The heavy sadness that clouded his usually bright emerald eyes made her stop in her tracks. He held a hand to the left side of his neck. Through his fingers, blood spilled down his shirt.

She started toward him. "Kody—"

He gingerly removed his hand. Deep cuts and bite marks covered his skin. Tegan sank to the ground, covering her mouth. *Oh, God.*

Kody looked down at his reddened palm and, through a watery smile, said, "Well, that's all, folks."

He worries me. He acts like it's nothing, like someone didn't infect him just hours ago.

Jag's words rang with mild exasperation in Mariah's head. *Sounds like Kody, alright. Let me guess, he's also cracked jokes about his situation?*

Not jokes. Puns. Awful ones.

That's the only way he knows how to cope with anything, which makes it harder to tell how he's really feeling. And you guys don't have the personal test kit anymore . . .

He's terrified out of his mind, Jag. It's in his eyes. It's like he's barely able to keep himself together but he doesn't want us to worry. He keeps saying 'At least I can't infect you guys!' It's insane.

I wish I could be there. Maybe—

I doubt you could've done anything. Really. Don't feel guilty. Marshall and Domi are already beating themselves up. Marshall cleaned out Kody's wounds and put a dressing on his neck with some of the Dema-Ki powder; he looks so miserable, as if he's failed us. And Tegan's on a major guilt trip.

Teegs? Why?

Mariah glanced at Tegan, who, with the Sentries, had led the march south of Khartoum through the fields and dirt roads toward a fenced, seventeen-acre estate surrounded by empty farmland. They approached the black padlocked gate with a sign that read 'Sigmund's Air Adventures' hanging on one side. Dominique hit the buzzer.

Mariah? Jag prodded. *Why does Tegan feel guilty?*

Because she made the call for us to go into the city instead of camping out in a field last night. She hasn't spoken much since the attack. If you could talk to her—

I will.

Thanks, Jag. So . . . how's your leg?

It's mending pretty fast, but Danny took a look at it and said it'll still take some time.

At least you're on track to recovery. And you're positive no one's on your trail?

As far as we can tell, we're good. The safe house is in the middle of a desert, so it would be hard to sneak up on us. Plus, Danny patrols the perimeter often. He's not a Sentry but, man, he's got a heart like one. We've been playing card games and sharing stories. You wouldn't believe some of the things he and Marshall used to do. They kind of remind me of us when we were a little younger.

I'd love to hear those stories sometime. Sounds like you're with good company.

Yeah, Danny's cool. Still . . . I know it's just been three, four days since you left, but I miss you knuckleheads.

Mariah smiled despite herself. *We miss you too, you macadamia nut.*

And you guys are sure you're not being followed?

We shook them before we got to the airport. There's no way Reyor's dogs know where we are.

Dominique hit the buzzer a few more times but got no response. Frowning, she snaked her arm through one of the gaps in the gate, pinched the sturdy padlock loose as easily as if she were snapping a pea, then led the group up the sandy pathway toward the redbrick bungalow.

Something's been bugging me, 'Riah, Jag said.

Mariah tilted her head up to feel the sun on her face. *Hm?*

The seeds.

What about them?

It's been on my mind for a while but I didn't really get to dig into it. Since you left, I've had time to turn it over and . . . well, the whole story bothers me.

Go on . . .

Think about it. So the siblings, Carmel and her brother, have the seeds to the Tree of Life, a tree that's supposedly able to cure basically every kind of sickness. Yet they guarded it with their lives and with so much secrecy instead of making this gift available to the world. I mean, when they thought they were going to die in Masada, they buried the box. Why was there a need to keep those seeds hidden away?

Maybe it was part of their mission? They were descendants of the Keepers of the Seeds, weren't they?

It still doesn't make sense to me.

There's so much that even the people of Dema-Ki don't know about the seeds, Mariah pointed out, and the little we do know came from the discovery of that old journal. Maybe it was just a safekeeping ritual or something.

I don't know. Something's not adding up.

Why don't you keep digging, see what you can find? Reach out to Elder Nageau. He might have some insights.

Yeah, I think I will.

We're about to enter the house. Catch up later, okay?

Sure. You guys stay safe. And keep a close eye on Kody.

Of course. Mariah severed the connection as the group headed up the small concrete patio. Dominique knocked on the door. They waited a few minutes but no one appeared to welcome them.

"That's odd," Dominique said. "His truck is still here."

She tried turning the knob and to everyone's surprise, the door swung inward. They filed into the sparsely decorated house. The single-story home had a spacious feel, with the kitchen and dining area to the left and the living room on the right.

"Sigmund?" Dominique called. "Siggy? It's Domi Mboya!"

Her words were met with silence.

"Domi," Marshall murmured.

The group turned to see him in the living room, looking at an old leather chair facing away from them. They approached hesitantly, Mariah trailing behind the rest. When Dominique reached him, Marshall had to hold her up with both arms to keep her knees from buckling.

A Caucasian man, deeply tanned from years of living in the desert, sat in the chair. His eyes were closed but sunken, and he was bony and frail with a few wisps of hair on his liver-spotted head. The skin around his cheeks and jowls sagged. A faint, foul odor forced Mariah to breathe through the sleeve of her T-shirt. *Oh, goodness.*

"Looks like he's been here for a couple of days," Marshall said, still holding Dominique steady. "Domi? Here, let's get you seated."

She pulled away from him and knelt beside the old man. Kody rested a hand on her shoulder; Mariah noticed the tenderness on his face. "I'm sorry," he murmured.

Dominique squeezed his hand, then lightly touched the deceased man's knee. She took a quavering breath. "He was . . . he was a good friend of my father's. I've known him since I was a child. He left Germany decades ago and had lived here this whole time. He loved Africa and her people so much. I . . ." Her voice shook and she went quiet.

They stood in silence for a time until Tegan said, "I really don't want to be the one to bring this up, but—"

"The plane," Dominique finished. She dried her eyes with the back of her wrists.

"Do you know what kind it is?" Kody asked, unconsciously tracing the edges of the square dressing on his neck. "Single or twin-engine?"

"I have no clue, but we should find out." The Sentry took a few more breaths, then led them outside. They found a barn-style aircraft hangar north of the house, beside a grass landing strip. As Kody studied the airstrip, Mariah heard him say to himself, "That's about twelve hundred feet. Which means . . . yeah, probably. Need to check out the plane first, though."

Dominique snapped off the chains and singlehandedly pushed the two hangar doors apart. They slid open with a screech, revealing a small white plane. Kody circled the pristine aircraft appreciatively. "Cessna 206. Single-engine, stretch version with six seats, large cabin. Built tough. Nice. I can work with this."

"You sure you're up for it?" Aari asked.

Kody gave him a sore look. "Dude, I'm fine. Besides, does anyone else here know how to fly one of these?"

"Point taken."

Kody picked up a thick binder from an office desk at the far side of the hanger. "Ah, maintenance records." He flipped through the pages. "Wow. Sigmund was super organized."

The hangar was stocked with tools, spare parts, and six fifty-five-gallon fuel drums sitting on wooden pallets. Poking around a dead man's property didn't sit well with Mariah especially since, if Kody could fly the aircraft, they'd be taking his plane.

Kody moved to a chart table filled with maps, taking measurements and doing some calculations on a piece of scrap paper. Aari wove between Tegan and Mariah and whispered, "How does he do that, take everything in stride after what happened last night?"

"I wish I knew," Mariah said. "I'm worried sick about him. How long does it take for the symptoms—"

"Shh," Tegan warned. "Later."

"We should be able to get to Kilimanjaro in eight or nine hours, but we can't make it without refueling." Kody tapped a spot on one of the maps with the eraser on his pencil. "Best shot would be somewhere in Ethiopia. Their airspace seems to be open, unlike Tanzania where we'll have to literally fly in under the radar. Which means we'll need to factor an hour's delay into the trip. I'll have to make a call to see if they're still up and running before inspecting the plane."

"But the plane can be flown?" Marshall checked.

"It looks like it's in great shape, so I'm thinking yes. Give me about forty minutes."

"How can we help?" Tegan asked.

"By leaving. I just need Domi's help topping up the fuel, but after that I need to be on my own."

Once Dominique had given her assistance, she and Marshall

left with Aari. Tegan watched Kody as he worked, plainly remorseful, before following the others to the house.

Mariah hung back, scuffing her shoes against the ground. "You sure you don't need us to lend a hand?" she asked.

Kody, standing underneath the plane's starboard wing with a clipboard in hand, shot her a lopsided smile. "You know, it's amazing how aware you become of other people's anxiety when they're worried about you. It feels like at least one of you has eyes on me at all times."

"Can you blame us?"

"No, I guess not. But honestly, this is on me. I should've been scanning our surroundings for any infected. I was tired and didn't think straight."

"You can't be constantly accessing your abilities, Kody."

"But I should have checked Atif's and his uncle's heat signatures. Look, I appreciate the concern, but it doesn't help. What happened, happened. All we can do now is hope we find the seeds soon."

"You're not scared?"

The joviality dissipated from his smile. "Does it really matter?"

Mariah stomped her foot. "You're unbelievable! It *does* matter to us, you jack—"

"Okay, fine, I hear you. You want the truth?" He dropped the clipboard, the metal casing clanging loudly, and strode over to her, all semblance of liveliness gone. "I *am* scared. I'm petrified. I think I might have even had a panic attack at some point. But what good does any of it do? I'm just trying to get myself into a space that lets me think 'Alright, if it comes down to it, I'm ready to die.'"

Mariah glared at him until tears formed in her eyes and he blurred in her vision. He reached out to her, alarmed. "Oh, jeez. I'm sorry. I didn't mean to upset you." He put his arms around her. "See? This is why I didn't want to say anything."

"Why in the world are you comforting me when I should be the one comforting you?" she spluttered.

He pretended to gnaw on her head like a zombie. "Because you have no braaaain."

She pushed him away, sniffling. "You're dumb."

"Maybe so, but do I detect a smile on your face?"

"Shut up."

"Never. Now, if you'll excuse me, I've got a plane to get acquainted with."

She gave him a tight hug and left him to his work, mopping at her eyes with her T-shirt as she slunk back into the house. *I'm such a wuss. Look at how he handles all of this, like some kind of superhero.*

Marshall, Tegan, and Aari stood together by the front door, conversing urgently; they looked on edge, ready to burst.

"How long do the symptoms take to show?" Tegan was asking.

"Anywhere between two to seven days," Aari said. "I'm keeping track of everything to the minute. So far it's been fifteen hours since the, um, incident."

Tegan rubbed her forehead. "Even if we find the seeds within the next day, it's not going to help. The trees take four weeks to mature. As far as we know, no one's lasted that long with either the Alpha or the Omega strain. And with the way Carmel and Lucius had been trying to escape the Empire, the seeds could be on the other side of the continent for all we know. What if we're chasing a ghost? What if the seeds are gone, lost for good? We're literally pursuing a memory, and in all this we sacrifice Kody?"

"That's a lot of what-ifs," Marshall said. "It'd be better to not go down that line of thought. But if we *do* find the seeds, there may be a way to slow the symptoms until a tree's fully grown. I can check with the Elders. Maybe harvesting a bit of the sap when it sprouts will buy Kody time."

"That's really wishful thinking."

"What else do you want me to say, Tegan?" the Sentry snapped.

Tegan threw her arms up. "I don't know!"

Mariah cleared her throat, making them jump. "Where's Domi?"

Marshall answered, visibly trying to calm his temper. "She wanted to do one last service to Sigmund. His wife's grave is nearby, so she's laying him to rest beside her."

"He must have known he was dying. Why did he just stay here?"

"What else could he have done?" Aari asked. "Get help? Who could've helped him?"

Mariah's shoulders slumped. She headed into the living room and sat on a sofa across from Sigmund's empty chair. *How many people are seeing something like this? Spaces that are now just a painful reminder of lost family and friends?*

Dominique returned a while later and busied herself with organizing the house even though it was already excruciatingly tidy. Mariah caught her breaking into quiet tears again and turned away to give her some privacy.

Kody finally joined them. "Okay, here's the deal. We'll be stopping to refuel in Jimma, Ethiopia, about four hours after takeoff. There was dead air when I tried to call the people at the airport, so let's cross our fingers that it's still functional. From there, it's another four, maybe five hours to Kilimanjaro. We'll land after sunset, and in radio silence, to avoid detection. I'm gonna turn off the transponder for extra measure and we'll be flying real low into Tanzania."

Mariah took in the haggard faces of the group. Since landing in Africa, they'd been shot at, nearly eaten, and one of their own had been attacked. They'd hardly gotten any rest except for a couple of hours here and there, and after what happened the night before, none of them had been able to sleep. But they were ready to push through, now more than ever.

Kody held the front door open. "All aboard the twelve o'clock flight to Kilimanjaro."

49

Victor sat up, holding his head in one hand and slapping the ground beside his mattress with the other until he found a bottle of painkillers and a glass of water. *That's what you get for abusing your body for years*, he seethed.

The view out of the wide, triangular window of his loft room at the Lodge boasted a mountainous view. Fresh snowfall that morning had carpeted the peaks. As the afternoon came around, the flurries had settled, and a light gray sky covered the region. Chief, curled up by the heating vent near window with his tail covering his nose, was fast asleep.

Victor absently felt his stubble up to his ear, finding the stitches on his torn helix. *At least it wasn't completely shot off . . . guess there's that to be grateful for.*

He grabbed a shirt and slipped it on as he headed downstairs to the airy common room. He found Deverell brooding on a sofa, his arm in a cast, looking toward the kitchen with his mouth turned down. Victor followed his gaze and saw Anya on the kitchen counter, where Gareth tried to entertain her with origami cranes.

Poor kid, Victor thought. *He's trying so hard to take care of her. He glanced at Deverell. And he's worried about his brother.*

Anya took one of the paper cranes, stared at it, then hurled it away with a sob. She slid off the countertop before Gareth could catch her and ran toward the living room. Gareth fell back against the island behind him and hung his head.

As the girl darted past Victor, he swept her up and sat her down on one of the sofas. She ripped out her hearing aids and chucked them to the floor. Victor held her cheeks, wiping the tears away and making her look at him, then signed at her to ask what was wrong.

She placed her thumb to her chin, the rest of her fingers extended. "Mommy."

He settled on the ground. *How are we supposed to tell her why her mother won't ever come back? He held out a hand.* Anya hesitantly grasped his pinkie through her blubbering, her hand tiny compared to his. *Being an orphan sucks—I know. But we won't let you go through this alone.*

Anya's sobs eventually quieted as exhaustion took hold. She snuggled against a throw pillow, eyes drooping. Victor waited until she was asleep before stepping into the kitchen to join Gareth, who looked up as he approached.

"I don't know what I'm supposed to do," the younger man whispered. "I want to take care of her but she hates me now. Which is fair. I may as well have killed Ina with my own two—"

"First of all," Victor said curtly, "she doesn't hate you. She's hurting. Kids are pretty perceptive so she can probably sense that something's happened to her mother. Second, you can't blame yourself for what happened."

"But I *am* to blame. I asked Ina for help and I waited too long to get her. You can't tell me my fingerprints aren't on this."

Victor leaned against the counter beside him. "That's not what I meant. I understand guilt. I understand regret. I'm not going to dispute what you're feeling. But if you let the guilt and the regret fester . . ." He looked down, jaw tight. "It'll eat at you from the inside and you'll find yourself running down a road you never wanted just to make the pain go away."

"I've never not been able to save anyone, Vic." Gareth's voice cracked. "I failed."

"I . . . yeah. It's a heavy weight on your shoulders."

"Does—does it—"

"It doesn't get easier. Not really."

"What am I supposed to do?"

"To start, don't do what I've been doing for the past few years.

It feels good for a short time, but you'll keep needing more and more to numb everything. What *you* need to do is look after that little girl. She needs someone."

"I don't know the first thing about raising a child, Vic. I'm not a father."

"Then don't be one. Just watch over her. Keep her on the straight and narrow. Take what you're feeling right now and make use of it."

They looked to Anya as Deverell slid a blanket over her with his functioning hand. Gareth shook his head. "Maybe you should just take over. She responds to you. And you know sign language, so that already makes her feel more comfortable."

Victor exhaled a short laugh. "If you don't think you're father material, then I most definitely am not. And with your smarts, you should be able to pick up sign language fast. It's a lucky thing she was taught the American version along with the Indian and Russian ones. You should keep trying to bond with her—you can help each other."

"Maybe." Gareth hoisted himself onto the counter and slouched over. "*Ach-y-fi*. I can't believe Reyor had Ina killed."

"Alright, I don't want to be an ass, but Reyor's killed over a million people as of today and the body count is rising. As horrible as it is, Ina was a casualty in this war. A war that she helped create."

"She destroyed lives. I'm not defending that. But she sought atonement. Maybe if she'd really gotten the chance . . . I don't know. I couldn't help but see her as a monster, but after talking with her I realized she was just human. And humans are always the ones who do the most damage to each other. It doesn't excuse her actions, but—bloody hell, I wish life was devoid of gray."

"Me too," Victor murmured.

"I swung by her house after I . . . after I'd buried her, to see if I could find anything that could help us, but they'd burned it down. Phoenix had burned the entire place down. Everything of hers, gone. It was surreal."

Deverell joined them, briefly grasping forearms with his twin. "Have you heard from the others, Vic? How is Kody faring? Are they in Tanzania already?"

"It's a real good thing they picked up the trail for the cure after mine went cold," Gareth muttered.

"That's partially why I came downstairs," Victor said. "Sawyer reached out while I was trying to grab some shut-eye, said that they're en route to Kilimanjaro and that Kody's holding up fine, no symptoms so far. But listen. Elder Nageau told him that it's time."

"Time?" Gareth repeated. "For what?"

"To move the kids' families to Dema-Ki. There are two Sentries already guarding them but the Elders want a few others to go along as security. There's fifteen people to transport and anything could go wrong."

"And they want *us*? Aren't there still a few Sentries in the U.S. and Canada who can help? We're on a completely different continent."

"And we'll have to drive to either Italy or Germany just to find an airport that hasn't grounded all its flights," Deverell added.

Victor pointed at Deverell's arm. "Oh, you're not going." He turned to Gareth. "I volunteered us."

"I get what you're doing," Gareth began, "but—"

"Let me rephrase: I'm going, and you're coming along." Victor gave the younger Sentry a hard, no-nonsense stare. "I'd advise packing light."

Gareth raised his hands in submission and stole down to the main floor. Deverell lightly bumped Victor's shoulder with a fist. "Thanks, mate. He needs this mission."

"You sure you'll be okay with Anya?" Victor asked.

"'Tis but a scratch. If the Black Knight could fight with all his limbs cut off, then this should be a breeze for me."

"You're ridiculous. For the record, the Black Knight couldn't fight. He was just extremely persistent to the point of absurdity."

"To-may-to, to-mah-to."

"Dev, before you go, there's one more thing. While we're gone, could you look up Phoenix's worldwide subsidiaries? Anything from mining to construction."

"Aye. Anything specific you want me to be on the lookout for?"

"When I listened in on Tony's meeting with Reyor and the Heads of Sanctuaries last month, there was mention of four other Sanctuaries apart from the ones in New Mexico and Kazakhstan—Brazil, New Zealand, South Africa, and some place called the Heart."

Deverell furrowed his brow. "The Heart? Where is that?"

"That's what I need you to find out. With a name like that, it has to be significant."

"I'm on it." As the Welshman turned to leave, he added, "By the way, do Kody's parents know what's happened to their son?"

Victor slowly bit the tip of his tongue, taking a moment to answer. "No. And we can't tell them. Not now."

"*Unidentified aircraft eighty kilometers northwest of Kilimanjaro International, this is Tanzania Air Force on guard. Identify yourself immediately.*"

Marshall, fiddling with his headset, shot a frown at the teenager in the pilot's seat beside him. "I thought you said you turned off the transponder?"

Kody's face puckered as he tapped on his own headset. "I did. I just didn't expect them to detect us this far out."

The Cessna banked right and flew west of Mount Kilimanjaro. The glistening white peak glowed in the sunset, its monumental shadow throwing the savanna and forests around it into darkness.

Kody blew a raspberry. "We'll have to get down in the weeds."

"We'll have to what?" Dominique's voice entered Marshall's ears; she had the only other headset aboard the plane.

"Fly low to avoid detection. Keep your seatbelts on!" Kody drew the throttle back and pushed the control column forward, putting the aircraft into a steep turning descent. Though securely strapped in, Marshall felt himself being lifted off his seat as they dove. Startled yelps rang out until Kody leveled the plane.

"Everyone okay?" Marshall demanded.

"Yeah," Tegan wheezed, "but what's the maniac doing?"

"We've been spotted by the Air Force," Kody called over the engine. "I had the transponder turned off so we'd be invisible to ATC radar, but it looks like they're using their primary one. I didn't think it would still be operational."

"And we really can't just fly to the airport?" Mariah squeaked.

"Definitely not. Tanzania closed its airspace, so all flights are grounded. If it were normal times, they'd seize the plane and detain and interrogate us. Now they might think we're carrying the virus, so who knows what could happen."

"What will they do now that they've spotted us?" Aari asked, yelling to be heard.

"Depends how frayed their nerves are!" Kody answered.

"Protocol usually dictates the Air Force checks it out," Marshall added.

Tegan raised her voice. "And where does that leave us if their planes do show up?"

"I'll have to use the terrain to mask our radar signature," Kody said. "Which means we'll have to fly even closer to the ground."

Marshall gripped the aviation chart they'd taken from Sigmund's hangar. "How close?"

"Over the treetops."

"You can do that?" Dominique sounded politely skeptical through the headset.

"Watch me."

Marshall wondered for the umpteenth time if he was out of his mind letting Kody pilot the aircraft into unknown territory. Then he shook his head, reprimanding himself. *You really need to let go and trust them. You can't protect them every step of the way.*

As they crossed over the savanna, Kody aimed the plane toward a spine of hills to the south, staying low and following the contour of the land. They flew in silence for several minutes until Kody leaned forward. "Here we go . . ."

"Spotted something?" Marshall asked.

"Yeah. Flyboys are out."

"How many?"

"Two. Hang tight, I'm taking us lower."

Baobabs and umbrella trees rolled by below them as the darkness overhead grew. The underbelly of the plane glided so close to the treetops that Marshall unwittingly held his breath. *Okay, Kody, you got this. You got this.*

The plane obeyed its pilot's steady, focused hands and

maneuvered easily through the hills. Eight thousand feet overhead, two jet aircraft thundered past the Cessna. The group rubbernecked to get a better look at the newcomers.

"I don't believe this!" Kody exclaimed. "How is the TZ Air Force flying those fossils in the twenty-first century?"

"I'm assuming you're using your abilities to ID 'em, because I can't see squat," Marshall said. "What are they?"

"Russian MiG-17s. They don't have lookdown capability in their radar systems, so they can't see us this close to the ground. And I've turned off our nav lights, which means we're practically invisible in the shadows. But the sooner we land, the better."

"Yeah. That's still the Air Force, and we're in a civilian tin can."

"Where was that airstrip again?"

Marshall peered down at the map. "Sigmund had marked it to be somewhere between Mount Meru"—he nodded to the smaller peak on his right as Kilimanjaro ruled the terrain to the left—"and that crater straight ahead, in the green belt."

"Uh . . . uno momento. Hey, yeah, I think I see it."

"You're really making good use of your enhanced vision, huh?"

"You know it."

The MiGs roared high over the small plane once again, sweeping past the mountains. Kody pulled back on the throttle, slowing the Cessna considerably.

Dominique spoke up. "Ah, um, Kody? What are you doing?"

"I'm trying to avoid visual sighting from the pilots up there," he said. "They may not have radar, but they probably have good eyesight if they're flying."

Marshall looked over at Kody. He'd been keeping a close watch on him since Khartoum, trying to discern symptoms of the Omega strain, but so far nothing seemed out of the ordinary. He dared to hope that the teenager wasn't infected.

It took them ten minutes to reach the landing strip. Touchdown was rough, and Kody brought the plane to a stop at the end of the unkempt grassy track. Dominique pushed the aircraft into a thick grove of trees and they covered it with foliage to disguise it from prying eyes. Quickly donning long-sleeved clothes to protect themselves from ferocious mosquitos, they embarked on the two-hour trek to the Nyika Wildlife Inn at the eastern foot of Mount Meru.

As they traversed the savanna, scattered with anemic trees that cast stretched-out shadows, a herd of elephants out of sight trumpeted into the dusk. The friends gaped at the land around them, eyes glimmering. Marshall watched them with a small smile, followed by a sharp wrench in his chest.

They may be the prophecy's fulfillment, but they're still so young. His throat constricted for a moment. *Victor was right. This isn't fair. And Kody—*

A soft hand rested on his arm. As if reading his thoughts, Dominique quietly said, "Don't think about it, Marshall."

He looked at her, pained. She gripped his arm tighter, then ushered the group along until at last they found the main dirt road that led the rest of the way to the inn.

Mariah crushed a mosquito on her arm. "Remind me again why we couldn't have just walked into a town."

"In my last vision, Lucius and Carmel were between Kilimanjaro and Meru," Aari said. "Better to stay the night close by so we can start the search quicker in the morning."

"That was rhetorical, Brainiac. I just hate walking through a wall of bloodsucking insects."

They trooped toward the standalone reception building, which was surrounded by numerous, round white huts with thatched roofs—*bandas*, Dominique called them—and timber cottages, all spread out. Inside the lit reception area, a long but simple wooden counter was unattended. Just as Marshall reached to ring the bell, a tall Tanzanian woman with close-cropped black hair, maybe a year or two older than the teenagers, rose from behind the desk. She eyed the group with calm curiosity. "Hello."

Marshall dipped his head. "Hi. We're looking for a couple of rooms?"

The young woman held his gaze for several long moments,

then said, "I will do you one better. We have a few two-room cottages available and, since we haven't had visitors in a while, I can give it to you for the price of a regular room."

"That's great. Thank you."

"I hope you're not looking to climb Meru. We no longer have rangers to guide you."

"Rangers?"

"Yes. They take you up and protect you from animals, like leopards."

"Oh." Marshall narrowed his eyes questioningly at Aari, who shook his head. "No, I don't think we'll be heading up there."

"Good. Also, during the mornings, you may find harmless wildlife roaming the grounds, so do not be surprised if you wake up to a giraffe looking through your window."

"As long as they don't steal my breakfast, I'm good," Kody said, pointing finger guns at her and grinning.

The receptionist didn't laugh. Wracked with secondhand embarrassment, Marshall thanked her and steered Kody outside, feeling the woman's prickling gaze on them as they left the reception and made their way to one of the cottages. *What's her problem?* he wondered.

Beside him, Tegan shuddered and scratched the side of her head. Marshall playfully tugged her earlobe. "You good?"

"Yeah. That woman had a tattoo behind her ear and I just—agh, I can't imagine the pain of getting one back there."

Marshall raised his wrist, where *Semper Fi* had been inked. "Guess it depends on your tolerance. But there's less fat behind the ear, so it would definitely be more sensitive."

Aari, marching ahead with Dominique and Mariah, stopped abruptly, his mouth forming an 'O' as he took in the sight of Mount Meru under the moonlight.

"We're close to the geo-marker," he said. "See how the entire eastern side of the peak is concave? In my vision, Lucius and Carmel were closer to that than we are now, and they were looking at Kilimanjaro from that vantage point."

"Good," Mariah said. "Shouldn't be too much exploring to do tomorrow."

"Huh," Kody mumbled. "There's another inn about a quarter mile northwest. Looks real nice, like a resort."

"Which means it probably costs an arm and a leg," Marshall said. "We got a reasonable deal with this place."

They arrived at their cottage, flanked by breathtaking views of Meru and Kilimanjaro, and Marshall told the rest to head in without him. He established a telepathic connection with Nageau. The Elder greeted him with his usual warmth, though there was an underlying tension.

Marshall.

Elder Nageau. We've landed in Tanzania and found the inn we told you Kody located on the map. Aari believes we're already close to the next geo-marker.

That is good news. And I trust all is . . . well?

As well as can be. Kody is holding up, and we'll head out first thing in the morning to search for the marker.

What of Gareth and Victor?

They're on the move. They should arrive in Montana within twenty-four hours and arrangements will be made to leave for Dema-Ki as soon as possible. Have the Sentries there prepared the families for this?

They have been speaking with them about this eventuality, but it will rest upon Gareth and Victor to convince them to act. On our part, we have been preparing for their arrival.

If you don't mind my saying, Elder Nageau, you sound apprehensive.

Oh, my boy . . . I am apprehensive. It will be hard for the families to adjust, and I am certain the people of Dema-Ki will be intensely inquisitive. The only outsiders we have entertained for centuries were the younglings. Even the Sentries have never been to the village. This will be . . . interesting, to put it mildly.

I'm sure it will be. But that's not all that's bothering you, is it?

The harbinger of darkness weighs on my mind every hour I

am awake, Marshall, and even in the hours when I am not. It is nothing new.

I have faith that you and the rest of the Elders will handle whatever is thrown at us with wisdom and steadfastness, just as you always have.

Nageau's warmth bloomed, enveloping Marshall in tranquility and comfort. *Your words are kind. We are blessed to have you with us. Now go. Rest. You will need your strength.*

Take care, Elder Nageau.

Marshall entered the cottage and found that, to remain within the safety of the mosquito net, he and the boys had to share the king-sized bed in one of the rooms. Dominique and the girls had already settled in next door; he could hear them chatting softly through the wall.

"Make way for the big man," Kody said as he and Aari rolled to the sides to give the Sentry room.

"You make me sound like I'm Jabba the Hutt." Marshall settled on the edge of the bed and patted Kody's calf. "How you doing, kiddo?"

Kody sat up, rubbing his eyes. "I don't feel any different. No fever, no headaches, no discomfort."

Marshall looked up, thanking the universe silently. "Glad to hear it. Here, let's get you a new dressing."

He cleaned the wound, added another layer of Dema-Ki remedy, and taped the gauze on Kody's neck, then fell into the middle of the bed with his face buried in a pillow. "I'm spent. You guys don't stay up too late. We're heading out early in the morning." He kicked off his shoes. "Great piloting today, Kody. I'm really impressed."

"Shucks. Thanks, Jabba. We have my dad to thank for that."

Marshall reached out telepathically to Dominique. *Everything okay with you ladies?*

Mariah's journaling and Tegan's just lying still, staring at the ceiling, Dominique answered resignedly. *I think the only thing on our minds right now is Kody.*

He's alright so far.

You think we got lucky?

I don't want to jinx it by giving a response.

That's fair. It's been a long few days . . .

Dominique conversed on but Marshall, unable to stave off the fatigue, slipped into a much-needed sleep.

* * *

The digital clock by the bed flashed midnight. Aari stifled a yawn. *Should sleep . . . but I wanna test something first. If I'm an omnilingualist through retrocognition, shouldn't I understand other languages by listening or reading when I'm not using retrocognition?*

Beside him, Marshall snored softly. Kody was on his phone, his eyes barely open. Aari picked up a letter from the canister and, as he rolled it out, an unexpected flash in his mind hurled him into the past. *What? But I'm not at the geo-marker! How can I—unless . . . unless another significant event happened here?*

Carmel flounced ahead of Lucius, using sprawling fig tree roots to navigate a path through the montane forest. Aari noted how easily Lucius kept up with her and how much surer his footing was, and wondered how long they'd been on the run now. The vast canopy broke in places and the sun's rays shone through like spotlights upon the pair. Joy fought to burst free from the confines of Lucius's chest as they ran. Aari recognized it as a new feeling; it was the Roman's first taste of real freedom, far away from the grasp of the Empire.

Carmel halted by a rocky stream that gurgled past, stretching some thirty feet across. She gracefully leapt onto a wet outcrop, working her way effortlessly across the water. As Lucius readied to take a bound, a prickling sensation made the hairs on his arms stand up. He tried to ignore it, but the sensation crawled up the back of his neck like an army of fire ants. He slowly turned—and threw himself sideways just as the open jaws of a leopard snapped shut on empty space.

The predator landed where he'd stood only a second ago. Lucius wanted to yell out to Carmel, but her name died on his lips as terror took hold. The leopard bounded across the stream toward her as she balanced unsteadily on a log.

His voice finally returned to him. "Carmel!"

The young woman looked over her shoulder and screamed. She attempted to face the leopard and displace it with her ability but couldn't pivot fast enough. The animal hurled itself at her, claws outstretched. They toppled off the log, splashing into the stream. The back of Carmel's head smacked against a jagged boulder and she slumped against it, her bag containing the seeds keeping her latched in place.

Lucius unsheathed a sword-like sickle from his scabbard. Aari remembered the weapon all too well; Lucius had killed a bandit with it in Khartoum. The Roman tore over the stepping stones to where the leopard paddled furiously against the current toward Carmel. He let loose a battle cry and leapt, sinking the blade deep between the predator's shoulders. The stream turned red as he yanked the weapon out and kicked the lifeless body downstream.

As he sheathed the blade, a compact force threw him face-first into the water. Claws pierced his tunic and he cried out, an explosion of bubbles erupting from his mouth. Deadly incisors closed around his neck but the weight on his back suddenly went limp before sliding off.

A hand gripped Lucius, like a cat grabbing a kitten by the scruff, and pulled him up. He gasped, lungs grateful for air, and came eye-to-eye with a black man wearing a half-face tribal mask. Behind him were others, similarly garbed in masks and loincloths. The man indicated downstream to where a second leopard floated with the current, an arrow shot through the base of its skull.

There was a brief spell of darkness accompanied by a bright flash, throwing Aari forward in time. Though jarred, he stayed connected to the memory as Lucius followed the tribesmen. They carried Carmel in a makeshift litter into a village that lay within a clearing in the forest. Curious faces popped out of huts, while others peered inquiringly from around a large fire pit. Lucius eyed the unfamiliar people with cautious trust.

Another flash. This time, they were sitting around the very same fire pit with the tribe. Carmel, beside Lucius, seemed to have aged a few years. When Aari first saw her she'd appeared to be in her late teens, and now she'd come into the full blossom of womanhood.

I'd peg her at mid-twenties, he thought. *I guess she survived the head trauma. And it looks like they've been living here all this while. Look at them, enjoying the company of the tribe. Is this where they settled? Did they live out the rest of their lives here?*

A young boy with a big afro sat by Lucius's feet, his mother looking on warmly from afar. He and Carmel played a game, each holding a certain number of twigs. Sometimes she passed him a twig, sometimes he passed her two or three. Lucius plunked the boy on his knee, hugging him snugly. The boy wiggled in delight but remained focused on his game.

A blurring of vision and a third flash.

As the haze lifted, Aari observed the village in shambles. Several tribespeople lay on the ground, motionless on grass mats, while others carried bodies into the forest to be buried. Lucius, his arm around Carmel as they watched, softly said, "Let's go back inside."

She pulled away from him. "These people cared for me—for us—when I was on the brink of death. They didn't have to, but they did. There must be something we can do, Lucius. I cannot watch more of them die. It's been days already."

Lucius touched the back of a finger to her cheek. "We don't know what this sickness is. None of the medicine man's cures have worked. I *know* you want to help. So do I, believe me, but there's nothing we can do."

"Exhaustion, vomiting, colds, sweats, coughs, pain . . . What *is* this illness?"

Malaria, maybe? Aari wondered. *But it could also literally be a bunch of other diseases.*

"I don't know," Lucius said. "And I fear the longer we remain exposed, the higher the chance we will contract whatever it is. Let's go back inside, love."

She reluctantly allowed him to guide her back into their hut, whereupon they curled together on their mats. Lucius stroked her hair until her breathing evened and her body had softened in his arms. Then pitch-darkness overtook Aari's vision.

What is this? What's hap—

Gently, the darkness gave way and his vision returned as Lucius awoke. The Roman felt around in the dimness of the hut but found the space next to him empty and cold. He twisted out of his sleeping pad and scrambled toward the entrance, only to collide into a figure striding in.

"Carmel!" he groaned. "Where did you go?"

She looked dazed. Lucius noticed her hands were covered in dirt and—

Is that blood?

"What happened?" he asked, sitting her down on the mats. She was still out of it so he cleaned her hands for her. Most of the blood came from a long cut on her palm that he wrapped in a strip of old cloth. His bafflement melded with Aari's.

Carmel gradually returned to herself. She looked down at her hands, befuddled. "Thank you, Lucius. I . . . I must have been sleepwalking. I suppose the stress of the village has even taken over my time of rest."

They lay together again, and this time Carmel slumbered almost immediately.

A fourth flash. Judging by his growing fatigue, Aari was sure this was the longest he'd been in the hold of retrocognition.

Carmel fell on top of Lucius and dragged him toward the exit of their abode. "Lucius!" she hissed. "Lucius, you need to see this!"

"Mmm, what are you—agh! Please don't yank off my arm!"

"Then get up!"

Lucius, barely awake, trudged outside after her. When they rounded the back of their hut, he stopped short. A sapling unlike anything he'd ever seen before hailed them. He pulled on his eyelids to clear his blurred sight, but the infant tree was still there, thin and waist-high, with ivory stems and luminescent violet leaves.

Carmel had a hand on her hip and the other over her mouth. "This was not here the last time I came to clean."

"And that was . . ."

"Six days ago."

"That can't be. Trees do not grow that fast. And no tree I have ever seen looks like this."

"Lucius." Carmel locked her turquoise gaze on his. "Do you remember when you found me sleepwalking that one night?"

He lowered his head once in cautious affirmation. "Yes. That was . . . six days ago."

She licked her lips. "Before I woke you just now, I checked my bag. There have always been five seeds in the box. But now, I only have four."

Before Aari could fight it, the memory booted him back into the present. He jolted, hearing his body crackle and pop as his joints released their stiffness. The clock indicated that he'd been sealed away in the memories for almost two hours. He extended a finger to the parchment again but withdrew at the last moment. *I don't have the energy to keep going. But. What. A. Revelation! So much happened right here! This might have even been Carmel's and Lucius's final stop. And that has to be the Tree of Life. Could it still be around?*

Marshall was fast asleep, and Aari didn't have the heart to pounce on him and divulge his discovery. Kody, though, was nowhere to be found, but his phone was on the bed. Aari checked the entire cottage before spying his friend through a window, sitting on the steps of the porch. He joined him, instantly wishing he'd brought a sweater to combat the cold. "Hey."

"Hey," Kody said. "Did you finish your trip down literal

memory lane? I noticed you'd spaced out a couple of hours ago."

"Yeah. I'm exhausted. But you're not gonna believe this. Right here, where this inn is? It's ground zero. And dude, *this* is where Carmel planted the Tree of Life!"

Kody, who'd been staring off into the distance with perturbed focus, faced Aari with a budding glow about him. "Don't pull my leg, man."

"I wouldn't. Not about this." He bumped Kody's arm. "We're so close to getting the cure for you."

"And for the world."

"But first for you. Don't ever doubt that you're our priority."

"That means a lot, Brainiac. Thanks."

"I thought you'd be a little more thrilled about this news."

"I am, really." The perturbed focus returned as Kody looked to their left, where he'd mentioned the fancier inn was located nearly five hundred yards away. "Could you give me a quick rundown of who exactly knows we're here?"

"It's just Gareth, Deverell, Victor, Magèo, and the Elders."

Kody rubbed his mouth. "Hmph."

"Is something wrong?"

"Some people pulled into the resort a half hour ago. The cars were in the way so I didn't get a good look, and for some reason my senses are inconsistent, but I got a quick glimpse of one guy . . ."

"No. No, please. Don't say it. Don't."

"Reyor's people have found us. Someone sold us out."

51

Ashack stormed into Dema-Ki's old community hall-turned-youth center; the fire of his fury could have lit a blazing trail in his wake. Two guards stood near Hutar, who looked up from where he was cleaning a countertop in the partially restored building. He wiped the sweat from his tanned brow. "Elder Ash—"

His words strangled as the muscular Elder grabbed him around the throat with one hand and slammed him against a wall, raising him high so his feet dangled off the ground.

"What have you done, filth?" Ashack snarled.

Hutar struggled against the older man's grip, barely able to get a breath out. Ashack tightened his hold. "Traitor! We took you back into our care and you repay us by funneling information to Reyor?"

"I . . . I never did," Hutar gasped, face turning a dark purple.

"Liar!"

"Stop!" Tayoka bellowed behind Ashack.

"We knew of his abilities!" Ashack roared. "We knew he could eavesdrop and yet we allowed him to recuperate in the convalescence shelter, close enough to listen in on our meetings!"

"It was only for the first few days after his arrival! That is why we moved him to the other end of the valley!"

"He could have slipped away!"

"Not with Nageau's grandson there. You know how Akol watches Hutar like a hawk." Tayoka moved toward him and said in a more soothing tone, "You're choking him, Ashack. Let him go. Please."

Ashack gnashed his teeth. He searched Hutar for a sign of

remorse or guilt or even pride, but the youth only stared coldly as stark red veins appeared in the whites of his eyes. The Elder further constricted his grip, fingers contorting flesh.

"Enough!" Tayoka hooked an arm around Ashack's waist and pushed him away. Hutar, now free, tried to slink past the men but Tayoka struck at his chest with an open hand, pushing him back against the wall. "Not so fast."

Hurried footfalls sounded behind them. Saiyu and Nageau appeared on either side of Ashack, giving the black-haired Elder beseeching looks paired with imperceptible shakes of their heads. Tikina hurried in after them, taking in the situation gravely.

Ashack stalked back to Hutar, but Tayoka kept him at arm's length. Hutar, pinned in place, bristled. "Elder Ashack, I have been working hard to earn back my standing among my people. I do not appreciate false accusations—"

"You will *never* regain your standing," Ashack snapped. "Mark my words. Our people have no faith in you. You demolished their trust when you nearly murdered—"

"Ashack, stop." Nageau, a mask of pain welded on his face, thrust the other Elder back.

"We gave him a chance, Nageau. No one except a handful of Sentries, Magèo and us knew exactly where the younglings were. And now the harbinger knows, too? This *boy* just happened to show up back in our lives and you think there might not even be a sliver of a chance that there is a connection? There are no coincidences, not in a matter like this. Even you of all people cannot argue that."

"I swear on my father's soul," Hutar said, his words stinging with acid, "I did not feed Reyor this information."

"Then who did?" Nageau asked.

Ashack was more aghast than angry now. "You cannot possibly believe anything he says!"

"I swear on my father's soul!" Hutar shouted. "And you know what else? I swear on my uncle's soul as well!"

It went so quiet, Ashack could hear the tap behind the

counter trickle drops of water into the sink. Hutar glowered defiantly at the Elders. "Is that good enough for you?" His voice cracked. "I swear, on the two most important people in my life whom I have *lost* . . . I was not the one who fed Reyor the location of the Chosen Ones."

Tikina stood toe-to-toe with the young man and pierced his sapphire eyes with her jade-green stare. After a long pause, she said, "I think he is telling the truth."

Ashack turned his back to them. Saiyu held his face in her hands, but he moved away and jabbed a finger in Hutar's direction. "You better be honest with us, boy, or so help me I will make you wish you had never returned home."

He swept out of the building and crossed the river to the stable. He mounted the first horse he saw, not bothering to saddle it, and raced out of the valley to clear his head.

If something happens to the younglings . . . He grasped the stallion's mane as they carved a trail through the snow, leaving Dema-Ki behind them. . . . *I* will *make him pay.*

The erratic flight of a yellow-and-black dragonfly distracted a group of gruff men seated at the polished bar. One with auburn hair and a square face swatted at the insect, grumbling something in Russian. To his left, a tattooed hulk with a satellite phone pressed to his ear imperiously blew a ring of smoke at the tiny creature. He chuckled as it thrashed away from the smog.

Jerk, Tegan complained as she completed her mindlink with the dragonfly. She guided the insect onto the wooden rafters over the bar. *Steady does it . . . There! Perfect landing. Now, let's see what these brutes are up to.*

The last time she'd utilized a dragonfly, the insect's three-hundred-and-sixty-degree vision had produced instant nausea. This time, her grasp on her environment proved stellar, although working each of the four independently operating wings was still a challenge.

Below her, Hajjar continued his conversation over the phone, his voice like the rumble of an approaching storm. "Whatever it is, you and your men need to be ready. We paid a lot of money for your service, so you move in the second I call. Understand?"

As he hung up, Ajajdif asked, "Are we good?"

"These guys are the best there is around here. We better be good."

"Are our birds in place?"

"Three choppers, set to go. The Osprey's been refueled and we can definitely get past the country's no-fly restrictions."

Ajajdif took a sip from his glass. "Money talks."

"Of course it does. Especially in times like these." Hajjar eyed the other man's drink. "A little early for that, wouldn't you say, sir? Sun's barely up."

"It's never too early when this is my only shot to right our last failure. Relax, Elias. It's just one drink."

The giant appeared unimpressed but didn't push further. He pinched the ember from his cigarette into an ashtray and returned it to his pack. "There's something to be admired about the quality of intel from the Boss. Always impeccable. And now we know for sure that it's definitely those kids at Nyika Inn."

"And we know that *they* know we're here."

Hajjar stretched, bulging biceps straining against his tight Under Armour T-shirt. "That young buck with the Boss is shaping up to be a perfect addition to our humble little family."

"Mmph." Ajajdif took another sip of his drink. "Yes. Perfect."

"Aw, sir, is that envy I hear?"

Ajajdif threw a disdainful look at the giant. "I have never seen anyone become so attached to the Boss's hip within a matter of months. It's unnatural."

"It's alright, I understand. It's hard when the head of a family has a new favorite son."

New favorite son? Tegan walked the dragonfly closer to the edge of the wooden beam, wings twitching. *I thought Tony Two-Timing Cross was Reyor's lapdog. Who's the new player?*

Hajjar waved away the three other mercenaries with them. Once they were gone, he said, "I still don't see why we can't just move in right now. Shoot the adults, grab the rest, and put a noose on the redhead until he leads us to the seeds."

"You're too trigger-happy," Ajajdif said. "There's a reason most ambushes are done at night. You know that."

"I am *not* trigger hap—okay, yes I am. But right now, as much as I like being out of the Sanctuary and mining operations, I'm tired of playing catch-up with these brats. And I really want to test out our new toys."

"Patience, Elias. We know they're getting close. The redhead's the only one we actually need. He's somehow got the nose for tracking the seeds. We can't jump the gun and risk screwing this up. Just have to wait until nightfall."

A growl came from deep within Hajjar's throat. "It's like we're stuck in a variation of cat-and-mouse and I hate it."

"*Da*. And this cat is hungry for a win."

Hajjar turned around on his stool to survey the modest space with warm lighting and glossy floors. "Is the little salamander on the move?"

"Jesus, Elias! I don't care for Tony, but you need to stop name-calling. Besides you being terrible at it, we can't keep egging each other on like this. And I should add that he can fight a *lot* better than you."

"That remains to be seen."

"He broke your arm at a company gala when he first joined!"

"I was drunk. That doesn't count."

"You're ridiculous." Ajajdif proffered a meager smile. "But, yes, Tony's in place."

"Is he going after *them*, then?"

Ajajdif shrugged. "I'm not being told much, but if he is, it would be the perfect leverage. My concern right now is for us. There are only so many times you want to get on the Boss's bad side."

"That's true." Hajjar swiped Ajajdif's drink and slid it to the far side of the counter. "How about we get you a proper breakfast, sir?"

As the giant guided Ajajdif toward the tables, Tegan backed the dragonfly away from the lip of the rafter. *Not good. Not good at all.*

She suddenly screamed, though without her physical body no sound came out. She'd been so focused on the discussion below that, despite having excellent wraparound vision, she'd failed to notice a gecko creeping up behind her. Just as it made a leap for the dragonfly, Tegan propelled the winged creature into flight.

I nearly got you killed, little guy! I think you're better off escaping geckos on your own.

She disengaged the mindlink and returned to her shared room, inhaling sharply. Dominique and Mariah sat cross-legged on the bed on either side of her while Marshall and the boys gathered around.

"They've got three mercenaries currently with them and more ready to move in from who knows where, plus two choppers and a plane," she said, sitting straighter. "They've been waiting for us to find the seeds but, because we're so close now, they're preparing to make a move *tonight*. And if I heard right, they plan to, uh . . . eliminate . . . Domi and Marshall, then capture the rest of us and put Aari on a leash until he brings them to the seeds."

The Sentries cocked their brows at each other.

"That's just great." Mariah rubbed her eyes wearily. "How do they know about the Tree of Life?"

"Maybe Reyor knew about it," Kody said. "Then again, their seeming to know where we are at all times kinda points to the fact that there's a snitch somewhere along the grapevine. I don't care what the Elders say about their confrontation with him, my money's on Hutar."

"I wouldn't be so quick to discount the Elders like that," Dominique warned.

Tegan lifted a finger, stopping their discussion. "There might be another problem." All attention turned back to her. "Tony's back in the field."

Marshall prickled. "Son of a—"

"I'm not quite sure what he's doing, but from what I heard . . ." Tegan addressed her friends directly. "What's our biggest weakness right now? What would get us to willingly turn ourselves in if they had this one thing over our heads?"

Mariah blanched. "Our families."

"Exactly."

"There are two Sentries with them," Aari said, picking fitfully at his nails. "And Victor and Gareth should be there in a matter of hours. And—"

"I'll warn all four of them to be on alert." Marshall's initial sweep of anger seemed to have thinned a little. "There's nothing else we can do as it is. But we do need to figure out how to find the seeds without Reyor's men following us. Before nightfall."

"I'll walk around the area to see if I can locate another emotional geo-marker," Aari said. "Since the village had been located here, I'll bet the grounds are chock-full of them."

"I'll come with you," Dominique offered.

"You two get on that," Tegan said. "The rest of us will find a way to get out of here."

She saw Kody peering out of the window, the side of his head resting on his shoulder. "Kody?"

He didn't turn. "I thought I couldn't really hear the men at the other resort last night because they were too far away." His throat worked. "But I just tried again, and . . . my range has decreased since then. Significantly."

"What are you saying?"

"I think the virus has started to take over."

* * *

"Are you alright, Aari?"

Aari strode between the numerous *bandas*, one of Lucius's letters in both hands, feeling the historical weight of the inn's grounds with every footfall. Dominique kept pace, having to shorten the steps of her longer legs to match his gait.

"Oh, yeah," he said. "Just peachy. One of my best friends is dying, our families are most likely in danger, we're being tailed by nutjobs who get orders from a bigger nutjob bent on destroying humanity . . . Yeah, life's fan-freakin'-tastic."

The laughter that escaped Dominique surprised him. "I've never understood these snide answers that young people today seem so fond of. A straight 'no' would suffice, I think."

"It might be our defense mechanism when things aren't going well."

A silence hung between them. Guilt poked at Aari like a cattle prod. "I'm sorry, Domi. I know you're just trying to be here for us."

"It's alright. I get it."

As they traversed over the pale green grass, he said, "So . . . you know Marshall well?"

The Sentry relaxed. "Well enough. He and my cousin used to work closely in the States. She introduced us when I was visiting her, about ten years ago. I look to him as a brother, but I think she might have seen him in a different light. He was completely oblivious, though. He usually is." A soft smile graced her face. "He was a good friend to Gwen when I couldn't be around, which was often, as my home base is Africa. For that, I am forever grateful."

The name sounded an alarm in Aari's head. "Gwen?" he repeated. "She—"

Dominique met his eyes, delicate understanding in her own. "Yes."

He didn't know what to say. *Gwen gave her life trying to save Tegan and Mariah when they were kidnapped. And now I'm talking to her cousin and no one thought to mention a word about this? I get that relationships aren't a priority given what's happening in the world, but . . . Gwen died. For us. And we never even got to meet her.*

Before he could push out a flimsy condolence, a flash erupted behind his eyes.

His last memory of the tribe who'd taken in Lucius and Carmel was of diseased villagers lying on the ground, dying or in pain. Now they danced around a fire pit bigger than anything he'd ever seen. They hollered into the night, sang at the top of their lungs, and feasted like there was no tomorrow.

Lucius's sight fell upon the radiant woman swaying around the glowing flames with the others, her blonde hair in a braid that encircled her head like a crown. Her laughter echoed above the other voices, and Aari couldn't stop a wave of emotion that tugged at every fiber of his being, nor the bliss that fueled the beating of his heart.

Is this what love feels like? he thought, bewildered. *Jeez, how can people stand being this happy? I feel like I'm gonna explode.*

Carmel caught Lucius's gaze and skipped over. Despite his weak protests, she pulled him closer to the fire and they danced in the flickering light, heat pressing against their bodies.

Lucius leaned in to catch her lips between his, but a sudden prodding made him look down. A little boy with a big afro—Aari recognized him as the one Carmel had been playing a game of twigs with from an earlier memory—beamed up at the two of them.

Lucius scooped him into his arms and nuzzled him. The boy proudly turned his head and pushed the top of his ear forward, displaying a fresh tattoo of three small triangles behind it, then pointed at an old, hunched woman with a toothless smile at the opposite side of the fire giving similar tattoos to others. Lucius nodded, approving.

The boy held the Roman's face between his hands, squirming happily. Lucius spun around several times, eliciting dizzied giggles from the child when he put him down. As the boy tottered around and worked on regaining his bearings, Lucius drew Carmel to him.

"That tree," she whispered, "saved so many lives. I know you still have questions about my possession of it, and I am sorry that I don't have the answers, but that tree was a blessing and, because of it, our tribe has flourished. Look at what we've been able to do, Lucius. People near and far know of us and trust us enough to heal them."

Lucius pushed her hair away from her face. "I will not deny that. But we both have seen the envy and greed in the eyes of some of the other tribe leaders."

"Sometimes those who are driven to make things better are required to take the risk of trusting others. I have faith, Lucius. You should, too."

"As you wish," Lucius said, then added teasingly, "I suppose it would be unwise of me to disobey the command of someone viewed as a legendary healer by the people."

"Oh, stop it."

He grinned and pulled her against him. As they danced together, she looped her arms around his neck and gazed up at him with tender adoration. He rested his forehead against hers. "There is something I have been meaning to ask. Back in Masada, why didn't you use your ability to fight off the soldiers?"

Pain flitted across her face. "I didn't possess it at the time."

Lucius cupped her cheek. "I'm so sorry. About what my countrymen did. About your brother."

She pressed a kiss against his palm. "He would have liked you, so long as you could have handled his teasing."

A flicker of something gray emerged from the forest around the village. A herd of elephants had convened at the fringes, watching the humans serenely.

"The newest additions to our family are here," Lucius murmured.

Carmel looked behind her and lit up when she saw the herd. "They grow more trusting every day. But this connection they have with the tribe is only in its infancy. Over time, the bond will grow stronger. You'll see."

"Again, this is because of you. You have a magical effect not just on people, but all of nature. The same way you have an effect on me."

She blushed fiercely as he slid his hand to the nape of her neck. "Carmel, I—"

Manic shrieks erupted from everywhere at once. Dark shapes burst through the trees, wielding spears and arrows and knives. Screams ravaged Lucius's ears as one by one the tribespeople fell, weapons protruding from their bodies. The elephants trumpeted hysterically, galloping into the forest. But one, the matriarch, remained to help fight off the intruders. Men and women ran for safety while others stayed to fend off the attackers.

Carmel dove into action, hurling the invaders back. Lucius frantically scanned the horde and almost yelled when he saw the little boy—*his* little boy—being trampled in the commotion. Like a rampaging ox he fought his way through the masses and flung himself onto the child, using his body as a shield. A foot stomped on his back and another on his calf. He cried out but refused to move. The boy under him quivered, tightly clutching his tunic.

Aari gasped and stumbled. He could feel Lucius's phantom pains on his lower back and his leg. Before Dominique could ask what he'd seen, he'd marched off in search of another geo-marker, weaving between cottages and *bandas*, working toward the reception building. The woman who'd checked them into their rooms watched him keenly from where she swept the entrance, her face unreadable.

As he made a turn to the back of the building, another flash yanked him away from the present. If it could, a bellow would have ripped from his throat at the sight that met him.

Lucius cradled Carmel in his arms. An arrow punctured her chest and the wound stained her clothes. Her eyes glistened as she looked up at him, her uneven breaths coming out in quiet whimpers.

"Two weeks," Lucius said, over and over. "Two weeks. We survived two weeks of warring over that damned tree. You will not stop now."

"I am sorry," she rasped between coughs. "I should have seen the archer."

"Shh, shh. The tree. Its sap. It can help you. It can—"

"The tree only cures the sick, Lucius. It does not heal a mortal wound."

"There has to be something. I'll—"

"Lucius. Listen to me. Listen!" Blood dripped from her mouth, and her face contorted in pain. "I can . . . I can remember now. The tree . . ."

"Shh, don't talk." He wiped the tears that slid down her cheeks. "Just hold on. I'll get the medicine man."

"My memory is returning, Lucius. All of it. I need you to *listen*."

He tried to sound gentle, strong, but suppressed emotion

clogged his throat. “Carmel—”

“No. Lucius . . . the tree. It is not a blessing. It is a curse. The people are not ready for it. You must destroy it. Burn that tree down. Plant no more. The seeds must be safeguarded.”

She stopped, wheezing for air; the sound grated in Lucius’s ears and made Aari want to curl into himself.

“When humankind is ready,” she managed to whisper, “the right people will come for it.”

“Don’t. Don’t speak like that. If you want me to burn the tree, I will do it. But you have to be there with me.”

Carmel weakly rested her hand on his jaw. “I haven’t much energy left, my love.”

With trembling lips, Lucius placed a long kiss on her forehead, shaking as he fought back the looming swell of grief.

“Burn the tree, Lucius,” Carmel murmured, her words ebbing. “Not just because of . . . greed. It must not be planted . . . by . . . anyone else.”

Aari felt it.

He felt the moment her life left her body.

Lucius didn’t need to look down to know she was gone. He held her limp form against him, rocking back and forth as he sobbed into her hair.

Having driven away the invaders, the surviving tribespeople surrounded him and knelt. They touched their brows to the ground, then threw their heads back and wailed to the heavens.

Aari snapped to the present. He was on his hands and knees in the dirt, weeping. The letter, Asa’s precious artifact, had fallen from his grasp and was speckled with soil but he didn’t care. His heart ached in a way he’d never felt before, a twisting, guttural sensation that hurt as it beat in the confines of his ribs, making him nauseous. He angrily wiped the tears away.

A warm hand cupped his chin. Dominique, crouched beside him, turned his head toward her. The concern she wore made him feel foolish but his emotions were out of his control.

“I don’t know what’s happening,” he stuttered. “I . . . I’m

feeling everything he's feeling."

"Are there any more memories here?" she asked.

He shook his head, unable to bring himself to speak again.

"Then let's go back."

The cottage door banged open and Aari staggered in, disappearing into the boys' bedroom. Dominique followed, closing the door quietly. Kody, sitting with the others around a table, pointed after Aari. "Um, is he okay?"

"He's shaken," Dominique said, joining the group. "He saw Carmel die, and everything Lucius felt, he felt. I've never witnessed anything like it. This new ability of his . . . it is a gift, but a gift I fear may take a toll if an emotional memory is too harrowing."

As she gave them a rundown of what had happened, Kody pulled the brim of his baseball cap low over his face and mulled. *So, Aari's felt what it's like to kill a man and what it's like to watch a loved one die in his arms. That's cruel.*

Aari emerged from the room, seemingly more in control of himself. Kody passed him a cup of water and an apple; the other boy took them half-heartedly.

"So much happened here," Tegan said once Dominique had finished. "Did you manage to get a flash forward to the next marker, Aari?"

"It came as we were walking back." Aari sounded hollow, tired. "Lucius was laying a slab of stone on Carmel's grave, and he spoke with the village's medicine man afterward. The tribe had wanted to build a monument in honor of Carmel for the lives she saved, but Lucius didn't think it would be appropriate. He wanted her to have a quiet, unmarked resting place. He found a spot by a stream near the foot of Mount Meru, the same place where the tribe first found her and Lucius when the leopards attacked."

"That's still a pretty wide search grid," Marshall said.

"And who's to say the stone is still there?" Mariah added.

Aari bit the rim of his cup. "It's all we have to go on. Oh, and there was this massive hunk of granite behind her grave; its shape matched the mountain's outline, like someone had carved it that way. That's a good landmark."

"It's something," Tegan agreed. "What did the stone slab look like?"

"It was the size of a pillow and had tribal markings on it. Carmel's name was etched in Hebrew at the center."

Dominique retrieved two bags from their rooms and pulled Aari's laptop from one and her portable satellite modem from the other. Together she and Aari set up the devices.

"Okay." He turned the laptop so it faced the group. "Here's a satellite image of Meru. All we need to do is find streams or dry riverbeds and follow them to where the grave should be."

Kody swept the screen. "I see lines cutting through the greenery, so those are probably streams, but there are a lot of them."

"We're just looking for the ones on the western side of Meru," Aari said, "where the ash cone is. That's what I saw in Lucius's memory."

"In that case, I've found three—here, here, and here."

"We'll split up," Tegan said. She looked at each member of the group and Kody noticed her eyes lingered on him a little longer than the others. He could see her deciding who best to pair him with. *I may be weakening,* he thought, feeling a touch of frustration, *but I don't need to be coddled, Teegs. You better not put me with a Sentry.*

"Domi and Aari, you guys scout the stream to the south," she said. "Kody and Mariah, you'll take the center stream while Marshall and I will check out the one to the north. This way, we have at least one telepath on each team. And take a photo of the satellite image with your phones so we can refer to it later."

Kody, rigid with anticipation, relaxed. "Yes, ma'am."

"Did you guys figure out how to distract Reyor's men so we can get past them?" Aari asked.

Kody grinned, sharing eager looks with Tegan. "Oh yeah. We're gonna throw a major monkey wrench into the works."

* * *

The group made their way over the inn's grounds toward Mount Meru, as casually as if they were taking a walk in a park. Kody, strolling arm-in-arm with Tegan, whispered, "We're coming up about four hundred yards to the left of the other resort. Is everything in place?"

"Almost," she whispered back. "It's a lot of pieces to coordinate, and they're all spread out so I have to bring them closer. Ahh, it feels so *good* to not have to sit still for stuff like this anymore." She squeezed his arm. "Now, be honest. How are you feeling?"

He considered lying but decided against it. "My powers are definitely weakening," he admitted. "At this range I should be able to listen in on anything in that resort, but my hearing keeps fading in and out and my sight is how it used to be before I got my abilities. All my senses are fading. And . . ."

"And?"

"I'm starting to feel a headache coming on."

Tegan gazed up at him, then at the gauze on his neck. Her fight to not show fear was as clear as day. Turning his baseball cap backward, he lowered his height and gave her a quick kiss on the tip of her nose. She broke into a laugh, pulling back. "Hey!"

"See? The virus has nothing on me, and I'm gonna keep fighting it. So let's just work on finding the seeds and not be concerned about the nutty brother of the group."

"You're a butt."

"Yes. Yes I am."

When Tegan looked away, he dropped his breezy grin, thoughts turning inward. *It's the strangest thing, to live with the knowledge that you're walking toward death while it walks toward you. When it's this close, and you know it's coming . . . It's fine. It's fine. I'm fine. I'm ready for it. I'm ready. I . . . I . . .*

I'm not ready.

A chorus of guttural roars exploded from the acacia trees surrounding the resort. A gang of colobus monkeys with shaggy black-and-white pelts burst from the foliage. They swung onto the wooden frame of the building and threw themselves at the windows until they shattered. As the simian troop clambered through, Kody, even with his fading hearing, picked up the yelps and expletives from the mercenaries inside.

Then his ears registered the faint pounding of hooves. He looked to his right and watched in amazement as a herd of two dozen buffalos thundered over the savanna. Their dark coats shone under the sunlight as they pulled their massive bodies, each easily weighing fifteen-hundred pounds, toward the resort.

"Look at the horns on them!" Kody shouted over the fray. "And—*holy cow!*"

The buffalo leading the charge slammed into one of the cars parked in front of the resort. Another larger bull lowered its massive head and gored a truck with its horns. The first buffalo joined in the effort and together they lifted and flipped the crumpled vehicle onto its side, the grinding of metal a foreign din to the livid rumbles of the wild beasts.

"I feel like I'm in *The Lion King*!" Mariah cackled gleefully as one of the buffalos turned to the resort's entrance and rammed the doors down. "This is insane!"

"I'm not done yet!" Tegan yelled.

From the shrubs around the inn, a war cry of furious squealing announced the stampede of reddish-brown animals with two pairs of tusks. They sprinted at unbelievable speed, filing through the building's decimated entrance.

"*Warthogs!*" Marshall doubled over in laughter. "Are you kidding me?"

"It's for good measure!" Tegan ran toward the main road. "Come on, while Reyor's men are distracted!"

She'd only taken a few bounds when she suddenly sagged forward. Kody caught her just before she fell. "Whoa," she mumbled, holding her head. "Guess I have my limits, too."

Kody lifted her up. "Are you okay? Can you walk?"

"Sorta. Just . . . wow. Sudden drain. I didn't realize jumping through so many animals so quickly would hit me this hard."

"The fact that you could do that at all is mind-blowing," Aari said.

Kody offered Tegan his arm again and she hooked on gratefully until they reached the main road, where Marshall took over and the group split up. With the satellite picture he'd snapped displayed on his phone screen, Kody fell in step with Mariah as they entered the rainforest and found the stream they were to follow.

"If I remember correctly," Mariah said, skirting a root, "the woman at the reception told us that coming up here requires a ranger. Because of, you know, leopards."

Kody glanced up from his phone. "Are you saying you can't fling away an overgrown housecat?"

She groaned. "Gah. I keep forgetting that I've grown in my abilities, and I don't have to fall into the habit of being afraid of . . . well, a lot of things."

"You're lucky like that, 'Riah. You and Jag, and Tegan, kind of. Aari and me, our abilities aren't exactly great when it comes to protecting each other or even ourselves."

"That's why we were trained in self-defense. And I saw you having a go with that staff in the Lodge before we left for Israel. You really flowed with it, like it was a part of you. And your abilities *are* useful, Kody."

"I'm a glorified bloodhound who provides slapstick comedy at best." When he saw her stiff look, he added, "Not that I'm complaining, of course."

"You don't know how important you are, do you?" she asked, sounding small.

Kody, armed with a deflective one-liner, swallowed his joke when Mariah stopped him from speaking.

"Jag and Tegan are leaders, putting aside Jag's ongoing self-doubts," she said. "Aari's got a mind that exceeds every one of us. I don't know what I am in this saving-the-world dynamic. But you . . . Kody, you're the glue. You do what you can to make everyone feel okay, feel like things aren't necessarily as bad as they seem. Honestly, without you, it would be harder for the group to function. And I'm not talking about just now. It's been like that all our lives. Yeah, maybe your abilities aren't so great when it comes to self-defense, but I'm convinced your real power is who you are as a person."

Kody focused on his shoes as they trekked among the fig and cedar trees, continuing upstream along the calm waters, exchanging no more words. He wasn't sure what to make of her statement and, from his point of view, she was being overly generous with his importance.

In the forest canopy blue monkeys chattered at each other, nosily following the humans from the trees for a time before losing interest and acrobatting away. The other teams checked in telepathically with Mariah to say they were on their assigned trails. One false alarm came from Dominique; the stone slab she and Aari unearthed had no etchings.

Kody found that he had to squint as his headache hammered harder inside his skull, demanding to be acknowledged like a child throwing a tantrum. He let Mariah take the lead, pretending he didn't catch her troubled expression. Little things began to annoy him, like the jabbering of monkeys, the trumpeting of distant elephants, even the general hum of the forest.

Cool it, he thought. *It's okay. You're fine. What did Victor say when you met him? Eyes forward. Yeah, that's it. Eyes forward.*

Determined to push past the sickness festering in his body, he overtook Mariah, giving her two thumbs-up and a big grin. "Hurry up, slowpoke!"

One look at his beaming face and she broke into a smile and darted after him.

Huh, he thought. *Maybe she was onto something with her little speech back there . . .*

They jogged side by side in comfortable silence, vaulting

over mounds and fallen trees while the stream gurgled next to them. Search as they did for any shape or clue in the landscape that might mark Carmel's grave, the forest seemed intent on keeping its secret.

As they split around a particularly wide cedar, Kody thought he heard something overhead, above the canopy. He fought to hone his hearing and magnify his sight. When he located the source of the disturbance, he rolled his eyes. "Reyor's guys found us."

Mariah whirled around. "Where are they?"

He pointed through a break in the canopy. "Over there, coming in lower. A drone."

"Oh . . . oh, I see it. But how did they track us through the trees?"

"It's probably got infrared, picks up heat signatures."

"Well, I'm not putting up with this garbage." Mariah, striking a sass-filled pose, placed a hand on her hip and lifted her other hand to the sky. With a swipe of her finger she brought the drone plummeting through the treetops before smashing it into the ground.

Kody loped over to the mangled quadcopter and prodded it with his foot. "The more I think about it, the more I realize just how unfair of an advantage we have."

"I think it's perfectly fair," Mariah huffed. "We have to deal with them having resources literally everywhere while we—"

She halted mid-sentence and grabbed Kody's wrist, hauling him along with her. A strange protrusion swathed in vines and moss, about eight feet long and six feet high, stood on its own between a couple of fig trees. She pulled at the clingy foliage and Kody helped until the uppermost layer of overgrowth had been peeled off, displaying the top of a jagged rock.

The pair ran backward a few steps, then turned to each other with elated grins.

The outcrop, though mostly covered in plant growth, still resembled the outline of Meru as the mountain peeped in the background through a bald patch in the canopy. Kody directed his attention to the ground, now searching for the slab of stone that marked Carmel's resting place. The headache continued to pound but his eagerness provided a modicum of distraction from the pain.

As they combed the forest floor, Mariah let out a giggle. "I told the others that we've found the landmark so they're heading over, but I also warned them about possible drones following them. Tegan said none were following her and Marshall, but Domi . . . Domi threw a stinkin' *rock* at one and completely destroyed it."

"Boy, I wish I could've seen that." Kody lightly stomped on the ground until his sole struck something hard. "Bingo."

He pulled away clumps of dried foliage, revealing a square stone block with rounded edges. A thick coat of grime on the surface, probably nearly two thousand years old, made it impossible to positively identify the grave marker. He stroked the gauze on his neck, wondering how best to clean the slab. A sudden flashback to a documentary his younger brother once forced him to sit through came to mind.

Thank you, George!

He hurried to the stream, picked up double handfuls of fine sand, and worked on exfoliating the slab. He was sweating by the time most of the accumulation had been scrubbed off. The sand easily filled in the markings on the dark stone, displaying several peculiar motifs. But one thing stood out to both him and Mariah: the Hebrew script at the center.

"Look at you go!" Mariah high-fived him. "Where did you learn to do that?"

"I—"

Kody's smile fell. A sudden rush of blood to his head made the agonizing beating within unbearable. He stretched a hand to Mariah but before she could grab it, he collapsed.

"Kody!"

Mariah dropped beside him, patting his cheeks and shaking his shoulders. "Hey, don't do this," she pleaded. "Up! Get up! Kody, get up!"

He was comatose and warm to the touch, warmer than he should have been. She sent out a telepathic blast to the others, telling them to hurry, then carefully pulled Kody aside. "I won't have you lying on top of a grave," she muttered. "No sir, none of that foreshadowing business here. I won't have it."

She positioned herself so his head rested comfortably on her lap. His breathing had quickened, but otherwise he remained unresponsive. Dominique and Aari arrived within minutes; there was a rush of air as they pulled to a stop beside her. Aari scrambled off the Sentry's back, looking uncomfortable that he'd had to cling on like a baby chimp as she'd sped through the forest.

"He just collapsed," Mariah told them, hating how her voice came out so tiny. "It was so sudden, I . . . I didn't see it coming."

Dominique leaned her head against Mariah's. The brief gesture and the Sentry's earthy scent delivered a morsel of composure. Dominique then moved to do a full-body check on Kody before sitting back on her balls of her feet. "No physical injuries, but he does have a growing fever. I don't know how to wake him."

Mariah stroked her friend's cheek. "Hopefully he'll come out of it on his own," she murmured. To herself, she thought, *This can't be happening.*

Marshall and Tegan reached them fifteen minutes later, drenched in perspiration. The forest had gone still apart from the pair's heaving gasps, as if every creature had left the humans to themselves. Once they'd caught their breath, Marshall tried to wake the unconscious teenager.

Tegan turned to Aari. "The letters!"

Aari tentatively stepped onto the grave, as if trying not to rouse the remains that rested underneath, and withdrew a parchment from the canister. Mariah watched him closely until she felt movement on her lap. Her heart skipped a beat as Kody's eyes eased open.

"Hey, kiddo," Marshall said quietly, brushing some dirt off the boy's ear. "Take it easy."

Kody sat up with Mariah's help, resting against her. She circled her arms around him, afraid that if she let go, he'd fall to pieces. He weakly grabbed his baseball cap, which had tumbled off his head. "H-how long was I . . . was I out?"

His speech was jarred, uneven. Before Mariah could respond, Aari yelled. "Nothing! I'm getting nothing!"

"You said this was a geo-marker!" Tegan snapped.

"I know what I said!"

Marshall held his arms out at the two of them. "Getting riled up won't help. Aari, try again."

Aari turned back to the grave; he held the letter so tightly, Mariah worried it would tear. He stood motionless, letting out small hisses of frustration every few moments, then spun back around, flushed red. "It's like the artifacts just *died!* They're not giving me anything! No flash, nothing!"

Mariah felt Kody go rigid in her arms. "The trail's gone c-cold?" he asked. "Right n-n-now?"

Aari couldn't meet his gaze. The group remained stock-still. Kody folded into himself, hiding his face with a hand. Mariah held him closer, her mind a panicked blank. *This—no—it can't—Kody—no—no—*

"The slab," she suddenly whispered. The others looked toward her resignedly. She pressed them. "The stone slab. Did Lucius carve it?"

Aari knelt by the freshly unearthed marker. "I don't know.

Maybe? I think he carved her name and the tribe symbols . . . if he did etch it, there could be enough emotional connection—"

"Try it," Tegan said.

As Aari's fingers neared the stone, Kody sat up so quickly his head struck Mariah's chin. "Ow!" she cried. "Kody, what—"

"I hear them," he said.

"Hear who?"

"Reyor's men. They're trying to be real quiet, but someone stepped on a b-b-branch. I think they're s-sweeping the forest."

"We demolished their trucks," Aari protested. "How'd they get here so fast?"

Marshall banged his fist against his forehead. "The drones gave away our location. And they've got local mercenaries waiting to move in with their own vehicles, people who most likely know this forest like the back of their hands."

"Guys." Kody tried to stand but was too frail to hold up his own weight. "L-look at me. If I can hear them in my state, t-then they're close. Less than a half a m-mile."

"You think they're moving up their kill-and-capture schedule?" Aari asked.

"Maybe." Dominique threw Kody over her shoulders in a fireman's carry. "We need to move."

Marshall covered up the stone slab and, together, the group disappeared deeper into the rainforest.

"I still can't believe we're playing for sugar cubes."

Jag glanced up from his cards and grinned. "I appreciate you humoring me, Danny."

Daniel chuckled. "The last time I joined a poker game with Marshall, it was with his army friends who were between deployments and we played for MREs. I nearly walked out of there. At least they threw in kosher rations. But sugar cubes . . ."

"It's sentimental. First time Aari, Tegan, Mariah, Kody, and I tried to play poker, we were eleven. We only had sugar cubes to bet with and it's been our thing ever since."

A rumble in the distance made them both look out the window next to their small table. Sprawling black clouds rolled toward them, throwing the desert around the safe house into gloom. Sand dunes painted the landscape every which way.

Jag's forehead crinkled. "You get rain out here?"

"The desert does bloom, Jag. But this kind of storm is rare."

Daniel's safe house was no more than a distant family member's cottage located in the Negev Desert. It was only spacious enough for three occupants at most, with a single open area on the main floor hosting a makeshift living room and bedroom combo, as well as a kitchenette. Wooden steps led to a small loft with an air mattress, a tiny table, and two chairs. Jag and Daniel spent most of their time there playing card games and conversing; the higher ground was also easier for surveillance. Daniel had set up his military grade spotting scope on a bipod by the window and checked it often.

The former commando tossed a couple of sugar cubes into the center of the table. "It's amazing how quickly your leg's healing. It's been ten, eleven days since your accident, and you already have more mobility than you should. What is *in* that remedial powder Mars left us?"

"Magic, probably." Jag looked down at his left leg. Daniel had removed his cast two days prior and wrangled a functional brace from Beersheba, the closest city to the safe house. The brace went up to Jag's knee and allowed him to put some weight on his injured leg when he walked, but he still favored his other foot.

The pair played on as the storm approached, the patter of rain like fast-falling pebbles on the roof. A streak of silver split the sky, followed by the crack of thunder. Jag unwound with the storm, but the contentment tasted more bitter than sweet in his mouth.

How can you enjoy something when the person who taught you to love it is . . . gone?

He fancied that he saw his grandmother's reflection in the window. Julia's tanned face glowed, her graying hair was in her signature side bun, and she looked healthier than she had her last days alive. She smiled at Jag. His heart fluttered and softened. Then lightning flashed again, and her face disappeared.

"Tell me more stories about Marshall," Jag said, fixing his attention back on his cards.

"Mmh, I don't know what's left to tell. I only lived in the States for six years, so my stories are limited." Daniel rubbed his jaw. "Wait, I got one. So you know how Mars was one of the smallest people in school, even as a teenager, and everyone picked on him?"

Jag grabbed his root beer from the table. "I still can't imagine him getting bullied."

"Mmhm. He had this weird need to please everyone and took it as a personal failure if people didn't like him. Even now, he has it."

"Yeah, I get that vibe sometimes."

"I think it might be a byproduct of being an only child to a single dad or something. Anyway, we had P.E. together in eighth grade. This one time, the class played prison dodgeball. Mars had a crush on this cute girl on our team but she got hit and had to stand behind enemy lines, and Mars kept throwing balls for her to catch so she could come back to our side, and"—Daniel had to put his cards down so he could cover his eyes, his shoulders shaking with suppressed mirth—"this *moron* gets so frustrated he *launches* the ball like a rocket and it hits the poor girl right in the face. The whole gym stops and looks at him. Nobody expected this scrawny kid to have that much arm-power. And at this point Mars is completely mortified. I'm talking red as a tomato. As the girl leaves with the nurse, he runs over to apologize but his shoe gets caught in the hem of the oversized sweatpants he loved so much, and he slips and smashes into the corner of a concrete wall. So they both end up heading for the nurse's office, her with a black eye and him needing stitches on one eyebrow. They never talked again after that."

Jag nearly choked on his drink as he spluttered a laugh. "Oh, I'm definitely gonna bring this up next time I see him."

Daniel reached over the table and lightheartedly smacked him on the head. "You are *not* allowed to say a word about anything I shared the last few days. Mars will kill me if he finds out."

"I thought you said you were a tough kid in school?" Jag teased.

"I was. Except I had Marshall—the Boy Scout would literally slap cancer sticks out of my mouth—who'd risk getting grounded for leaving his house to stop me when I snuck out to late-night parties. He's a hell of a friend . . . but as a kid, I called him a killjoy."

Thunder boomed, this time sounding like it was right above the safe house. Neither occupant inside flinched. Daniel shoved his sugar cubes to the center of the table. "I'm all in."

Jag narrowed his eyes at him and played the hand. Daniel chortled, slapping down his cards. "Four of a kind! I'll collect my winnings, thank you very much."

"No, you won't." Jag smugly laid his cards right-side up. "Straight flush."

"Oh, come on!"

Jag gathered the sugar cubes and popped one into his mouth. Daniel pulled a face. "That's nasty."

The teenager responded by throwing in a second cube, then pushed his chair to the window and looked out at the desert through the lashing rain. Daniel joined him, kicking up his feet onto the windowsill. "Hey, you know the deal. I talk, you talk. And no more stories about you getting into fist fights. I can't believe how many of those you've had. You're worse than I was."

Jag linked his fingers behind his head. He liked how easy it was to chat with Daniel. "Alright, we'll switch it up, then. Nearly two years ago, Tegan and I tried dating. Didn't last a week. It was *really* weird for the both of us. We grew up like family so romantic relationships aren't in our cards, I guess. We did it because people around us thought it would be a good idea. It wasn't."

"That's a bad way to go about it," Daniel agreed. "But it's nice to see how close you and your friends are. It's a solid support system to have."

"Amen. And good for keeping each other grounded. Which reminds me, one time—"

Daniel snapped up from his chair, peering through the spotting scope. He stood rigid for several heartbeats then turned around, brows raised. "Thought I saw something glint on a dune."

"Well, that's a first. The last eleven were false alarms. It's probably nothing."

"Yeah . . ." Daniel fidgeted with his wristwatch. "Maybe I should do a patrol."

"Wouldn't that be pointless in this storm?"

"A storm would be a good cover to move in. Better to be safe than sorry."

Jag closed the curtains over the window and followed the Israeli down to the main floor to do the same with the rest. Daniel grabbed a jacket and slung his bullpup assault rifle across his back, then pulled on a pair of goggles. As he and Jag tested their handheld radios, he said, "Emergency contacts are on the fridge, and—"

"—and if the cell signal is as spotty as usual, I should go to Beersheba, find a crowded place, blend in, and call for help. I got it, Danny. Really. Pretty sure you don't have to repeat it every time you head out."

The man ruffled Jag's dark hair and walked through the door connecting the cottage to the garage. Jag hobbled upstairs and pulled the curtain back slightly in time to see Daniel emerge in his blue dune buggy. He followed the vehicle with the spotting scope as it went over the undulating terrain, appearing on top of a sand dune, then disappearing, then reappearing on the next one. In sight, out of sight. In sight, out of sight.

That looks like fun, he thought before scoffing at himself, amused by how much he sounded like a five-year-old.

The buggy rematerialized on top of another dune. As it moved to disappear down the incline again, Daniel's head jerked violently to the left. He slumped sideways, the buggy's framework keeping him from falling out, before the vehicle slid down the dune.

Jag felt like the air had been punched out of him. He waited for Daniel to pop into sight, but he never did.

The storm struck out with all its might, the rolling crackle of thunder striking fear in Jag for the first time in years. He stumbled back and gripped the pendant hanging around his neck, pressing its sharp edges into his palm to slow the maelstrom in his mind. He considered radioing Daniel but was worried someone else would answer instead.

Help. Call for help first. God, Danny—focus! Focus!

He hurried back to the main floor as fast as his leg brace allowed. As he dialed the emergency contact on the fridge with Daniel's cell phone, he tried and failed to scrub away the image of the man crumpling.

As expected, the signal wasn't good enough for the call to go through. He stuffed Daniel's phone and his own into his backpack with some essentials, hooked his full-face mask to his belt loop, then limped hastily into the garage where the truck they'd arrived in was parked. He scowled down at his leg. *I can barely move with this thing!*

Knowing he'd regret it later, he removed the brace and threw it onto the passenger seat. The engine rumbled to life and the black truck roared out over the gravel driveway, swinging onto a long, winding dirt road that led to the freeway.

Jag reached out telepathically to Marshall. *Mayday!*

The Sentry connected with him. *Jag!*

Marshall, Danny—he was out on patrol. I think he was shot. It was hard to tell. He never reappeared. I think he's . . . The image of the Israeli flashed behind his eyes again and he shoved the knuckles of one hand into his mouth, biting down firmly to ground himself.

Marshall was incoherent for a few moments until he asked, *Is anyone after you?*

Not yet. I'm heading to Beersheba. Danny said I could blend in safely there.

Good. You do that. But be careful. Keep your mask on hand. And keep me posted, okay? We're dealing with stuff here, too. Reyor's men found us. And Kody's not doing great.

What?! And no one thought to tell me?

I'm sorry. We've been dodging the enemy for the past two hours. At least Kody's still holding up. I'll fill you in later. Did you manage to see anything at all? Or anyone?

No. But . . . Marshall? I'm sorry. About Danny. I'm really sorry.

Marshall tried to speak but his words came out haltingly. *Just stay alive, Jag. Please.*

You too.

As Jag was turning from the desert road onto the freeway, a dark vehicle swerved out from the dunes behind him and closed in. He punched the gas and the truck battled through the torrent, its wipers feverishly slashing to and fro. *Who is that?*

Distracted by the ambush, he nearly missed the appearance of another van as it veered out of the wet sandbanks in front of him, boxing him in. His eyes darted from the windscreen to the rearview mirror. *They're not shooting. And they're not making a move to draw even with me.*

Before he could get any further in his thought, the vehicle behind him nudged his bumper. Jag fought with the steering wheel as the truck veered off the road and rumbled toward a dune. It slowed as the tires dug into the sand and came to perch at the dune's peak. He tried to glimpse the drop below, but the hood blocked him. *Oh, crap.*

The van that had tapped his truck revved and sprang toward him. Like a bull it rammed against his vehicle, pushing it closer to the edge. Jag stomped on the brakes. The second van joined the first, and the truck was no match. Unable to stop what was coming, Jag held on to anything his hands could grip.

The truck creaked, then toppled over the mound. It flipped once and slid all the way to the bottom on its roof. Jag's fractured leg jarred horribly on the way down. His mouth opened in a silent bellow until the vehicle came to rest. With his vision swimming, he undid his seatbelt, careful not to fall on his neck. His backpack had disappeared into the darkness in the depths of the truck. Unable to maneuver to search for it, he shattered the windscreen with an easy kick from his good foot and heaved himself out into the rain. The cold drops splattered on his face and soaked into his skin.

He quickly assessed his options. *I could push the truck upright, but then what? It can't go over the dunes. I could try to take those guys out but . . . what am I up against? Maybe I should just run. But that's so cowardly.* He grimaced as the tingling pain deepened. *No, not cowardly. Smart.*

As he forced himself up, lightning lit up the sky and he caught sight of two figures looking down at him from the top of the mound, their faces covered. One of them had a gun trained on him. The moment the trigger was pulled, Jag's instincts kicked in and he jumped into hyperspeed. Everything slowed enough for him to watch the projectile leave the muzzle of the weapon, its tufty red tailpiece rustling in the wind.

Tranquilizer!

He ducked. The projectile sailed harmlessly over his head,

and the world eased back to its normal speed.

Before the attacker could launch another dart, Jag turned and hightailed it through the desert, kicking up a trail of wet sand as he ran north toward the city. He'd only gone a short distance before searing agony flared white-hot in his left leg, making him stumble and roll. He got up and made another attempt but couldn't get more than a few dozen yards. Dropping to his elbows and knees, his fingers ripped into the desert floor. He was drenched to the bone. His teeth chattered from the cold and the pain. He was terrified. And alone.

I can't. I can't.

Headlights appeared behind him, casting his shadow on the sand ahead. He looked back, blinking raindrops from his eyelashes. The vans raced toward him, somehow able to travel over the terrain effortlessly. Jag roared at them like a wounded animal, his voice dwarfed by a clap of thunder, and pushed himself up. He sped in short bursts, spitting curses every time he fell and had to power himself back to his feet.

At last, Beersheba's skyline emerged through the downpour. As if to reward Jag for nearing the finish line, the rain eased and a small break parted the black clouds to let the sun shine on the city. Jag looked back at his pursuers, now half a mile behind him as they maneuvered out of the dunes and onto the freeway. He wasted no time. Bounding across the asphalt, he entered the safety of the city.

A youngish man in a navy blue coat with a beanie pulled over his tousled, honey-colored hair stood atop the roof of a five-story office building, a pair of binoculars glued to his eyes. He'd witnessed the pursuit and radioed the drivers of the vans to leave the rest to him. As soon as he saw the teenager lope into the city, he calmly walked to the elevator and, moments later, perused an outdoor market in Beersheba's Southern District. The aromas of an array of food and spices fragranced the air. The rain had not deterred the vendors, who came back at full force once the storm had eased. They conversed loudly in Hebrew and Arabic, trying to get rid of the last of their produce.

Every man, woman, and child wore a mask, prompting the young man to do the same though he didn't have to. He purchased an apple and tossed it into the air as he ambled, catching it easily. His eyes flicked to the tall, well-built teenager limping ahead of him, the hood of a black sweatshirt pulled over his head.

A gruesome smile split the man's face. *Just where I want him. Oh, it's good to be back in the field.*

Mariah slumped against a fig tree, breathing hard. Tegan came up behind her and pushed her on. "I know you're tired, 'Riah, but we have to keep going."

Groaning, Mariah jogged ahead and grabbed Marshall's outstretched hand, letting him pull her along. "It's been over two hours and those brutes are still trailing us," she puffed. "Why haven't they just busted in with guns blazing?"

"For one thing," Marshall said, "it's pretty clear Reyor wants the five of you alive. Who knows what else is at play."

Behind them, Dominique still had Kody slung over her shoulders. The teenager looked resentful about being carried, but he'd asked to be put down only twice. Mariah didn't take that as a good sign.

"You hear anything, Kody?" Aari asked.

Kody lifted his head so his ear perked upward. "Yeah. They're keeping some distance between us, but it's like they've spread out. A rustle here, a rustle there." He screwed his eyes shut, digging the heel of a palm against his temple. "Let me see how many there are."

"You've already tried a few times," Dominique said soothingly. "Your thermal vision isn't at full capacity and using it drains you. Just rest."

"Let me try!" he snapped.

The group jerked to a halt and stared at him. He glared back, then seemed to realize he'd lost his temper. "I'm sorry. This headache, it's—it's killing me. Just, please, let me try."

As Dominique lowered Kody to the ground, Mariah went to

join him. A certain darkness begrimed his eyes and perspiration dripped down his forehead and neck.

He's sweating as much as we are, and he hasn't even been running, she thought.

"Thirteen," Kody said. "There's thirteen of them. That's not a lucky number. They've separated into smaller groups. It's weird. Sometimes a sound will come from one, sometimes another. It's like . . . I don't know. It's like they want us to hear them."

"At least we have a head count now," Marshall said. "Let's keep moving."

With Kody listening and guiding them away from their pursuers, they climbed the rising incline of Mount Meru. The vegetation around them gradually changed the higher they went and soon the rainforest gave way to pine trees. The sound of water percolating through rocks was faintly audible. The air grew noticeably cooler, a welcome change for the group.

They eventually emerged from the tree line into a secluded U-shaped gulch the size of a football field. A clear stream flanked by muddy banks gurgled the entire length of the declivity, meandering past the group and disappearing down the side of the mountain. At the far end of the gulley, a small waterfall cascaded down a two-story high volcanic rock face into a pool. To the left of the pool lay a cluster of boulders.

The rock face, covered sporadically in thick vines, extended to either side of the gulch and tapered to the ground, defining its borders. The tops of the walls were overgrown with coniferous trees and shrubs. Mariah spotted an almost perfectly spherical boulder perched near the lip of the right incline of the wall. In a brief moment of absurdity, she was reminded of the marbles she used to play with as a child.

As the group neared the entrance to the gulch, she saw Marshall's eyes flick around and realization creep into them. He lifted a fist, stopping the others. "They've been herding us." His jaw clenched. "I should have known better."

Dominique stepped into the gulch to take a look. "So they

know where we were *and* somehow shepherded us toward a trap without physically seeing us? How?"

"They might have another drone," Kody said resignedly, "and probably kept it out of my range."

"I am so done with this!" Mariah fumed. "Every time we think we have the upper hand, they leapfrog over us!"

Tegan rubbed her eyes with a sigh, not offering any words.

"We can use this place to our advantage," Aari ventured. "I'm sure we can. Like . . . the mud. If we cover ourselves with it, we'll be invisible to the drone."

"Only until our bodies warm the mud," Marshall said. "But I like where you're going with this."

"Those boulders to the left there, near the pool. Good for cover. And there's a great vantage point up on the ledge, to the right of the waterfall."

"Are you suggesting we use their trap against them?" Tegan asked.

Aari only answered with a devious grin. Marshall took stock of the dead end, then nodded. "If we plan this right, we just might be able to do this."

* * *

"That's it." Marshall dumped their backpacks into some nearby shrubbery. "If Reyor's men do have a drone with infrared sensors, it'll look like everyone but Mariah and Tegan have disappeared."

Tegan inspected the group as they convened in the gulch, ensuring that the Sentries and the boys were properly covered from head to toe in mud. "Looks good. Now, you guys vamoose while Mariah and I become the perfect bait."

"Of *course* the women do all the work," Mariah quipped.

Marshall and the boys started to stutter but were shooed away. Leaving the girls and Dominique in the gully, they went to the entrance where the ends of the rock wall tapered. With Aari leading, Marshall helped Kody scramble up the right-hand incline. They moved between trees and bushes until they reached the ledge beside the waterfall, the vantage point providing the visibility needed for their plan to succeed.

As they lay prone, Marshall said, "Don't forget. At the speed that Domi moves, the mud might slide off her and she'll reappear on the drone's sensors. Aari—"

"I'll keep my eyes on her at all times," the teenager promised.

"Kody?"

"I've got some strength back," Kody said. "And my abilities seem to be holding up. I should be good for a while more."

Twenty feet below them, Mariah and Tegan darted to the boulders near the foot of the waterfall, both yelling when they nearly slipped into a deep hole behind the rocks. *Yikes, that was too close,* Marshall thought.

Farther ahead of the girls, Dominique positioned herself beside the stream at the center of the gulch. Aari diverted the light to render her invisible, and they waited for their hunters to appear. It didn't take long.

Thirteen men emerged from the tree line; Tanzanian mercenaries led by a tattooed giant, their weapons trained. Marshall felt Tegan reach out telepathically. *You see them?* she asked.

Clear as day, he replied. *Hajjar's leading. Guess Ajajdif decided to hang back at the resort.*

What kind of weapons are they carrying?

Looks like SMGs—submachine guns. Good for close-quarter combat. I think I see other guns in their holsters. Tranquilizers for you guys, probably. If Phoenix provided them, they could be using fast-acting drugs.

Best not to find out.

Exactly. And you two chipmunks need to stop poking your heads around the boulders or they'll see you!

At the mouth of the gulch, Hajjar used hand signals to order two men to climb each incline to the top of the rock wall. As the pairs moved out, he looked down at the electronic tablet he held, then pointed directly at where Dominique stood—or rather, past her at the cluster of boulders where the girls hid.

"They seem confused," Kody said. "And Hajjar has definitely got to be using a drone."

The hulk of a man dropped back, letting the remaining eight mercenaries split evenly on either side of the stream. In both groups, the two men in the middle readied tranquilizer guns while the other two kept their SMGs.

Without taking his eyes off them, Marshall asked, "You ready, Aari?"

"Yup," came the reply.

Marshall reached out to Dominique. *Showtime.*

The first mercenary suddenly choked as his shirt collar scrunched. He was lifted off the ground, feet hanging. Then his head jerked and lolled limply as if he'd been punched. As he dropped onto the dirt, the rest of the men looked back at Hajjar.

Kody wiggled closer to the brink of the ledge. "Hajjar's surprised, but he also looks like he *knows* something."

Two seconds after the first man's struggle, the pair of mercenaries with tranquilizer guns found their weapons swinging toward each other. Before they could pull back, their triggers squeezed. Both fell, darts sticking of their stomachs.

The last man standing on Dominique's side of the gulch yelled in Swahili and unleashed his weapon. The others prepared to join in but Hajjar shouted at them to stop. The mercenary firing away had his gun ripped from his hands by the invisible force, and the butt slammed into his head. He dropped to his knees and was struck again. The instant he was down, one of the four men on the other side of the stream yelled out and the rest started shooting.

"It's *not* a spirit!" Hajjar boomed. "It's one of them! Our targets!"

Beside Marshall and Aari, Kody chuckled. "The looks on these guys' faces, man. I think they're starting to wonder what they got themselves into." He slowly stiffened. "Oh, no."

"What?" Aari asked.

"There's blood on the ground. And the mercs just spotted it."

Dominique's voice sounded in Marshall's head, breathless from panic. *Marshall. Marshall, they got me. Too many bullets flying. I couldn't get away fast enough.*

Where are you hit? he asked, hoping he sounded calm.

My . . . my thigh.

Did it go clean through?

No.

Marshall watched, mind racing, as the ring of blood grew. This was not how the plan was supposed to go. *Domi, you need to put pressure on it. Hang tight. We'll get you out of there.*

Marshall, they see the blood. They're moving toward me.

The mercenaries had waded halfway across the stream. From the other side of the gulch, Hajjar gave a firm command to hold their fire. To Aari, Marshall said, "As long as they don't know who it is, they won't shoot to kill. Don't lose your hold on Domi."

Dominique's voice was in his head again, pleading. *It hurts so much to move.*

He tried to form a response but his mind went blank when he saw Hajjar whip out his tranquilizer gun and level it. Then, a powerful, shrill whistle came from above.

A crowned eagle soared over the mercenaries. It tucked its six-foot wingspan and dive-bombed Hajjar, talons raking the giant's arm until scarlet trailed over his tattoos. The bird yanked the gun away from his weakened grip and flew to Dominique's position. As the other mercenaries fired at the winged attacker, the eagle released the weapon.

Nice one, Tegan! Marshall said.

Thanks! she replied. *I enjoy being a menace!*

When Hajjar saw the gun rise from the ground, seemingly out of its own volition, he dove into the stream. The dart flew past, hitting one of the mercenaries. He dropped like a fly.

The gun only had one round! Dominique cried.

They have to be loaded each time, Marshall said. *I know it hurts, Domi, but can you move toward the incline behind you?*

I'll try!

The three men kept firing at the eagle as it maneuvered around them. Out of the corner of his eye, Marshall saw the immense spherical boulder on the lip of the rock wall tilt over the side and roll down the rock face, gaining momentum. At the rumble of the approaching threat, the mercenary closest to the danger yelled a warning. He made a jump to safety but was too slow. The boulder rumbled over him, pinning one of his legs. He brayed, the sound amplified by the gulley. His two comrades rushed to help but Hajjar shouted, "Worry about him later!"

Was that your handiwork, Mariah? Marshall asked.

Yup, she said. *Although gravity did most of it, thankfully.*

The eagle circled around, grabbed the pinned man's sub-machine gun, and flew toward the waterfall. The two pairs of mercenaries on both flanks of the rock wall fired at it, bullets crisscrossing but never finding their mark. Marshall looked up at the approaching raptor and scrambled out of the way as the gun was dropped where he had just lain.

Delivery for probably the only person here who knows how to use this, Tegan said. *I've only ever fired my dad's pistol when he let me. This thing is a beast.*

You're a wonder, Tegan. Marshall picked up the futuristic-looking gun, feeling the weight of it in his hands, then thought to himself, *Never seen this before . . . maybe Phoenix's armaments or defense subsidiary supplied them? At least the poor shmuck reloaded before his leg got crushed.*

Out loud, he asked, "Kody, you got a head count?"

"Six down, three remaining in the gulch, two coming up the rock wall on our right, and two more on the left but I've lost sight of them," Kody reported. "And my thermal vision is completely gone now. *Also*, just heard Hajjar on his radio telling the guys on the right flank of the wall to check out the heat signatures behind the boulders. And . . . oh. He just told the other two in the gulch to tranquilize Domi."

Marshall ensured the selector switch on the gun was set to fully automatic and that the suppressor was screwed on properly.

"You guys stay low. I'm gonna cross over to the other side of the waterfall so that when I start shooting, it'll give away my position and hopefully not yours."

Keeping low, he rock-hopped across the water and crouched down. Scooping mud off various parts of his body, he packed it against his ears into makeshift earmuffs, then looked down the gun's sights. He tapped the trigger in short bursts, steadying himself from the rapid recoil against his shoulder. Hajjar and the two mercenaries dodged behind the boulder that had pinned their now-unconscious comrade.

Tegan, a couple of guys are coming up on my right, Marshall said. *They're looking for you and Mariah, but now they'll come for me too. Can you take them out?*

In response, the eagle swooped over his head. He stole glances at it as he kept suppressive fire on the men behind the boulder, refusing to allow them near Dominique.

The raptor seized one of the mercenaries by the shoulders and dragged him toward the edge of the rock wall. The man, hysterical, tried to pull away. Unable to gain purchase, his feet left the safety of the ground but as he fell, he grabbed the eagle, pulling it down with him. The eagle screeched, wings flapping madly. It scratched the man's face and he let go, falling the rest of the way and landing in the bushes; he didn't get up.

Tegan couldn't get to the second man in time. Marshall fired the last of his ammo and, in the next breath, turned and hurled the gun at the mercenary ten feet away from him. The man reflexively dodged and Marshall used the diversion to tackle him. As they tussled, a dart slipped out of the mercenary's pouch. Marshall snatched it up and jabbed it into the man's chest, then pushed off.

He was torn. The boys wouldn't be able to defend themselves if he left; Kody was weak and Aari had to focus on giving Dominique cover. But a ghost from the past haunted him; Gwen's failing voice as she lay dying echoed in his ears. She'd been shot trying to rescue the girls from their abductors a few months before. Marshall had been too far behind her to save her. And Dominique's tears when he'd explained what had happened to her cousin . . .

No.

He wouldn't lose Dominique too.

Gathering up the mercenary's SMG and additional magazines, he made his way along the rock wall, peppering the boulder that sheltered the mercenaries with occasional shots. He knew it wouldn't last long.

If this was Hollywood, I'd never run out of ammo, he griped. To Tegan, he said, *There are two mercs unaccounted for on the left flank. Make sure they don't get to Kody or Aari.*

On it, she replied.

Marshall reached out to Dominique. *I'm coming for you, Domi. I think I know where you are.*

The blood would be a good indicator, she told him.

You're in pain. Stop being sarcastic.

I think I picked it up from the Chosen Ones.

Marshall trekked down the wall's incline and went prone behind a few knee-high rocks. Dominique was at least a dozen feet straight ahead, and he was down to his final magazine. It wouldn't last him half a minute. *Can you drag yourself closer?* he asked.

I-I'm trying.

Tegan knocked on Marshall's thoughts. *I'm still searching for the two mercs, but the boys are safe.*

Good. Keep at it. I'm gonna get Domi.

What? Not on your own, you're not.

The eagle's silhouette blocked out the sun as it flew toward the mouth of the gulch. Marshall waited for it to swoop over the mercenaries, readying himself to run into the open. But, when he glanced at the growing pool of blood, the space near it started to shimmer—and Dominique became visible.

They stared at each other; their terror reflected in the other's face when they realized he could see her. Marshall's head snapped up toward the ledge by the waterfall. Instead of mud-covered teenagers, two muscular mercenaries stood in their place. He cried out as they threw limp forms over their shoulders and hurried out of sight.

Tegan! he blasted. *They got the boys! You need to help them!*

I can't leave you!

Yes you can! I got this! Get our boys!

Marshall bolted out, firing at Hajjar and his men, keeping his bursts short to conserve ammunition. As he neared Dominique, he held his hand out and she grabbed it. He dragged her back toward the rocks, hearing her groans of pain in the quiet between eruptions of gunfire.

He pulled her to safety and located the eagle nearing the boys' last position, then looked at Dominique as they lay behind the rocks, both of them covered in mud. An apology brimmed in her gray eyes. He shook his head. "Not your fault," he murmured.

As he kept suppressive fire on the mercenaries, Mariah connected with him telepathically. *The guys you're fighting are distracted. I think I can step out of cover and deal with them. Okay?*

I just ran out of ammo. Do it. But stay close to your cover.

Alright. I've got an idea, but it's gonna give me a ginormous headache.

The massive boulder the mercenaries hid behind started to vibrate, slowly at first. It rose into the air as if a giant hand had picked it up, wobbling precariously over their heads. The crouching men scattered, gaping up incredulously. The boulder hovered, suspended high in the air for several moments, then dropped. The earth shook like it had been struck by a god.

As the mercenaries flinched, their guns were torn away one by one and lobbed over the rock wall behind them. Marshall saw his break. He scrambled toward the stream where the mercenaries Dominique had rendered unconscious lay. He picked up one of the submachine guns, aiming at the now-unarmed men. He hesitated, finger twitching on the trigger. Then he threw the weapon aside, scooped up two tranquilizer guns, and shot the remaining Tanzanians in the gulch. He didn't wait to watch them drop before fishing around for more darts.

A shot rang from afar and a scream came from behind the boulder where the girls hid. Marshall looked up just as the crowned eagle above the rock wall plummeted. One wing worked to keep itself in the air but it crashed to the ground.

Tegan! What happened?

The teenager's voice trembled. *One of the mercs shot the eagle in the wing. It hurt . . . it hurt so much. I had to let go of the mindlink.* He could feel her working to steel herself. Then she said, *Mariah and I are going after the boys.*

Be careful.

We will.

As Marshall finally found a dart, he sensed movement ahead. Hajjar charged over the stream toward him. He fought with the tranquilizer gun that refused to load properly. *Get in, dammit!*

He jumped out of the way but Hajjar clipped his hand, knocking the weapon out of reach. The giant was too close to the mercenaries' guns for Marshall's liking. The Sentry flicked out his tactical switchblade. As he wiped the filth off his face, a disconcertingly pleasant smile grew on Hajjar's lips and his black irises glinted. The dark, jagged scar from his forehead to his chin complimented his eyes. When he spoke his voice was deep, cavernous.

"Well, hello again, hero."

Marshall said nothing.

Hajjar's gaze darted to the guns a few feet away, then back to the Sentry. "I nearly ended you in New Mexico during the summer. Remember that? I've been looking forward to meeting you again ever since."

"As have I." Marshall flung his blade and it embedded itself into the hulk's bulletproof vest. Hajjar tutted, looking down as he pulled the knife out. "For a former Marine, I thought you'd know better."

A fist to his meaty throat sent him stumbling back. Marshall, his arm extended, smirked. "I do."

He struck out with his foot, catching the giant in the stomach, followed by a deft uppercut. He knew brute force wouldn't work with Hajjar, his assumption confirmed when the man socked him in the face. Marshall shrank back. *Gonna have a pretty black-and-blue soon. Need to play smart. And keep him away from the guns.*

He moved on his toes, increasing distance every time the giant came in for a strike.

"I see what you're doing, hero," Hajjar rumbled, "but I promise, you'll wear yourself out before you do me."

Marshall hopped farther back, closer to the guns. When Hajjar followed, the Sentry sprang upward and grabbed the giant around the neck. Locking his arms, he used his momentum to flip himself over the bigger man's head. He pulled Hajjar down with him, making the ground quake with their combined impact. Hajjar, short of breath, struggled to get up but wasn't fast enough. Marshall swung on top of him, winding his arm back to deliver a knockout blow, but was thrown clear off when Hajjar bucked.

He tumbled a few times before coming to a stop. Dazed, he pushed himself up and rested on all fours. At the far end of the gulch, he saw Tegan and Mariah using the vines to scale the rock wall. They pulled themselves over, then hurried across the water. He swallowed, relieved.

A massive arm hooked around his neck and another around the back of his head, squeezing. The force cut off the air in his windpipe, choking him. Hajjar sneered into his ear. "I could do this the proper way and have you asleep in five seconds, but then there'd be no suffering. We've been watching you since Israel, you know? We see how those kids dote on you. Maybe I should wait until we capture all of them, then make them watch as I put a bullet between your eyes. That'd be fun. I'd love to hear them scream."

Pressure grew in Marshall's neck and built up in his head. His chest tightened and his sight darkened. He feebly tried to sink his teeth into Hajjar's arm, but the giant constricted his hold. "None of that."

Losing what little air he had left, Marshall desperately kicked his foot back twice, rapidly, catching the giant in the groin and the kneecap. Hajjar wheezed, his hold loosening slightly. That was enough for Marshall. He twisted away, gripping the other man's wrist, and torqued the outstretched arm before driving himself into Hajjar's shoulder.

The giant roared as his arm popped out of place and hung uselessly. His eyes gleamed with frenzy. The Sentry withdrew. As Hajjar leaned in to follow, Marshall lunged toward him, grabbed his drooping arm, and yanked it back. The giant lurched forward and tripped over one of Marshall's extended legs, landing roughly.

The second Hajjar rolled onto his back, Marshall was on top of him, punches flying. The frustration of everything—failing Gwen, the never-ending chase for the seeds, the rampaging virus, Reyor, the teenagers being forced into a prophecy they never wanted, Dominique, Kody sinking deeper into the grips of the disease—all came out in every blow he landed.

At last he sat back, staring down at Hajjar's barely conscious, battered appearance. He had trouble breathing; the giant's neck hold had taken a toll. His vision faltered, still dark around the edges. He toppled off Hajjar and onto his side, most of his energy gone. The only sound to be heard over his ragged breaths was the waterfall. He closed his eyes, taking in the reprieve, and hoped the girls were okay.

Tegan and Mariah shadowed the two mercenaries through the trees, moving quickly and quietly. Even with the boys on their shoulders the men were fast, running as though they'd just seen specters. Tegan couldn't blame them; she'd be unnerved, too, if she had to fight an invisible enemy.

Beside her, Mariah mopped up blood from her nose with her sleeve. She'd said that lifting the boulder hadn't been as hard as she'd thought it would be, especially after her feat with the buses in Egypt, but clearly it still hurt.

Tegan was almost spent as well. Her stunt with the wild animals at the resort had severely drained her, but she was determined to push on. In the back of her mind, she hoped Marshall was alright. She'd connected to him telepathically; he had faded in and out as he assured her that he was fine and was going to Dominique's aid.

The girls communicated through thoughts to keep their presence hidden from the mercenaries. *Tell me when you're good to go, 'Riah,* Tegan said.

Mariah pinched her nose and tilted her head back. *Give me another minute.*

The two men retreated down the slope behind the gulch, evidently content enough with their catches to not check for pursuers. *They must've had a rendezvous point preestablished,* Tegan said, *in case things didn't go as planned.*

Probably. Okay, I'm ready.

They broke into a run, rubber-soled shoes hardly making a sound, until they were within a few yards of the mercenaries.

Mariah held up a hand and the gun that was slung around the body of one of the men jerked, its strap pulling him backward. He yelped as he fell, his hold on Kody lost. The boy dropped with a thud.

The second mercenary turned to help his partner but, when he noticed the girls, he made a move for his tranquilizer. Mariah flicked her fingers and the weapon flew out of his holster toward her. She caught it, aimed, and fired. He collapsed and Aari rolled off limply.

The first man recovered and jumped up but couldn't withdraw his own tranquilizer in time. Tegan flung dirt into his face. As he angrily dusted it off, she grabbed one of his wrists and yanked it backward until he yelled. The gun dropped and he swung his other fist at her temple. She dodged beneath his twisted wrist and drove the top of her head under his chin. His head jolted back; she heard his teeth crack together. Sharp pain exploded in her dome and her eyes watered. Through the haze, she jammed the heel of her palm against his nose.

He staggered, recovering his footing, but by the time he made a grab for her she'd already scooped up his tranquilizer. Her confidence skyrocketed at the unamused look he wore as she shot him in the shoulder. His legs buckled and he fell, face-first.

The girls scurried over to Kody and Aari, grabbing them by their arms and dragging them toward the mouth of the gulch. On the way, Tegan found her downed eagle. She ran to it, hoping it was still alive, but the bird had succumbed to its injuries. She thanked it sorrowfully and continued on. By the time they arrived at the gulch, their upper bodies were almost numb.

The Sentries were barely back on their feet. Marshall, his neck displaying red welts from strangulation, was busy patching up Dominique with healing powder and a first aid kit. He got up when he saw the girls and pulled them into a tight hug. Mariah lightly touched the bruise forming around his left eye. He smiled wanly.

Tegan knelt beside Dominique. "How are you holding up?"

The Sentry rocked her open hand from side to side. "Eh, I'm okay."

Marshall was hoarse when he spoke. "Don't even try." To the girls, he said, "I don't think any major artery or bone was hit, but she did lose a lot of blood. The bleeding's slowed, though, so the bullet might be helping to clog the wound. I told her I'd rather not remove it just yet."

"Now we just have to figure out what to do with the mercenaries," Dominique said.

"We have an idea," the girls piped in unison, and Tegan added, "There's a hole in the ground behind the boulders. It opens up to a huge cave thingy. We could plunk them in there."

Dominique grinned. "A lava chute. That's perfect."

"That means we have to drag back the two mercs we left behind," Mariah bemoaned.

"Three, actually," Marshall said sheepishly as he finished bandaging Dominique's leg. "I dropped a guy on the rock wall."

Tegan grabbed Mariah's arm and they ran out of the gulch, Marshall in tow. By the time they returned with the men, Dominique, using a stick to help her get around, had destroyed every submachine gun except one, which Marshall took. He stuffed his cargo pants with all the ammunition he could find while Tegan tranquilized the thirteen mercenaries.

Dominique offered to push a boulder over the lava chute opening once the men had been slid in, but Marshall and the girls refused. They destroyed all the radios except Hajjar's. A man's voice crackled from the speaker, demanding a situation report. They didn't respond.

"When we've got the seeds," Marshall said as they headed back to the mouth of the gulch where Dominique had returned to rest, "we'll tell Ajajdif where his men are."

"Hey." Mariah held up Hajjar's electronic tablet. "This thing controls the drone. What should we do?"

"How much battery's left?"

"Very little."

"No use keeping it, then. Bring it down, we'll destroy it."

When the gray quadcopter landed in front of them, Tegan carried it to Dominique and the Sentry crushed it in her hands like paper.

"Okay," Mariah said. "What now?"

"We need to return to Carmel's grave so that when Aari awakes, he can look for the seeds," Dominique said, shaking her hands clean of drone bits. "We shouldn't waste time."

Marshall snatched her walking stick away before she could use it to stand. She glared up at him and he returned the look. "You can't go back down, Domi. You'll worsen the injury. Please, just—just don't argue with me on this one."

Tegan heard a heavy, underlying emotion in his words. *Is that . . . guilt?*

The Sentries stared each other down, then Dominique grunted. "Fine. But you're not well, either."

"I'll manage. It was just mild asphyxiation."

"Mild, he says."

Tegan rubbed Kody's and Aari's heads affectionately. "How long till they come around?"

"Dunno," Marshall said. "Maybe an hour or two? But we can't sit here and wait."

"Leave Kody with me and take Aari with you," Dominique instructed. "Don't worry about us, I'll find somewhere we can lay low."

"I'll stay," Mariah volunteered. "Teegs, go with Marshall. He'll need help carrying Aari."

They quickly scrubbed themselves and the boys clean in the stream, then parted ways with the others. Tegan kept a watchful eye on Marshall as he carried Aari, and together they descended toward Carmel's resting place.

From behind the driver's seat of a sleek Buick parked by the packed shopping mall, Tony monitored his team's chatter through his earpiece. The time on his cell phone read fifteen minutes to six.

Come on, Jag. You can't hide in there forever.

The kid was smart—and seriously paranoid. Instead of loitering around the streets, he'd dodged into the mall an hour prior, preventing potential stalkers with weapons from following him through the security checks at every entrance. Tony cursed Israel's uptight safety measures. It would have been impossible for his team to get past the metal detectors with their tranquilizers, so he'd sent in an unarmed operative to tail the teenager while the rest hung back outside and watched every exit.

He also cursed the fact that Beersheba was one of the safest cities in Israel, and probably the world. The country had already instituted stringent methods to contain the virus. With Beersheba tucked away in the Negev Desert, chances of infection were even lower, allowing the locals to carry out their daily lives with some semblance of normalcy. Precautions were still taken and businesses sometimes closed earlier than they otherwise would, but for the most part life continued as usual.

Which meant plenty of crowded public spaces where Jag could blend in to avoid capture.

A woman's voice sounded quietly in Tony's earpiece. "He's skittish, Mr. Cross. Always looking around. He's like a frightened animal."

"Obviously. Just don't lose him. And *don't* engage him."

"Understood. And, Mr. Cross? The mall closes in ten minutes.

What if he decides he has nothing left and approaches one of the guards at the exits? Tells them he thinks he's in danger?"

"I may not have the entire picture," Tony said, "but I have full assurance from the B—I have full assurance that he will not involve the authorities."

The operative acknowledged him doubtfully and returned to her duty. Tony rubbed his fingers over his bottom lip, eyes half shut. He was an inch away from either being reinstated to his original position by the Boss's side or being in the Boss's iron sights. Yet, despite the magnitude of his mission, he felt oddly calm . . . and just a bit livid.

Jag had humiliated him the last time they'd met, locking him and his men in a shipping container on the Sanchez farm in Kansas. Then he'd been taken north to Canada and interrogated for weeks; he could still see his captor's penetrating hazel eyes. He flinched involuntarily.

And then the Boss thought it best to demote me when I returned . . . Come out, Jag. We've got unfinished business.

In the driver's seat of the Buick, a burly American not much older than Tony checked and rechecked his tranquilizer gun while speaking into his phone. He ended the call a minute later. "We're good to go, Mr. Cross."

"Is the pilot ready to leave the moment we arrive?" Tony asked.

"Yessir. And your employer's Gulfstream is fueled and waiting at Beersheba Airport."

"The papers have been filed correctly? Israel's insanely tight with security. We can't afford any slipups."

"All done, Mr. Cross. We're lucky Israel's airspace is still open. Restricted, but open."

Beside Tony, another man, an Israeli, readied some nylon ropes. Tony watched him, then jumped when the woman spoke into his ear again. "You're right, Mr. Cross. He bought a prepaid phone and made a call, but he's not going to the guards. He's leaving. South exit. Moving fast."

"South exit!" Tony barked.

The driver tapped on his own earpiece and the Buick took off past groups of people straggling out of the shopping center. Tony instructed his team to remain at a distance until the teenager was out of view of the mall's security personnel. "Remember, we do this clean and quiet."

Just as the full-sized car braced to turn left, a man panted into Tony's earpiece. "He's quick for someone with an injured leg! I think he's making a break for the train station!"

The driver of the Buick pulled back from the turn and sped onward, racing past startled drivers. Tony rubbed his forehead. "Where would the train take him?"

"Nahariya, Tel Aviv, Haifa, take your pick," the Israeli operative said. "It's all direct links. Maybe he's going for Ben Gurion Airport, fly out of the country from Tel Aviv."

Tony clenched the driver's headrest as the car swung left. "If he gets on that train, we're done. He'll get off inside the airport with security crawling all over the place. We need to take him, *now*."

"So much for clean and quiet," the American said.

Another operative chimed into Tony's earpiece. "I'm on your six, Mr. Cross."

Tony looked through the back windshield at a lime green sport bike catching up to the Buick in the empty lane. "Visual," he confirmed.

The white-and-tan train station came into view on their right. A handful of locals strolled over the pedestrian crossing toward it. Tony picked out Jag a few yards behind them, limping fast. As the Buick neared the crossing, the driver powered down his tinted window and grabbed his gun. Tony's hand touched his door handle, ready to pounce the moment Jag was tranquilized. Beside him, the Israeli's door was already ajar.

The driver hit the brakes. The Buick screeched to a halt in front of Jag as he passed the middle of the crossing. The teenager's eyes widened when he saw the barrel of the gun pointed at him. It was a clean shot.

Tony heard the pop as a dart left the gun. The projectile should have embedded itself in Jag's chest. Except it didn't. If Tony had blinked, he would have missed the teenager flicker into a split-second blur. The dart sailed past Jag and struck a chubby man about to cross the road; he collapsed moments later.

The driver of the Buick started. "What the ever-loving—"

He didn't get to finish. Jag stuck his hands into the open window, snarling, and hauled the beefy man out as easily as if he were pulling an oversized stuffed animal. The Israeli beside Tony dropped profanities.

"I got him!" someone hollered in Tony's earpiece.

Tony turned to see the operative on his sport bike skid to a stop behind the Buick, take aim at Jag, and shoot. But the teenager moved impossibly fast, spinning the big American into the dart's trajectory. The driver sagged. Jag hurled him at the motorcyclist, knocking the man clear off and toppling the bike, then ran between the vehicles.

Tony was halfway out of the car when Jag saw the entire team of operatives converging on foot, blocking his route to the train station. The teenager swiped the black helmet off the dazed motorcyclist, picked up the fallen but idling bike, and roared past the Buick.

Whatever composure Tony harbored dissipated in an instant. He leapt behind the car's steering wheel and tore after Jag, trusting his team to clean up the mess at the crosswalk. The Israeli clambered into the passenger seat. "Did you *see* how he pulled Anderson out like he weighed nothing?"

"No, I was busy giving myself a pedicure," Tony snapped. "The hell kind of question is that?"

"Who *is* that kid?"

"Someone you don't want within arm's reach of you if you can help it."

Jag followed the line of vehicles turning at a traffic circle before going around it and exiting to a road on the left. Tony pulled the wheel to intercept him before he got onto the main road. He cut past the splitting island and into the path of an oncoming transit bus. The bus blared its horn and swerved, narrowly missing the Buick. It sideswiped a thirty-foot tall lamppost on the corner. The post buckled with a groan and tilted slowly toward an open parking lot. It landed with a resounding bang, destroying cars, and would have crushed a family of three if they hadn't evacuated their minivan in time.

Jag saw the Buick about to cut him off. Instead of plaiting through the line of cars he veered onto the sidewalk, brushing against a bright orange lotto stand. The bike wobbled, but steadied as he accelerated. Tony pursued closely from the road.

As they neared the junction Jag suddenly pulled away from the pavement, toward a small park with wooden benches in front of several office buildings, leaving an unsightly trail in the grass. Tony wove surgically between the double lanes before screeching right at the junction. Just ahead, Jag whizzed past a row of parked cars, constantly checking over his shoulder.

"Where's he going?" Tony muttered.

"He might be trying to get to the 406," the Israeli said, loading another dart into the tranquilizer gun. "When we get out of the city, it's all highway to Tel Aviv."

"But 406 is parallel to us. Where is this kid going?"

The Israeli lowered his window. "If you're able to pull closer, I could take a shot."

"Negative. I need him alive. You shoot him on that bike and he might—"

The window closed. "Got it."

An apartment and office complex appeared ahead. Jag jerked left and Tony stomped on the brakes to make the sharp turn, only to overshoot when the teenager made a sudden right into a lane between the two buildings, smashing through a meager boom gate.

The Buick's tires squealed as Tony brought the car to a jarred stop, cursing. A couple seated at a dingy sidewalk café at the bottom of the office building nearly spilled their drinks.

They watched, openmouthed, as he reversed and entered the downward-sloping narrow lane. The car fishtailed against the two buildings until he regained control.

The alley opened up into a parking lot. Tony spotted Jag as he raced past empty stalls and steered the bike up a set of stairs leading to a road. Bottling his frustration, Tony backed out through the narrow lane and rounded the complex. As he neared another junction of a semi-busy road, the Israeli grunted. "Mr. Cross, this is the 406. Either the target knows what he's doing or this is dumb luck."

"I'm betting it's the latter. Either way, we can't let him get onto the open highway."

The teenager had a two hundred-yard lead. Both he and Tony vied at breakneck speed, neither one gaining ground or losing. Tony drifted back and forth between traffic in the four lanes with practiced ease. The Israeli operative seemed unperturbed by the speed at which they maneuvered, but he'd firmly seized the handle above his door.

Jag squeaked through just as a traffic light turned red. *Oh, no you don't,* Tony thought. His speedometer climbed ever so slightly as he ran the light. Angry honking blared around him. *You can't keep it up, Jag. I see that leg hurting you.*

They entered a bare section of the city with wide spaces on either side of the roadway, some with tall buildings in mid-construction. No other vehicle was between them. The looming traffic light flipped to red and as Jag neared the intersection, Tony saw him hesitate. He leered. *No way he's gonna—*

Jag throttled forward. Surprised, Tony punched the accelerator in response. From his peripherals, he caught a colossal shape bearing down the intersection, directly at the teenager. He uttered a strangled sound.

A deafening horn wrenched Jag from his tunnel vision at the last second. He saw the oncoming semitruck and braked, leaning and straining the handlebars sideways to avoid impact. But as the semi rolled into the motorcycle's path, momentum pulled the bike down. It slid under the belly of the giant vehicle. Jag fell off, rolling viciously while the motorcycle skidded ahead. Sparks flew as metal ground against asphalt.

The semi moved forward a few feet then came to a standstill. Tony brought the Buick to a screaming stop in the middle of the intersection, his heart thundering. He looked at the rampant sparks. *Better not be a fuel leak . . .*

As if on cue, the bike exploded. Jag curled into a ball as pieces of framework blasted every direction and rained down. Flames cannibalized the motorcycle and burned hot along the trail of fuel leading to him.

No! Tony snatched the gun from the Israeli and burst out of the car, sprinting toward the accident. As he reached the scene, relief flooded him when he saw the boy stir. Dazed, Jag lifted his head at Tony's approaching footsteps and pulled off his helmet. His amber gaze, distant and unfocused, grew clear and sharp when he registered the young man's face.

Tony held up the gun, his lips pulling back into an animalistic smile. "You're mine, kid."

The dart sank into Jag's chest.

When Aari came to, all he could get out was a disoriented "Hng?"

Two faces appeared above him. Neither smiled, but their expressions softened upon seeing his eyes open. He lay on the ground; a rainforest surrounded him. *Why am I here? What—*

His memories rushed back like a train hitting him. He bolted upright, though it was really more of a sluggish wiggle into a sitting position. A strong hand kept him from flopping down again.

"Careful," Marshall said.

"Buh?"

The Sentry looked at Tegan. "I don't want to know what they put in those tranquilizers."

Aari tried to articulate his thoughts slowly. "Wuh huppen?"

Marshall and Tegan took turns filling him in as his muddled brain returned to its normal state. He didn't need Tegan's perceptiveness to notice the shame on Marshall's face. He nudged the Sentry. "Hey, you couldn't leave Domi to those guys. I'm just sorry Kody and I didn't get a chance to fend for ourselves. But what matters is that we're all still here."

"Maybe not," Tegan said heavily.

"What does that mean?"

"I got a telepathic blast from Jag," Marshall answered, running a hand past his black eye and through his hair. "All that came through was a name: Tony. Tegan and I have been trying to reach him but he's gone dark in the novasphere. We can't find him."

Questions stumbled out of Aari's mouth. "Tony? *Tony* was hunting Jag? You think he got him? Jag went black but that doesn't mean he's dead, right? Right? Marshall?"

"Reyor wants the five of you alive, so I doubt they'd kill him. He could've been tranquilized. Or maybe there was some kind of mishap and he's unconscious. I just don't know."

Marshall was frustrated and battered. Tegan sat cross-legged on the dirt, silent. Aari turned his head from one to the other. "So Tony wasn't after our families, then."

"Apparently not," Marshall said. "I've told Colback what happened, but your families will still be moved to Dema-Ki. He and Gareth are trying to convince them to leave as we speak, but it's not an easy task. And they haven't mentioned a word about either Kody's or Jag's situations."

"Smart," Tegan said.

"Deceitful," Aari retorted.

"It's called strategy, Aari. All we can do is move things on our end and find those seeds, and hope that Jag . . ." She wavered. "You good to enter Lucius's memories again? We brought you back to Carmel's grave and waited for you to wake up."

Aari gawked at her. *How is she doing that? Continuing like . . . like some kind of machine?*

She stared back, prompting him with her eyes. He stood up. "Yeah, I'm good."

"Perfect. That grave marker had better work."

"I wonder why the letters stopped functioning to begin with," Marshall said.

"Carmel's death was a huge blow to Lucius." Aari knelt by the stone slab. "Maybe it erased everything after that? Or maybe there was nothing emotional enough to constitute another geo-marker? It could be anything."

He touched the Hebrew script at the center of the slab surrounded by various tribal markings, beseeching quietly, *Please work.*

He saw the flash and would have leapt for joy if he could. The feeling fled when Lucius held up his deeply tanned and wrinkled hands. *He's aged!*

Lucius sat in front of Carmel's resting place in the wide clearing. The box of seeds lay in his lap, the brass engravings on the lid dulled with time. In a voice roughened by years passed, he said, "I kept my promise to her. I kept the seeds safe."

A black man in a long loincloth, perhaps forty years of age, was seated beside him. He took one of the Roman's hands in his own, holding it tightly. Aari tried to remember why he seemed familiar and realized that this was the little boy he'd often seen with Carmel and Lucius.

"You were faithful to her in more ways than one," the man said tenderly. "You've lived your whole life as though she was still by your side." He touched Lucius's face and his eyes welled. "And now . . ."

Lucius brought his forehead to the younger man's, his own eyes dampening. "Do not cry."

"You and Carmel looked after me as if I was your own child, even when my mother was still alive. Then both she and Carmel died defending the Tree of Life and you took me in." The man broke down, quivering with each new wave of tears. "I know that we do not have long together. You will join Carmel soon. The selfish side of me wants to beg you to fight to stay, but it isn't my place. I want you to be free. To be whole."

The Roman's eyelids slid shut. "You were one of the best things that happened to me," he whispered. "You gave me reason to get up every morning after my heart was broken. You may not be my blood, but I am proud to call you my son."

They held each other, taking a few moments to gather themselves. Then the younger man pulled back and tried for a smile. "I want you to go in peace, Lucius. I've already given you my word that I will protect the seeds. I know a safe place in this mountain to hide the box from unwelcome hands. The tribe and I will not let you down. I promise."

At the sound of a quiet trumpet, they looked behind them. A

herd of elephants stood watching them with the rest of the tribe. The largest female approached Lucius and caressed his head with her trunk. Lucius beamed tiredly at the immense creature.

"Thank you for carrying me all the way here," he said. "You have been a blessed addition to our big family over the years. Not just as protectors, but as friends."

The elephant gently wrapped her trunk around him, as if hugging the frail man. Her eight-foot-long tusks and massive ears threw curved shadows on the ground on either side of him. Finally, she stepped back and bowed, the elephants behind her doing the same. The tribe followed their lead, some of them trying to hide their weeping.

Lucius looked at all of them with a lump in his throat, and Aari felt an entrenched sense of finality. The Roman's adopted son took the box of seeds and rested it by his side. When the man turned his head, Lucius saw the three small triangles tattooed behind his ear. He smiled and softly ran a finger over it as the younger man made room for Lucius to lean against his chest, holding him close. Lucius didn't fight the growing fatigue. As his vision dimmed, he felt two wet drops on his cheeks.

"Do not cry, my son," he murmured. The arms tightened around him in response.

The darkness became whole. There was a feeling of levity, as if the weight of the world had been shed. Then—

Light. An all-encompassing brightness. And warmth like nothing Aari had ever known. It lingered as though time didn't exist, then slowly faded into nothingness.

He returned to himself gradually. His head was cradled in someone's arms and for a moment wondered if it was he who had died, not Lucius.

"Aari?" Tegan whispered.

She looked overwrought. Beside her, Marshall wore the same expression. Aari gazed past them at the blue sky through breaks in the canopy, unblinking. A few tears eased out.

Tegan lightly shook him. "Aari, talk to us. Please."

He sat up and dried his eyes. "Lucius passed away here."

"He . . . you mean, you . . ." Marshall faltered.

"Yeah. I experienced it." At their perturbed looks, Aari gave a little smile. "But I'm okay. At least, I think I am. It was . . . I guess peaceful is the word. There was darkness, and then this intense illumination and all I felt was—I don't know how to put it. The only thing I can think of is love. Love in the purest form."

Tegan and Marshall stared at him for the longest time. Aari nodded toward the peak of Mount Meru. "The seeds are here, but I don't know where, exactly. It looked like they had a plan in place to guard the box for however many years. And at some point, they even managed to tame some African elephants. Do you know how hard that is to do? And they knew Lucius was dying, too. They *bowed.*"

Marshall listened, awe-struck, but Tegan was occupied, running her fingers over the inscription and etchings on the grave marker. She suddenly went rigid. "Those things right there," she said, "to the right of the inscription. Do those look like three triangles to you?"

Aari examined the slab. It was difficult to identify much after centuries of weathering. "Umm, kinda. It was the tribe's symbol or something. The boy that hung around Carmel and Lucius had it tattooed behind his ear."

"*What?*" Tegan yelped. "Why didn't you say that earlier, you baboon?"

Aari flung his arms up to protect himself, almost certain that she was going to smack him. "Why are you getting mad at me? It didn't seem like a big detail to talk about!"

"It *is* a big detail! The girl running the inn—she had three triangles behind her ear! I saw it when we first arrived!"

Aari gawked.

"We should definitely go talk to her," Marshall said. "She may know something about the seeds. Tegan, can you scout ahead and see if she's at the inn?"

Aari kept his arms up, still convinced he'd get smacked, but when Tegan closed her eyes to find an animal to use, he lowered his defenses. A rampant itch made him scratch his calf; when he pulled up the hem of his cargo pants, he found a minute hole surrounded by red skin. *Guess that's where the tranquilizer hit. Jeez, by the time I felt it, I couldn't even move.*

Tegan returned to them a while later. "I've looked everywhere but I can't find her."

"Maybe she's on a break," Marshall said.

"No, you don't understand. The entire place was closed. Shut down. Like she'd up and left."

The Sentry let out a long breath. "I honestly have nothing to say now. It's been one roadblock after another."

Tegan muttered an agreement, then lasered in on the grave marker. "Aari, if Lucius died, there wouldn't be any more memories, would there? No way to find the seeds."

"Probably not." Aari stared at the dirt, then his face hardened. "But I need to try. I have to. People are dying every day by the tens of thousands, if not hundreds. The body count could be close to three million by now. Entire families just *gone.* And Kody . . ."

He turned back to the slab. *Can you pull off a miracle for me?* he coaxed. *Give me anything. Anything at all. The trail can't stop here.*

Bracing himself, he touched the stone. No flash greeted him this time. He stubbornly pushed his hand down harder, the skin on his palm pressing into the rough center engraving. *Something. Anything. Please.*

Brightness flared behind his eyes, and it was as if something had pulled all the air and sound out of the world with a cosmic inhale. The only words Aari could use to describe what he felt was a sensation of floating, of being but not being. He found himself on a mountain face with a forest just below. Above him, the tree line ended abruptly, instead becoming an uneven incline of hardened lava and ash that had flowed as molten rock from the mountain's peak ages ago. In the distance behind him, half of the sun was hidden beneath the horizon.

He had no control as he drifted past the forest toward the edge of the tree line and entered a shallow cave hidden by foliage. In the center, atop a chest-high granite pedestal, rested a box. At least, it looked like a box. It seemed to be entirely made of clay. As he moved closer, he smiled inwardly.

On the surface of the case, three triangles were etched in a row.

He floated around the granite stand until he faced the mouth of the cave. The sun had disappeared, leaving behind a reigning night sky. Inexplicable contentment swelled in him even as the vision faded, contentment that wasn't his.

He removed his hand from the grave marker, noting the red impressions left on his palm, and shot the others a jubilant grin. "I know where the seeds are."

"You found them?" Tegan sounded cautious, as though she didn't dare to believe.

Marshall looked exultant as well as startled. "You . . . saw? But Lucius died, didn't he?"

"He did," Aari affirmed.

"So what are you saying?"

"I have no idea. I just know what I saw. Teegs, can you find a way to scout the western face of Meru? The seeds are in a cave on the other side of the mountain, somewhere along the boundary where the tree line meets the rocky surface at the top."

She sat back, immobile. Aari and Marshall waited, giving her space to mindlink. Many long minutes later, her eyes flickered open in disappointment. "There's nothing there. I've searched the entire tree line. There's no opening."

"It's a cave, Tegan," Aari said. "How can it not be there?"

"You tell me, Brainiac. We know this isn't just a mountain. It's a dormant volcano, which means it was once active. Which *means* at some point in the past nineteen-hundred years, it probably erupted."

"And lava could have covered the cave entrance when it solidified," Aari moaned.

"Doesn't matter," Marshall said firmly. "We'll destroy the

mountainside if we have to. We just need to get as close as possible."

"Aari, do you remember anything that could help pinpoint the location?" Tegan asked.

He covered his face, thinking hard and muttering to himself. Then he jerked up. "Ravines! There were three of them leading down the mountain. The cave was located right above the ravine in the middle on the edge of the tree line."

It took only moments for Tegan to confirm the landmark. She grabbed her tranquilizer gun and sprung to her feet. "We should get moving. Sun sets in a couple of hours."

There were no real trails on the western face of Meru, prompting Tegan to utilize both four-legged and winged creatures to guide them through the forest. As they climbed higher, Marshall communicated with Dominique, who informed them that Kody was awake. She insisted she had rested enough in the past three hours and both she and Kody demanded to join them. When Marshall reluctantly gave in, Tegan sent a bird to escort the African Sentry and the teenagers. The two groups met an hour later at the exact spot Aari had seen in his vision. Dominique refused help as she limped determinedly along. Aari hoped her wound wasn't going septic.

He chugged the last of his water, then bent over with his hands on his knees. His legs were on fire from the grueling trek and he was sure he'd left a lung halfway down the mountain. He looked over at Kody, worried. *If it was this hard for a healthy person, it couldn't have been good for him. Or Domi. Or Mr. I-Was-Just-Lightly-Choked. Man, we are not in good shape.*

The six of them spread out, searching for hints of a cave opening until the sun started to disappear. They reconvened, exhausted, sweaty, and hungry. None of them had the energy or the mood to soak in the breathtaking view of the savanna's vanishing glow in the last minutes before nightfall. Kody's worsening headache made him more irritable; he'd lashed out at least once at everyone. He sat beside Dominique now, head between his knees, as the others gathered wood for a fire. Mariah massaged the back of his neck to try to ease his tension.

By the time the stars made their appearance and the temperature dropped, the group was huddled together near the flames. Aari couldn't believe their rotten luck. *Every step of the way, we've had one obstruction or another. Jag's gone. We're literally right on top of the very thing that could save Kody, save the rest of humanity, and even that's blocked! Why are we tested over and over and over? Why can't we just get a clean break for once? Why are we the ones with this weight on our shoulders? Why us?*

Too drained to carry on his internal tirade, he fell into the blackest of sleeps on his makeshift bed of twigs and dried leaves.

* * *

Cacophonous trumpeting awoke the group. The fire had turned to embers, but the moonlight illuminated everything with perfect clarity. Aari, ears ringing and heart racing, gasped at the sight only yards away from the group.

Three African elephants, all at least ten feet at the shoulder, glared down at them. They trumpeted again and, from behind, twenty silhouettes emerged, brandishing flaming torches.

Aari watched as one shape approached the six of them. The light from the torch danced off a half-face tribal mask. A hand lifted the mask back so it rested on top of the head, and Aari's eyes widened.

It was the young woman from the inn.

As the rest of the silhouettes circled them, she pointed a finger at the group and snarled. "You are not welcome here."

Nageau didn't need his hypersenses to hear the loud voice coming from the Elders' assembly *neyra* as he passed. He raced inside and clambered down the stairs, where he found Magèo and his apprentice raiding the cellar. Books and scrolls lay askew on tables. Wincing at the mess, Nageau strode up to the older man as he perused a shelf. "Magèo!"

The scientist looked up, agitated. "What?" he snapped.

Nageau tempered his approach. "You know the archives are off-limits without an Elder present in the *neyra*."

Magèo waved him off. "If that is your biggest worry, old friend, then I have nothing to say to you."

"Actually, my biggest worry is for these precious artifacts."

Magèo's black-and-ginger-haired apprentice scurried over to clean up a stack of volumes on a table. "We apologize, Elder Nageau! I have been telling him to take it easy, but you know how he is once he has locked onto a particular task."

"All too well, unfortunately," the Elder said. He helped the girl put another stack of books onto a nearby table.

Magèo grumbled. "Nal, have you got one of those things you tie your hair with?"

"Do you mean this?" Nal passed him a hairband from her wrist.

The old man tied his flowing gray beard into a knot. "Much better. Thank you." He marched to a table and upturned a crate of ancient scrolls.

"How goes the search?" Nageau whispered to Nal.

The girl sighed, and he noticed how worn and strained she seemed. Her cheeriness had vanished in the past weeks, and she hardly smiled anymore. Without meeting his eyes, she said, "We have looked through half of these texts and are yet to find the missing piece of the scroll about the Tree of Life. I cannot say that it goes well at all."

"That boy just *had* to inquire about the seeds," Magèo ranted from the other side of the cellar. "And now the Chosen Ones are inches away from finding the box, and we *still* have no inkling as to why our ancestors did not want to share this gift with the world! *What is the big secret?*"

He slammed another crate onto the table and paused to collect himself, then faced Nageau. "I ask that you do not mistake my frustration for anger at Jag. Truthfully, I am amazed that he saw this entire mess from an angle no one else did. Not me, not even the Elders."

Nageau pushed back his short, wispy hair and avoided looking at the older man. Magèo noticed his change in posture and gave him his complete attention. "Nageau? What is it?"

"We have just received news from Marshall." Nageau almost couldn't bring himself to speak. "Jag may have been captured."

Magèo blinked at him once, the lines on his face scrunched, then spun on his heel and emptied another crate. Nageau continued halfheartedly. "For whatever reason, the harbinger of darkness has been restrained when it comes to harming the Chosen Ones. The Elders and I have reason to believe that Jag should, for the time being at least, be safe."

"And how long will that last?"

Nageau had no answer to give. Magèo kept his mouth firmly closed, so the Elder took his leave.

Outside, under the cover of dark clouds and snowcapped pine trees, he rested heavily against the log wall of the *neyra*. He'd felt powerless many times during his leadership of the Council of Elders, but nothing matched the burden he now experienced—except when he had banished Reyor from their home.

The younglings have their path to walk, but are we not supposed to protect them where we can? What are we supposed to do?

What am I supposed to do?

"Grandfather!"

Two youths in buckskin tunics hastened out from between the trees. Nageau hurriedly righted himself and smoothed his cloak. The pair came to an abrupt stop in front of him and Huyani took his face in her hands, her warm brown eyes already asking the question.

"Is it true, Grandfather?" she demanded. "Has Jag really been taken?"

Nageau covered one of her hands with his and gave a barely perceptible nod. Akol raked his fingers into his scalp, shaking his head uncontrollably. "I could not believe it when Grandmother told us. How did this happen?"

Huyani let go of Nageau and put her arms around her brother. He buried his face in her raven locks, head still shaking. Nageau watched them with a pang. He knew his grandchildren had a special bond with the Chosen Ones—it was Huyani who'd nursed the friends back to health after their plane crash a year and a half ago, and it was Akol who'd found them when they had run away in an attempt to return to their homes, and it was they who'd kept the younglings company when Dema-Ki was a foreign place.

He enfolded the siblings in an embrace. Their arms slid around him and he pulled them closer. "We will get him back," he promised quietly. "We will find out where the harbinger has taken him and we will get him back. In the meantime, pray. That is all you can do."

"Grandfather, I am willing to go into the outside world and do more than just pray," Akol said, pulling away from the hug. "Let me join the Sentries. Let me help bring Jag back."

"I commend your resolve, my boy, but I do not think the outside world is where you need to be in the coming months."

"Why not?"

"Please, Akol, do not dispute me."

The youth held his chin up, then bowed stiffly. "I should go. My shift begins soon."

Nageau watched his grandson's broad back retreat into the trees. Huyani sidled up to him. "You know he does not mean to defy you. He just wants to help."

Nageau kissed her cheek. "I know, and he will. Just not out there. Not yet, at least."

She patted down his cloak and fixed his hair, then jogged after Akol. As she disappeared, Nageau thought, *They would both make fine Elders one day.*

He rounded the assembly *neyra* and headed toward one of the wooden bridges crossing the river. He found Ashack leaning against a railing, overlooking the frozen water. The man surely heard his approaching footsteps but didn't stir.

Nageau propped his elbows on the railing beside the muscular Elder. "Sometimes I come here to clear my head, too."

"Are you here to talk about what happened yesterday?"

"I had not intended to cross paths with you, but yes, at some point we will need to speak about the incident. Ashack, that was not—"

"Hutar was evasive with his answers."

"He swore on the souls of the two people he cared about most. Do you really think he would desecrate the names of his father and uncle?"

Ashack finally turned to him with a hard gaze. "Daltair and Aydar were two of the best men I ever knew. I would like to think Hutar would not stoop to such vile levels to deceive us, but I do not know what to believe."

"Ashack, you were there. Tikina looked him in the eyes and believed he was telling the truth. You know how perceptive she is."

"Maybe so, but did we ask the right questions?" Ashack pressed.

Nageau's mouth tightened. "What are you saying?"

Elated yelling rang from the direction of the Elders' assembly *neyra* to their left. Magèo and Nal scampered into the trees away from the river toward the old man's laboratory.

"Magèo!" Nageau boomed.

"We found the missing piece of the scroll!" Magèo hollered, turning around so he could address the Elders while walking backward in a hurry. "But most of the writing has faded so we must restore it! We have no time for idle chitchat!"

Nageau couldn't get a reply out before mentor and apprentice scurried into the laboratory and locked themselves in. *This is good*, he thought. *Hopefully we can soon see if we truly have cause to be concerned.*

He touched Ashack's forearm. "Please, my friend, continue."

Ashack looked at the river again, picking at the slivers of wood on the railing. "I have a hunch I am working on. And if I am right, I will bring this back to the Elders."

"What hunch?"

"Afford me this one ambiguity, Nageau. That is all I ask. When I have reached some level of certainty, you have my word that I will come forward with it."

Nageau clasped his fingers together, deliberating. "Alright. But your actions yesterday—"

"*If* I am wrong about Hutar, then I will apologize to the boy. For now, I am not convinced that he is innocent."

"Ashack, given what has transpired, an apology may not suffice. You know this. We do not assault the people we are meant to guide. It is not who we are. If you come back without evidence . . ."

The black-haired Elder shifted his head just slightly toward Nageau, but didn't take his eyes off the river. "What?"

"If you come back without evidence, I will have no choice but to call for council about your position as an Elder."

"You are not welcome here."

Marshall and the others scrambled to their feet. The masked men and women strode toward them, and the group moved back. There was nowhere to go. Behind them was only a mile-long incline of basalt and hardened lava leading to the top of the mountain.

The young woman who'd lifted her tribal mask raised a hand, and the looming elephants retreated a short distance, keeping watchful eyes on the humans. Two men stood beside the woman, holding up torches capped by twisting flames. All twenty silhouettes wore embroidered cotton vests and black pants with what resembled utility belts around their waists. Knife sheaths clung to their hips. They were lithe and toned, and their masks glimmered under the moonlight and the glow from their torches.

"Who are these people?" Kody muttered, a little louder than he must have intended.

"I am Subira," the woman said, her voice rich and strongly accented, "and as leading Watcher of Meru, I must ask you to leave."

Before Marshall could stop her, Tegan went toe-to-toe with the woman. "Last I checked, this isn't exactly off-limits."

"This is hallowed ground for my people. No one is allowed here."

"Folks go up and down this mountain all the time."

"Not this side." Subira's face was as icy as her tone. "I knew the moment I saw you that you were trouble. I've seen your type; American tourists who walk like you own these ancient grounds, desecrating it with your arrogant footsteps."

"We're not tourists!" Tegan asserted. "We have reason to believe—"

"If you're not tourists, then you're here for the scarce blue garnet of Meru. The mountain has no more to offer. You and your people have stolen enough."

"What blue gar—"

"There is no more left! Now go! All of you! Leave!" Subira raised her arm again and this time the elephants lifted their trunks and trumpeted in an angry chorus.

Marshall balked at the titanic display but kept his voice soft and even as he addressed the young woman. "Please, we mean no disrespect. We have no interest in any treasure." He thought he saw a flicker of understanding on Subira's face, and took a few wary steps toward her. The men on either side of her reached for the knives on their belts. The Sentry held up his hands. "Whoa, hey, easy. We don't want any trouble. We—"

Subira whipped out her own blade and swung it under his chin. "I don't care what you are or aren't. You *will* leave, cooperatively or otherwise."

The flat edge of the cold steel pressed against Marshall's skin and its tip nicked his throat. Subira locked eyes with him. Despite how fierce she was and how royal she appeared, he couldn't help but be taken aback by her youth.

"Put the knife down," Tegan warned.

"Are you giving me an order, girl?" Subira jerked her blade away from Marshall's throat and hoisted it high above her head. The elephants flapped their ears and stomped, the tremors sending vibrations up his legs. The ring of torch-bearing Watchers parted, creating a flickering path from the imposing animals to the teenagers and Sentries.

"Uh, guys?" Aari said under his breath. "I don't like this."

The leading elephant tossed its trunk and all three reared up on their hind legs. Marshall instinctively herded the group up the rocky incline. He kept a grip on Kody so the sick boy wouldn't lag behind. The elephants collectively slammed the ground, sending out another quake. Marshall didn't get the chance to shout a warning before the massive animals charged. The group yelled, trying to scramble up the incline, but none of them moved fast enough. The elephants were within striking distance when Tegan suddenly broke away from the others.

"What are you doing?" Mariah screamed.

Tegan swept forward, unleashing a wordless roar. The leading animal slowed, as did the other two, and stopped directly in front of her. She stared up at them. They drew themselves to their full height and peered down at her as if confused. Then Marshall watched with unbridled astonishment as the first elephant kneeled. Behind it, the other two followed its example.

"Attagirl, Teegs," Aari said, barely above a whisper.

Tegan's reply carried an air of shock. "I didn't do it."

"You . . . you're not controlling any of them?"

"No. I was too slow to mindlink. They—they bowed on their own."

The Watchers seemed at a loss. Subira's dark eyes widened but she quickly smoothed her features and went up to the leading elephant, commanding it to stand tall once more.

"It seems our companions have decided to spare you," she said. "But it's only a short reprieve. You cannot stay here. If you don't leave, then this time *I* will make sure they don't stop."

She finished her statement with a flourish and turned her back to the group. As she did, the torches illuminated the three triangles behind her ear. Marshall heard a strangulated gasp from his right. Dominique came forward with her walking stick. He connected telepathically with her. *Domi, what are you doing?*

I know that symbol—that tattoo.

What?

Out loud, Dominique repeated, "I know that symbol! Behind your ear!"

Subira stopped, head tilting, then pivoted to stand eyeball-to-eyeball with Dominique. Disbelievingly, almost threateningly, she pointed to the ink on her skin. "You claim to know this?"

Dominique widened her stance. To anyone else she would have appeared confident, but Marshall knew her well enough to notice the slightest tremor of uncertainty in her movements.

"*Adiha kilazi,*" she whispered.

Subira looked as if she couldn't believe what she'd just heard. "Say that again?"

"*Adiha kilazi.*"

Subira echoed the words, breathless. She stared unblinkingly at Dominique for the longest time, then gathered her people away from the group. Marshall couldn't hear anything save for a rustle of urgent words foreign to his ears. He sent a thought to Dominique. *What's going on? What did you tell them?*

Marshall, I don't know how, but it may have come full circle.

That's not clearing anything up. Whatever you just said, it shook Subira. And her friends.

Do you remember when I served in the village in the DRC? Where the disease first broke out?

Yes . . .

The medicine man whispered those words to me, but I had no idea what it meant. He had contracted the disease so I thought it was his fevered mind spouting gibberish. He said that he wished he hadn't deserted his ancestors and prayed for them to forgive him. A few days later, he went into a coma and succumbed to the disease. He had the exact same symbol behind his ear—the three triangles. I had no clue what he meant, but after seeing Subira's tattoos I'd hoped that maybe . . . maybe the phrase would trigger something.

You were betting on two words no one knows the meaning of?

It was worth a try. At this point, we have nothing to lose.

The Watchers fell back into a semicircle around the Sentries and teenagers, Subira at the center. "A stranger who knows this treasured phrase that belongs only to our people is not to be taken lightly." Her posture softened only a little, and in a tone that said she suspected the answer, she asked, "Why are you here?"

"We're searching for a box of ancient seeds," Tegan said

cautiously. "As far as we know, its last location was somewhere here, in a cave."

Subira considered the group thoroughly, her fingertips pressed against her lips. "This knowledge is not known to anyone but our people. Maybe you *are* the ones our ancestors spoke of."

"You were expecting us?"

"We didn't know who to expect, or when. For scores of generations, all my people knew was that we had to guard an artifact entrusted to us by—"

"Lucius?" Aari cut in.

Subira spun toward him. "I was going to say a revered soul. How do you know this?"

"I-I don't think it's my place to explain. But I know about Lucius. And I know about Carmel, who grew a tree that could save—did save—many lives. She died protecting it. Lucius burned the tree to honor her last wish, and lived on for years before passing the seeds to a man he considered a son, with instructions to keep it safe and never plant another tree."

The men and women beside Subira removed their masks, mesmerized. Subira lifted her head to the sky and Marshall thought he saw tears shimmering in the moonlight. She dragged in a long breath. "For nearly two thousand years, our people wondered if there would ever be a day when what we have protected would come to light. We've never wavered a hair's breadth from the promise we made to Carmel and Lucius."

Marshall was floored. *Carmel and Lucius must have had an incredible impact to have been worthy of a promise that spanned centuries. Not just for the seeds they brought, but the people they were. Pride stirred within him at the notion that he was, in some way, distantly related to Carmel. I wish I could know more about her, the final Keeper of the Seeds.*

"Will you help us, then?" he asked. "More and more people are dying every day and these seeds are our last hope."

For the first time, Subira smiled. It wasn't bright or wholly warm, but it was a smile and Marshall could get behind that.

"Yes," she said. "We can help."

* * *

The western face of Meru trembled with every impact. A large log, the trunks of two of the elephants coiled around it, rammed the rock again and again. Subira had guided the group to a spot not far from where they'd made camp, claiming that the concealed cave lay just below the surface.

The elephants worked tirelessly until at last the basalt cracked and loosened, revealing a gaping black hole. Subira, torch in hand, reverently led the teenagers and Sentries inside while the rest of the Watchers stood guard near the entrance. Marshall brought up the rear, following Subira's measured pace. The cave was musty and oddly warm, barely big enough for the seven of them as they encircled a granite pedestal at the center. Upon it rested a tan, clay-like box. Carved into the top was a row of three triangles, matching Subira's tattoo.

Firelight swayed on the walls, warping shadows. Marshall stood behind the rest, arms crossed, wanting to believe that they were at the end but too wary to be optimistic. *Is this really it? After everything—Israel, Egypt, Sudan, now Tanzania—is this the final stop?*

He regarded the teenagers and figured they were wondering the same thing. They looked on, hushed, as Subira removed a small reed tube from a pouch on her belt and uncorked it. Her hand hovered above the clay case, shaking. Dominique touched her shoulder, and Subira's hand steadied. She tilted the tube and clear liquid poured out. The case began to dissolve as the drops hit, crumbling like wet sand, until all that remained was a wooden box clad in brass with faded engravings. Marshall immediately recognized the carvings as those on the teenagers' pendants.

Subira delicately lifted the box. "If what lies within this is truly destined to save humanity, then Carmel's vision for the seeds and Lucius's unwavering commitment after her passing will not have been in vain. Under the watchful eye of Kilimanjaro, in the bosom of Meru, this box has been hidden for nearly two thousand years. Now, it will see the light again. We never thought this day would come, not in our lifetime."

Her gaze glided across the group, alighting on Dominique. "*Adiha kilazi,*" she whispered, handing the box to the Sentry. "Bound by providence."

Dominique took the box as if it was the most priceless of gemstones. "Thank you, Subira."

The young woman led them back outside. Her people clamored to catch a glimpse of the box, speaking in elated undertones. No one could peel their eyes from the treasure until Tegan snapped out of the trance. "We need to plant one of the seeds. Kody needs this."

Marshall eased back to himself. "But we can't wait here for it to grow. We need to head to Dema-Ki and hand the seeds to Magèo." He located Kody watching them mutely behind the throng, then said, "What if we plant a seed in one of our bags? Then we can take it with us while we find a way out of Africa."

"That Cessna isn't gonna carry us across the ocean," Aari pointed out.

"If I may," Subira interjected, "Cape Town still offers select flights out of the continent. I don't know where you intend to go, but that would be your best option."

"Kody?" Tegan said. "Would you be able to figure out—"

The boy made a shushing gesture, and he and Subira conversed rapidly. He pulled a map from Aari's backpack and studied it, eyes squinting against what Marshall suspected was a continuous headache. Then he cleared his throat. "If I'm right, it'll probably be a twelve-hour flight to Cape Town in our little plane. Maybe throw in a couple of hours for fuel stops."

"Fifteen hours for the seed to grow," Tegan said. "How many days will we need before we can use it to treat Kody?"

"According to my, um, earlier *exploring*," Aari said, glancing furtively at the Watchers, "it took six days for the sapling to come up to waist height after Carmel planted it. Maybe someone can reach out to Elder Nageau and see if Magèo knows what to do."

"In the meantime," Mariah said, unzipping her backpack, "we can use my bag to carry the seed once we've planted it."

The group scrambled to empty the contents of her bag into the others, then filled it with black, nutrient-rich volcanic soil. Dominique gingerly opened Carmel's box. Inside, four seeds in separate glass vials rested on indented velveteen beds. Tegan carefully removed a vial, holding it so close to her face that her breath fogged the glass. Around the group, Subira and her people began chanting a lush, unknown hymn, dense with devotion. Their voices lilted together like liquid gold under the gloss of the full moon. Marshall's skin tingled as he slipped into what felt like another realm.

A familiar prodding pushed against his mind. *Marshall!*

Elder Nageau! The Sentry moved to a quiet distance from the impromptu ceremony. As he listened to the Elder, the chanting faded entirely into the background. He went rigid, horror pressing down as Nageau's message sank in. He looked up in time to see the seed about to leave Tegan's fingertips. An unearthly sound tore from his throat. He sprinted to cross the ten-foot distance and as the tip of the seed disappeared into the bag, he dove, hand outstretched, and snatched it away, landing roughly.

The chanting stopped. Twenty-five pairs of stunned eyes gouged into him.

"Have you lost your mind?" Tegan stormed. "Give the seed back!"

Marshall opened his hand to make sure that the kernel was in fact in his grasp, then picked himself up. "There was a reason those seeds were in vials," he said, exhaling deeply, "and a reason why Carmel said they should not be planted. It wasn't just to keep them airtight for millennia after millennia. It wasn't just to keep them away from people's greed."

Mariah's forehead pinched. "Then why?"

"The Tree of Life has another name. It's also known as the Tree of Death."

Convoluted emotions competed on every face he saw. He gazed down at the kernel in his palm. "The moment a seed touches soil, it grows into a malignant fern-like tree within days. Its spores spread like wildfire in any climate, in any terrain, and is indestructible even by fire. Worst of all, a breath taken by any living being under this tree will lead to an instant and painful death."

The friends nearly collapsed. Screams simmered plainly just below the surface. "So then what?" Mariah exploded. "Another godforsaken dead end?"

Marshall lifted his free hand when he felt Nageau attempting to reconnect with him. The others fell silent. He opened his mind, listening closely, and his expression slackened into a thousand-watt smile. He clutched the seed over his heart.

"No," he said. "This isn't another dead end. This is the start of salvation. To become the Tree of Life, the seed needs Dema-Ki blood. Islander blood."

The underlying screams evaporated. Kody slumped onto his knees, shielding his eyes, but Marshall still saw his tears hit the ground. His friends were at his side in the next second, holding him tight.

Marshall lifted the seed toward Dominique. "If it weren't for you, we wouldn't be here right now. Dominique Mboya, would you do the honors?"

Overwhelm and veneration set her face aglow as she delicately took it.

Marshall flicked out his switchblade and passed it to her as she crouched by Mariah's bag with some effort. The crowd around them pressed in. Dominique rested the knife against her palm and drew a line, staving off a grimace as her skin tore. She curled her fingers into a fist, covering the seed, then dropped the reddened germ into the bag. Mariah brushed the soil over it and they all watched; the teenagers and the Sentries, Subira and the Watchers. Even the elephants towered behind them. Soundless minutes passed as the moon and torches illuminated them in the chilly air.

The soil quivered. An inch-long shoot pushed out, bearing a single, luminescent violet leaf.

Marshall grinned. *We did it.*

Victor shifted in the jump seat of the red charter bus, trying to fit his broad-shouldered frame into the small bench. Beside him, Gareth absently controlled the steering wheel, staring at the empty stretch of road flanked by ditches. His shaggy hair fell over his eyes. From the uncharacteristic tension in his shoulders and hands, Victor knew that the younger man was steeping in a toxic vat of emotions. Not one for offering empty platitudes, he kept his mouth closed.

A white Dodge Ram led the way ahead and a second gray pickup tailed them, each vehicle carrying one American and one Canadian Sentry. The only source of illumination on the road came from the convoy's headlights. They had left Great Falls, Montana, an hour before midnight to avoid traffic and have better situational awareness. They'd crossed the border into Alberta, a province nearly the size of Texas and Victor's place of birth. His role as a Sentry often took him away from home but he was glad to see the familiar, wide open countryside that made up nearly one-third of Canada's farmland.

He'd gotten word around noon from Marshall, who was ten hours ahead in Tanzania, that the seeds had been found. Rarely anything fazed him, but hearing the Tree of Life's twisted dichotomy sent his gut roiling.

He chased the thought away, and, having had enough of Gareth's atypical silence, nudged him. "Be here, kid."

The Welshman started to roll his eyes but thought better of it. "I am."

"Really? Because you've had that look on your face since we left the Lodge. You need to put your regrets and guilt in your back pocket and sit on them. We have fifteen individuals in here who need our full attention. And if we can't give it to them, this mission has already failed."

Gareth sat a little taller and looked into the rearview mirror. "Happy bunch we have back there."

Victor checked the side mirrors instead, something he'd been doing the entire time to make sure they weren't being shadowed. "They're leaving everything behind. Jobs, homes, friends, families. I wouldn't expect them to be dancing and singing Kumbaya."

"True. I'm sure it helped that you offered to move their relatives in with other Sentries until everything blows over. Not to mention telling them that staying behind would turn them into a liability for their kids. But it would've been nice if we hadn't had to go that far."

Victor gave a half shrug. "It had to be done. It made them cooperative."

"Mmh. At least Kody's father was a huge help. Sam's a good voice of reason. Between you and me, I'm glad we had him on our side. Tegan's father, on the other hand . . ."

This time, Victor did glance up into the rearview mirror. Curtis Ryder sat at the far end of the bus with his wife and twenty-one-year-old son. His blown-back ebony hair contrasted with the medium tan of his skin and his piercing gray eyes. He was the picture of a man whose duty was to protect his city and was upset that he had to leave it behind. Across the aisle, Samuel Tyler's short-afro head bobbed all over the place as he and his wife tried to stop their second-eldest son from apprehending their overactive youngest.

Mariah's mother sat by herself in one of the window seats, apparently not inclined to mingle; she was so petite Victor could barely see the top of her head. Aari's and Jag's parents spoke quietly, while Jag's older siblings entertained the Barnes' four-year-old daughter.

"Fifteen lives entrusted to us," Victor observed again, loud enough for only Gareth to hear. "And forty more hours until we get to Yukon with all the rest stops. And then, Dema-Ki."

The radios clipped to the Sentries' belts crackled. "*Sheepdog One to Flock, radio check, over.*"

"Read you loud and clear, Sheepdog One," Victor said. "And I am never letting you pick our call signs again. Out."

The white pickup in front of them wiggled side to side in response. Gareth snickered. "It's hard to believe you're friends with them. They seem too cheery for your speed."

"I'm friends with you and Dev, aren't I?" Victor retorted.

"Should've seen that coming." Gareth checked the GPS near the steering wheel. "We're less than an hour away from Lethbridge. That'll be the last big town until Calgary. Vic, I'll say it again, this trip would've been so much faster if we'd taken a plane."

"I know, but given the situation, this was the best option. Besides, we have better control over everything this way."

Gareth paused to listen to the radio chatter between the two vehicles sandwiching them, then said, "I can't believe we're going to set foot in Dema-Ki. I've been dreaming about this my whole life—well, who hasn't, really—but nothing ever warranted a visit. I wish it wasn't such a big secret to be kept hidden. Och, but the mere thought that we'll be there in a couple of days . . ."

"Yeah. I'm sure it'll be something."

"You don't seem eager, mate. What's the matter?"

"Nothing. Focus on the road."

Gareth gave him a sidelong stare. Victor twisted the silver rings on his middle fingers, refusing to look anywhere but the endless farmland. He regretted leaving Chief at the Lodge. He needed to grasp the wolfdog's fur, scratch his head, anything that would give a sense of reassurance to quell the anxiety rising in the pit of his stomach at the mention of Dema-Ki.

Knock it off. Anya needs him more than you do. He's giving comfort to an orphaned little girl. God knows you needed a companion like him when you were younger.

He was grateful when Gareth switched topics. "So many

acres of farmland, barely a soul to see. There've been no cars on this road. Aye, it's one in the morning, but still. It feels *dead*."

"The nanomites did their job," Victor said. "Most of the barley, wheat, and canola crops were destroyed, so a lot of people packed up and moved. It's something I never thought I'd see. I remember running around my cousin's farm when I was a kid. Now it hurts just to look at this."

Gareth dug his nails into the leather wheel. "Reyor's attack is so well thought-out. Makes you wonder what else is planned. After famine and disease, there can't be much left for the next hit."

Victor grunted. His phone buzzed against his leg and he pulled it from his pocket. A name flashed on the screen: Kenzo. The silver-haired teenager from the New Mexico Sanctuary; his informant within the ranks. The phone pulsed as texts appeared one after another.

The phone pulsed as texts appeared one after another.

> IS THIS WORKING?

> VICTOR?

> THE RECEPTION IS SO WEAK! IS THIS WORKING??

> TELL ME IF YOU RECEIVE THIS, PLEASE.

The Sentry typed a quick reply.

> SHOOT.

Kenzo gave a rundown of Reyor's address a few days prior, everything from the establishment of the five echelons dividing the Stewards of New Earth, to Reyor's willingness to use extreme measures if thwarted, to the distribution of a group of rare individuals among the Sanctuaries. When Victor pressed him for more, Kenzo said that was all he knew and would keep him abreast if he learned anything else.

"Who's texting you this time of night?" Gareth asked.

Victor scanned the messages a few times over. "My inside source in New Mexico. He just gave the details of Reyor's latest speech. One thing stuck out."

"What?"

"That people with unique blood will eventually be distributed in the Sanctuaries, and they'll give the next generation of SONEs a quote-unquote, array of remarkable abilities."

Gareth pushed his hair back, stunned. "Unique blood? Remarkable abilities? That's us, right? Anyone with Dema-Ki in their veins, maybe even the Chosen Ones."

"That's what I'm thinking. I should—"

One of the Sentries at the back of the convoy interrupted the chatter on the radios. *"Break, break, a vehicle just appeared half a klick behind us. Came out from the fields. Stay sharp."*

Victor sat ramrod straight as he and the other Sentries gave their acknowledgments. Gareth looked into his side mirror at the dark SUV behind the convoy. "Could just be a farmer."

"Could be." Victor's fingers twitched by the buckle of his seatbelt.

"You really think Reyor's people waited for us all the way out here?"

"They found Jag. I'm not taking any chances."

Ahead of them, a second SUV raced over a field from the right, barely distinguishable in the darkness with its headlights off. It bounced along the depression of the deep ditch flanking the road and rolled up onto the asphalt five hundred yards in front of the convoy. It slowed as the SUV in the back accelerated.

Victor unbuckled himself. "I don't like this."

There was shuffling behind him. He turned to see Tegan's and Kody's fathers; the cop and the retired Air Force pilot must have been listening in on the radio chatter from the back.

"Trouble?" asked Curtis.

"Looks like an intercept," Victor said.

Gareth's grip on the wheel constricted. "It's just two trucks. We've got six Sentries with abilities. We can handle this."

Distant staccato thumps grew louder until Victor felt it in his chest like the rapid beating of a colossal heart. An immense, dark shape eclipsed the bus. Disbelief shot through him as the source of the shadow descended into full view directly ahead of the convoy.

A V-22 Osprey flew over the white pickup truck in front of the bus, its loading ramp open. Dim lights inside outlined a figure in full combat gear behind an M2 machine gun pointed directly at them. The rotors of the aircraft tilted up until the plane hovered a short distance from the vehicles. The commando adjusted the gun lower. In a breathless second, Victor knew what was going to happen but his lungs were a vacuum and he couldn't scream.

The white pickup in front of the bus exploded.

Gareth yelled, swerving around the flames and smoke that poured from the scorched wreckage, but Victor's focus was entirely on the two young Sentries who lay dead inside it. He didn't register the bus's front tires being shot out, nor the Osprey swinging around and landing on the isolated freeway facing the convoy. He only snapped back when he felt their big vehicle tilt perilously to the right. Shrieks followed as the bus tipped and plummeted into the ditch. Victor's head struck something hard and he blacked out.

When he came to, he was askew against the dashboard, and found that the left side of the bus was now the ceiling. Groaning, he peeled himself off and wiped the blood dripping down his temple. Whimpers and crying trailed from the back of the vehicle. A sharp pain in his side signaled that he had at least a couple of bruised ribs.

That's fine. Dealt with worse.

As he pulled Gareth from his slumped position against the steering wheel and ensured that he was conscious, he telepathically connected with one of the Sentries at the back of the convoy. *Talk to me, Gabby.*

The plane shot our truck after you guys fell, she said, an ache in her words. *Ryan and I managed to bail out before the car exploded. I'm some ways behind you in the same ditch your bus fell into. He's in the one on the other side of the road.*

And the SUV that was behind us? Victor asked, helping Curtis and Samuel sit up.

Two men just got out. They're splitting up to check the ditches. They've got tranquilizers but I see handguns, too.

Can you guys manage?

Ryan has the bag with the explosive gels, but I can handle one guy. There's enough light scattering from the cars that I can use my abilities to blind him for a bit.

Good. Gareth just did a roll call. Apart from some injuries, everyone here is fine.

What about Duke and Beth?

Victor screwed his eyes shut. *They're dead.*

The other Sentry let out a choked curse.

We'll make Reyor pay, Victor said. *But we need to get the families to safety first.*

Vic, the men up front are moving in on your position. Full tactical gear with masks, trying to open the emergency hatch on top of the bus. I'd blind them, but they're not facing me.

Victor heard a loud pop from the back, confirming the opening of the hatch. *I hear them.*

Cover your face. They're about to throw in smoke grenades.

Before Victor could yell a warning, there were two distinct clinks followed by the hiss of released smoke. Coughing erupted as the suffocating cloud spread toward the front of the bus. Victor pulled Gareth, Curtis, and Samuel into a crouch facing the cracked windshield. Through it, he saw two armed men slide into the ditch from the road and run toward them.

Victor bared his teeth and swept one hand out, forcing a concussive blast that tore the windshield apart. Smoke rushed out of the opening. Glass shards hurtled toward the commandos and they fell. Victor tuned his hearing to their comm units, picking up chatter as the rest of their team wondered what had happened. A throaty voice assured that it would be checked out. At the top of the ditch, Victor spied two more men. One wore an eyepatch and, by his commanding posture, the Sentry pegged him as the man leading the ambush. The other was smaller, possibly the second-in-command.

When he honed in on the one with the eyepatch, he heard the man supplying a play-by-play of the situation to someone in his earpiece; Victor could recognize the irritatingly honeyed voice of Tony Cross anywhere.

He's overseeing this capture, too? Must be pulling double to get on Reyor's good side.

The commotion of people screaming as they were dragged out of the bus via the emergency hatch made Curtis and Samuel turn to help, but Victor grabbed their arms in a vice grip. "Don't do anything," he whispered. "Gareth and I will take care of it."

"By letting them take our families?" Curtis growled.

Victor leveled his gaze. "No. By going with them. Gareth and I will blend in, act like we're part of your families. We'll strike when we're ready, so *don't* do anything."

Curtis looked angry but Samuel urged him toward the back of the bus. Gareth tailed them as he turned off his radio and covered it with his blazer, Victor doing the same. Two men in black stood above them atop the side of the transport vehicle, rifles pointed downward to prevent anyone from fleeing through the windows.

Victor was the last to be roughly pulled out. He bit back a cry as arms tightened around his bruised ribs and threw him to the ground. Four commandos quickly herded the group of seventeen onward, keeping the families pinned between them and the bus so there would be no escape. The men on top of the overturned vehicle moved closer, weapons ready.

Victor stayed close to the families, as did Gareth. He did a mental count: Six men were focused on them. Eyepatch and his second-in-command were by the ditch at the front of the bus, and two men were at the back of the destroyed convoy. He heard struggles elsewhere but didn't have time to check in with the other Sentries.

As they neared the midpoint of the bus, Victor caught Gareth's eye. Understanding passed between them. In one voice they shouted for the families to duck. Gareth faced the two men on the flipped vehicle and Victor launched a concussive blast that threw the four commandos to the ground, thirty feet away.

The families gazed around, wide-eyed. Victor looked up. The men on top of the bus suddenly screamed before dropping their weapons, tendrils of vapor rising from their heating bodies. Gareth pushed on with dogged fixation until they toppled off the vehicle onto the road behind them. Whimpering could be heard as they lay on the asphalt, their fevered bodies weakened by rapid dehydration.

Two of the men Victor had flung got to their feet, disoriented. Victor forced himself away from the bus and ran toward them. He needed to recharge just a bit more before he could send out a blast strong enough to knock them back down. He heard Gareth on his heels as they tore over the field.

Just as the men reached for their weapons, both Sentries bowled them to the ground. Victor was quick, slipping behind his target and locking him in a sleeper hold. Once the commando was out, he fished around the man's ammunition belt, found a tranquilizer dart, and stuck it in his neck.

The commando Gareth fought had gotten the upper hand. He trapped the slimmer Welshman below him, crushing him until the Sentry had turned a sickly shade of blue. As he pressed his pistol to Gareth's forehead, Victor struck out with a kick that would have made any pro soccer player proud. His boot caught the commando across the head, knocking him out and stamping a massive bruise on his face.

Gareth rolled upright, gasping for air. "Thanks!"

Gunfire responded in Victor's stead. The Sentries spun around. Eyepatch and his second-in-command fired over the heads of the families and into the ground at their feet, shouting for them to hurry forward. Tegan's father tried to fight back, receiving a bullet through his shoulder for his effort. He cried out, blood splattering the bus behind him, and was shoved up toward the road with the others.

Gareth took off at a sprint, leaving Victor to race after him.

They rounded the front of the bus and climbed over the ditch. The families were being steered toward the Osprey, its propellers still rotating in preparation for takeoff. Victor drew in his energy and readied another concussive blast. Before he could unleash it, the road rocked as an earth-shaking boom threw everyone in the vicinity to the ground. A gust of wind blew the smoke from the Osprey's destroyed wing toward Victor until he could taste the acrid tang in his mouth. Through the ringing in his ears and the sting in his eyes he saw the families scatter from the plane, voices muffled as they yelled.

As the curtain of smoke churned past him, the Sentry at the back of the convoy reached out with her mind. She sounded exhausted. *Vic, Ryan stuck the explosive gels onto one of the plane's wings.*

Victor got his feet under him, forcing the distorted world to steady up. *So I noticed. Remind me to buy that guy a cake when this is all over. You okay, though, Gabby?*

Yeah. Just took care of the two guys in the back. They were tough, but I got 'em.

Good. Some of the families are headed toward you. Corral them while I get the others.

A few feet ahead, Gareth struggled to get up. Just past him, the Osprey tilted, off-balance, with its right nacelle consumed by fire. Victor traced a line from the remaining wing down to Camilla, Jag's older sister, who'd been knocked to the ground by the detonation. He leapt over Gareth's hunched form and ran to her, lifting her into his arms. She held onto him like a lifeline.

The sixty-foot-long Osprey tilted further, its spinning propellers listing toward the road. Victor made a break to safety but knew he was too late when the thumping of the rotors turned into a tornado of metal projectiles. He threw himself to the ground, using his body to shield Camilla from the fragmented blades. Something sliced across his back, not deep but enough to carve through his shirt and skin, leaving a hot gash. He roared, curling his hands into fists so tight his nails cut into his palm. The clanging and high-pitched whine of the shredded propellers flying echoed around them, followed by the low, heavy *thump* of the burning Osprey hitting the ground.

The sounds of a child crying and a woman shrieking, proceeded by car doors slamming and tires squealing, made him drag himself off Camilla. He twisted around, suppressing a yelp as the skin around his wound contorted. He could just see the taillights of a vehicle flying past the wrecked Osprey. Another SUV took off after it. Victor blinked through the haze but couldn't find Gareth anywhere. He unclipped his radio and turned it on. "Gareth!" he barked.

The Welshman answered a moment later. *"They took Sam and his child! And Mariah's mother! I'm going after them! Take care of everyone else!"*

"Don't do anything stupid!"

"I'll do what I have to! I'm not losing them!"

Victor jammed his radio back onto his belt and offered Camilla his hand. She didn't take it and stared up at him instead, her dark hair a mess, a gash on her cheek, fear lancing in her amber eyes. Fear and realization. Realization that it was all real. The danger her youngest brother and his friends faced, the threat of an enemy bent on doing whatever it took to win.

The Sentry knelt, ignoring the sting in his back. He held out his hand again, and this time she took it. Victor squeezed gently. "We'll keep you all safe," he said. "I promise."

Marshall rested against a tree, heedfully watching Kody as the group hid from the late morning sun under some sparse foliage. The teenager turned his red cap backward and paid his friends no mind as he inspected the Cessna. Perspiration dotted his face; Marshall had to squash the impulse to mop his forehead and sit him down with a water bottle. Not that he could have; in the state Kody was in, the boy was likely to snap Marshall's fingers off with his teeth. Besides, they had limited water and no one felt like making the long run to Nyika Wildlife Inn. Tegan had scouted the area and said that Ajajdif and his men had cleared out of the neighboring resort.

After finding the seeds the night before, the six of them had headed down the mountain on the backs of the elephants. Subira's people had become more open in their conversations, but the young leader herself did not partake much in the dialogue.

Upon reaching the base of the Meru, the sounds of gunfire drifted to their ears. Subira informed the group about the government's frequent nighttime sweeps of towns for rebels and rogue soldiers, something now commonplace in the region since the famine. She'd advised them to stay put until morning. They acquiesced, taking the time to rest and converse with the Watchers. When morning arrived, Subira had bid them goodbye and good luck as she and her people disappeared into the forest.

Marshall jumped when Dominique's head dropped against his shoulder, then smiled at her sleeping form. He gave her leg a once-over, making sure blood hadn't soaked through the fresh gauze he'd tied over her wound. Tegan, Aari, and Mariah were perched on a hefty log to his left, sharing a bag of stale chips. He would have liked to eat something to quiet his stomach but his neck and throat were still sore from his fight with Hajjar.

"You sure you don't need help, Kode-man?" Aari asked.

"I've got it, thanks," came the curt reply.

The friends on the log cast grimaces at one another. Marshall sympathized. Kody's temperament had worsened to match his pounding headache. There was nothing anyone could do except wait for the seedling in Mariah's backpack to grow and hope that the sapling could heal Kody somewhat, even if it wasn't fully mature.

Marshall repositioned himself so Dominique would be more comfortable against him, then saw something black-white-and-red. He opened and closed his eyes a few times. "Is something wrong with my vision, or is that tree directly ahead alive and moving?" he asked the others.

The friends quirked their heads at said tree a few hundred yards away. Tegan grinned. "Neither! Those are birds. Hornbills, I think, and hundreds of them by the looks of it."

"I know we've been globetrotting for a reason," Aari said, tossing a chip into his mouth, "but it's nice to finally just pause and take it all in. We're in *Africa*. Who would've thunk?"

Marshall drank in the sight of the savanna and the grand peaks of Kilimanjaro and Meru on either side of the group. It was deceptively tranquil given the state of the world, but he rarely passed on an opportunity to stop and smell the roses. It was a nice moment of serenity.

A moment that was quickly and rudely disrupted by the thumping of aircraft rotors. The teenagers scrambled out of the shade to get a view of three helicopters coming from the north. There was no mistaking their target.

Kody closed the fuel cap on the wing of the Cessna and hurried to join them. "Those are Mil Mi-17's," he informed them monotonously. "Russian-made transport choppers."

The gray helicopters hovered low over the savanna. They spread into a half-circle and kept a distance of a city block from the group. As they hung in the air, a rough, Russian-accented voice boomed over a loudspeaker. *"Before you get any smart ideas, I will warn you only once: Don't try anything. We have your families."*

By this time Dominique was completely awake and the Sentries were by the teenagers' sides. Mariah raised a hand, as if determined to bring down one of the helicopters. Another voice came over the speaker and the girl's hand dropped weakly to her side.

"Stop! Please, stop!" The shriek swept across the plains. *"Why are you doing this?"*

Mariah would have fallen if Dominique hadn't caught her around the waist. "Momma," she whispered.

The voice of a man both furious and terrified followed. *"Stop the car or I swear I'll—"*

He was cut off by a child's wail. *"Daddy!"*

Kody stepped in front of the group, hands curling into fists. His chest heaved dangerously. "That's my dad and kid brother!" he roared. "If you hurt them, I'll rip out your spine and strangle you with it!"

The powerful thumps of helicopter blades drowned his threats. He started to run toward the enemy but Marshall leapt for him. They fell, and as the Sentry rolled them upright, Kody flew into a fit of blind rage, pummeling his fists against Marshall as he tried to writhe away. The boy burned to the touch, his aggravation accelerating his fever. Marshall held him closer.

"Kody," he murmured. "Stop, kiddo. Stop."

"They have my family!"

Kody jerked his head, catching the Sentry under his jaw. Pain exploded from the contact but Marshall hugged the teenager closer, one hand cradling the back of the boy's head. Kody choked back a sob before allowing himself to go limp in Marshall's arms.

Ajajdif returned to the speaker. *"Now that I have your attention, I want the four of you to listen carefully. Come quietly with the seeds and you have my word that I won't harm your families.*

Better yet, I'll throw in a little bonus. Come without resistance, and I will let Mr. Sawyer and Ms. Mboya live."

The helicopters descended, landing on the plain and kicking up a dust storm. Two dozen heavily armed Tanzanian mercenaries poured out from the open ramps at the back of each aircraft, forming a crescent perimeter that still gave the group space. Marshall eyed them, then reached out telepathically to Victor. *Colback! What's going on?*

Ambush, the Canadian Sentry responded. *They made off with Mariah's mom and—*

I know! Reyor's people are giving the kids an ultimatum!

Victor growled. *Crap. Gareth just took off after them, but he's on his own.*

We've already lost Jag. I won't lose these four.

Trust me, none of us want to. But it's not looking good. I . . . I'm sorry.

Marshall severed their connection viciously but his grip remained gentle as he hoisted Kody up. The rest of the group clustered around them. Mariah, her voice still a cracking whisper, said, "They have our families. Look at us. We're in no shape to fight fifty fully armed men, and if we try anything they'll kill Marshall and Domi. What do we do?"

Marshall met Tegan's eyes. He could see the gears in her mind spinning. His own thoughts whirlpooled to find a solution but he drew a blank. They still had the submachine gun and the tranquilizers, but those would never subdue the army before them. He saw Tegan reach the conclusion the same time he did. His heart clenched. Stuttered. Screamed.

Tegan rested a hand on Aari's shoulder, another on Mariah's. With her chin held high, she said, "We're not winning this one."

Her friends didn't argue, though a part of Marshall wished they would have. But he knew them; they would not risk the lives of their families and the Sentries.

Mariah rushed into his arms. He enfolded her tightly, letting his shirt soak up her grief. "I'll find you guys," he whispered. "I promise I'll find you."

She looked up at him, mouth open as if she wanted to say something, but all that came out was a broken whimper. Going onto her toes, she brushed a kiss on his cheek and slunk toward Dominique, who tugged her into an embrace.

Aari solemnly extended a hand to Marshall. The Sentry grabbed it and yanked the redhead toward him. Aari hugged him firmly. No words were exchanged, but none were needed. The teenager attempted a smile, then moved aside.

Kody's silence didn't fool Marshall. The boy was sick, angry, and scared. He refused to be grabbed in an embrace so the Sentry clasped the back of his neck reassuringly, lingering. The only thing that gave him a shred of hope for Kody's health was that Reyor wanted the teenagers alive. Phoenix had to have Dr. Deol's cure somewhere.

Lastly, Marshall turned to Tegan. To her credit, she hadn't shed a tear, but there was a sheen brimming, threatening to spill over. She remained unblinking until the glistening dried, then wrapped her arms around his neck.

"Thank you," she said. "For everything."

"I couldn't protect the five of you from this. I'm sorry."

"You have nothing to be sorry about. You've been helping us since we met, guiding and supporting us. Heck, you even put up with us, and that's saying something." She gave a sheepish smile. "But protecting was always meant to be our job. The five of us. That's our duty. And that's what we're doing now."

Marshall pressed his lips to the top of her head. "The Elders would be so proud of you. I know I am."

They shared a secret fist bump. Aari had already grabbed the box of seeds but left Mariah's backpack with the Sentries, as well as Lucius's letters that needed to be returned to Asa. "Reyor's people don't have to know that we've already planted one," he said.

Dominique leaned against her walking stick, the fingers of her free hand pressed against her closed eyelids. "The tree will save so many lives. You will save so many lives."

"No way could we have done this without you," Mariah said, taking her hand. "You had the missing piece that unlocked everything."

"We'll make sure the tree gets to Dema-Ki," Marshall said. His gaze shifted to the increasingly restless mercenaries. "Probably best not to keep them waiting any longer."

He placed his right fist over his heart and bowed. Dominique did the same and the teenagers returned the gesture. Then, with one last look at the Sentries, the friends turned and walked shoulder to shoulder toward the helicopters.

"Gareth! Sitrep!"

Gareth clicked his radio, keeping his other hand firmly on the wheel. "I'm closing in, Vic. Quarter mile between them and me."

"The kids know about the situation. They gave themselves up."

Gareth's radio should have snapped from his death grip. "What?"

"They just got into a chopper. With the seeds. It's over, Gareth."

The Welshman flung the radio into the passenger seat. A cyclone of obscenities and pleas spun until they were nothing more than blinding thoughts. It wasn't fair. It wasn't fair that he'd failed Ina Deol and her daughter. It wasn't fair that he'd failed the Chosen Ones. It wasn't fair that something always went wrong just when something else started to go right.

Shadowed fields blurred past the windows. Cloud cover concealed the moon. The speedometer topped out at a hundred-and-twenty miles per hour but the other SUV, just slightly slower, managed to stay out of Gareth's reach. The Sentry shuffled through his options. Melting the asphalt to trap the abductors wouldn't work at this distance, and doing the same to the tires could lead to an accident.

A sharp *crack* reached his ears as a bullet buried itself in the fender of his SUV. One of the two hostage-takers leaned out of a rear window, firing at his tires. Gareth swung his vehicle to the assailants' other side, but the gunner followed to the left window. The Welshman kept a hand on the gearshift and maneuvered instinctively, dodging a few projectiles while others skinned the body of his vehicle.

He assessed the situation; it would either end with his tires shot or the gunner running out of ammunition. *There has got to be a way to beat this*, he seethed.

He narrowed in on the two tailpipes by the SUV's rear right tire. A memory flickered amidst his thoughts: He saw himself and his brother, thirteen years old—experimenters, troublemakers. Gareth had a potato in hand and Deverell held the keys to their father's car. Swapping mischievous grins, Deverell jumped behind the steering wheel, ready to turn the ignition. Gareth shoved the potato into the tailpipe, somersaulted to a safe spot, and waited eagerly to hear some kind of boom. To the brothers' disappointment, the car only stalled.

The memory winked away. Gareth leaned on the gas as he avoided the bullets, knowing it barely brought him closer to the SUV ahead. He focused on the first of the vehicle's tailpipes. The metal began to glow from red to orange, to bright yellow. Before it hit white-hot, the pipe melted in on itself, sealing the opening.

The SUV jerked and sputtered, slowing but stubbornly pushing on. Gareth concentrated on the second tailpipe as he drew closer. As soon as the metal had fused closed, a dull boom reverberated across the empty freeway. Smoke rolled out from under the abductors' vehicle as it came to a rough stop.

Gareth barely had a second to revel in his success. The two abductors leapt out, growing brighter under the headlights of his SUV, their rifles spitting. Gareth knew he'd lost his front tires when the car started to swerve and kick without his permission. In a split-second decision he grabbed his radio, shoved the door open, and threw himself onto the road. His tumble was wild and reckless. He scraped his jeans, hands, and head, but his leather jacket protected him from further injury. Adrenaline was his friend, keeping him from gauging just how badly he was hurt.

With shaky arms, he pushed himself up and watched his ride skid at an angle before flipping onto its side. He leapt toward the overturned vehicle for cover. The reek of burned rubber permeated the air.

Peeking past the vehicle's hood, he found the lead commando with the eyepatch coming from the left. Gareth shrank away just as two bullets whizzed past his face. He couldn't hide forever. It needed to end, one way or another.

He took a second to steady his pulse, then launched himself into the ditch beside the road. Keeping low, he zoomed in on the leading commando's rifle. The weapon heated in moments. Eyepatch dropped the gun, hissing, and ripped off his blistering tactical gloves.

In his peripherals, Gareth saw the second commando putting him in his sights. Before he could act, a silhouette appeared behind the man and delivered a blow to the back of his head. The commando stumbled and spun to face his attacker but was promptly met with an elbow to the face. He buckled. The silhouette tore the rifle away and slammed it against his temple. The commando fell sideways.

Realizing he'd been distracted, Gareth snapped back to the man with the eyepatch. He was too slow. The commando had pulled out his pistol, firing rapidly. Three bullets missed and the fourth clipped the side of Gareth's abdomen but he barely felt it. He stretched his hand out, using it to bring his ability to bear.

The commando trembled, skin paling in the darkness. He fell to the road as though his legs were ice smashed by a pickaxe. He shivered, each judder shaking his body. "What's hap . . . happening?" he gasped.

Gareth straggled over, towering over him. The commando could barely look.

"What's happening?" the Sentry repeated, kneeling so he was at eye level. "Instant cold shock response, mate. You're freezing too fast and your heart is working overtime to pump enough blood to keep your body warm."

"Make it s-stop," the commando groaned. "I c-can't . . . I can't f-feel . . ."

Gareth despised imparting threats, but his turbulent emotions did a wondrous job chasing the sentiment away. "If I keep this up," he said, "you'll get colder. More confused. Your heart will stop working. So, that being said, if you come after any of us again, I will not hesitate to end you. *Don't* test me."

The silhouette of Gareth's savior appeared by his side. Samuel Tyler gave him a hand up. "Thank you," the man said. "Thank you for coming for us."

Gareth couldn't bring himself to say anything. All he could think was that he'd been too late. The teenagers were already in the chopper that would take them right to Reyor.

The friends sat on fold-away canvas seats attached to the side of the chopper's hot, musty cargo hold. Mariah, Aari, and Tegan were near the cockpit, and Kody was closest to the sealed ramp. Across from them, Ajajdif held the box of seeds, his square face set in a cautious smile as the helicopter ascended. A branded white dress shirt and black slacks covered his mesomorph form, and a handgun glinted in his thigh holster.

Mariah had trouble discerning his age but decided to pin him in his mid-forties. His visage, marred by faint scars, carried the gravity of a man who'd experienced his fair share of life's struggles. His somewhat subtle accent proved his Russian heritage, but there was something about his appearance that bespoke another ethnicity as well.

"So, we found our missing men in a lava chute up the mountain," Ajajdif said, almost conversationally. "Well done overpowering them. It's a good thing I had a lock on their positions before we lost connection. They're waiting for our arrival now, with a plane that will take us out of Africa. I'm sure they'd love to see you again."

He pointed at Mariah. "I remember you. You and that woman. One of you sent me through the roof of my office back in the Canadian mining site. I was in a neck brace for weeks and had to get my nose reconstructed." He called to one of the four mercenaries riding with them. "Sedate her first."

"You said if we came quietly—" Tegan began.

"All I said was that I'd spare lives. The sedatives are to make the ride smoother for *us*. I'd let my men shoot you with their darts, but at this range it would hurt. A lot. Still, if you don't cooperate, I will give them the order to fire. I can be nice, see?"

Three of the mercenaries hefted their pistols at Mariah. She worked down the lump in her throat, pulse racing. The fourth mercenary readied a syringe and knelt in front of her. She clenched her hands but Tegan lightly tapped a knee against hers, cautioning her not to act impulsively. The needle had barely touched her skin when Kody stomped his feet and thrashed, a wild gleam in his eyes.

"He's sick!" Ajajdif glanced at the box of seeds in his hands, then at Kody. "Never mind the girl. Sedate him first!"

Kody's mouth had adopted a foul vocabulary distressingly unlike him. Mariah, alarmed, listened to the sickness toying with his mind. He shouted and screeched, fighting against the safety belt around his waist as the mercenaries turned to him.

Tegan, they're gonna sedate him! Mariah blasted telepathically. *We need to do something!*

Don't jump in, Tegan warned. *If we try anything, we'll be risking our families.*

So we just let them put Kody under?!

I think the stress is accelerating the infection. Listen to him. He's yelling that he's burning up. The fever's getting worse, Mariah. It's best to let them sedate him. That way he won't hurt anyone. And more importantly, he won't hurt himself.

Mariah dug her heels into the floor, forcing herself to accept Tegan's words, then twisted to look out the oval window behind her. They were a hundred feet in the air; on either flank at ground level, the other two helicopters were lifting off. Beside her, Aari leaned into her shoulder and she pressed back against him, both of them searching for some comfort to shore themselves up.

Then a presence like the sun melting away a cold winter knocked on Mariah's mind. She recognized Dominique instantly and opened up. *Domi, we—*

The Sentry didn't let her finish. *Your families are safe! You can fight, Mariah! Fight!*

She didn't need to be told twice. From Tegan's expression,

Mariah knew she'd gotten the news from Marshall. The girls coughed until Aari noticed the change in their demeanor. He nodded. Facing the man who'd finally managed to slide the syringe into Kody's neck, he goaded, "You know he's contagious, right? We all are. And you're stuck in here with us."

The mercenaries shared uncertain looks and started to slowly put distance between themselves and the friends as Kody slumped, unconscious. Ajajdif snarled. "What are you doing? Sedate them!"

As the man with the syringe reluctantly prepped another dose for Aari, Mariah looked out the window again, trying to hide her frenzy. She located the large log the friends had sat on and tunneled her energy toward it. The log took off like a mortar, striking the tail rotor of a chopper below them. The aircraft went into an uncontrolled spin before plummeting to the ground not far below. Mercenaries scrambled out from the back of the broken but still upright chopper, some injured, but there didn't seem to be any fatalities.

A shout came from the cockpit as the pilot relayed the crash to a dismayed Ajajdif. Emboldened by her feat, Mariah aimed the remnant of the log at the second helicopter's tail. Realizing belatedly that the chopper fifty feet in the air had begun to turn, she couldn't readjust the log's trajectory in time. It slammed into the front of the aircraft, embedding half of its ten-foot length in the cockpit. She stifled a horrified shriek.

The chopper tilted perilously to its right, its controls most likely jammed. It floundered, scraping the ground before smashing into the thorny foliage of an acacia tree. The collision didn't result in an explosion, but the helicopter landed hard on its underside.

With two choppers down, Ajajdif swore wildly. Aari unbuckled himself and charged, throwing one of the mercenaries down. Mariah disarmed the others with a flick of her fingers and Tegan grabbed a dislodged weapon as Aari picked up another. Muffled pops preceded two men dropping to the floor.

Outmaneuvered and now outnumbered, Ajajdif seized Tegan around her neck and pulled the pistol from his holster, pressing it against her temple. "I will end her right here, right now," he promised, voice frighteningly soft. "I think I'll be forgiven if I return with just three of you alive."

"You wouldn't dare," Aari snapped.

"Want to test that? You have uncanny talents, yes. But you never should have tried this."

"You don't have our families anymore," Mariah hissed. "You've lost your bargaining chip."

"How did you—" Ajajdif cut himself off and struck out with his leg, kneeing Mariah in her abdomen and throwing her back into her seat. "Forget it. *Poshel ty.* Screw you kids and your witchcraft. We may no longer have your families, but we have you. That was all we needed."

He barked an order at the remaining Tanzanian. The mercenary picked up a fresh syringe from a compartment under Kody's seat and loaded the sedative.

"One slight move," Ajajdif said, squeezing his arm harder around Tegan's neck, "any inkling of your magic, the slightest hint, and my trigger-happy finger will blow a hole in her head."

Mariah yelled telepathically. *Teegs!*

Don't do anything, Tegan said. *Just wait.*

"Mr. Ajajdif," the pilot called uneasily, his accent slathered on every syllable. "You might want to see this."

"What is it?" Ajajdif shouted.

"Please, sir, come here."

Ajajdif dragged Tegan along as he ducked past the bulkhead. There was a moment of quiet. Then he asked hoarsely, "Is that a swarm?"

"Yes, sir. And it's coming right for us."

Mariah craned to see what they were talking about. Ajajdif shifted to the side, and her mouth dropped open. Her reaction caused the remaining mercenary to peer into the cockpit as well. His face mirrored hers.

A black-white-and-red cloud of birds spanning a hundred yards soared toward the helicopter, slightly above the aircraft's flight path. Ajajdif gestured irascibly at the blockade. "Just go higher!"

"I can't," the pilot said. "The birds are too close. If I bring us higher, they'll fly right into us, hit our rotors, and get ingested by the engines."

"Fine. Fine! Wait until they pass, then." Ajajdif eyed Mariah and Aari suspiciously, gun still pressed against Tegan's head. They stared back, wearing masks of innocence.

The birds were on top of them in seconds. They all strained to look out the windows, gawking. The chopper hung in the eye of the storm as the creatures trapped them in a tornado of feathers and wings. Mariah reached out to Tegan. *This is you?*

Her friend was the picture of defiance and smugness. *Yep. Remember that tree full of birds Marshall saw? Turns out hornbills can play follow-the-leader pretty well.*

All at once, the chopper started to lose altitude. Ajajdif, thrown off by the motion, demanded, "What are you doing?"

"They're forcing us to land!" the pilot shouted.

"Fly through them!" Ajajdif ordered.

"I can't! We'll destroy the chopper and crash!"

As the birds formed an enormous umbrella over the aircraft, now just forty feet off the ground, Ajajdif returned to the cargo hold with Tegan. "I know one of you is doing this," he accused, then cocked his chin at the mercenary. "Put them under. Right now."

Without warning, Tegan clamped her teeth into Ajajdif's arm. He yowled and crushed his gun-wielding fist into her temple. Mariah saw her chance and telekinetically jerked the pistol out of his hand, pointing it at his head.

"Don't," she said. "Don't touch her again."

Ajajdif scowled down the barrel of his gun but didn't make a move, allowing Tegan to squirm free just as the chopper landed. Aari hurled himself at the lever at the back of the aircraft and the ramp dropped. Mariah undid Kody's seatbelt and pulled him up. Aari helped, and together they half-carried, half-dragged the unconscious teenager down the ramp. Tegan grabbed the box of seeds from Ajajdif, snatched the levitating gun, and smashed it over the man's head. He fell, unconscious, with an unceremonious *thunk*, and Tegan hastened to catch up to Mariah and Aari.

Kody's head lolled against Mariah. She could feel the fever coming off him in waves. *Hang on, Kody,* she thought. *Just hang on.*

On either side of the aircraft, two groups of twenty or so mercenaries advanced in the direction of the helicopter. A breakaway group of half a dozen men on the teenagers' right was firing at a rocky outcrop a hundred yards away. Mariah saw Marshall returning fire but the Sentries were clearly pinned.

Ajajdif's groggy voice suddenly blasted on a loudspeaker. "We have four runners!"

"Ugh!" Tegan groaned. "Should've hit him harder!"

As the friends raced across the savanna, Mariah pinpointed the log she'd used to take down the other choppers, then launched it at the last aircraft standing. It rocketed over the golden grass, past the mercenaries, and hit the main rotor. The blades snapped off, one wheeling past the friends. The smell of smoke filled the air but dissipated as the pilot shut down the engine.

"Thanks, 'Riah!" Tegan called. "Don't need the birds now!"

"Anytime!" Mariah chirped.

"Don't get hit by the tranqs!" Aari yelled.

Darts hailed around them, each one missing the group by some stroke of luck. Mariah's eyes flicked to where the Sentries were pinned. The breakaway mercenaries were moving toward the rocky outcrop.

"I can help them!" Mariah cried.

"No!" Tegan shouted. "Just get to safety first! Fifty yards to go!"

Marshall couldn't believe his eyes. Somehow the teenagers had managed to bring down the helicopter and were halfway across the battlefield, nearing the Sentries. But why were they dragging Kody?

He started to move but Dominique used her strength to hold him against the outcrop. "Might I suggest that you *not* turn kamikaze?" she said sternly.

"The kids—"

"I know, but it won't do for you to get gunned down when they've made it this far."

Marshall pushed her arm, more to tell her to let go than actually putting up a fight against her abilities. She complied. Bits from the top of the rock blew off as bullets struck. He leaned out to get another look. The teenagers were so close, he could almost see their features. He hollered encouragements and they waved wildly, yelling his name.

Then one form dropped, followed by another, and another, then the last one.

Marshall's mind blanked from every logical thought. He ran into the open, not getting more than a few feet before Dominique walloped the back of his legs with her walking stick and dragged him into the safety of the outcrop. Marshall, stomach-down in the dirt, tried to get away but Dominique pressed her good knee into his back.

"You think I don't want to help?" she hissed. "You don't think I'm angry, like you? That I don't feel *useless*, too? The bullet in my leg stops me from being at full capacity! But we cannot make martyrs of ourselves, not now when no good can come of it!"

Marshall knew she was right, and he knew he was in a precarious place in his mind. He couldn't think straight anymore and emotions drove his decisions. But he didn't care. When Dominique yielded her strength, he squirmed free and tore toward the teenagers. A bullet struck him somewhere, then another, and another. He fell, yards from the unconscious friends. Hot blood clotted his throat, but he pulled himself toward them.

Not my kids, you bastards. Not my kids.

He was within arm's reach of the teenagers when his strength gave out and he collapsed. His body worked against his short, rapid breaths that seemed to make the very earth shake. Slight spasms twitched his fingers and the muscles in his back.

It took him longer than it should have to grasp that his laboring lungs weren't the culprits behind the quaking ground. He lifted his head a few inches just as a war cry rolled across the savanna, followed by an orchestra of infuriated trumpeting.

From behind Marshall, three groups of Tanzanians charged onto the battlefield, each one led by a group of elephants. The leading pachyderms had triangles painted from their foreheads to their trunks, and riders in tribal masks sat atop them like royal warriors.

If Marshall hadn't been weakening so fast, he would have laughed maniacally and whooped until he'd cheered his throat raw. Instead, he managed a wet snicker, blood spattering out from between his teeth.

The Watchers of Meru. Subira and her people came for us.

Each of the three groups were at least a hundred strong, all armed with drawn bows. They raised another call of challenge to the enemy. The battlefield was charged with such an abundance of energy that even Marshall felt more alive than ever.

He wished he could have howled with laughter at what happened then.

Across the entire battlefield, mercenaries dropped their guns and went onto their knees, some with their hands behind their heads, others with their arms up in surrender. To Marshall's amazement, a few even prostrated themselves.

The last thing he heard before losing consciousness was the elephants as they trumpeted to the sky in victory.

In a cottage at the Nyika Wildlife Inn, Aari lounged on an ancient bergère chair beside a bed, scrolling through his phone as he kept vigil. Marshall slept peacefully save for an occasional sound of discomfort. Sunlight filtered through the thin curtains onto the blue covers, and mild scents of flowers and wood drifted through the bug screen covering the open window.

One story permeated all of Aari's social media, rendering him numb. The U.S. had been hit by the virus, hard, and authorities were scrambling to figure out how that could have happened with the safety measures in place.

Phoenix must have had the virus in the States for weeks already, just waiting to unleash it these past couple of days, he thought. *So much for closing our borders. And now three and a half million people are dead worldwide with mortality doubling every two days. All those lives . . . snuffed out, just like that.*

He read on, barely taking in the articles about economies around the globe going into a tailspin, some being propped up by central banks to prevent total collapse. People were locked in their homes, terrified, hoping and praying that they and their loved ones would somehow survive. A lump formed in Aari's throat, and he felt sick.

Marshall let out a quiet groan and opened his eyes groggily. Solace washed over Aari, superseded by a flare of anger. "Morning," he said brusquely.

Marshall stirred, failing to notice the boy's tone. "Ech, my breath is rancid."

"I don't doubt it. You've been in and out of it for almost three days."

"What?"

Aari glared. "You're an idiot, Marshall. You were shot three times. You're lucky some of the Watchers are great healers and a couple are certified doctors."

He could sense a justification forming on the Sentry's tongue; then Marshall sighed and shoved his blanket down to expose his bare chest and shorts-clad legs. He had sutures on his right deltoid, another above his right hip, and one down the middle of his chest.

"Huh," he said. "I feel pain, but it's not as bad as it should be. Remedial powder?"

Aari nodded. "Domi's. The healers applied it after the bullets were removed."

The door swung open with a creak and Tegan and Mariah barged in, trapping Marshall in a bear hug. "You're awake!" Mariah squealed. "We thought we heard voices in here. We were in Domi's room, beside yours. She's resting. The Watchers took you both to a nearby hospital and removed the bullet from her leg and took care of your wounds."

Marshall mussed her hair, then jerked upright. Aari's arm snapped out to stop him from popping his stitches. The Sentry took in the faces of the teenagers. "Where's Kody?"

"He's being cared for," Tegan said, sitting on the bed. "Marshall, it's bad. It's day six of his infection. He's gotten more . . . uncontrollable . . . but it's weird. He should be bleeding but he's not. For some reason, his reaction to the Omega strain is different from what we've heard about. Aari thinks it could be because of our physiology. We don't have Dema-Ki blood, but there might be something in our system that has some resemblance to it."

"It might explain how the five of us have our abilities," Aari added. "But as long as Kody hasn't started to bleed, we still have time."

A weary quiet fell upon them. Aari stared at his shoes for a while; then, without looking up, he said, "Hey, Marshall?"

"Yeah?"

"You know how my retrocognition works, right? Touch an object, access whatever memories belong to the object's owner or maker when they were alive. But with Lucius . . . I witnessed him die. How is it possible that my connection with his memories continued after that? And I know it was him because his presence felt the same. I guess what I'm trying to get at is, what exactly did I experience?"

Marshall drummed his finger on the bed, blinking slowly. "I've been wondering that myself. To be honest with you, Aari, I'm really not sure. Some of the things you guys do are beyond me, and apparently beyond the Elders. You're the Chosen Ones of the prophecy. This is new territory for all of us. We're learning as we go. As for Lucius, maybe the essence of his being lingered on in the novasphere for whatever reason, and perhaps you were destined to tap into that. But I don't think there's a way to know for sure. Truth is, we'll probably never get all the answers we want."

"That's immensely frustrating."

"I know."

There was a knock on the door and Subira entered. She was back in her jeans and white camisole but, to Aari, she didn't look any less regal or fearsome than when she'd donned her tribal ensemble. He lifted his hand in greeting. "Hi."

She inclined her head at him, then addressed Marshall. "You're up. Good. You've missed a lot."

"I'd like to ask some questions, if you don't mind," he said. "All I remember is the mercenaries giving up when you came. Why? They were armed and could have fought back."

Pride colored Subira's words when she spoke. "My people are—were—no more than myths. Stories of who we are and what we do have been exaggerated for centuries. Those mercenaries, they had no higher loyalty besides getting paid for a job done. Present them with the legendary Watchers and spirit elephants they've heard of since childhood and they were more than co-operative. We warned them that if they meddled with the affairs of foreign powers again, we would come after them until no one was left. They've since slunk back to their towns and villages. We did get visitors shortly after, led by a giant man called Hajjar. He was searching for his superior, the one we apprehended. Vladimir Ajajdif."

Marshall goggled. "We have Ajajdif? And Hajjar—"

Aari patted the Sentry's forearm. "Ajajdif is tied up in another cabin. He told us in the chopper that Hajjar and his mercs had been found and were waiting in a plane at another location to take us off-continent. We figure that when Hajjar learned about the raid by the Watchers, he probably decided it was best to live to fight another day."

"Guess he isn't all brawn," Marshall quipped, bemused. "Subira, I need to contact someone to see where we go from here, but if you could keep an eye on Ajajdif until then . . ."

"We can do that," she said. "Now, if you're up to it, we could visit your sick friend."

Marshall removed his covers in response and grabbed a T-shirt from his bag. As the group followed the young woman out to the warm grounds, he called, "Subira?"

"Mmh?"

"Thank you. For all that you and your people have done to help us."

She raised her eyes heavenward but smiled. "Do you know how many times we've heard that while you were in and out of consciousness? You woke up when a bullet was being removed from your shoulder and told the doctor that she was a beautiful soul for helping a rascal American like you. It's made my people keen to know what you'd be like drunk."

Aari snorted a laugh so hard it hurt his throat. "You're a regular Clark Kent, aren't you?"

Marshall made a move to cuff Aari's head, but the teenager dodged easily. They passed a few Watchers, all in civilian clothes, who greeted them with different levels of candidness.

"Where's the tree?" Marshall asked, waving bashfully at the onlookers. "And the box?"

"The box is safe," Mariah said. "So's the tree. It's getting some sun right now. You won't believe how *fast* it's growing!"

Subira led them into a single-room cottage near the reception building and Aari tried to shut his ears to the clamor within. He saw Marshall falter upon seeing Kody on the mattress.

Each of the boy's limbs were secured to separate bedposts by ropes wrapped in fabric to avoid burning his skin when he thrashed. Multiple fans hummed, and buckets of ice water surrounded the bed. Two Watchers battled Kody's fever by drenching strips of cloth in the buckets and resting them on his face, neck, and upper body. He looked like a mummy, which Aari would have found hysterical at any other time. Now, it made every part of him hurt, his emotions twisting into a giant knot.

Marshall sat on the edge of the bed by Kody's side. Kody gnashed his teeth, his normally bright eyes manic and darting. His nostrils flared with every rapid breath. The Sentry hesitated, then rested a hand on the teenager's forehead, murmuring soothingly. Aari watched, astonished, as Kody's struggling eased and the frenzy retreated from his eyes. For a few seconds, peace breathed into the room.

Then Kody screeched and Marshall shot off the bed. Subira clicked her tongue, assertively steering the group outside. "Maybe that's enough excitement for him today."

"Probably," Marshall agreed weakly.

A Watcher on the other side of the grounds called to Subira. She excused herself, leaving the friends and Sentry alone.

Tegan kicked a pebble over the grass and, after a few beats, said, "Elder Nageau reached out yesterday. He told me the sap from a mature tree can be harvested by tapping the trunk, but since we're running out of time for Kody, he said to wait until the sapling's at least four days old. That's tomorrow. At this stage, the sap evaporates within moments, so we'll need to bring the tree to Kody, tear off a leaf, and have him inhale the sap from the stem. It should buy him some time but, for now, there's nothing more we can do."

Aari wanted to claw to shreds the powerlessness that came with the tedious ticking of the clock. The group stayed together until the sun dipped below the horizon, when Aari decided the best way to make time pass was to turn in early. Subira had given them the run of the place, so he retired to the suite he'd staked out for himself.

Peculiar dreams plagued his subconscious through the night, only ending when he arose at the crack of dawn. Tired and off-kilter, he lumbered into the shower until he felt more human than zombie, then wandered out into the cool morning. *I could do with coffee right now,* he thought. *Maybe even pour some Red Bull in there and create the Unholy Cocktail. Ha, Tegan would definitely kick my butt across the continent if I tried that nonsense again . . .*

His feet mechanically took him to Kody's suite, where a small lamp on the bedside table lit the room. Some of the Watchers had taken shifts through the night to keep an eye on him. Kody was fast asleep; aside from his ragged breathing, all was well. Aari thanked the Watchers, earning him drowsy smiles. As he opened the door to leave, a snuffle sounded. He turned.

Kody had lifted his head to stare at him.

In the silence, Aari's flesh crawled at the violent glint in his friend's eyes. "H-hey, you're up. You . . . you okay?"

Drops of scarlet started to trickle from Kody's tear ducts, rolling down his cheeks. The Watchers tried to wipe the blood but he screamed at them and fought against his restraints. Aari dashed outside, shouting at the top of his lungs. Marshall and Dominique emerged from their cottage, frazzled. Tegan and Mariah ran out from their own suite in their tank tops, sweatpants, and bedheads; Mariah had her backpack with the knee-high sapling sticking out.

"He's bleeding, isn't he?" Marshall asked as they rushed to Kody's cabin.

"Just started," Aari panted.

Subira appeared from her suite and caught up with them as they entered the room. The mattress was stained red around

Kody's head. A steady stream of blood dripped from his eyes, ears, and nose, and he shrieked at anyone who attempted to get close. He pressed himself into the bed, as though trying to sink into it and escape.

"He sees us as the enemy," Tegan whispered.

Dominique shouldered the Watchers aside and sat over Kody, using her strength to hold his head still. "Get the sap!" she ordered. "Hurry!"

Mariah set her bag on the bed, face wan. Her fingers trembled as she touched one of the sapling's luminescent violet leaves. Beside her, Kody thrashed as he screamed, his tears mingling with blood. She looked down at him, then wrenched the leaf free and held the stem in front of his face, letting the silky sap evaporate into his nostrils in a mist.

Kody grew still, eyes staring blankly at the ceiling. His chest stopped moving. Aari inched closer, frantic. "What's going on?"

Dominique placed two fingers on the teenager's neck. "His pulse is there," she said. "But I don't know why he—"

Kody's mouth opened and he drew in a deep, grating breath, exhaled, then went still once more. Aari picked at his nails. *What is this? Should this be happening?*

Beside him, Tegan and Mariah looked on helplessly, arms folded, eyes welling.

Kody labored in a second breath. As he released it, the sharp creases on his forehead eased and his eyelids slid shut. He took in another breath and stilled again. The group watched. Waited. Hoped.

Moments passed before Kody slowly opened his eyes. He seemed confused, as though he didn't recognize the people in his company. Tegan moved in, Aari and Mariah following. Kody wasn't able to focus on them, but Aari saw the veins in his bloodshot eyes recede until his sclera cleared completely. His mouth opened again. Instead of howls of agony and rage or abysmal, rattling breaths, Kody squeaked, "Domi, could you please get off me? I can't breathe."

The group gaped, then let out a meager laugh. Dominique beamed and patted Kody's cheek as she got off the mattress. While one of the Watchers dabbed the blood from his face and ears, Tegan sat beside him. "Do we have you back?" she murmured.

When Kody answered, it sounded like his vocal cords had been flayed. "Well, I'm not burning up and the pounding in my head has faded. Also, um, could someone kindly untie me?"

As the Sentries undid the bindings, Aari rubbed his knuckles against Kody's scalp. "You're okay? In the noggin, I mean."

"Why wouldn't I be?" Kody replied cheerfully. "I'm still alive."

Aari didn't buy the charade and knew the girls didn't either, but they wouldn't question it. Not yet, anyway. Mariah smiled. "We're glad you're still here, brickhead."

Kody smiled back. "Me too."

"Now that that's settled," Subira said, not unkindly, "I recommend you stay today and tomorrow. If Kody is flying you to South Africa, he should have a few proper meals and rest."

"Oh boy," Kody hummed. "I'm *starving*."

"Er, we might have a problem." Mariah held up her backpack. "I don't think we'll be able to take the tree with us on any flight out of Africa. It grows a lot every day."

"There is a courier south of the border that may still be open," Dominique said. "I can have the tree dispatched to the go-between Sentry in Yukon, who'll deliver it to Dema-Ki. And I might as well tell you this now and get it over with . . ." She cleared her throat. "Elder Nageau reached out to me last night. He instructed me to take Ajajdif back to the DRC and hold him there."

Mariah wheeled around to face her. "DRC? But that means—"

"I won't be going with you to Dema-Ki," she affirmed.

Before the Aari and the others could complain, Marshall said, "One more thing. Subira."

The leader of the Watchers regarded him crabbily. "If you're going to thank my people again, I will personally feed you to a leopard."

"Heh, don't worry. Actually, your people is what I wanted to talk about. Yours and ours. You, Dominique, and I are really not so different. Domi and I are Sentries, descendants of an uncommon group of people with a duty that we can't forsake . . . quite like the Watchers."

Aari could see Subira's curiosity pique. "Interesting," she said, "though something in your tone tells me you won't share more than that, most likely because you can't."

Marshall grimaced. "Guilty as charged. But I'd like to think that there's a kind of kinship between the Watchers and the Sentries."

"I don't know about 'kinship,' *Sentry*, but let's start with this: Should you need aid, or even if you drop by this region for a visit, know that you have allies here."

"That's a better start than I could've hoped for, Watcher."

Subira nodded at the teenagers. "And what of these four? Are they Sentries too?"

Marshall smiled fondly at the friends. "Actually, there's five of them. And they've got a bigger role to play than any one of us."

"Love you too, big guy," Kody said, "but I could *really* do with a meal right now."

* * *

Two mornings later, the friends and Marshall saw Subira and some of her people one last time as they prepared to take off for South Africa. The Watchers wished them well, each touching the box of seeds before Tegan zipped it in her bag.

Parting with Dominique was difficult, but the Sentry assured the friends that they would see each other again. They gave her long hugs and boarded the Cessna, waving as she and the Watchers grew smaller in the vast savanna as the plane ascended. Flying south and under the radar until they were out of Tanzania, they refueled at a small town on the shore of Lake Malawi that Subira had recommended.

The leader of the Watchers had been on the money about the availably of flights out of Cape Town. However, the only connections they could find involved a circuitous route through painfully slow transits to their destination. Three days after leaving Tanzania, they shivered in the chilly air of northern Canada as they neared the fringes of Dema-Ki on horseback.

I'm packing a heated blanket next time, Aari groused to himself. *Guh, I hate the cold.*

Huyani and Akol had met them at the edge of the forest, gathering the friends in one massive cuddle while Aari made a muffled comment about there being a lot of physical contact the entire week. Marshall was instantly overwhelmed upon being introduced to the siblings; he had never met anyone from Dema-Ki apart from Nageau. Huyani and Akol welcomed him, arms wide open and eyes damp from emotions the friends would never understand. The Sentry responded in kind, hugging them fiercely. He was still in awe and trying to come to grips with the whole experience as their horses climbed the incline at the open end of the valley to enter the snow-covered village from the east.

Akol, riding beside Marshall, grinned. "You wear the same expression the other Sentries did when they arrived a few days ago."

"We hear about this place from family members who heard it from Sentries before them," Marshall murmured, taking in the pine trees, clusters of *neyra*, and assortment of structures. "But to actually be here? It's like retuning to a home I never knew was mine, but it feels just right."

"I hope you are well-versed in our language," Huyani said lightheartedly. "Not all of us are omnilingualists."

"My dad made sure of it, but my accent's gonna be atrocious. I apologize in advance."

Aari wondered at Marshall's reaction. *Funny,* he thought. *The five of us take this whole place for granted, but for a Sentry . . . it's almost like a pilgrimage.*

Beside him, Mariah patted her mare's neck. "It feels so good to be back in the saddle."

On Aari's other side, Kody grimaced. "Of course you'd say

that. Meanwhile, I've got a nasty saddle sore."

"Weakling."

"Don't joke," Tegan sighed. "He *has* been weakening again. We'll need to get another leaf for him to inhale."

They kept to the left bank of the river that divided the village, riding past the community square, the greenhouse, and finally to the barn and stable. The friends swiftly dismounted and Tegan looked to the siblings. "Is it okay if we—"

"Yes, yes," Huyani beamed, waving them away. "Go! We will take care of your steeds."

The friends took off, jogging upriver through the trees until they came upon Dema-Ki's new community hall, where they knew their families and the Elders awaited their arrival.

Tegan gripped the handle but didn't turn it. Aari tilted his head. "Hey, what's wrong?"

"We're going to see our families again after more than three months." Her every word shook. "But this time we don't have Jag with us."

"They already know he was taken," Kody said. "And they know I'm sick. The Elders told them when they arrived."

"I know that. It's just . . . it's going to be hard to look at the Sanchezes."

Mariah rubbed Tegan's back. "Jag wouldn't want us to feel like this, Teegs. Come on. Let's head in."

Tegan's jaw stiffened, and they entered the spacious community hall. It was identical to the old one, right down to the fixtures and amenities, the prominent log beams that held up the roof, and the many round, wooden tables. Aari shuddered at the familiarity of the place. He recalled too clearly how the old hall had nearly burned down when Hutar tried to kill the friends.

Then he spied the families and Elders by the stained-glass doors at the other end of the building, and the memories dispersed.

The reunion was semi-chaotic, filled with sobs and cries of relief, just a blur of motion as families rushed to envelop each of the friends. Aari's father crushed him in an embrace, lifting him off the ground. Aari tried to pull away from the stubbly face. "Oy! I like affection as much as the next guy, but do you know how much *hugging* we've had recently?"

"William, be careful, please," Aari's mother tutted, tears drying on her cheeks.

William Barnes' freckled face lit up as he let his son go. Aari picked up his four-year-old sister, swinging her into the air. "Hey, you little stinker. Missed me?" When the smaller redhead poked his nose, he laughed and peppered her with little kisses. "Yeah, I missed you too, Leah."

As the buzz died, Tegan motioned for the friends to join her. They approached the Sanchezes. Neither party spoke, but when Jag's parents held out their arms, the friends rushed into their embrace. It was a long minute before the family would let them go.

Tegan pulled out the brass-clad box from her backpack and the group followed her to join the Elders, who'd watched the proceedings in courteous silence. She presented the box and Nageau took it reverently, fingertips feather-light as he traced the patterns on the lid.

"The Saplings of Aegis have returned," he said. "And with them, the cure for humanity."

66

Kody, Tegan, Aari, and Mariah looked out over Dema-Ki from a hill at the west end of the valley. Gareth and Marshall, having updated each other on recent events, joined the friends on the slope. Even Victor decided to mingle, though he didn't speak much. That was perfectly fine with Kody as he still couldn't decide what to make of the man.

It turned out that, after losing their charter bus in Alberta, two of the remaining Sentries in the convoy had trekked to the nearest town to secure a pair of RVs while Victor and Gareth interred the bodies of the young Sentries killed in the assault. The entire group arrived at Dema-Ki later than scheduled, but all in one piece. Tegan's father had his gunshot wound looked at by Victor and he'd patched him up just enough to get to Dema-Ki, where Huyani and Tikina had then tended to him.

Kody tugged his jacket tighter around himself. It wasn't smart to loiter in the cold in his state, but he wanted to take in the pristine mountain air, to allow its freshness to seep into his ailing body. He tried not to think about what he'd been through, how the sickness had invaded him and pervaded his mind, driving him to see things that weren't there and feel things that made him want to—

He thrust the thought away. *Don't think. Eyes forward. You're fine. You'll be fine. You're not messed up. You're fine.*

He bopped his head against Marshall, harder than intended. "So! How long are you staying?"

"Dunno," Marshall replied, grabbing him in a headlock. "Depends what the Elders need from us."

"Speaking of," Gareth said, "it's the end of the evening. Don't you four have a meeting?"

"Yeah," Tegan mumbled from where she rested against Mariah, half dozing. "We should get going."

The friends pulled each other up and bid the Sentries good night. They headed across the river and up another incline to the temple, passing the open marble foyer with the center cauldron flaring its vibrant-colored flames, and turned down the hall. Nageau, Tikina, Ashack, Saiyu, and Tayoka welcomed them as they entered the alcove where the Elders met to discuss matters with the friends.

"Let us address the concern that is at the top of our minds," Nageau said once the greetings were over. "Jag."

"We've tried but we still can't sense him in the novasphere," Tegan said.

"Unfortunately so. From what we have ascertained, the harbinger wants him alive, so perhaps his abilities have been curtailed. Tony seems to have returned with a vengeance and remains utterly loyal to Reyor. We have no inkling as to where he would have taken Jag but, rest assured, every Sentry out there is keeping an eye out and an ear to the ground."

"Keeping an eye out?" Mariah echoed. "Is that all we're doing?"

"No," Tikina said delicately. "Younglings, we know this is hard, especially for Jag's family and the four of you. It is not easy on the Elders and the people of Dema-Ki, either. Know that we will not rest until we find him. Still, there is a spark of hope. Victor gave us the name of a location known as 'the Heart.' We speculate that it may be a Sanctuary. Victor believes a place with such a name must be significant, and Deverell is looking into it. We have other Sentries helping as well."

Tayoka pulled at his red beard, his face weighed by grief, and murmured a few words. Tikina and Nageau, who'd been telepathically translating for the other Elders, both squeezed his arm. A knot formed inside Kody and he found himself wanting to comfort Jag's mentor.

"Elder Tayoka wishes us to recognize something important," Tikina said. "Jag's role."

"His timely and relentless questioning about the Tree of Life's secrecy gave us cause to delve deeper into our archives." Nageau smiled ruefully. "None of the Elders probed into that aspect of the Tree because that same secrecy is a mantle in our world. As such, we accepted it without question. But Jag would not have it. If not for him, Earth would be consumed in hellfire worse than what Reyor has already spawned."

Kody folded his arms and let his gaze wander through the assortment of flora around him, taking in the scents that were uniquely Dema-Ki. *Jag, man, you don't know what a hero you are. I hope you're okay, brother.*

"So our boy averted a crisis," Aari said, "but what about the current one? Elder Nageau, as of today, at least fourteen million people are *dead*. And that's just from the violent strain."

Nageau sat back. "The Tree of Life arrived yesterday and was replanted in the greenhouse. Magèo and Nal have already sowed the remaining seeds. The first tree is nine days old now, and for full potency in large doses it needs to be at least four weeks old. If we rush to administer the cure, the sap's effectiveness will be reduced drastically."

"But three more weeks." Aari tucked his chin to his chest. "The number of lives that will be lost while we wait . . ."

"I understand, Aari. It is devastating. So, given the situation, this is what the Elders have decided after discussing with Magèo: While we cannot afford to risk tapping into the sapling just yet, we will try when it reaches the two-week mark. At that time, the sap can be harvested but its potency will be halved. We will tap into the tree again when it reaches maturity. It is the best we can do."

"Is there a plan to distribute it to the masses?" Tegan asked.

"Since the sap is highly concentrated and evaporates readily into the atmosphere, Magèo believes that it would take a minute quantity to permeate the air in the form of mist. He has worked out three stages in the delivery of the cure."

"Sorry, I don't mean to cut in," Kody said, "but if we can get the cure from the tree at the two-week mark, does that mean . . ."

Nageau leaned forward to briefly cup the boy's chin. "Yes, Kody. We can administer it to you and heal you completely."

Kody forced back the wetness that edged from the corners of his eyes and beamed at his mentor. "Awesome. So, you were saying about the three stages?"

Nageau removed a piece of paper from his cloak. "This is Magèo's writing; do forgive me if it takes a moment to decipher his scrawl. He and Gareth worked out the mathematics. Ah, here it is. When taken from a two-week old tree, the sap is effective at a concentration level of one part per billion. The tree is expected to yield one large bucket of sap equivalent to three gallons, as you call it. The sap will then be diluted with a billion parts of distilled water, which will produce three billion gallons to release as mist over cities and towns around the world."

"Cities and towns vary in size and population," Aari said. "How do we account for that?"

"The short answer is, this is an average figure that we are using based on research Gareth has done. There are several factors to consider, like total population, land area, and density. We have been told that there are close to three thousand cities in the world with a minimum population of one hundred and fifty thousand people. Some of them have extremely high densities. Gareth gave examples of Mumbai, Seoul, and Lagos."

Aari nodded. "Mumbai has something like seventy thousand people per square mile."

"Yes," Nageau said. "Such cities will lend themselves well to the aerosol method of delivery. On the other extreme, there are sparsely populated areas flung across larger regions. For these, ground delivery—as in inoculation centers—and even the door-to-door approach will be required."

"This all sounds hopeful, but who's gonna get this rolling?" Tegan asked. "I don't think we're equipped for this, are we?"

"We are not. Your Centers for Disease Control will receive the sap anonymously, with a letter detailing everything. They may even synthesize it eventually, but it would take a while to recreate some of the sap's more unique elements . . . In any case, we will task Gareth and Victor with the deliveries."

"Why would the CDC believe anything in an anonymous letter?" Mariah asked.

"We will request that they test the cure," Tikina answered. "They will have no choice but to follow through with the rest of our instructions when it works. If all goes well, they will receive the sap in six days, and once they have tested it and found a means to disperse the mist, we estimate it might take a few more days before the first round of the cure begins to descend from the skies."

Aari blinked fast, something Kody had learned he did when engaged in rapid mental calculation. "That's anywhere between eight to ten days before the world receives the remedy, and that's the optimistic route. We're talking about four hundred million lives lost in that time span. This is nuts! And it doubles every two days that it's delayed!"

Kody linked his fingers over his head and stared glassily at nothing. *Nearly half a billion people.* Mariah curled against him. He felt her shaking slightly and put his arms around her, rubbing his cheek against her hair.

"Alright," Tegan said. "At least others can still be cured. What's next?"

Aari shoved his face into hers, lip curling. "Are you serious? Stop being a machine, Tegan! *Feel* something!"

She bristled. "I feel *everything.* I'm just not letting it distract me from what needs to be done."

Kody got up and fell into the tiny gap between the pair, forcing them apart. "Nope. Cool it. We're not doing this right now." He politely signaled for Nageau to continue.

The Elder gazed at them, a twinge of sadness passing over his eyes. Kody had seen that look all throughout his training;

his mentor was aggrieved by the burden of responsibility that had been laid on the friends. He wished he knew how to console the older man.

"I know this is a difficult situation," Nageau said. "Many lives will be lost. But the five of you, the Bearers of Light, the Saplings of Aegis, *you* will save innumerable others. The harbinger will not bring humanity to its knees, not as long as you stand together. Not as long as you follow your spirit, and not as long as you carry the light that the prophecy has charged you with."

"Speaking of light," Tikina said, bumping shoulders with Nageau, "there is something else we want the four of you to know. Something special regarding the Tree of Life."

Nageau's mood visibly lightened. "Yes, of course. I think you will be quite thrilled to learn that, in addition to healing victims of the harbinger's virus, the tree will protect humanity from all diseases."

"*All* diseases?" Mariah echoed, disbelieving.

"I should clarify. It will protect humanity from diseases caused by external organisms that invade the body—pathogens such as viruses and bacteria."

"This is going to change the lives of so many people around the world! But why won't it cure other diseases?"

"Everything in the universe exists in cycles and a state of equilibrium, our bodies included," Tikina said. "Sometimes there are deviations that occur for reasons that we are yet to understand. Other times, this equilibrium is upset by our own doing. The choices we make for the sustenance and maintenance of our bodies have far-reaching implications that are beyond the power of the Tree of Life to prevent or cure."

"Hey, if I never have the stomach flu again, that's enough for me," Kody said. "This tree is a blessing."

"You're right," Tegan said. "It *is* a blessing. A gift from Dema-Ki to the world."

"Well, from our ancestors," Nageau amended. "This gift has remained hidden for centuries until you, the Chosen Ones, found it. And now it will be the beginning of your legacy to humanity."

In the ensuing silence, the immensity of the discovery of the seeds, their history and now their future, started to fully dawn on Kody. *The effect this will have on each person that survives the pandemic . . . holy smokes. It doesn't matter who wins, Reyor or us—the world won't be the same after this.*

"Moving on to a focal subject," Nageau continued. "The head of the hydra itself."

Kody twiddled his thumbs. "Even when the cure goes out, there's not a chance Reyor will stop, is there?"

Nageau indicated no and apprised the friends of Victor's gleanings from his contact in the New Mexico Sanctuary. They listened attentively, then Aari raised his hand. "If they need your blood to populate the Sanctuaries, then is an attack on Dema-Ki imminent?"

"We are unsure," Tikina said, "but even if it is not imminent, it is a certainty."

"At the risk of coming across selfish," Tegan said, "is Dema-Ki safe for our families?"

Nageau seemed to weigh his answer carefully. "This is the safest place for the time being. The Elders and I are already working on a contingency, so please do not let this trouble you."

"Reyor's probably coming here to build a breeding farm," Aari said. "And that's all there is to it?"

The other Elders raised their eyebrows at Nageau expectantly. The tall man rose from the divan and paced between the two groups. Kody narrowed his eyes. *Uh-oh. He never paces.*

"There is something else," Nageau relented. "It is an ancient quartz known as the black crystal. Mind you, this information is meant only for the Elders and Magèo. And soon Nal, as she is the one appointed to succeed him. This crystal can alter a person's lifespan, extending their longevity over centuries. As it is, our people live for a hundred-and-thirty years on average. We believe this is the other reason Reyor intends to infiltrate Dema-Ki. It seems to fit the harbinger's plan to reshape the world and to live long enough to revel in it. This is all we know for now, but it is imperative that you never speak of this to anyone."

"Hold up, rewind, and pause," Kody said. "You live for *how long?*"

"Focus, Kody!"

Nageau's reprimand didn't stop the friends from eyeballing each other, thunderstruck. The Elder resumed his pacing. "We must halt this scourge at its source. We need to learn what it will take for you to defeat Reyor. The *lathe'ad* is an astoundingly powerful object. Too powerful for this fiend to possess. I should have been more careful . . ."

"More careful about what?" Mariah asked.

"About ensuring that nothing had been stolen when I banished that monster. But it no longer matters. Reyor has it—has the *lathe'ad*. A terraforming device that can either bring life to a dead planet or death to a living one. And, obviously, we reside on the latter."

Tikina grabbed Nageau by the arm and gave him a pointed look. He expelled a lengthy breath, then smiled tiredly. The other Elders stood and the friends followed their lead. "We have kept you long enough from your families," Nageau said, apologetic.

"But where do we go from here?" Mariah pressed.

"For now, stay with your parents and siblings," Tikina advised. "We do not know how long this reprieve will last before the next wave begins."

Aari stuck his fists into his pockets. "That can't be all. Maybe we can help the Sentries locate the Heart. If we find it, we could find Jag."

"It feels like we're playing defense," Tegan said. "Which I get, but I can't sit on my hands and wait for news to come."

As his friends and the Elders conversed, Kody sat back down, elbows resting on his knees. The destructive images, the fearful thoughts swarming in his mind were still trying to break through the barrier he'd put up. He could feel them, each strike weakening his wall. He followed a pattern on the marble floor to distract himself, but the sickness yanked at his nerves and he couldn't fight its pull.

"What if Reyor's right," he said.

The conversation stopped. He felt all eyes on him.

"What was that, Kody?" Tikina asked softly.

"What if Reyor's right?" he repeated. "That as a species, we *are* inherently destructive? That we deserve what's coming to us? That . . . that we're Midas, except everything we touch becomes rotten instead of gold?"

Aari was aghast. *"Dude."*

"Let me speak to Kody on this one, Aari," Nageau said. "The answer to your question, youngling, depends on how you choose to view the world."

Kody rubbed his arm. "How do you view it, Elder Nageau?"

"I choose to believe that human beings, as imperfect as we are, are remarkable creatures capable of love, sacrifice, and compassion. Yet we also bring so much strife and devastation upon ourselves. But sometimes it is through these imperfections, these cracks, that the light gets in. We are still evolving as a species and I know our best days are ahead of us. I do not necessarily mean this in the sense of our physical evolution, but rather an evolution of the mind and spirit. What is the point of attaining higher physical progress if we do not have strength of the mind and wisdom of the spirit to guide us?"

"It is *this* evolution that we believe will turn the tide for humanity," Tikina chimed in. "The understanding, acceptance, and nurturing of our higher nature. The knowledge that we are all interconnected, living our fleeting material lives on a tiny blue speck in the universe in preparation for the next stage of our journey. The question that remains then, Kody, is this: How do you view the world?"

"I don't think I have an answer," Kody said.

"Yet," Nageau added. Kody, though disbelieving, admired his mentor's confidence.

The Elders left shortly after, and the friends trickled out after them. The four of them gathered around the colorful bloom of fire in the foyer, looking out at Dema-Ki as it glowed in the ambience of the night.

"Aari?" Tegan said. He hummed in response. "I'm not heartless. You know that, right?"

Aari shuffled closer to rest his chin on her shoulder. "I know. I'm sorry for what I said. I just don't understand how you're able to troop on, but I guess with your new role you have to figure out how to go about this whole mess the best way. Your way. And truthfully, logically speaking, your path does make sense given the situation. Just don't turn into the Terminatrix, okay? She spooked the bejeebers outta me in T-3."

"I'll do my best, Brainiac."

Kody noticed Mariah pointing her phone at the pair and he sidled up to them, shoving his face between theirs. He stuck his tongue out at Mariah, one eye closed in a wink. She gave a lopsided smile and snapped a photo of the flames and her friends. As she gazed affectionately at the picture on her screen, she murmured, "Well, what now?"

"Now," Kody said, "we do what the Elders told us to. We enjoy the time we have with our families. Then, we strike Phoenix at its heart and get our brother back."

Epilogue

The silence was unbearable, and though the room was scentless it still smelled *clean*. Overhead, an ultrahigh-definition screen took up the entire ceiling, displaying cotton-like clouds floating without a care against a cerulean backdrop.

Jag wanted to punch it.

Strapped to a white reclining chair similar to the kind found in a dentist's office, he was completely powerless in what Tony called the CUBE—the Center for Understanding, Betterment, and Enlightenment. Or an indoctrination chamber, as Jag knew it really was. From what he understood, it was one among many.

He had awoken three days before with a silver silicon band fastened around his head. It locked together and extended down the back of his neck to wrap around his throat like a collar, making it impossible to remove. He could still turn his head from side to side but he hated the device's constrictiveness. Tony called it an inhibitor, a tool Dr. Nate had recently perfected that suppressed special abilities supposedly without the use of drugs. Jag didn't feel any side effects but the device certainly worked; he couldn't break out of the leather restraints binding his wrists to the armrests, or use telepathy.

The floor-to-ceiling steel door opened and Tony strolled into the ten-by-ten room. He wore a beige blazer, dark skinny jeans, and penny loafers. His jeans were rolled up at the hems to show off different-colored striped socks. He took a seat on a chair to Jag's left, just a couple of feet away, and his eyes flashed with something the teenager didn't like.

"You look like a cat that ate the canary," Jag commented.

Tony smirked. "I have just been massively enlightened.

Capturing you catapulted me a notch higher in the pecking order."

"I'd catapult you into something if I didn't have this thing on me."

"Oh, I know. And now I know all about you and your friends, and your mentors in . . . what's it called? Dema-Ki? You told me about it during the summer but left out some crucial details."

"You're kidding."

"Hardly. It makes sense now, how you moved so fast back at the Kansas f—"

"No. I meant, you're just learning this now? Guess you really were nothing more than a lapdog licking dirt off Reyor's shoes."

Tony's foot snapped up, delivering a kick to Jag's mending leg. A shockwave slammed through him and he gasped, rapidly blinking back tears.

"Watch your mouth," Tony warned. "You're in my world now."

Jag breathed hard through his nose. "Little big man," he jeered. "Let me out of this chair and I promise my mouth will be the least of your worries."

"Where is this appetite for violence coming from?"

"You mean aside from pretending to be a good guy and then kidnapping my friends? Aside from killing the man guarding me in Israel? Aside from holding me hostage?"

"Wow. You're an emotional one, aren't you?"

Jag spat at him. "You killed my grandmother!"

"I never laid a hand on her."

"You work for the person whose actions dealt her the coronary. Guilt by association is enough for me."

Tony crossed an ankle over his knee and rubbed his nose. "I suppose that's fair."

Jag curled his hands, nails biting into his palms. *The casualness. He doesn't care.*

"What do you people want from me, Tony? Why am I here?"

"You ask that every day," Tony answered, "and every day I say you'll find out soon."

"How did you find me in the middle of the Negev Desert?"

Tony looked offended. "Now you're getting ridiculous. Jag, an organization like this, we have our ways. It was just a matter of narrowing down names and properties. You think we wouldn't have such capabilities with the direction we're heading? You don't know what else we've got. During the summer, I had to get assets on my own. I was at a disadvantage. This time, I've got the Boss fully behind me. That's why you're sitting where you are."

A muffled buzz came from the phone in Tony's hand. He looked at the screen and froze, then jumped up. "Looks like it's time for me to go," he said, heading toward the door. "Man, I wish I could be a fly on the wall for this one."

Jag tugged at his restraints once he was alone in the CUBE. The metallic fragments of the bindings rattled, laughing at his attempts to break free. He gave up, jaw ticking. *This is useless—I'm useless. I lose my abilities and that's it. I'm nothing.*

The door clicked and swung inward. A tall figure in a knee-length black coat stood in the entranceway, a gold hood shielding a shadowed face. The room's temperature seemed to drop. Jag's stomach knotted and his mouth dried instantly.

The figure stepped in, coming to a halt by his elevated feet as the door behind closed firmly. Jag had never seen Reyor but there was no mistaking the weight of the presence before him.

He exhaled his jitters. "*You.*"

"Jag Sanchez." A concealed modulator deepened and distorted the voice. "I don't believe we've had the pleasure of meeting."

"We haven't. But I know who you are."

"You've been a hard nuisance to catch, but I always get my way. If you don't know that by now, you will learn it soon enough."

Jag kept his head high. "What do you want from me?"

"Nothing. At worst, you're a freak. At best, you're a pest. But there's someone who wants to see you, who believes you're important. I think this is all a waste of time but, if we can't be rid of you, maybe we can put you to good use, give you a higher purpose."

"Who wants to see me?" Jag asked. "Where am I? What is this place?"

"You'll meet him soon," Reyor said. "As for this place . . . this is ground zero from which a new world is being built. A world unlike anything humanity's ever seen."

"Spare me the elevator pitch. You think murdering the whole population justifies your actions? You're gonna model the new world after, what, yourself? Evil incarnate?"

"Evil is a matter of perspective. From where I stand, evil is what's out there. Look at what humans have done to themselves with their greed and corruption and waywardness. The new world I'm building will be better. Healthier in every sense of the word. Earth will finally have stewards who respect her and each other. They've been taught to be the ideal—"

"Taught? You mean brainwashed. Or what's that word you guys use . . . repurposed?"

Reyor reached into one of the coat's pockets and withdrew a violet sphere. The *lathe'ad* rolled over long fingers. "It takes a strong hand to alter the course of humanity. To save it from itself. And if that strong hand needs to be iron, then so be it."

"You think the end justifies the means," Jag accused. "Who gave you the right to play God?"

"Why *shouldn't* the end justify the means, if the end is noble?"

Jag tried to answer, but to his horror realized that on that single point he might agree with the monster before him. Reyor's ends weren't noble, but what of the friends' fight against the harbinger? If it was to safeguard the world, wouldn't it be honorable to do anything necessary to ensure its security?

"That's what I thought," Reyor said, slipping the *lathe'ad* into the jacket. "Coming back to your second question. What is this place? I call it the Heart. This is where it all began. A majestic island stood here once, surrounded by shimmering turquoise waters. This Heart now beats in the same spot where that island used to be. Well, close enough, anyway. So, Mr. Sanchez, what is this place? It's home."

The door opened again and a statuesque older man in a short-sleeved, royal purple tunic strode in. A tribal tattoo wound around his left arm. His curly dark hair was frost-tipped with age, his full beard similarly colored. Only his amber eyes cracked his stern countenance; they were inquisitive. Light, even. But Jag still knew a dangerous man when he saw one.

As the newcomer took his place beside Reyor, his gaze never leaving Jag, the hooded figure bowed slightly. "Mentor."

The corners of the man's mouth pulled up just a bit. "Reyor."

Jag looked from one to the other. "There's *two* of you? I thought we were only dealing with one Satan."

The old man started to smile fully. "Jag seems to think you're the devil himself, Reyor. He thinks you're a . . . oh. Interesting." His smile took on a mysterious shade. "You know, Reyor, you're quite right about what you said earlier. We *are* home. You needn't conceal yourself behind that hood anymore. At least not in here."

For a moment, the hooded figure didn't move. Then one tanned hand reached into the shadows under the cowl, pulled out the vocal distorter, and pocketed it. Then the hand grasped the gold hood and pulled it down. Jag went slack.

Reyor's a woman.

High cheekbones, full lips, and a strong chin accentuated her features, all framed by wavy burgundy hair tucked into the jacket's tall collar. A lock of white to the side of the center parting fell across one of her mauve eyes. She observed Jag with catlike focus; if she was amused by his reaction at her reveal, she made no indication of it.

In a crisp, husky voice that hinted a Dema-Ki accent, Reyor said, "We will see each other again, Mr. Sanchez. For now, I must take my leave. I ask that you be on your best behavior."

Jag was still reeling. *I never realized . . . Not only did the Elders try to avoid saying Reyor's name whenever they could, they avoided pronouns. Like they completely wanted to erase her from their lives. Like not attaching her to anything identifying would bring them comfort.*

The old man waited until Reyor departed, then took a seat

in the chair beside Jag. "Now, young man," he crooned. "We have much to discuss."

* * *

At the center of the circular island, on a grassy knoll overlooking an eighteen-hole golf course, Reyor lowered herself onto a park bench. Her long tresses flowed with a breeze from the sea. Behind the knoll, workers were engaged in reforesting the rest of the thousand-acre island. The place was a private resort, complete with a luxurious hotel by the fairway and a circus hippodrome next to it. Beneath the legitimate operations lay the Heart, the largest of the six Sanctuaries.

The bench creaked as the old man slid next to Reyor. They watched a gull ride the thermals. It lazed in the sky for a time then straightened, diving into the water to snap up a fish.

The man sighed contentedly. "It is a sight to behold."

Reyor pinched some soil underfoot and rubbed it between a thumb and forefinger. "Surely a bird catching its meal is barely noteworthy."

"The island, Reyor. The island is a sight to behold. Through land reclamation, you brought our home back." The man pressed his palms together, fingers against his lips. "I lost my wife and two daughters to the volcano that claimed the original island."

"I know, Mentor."

"That day never ceases to haunt me. Much of the pain has ebbed over the centuries, but sometimes thinking about it brings the ache back, as fresh and raw as if it had just happened."

"The past cannot be changed, but we can grow from it."

"Indeed. And grow we have. This island has risen again, like a phoenix. All thanks to you."

"Mentor, please. If it weren't for you, I wouldn't have known which outcrop to purchase from the Italian government. You hold the key to a trove of important information."

"Your words are gracious but carry impatience, Reyor. Get on with it, then."

Reyor flicked the soil away. "You spent an hour with the boy. What do you think of him?"

The man looked out at the turquoise sea. Distantly, he said, "Evolution is a funny thing. An enigmatic force. Just when you think you know all there is to know about it, it will throw you a surprise, much like the universe itself."

Reyor was careful to avoid any telling motions. "What does that mean?"

"I'm not sure, exactly. I'll need more time with Mr. Sanchez. But there's something about him . . . a fire. He's a fighter. And as much as he tries to deny it, he wears his heart on his sleeve. Dangerous combination, but there is certainly something special about him."

"He's a freak of nature, Mentor, an anomaly. Him and his friends. They aren't proof that humanity is capable of our kind of evolution."

"You've made how you feel about this abundantly clear, Reyor."

She turned away, the sole of her boot mincing into the grass. *It sounds as though he's starting to take a liking to the boy,* she thought.

"It would have helped greatly if his friends had been delivered as well," the man said. "And the seeds."

"You have one in custody," Reyor responded brusquely. "I do have other priorities, you know. Why not figure out if Jag's what you suspect he is. I have pressing work that demands my attention, and I will not expend more time and energy on capturing the others. As for the seeds, it doesn't matter now. We've unleashed two waves. The nanomites have done tremendous damage, and the virus is on a warpath. The Elders may have the Trees of Life but the extent of the devastation is far-reaching and will continue to be so."

The man yielded. "And what of the next wave?"

"It will need to be moved up." Though furious about that fact, it took effort to quell the smile threatening to crack Reyor's taciturn exterior. "Quest Defense has been working hard to set this up, our *coup de grâce.* It will send humanity back to the Stone Age."

"Through all this, many will still survive."

"That's why our newest creatures are being mass-produced in double time. We acquired a fleet of merchant vessels several months ago as well; they will prove helpful in the distribution process. This will clean up the stragglers."

"Mmh . . . It's been a long time coming. Still, I wish this needn't happen."

"You have been around far longer than I have, Mentor, and you've done everything in your power to help, to make a difference. Yet look at where humanity stands now."

"I did try," the man said thickly. "For over two millennia I traveled the globe. I witnessed the rise and fall of civilizations. I tried to impart wisdom. Whispered in the ears of emperors and monarchs, presidents and generals, but to no avail. They invariably turn into cruel beasts that slaughter each other. I beheld rivers of blood flowing in the four corners of the world, all for a fleeting sovereignty, a handful of dust. How foolish. None of them heeded my counsel and warnings. At the time, I was averse to taking lives. I could have saved countless souls if I had. But to what end, I ask. Are humans capable of achieving a higher evolution? Humankind has walked such a long road, and it seems this species is doomed to be trapped in a loop of division and destruction. And now their corrosiveness is beginning to destroy the planet itself."

"And this is why we do what we do," Reyor said. "We need to stay the course, Mentor. Ours is the righteous path. We are the healers. We protect all that is good."

"And that will always be our belief." The man sighed as he brought his knuckles to his lips and softly touched them to Reyor's cheek. "I know you have things to attend to. I'll see you at dinner. Will your shadow be joining us?"

"Tony is getting ready for another mission."

"It isn't Tony I'm talking about."

Reyor's lip curled in a twisted smile. "Ah. No. That one is still confined to his quarters as a security measure, working on perfecting the ability we helped him unlock. He laid some satisfactory groundwork before returning to us. But if the situation in Dema-Ki cannot be handled, he will dine with us once before we make proper use of him."

"Very well. Give him my greetings when you do see him, hm?"

He left, and as he grew smaller against the golf course, the prickle of suspicion that had invaded Reyor's thoughts earlier returned. *He's grown soft. He was the first architect of this creed, but now . . . if he slips, if he becomes an apostate . . .*

She pulled the hood on, stood up, and followed the old man's footsteps toward the Sanctuary.

. . . I'll have to take matters into my own hands.

List of Characters

The Five:

Aari Barnes
Jag Sanchez
Kody Tyler
Mariah Ashton
Tegan Ryder

The Elders:

Ashack [Ay-SHAK]
Nageau [Nah-GO]
Saiyu [SAY-yoo]
Tayoka [Tah-YO-ka]
Tikina [Tee-KEE-na]

The Villagers:

Aesròn [Ay-zuh-RON]
Akol [AY-cole]
Hutar [HYOO-tar]
Huyani [Hoo-YA-nee]
Magèo [Ma-JAY-oh]
Nal [Nahl]

Sentries:

Benny Kumar - India
Deverell Vaughn – Wales
Dominique Mboya – Democratic Republic of Congo
Gareth Vaughn - Wales
Lei Shao – China
Marshall Sawyer – USA
Victor Colback - Canada
Zoe King – Australia

Related to the Five:

Camilla Sanchez — Jag's older sister
Jennifer Sanchez – Jag's mother
Roberto Sanchez — Jag's father
Tristan Sanchez — Jag's older brother
George Tyler — Kody's second-youngest brother

continued...

Rachel Tyler – Kody's mother
Roshon Tyler — Kody's youngest brother
Samuel Tyler — Kody's father
Krystal Ashton – Mariah's mother
Ellen Barnes – Aari's mother
Leah Barnes – Aari's younger sister
William Barnes – Aari's father
Curtis Ryder – Tegan's father
Damian Ryder – Tegan's older brother
Genevieve Ryder – Tegan's mother

Supporting Characters

Carmel
Ezra
Lucius
Anya Deol
Asa Abramson
Daniel Cohen
Kenzo Igarashi
Subira Nyamba
Chief – Victor's wolfdog

Phoenix Corporation:

Adrian Black — CEO, Phoenix Corp.
Dr. Albert Bertram — Chief Scientific Officer, Phoenix Corp.
Elias Hajjar — Head of Security, Quest Mining and New Mexico Sanctuary
Dr. Ina Deol – Lead Scientist, Quest Biotech
Jerry Li — Chief Financial Officer, Phoenix Corp.
Luigi Dattalo — Chief Executive, Quest Defense and Quest Aerospace
Dr. Nate — Director of Human Resources, Global Sanctuary Projects
Tony Cross — Personal Assistant to the Boss
Vladimir Ajajdif — Chief Executive, Quest Mining and New Mexico Sanctuary
The Boss — Owner and Founder, Phoenix Corp. and all subsidiaries

We hope you've enjoyed *Aegis Evolution*. To continue the Aegis League series, follow the link below for Book Four - *Aegis Desolation*
https://www.amazon.com/gp/product/B08PPX8SPK

Have you joined my Insider reader group? Sign up at the link below to receive three Aegis Chronicles short stories plus exclusive advanced reader opportunities.
https://www.sssegran.com/insider

Acknowledgments

To say that *Aegis Evolution* was a monster of a book to reel in would be an understatement. This novel challenged me in many ways and showed me that my capacity is not fixed, and that the more we push ourselves, the more resilient we become.

I began working on this manuscript in March 2016 and completed the first draft around the spring of 2017, if memory serves. Then it went through a couple of edits to slim down, but this story refused to be corralled into fewer pages. It openly defied its creator, who spent countless nights engaging in bleary-eyed staring contests with it while her tea went cold beside her. Guess who won.

There are many wonderful people to thank for getting this book ready for you, the reader. First and foremost, my mom and dad as always, though I'm not sure where to begin. There's just no way to fully articulate how much their support and love was crucial to the publishing of this novel.

A HUGE thank you to my amazing beta readers! Oluwatobi Martins, Julie Kuhn, Marco den Ouden, Kathrynne Creecy, Danny Coons, Don Simpson, Judith Avent, Dr. Michael Higgins, Linda Barnett, and Dr. Anthony Zehetner (who was also my medical and scientific advisor)—I have no words to properly express my deepest gratitude to all of you. Your insights, sharp eyes, and friendship helped make *Aegis Evolution* what it is.

Thank you also to my dear editor, Gordon Williams, for cleaning up the frazzled messes I sometimes left in my wake. We've been working together for about four years now, and I'm so thankful for all he's done to help shape and polish this series.

Lastly, I'd like to give my appreciation to Captain Jim Tang, my aviation technical advisor who was a remarkable resource and guide for chapters dealing with things that fly!

The next couple of years will be a period of hustling hard with two more books to go. I hope you will stick around for the big conclusion of the *Aegis League* series, and perhaps even begin a new adventure with me. I'm excited for the future and look forward to sharing in this voyage with you.

S.S. Segran
Vancouver, British Columbia
March 2018

About the Author

S.S. Segran's journey to becoming a bestselling novelist began in elementary school when she wrote extensions to books she loved. Her attempts to keep her favorite tales alive eventually led to the creation of her own characters and stories. Now, years later, her genre-defying novels are enjoyed by readers all over the world.

Even as she delves into her creative endeavors, Segran intends to help youth in less fortunate circumstances explore their potential through her non-profit, the Aegis League Youth Empowerment Program.

She's an ardent fan of horseback riding and parkour, and having enjoyed jumping out of a perfectly fine airplane at fifteen thousand feet—perhaps skydiving.

Segran lives in British Columbia and enjoys fall and winter in the Great White North. She loves to hear from her readers. You can reach her via her website at **www.sssegran.com**

www.ingramcontent.com/pod-product-compliance
Lightning Source LLC
Chambersburg PA
CBHW020344310726
48979CB00015B/2494/J

* 9 7 8 0 9 9 1 0 8 1 3 6 3 *